Praise for *Summer Rental*

"Mary Kay Andrews spins a beach-blanket sizzler around three lifelong friends . . . a warm-weather treat that has a lot going for it, not least the sunny forecast that summer love can blossom into a four-season commitment."
—*Publishers Weekly*

"Andrews writes another charmer with a picturesque Southern setting and winsome female characters."
—*Booklist*

"[R]eaders of *Summer Rental* will stay glued to their sandy beach chairs waiting to see what happens next."
—*The Christian Science Monitor*

"Secrets are shared, a mystery woman appears, love may be in the air."
—*People* magazine

"[T]his is prime beach-read material." —*Daily Record* (Gannett newspapers)

"*Summer Rental* is like a great day at the beach. You don't want it to end. Enjoy a vacation any time of the year with the ever-delightful Mary Kay Andrews." —Susan Elizabeth Phillips, author of *Call Me Irresistable*

"The bright and breezy plot of *Summer Rental* delivers just the right combination of sexy romance and warm friendship." —*Chicago Tribune*

"*Summer Rental* is just a delight to savor. The lively cast of characters is complex, genuine, and strong, and the interplay between the long-term friends is heartwarming." —*Times Record News* (Texas)

"You will relate to the women and their relationships as you laze through the pages . . . and you will smile, chuckle, and maybe even get a little misty eyed."
—*Examiner.com*

Praise for *Spring Fever*

"If you are making a list of 'must-read' books, this one should be at the top of your list. It has romance, comedy, and drama as well as a surprise here and there. Mary Kay Andrews is a people pleaser as an author, and this is one of her very best efforts."
—*The Huffington Post*

"This popular Georgia-based author (her hit last year was *Summer Rental*) brings us to Passcoe, North Carolina, where feisty heroine Annajane is reluctantly witnessing the wedding of her ex-husband, Mason, to the beautiful but evil Celia. This novel is full of intriguing plot turns by colorful characters with equally colorful names, like Mason's sister, Pokey. Most of those characters are conniving, larcenous, libidinous, and otherwise up to no good. And up to the very least good of all is the dreadful Celia, whose awfulness is so downright cinematic that you're rooting for this book to be made into a movie."
—*The Seattle Times*

"Andrews deftly combines a winsome love story and compelling family drama, and the idyllic small-town setting and surprising twists and turns are tailor-made for laid-back summer pleasure reading."
—*Booklist*

"Andrews delivers a satisfying read that will leave a taste as tangy, delicious, and sweet as an ice-cold bottle of Quixie soda."
—*Kirkus Reviews*

"A book you will want to sink your teeth into."
—*Altanta Journal-Constitution*

"Beach-read favorite Mary Kay Andrews delivers her delicious new escapist novel about small towns, old flames, and deep secrets."
—*Deep South* magazine

"Mary Kay Andrews fills the book with all the charm you'd expect to find in the inhabitants of a sassy Southern town, plus a whole lot of scandal for good measure!"
—*Chatelaine*

ALSO BY MARY KAY ANDREWS

The Weekenders

Beach Town

Save the Date

Christmas Bliss

Ladies' Night

The Fixer Upper

Deep Dish

Savannah Breeze

Blue Christmas

Hissy Fit

Little Bitty Lies

Savannah Blues

Summer Rental
&
Spring Fever

Mary Kay
Andrews

 St. Martin's Griffin ⚐ New York

SUMMER RENTAL. Copyright © 2011 by Whodunnit, Inc. SPRING FEVER. Copyright © 2012 by Whodunnit, Inc. All rights reserved. Printed in the United States of America. For information, address St. Martin's Press, 175 Fifth Avenue, New York, N.Y. 10010.

www.stmartins.com

The Library of Congress Cataloging-in-Publication Data is available upon request.

ISBN 978-1-250-14056-2 (trade paperback)

Our books may be purchased in bulk for promotional, educational, or business use. Please contact your local bookseller or the Macmillan Corporate and Premium Sales Department at 1-800-221-7945, extension 5442, or by email at MacmillanSpecialMarkets@macmillan.com.

First Edition: June 2017

10 9 8 7 6 5 4 3 2 1

Summer Rental

Dedicated with love to Molly Hogan Abel,
who actually did *hang the moon and the stars*

Acknowledgments

The author wishes to express heartfelt thanks to all those who patiently answered her questions, offered her advice and/or Diet Coke, or just put up with her whining and complaining during the writing and research of this novel. Any errors or misstatements of fact are my own and not theirs.

Huge thanks go to the Weymouth Center for the Arts and Humanities of Southern Pines, North Carolina, where large portions of this novel were plotted, and to my precious, invaluable writer buddies, Diane Chamberlain, Margaret Maron, Katy Munger, Sarah Shaber, Alexandra Sokoloff, and Bren Witchger, who trounced me at Scrabble and Balderdash and helped in more ways than I can say. Thanks to Anne Needham for helping me with foreclosure info; to Beth Fleishman, who helped me scout Nags Head; Frank Jones, who told me about day-trading; Sascha Springer, my source on location scouts; and Bobbie Murray of Pelican Cottages of Nags Head, who rented me the adorable Windswept cottage and connected me with longtime Nags Head residents Jean and Edward Griffin and Nancy and Peter Rascoe.

To my editor, the amazing Jennifer Enderlin, I offer everlasting gratitude for whipping me, and the girls of Ebbtide, into shape. Many thanks also to the team at St. Martin's Press, including but not limited to the fabulous Sally Richardson, Matthew Shear, Matthew Baldacci, John Karle, John Murphy, and Dori Weintraub. The best damn agent in the whole world, Stuart Krichevsky, guided and presided, and was, as always, a beacon of light when things got funky, so huge thanks to him and the girls of SKLA.

Family might be listed last, but they come first in my heart, and in my thanks—to Tom, Andy, Katie, Mark, and yes, Molly, all my love, now and always.

1

It was not an auspicious beginning for a vacation, let alone for a new life. The rain chased her all the way down the East Coast, slashing at the windshield, pounding her car from every angle. Between the backwash from a continuous stream of eighteen-wheelers blowing past her at eighty miles an hour (in contrast to her own sedate fifty-five mph) and violent gusts of wind from the storm, it was all she could do to stay on the roadway.

It was her own fault, Ellis decided. She should have stuck to her original plan. She should have gotten up at a sensible hour, at least waiting until daylight to start the drive from Philadelphia to North Carolina. Instead, on some insane impulse, she'd simply locked up the town house and driven off shortly after midnight.

It was a most un-Ellis-like decision. But then, her old life, back there in Philly, was gone. And somewhere, on that long drive south, she had subconsciously decided that the seeds of a new life must be waiting, at the beach. In August.

Ellis took a deep breath and rolled her shoulders, first forward, and then backwards, trying to work out the kinks from six hours of driving. She reached for the commuter mug of coffee in the Accord's cup holder and took a long sip, hoping it would clear the fatigue fog.

An hour later, she saw the sign: Nags Head, 132 miles. She smiled. The rain had slowed to a light drizzle. She should arrive at the house, which was called Ebbtide, by around seven.

Her smile faded. What had she been thinking? Check-in was at 2 P.M., according to the renter's agreement she'd signed.

She composed a mental e-mail to herself: To: EllisSullivan@hotmail.com. From: EllisSullivan@hotmail.com. Subject: Failure to plan = plan to fail.

But the memo would have to wait. The highway rose and she found herself on a long, gently arching bridge. One more damned bridge. Surely it was the last. The Chesapeake Bay Bridge had nearly done her in. She felt her jaw clench tightly. Her fingertips clamped the steering wheel, and her heart raced. A bead of sweat trickled down her back.

Nags Head was on the Outer Banks of North Carolina. She'd studied her guidebooks, maps, and AAA Triptik for weeks now. She knew the island's geography, even its topography, intimately. But she'd refused to allow herself to focus on the bridge issue. Because the fact was, as the girls knew all too well, bridges—even wimpy little bridges like the Sam Varnedoe that separated Whitemarsh and Wilmington islands back home in Savannah—scared the living bejeezus out of Ellis Sullivan.

She kept her eyes straight ahead, not daring to look right or left at the water flowing under the bridge. When she'd finally crossed the bridge, her hands were clammy, her T-shirt sweat-soaked.

Now she was on the Outer Banks proper. Signs for the little towns flashed by: Corolla, Duck, Southern Shores, Kitty Hawk, Avalon Beach. The sun rose, and she was somehow shocked at how densely developed the beach-front was here. She'd expected to see clumps of sea oats silhouetted against sparkling blue water; sailboats bobbing at anchor; great, gray shingled houses staring moodily out to sea; the occasional lighthouse. The reality was that, so far, what she'd seen of the storied Outer Banks could just as well have been the Jersey shore, Myrtle Beach, Fort Lauderdale, or any other East Coast tourist resort—meaning miles and miles of hotels and motels, restaurants, and strip shopping centers lining both sides of the road, and a shoreline packed with cheek-to-jowl condo complexes and huge, pastel-painted beach houses.

She followed Route 12 south, and when the GPS computerized voice instructed her to turn left and then right, she knew she was getting close. Virginia Dare Trail was the beach road. Here, at least, there was a little bit of elbow room between the houses. Once or twice she actually caught a glimpse of sand dunes and sea oat plumes. Finally, the well-modulated woman's voice announced cheerily, "Arrive at destination, on left."

Ellis slowed the car and stared. A long crushed-shell drive led through a weedy patch of sand. There was a mailbox at the curb, with a sun-bleached cedar sign in the cutout shape of a whale. EBBTIDE was painted on the sign in faded white letters. The driveway ended at what looked like a two-story garage. The wood-shingled structure was a weathered grayish-brownish affair. Through a set of open wooden garage doors, she spotted a beat-up tan Bronco with a red surfboard strapped to the rooftop rack.

To the side of the garage, a rambling three-story wood-frame house arose from a set of wooden stairs. Stretched across the front of the house was a long, open porch. A row of rocking chairs marched across the porch, and a gaudy striped beach towel was draped carelessly across a railing. From the sandy side yard, a wooden walkway led up and over a towering sand dune.

On an impulse, she pulled the car into the next driveway. Here, there was no house at all, only the charred remains of a concrete-block foundation, along with some blackened timbers. A black-and-orange NO TRESPASSING sign was posted on a block wall. Ellis put the Accord in park and got out of the car, her cramped legs and back screaming in protest. The air was already hot and muggy. She did a couple of deep knee bends, scanning the yard next door for any signs of life. Had the earlier renters already checked out? Or did the Bronco in the garage belong to somebody who was still enjoying a last hour or two on the beach before it was time to head home?

She strolled over to the mailbox and peered up at the house. Their house, at least for the month of August. Ellis intended to make every hour of this month count.

"Ebbtide," she said aloud, satisfied that the exterior of the house, at least, seemed to match the photo she'd spotted in the Vacation Rentals by Owner listing. Of course, that photo had also shown an inviting green lawn dotted with billowing blue hydrangeas and a hot-pink bicycle built for two with a charming wicker basket leaning up against a rose-covered picket fence. None of these were in evidence now. In fact, the only thing in evidence in what passed for a yard, besides a bumper crop of weeds, was a busted-up Styrofoam cooler full of empty malt liquor cans and a sodden heap of yellowing newspapers, still in their plastic wrappers.

She glanced down at her watch. She had half a day to kill until check-in. Being Ellis, she'd already planned to arrive hours before the others. The extra time would give her a chance to go to the grocery store, prepare their first night's dinner, get the house situated. Linens were not included in the house rental, so she'd brought enough sheets and towels for everybody, just in case. And yes, she would have first crack at choosing her bedroom, but since she *had* done all the legwork finding the house and planning this trip, would anybody really mind?

Well, maybe Willa would mind. She was only older than the others by twenty months, but really, she could be so pushy and bossy. It would be just like Willa to accuse Ellis of hogging the best bedroom. Which she had no intention of doing. She just didn't want a bedroom facing the street and a lot of noise. She was a light sleeper—and she had a lot of thinking to do. And anyway, as the only single woman in the group, she was used to her own space. Too used to it, she thought wryly.

She was dying to see Ebbtide up close. She glanced up and down the road. There was no sign of traffic. Just another sleepy summer morning at the beach. Maybe it wouldn't hurt to walk up the driveway of the burnt-out house to see what she could see. Technically, she knew, it was trespassing. But it wasn't like she was looting the place. What was left to loot?

Quickly, before she lost her nerve, Ellis trotted up the crushed oyster-shell drive. Another wooden boardwalk and a set of stairs leading up and over the sand dune, just like the one at Ebbtide, seemed to have survived the fire that had taken this house. She trod the steps quickly, not wanting to be seen from the road.

There was a shed-roofed deck at the top of the dunes. At one time it would have been an amazing place to sit and sip a cocktail and enjoy the ocean breezes. But not now. Some of the decking had rotted out, and the railings missed pickets in several places. A couple of broken plastic lawn chairs lay sprawled on their side, but it was the view that captured Ellis's attention. From here she could see the Nags Head she'd imagined. The dunes, covered with sea oats, beach plums, and shrubs whose names she didn't know, sloped down to meet a wide, white beach. The tide was out, and the Atlantic Ocean sparkled gray-blue below. Here and there, people walked along the shore, stooping to pick up shells.

"Perfect!" Ellis exclaimed. Just then, she heard the slap of a wooden screen door. Turning, she saw movement from the second-floor apartment over the garage at Ebbtide. That apartment had a small wooden deck wrapping around the sides and back of it. As she watched, a man walked out onto the deck. She could see him clearly—good Lord—he was in his underwear.

The man was barefoot, deeply tanned, with unkempt sun-bleached brownish hair. A pair of baggy white boxer briefs hung low on his slim hips. He turned, faced the water, yawned and stretched. And then, while Ellis watched, slack-jawed with amazement and disgust, he quite casually proceeded to pee off the edge of the deck.

He took his own good time about it too. Ellis was rooted to the spot where she stood, her face crimson with embarrassment. When he was finally finished, he stretched and turned. And that's when he spotted her, a lone figure in hot pink capris and a white T-shirt, her long dark hair blowing in the breeze coming off the beach.

The man gave her a nonchalant smile. His teeth were white and even, and from here she could see the golden stubble of a days-old beard. He waved casually. "Hey," he called. "How ya doin'?"

Ellis managed a strangled "Hey." And then she fled down the stairs as fast as her flip-flop-shod feet would take her.

2

Ellis jumped in the Accord and backed out onto the roadway so quickly she nearly mowed over the Ebbtide mailbox. That's what she got for trespassing, she thought. A bird's-eye view of a pervert. She checked over her shoulder, back towards that garage apartment, to see if the man would reemerge from the deck to see where she'd gone. But there was no sign of him now.

Hopefully, she thought, he was the owner of that Bronco parked in the garage. Hopefully, he would be checking out of Ebbtide any time now, and he would be long gone by her check-in. Hopefully.

But what was she going to do with herself until then? There was an outlet mall down the road, but it probably didn't open until ten. And she needed to get groceries, but she didn't want her refrigerated goods to sit in her hot car for the hours until check-in.

She drove aimlessly down the road until she came to a restaurant whose marquee promised BREAKFAST SERVED ALL DAY—EVERY DAY. The parking lot was full. She even spotted a couple of UPS trucks, which, her father had told her years ago, meant the joint must be half decent.

The hostess showed her to a table near the window, and Ellis ordered scrambled eggs, turkey sausage, and an English muffin. Unbuttered. No coffee. She was wide awake now. Instead, she asked for ice water and grapefruit juice.

When the food came, she ate slowly, willing the time to pass quickly. The restaurant was noisy with small children laughing and running between the tables and the excited chatter of vacationing families and friends. When she'd finished eating, Ellis took out her iPhone to check her e-mails.

The iPhone was new. All those years she'd worked at the bank, the Black-Berry clipped securely to the outside of her pocketbook had been her lifeline to her workday world. It was the first thing she touched every morning, weekends included—even before she brushed her teeth and showered—and it was the last thing she checked at night, before drifting off to sleep.

But two weeks ago, an e-mail on that BlackBerry had summoned her to a meeting with Phyllis K. Stone in human resources. Around the company, Ms. Stone was known as "the grim reaper" or "Stonehenge." But she'd always been perfectly nice to Ellis on the rare occasions they'd had dealings. On that particular day, Ellis had assumed she was going to be given her new health-care packet. But the packet which Ms. Stone silently slid across her desk to Ellis had nothing to do with deductibles or co-pays. BancAtlantic, her employer for the past eleven years, was, Ms. Stone said blandly, being swallowed up—no, *acquired* was the exact word—by CityGroup, Inc.

"Obviously, CityGroup has its own marketing department," Ms. Stone went on. "And because their concern at this time is in cost savings and maximum efficiency as well as financial stability for our stockholders, the executive committee has decided that BancAtlantic's marketing group will be extraneous."

Ellis wasn't sure she understood what Ms. Stone was saying. "Extraneous? Does that mean I'll be transferred over to the CityGroup side?"

Ms. Stone slid the packet a millimeter closer to Ellis. "I'm afraid not."

Ellis felt her mouth go dry and her palms begin to sweat. She liked her job, liked the people she worked with, loved the lifestyle it afforded her: the town house in a good neighborhood, business travel with a generous expense account, a new car every three years. "Then," she said, her voice quavering a little, "I'll be offered another position within the bank? I mean, it's not like I was born into marketing. My degree is in finance, and before I joined Banc-Atlantic..."

Ms. Stone's lips pursed slightly. Her fuchsia lipstick had feathered into the deep creases in her upper lip. She had a mustache too. Ellis wondered why she didn't wax it, or at least get it bleached.

Now Ms. Stone was tapping the file folder again. It had a glossy photograph of BancAtlantic's granite-and-chrome headquarters building on it, and the words TRANSITIONS FOR TOMORROW were superimposed across the photo.

There was a clattering outside the window of Ms. Stone's seventh-floor office. Ellis looked up and saw a window-washing apparatus glide slowly past. But the men on the apparatus were not window washers. They wore dark jumpsuits, and they were wrestling with a huge chrome logo, consisting of eight-foot-high letters: CG, in flowing script.

It occurred to Ellis that the bank's new owners were not waiting until tomorrow for transitions.

"This is your separation package," Ms. Stone said quietly. "You'll find it's quite generous. You'll have your pension, of course. Your buyout will give you two weeks' salary for every year of your service with the institution."

"Institution?" Ellis said dully.

"BancAtlantic," Ms. Stone reminded her. "Although," she said, glancing down at the wristwatch strapped to her unnaturally narrow wrist, "as of three minutes ago, BancAtlantic ceased to exist. We're CityGroup now. It's an exciting time, isn't it?"

Somehow, Ellis thought, she would not have chosen "exciting" as the adjective to describe this moment. She finally reached over and picked up the file folder which Ms. Stone had been inching towards her. She rifled through the contents. It contained legal forms and memos, and just looking at the fine print of the documents made a vein in her forehead throb. She had to get back to her office, read the documents, and try to process everything.

She stood up. "How long?" she asked. "I've got a big project I've been working on, and the report should be done by next week."

Ms. Stone blinked. Ellis could have sworn she hadn't seen the woman blink before. Ever.

"Oh," Ms. Stone said. "I thought you understood. Your termination is immediate."

"Like, right now?"

"I'm afraid so," Ms. Stone said, holding out her hand, palm up, expectantly.

Ellis Sullivan was not normally a woman given to sarcasm. But somehow, the occasion seemed to cry out for . . . something.

"What?" Ellis said hotly. "It's not enough you just *fired* me? You took my job, my career, eleven years of my life? And for that I get, what? Twenty-two weeks of pay? Are you *freakin'* kidding me? What do you want now, lady? A kidney? My spleen maybe?"

Ms. Stone's mustachioed upper lip twitched. "That's entirely uncalled for," she said, her voice tight. "This is purely a professional business decision made by the executive committee. Please don't try to make it personal."

"Not personal?" Ellis cried, fighting back tears.

"Not in the least," Ms. Stone said. She stood up now. She was a good six inches shorter than Ellis. She was holding out her hand again. "I'm going to have to ask for your employee security badge."

Ellis ripped the laminated badge from the beaded silk cord that hung around her neck, and flung it right in Ms. Stone's face. The woman blinked again, and then ducked, but the badge glanced off her chin before falling onto the desktop.

"The cord's mine," Ellis said. "It's not company property."

"Fine," Ms. Stone said. "Understood. And now I'll need your BlackBerry. The company's BlackBerry, that is."

Ellis winced. "I don't have it with me," she admitted. "It's in my office. I'll drop it off here after I clean out my desk."

Ms. Stone smirked. "Your desk has already been cleaned out." She crossed to the door and opened it. A security guard in an unfamiliar charcoal gray uniform stood in the hallway, clutching a large cardboard carton. Sticking out of the top of the carton was a goofy red-plush stuffed bear wearing a T-shirt with the BancAtlantic logo stitched in green script. Ellis had won the bear two years ago at the department's Christmas party. Her Louis Vuitton pocketbook, the one she'd splurged on after her last promotion, was draped across the security guard's arm.

Ms. Stone jerked her head in the direction of the pocketbook. Ellis took it from the guard, reached inside, and unclipped the BlackBerry.

Ms. Stone ducked, but all the fight had suddenly drained from Ellis. She put the BlackBerry on the edge of the desk, turned and followed the waiting security guard down the hall and into the elevator.

There she held out her arms for the carton. "I can take it from here. Don't worry. I won't come running back upstairs with an Uzi or anything."

The guard shrugged. "Sorry I've gotta escort you all the way out of the building. It's policy."

She punched the "B" button on the control panel, and they rode the elevator down to the basement parking garage in silence. The guard followed her to the Accord. She opened the trunk and he put the carton inside it, handing her a slip of paper that had been lying on top of the contents.

"It's an inventory of everything from your office," he said apologetically. "If you could just initial it, you know?"

She scrawled her initials at the bottom of the page without even looking at the list and handed it back to him.

He nodded. "This really sucks, man. I hate this part."

"Not your first termination of the day?"

"You're my eleventh," he said gloomily. "After lunch, we've got commercial loan. The whole stinkin' department."

Ellis nodded. It was no consolation to know that the rest of her company was being disassembled and discarded, one department at a time. "See ya," she said, knowing she wouldn't.

She hadn't known what to do with herself for the first two days after what she'd come to think of as T-day. The first morning, she'd gotten up at her usual 6 A.M. and groped in the dark for her BlackBerry. After a brief moment of panic, she'd remembered that the bank had repossessed it, along with her former identity. Then, groaning, she settled back into the bed, realizing she really had no pressing need to get up.

What followed was a week of bereavement. She went two days without bathing, lived in grungy yoga pants and sweatshirts, subsisted on a steady diet of cold cereal and daytime television because she couldn't bear leaving the town house. Anyway, where would she go? After seven straight days of therapy courtesy of Dr. Phil reruns, she'd forced herself to go out and buy the iPhone. She even bought a perky pink rubber jacket for the thing.

Since she'd never had any e-mail address other than her BancAtlantic one, she set herself up with a Hotmail account and e-mailed everybody she could think of that she had a new e-mail. There had been the inevitable flurry of replies from friends wanting to know what was up.

She couldn't stand the idea of anybody pitying her, especially since she already had enough self-pity to go around, so she made up a peppy reply: "Midlife career adjustment! Time to stop and smell the roses! Details to follow."

But there were no details. Not yet. This trip with the girls, which she'd been plotting since April, when they'd all been together down in Savannah for Julia's mother's funeral, was the only thing that had kept her going since she'd lost her job. A small, insistent voice in the back of her head kept telling her she should have canceled the trip, should have saved her money, should have put herself right back out there on the job market.

And she'd replied to that small, insistent voice. Shut. The. Hell. Up.

It was almost August. No way was she canceling this beach trip.

So here she was, sitting in a restaurant in Nags Head, North Carolina, and two weeks' worth of her severance package had already been eaten up. She didn't care. In the past five years, she'd taken exactly one week of vacation per year, spending Christmas with her mother and aunt at the condo down in Sarasota, listening to her mother bicker with Aunt Claudia.

In April, Ellis had sat next to Julia in the front row of Blessed Sacrament Church in Savannah. Dorie sat on the other side of Julia, and Willa sat beside Dorie. Booker, Julia's boyfriend of many years, couldn't make the trip from London. All four of the girls clutched each other's hands as a young priest none of them recognized, Father Tranh, said the Mass of Christian Burial for Catherine Donohue Capelli. Later, back at the Capelli house, after all the funeral-goers had finally cleared out, the girls had taken off their funeral dresses, climbed into pajamas, and sprawled out on the double bed in Julia's old bedroom, just like they'd done all those Friday nights in the old days. Only this time, instead of sipping Pabst Blue Ribbon stolen from Mr. Capelli's beer fridge in the garage, they'd gotten shit-faced on a pitcher of cosmos.

And that's when they'd hatched the plan. No more catching up at funerals. Ellis's father had died two years earlier, and Mr. Capelli had been gone, what? Six years? No more of that, Julia had declared, waving the empty pitcher in the air.

"We're gonna go away together," she announced. "To the beach. All of us." She'd looked over at Dorie, the newlywed of the group, and added, meaningfully, "Just us girls."

The group had elected Ellis, the planner, the organizer, ruthlessly efficient Ellis, to put the trip together. And that's what she'd done. And now here she was, jobless, but with the whole month of August to spend in a summer rental with her best friends. Plus Willa, Dorie's sister, who'd invited herself along.

She felt positively giddy at the prospect. The amber-hued summers of her girlhood had been the sweetest of her life. She and Dorie and Julia had been inseparable, spending weeks at a time at Julia's grandmother's rambling cottage on Tybee Island, lazing around the beach during the day, spending hours getting ready to go out in the evenings.

Dorie always trailed a wake of would-be boyfriends, so they'd traveled in a pack, cruising the beach road in Julia's mother's big Fleetwood Caddy. It hadn't mattered that Ellis didn't have her own boyfriend. The Caddy was white with a moonroof and the fifth tire mounted on the trunk, a total pimp car, which they all thought screamingly hysterical—that Julia's churchgoing mother drove a pimpmobile. They loved the Fleetwood because it could fit six or seven people on its big leather bench seats. They'd roll the windows down and blast their favorite song, screaming the tagline—"WHOOMP, There It Is!"—over and over again, and the Fleetwood would rock with the heavy bass beat.

They'd dance at a club whose name Ellis had long since forgotten, but she could still remember the boy she'd met and danced with all night long the last summer weekend before her sophomore year of college. His name was Nick, and he went to Boston College, and she'd gladly let him grope her while they swayed to "I Swear," and she'd allowed herself to fantasize that it was Nick who was promising—by the moon and the stars above—to love her forever. Then school had started, and he'd e-mailed a couple of times, and then nothing.

Ellis looked down at the iPhone. She opened an e-mail window and typed in the address:

Mr.Culpepper@Ebbtide.com.

Dear Mr. Culpepper. I realize that my group's check-in time for Ebbtide technically isn't until 2 p.m. today, but I find myself in the area earlier than planned, and wonder if it would be possible to have access to the house any earlier. Say around noon? I'd be totally grateful. Sincerely, Ellis Sullivan.

She pushed the send button and a moment later heard the soft whooshing noise that notified her the message had been sent. Not for the first time, she pictured Mr. Culpepper as a wizened but kindly old duffer. She imagined him in a faded but starched Hawaiian shirt, with knobby knees protruding below madras Bermuda shorts, and wearing high black socks and beat-up sandals. His face would be weathered, his head nearly bald. He would take an instant liking to her and the girls, calling them "sweetheart" and "dearie."

She couldn't wait to meet Mr. Culpepper in person.

3

Maryn drove south, switching between the interstate and winding back roads, with no specific destination in mind. Away. That was the only place she knew she was going. Away from her home, what little family she had left. Away from Biggie; that one really hurt. But there was nothing she could do about that. She could still see Biggie's melting brown eyes watching as she rushed around the house, throwing her things in a duffle bag. He'd followed her from room to room, and then, when she was about to leave, he'd met her at the back door, his red leather leash in his mouth, convinced they were going to the dog park.

It broke her heart to leave Biggie behind. She told herself the aging golden retriever would be all right. He would never harm Biggie, not even to get back at her. He adored Biggie, had raised him from a puppy. Biggie had been there before her, and he would be there after her. Wouldn't he? Anyway, the main thing was that she had to get away. From him. And that meant leaving Biggie behind.

Thinking of him, she twisted the diamond solitaire on her ring finger. She'd wanted to fling it at him so many times, tell him yes, he'd bought her with it, but he'd gotten the deal of a lifetime. She'd almost left it behind, along with her other belongings. But at the last second, she decided she would keep wearing it, a reminder—as if she needed one—of how easily and cheaply she'd sold herself to the devil.

Maryn glanced down at her arm. Her sleeve hid them, but she could still feel the bracelet of ugly purple bruises on her left forearm. Another reminder of the real Don Shackleford. The bruises would fade, she knew, but she doubted she would ever forget his icy rage, the way he'd so easily clamped a hand around her arm—squeezing until she'd cried out in agony, his expression never changing as he told her exactly what he'd do to her if he ever caught her snooping around in his private business again.

"I'll bury you," he'd said, a strange light coming into his pale blue eyes. "Someplace where you'll never be found. Nobody will even know you're missing until it's too late. Not Adam, not your mother, nobody will know what happened, where Maryn has gone." He'd smiled at the thought of that. A moment later, he'd released her arm, but not before bending his head to her forearm and tenderly kissing the angry red welts he'd left there.

By the time she heard his Escalade roar out of the driveway, she'd already started planning her escape.

She locked the front door and ran to her bedroom. When she retrieved the money from the Ugg boots at the back of her closet, she was startled to discover that she'd amassed nearly six thousand dollars. Her seed money was twenty-seven hundred dollars in winnings from an April trip to Atlantic City, money she'd won at blackjack, and which she'd told Don she'd spent on clothes and shoes. Lying to him came easily to her and didn't seem wrong. The rest of the money was added in spurts: a twenty picked up from the wad of bills Don tossed on his dresser at night, a hundred saved back from the money she told him she needed for a new jacket, five hundred dollars realized when she exchanged the ridiculously expensive (and ugly) watch he'd given her for her birthday for a more suitable model.

Maryn couldn't say why she'd been squirreling away those twenties and fifties. Was it really for that Hermès Kelly bag she'd been eyeing, or was it more the vague memory of her mother's cynical advice, delivered with a cigarette dangling from colorless lips? "A woman always needs to have her own money. Always. Get-outta-town money."

Thank God for the one good piece of advice her mama had given her. The packing hadn't taken long. Twenty minutes? She'd changed blouses, putting on a long-sleeved silk top to hide the bruises on her arm. So here she was, back on the road. Again.

How long had she been driving? Her eyes burned with exhaustion, her arms and shoulders ached. She should stop soon. Stop for sleep. For food, although her stomach roiled at the thought of eating.

She'd crossed the Virginia line, saw that she was in North Carolina now. The sun was coming up. She flipped the Dior sunglasses down over her eyes and squinted at a billboard advertising a place called The Buccaneer, a motel on Nags Head.

Nags Head. Her parents had taken her to Nags Head the summer after her father was transferred to Fort Bragg, in Fayetteville, North Carolina. She'd been what, twelve? They'd stayed in a tiny motel, right on the beach, and her father took her fishing on the pier, just the two of them. The motel had a pool and a little coffee shop, and they'd eaten out every night, a real treat. One night they'd played putt-putt golf, another time they rode bumper cars in an amusement park.

Had that been the last happy summer? The divorce came a year later. Just as she was settling into her new school. Not that she'd made many friends there. She'd been a goofy-looking kid, all knees and elbows, with hair the color of dirty dishwater and a head too big for her body. Maryn had been appalled when she became the first girl in her sixth-grade class to need a bra. Her mother, of course, had celebrated this fact by buying Maryn the tightest-fitting tank top she could find. "If you got it, flaunt it," Mama told her. To avoid a fight, Maryn wore the tank, but topped it with a baggy shirt the minute she left the house for school.

She'd just started cracking the social code of her new school when Mama loaded her into the faded blue Buick that May and announced they were going to visit Aunt Patsy in New Jersey. "If you think I'm stayin' in this godforsaken excuse of a town while your daddy parades around with that whore girlfriend of his, you've got another think coming," Mama said, throwing the car into reverse and slamming into the mailbox at the end of the driveway. She didn't even stop to look at her crumpled rear fender.

Visit? How about move in with her mother's older sister, Aunt Patsy, a part-time hairdresser and full-time alcoholic? By fall, Maryn had emerged from puberty and entered junior high, two inches taller, wearing a B cup, tight-fitting new acid-washed Jordache jeans, and a glamorous blond hairdo courtesy of Aunt Patsy. Also by fall, Maryn's mother had joined Aunt Patsy at the hair salon—and the liquor store.

Maryn's first few weeks of junior high had been a triumph. A petite brunette named Brooke sat in front of her in homeroom and took pity on the new girl, inviting her to sit at the cool girls' table at lunch. She'd gotten invited to sleepovers and skating parties and spent hours on the phone with Brooke every night, rehashing who-likes-who, with her mother and aunt relishing every second of Maryn's newfound popularity.

In October, she'd gotten invited to her first boy-girl function: a Halloween party. The invitation threw her mother and Aunt Patsy into a frenzy of sewing and thrift-store shopping. On the appointed night, Maryn slithered into Heather Palumbo's basement rec room dressed in a towering black wig and a flowing, long-sleeved black sheath with a deeply plunging neckline. Her face had been whitened with pancake makeup, her eyes rimmed and outlined with stark black liner, her lips lacquered bloodred, matching her inch-long fake red fingernails.

All these years later, Maryn could still remember the impact her entry had on the party. Brooke and Heather and Colleen, dressed in '50s-era poodle skirts, bobby socks, and letter sweaters, gathered in a circle around her, staring at her as though she'd just been beamed down from another planet. "What are you supposed to be?" Colleen demanded, hands on hips.

"You know," Maryn said, taken aback. "Elvira. Mistress of the Dark. Like from TV?"

"You look," Heather sneered, "like a prostitute."

Maryn's cheeks burned with shame. She'd slipped upstairs to try to call her mother and ask her to come pick her up early, but Mama and Patsy had dropped her off and headed straight to Harlow's, their favorite bar.

When Maryn got back to the basement, she'd found that the girls had turned on her. The boys, however, had been a different story. They'd swarmed around her, laughing and talking too loud, bringing her Cokes and asking her to dance. In what seemed like an instant, she'd simultaneously become both the belle of the ball and the school skank—depending on your gender.

If Brooke and Colleen quit calling, Alex and Nathan and Jordan (an eighth-grader) took up the slack. At first, Maryn was devastated at the loss of Brooke's friendship. But her mother and aunt reveled in her sudden status as a femme fatale.

"You don't need those silly little bitches," Aunt Patsy advised. "Every single one of them is jealous of you because you're cuter and the boys like you better than them." As the weeks and months passed, and it became clear that she held a surprising new power over the opposite sex, Maryn decided she liked boys just fine.

Not that she didn't miss having a best girlfriend. When Aunt Patsy lost her job at the Stylesetter Salon at the beginning of Maryn's sophomore year of high school, forcing them to move to a smaller rental house in a different school district, Maryn made a conscious decision to reinvent herself.

Before school started that year, Maryn hung out at the mall, studying what the other girls were wearing. She bought button-fly Levi's 501 jeans and pastel Gap tees, quit bleaching her hair, and toned down her makeup.

And for what? Despite her best efforts, Maryn found herself frozen out of the cliques and circles in her new school. So when Wesley Bates, the cute, dumb jock who was her chemistry lab partner, asked her out for the third Saturday in a row, Maryn had finally agreed to go, even though she'd heard through the school grapevine that Wesley was supposedly dating a girl named Janelle Rivenbark.

One date. She'd gone out with Wes exactly once, but to Janelle Rivenbark and her coven, that had been more than enough to seal her fate. The next Monday, she'd found hate notes stuffed into her locker. Every night, there were crank phone calls and hang ups. Bags of flaming dog poop were left on her doorstep, her mother's car was egged, her aunt's yard festooned with toilet paper on a weekly basis.

"Screw 'em," her mother advised, and finally, Maryn had come to the same conclusion. From that point on, Maryn made her own rules. She was never without at least one boyfriend and wasn't shy about stealing a boy, especially if his previous girlfriend was friends with Janelle Rivenbark.

All the while, her mama and Aunt Patsy cheered her on, living vicariously through her romantic conquests. No matter how late she came in on a Friday or Saturday night, her mother waited up, eager to rehash the night's events.

Thinking of her mother now made Maryn wince. When had they last talked—three, four months ago? Maryn's eyelids drooped, then fluttered. She had to get off the road. She hit the button to open her window, let in some fresh air. Nags Head, she decided. She would stop in Nags Head. It was far enough away from New Jersey. Far enough away from him.

4

Ty Bazemore went around to the back of the house and tried the door-knob. Good. It was locked. God knows, there was nothing really valuable in the house, but it was better to make sure about stuff like this.

He unlocked the door and stepped inside the kitchen. "Christ!" he muttered, looking around. The place was a disaster. Dirty pots and pans were piled in a sink full of sludgy gray water. Every dish in the house seemed to be piled on the countertop. The trash can in the corner was overflowing with empty beer cans and wine bottles, and there was a distinct fishy smell.

He peered down into a pot that had been left on the stove top. Yup. It was full of shrimp peels, and it had been there a day or two. He picked up the pot and went to dump it out, and for the first time, noticed the slurping sound his flip-flops were making on the linoleum floor.

He looked down and lifted his right heel slightly. The flip-flop stuck to the floor.

"Fuckin' college punks," he said aloud.

He should have known better. The e-mail address for their reservation had been Cooter@Gamecocks.com. The VRBO and Craigslist ads clearly stated that rental of the house was restricted to adults. But Cooter and company had paid for a week in advance, and the American Express card they'd paid with had gone through with no problem. He'd had a bad feeling about it from the start, but, hey, thirty-four hundred dollars was nothing to sneeze at, not these days.

So when the caravan of cars had pulled into the driveway—first a stripped-down Jeep, then two pickup trucks and a lime green VW bug convertible carrying four half-drunk chicks—he'd made up his mind to ignore them. He'd watched with a sinking heart, though, as sixteen college kids piled into the house. And that was just the first night.

The ad specifically stated that the house slept a maximum of ten people—which wasn't totally accurate, since two of those people would have to be willing to bed down on the butt-sprung living room sleeper sofa he'd picked up off a curb back in March.

With a sigh, Ty went out to the back porch and dragged in the big-wheeled garbage can. He grabbed his janitor's bucket and mop and the battered Food Lion grocery cart some other little college pricks had left at the back door earlier in the summer, which now contained his cleaning supplies.

Not for the first time, Ty pondered the irony of his situation. Maybe his old man had been right. Maybe, if he'd stayed in law school, he'd be sitting pretty at some white-shoe law firm in Manhattan.

Maybe he'd still be with Kendra too. Nah, probably not. But maybe he'd have a fatty mutual fund, maybe he'd be driving a Jag, wintering in Cabo, or at least Key West. Maybe he shouldn't have sunk every last dime and mortgaged himself to the hilt trying to save Ebbtide. *Told you not to buy that dump.*

Maybe, if he'd listened to his old man, he wouldn't be living in a tiny garage apartment, staring at a computer screen all night 'til he was glassy-eyed and brain-dead. Maybe he wouldn't be cleaning toilets by day and worrying that the next phone call or e-mail would mean the end of all of it.

The clock was ticking. He had less than six weeks left to save Ebbtide. Otherwise, come September 15, the house would be auctioned off on the steps of the Dare County courthouse. He'd be out on the streets, jobless, homeless. And his old man would stand there, shaking his head. Kendra, his ex, and

Ryan, her new husband, aka Fuckface, would be right there with his old man, oozing phony sympathy. They might not say it, but they'd all be thinking it. *Told you so.*

Ty looked out the kitchen window. If he leaned out, he could see the waves rolling in on the beach. They had some size to them this morning. His stomach growled loudly. If he got this pigsty cleaned up, in say, three hours, he'd have just enough time to make it to Abigail's before they ran out of the Saturday lunch special: mahi-mahi tacos.

He pulled the grocery cart into the combined living/dining room at the front of the house and his eyes widened at the degree of destruction his tenants had wrought there. Armchairs, tables, and lamps were upended. The battered wooden floor wore a thick carpet of beach sand, and the sofa cushions were lined up end to end in front of the fireplace, where a trio of untwisted wire coat hangers suggested an impromptu wienie roast. Which would have been fine, if the fireplace damper had been opened, which it hadn't. Fingers of greasy black soot marred the white mantel, which Ty had repainted in June. His grandfather's huge, framed navigational map of Currituck Sound, which had hung over said mantel, was askew on its hanger, its glass shattered. Tufts of stuffing poked out of one of the sofa cushions, which had a baseball-sized hole burnt into it. The unmistakable odor of stale beer and cheap weed lingered in the air.

"Christ," he repeated. He yanked his iPhone from the pocket of his baggy board shorts and scrolled over to the last e-mail he'd gotten from his good buddy, ol' Cooter.

He typed rapidly, his fingertips flying over the tiny keyboard.

"Hey Cooter," he wrote. "Kiss your $500 security deposit goodbye. Asshole. Sincerely, Mr. Culpepper, manager, Ebbtide.com."

When he got the notification that the message had been sent, he looked down at his incoming message box and sighed. Another e-mail from another pain in the ass. The PITAs were the reason he always communicated with his tenants by e-mail and never gave out his phone number. As far as they knew, Mr. Culpepper was a cranky old bastard who resided somewhere in the Internet. They didn't need to know that their landlord was actually the guy who lived over the garage, just a door knock away if the toilet didn't flush or you couldn't figure out how to use the remote control.

This particular PITA's name was Ellis Sullivan. He'd been peppering Ty with nit-picking questions for weeks now. From the tenor of the questions— should he bring his own linens, were there beach chairs, bicycles, a grill—Ty decided Ellis was undoubtedly gay. Straight guys, like ol' Cooter, just wanted to know the location of the nearest liquor store.

Ellis Sullivan and his friends were supposed to check in later today. The later the better, as far as Ty was concerned. God knew how long it would take to clean up the kitchen and living room. His shoulders sagged as he realized he hadn't even taken a look upstairs yet.

He was headed for the stairs when he became aware of a faint gurgling sound. It was coming from the bathroom tucked under the stairs. Funny, the door was closed and it didn't want to budge. He braced one leg against the doorjamb and yanked hard. The door flew open, and a torrent of foul-smelling water rushed out into the hallway.

"Shiiiit," Ty said. And he meant that literally.

Ellis took her time finishing breakfast. She checked her e-mails repeatedly, finding nothing new except for sale offers from Bloomingdale's and more e-mails from old friends at the bank, who'd also had unpleasant termination sessions with Stonehenge.

In the days following her downsizing (which was how she preferred to think of it), Ellis had been consumed with the injustice of her situation. She'd spent hours, days really, commiserating with her former colleagues. She'd joined a "I got jobbed by BancAtlantic" Facebook group and chatboard and had even attended a meet-up at a bar in the suburbs, where everybody had gotten sloppy drunk and teary-eyed about their dire situations.

No more, though, Ellis had resolved. She'd been a saver her whole life. Her father had left her a little inheritance, so her town house was paid for. Her car was paid off, and she'd wisely decided years ago against investing her pension funds in her own bank's stock. She was by no means wealthy, but she had a little cushion, and she refused to panic. Or so she told herself.

So she scrolled down the messages in her in-box, looking in vain for a reply to her message to Mr. Culpepper.

Finding none, she got out the printout of the VRBO ad for Ebbtide. Strange, the only thing it lacked was a contact number.

She frowned and tapped out a follow-up e-mail, reminding Mr. Culpepper of her request for an early check-in, and suggesting that he call her on her cell phone, to let her know the house was ready.

Finally, there was nothing else to do but kill some time at the outlet mall. But first, she'd just take a spin past the house, to see if the previous guests had checked out.

She cruised down Virginia Dare Trail, slowing as she came to the house, but there was a line of cars directly behind her, so she pulled into the driveway at Ebbtide.

Damn! The Bronco hadn't moved from the garage. But the broken cooler and beer bottles had been picked up since her last drive-by, and now a large wheeled garbage can overflowing with trash had been parked in the weedy area beside the mailbox. She craned her neck to try to see if there was any activity around the house.

She checked her e-mail in-box one more time. Nothing. Reluctantly, she decided to head for the outlets.

At one, Ty loaded the last load of damp towels into the dryer. Straightening, he looked out the window of the ground-floor laundry room just in time to see the same silver Accord slowly cruise past. This was the Accord's third pass in the past hour. What was up with that? It couldn't be one of the assholes from the bank, right? It was Saturday, for God's sake. Not that he had time to worry about it too much. As bad as the first floor of the house had been, the second floor was worse. Much worse.

It was a horror show, is what it was. The bathrooms held piles of wet, mildewed towels, and somebody had barfed in the shower stall. He'd found what looked like a dog turd in the closet in one of the front bedrooms. How the hell had they snuck a dog past him? And it must have been a friggin' Great Dane from the looks of things. The twin-bed mattresses from the back bedroom had been dragged out to the sleeping porch and piled on the floor, where last night's rain had given them a good soaking. Trash was strewn everywhere, and the wood-slat shades in two of the bedrooms looked like somebody had taken a baseball bat to them.

Ty had never worked as hard, or as feverishly. He had to replace the ruined twin-bed mattresses with a double bed he'd dragged out of the attic. The window shades were a total loss, so he rigged up some faded flowery curtains he found on a shelf at the back of the locked owner's closet on the ground floor. He shoveled and mopped and scoured and plunged until his back and legs ached, and his hands were rubbed raw from all the bleach and disinfectant.

Check-in time was only minutes away. He knew that without looking at his watch, because he'd received three more e-mails from friggin' Ellis Sullivan, wanting to know why he couldn't have access to the house, like, now. He hadn't bothered to answer. He was too busy staving off disaster.

And now he heard the tap of a car horn from the driveway. Not a blast, really, just a tap. He darted to the window and looked out. Christ! The silver Accord was parked in the driveway, blocking him in. And somebody was walking towards the door. No. It couldn't be. But it was. Oh yeah. It was totally the dark-headed chick who'd caught him whizzing off his deck this morning. Ty Bazemore was having himself quite a day, all right.

5

O n her third pass by Ebbtide, Ellis decided it was time to take action.
She'd wasted half a day already. After all, it was five after two, so these
people were now, officially, encroaching on her time. She pulled into the driveway and stared daggers at the Bronco, which was still parked in the garage.
She gave two polite taps on the Accord's horn. But the tap brought nobody
scurrying out of Ebbtide. She glanced down again at her iPhone, but there
was still no reply from Mr. Culpepper.

She parked and walked briskly towards the house and up the front steps.
She hesitated a moment before stepping onto the porch—her mother hadn't
raised her to be the sort of person who just went barging up to somebody
else's house. Even fifteen years of living up north couldn't change that.

"Hello?" she called softly. All was quiet. She took a good look around. The
porch was broad, and although the clapboard frame of the house was brownish gray and unpainted, the trim was painted white. The porch railing had
built-in benches that raked outwards, and a clothesline with bleached-out
wooden clothespins was looped between the posts, just under the rafters. Four

white rocking chairs were upended, two on either side of the front door. There was a galvanized tin pail half-filled with water sitting right beside the steps. PROPERTY OF EBBTIDE was painted on it in bright blue letters. She made her footsteps on the weathered gray porch boards loud and deliberate—sort of an early warning signal that she'd arrived.

The hinges of the rusted screen door squeaked loudly when she pulled it open. There was no doorbell, so she knocked briskly on the periwinkle blue door. And then she knocked, and banged, and knocked some more. She walked over to the window, and cupping her hands, peered into the darkened room. The place looked neat enough, but there was no sign of life.

Just then, her cell phone dinged softly, notifying her that she had an e-mail. She pulled it from the pocket of her capris and looked at the in-box.

To: EllisSullivan@hotmail.com
From: Mr.Culpepper@Ebbtide.com
Subject: Check-in: Sorry, it is our policy not to allow early check-ins. After 2 pm, you'll find the key to the front door in an envelope under the front doormat. Be advised there is a $25 fee for replacement keys. Enjoy your stay.

"Prick," Ellis muttered under her breath. She found the key, unlocked the door, and stepped inside.

It took a moment for her eyes to adjust to the darkened room. She found a light switch by the door and flipped it on. A ceiling fan hummed to life overhead.

"Hmm," she said, looking around. "Not too bad." She was in a large combined living/dining area. The walls were varnished knotty pine that had grown dark with age. The wood floors were still damp from a recent mopping, and the familiar smell of Murphy Oil soap hung in the air. Ellis smiled. Her grandmother always mopped her wood floors with Murphy soap. She decided this was a good omen.

The place was not fancy, but then she'd seen that in the photographs on the website. There was a faded oval rag rug on the living room floor, a large, lumpy sofa, and a couple of '80s-era armchairs facing a soot-blackened fire-place. The walls were dotted with what somebody considered beach-appropriate art—paint-by-number scenes depicting lighthouses, fishing boats, tropical birds, and waving palm trees.

A nicely framed nautical chart hung over the mantel, but its glass was badly cracked. Ellis leaned in and examined it with interest. She loved the names of the rivers and sounds. Pasquotank, Croatan, Ocracoke, Currituck, and her favorite, Mattamuskeet. But then, Ellis adored anything with names and numbers and places: maps, graphs, charts. As a child, she'd traded a doll—an expensive Madame Alexander dressed as Princess Diana, sent to her by her godmother in Atlanta—for her older brother Baylor's light-up globe. Baylor had turned around and given the doll to his little fourth-grade girl-friend.

Reluctantly, Ellis turned away from the chart. She had a car to unload and a house to set up.

The dining area held a long, scrubbed pine table and was surrounded by eight mismatched white-painted wooden chairs. A hideous plastic flower arrangement in a fish-shaped ceramic bowl was centered on a plastic doily in the middle of the table. It looked like somebody's granny had just gotten up to fetch another cup of tea.

A smallish kitchen opened off the dining area. It was clean, yes, but it had definitely seen better days. Here, the board walls were enameled white. The cupboards were painted white, with green glass knobs, and the counters were yellow linoleum with aluminum trim. Instead of upper cupboards there was a pair of shelf units with scalloped trim nailed to the wall on either side of a kitchen window that looked out onto the sand dunes. A small stack of chipped plates, two plastic cereal bowls, and some plastic convenience store go-cups were lined up along the shelves. In the middle of the room stood a large wooden table with a chipped turquoise enamel top. The floors were of cracked and faded yellow-and-white checkerboard linoleum tiles. There was a four-burner electric stove with curious push-button controls and a white refrigera-tor with rust spots around the corners of the doors.

Ellis opened the refrigerator, which was empty except for a box of baking soda, and then she peeked inside the freezer, which held two miserly alumi-num ice cube trays, but no automatic ice maker. She congratulated herself for picking up a five-pound bag of ice to keep the groceries she'd bought cold until check-in time. She noticed, to her chagrin, that there was no dishwasher. How had she missed this during all the hours she'd spent poring over the pictures and description of the house?

Never mind, she told herself. It was only for a month, and after all, four women—not to mention Dorie's husband, Stephen—were sharing this house. Everybody would pitch in and make do. It would be like Girl Scout camp, Ellis told herself. But with air-conditioning and indoor plumbing.

Finally, August had come. The month they'd all been planning for was becoming a reality. Ellis could not wait for the fun to begin. As she left the kitchen, she did an impromptu skip-step.

Ty tipped the Corona bottle to his lips and sucked down the last drop of icy beer. He wandered around the corner of the porch to check on his new ten-ant's whereabouts. Whoa! The silver Honda was pulled up directly in front of the house now, and as he watched, a woman in pink pants and a tight white T-shirt hurried towards the house, her arms full of grocery sacks. Her dark hair fanned out behind her in the breeze.

No. It couldn't be. Could it? "Ellis, dude," he whispered. "You're not gay. You're a girl."

In fact, she was *the* girl. The one from this morning. He'd really only got-ten a glimpse of her this morning, but now, as he leaned up against the side of his apartment, watching as she ferried endless suitcases, boxes, and bags into the house, her sandals flapping madly, he liked what he saw. Her figure was what his mother would have called "sturdy," with a high, round butt that probably wouldn't be considered fashionable, but which Ty found fascinating. She had her hair pulled back with some kind of a headband, and her oval face was bright pink in the blazing afternoon sun.

Intriguing. But no, he told himself sternly. This Ellis person might have a cute butt, but she'd already proven herself a major pain in his ass, a distraction he totally didn't need right now. His cell phone beeped. He picked it up and read the alert. Hodarthe, a pharmaceutical company out of Topeka, was announcing that the FDA had approved a promising new cholesterol-busting drug. Maybe it was time to dump some of his Pfizer stock. Or maybe it was too late. He needed to do some quick research.

Ellis Sullivan was leaning into the trunk of the Honda, her head obscured from view. He allowed himself one last, lingering gaze, and turned to go back to work.

Ellis had just finished emptying the first bag of groceries when she happened to look down at the counter where she'd stacked the rolls of paper towels, toilet paper, and coffee. Ants! A small army of the tiny ones her grandmother called sugar ants made a thin black line leading from the window sill to the back of the sink. Gak! She grabbed a paper towel, wet it, and frantically wiped at the counters. She flung the under-sink cupboard door open, looking for bug spray, but all she found was a damp sponge and a plastic jug of drain cleaner.

Ellis ran to the laundry room and then the linen closet, opening and closing doors, but there was no sign of bug spray. She shuddered. She'd hated bugs her whole life, and although she loved Savannah and the South, she never once missed its bugs after she moved to Philly. She fought the impulse to run out to the car and drive over to the first store to buy an arsenal of Raid, Black Flag, or whatever. They were only harmless little sugar ants, she told herself. But if they'd been roaches, she *so* would have been out of there.

She made herself return to the kitchen. She soaked a paper towel with drain cleaner and dabbed it on the windowsill. That oughta put a hurt on the little bastards, she thought grimly. At least until she could get some proper bug spray. She put away the rest of the groceries, lining up the cans of Diet Coke, the white wine, skim milk, half-and-half, and bottled water in the fridge. She found an empty cupboard and decided it would be the liquor cabinet. Vodka, gin, rum, scotch, and oh yes, whiskey for Julia, who'd become a die-hard Jack Daniel's fan at the tender age of fourteen, when she'd begun snitching it from her father's liquor cabinet, refilling the bottle with water. She'd bought mixers too: tonic water, 7-Up, grapefruit juice, and cranberry juice for Dorie, who liked Cape Cods. Funny, she couldn't remember what Willa liked to drink. Dorie's sister Willa was two years older than the rest of them, which meant that she was the girls' go-to source for liquor when they were teenagers, since her boyfriend Ricky was legal. Of course, Willa always charged them five bucks extra, which Ellis thought was pretty pissy of her. But then, that was Willa for you. Even way back then, she had an angle or an agenda—and it was all Willa, all the time.

Finally, Ellis got the kitchen just the way she wanted it. There was a fugly amateur seascape hanging on the wall beside the stove. She took it down and put it on top of the fridge and replaced it with the whiteboard she'd bought at the office-supply store. She'd spent a happy forty-five minutes ruling off the Kaper chart, carefully listing the assigned chores, the days of the week, and everybody's names with color-coded Sharpies. It was truly a work of art.

She stood back and admired her handiwork. Now, she thought, it was time to head upstairs and get the bedrooms organized.

But when she'd lugged her big wheeled suitcase upstairs and opened the first bedroom door, her heart sank.

The room was painted white, with battleship-gray painted board floors. It was large and square, and two big windows gave a glorious view of the impossibly blue summer sky. But it was nearly empty. A lonely little double bed was shoved into a corner, covered with a limp and faded pink-and-blue floral quilted spread. A pair of wafer-thin pillows sat at the head of the bed, and there was an olive-drab army blanket folded at the foot of it. There was no nightstand, no lamps or mirror, no chairs or even a luggage rack. A rickety-looking three-drawer pine dresser was against the wall opposite the bed. There was a miniscule closet with no coat hangers, not even a wire one. A small window beside the dresser held a rusty air conditioner.

"A window unit!" Ellis cried. The room was hot and stuffy. She walked out into the hallway and opened up the other two bedroom doors. They were furnished just as sparsely, and yes, each had a dinky little air conditioner stuck into a window.

She switched on the air conditioners in each room. They were loud and they rattled the windows, but within a few minutes, she could feel the temperatures begin to drop and her own boiling blood pressure start to simmer down.

Wait until she got hold of Mr. Culpepper! Nothing upstairs was as it had been described on the Ebbtide website. Her room should have had a queen-sized bed—not the crappy little double bed that was in there now. Julia's room, which was painted baby blue, should have had a double bed, but it held only a narrow twin. And Willa's room, the daffodil yellow one, held yet another double bed. Ellis winced, anticipating what Willa's reaction would be to that. Willa had reluctantly agreed to pay an extra two hundred bucks if the girls would let her have the room with the king-sized bed, since that's what she and her husband were used to sleeping in at home. Arthur wasn't coming along, of course, but Willa had insisted she couldn't possibly sleep in anything less than a king.

Once she'd turned on all the air conditioners, Ellis trudged up the narrow staircase to the third floor. The stairs were steep, and the walls so close that she didn't see how anybody could get a full-sized suitcase up them. She had to stop to catch her breath when at last she'd reached the third floor. It was even hotter up here, she discovered.

She found herself on a small landing. Unlike the second floor, the walls up here were unpainted board. They smelled faintly piney. There were three doors. She opened the first and found the tiny bathroom, with its claw-foot tub and funny high-backed commode. She could only shake her head when she saw that the tub had no shower. Dorie wasn't the type to complain, that was her sister Willa's specialty, but even sweet Dorie wouldn't be happy about not having a shower.

Ellis tugged at the door on the facing wall. It was swollen from the heat and humidity, but she finally managed to yank it open, only to discover an unfinished attic space. The high-ceilinged room was stifling and full of dusty cardboard boxes, trunks, and dust-covered bits of furniture. Maybe, Ellis thought idly, between sneezes, she could find some spare end tables and chairs to make their bedrooms more habitable. Later.

She opened the third door to find the bedroom. Tucked up under the eaves of the house, it had a low, sloping ceiling, but a dormer window opposite the bed ran the length of the room, and Ellis could see an amazing view of the ocean below. The waves were rolling in, and children darted in and out of the water. She yanked the window open and a breeze wafted in, carrying the smell of saltwater with it. There was another window, high in the wall above the bed, and if she stood on her tiptoes, she could see out to the street.

The room was just as sparsely furnished as the others, the bed was a double, with a sad, thin mattress. There was no overhead fan as in the downstairs bedrooms, but there was a pair of nightstands, each with a twee little white milk-glass lamp. Instead of a closet, a white, mirrored chifforobe stood in a corner of the room. And the air-conditioning unit was stuck into a hole that had been cut in the wall right beside the bed, which meant that whoever slept on that side would have it blasting in her ear all night long. The sad thing was, this was the best bedroom in the house. Ellis was glad Dorie and Stephen would have it. Not particularly glad about the Stephen part. After all, they'd agreed, way back in April, at Julia's mama's funeral, that this would be strictly a chick trip.

But Dorie and Stephen had been married only a year. Since they both taught school, August was the last month they'd have for vacation. Nobody, not even Julia, had the heart to say no to Dorie. Anyway, Stephen really was very nice. He liked to cook, and he was quiet, and he'd probably spend most of his time at the beach reading, Dorie had promised. So they'd relented and agreed, just this once, that Stephen could be one of the girls.

At least, Ellis thought, Stephen wouldn't be in their hair downstairs. They wouldn't have to worry about running into him in their underwear, or keep having to put the toilet seat down on the second floor.

But she was definitely still going to give Mr. Culpepper an earful! It was probably too late to get out of the house now, since he had half the month's rent, but she was already calculating how much of a discount she was going to ask for, considering the crappy beds, the window air-conditioning units, and—oh yes, the ants.

There it was again, the nagging, insistent itch she could not scratch. Money. Would she have enough? What would happen when this month was over? And how long would it be before her money ran out?

6

Ellis heard the crunch of gravel outside. Then a series of short, loud blasts from a car horn. She stood on tiptoes and looked out the window over the bed. A dark red minivan had pulled into the driveway, and a familiar blonde was leaning halfway out the passenger window, hollering at the top of her lungs.

"Whoo-hoo! We're here!"

Ellis flew down the two flights of stairs, out the front door and off the porch, launching herself in the direction of the van.

"Oh my God!" Ellis cried, falling into Julia's outstretched arms. "You're here. August is here. I can't believe we're all finally here."

She held Julia at arm's length and looked at her critically. "And you're so much blonder. I love it, but when did you decide to go platinum?"

Before Julia could answer, Dorie had gotten out of the minivan, and then the three of them were hugging and shrieking and babbling and jumping up and down so hard that it sounded like a sorority chapter meeting.

"Excuse me," Dorie said, finally pulling away. "I can't wait to see the house and catch up. But y'all have got to excuse me. I had an iced tea an hour ago, and my eyeballs are positively floating."

"Go on," Ellis said, laughing. "You never could hold your water. Julia and I will start unloading."

She walked to the back of the minivan and groped around for the catch on the tailgate. "Where are the others?" she asked Julia. "Are Willa and Stephen driving up separately? Dorie didn't mention that when I talked to her the day before yesterday."

Julia raised one elegant eyebrow. "There's quite a lot Dorie hasn't mentioned. To either of us. They aren't coming, sweetie."

"At all?" Ellis said, bewildered. "What happened?"

"The bitch bailed on us! Dorie said Willa just rang her up last night, right before she was to pick her up, and announced that she couldn't go."

"Just like that?"

Julia shrugged, and the strap of her orange tank top slid off one sun-browned shoulder. "Willa told Dorie something had come up with one of the kids. Isn't that just like her? She horns in on our trip, and because we don't want to hurt Dorie's feelings, we agree that she can come, plan around her, go to the expense of renting the bigger house with the extra bedroom, then she just up and cancels. You want to know what I think?"

"What?"

"I don't think she ever really intended to come," Julia said. "She was just up to her same old games again, pushing Dorie's buttons, testing to see if Dorie would cave in and invite her. Willa's never had any real friends of her own. Why would she? The woman's a raving bitch."

"But what about Stephen?" Ellis pressed. "Is he coming later? I know Dorie said he's been working really hard all summer, trying to get his master's thesis finished before school starts up again."

Julia grabbed a battered leather suitcase from the back of the van and set it on the driveway. "Stephen's quite another puzzle. When she picked me up at the airport this morning, all Dorie would tell me was basically the same thing: 'Stephen's working so hard on his thesis, he has to meet with his advisor, he needs absolute quiet, he's heartbroken that he can't come after all.' Blah, blah, blah."

"You don't believe her? Why would she make up something like that? Dorie wouldn't lie. Not to us."

They heard the slap of the screen door and Julia glanced back at the house. "Shh. She's coming. I'm not saying she's lying exactly. But she's not telling us the whole story. This is not our Dorie. Not at all."

"Did Julia tell you the bad news?" Dorie asked, approaching the van. "I know you guys must hate me. Stephen feels awful about not coming. He was so looking forward to the beach. But he's just frantic with worry about his thesis. And Willa . . ." Her voice trailed off. "Annabeth, her youngest, was supposed to be at sailing camp this week. But she gets these terrible headaches. And she's only six. They got her glasses, but . . ."

"Willa is Willa," Julia said dryly. "You don't have to apologize for her, Dorie. She's been like this her whole life."

Dorie's cheeks flushed bright red. "I know she can be a pill sometimes, you guys."

Ellis gave her a quick hug. "We all have our moments. We understand. Anyway, I'm just really bummed for you, having to spend the month without Stephen. We're all going to miss him."

Julia, standing directly behind Dorie, crossed her eyes and grimaced. The last statement was an outright lie, and they both knew it. They'd had a spirited e-mail exchange as soon as Dorie had brought up the possibility of having Stephen join them at the beach.

"No way!" Julia had written. "This is our time together. Remember? No effin' boys. Anyway, if Booker finds out, the next thing you know, he'll want to come. And then it'll be couples. And that's not what this month is about."

Booker and Julia had lived together for years, first in New York, and then, for the past six years, in London. Booker was a photographer, and Julia was a model. Ellis didn't quite understand their relationship. Sometimes, the way Julia talked about Booker, you had to wonder what had kept them together all this time.

Ellis hadn't liked to conspire against Dorie behind her back, but for once, she was in total agreement with Julia. She liked Stephen, although they'd only met twice before Dorie's wedding a year ago. He was attractive and thoughtful and obviously wild for Dorie. As for Dorie, she was long overdue for a good man. But just this once, couldn't they leave men out of it? Especially since Ellis was so obviously without a man—and had been for more years than she cared to admit.

That had never been the case with Dorie. With her strawberry blond hair, freckles, and kittenish green eyes, not to mention her voluptuous curves, Dorie was the man magnet of the group. She had been since third grade, when every single boy at Blessed Sacrament School wanted to be her valentine. Nobody could remember a time when Dorie had been without a boyfriend. And it wasn't like she even tried. She was just Dorie.

Once, when she was a freshman at the University of Georgia, she'd started dating a doctor. An honest-to-God physician. A gynecologist, if you could believe it. Howard had been gaga for Dorie. He'd given her a pair of two-carat diamond stud earrings—which she didn't dare show her mother—taken her on a spring break trip to Vegas, let her drive his Mercedes all the way to Savannah and back just so she could hang out with her girlfriends for Saint Patrick's Day.

The fling had lasted nearly a year. And then Dorie, who was only twenty, after all, got tired of playing doctor with a thirty-year-old who wanted her to quit her sorority and instead spend weekends hanging out with him at the country club. It wasn't until *years* later that she got up the nerve to admit where she'd actually met Howard.

They'd all gone back to the Dunaways' house after Willa's bachelorette party; they'd been doing tequila shooters at Spanky's down on River Street. It was their own version of Truth or Dare. Of course, nobody else had a story near as cool as Dorie's.

"I went to the student health clinic, you know, to get on the pill, because Bo and I were getting pretty serious, and I thought only sluts used condoms, but I was terrified of getting knocked up," Dorie had said, giggling nervously. "And anyway, who do you think gave me my first pelvic exam? Howard! And he was really so sweet, so gentle, you know? Afterwards, he called me into his office, and he gave me this very serious talk about the dangers of STDs and all that. I almost died, I was so embarrassed! Then he handed me my prescription and a package with, like, six months' worth of Ortho-Novum, and he'd written his home phone number on the back of the prescription."

Howard had been one of the nicer guys in Dorie's constantly changing constellation of boyfriends. A lot of them had been rats. So when she'd started talking about "the new guy at school"—meaning, Our Lady of Angels, the Catholic girls' high school they'd all attended, and where Dorie taught English—nobody really thought much of it. Stephen was the girls' soccer coach, and he taught history. He was lanky and dark haired, with a deliciously dry sense of humor. He wasn't from Savannah, he'd grown up in Omaha. And he was Catholic, so Dorie's mother approved. He and Dorie dated for two years before he finally talked her into getting married.

Dr. Dunaway—Dorie's mom (she had a Ph.D. in English and always insisted that everybody call her "Doctor" instead of "Mrs.")—had been so relieved that Dorie was finally settling down, she'd even helped Dorie pay for the wedding.

"I still can't believe how cheap that woman is," Julia had complained at the reception, where the alcohol had consisted of jug wine and a keg of Natty Lite. "Remember how she used to make Dorie and Willa use their allowances to buy their own shampoo and tampons?"

So Stephen was nice, but he was still a man, and this *was* supposed to have been a chick trip. Ellis was glad he'd bowed out at the last minute. And she felt guilty for being glad.

"Come on, you guys," Ellis exclaimed, refusing to look Julia in the eyes for fear of laughing. "It's hot as hell out here. Let's get this stuff inside. I want to show you the house."

"Screw the house," Julia said dramatically, throwing a garment bag over her shoulder. "I don't know about you two, but I'm here for the beach. We've had a hideous winter in England, and no spring to speak of. Just rain and more rain. So no offense, Ellis, but right now the only thing I want you to show me is the ice, the bourbon, and the beach. In that exact order."

"You got it," Ellis said, grabbing a tote bag. "And don't worry, Dorie. I even bought you your own bottle of tequila. And I brought my blender from home, just in case, which was a good thing, 'cuz there wasn't one here."

Dorie wrinkled her nose. "Actually? Right now I'd settle for another big ol' iced tea."

Julia stopped in her tracks. "Seriously? Iced tea? Eudora Dunaway is turning down a margarita? Alert the media!"

Dorie gave Julia a playful kick in the pants. "Hey! You make me sound like a falling-down drunk. It just so happens that I had a serious case of tequila poisoning after a friend's Cinco de Mayo party, and I haven't been able to look at the stuff ever since."

"S-u-u-u-r-e," Julia said. "Dorie is breaking up with Jose Cuervo. You hear that, Ellis?"

Ellis heard, and she saw the barely disguised suspicion in Julia's eyes, and she thought—just maybe—Julia was onto something. Something about Dorie was . . . off.

7

To: Mr.Culpepper@Ebbtide.com
From: EllisSullivan@hotmail.com
Subject: WTF? Fleas!
Mr. Culpepper, you need to get an exterminator over here ASAP. This place is crawling with fleas. Also ants and mildew. And the kitchen faucet drips. Constantly. And the mattresses suck, bigtime. Your website specifically stated that our house would have a "fully stocked kitchen." In my mind, a fully stocked kitchen includes items such as a stove with more than one working burner and such basics as saucepans, silverware, and dishes. I do not consider five cracked, chipped, and mismatched plates and a collection of plastic NASCAR go-cups to be "serving-ware for eight." As this is my third e-mail in the past two days, I'd appreciate it if you would take care of these things, IMMEDIATELY.

Ellis tapped the "send" button and scratched her right knee absentmindedly. Both of her ankles, her calves, and the backs of her knees were dotted with angry red flea bites. She had flea bites underneath her breasts, and flea bites on the back of her neck.

Julia had only a couple of bites, on her ankles, and Dorie didn't have a single one. But the fleas must have made Ellis's bedroom their home office, because that first morning at Ebbtide she woke up scratching like a maniac. She'd stared down at the white sheet on her bed, and had been horrified to see a semimicroscopic insect hopping around. "Fleas!" she'd screeched.

She'd stripped her bed of all the linens, taken every stitch of clothing out of her suitcases, even picked up the throw rug on the floor, and washed and bleached the daylights out of everything. But the fleas didn't care.

When she'd gone downstairs that first morning, Julia and Dorie were already sitting at the kitchen table, sipping coffee.

"Ellis," Julia said, pointing at the Kaper chart on the kitchen wall. "You're not really serious about this thing—right?"

Ellis got herself a glass of orange juice and settled at the kitchen table. "Well, now that Stephen and Willa aren't coming, I guess I'll have to redo it, but I still don't think it'll be too much trouble, not if everybody pitches in."

Julia stood and pointed at the first line of the chart with her half-eaten piece of toast. She read aloud in a high-pitched schoolmarm voice: "Monday: Julia cooks breakfast. Dorie does dishes. Willa sweeps sand from floors. Stephen takes out trash. Ellis does laundry."

Dorie pressed her napkin to her lips to suppress a giggle, but after Ellis glared at her, she looked down innocently at her cereal bowl.

"Ellis, honey," Julia said, nibbling at her toast. "I'm sorry. It's ludicrous. It really is. This chart thing . . . what did they call it back in Girl Scouts?"

"A Kaper chart," Ellis said quietly.

"Oh yes, Kaper." Julia nodded. "Excellent for eight-year-olds who have to be reminded to scrub their teeth and gather wood for the campfire. But for the love of God! We're grown women here. I'm thirty-five years old. I don't need a chart to tell me to hang up a wet towel."

Ellis felt her face go pink. "I just thought . . . well, I thought it might help the month go smoother, if things were sort of organized. Unlike you guys, I'm used to living alone and doing everything myself. I thought the chart would be kind of fun, but obviously I was wrong." She pulled the whiteboard off the wall and walked rapidly out of the room, her back stiff. A moment later, she was back, but only to pick up her empty juice glass, rinse it out, and place it on the drainboard. Then she stalked out of the room. Doric and Julia heard the screen door open and then slam shut.

"Shit." Julia tossed the toast crust onto her plate. "I'd forgotten how prickly our girl can be. But really, Dorie, it had to be said."

Dorie picked up both their plates and coffee cups and put them into the sink full of soapy water. "It could have been said nicer. Ellis isn't like you, Julia. She didn't grow up fighting and fussing with a bunch of brothers. You really hurt her feelings. And after all the work she did putting this together for all of us. It wouldn't hurt to go along with her. At least for the first week or so."

Julia sighed. "Now you're gonna make me play nice, aren't you?"

Dorie grinned. "Either that, or you pick up your Tinkertoys and go home."

Dorie walked out to the front porch, with Julia trailing reluctantly behind. They stopped at the front door and peeked out. The whiteboard was poking out of the top of the trash can at the edge of the driveway, and its creator, Ellis, was sitting on one of the porch chairs, rocking rapidly to and fro, staring off into space. It was a gorgeous summer morning, sunny, not too humid, with banks of high, puffy white clouds overhead.

It was the second day of August, and already they'd started to bicker.

"Come on, Ellis," Dorie coaxed. "Don't be mad. Julia didn't mean anything by it." She turned and glared at Julia. "Did you, Julia?"

"Julia's a bitch," Julia whispered loudly, poking her head out the door. She tiptoed onto the porch and stood behind Ellis's chair. "And just for that, Julia's going to have to clean the latrines for the whole month, right, Dorie?"

Dorie sat down on the rocker next to Ellis's. "Absolutely. *And* she gets no s'mores. Ever."

Julia knelt down on the floor on the other side of Ellis. She wrapped her arms around her friend's waist and laid her head on Ellis's lap. "Julia's sorry," she said in a little tiny mouse voice. "She loves Ellie-Belly and doesn't ever want to hurt her friend's feelings."

Ellis suppressed a smile. She patted Julia's head and then gave it a sharp thump. "Get up, you nutjob. And don't think you're going to get out of cooking my dinner tonight, either."

Julia groaned. "Thank God. My knees are killing me." She flopped down into the other rocking chair. "So what should we do today? Our first whole day at the beach? Bike ride? Shopping? Hang gliding over at Jockey's Ridge? I saw a brochure for the most marvelous-looking school where they actually teach you to hang glide. Remember that time we all went bungee jumping at Myrtle Beach?"

"You and Dorie went bungee jumping," Ellis corrected. "I couldn't even watch. I was petrified you'd be killed, and I'd have to explain to your mothers what happened."

"Nah, you were just scared if we got killed you'd have to go home alone and drive over the Talmadge bridge all by yourself," Julia taunted.

"True," Ellis admitted.

"Why don't we just hang at the beach here?" Dorie asked.

The others turned to look at her in surprise. Dorie had never been one to pass up an adventure.

"What?" she said innocently, catching their meaning. "Why do we have to do anything at all? I'm just enjoying being here, spending time with you guys. Anyway, hang gliding is expensive. You forget, I'm living on a schoolteacher's salary. A private school too—which doesn't pay diddly, I might add."

Ellis jumped to her feet. "Dorie's right," she said. "This is perfect beach weather. I'm gonna go put on my suit. If nothing else, maybe the saltwater will heal my flea bites."

Julia looked at Ellis's outstretched legs. "Eww! Disgusting! Have you contacted our landlord?"

"Mr. Culpepper? Repeatedly," Ellis said. "I sent him another e-mail just before I came downstairs. If I don't hear from him by lunchtime, I'm going to just find an exterminator in the phone book and tell Culpepper I'm going to deduct it from the rest of our rent. And I told him how unhappy we are about the mildew and the ants."

"And the crappy mattresses, I hope," Julia added. "I haven't slept on a bed that lumpy since I went hosteling in Belgium after high school. We're paying enough rent for this dump that we should at least be able to expect a decent bed."

"About the rent," Dorie said hesitantly. "I really think Willa should offer to go ahead and pay her share, even though she did cancel."

"Did she offer to reimuburse us?" Julia asked.

"Not yet," Dorie admitted.

"Well, I wouldn't hold my breath waiting for her to offer," Julia said. "Even though good old Arthur is swimming in dough. It wouldn't occur to darling Willa that the rest of us might be out-of-pocket because of her."

"I could ask her," Dorie volunteered. "But you know Willa."

"We do," Ellis said briskly. "So we won't count on her chipping in. If she does, that would be great; if not, no biggie. Like I said, I'm seriously thinking of renegotiating our lease on Ebbtide. The place is totally not what he advertised."

"I think it's kinda sweet," Dorie said. "Did you know, in the daylight, you can look through the cracks in the floorboards in that bathroom under the stairs and see little fiddler crabs crawling around in the sand under the house?"

"Sweet Jesus!" Julia said. "I am never using that bathroom again."

"Oh, Julia, quit being so damned British," Dorie said impishly. "You grew up in Savannah, Georgia, just like the rest of us. It's not like you never saw a fiddler crab before. Or a cockroach or an ant."

Julia stuck her tongue out at Dorie. "Screw you. I might have grown up living around creepy-crawlies, but that doesn't mean I want to live with 'em as a grown-up."

Ty had been watching the waves off and on since sunrise. They weren't really that big, but it was a break—he'd been sitting at his computer for the past twenty-four hours, researching cholesterol and statin fighters in every online medical journal he could find. He was no scientist—hell, he'd barely passed high school chemistry—but this new drug Hodarthe had come up with sounded like it could be a winner.

He'd done well the previous day with a start-up company in California that was doing interesting things using recycled glass in commercial concrete applications, so he had some funds, and he was poised to take a position with Hodarthe. But damned if he hadn't just received *another* e-mail from Ellis Sullivan.

He chuckled to himself as he reread her latest missive. "WTF? Fleas!" Little old Ellis was turning out to be a real ballbuster. He found himself scratching at a phantom flea bite even as he read. She was right, though. He *did* have to do something about the fleas. If they got too out of hand, he'd never get rid of 'em, and they might just chase away Ellis and her girlfriends. He couldn't afford to lose a month's rent.

Much as he hated to, he picked up the phone and called an old high school buddy, Frank, who had gone into his father's pest control business over in Elizabeth City. After some idle chatter about prospects for Carolina football (sorry) and the economy (way sorrier), Frank promised to head over to Ebbtide for a little bug-bombing session that afternoon. They even worked out a trade: Frank would provide pest control services for three months in return for a week's vacation at Ebbtide.

Ty didn't have to tell Frank money was tight; Frank knew about the jam he'd gotten himself into. Hell, everybody on the Outer Banks knew that Ty Bazemore was in a world of hurt. The first foreclosure notice for Ebbtide had been published in the newspaper in July, and every week since, the notice had run in the paper's legal ads, rubbing salt into his already wounded ego. Six weeks. That's how much time he had to pull off a miracle. Until then, he needed to keep his tenants happy and, somehow, raise enough money to catch up on six months' worth of missed house payments and back taxes.

But it wouldn't do to let Ellis Sullivan get the upper hand. So he fired off a missive of his own.

To: EllisSullivan@hotmail.com
From: Mr.Culpepper@Ebbtide.com
Subject: Alleged fleas.

Ms. Sullivan, if the house has fleas, you must have brought them with you. Likewise the ants. I've never had complaints before, about bugs or the mattresses. But Frank from Bug-Off Pest Control will be out today, after 2 pm. You'll have to vacate the premises for at least two hours, unless you enjoy inhaling toxic fumes. If you don't like my dishes, there's a Walmart in Kitty Hawk. I'll send somebody to take a look at the faucet. Happy?

Through the open door, he could hear the waves rolling into shore. He could stand it no more. He got up and strolled out to the porch.

The women of Ebbtide had pitched camp on a stretch of sand directly below. They had a jaunty striped pink-and-yellow umbrella, three lounge chairs, and a large cooler. The brunette, Ellis, and a tall, elegant blonde were playing Pro Kadima, inexpertly slapping the little rubber ball around, dashing back and forth in the sand, laughing hysterically.

The blonde was a knockout, with long, slender bronzed legs and a bright orange bikini that left little to the imagination.

The third woman was a petite strawberry blonde. She was stretched out in her chair, a pair of sunglasses perched on her little snub nose, reading a magazine. Even the loose-fitting sleeveless cover-up she wore over her swimsuit couldn't disguise a body that was luscious—and that was a word Ty didn't just throw around. Her pale, freckled skin was already turning pink, and it wasn't yet noon.

But it was Ellis, pain-in-the-ass Ellis, he couldn't keep his eyes off of. She'd knotted her long hair in a goofy ponytail on top of her head, emphasizing the graceful curve of her long neck. Her modest, black one-piece bathing suit should not have been alluring, but somehow it was—the high cut legs showed off her great butt, the scoop neckline revealed a promising amount of creamy cleavage. And when she ran, as she was doing now, looking like a total klutz, the suit rode up in the back and down in the front, giving him a rewarding view.

Ellis Sullivan was not by any means the hottest thing he'd ever seen on this stretch of beach. That honor, he thought, ironically, would have to go to Kendra, whom he'd first spotted the summer they were fifteen, as she did a slow, taunting stroll past him while he painted his grandmother's Adirondack chairs on this same deck. He found himself scowling at the memory of that day.

Dorie had promised herself she'd go for a swim at exactly 11 A.M. She ran and dove into the waves, letting them take her out and under, again and again. The water was wonderful. She floated on her back and looked up at the clouds, trying to force herself to empty her cluttered mind and think of... absolutely nothing.

But the worries lapped at her as surely as the warm waves. Damn Willa for backing out on them! Dorie had budgeted this vacation down to the last nickel, counting on splitting expenses four ways. And now? Her budget was blown to hell. She had just barely enough money to pay for her share of the rent, let alone kick in her share for groceries. And then there was Stephen. It was all just too sad, too awful. He would have loved this place. The thought came to her unbidden, as did the unexpected wave, washing over her face. She stood up, sputtering and choking, the saltwater burning her eyes and throat.

She was running back to her chair when she spotted him—a man, standing on the second-floor deck of the garage right beside their house.

The other girls were opening beers when she got back. She opted for an icy bottle of water instead, and as she was toweling off, she glanced up and saw the man again. He hadn't moved.

"Hey," she said, running a comb through her tangled hair. "Who's that guy?"

"What guy?" Julia said, not bothering to look around. She twisted the cap from her beer and took a long drink. "Probably one of your old boyfriends."

"Wrong," Dorie said. "I've never dated anybody from North Carolina. I had a boyfriend who went to Wake Forest, but that doesn't count because he was from Charleston."

"Where is this guy?" Ellis asked, standing up.

"Right there." Dorie pointed towards the garage apartment. "He's totally been staring at us for the past ten minutes."

Ellis put on her sunglasses and looked.

"It's him!" she exclaimed.

Now Julia was looking too. "Him who?"

"That's the guy," Ellis exclaimed. "Remember? I told you, he was standing right there, peeing off that porch, yesterday morning when I got here."

"Gross," Dorie said.

"He doesn't look gross to me," Julia said. "He looks kind of, um, yummy to me. He's all tan and ripped. My God, look at those pecs!"

"Julia!" Ellis and Dorie exclaimed in unison.

"Excuse me," Julia said. "Can I help it if I've had my fill of looking at flabby white Englishmen in the past few years? Have you two ever seen European men at the beach? They all wear those nasty little Speedos with their schlongs waving around."

"Banana hammocks," Dorie said, giggling. "Disgusting. Booker doesn't wear one, does he?"

"Booker?" Julia said with a derisive snort. "Hah! Booker hates the beach. He always says if he wants to get sun poisoning or skin cancer, he'll do it someplace with air-conditioning and decent cable reception."

"Stephen loves the beach," Dorie said wistfully. "He'll drive out to Tybee in the middle of the winter, just so he can walk barefoot in the sand."

"It's just too bad he couldn't come after all," Julia said sympathetically. "Have you talked to him since we got here?"

Dorie's eyes filled with tears. "No. . . ."

Ellis shot Julia a warning look. Julia shrugged.

"Oh look," Julia said, turning back towards the dunes. "The guy! He sees us looking at him." She gave him a coquettish wave. "And he doesn't even care. Oh my God. He's waving back. Who the hell is he?"

"That's what I intend to find out," Ellis said.

8

Ellis marched herself right up the stairway over the dune, stopping only to slide her feet into a pair of flip-flops she'd left at the edge of the steps.

"Hey!" she called, standing at the covered deck at the top of the dunes, her hands at her hips. "Hey, you!"

"Who, me?" Ty called, leaning down over the porch railing. He could just barely see a bit of her nipples from this vantage point.

"Yes, you," Ellis retorted. "What the hell do you think you're doing?"

"Just taking in the scenery," Ty said innocently. "How about yourself?"

"My friends and I *were* relaxing on the beach," Ellis said. "Until we became aware that we were being spied on by some pervert."

"What makes you think I'm a pervert?"

"Yesterday I caught you pissing off that same deck. Today you're up there staring at us. What's your name, anyway?"

He was taken off guard by her question, and before he knew it, he was actually telling her. "My name is Ty Bazemore. Why do you ask?"

She nodded, seeming to memorize it. "Ty Bazemore. Is that it? Not Tyson, or Tyler?"

"Just Ty," he said. "What's your name?"

"None of your business," she said. "What are you doing up there on that porch?"

"I happen to live here," he said indignantly.

"Does Mr. Culpepper know you're staying up there?"

He managed to suppress a smile. "Culpepper knows all about me."

"Don't you have anything better to do with your time?" she asked.

"Come to think of it," he said, looking down at his watch, "I do." He started to go back inside, but then he thought of something.

She was halfway down the beach stairs.

"Hey," he called. "Why do you want to know my name?"

"So I can Google you," she called back, not bothering to turn around. "And I intend to run the tag on that Bronco too, Ty Bazemore."

"The perv's name is Ty," Ellis reported when she got back to the girls. "He claims he rents the garage apartment from Mr. Culpepper."

"What makes you think he's a perv?" Julia asked, thumbing through *Vogue*.

"He was peeing off that deck!" Ellis said. "Right there in front of God and everybody."

"That doesn't make him a pervert," Julia said, dog-earing one of the pages. "It just makes him a guy. My brothers used to pee off the second-floor porch at the house at Isle of Hope when they were kids. It was like a contest. Peeing for distance, they called it."

"My brother did the same kind of stuff. And sometimes, when Stephen's in the backyard mowing the grass, he'll pee behind the garage," Dorie volunteered. "He doesn't think I know. I think it's kinda funny. Didn't your brother ever do anything like that?"

"Baylor wouldn't have dared. My mother would have had a cat-fit," Ellis said. "I don't care what you guys say, I'm keeping an eye on Ty Bazemore."

"Mmmm," Julia purred suggestively. "I'll help."

"Me too," Dorie said. "He's adorable. He'd make the perfect summer fling for you, Ellis."

"As if," Ellis said.

. . .

At lunchtime, the girls trooped back up the dunes to the house.

"I'm starved," Julia announced. She was leafing through a thick booklet advertising local shops and restaurants. "Where shall we go for lunch? Seafood, right? The fish we get in England is crap. It's the one big thing I miss about living in Savannah. Do you guys remember my mom's fried grouper sandwiches?"

"I remember her she-crab bisque," Ellis said. Unlike her own mother, who was strictly a meat and potatoes, canned peas, and cherry Jell-O kind of cook, Catherine Capelli had been a fabulous cook. "And I'd give anything for another plate of her spaghetti with the Italian sausage that she'd make in the wintertime."

"And those little yeast rolls she'd make, dripping with garlic butter," Dorie put in. "And all the different kinds of cookies she'd bake every year at Christmas. She'd fix a huge plate for each of us to take home to our families. It's a miracle we all didn't end up fat little piggies after eating your mama's cooking all those years, Julia."

"She could cook, there was no denying that," Julia said lightly. "But you still haven't told me where you want to go have lunch." She rifled the pages of the booklet. "Awful Arthur's? Barefoot Bernie's? Dirty Dick's?"

Ellis picked up a manila folder she'd left on top of the microwave. "Let's see. I've got coupons for Mako Mike's and Freaky Freddie's. Buy one entrée, get a second free."

"You guys go," Dorie said. "Maybe I'll just fix myself a peanut-butter-and-jelly sandwich."

"Peanut butter and jelly? At the beach? Are you nuts?" Julia said.

"I prefer to think of it as being thrifty," Dorie replied. "I mean, c'mon, Ellis, aren't you the tiniest bit worried about your situation? I know you'll get another great job, but I just think I'd be crazy worried if I were you."

"I've got some irons in the fire," Ellis said blithely. "But I'll be all right. As long as I'm sensible about my spending, which I usually am anyway." She opened the refrigerator door, secretly relieved at the twenty dollar bill she'd save by eating lunch at home. "Look, I stopped at the seafood place up the street when I got in yesterday and picked up some shrimp. They claimed it was right off the boat. And I brought a can of Old Bay seasoning. We can steam some shrimp in beer."

"What else have you got in there?" Dorie asked, leaning in to look. She held up a head of romaine lettuce, a cucumber, and a tomato. "Great. I'll throw a salad together while the shrimp are cooking."

"Oh, all right," Julia relented. "We'll stay in for lunch. But tonight, we're going out for dinner so I can get my fried grouper fix. And it's my treat, so don't even try to argue."

They took turns showering, and when lunch was ready, they sat companionably around the enamel-topped kitchen table. They discussed plans for the afternoon, while Ellis checked her e-mail.

"Hey," she announced. "Old man Culpepper finally answered my e-mail. A pest-control guy is coming over to spray the house at two. But he says we've got to stay out of the house for a couple of hours afterwards."

"Suits me," Julia said. "I've got a new book, and the beach is calling me back."

"Guess I've had enough sun for one day," Dorie said, holding out her sunburnt arm.

"Me too," Ellis agreed. "I saw a movie theater up the street. Why don't we catch a matinee?"

"A chick flick!" Dorie's green eyes lit up. "I'll bring my biggest pocketbook and we'll sneak in our own Diet Cokes like we did in junior high. And we can stop and buy a giant box of candy at the Dollar Store."

"Well . . ." Ellis said. "You know they always have those big signs that say 'outside food and drink prohibited'. . . ."

Julia set her beer bottle down on the countertop. "Who cares? They just put those signs up so you'll have to buy their five-dollar Cokes and seven-dollar tubs of popcorn. Nobody pays any attention to those signs."

"I do," Ellis said stubbornly. "What if we got caught? How embarrassing would that be?"

"Who's going to catch you?" Julia wanted to know. "It's not like they have ushers in movie theaters anymore. And even if they did, what do you think is going to happen if they catch you sneaking in your own stuff? Huh? You think they're gonna revoke your driver's license? Seize your jujubes as contraband?"

"Never mind her, Ellis," Dorie said. "I'll carry the Cokes and Milk Duds in my purse." She paused then, remembering that her redrawn budget had no room for movies—let alone seven-dollar boxes of popcorn.

Ellis noticed Dorie's sudden look of concern. She opened the manila folder again. "I went online and downloaded some Movie Lover's passes. If we get there before 1:30, our tickets are only two bucks. And there's one for each of us."

Julia rolled her eyes. "What is with you two with the coupons and early-bird specials? We're on vacation. We've all worked hard and we deserve to be good to ourselves. If you're that hard up for money, just say so." She grabbed her pocketbook.

Ellis saw Dorie bite her lip and look away. "Thanks anyway. We'll pay our own way," she said, her voice deliberately even. "And if you don't want to be seen with a couple of coupon-clippers, we'll understand."

"Oh. Sorry. I didn't mean . . . well, you know." Julia hastily craned her neck to look out the kitchen window. "It's kind of clouding up out there. So if you've got a spare coupon, I guess I could go. Anyway, I figure I laid down a pretty good base coat this morning."

"You're half Italian," Dorie pointed out. "You were born with a base coat. Unlike me, with this darned red hair and freckles. I swear, I think I get sunburn from my night-light."

Ty saw the women load up into the red minivan and head off down Virginia Dare Trail. It was only a little after one. He waited five minutes, and then another five, just to make sure they weren't doubling back. Then he picked up his toolbox and key ring and, whistling, headed over to Ebbtide.

He stood on the porch, hesitant. Beach towels were draped over the rocking chairs, and three bathing suits—the orange bikini, a lime green flowered one-piece, and the black one-piece, were pinned to the clothesline. Three pairs of flip-flops were neatly lined up by the front door. He fit the key in the lock but still didn't turn it. It didn't feel right, somehow. But it was his house, damn it. He was the landlord. Ellis Sullivan had been nagging about a dripping faucet and fleas and ants. So he had a legitimate reason to be in the house.

Then why did he feel so creepy?

Because some neurotic chick accused him of spying on her and her friends? When did it become a crime to stand on his own deck and enjoy the sight of a pretty woman? It was a public beach, wasn't it? It wasn't like he'd taken a pair of binoculars to peep into some unsuspecting woman's bedroom.

He squared his shoulders, unlocked the door, and marched inside. He went directly towards the kitchen. He could hear the faucet dripping from the hall-way.

The kitchen looked a hell of a lot better than the last time he'd been in it. The floor was swept, the counters and stove top sparkled, and damp plates and glasses were neatly stacked in the dish drainer, a clean dish towel draped across them. He could smell the Old Bay seasoning they'd used to cook shrimp, but there were also faint undernotes of flowery perfume and coconut-scented suntan lotion.

Ty put his toolbox on the counter. He opened the cupboard under the sink and shut off the water. Then he dug out a pair of Channellocks from the tool-box and went to work. A washer. It just needed a washer. He was putting his tools away when he noticed the dishes stacked on the open shelves. Or what there were of them. He could have sworn there had been dishes for eight when he'd gotten the house ready back before Easter. Now, there were, as Ellis Sullivan had claimed, only five dinner plates. Five chipped, cracked plates. Three cereal bowls, none of them matching. What had happened to all the china he'd stocked the house with back in the spring? He opened one of two drawers. The silverware was pretty skimpy too. There were no knives to speak of. In the cupboard, he found a couple of small saucepans, none with a lid, and the world's smallest cast-iron skillet.

And what about the range? He turned all the burners to high and held the palm of his hand over them. Only the smallest eye, at the back of the stove, worked.

His shoulders slumped. His old man had taught him how to do basic plumbing and rudimentary electrical repairs, but he didn't have any idea how to fix this stove. It had been in the house since his grandmother lived here, at least since the 1970s. It was unlikely he'd find somebody who could fix it, since you probably couldn't even buy replacement parts for the thing anymore.

He was standing there, staring at the half-broken stove, when the doorbell rang.

"Ty Bazemore!"

He wouldn't have recognized Frank Patterson if he hadn't been wearing a BUG-OFF PEST CONTROL uniform shirt, with the name FRANK embroidered in script above the left breast. They'd gone to high school together, where Patterson quarterbacked for the football team and Ty had played tight end.

"Dude!" Ty said, pumping his old teammate's hand. "How the hell are you?"

They stood in the living room, chatting awkwardly. "You're lookin' good, Frank," Ty said. "Bug busting must agree with you."

"It's a living," Frank said. "How 'bout you? Are those your boards I saw out in that garage?"

"Yeah," Ty said. "I'm still surfing. When I get time, which I haven't lately." Finally, they got down to business.

"Fleas, huh?" Frank said, giving the living room an appraising look.

Ty's face darkened. "Friggin' college kids snuck a dog in here last week."

"You don't live here?"

Ty laughed. "No, man, I can't afford to live here. I live over the garage, in what used to be the maid's apartment. I rent out the house."

"Pretty cool old place," Frank said, running a hand over the wood-paneled wall. "It's one of the original ones, right?"

Ty shrugged. "This isn't one of the original thirteen, the ones they call the 'unpainted aristocracy.' My grandmother's aunt bought it in the 1920s. We've still got the original bill of sale. She paid eight thousand dollars back then."

"My dad used to have the pest control contract on the one right next door," Frank said. "The Lunsfords. Nice folks. Clark and Margaret? Maybe you knew them? After the last hurricane hit it so bad, they sold it to some people from Virginia."

"Haven't met the new owners," Ty said. "But Mrs. Lunsford, Miss Margaret, we called her, she was one of my grandmother's running buddies. They were classmates at Saint Mary's, back in the day."

"What was your grandmother's name?" Frank asked. "Not Bazemore, right?"

"No," Ty said. "This house belonged to my mom's family. She was a Culpepper. Edwina and Garrett Culpepper. My granddad died about ten years ago. And then Nanny, she passed two years ago. Everybody called her Winnie."

"I remember hearing your mom passed, some years back, right?"

"That's right," Ty said. "She died the year after Granddad. Hard to believe it's been that long."

Frank nodded his head in mute agreement. He picked up his canister of chemicals and, pointing a long-necked wand, began walking around the perimeter of the room, spraying as he talked.

"Your grandmother left you the house, huh? That's pretty awesome. House like this, right on the ocean. I mean, it's none of my business, but it's worth some bank, right?"

"It would be if it were fixed up," Ty agreed. "Anyway, Nanny left the house to my mom's only brother, my uncle, who lives in South Dakota. His wife hates the beach, and they never had any kids. He was gonna sell it, so I got the bright idea that I should buy it from them. You know, the place was a gold mine—or so I thought."

"Awesome."

"Place is a dump," Ty said, gloomily. "A giant money pit. That's the real reason my uncle was so glad to unload it. My grandmother never wanted to modernize anything. Wanted to leave things like they were when she was a little girl and they'd come up here from Charlotte and spend the whole summer. There's no central heat or air. Granddad finally put in window units, back in the '80s. No insulation, of course. In some places, you can see daylight through these old floorboards. I about froze my ass living here this past winter. In Nanny's day, they closed the house up every October and didn't open it back up until Good Friday. The plumbing sucks, too. Only two full bathrooms for this whole big house and only one indoor shower. And the taxes? The county thinks this dump is worth two million dollars! Don't get me started."

"Crazy," Frank agreed, moving into the dining area and then into the kitchen.

"Hey, look at this," he chuckled, looking down the room. "This is some old school, here."

"And not in a good way," Ty said, leaning on the doorframe. "That stove is shot. I just got new tenants for the whole month. Three women! Been here a day, and they're already bitching about the place."

"You need a new stove?" Frank asked casually.

"Yeah," Ty said, bending down to scratch his ankle. "I need a lot of new stuff for this house. But I can't afford shit."

"Reason I ask," Frank said, "is we just replaced all the appliances over at our place. We put the fridge out in the garage, you know, for beer and stuff. But the stove, it's just sitting on the back porch, gathering dust. My wife's kinda into cooking. Wouldn't let up until we got all new stainless-steel fridge and stove and dishwasher. The old stove's fine, she just had her heart set on stainless steel. You know how they get."

"Yeah," Ty said. "I guess."

"You and Kendra still together?" Frank asked, shooting him a curious look before squatting down and directing the pesticide to the kick plate under the counters. Frank knew Kendra from high school, of course. Everybody on the Outer Banks knew the Wilcox family. Kendra's father Boomer had been chairman of the Dare County Commission, and her grandfather had been a superior court judge. Kendra was the fourth generation of lawyer Wilcoxes.

"Nah," Ty said. "We split up a while ago."

"Sorry, man," Frank said. He opened the kitchen door. "You want me to hit the porch out here?"

"Everything," Ty said, following him out. "The place is crawling with fleas. And it all happened in, like, a week."

"Yeah," Frank said, walking up and down the length of the porch, "the little bastards run amok this time of year. You can't let them get ahead of you. I'm not trying to sell you nothin', but seriously, you might wanna think about signing a contract. Save you some money over the long run."

"I'll think about it," Ty said, but his voice said he wouldn't.

Frank stood and faced the ocean. A faint breeze ruffled the sea oats, and the plum-colored skies promised rain. Just beyond where the waves broke, he spotted a dolphin.

"I can see why you'd want to keep this house," Frank said, leaning on the porch rail. "My wife and kids are gonna go nuts about this place. Fall, huh?"

"I'm wide open in October," Ty said. "Unless the bank takes it back before then. You just name the weekend."

"Fishing oughtta start picking up about midmonth," Frank said. "My youngest one? That little girl flat loves to fish. She's her daddy's girl all the way."

"My granddaddy showed me how to bait a hook right out there," Ty said, pointing to the ocean. "I was probably about five. He used to catch the hell out of the red drum in the fall."

"October," Frank repeated. He looked over at Ty, who was still gazing at the place where he'd caught his first fish. Raindrops, big fat ones, began plopping on the sun-bleached walkway over the dunes. People on the beach started gathering up chairs and towels.

"Listen, Ty," Frank said suddenly. "You think you want that stove, we could run over to my place and throw it in the back of the truck. Might as well haul the old one outta here and drop it at the dump."

Ty held out his hand and the men shook. "You got a deal."

9

To: Mr.Culpepper@Ebbtide.com
From: EllisSullivan@hotmail.com
Subject: Thanks!
Dear Mr. Culpepper. I take back all the nasty stuff I said about you. The
fleas and ants are gone. The new stove is a huge improvement, and
I'm sure you'll notice a savings on your water bill since the leaky faucet
has been fixed. Also, the new (old) dishes are very sweet. My friends
and I just love china with pink roses. Dorie, who is one of our group, says
she thinks her grandmother had that exact same china pattern. So
again, thanks! Ellis. P.S. What can you tell us about the guy who lives in
the garage apartment here? He seems to keep very odd hours—we've
noticed the light stays on over there all night long. He's not a serial killer,
right? (Just kidding. Mostly.)

To: EllisSullivan@hotmail.com
From: Mr.Culpepper@Ebbtide.com
Subject: Garage guy

Dear Ellis: Ty Bazemore is harmless. He tells me he makes a living day trading, but maybe that's just a cover story for an international white-slaver. (Just kidding. Mostly.)

"Hey, you guys," Ellis said, putting her iPhone back into the protective plastic pocket of her beach bag. "Mr. Culpepper says that guy above the garage is a day trader. That's why he stays up all night."

"Interesting," Julia said. "I wonder if he literally stays up all night?"

"Julia!" Ellis said, not really shocked.

"Mmm," Dorie said drowsily. She was stretched out facedown on her canvas-covered chaise. Her fingers trailed in the sand, and her body was slick with suntan lotion and perspiration. "What time is it? I think I can only take fifteen more minutes on my stomach."

"It's three o'clock," Julia said, propping herself on one elbow to assess her friend's tanning progress. "You've only been like that for fifteen minutes, and you already look like a boiled lobster. I swear, Dorie, you are the whitest white girl I have ever known."

"Mmm," Dorie said. Moments later, she was softly snoring.

"Such a party animal," Julia said. "Come on, Ellis. I'm bored. Walk down the beach with me, okay?"

Ellis glanced down at their sleeping friend. "Should we just leave her like that? She is getting pretty burnt."

Julia took a beach towel from her bag and gently draped it over Dorie's motionless body. "She'll be fine," Julia said. She slung her beach bag over her shoulder. "Let's walk down to that ice cream shack near the pier. I'm starved."

Ellis pulled her cover-up over her bathing suit, tucked some money into the pocket, and, as a second thought, added her phone.

Julia, who never missed anything, rolled her eyes. "Another thing I don't miss about living in the States! You people and your mania for your mobiles. Do you ever go anywhere without that thing? Can't you just relax? At least while we're together?"

Four days of living in close quarters with Julia had taught Ellis to shrug off her friend's caustic comments. "What about you?" she countered. "Don't you supermodels have to keep in touch with your agencies to find out about bookings or whatever you call it?"

"I am so *not* a supermodel," Julia said. "Anyway, I told the agency I was taking the month off." She picked up the pace, and with her long lean legs had soon left Ellis a couple yards behind.

"Wait up," Ellis called, nearly sprinting to catch up with her friend. "I thought this used to be your busy time," she said.

"Things change," Julia said. "Anyway, I'm on vacay."

Ellis followed Julia up towards the boardwalk crossover and was walking as fast as she could, but even though she wore flip-flops the flour-fine sand scorched her feet.

"I thought I was doing a pretty good job of relaxing. As for worrying— well, I can't help it. I'm thirty-four years old. I've had some kind of a job since I was fourteen years old. I've been in banking since Daddy helped me get my first job at Savannah Bank when I was seventeen. Now, well, I just don't know what's going to happen next."

"Nobody knows what's going to happen next, ever," Julia said, gesturing wildly with her hands. "That's my whole point, Ellis. You've got no control over anything, so why not just sit back and take life as it comes?"

Now it was Ellis's turn to roll her eyes. "That's fine for you to say. I mean, I know you're not an heiress or anything, but at least you've got a nice inheritance to live on. And work that you can do anytime, anywhere. You've been all over the world. And let's face it, you've got Booker. Me? I've lived in three places in my life: Savannah, Charlotte, and Philly. And I've got me. And Mama. Daddy left her just enough to live on, if she's really careful. And she's not. It'll be me taking care of her eventually, not my brother. So yes, I worry. I guess if I had your life, I wouldn't have to worry. But I don't. So I worry a lot. But I'm trying not to let it ruin this month for us."

Julia walked on, three or four steps ahead of Ellis, who couldn't catch up with her friend's long-legged gait, no matter how hard she tried.

Ellis was already regretting her outburst. It was tacky to talk about Julia's money that way. It wasn't like Julia went around flaunting the fact that she was semirich or the fact that Ellis and Dorie were semipoor.

When they got to the paved road, Ellis trotted until she was right beside Julia. "You're mad at me, aren't you?"

"Nope," Julia said. "I'm not going to get mad at you for saying what you're thinking. At least, I hope I won't. It's just that you don't really have a clue what my life is like."

"I don't?"

"Not really," Julia said. They'd reached the open-air ice cream shop. It was a concrete block affair, painted with circus-bright red-and-yellow stripes. A dozen people stood in line in front of them, waiting to order, and the picnic tables, located in the shade of the shop's overhang, were full. Rock music blared from speakers mounted on wooden columns. Ellis and Julia crowded close together, seeking refuge from the searing ninety-plus heat.

The song was Bruce Springsteen's "Dancing in the Dark." Without thinking, they started swaying their upper bodies to the music.

"What's this song remind you of?" Julia asked, reading the chalkboard menu.

"Me?" Beneath two days' tan, Ellis blushed.

"I knew it!" Julia cackled. "Ellis and Mikey Cavanaugh, gettin' jiggy at my fifteenth-birthday party."

"Would you please shut up?" Ellis said. "People can hear you."

"So what?" Julia twirled around, juking right and left, humming the song that had been their junior high anthem. "Oh, you were so hot for Mikey Cavanaugh back then. My mother saw you making out with him behind the garage, you know. She was gonna call your mama and tell her, but Daddy told her to mind her own business. Oooh, Ellis, you were a bad little girl back in the day."

"Shut up," Ellis said, going pink with the delicious memory of kissing the cutest boy at the party.

"Take your order?" The girl behind the counter was Hispanic, and she wore a pained expression and a ridiculous paper cap made to look like an ice cream cone. "Ma'am?" she said loudly, to the oblivious Julia.

Ellis jostled Julia's arm. "Come on. It's your turn."

"Oh. Yeah. Let me see. All right. Do you have gelato?"

"Julia! This is Nags Head, not Rome," Ellis said. "It's ice cream, all right?" She leaned into the counter. "She'll have a single scoop of Rocky Road in a cup, and I'll have a single coffee chocolate chip in a sugar cone. And two large cups of ice water, please."

Before Julia could stop her, Ellis handed over a five-dollar bill, and plunked the change in a tip jar displayed prominently on the counter.

By mutual agreement, they perched at the end of a picnic bench at a table where a young mother busily spooned ice cream into her sandy toddler's wailing mouth.

"I can't believe you remembered about the Rocky Road, and the cup, no cone, after all these years," Julia said, dipping the tiny plastic spoon into the ice cream.

"And I can't believe you still won't let me live Mikey Cavanaugh down— twenty years later," Ellis said. "Did your mother really see us together, or are you just saying that to torture me?"

"She really did!" Julia nodded vigorously. "You know, until the day she died, she still thought you were a bad influence on me."

"Me?" Ellis hooted. "I was the voice of reason. The sane one. If it weren't for me, you would have gone to jail or hell, long ago."

"I know," Julia said. "Ellis Sullivan, designated driver for life. Mama always thought I was the angel and you were the devil, and I wasn't going to tell her any different. And you know, when you got out of college and got engaged, Mama told me she was glad, because you were finally going to settle down with that nice boy. She didn't even really mind that he was Jewish, and a Yankee."

Ellis sighed. "Bless her heart, your mama never did have a clue."

"You ever hear from him?" Julia asked, tilting her head. The three of them, Julia, Dorie, and Ellis, had all pledged, long ago, to never again speak the name of Ellis's ex-husband. "He's dead to us," Dorie had proclaimed at the end of the three-month-long marriage.

And his name, which was Ben Greene, and the wedding and marriage, as far as her friends knew, seemed to have miraculously faded from Ellis's memory. It was such an un-Ellis-like thing to have happened that she could almost persuade herself that it hadn't. Almost.

"I haven't heard from him in years," Ellis said, which was technically true. "Last I heard, he'd gotten remarried. I think they have a baby."

Through the magic of Google, where she'd found *Greene Acres,* his second wife's chatty blog, Ellis knew exactly where Ben was living (Winnetka, Illinois), what he was doing (running his family's furniture-import business), and the name of his new wife (Sherry). She knew they had two shelties (Lulu and Lucky) and a two-year-old son named Sam (after Ben's favorite uncle).

And she would have died if anybody, *especially* Ben, knew just how often she read *Greene Acres.*

"Well, thank God for small favors," Julia said vehemently. "He's somebody else's problem and not yours. Sweet Jesus! Can you imagine having a baby with ears like his? You'd have to put a sidecar on the baby buggy just to accommodate 'em."

On the contrary, Ellis had seen photos of little Sam, and she thought he was the most adorable toddler she'd ever laid eyes on. He had huge, soulful blue eyes, a thick fringe of pale hair, and a perfect, cupid-bow's mouth, which he must have gotten from his mother, because everybody in Ben's family had nearly nonexistent upper lips.

"Ellis?" Julia was looking at her strangely.

"His ears weren't that big," Ellis said. "You just never liked him from the get-go."

"And was I wrong? Did you have to file papers on him even before you'd finished writing the thank-you notes for the wedding presents?"

"You were right," Ellis said, wadding up her paper napkin and crushing it on top of her unfinished ice cream cone. She tossed both, underhand, into the metal trash basket, and took a long drink of ice water. "I hated you for it at the time, but you were oh, so right."

Everybody but Ellis had known just how wrong Ben was for her. And the day Ben realized it too, just three months into the marriage, he'd calmly, coldly announced, at dinner, two days before her birthday, that the whole thing had been a regrettable mistake. That was the exact word he'd used, too. Regrettable. There'd been no fight, no ugly scene, just Ben, in his pale-yellow golf shirt, pushing back from the table, setting his fork at the edge of his dinner plate, saying, his eyes serious but dry, "I'm sorry, Ellis, but we both know this will never work."

Pressed by his tearful—well, hysterical, really—bride, Ben had finally uttered the words that had stilled the tears and broken Ellis's heart for good. "I'm just not in love with you. I thought I was, I wanted to be, but I'm not."

Before the night was out, Ben had packed his clothes, his books, his CDs, and moved out of their apartment. And before Ellis could even really comprehend what was happening, the divorce was final and the marriage was almost, but not completely, forgotten.

Nobody but Ellis knew how she still grieved for what was gone. Her marriage was the first thing she'd ever really failed at. Afterwards, she'd packed away all the wedding china, silver, and crystal, which she could no longer bear to look at, and simply thrown all her energy and talent into her job, winning promotions, rave job evaluations, and raises. But the loneliness never subsided. She missed living with a man, having somebody to eat dinner with and buy shirts for. She missed having somebody waiting at the airport baggage claim when she came home from a business trip, and she missed slow, delicious Saturday morning lovemaking. Oh God, had it really been ten years since she'd had sex? More. Eleven and a half years, if you didn't count some heavy petting with a man she had dated in the year immediately following her divorce, when she'd been desperate to prove to herself just how over Ben she was.

Julia stood up abruptly. "Come on, we better get back to Dorie. I don't want to have to be giving her oatmeal baths like we did that summer at Myrtle Beach."

Ellis grimaced. "What were we thinking, slathering ourselves with that nasty baby oil and iodine mess? It's a wonder we don't all have skin cancer. "

"We weren't thinking. We were drinking," Julia reminded her. They strolled back across the street and over the dune to the beach below.

"Listen," Julia said suddenly. "What do you think is really going on with Dorie?"

"Dorie? Nothing. Why? What do you think is going on?"

"It hasn't struck you that we've been here over three days now and she hasn't once called Stephen?"

"Nooo," Ellis said. "I guess she hasn't. But maybe she's just letting him alone so he can concentrate on his thesis."

"Nuh-uh," Julia said. "He hasn't called her, either. I know, because her room's right next to mine."

"Maybe they had a fight. Maybe she's pissed he decided he was too busy to come. I don't know, Julia. But I don't think it's any of our business, whatever it is."

"This isn't Dorie," Julia said stubbornly. "Something really bad has happened to her. Listen, at the movie the other day? She cried all the way through it."

Ellis's brow wrinkled. "It was a comedy! Nobody cries at a Ben Stiller movie."

"She got up twice to go to the bathroom," Julia said. "Didn't want us to see her bawling her eyes out. Something is going on with them, Ellis. I can sense it."

"Then do me a favor, Julia," Ellis whirled and grabbed Julia's wrist to make her point. "Leave her alone. I mean it. If she wants to tell us, she will. If she and Stephen are going through a rough time, the best thing we can do for her is just be here for her. You hear me?"

"Of course," Julia said. "You act like I'm some kind of bully or something. I've known Dorie as long as you have. I love her as much as you do. I want her to be happy, that's all."

They were almost back at the beach. Something had been bothering Ellis. "Listen, Julia," she said, slowing down so her friend would have to also. "Since we're on the subject of happiness . . . What's going on with you and Booker?"

Julia stopped walking and made an elaborate gesture of adjusting the oversized silk scarf she'd casually knotted around her waist. "Nothing," she said. "Same old, same old."

"You lie like a rug," Ellis said. "Now come on, out with it. You're not breaking up, right?"

"Not exactly," Julia said. "It's gotten complicated. And you know how I hate complications. Really, I don't know why he wants to mess with a good thing. But that's Booker. He never has been able to leave well enough alone."

"What's he done now?" Ellis asked.

"Oh Gawwd," Julia said. "What hasn't he done? Well, for starters, he's gone and taken a real job."

"In England?"

"No, and that's the problem," Julia said, frowning. "He's head of the photo department at some magazine publishing company you never heard of in Washington. I mean, can you imagine? Booker, in a coat and tie? Actually punching a clock? It boggles the mind."

"In DC?" Ellis said, her voice only an octave below a squeal. "But, Julia, that's great. DC's only a hop and a jump from Philly! You know, if I manage to find another job and stay in Philly. But whatever, right? I mean, you'll be back in the States, that's all we care about."

"I wouldn't start buying Amtrak stock just yet," Julia said. She was walking, no, almost running now.

"What?" Ellis was out of breath from trying to catch up. "Hey, slow down. Julia!"

"Who says I want to move back to the States?" Julia turned and snapped. "Who says I want to give up my career for Booker? Who says I have to get married and start pumping out a baby a year like my poor mother? She basically lived in those fugly maternity clothes for seven years, all before she was twenty-five, and I never remember a time when she did anything for herself, her whole life. I'm only thirty-five, for God's sake! I like my life just the way it is. All right?"

Ellis blinked. What would be wrong with having a life like that, like the one Julia's mother had—with babies and a loving husband, and yes, spit-up and drool and even stretch marks? Julia said she couldn't remember her mother having any time alone—Ellis had practically lived at the Capellis' during her teenage years, and she couldn't ever remember seeing Catherine Capelli when she wasn't singing or laughing or telling a joke—surrounded by her noisy, adoring family.

"Nobody's saying you have to do any of that," Ellis said quietly.

"That's what you think," Julia said, her shoulders sagging. "Look, we're at the beach. Can we not talk about this right now? I'm going for a swim."

Ellis stood on the tide line, the place where the burning sand met the wet sand. It was strewn with broken shells and dried seaweed. She stepped out of her sandals and dug her toes into the cool sand. Her hand closed around the cell phone in the pocket of her cover-up. She had résumés out at a couple different places. A former colleague had sent her a promising lead about a job at a start-up financial services company in Pittsburgh.

Pittsburgh. She didn't know a soul in Pittsburgh. Starting over in a new town? At a new company, a new job? Unbidden, she pictured herself, alone, in a new apartment, studying a stack of takeout menus, with an empty evening, an empty weekend, stretching out before her, in appalling, *regrettable* aloneness.

Worry, Ellis thought, hell yes. Worry didn't begin to cover what she was feeling right now.

10

It wasn't until her stomach rumbled that Maryn realized how hungry she was. She pulled the car into the next strip shopping center she passed. The place was called The Picky Pelican. Stupid name for a restaurant. But she was really, really hungry.

And she was desperate to talk to Adam. Her one friend. Funny, when you thought about it. Adam Kuykendall was the least likely candidate for a best friend that Maryn could think of. Short and stocky, with thinning blond hair, geeky glasses, and a scraggly soul patch on his chin, Adam and Maryn had bonded as soon as she'd started work at Prescott and Associates, a midsized family-owned insurance agency in Cherry Hill.

The other women in the office wanted nothing to do with Maryn, giving her disapproving sideways glances, pointedly excluding her from their lunchtime cliques and after-work drink outings. Most were older, married, with kids, even grandkids. Adam was the only male nonagent in the whole office.

So they were both outsiders. At first, Maryn had just assumed he was gay. But he was surprisingly good company, and he'd won her over her first week at work with his wickedly cutting comments about their bitchy female coworkers. Within a week of meeting, they'd established their rituals—lunch from the Italian deli around the corner, Friday night happy hour, Sunday movie matinees—chick flicks for her, slasher movies for him.

And then Don came into her life eighteen months ago. And everything changed.

She had to talk to Adam right away, warn him. Don knows. I'm gone. I'm afraid. Afraid he'll come after me. Afraid he'll come after you. Be careful. I'm gone.

Adam would have to wait, though. She yawned, got out of the car, locked it, and looked around, automatically tensing at the sight of a black SUV and, quickly, rebuking herself. This SUV was an Explorer, not an Escalade. Don Shackleford did not know where she was. Yet.

Inside the restaurant, all the tables were full. There was one seat vacant, at the counter, between a guy who looked like a construction worker and a young woman her age, with a sunburnt nose, who looked to have just walked in off the beach.

The restaurant smelled like hamburgers and French fries. Maryn's stomach growled again. She needed food, a bed, a new name, new identity, new life. But for now, a seat at the counter at The Picky Pelican would have to do.

11

Dorie sat alone at the luncheonette counter. Even though it was nearly two, the place was still mobbed with a late lunch crowd. "Here ya go, hon," the waitress said, as she carefully poured the chocolate shake from the stainless-steel shaker into the tall, frosted glass and then placed it on the fluted white-paper place mat. "Wait," the waitress said. She turned to the back bar and returned with a can of whipped cream in one hand and a maraschino cherry in the other. "There now," the waitress said, plopping the cherry atop the mound of whipped cream.

"Thank you so much," Dorie said, shooting the waitress a smile. "This looks awesome."

She plunged the straw into the shake and took a deep sip. The sensation of the ice-cold chocolate sent a chill down her sunburnt back, but that didn't slow her down. When she'd woken up back at the beach, Ellis and Julia were gone, and she was starving. Again. She'd washed the sand off at the outside shower, slipped into her cover-up, and gone in search of something to eat. The little luncheonette was called The Picky Pelican. It sat in the middle of a strip shopping center only a few blocks from Ebbtide, and it reminded her of Clary's Soda Fountain, back home.

So she'd found the seat at the counter, but when the waitress brought the menu, nothing really appealed to her. Except a chocolate milk shake.

Dorie tried to take her time finishing the shake. She'd felt a little guilty, leaving without telling the girls where she was going, but then, hadn't they gone off without her while she was sleeping on her lounge chair?

She pulled a magazine out of her beach bag and flicked idly through the pages.

"Ah-hem." A woman in expensive-looking designer sunglasses cleared her throat.

Dorie looked up from her magazine. "Hello," she said.

"Would you mind if I sat here?" The woman gestured at the empty stool beside Dorie's. It was the only vacant one at the counter.

"Not at all," Dorie said.

"Thanks." The woman sat down and silently picked up a menu. She was attractive, maybe a little younger than Dorie, and with her tailored black slacks, black sling-back stiletto heels, and clingy silk leopard-print blouse, she looked distinctly out of place amongst the T-shirts-and-shorts-wearing beach crowd in the restaurant. Dorie went back to her magazine, forcing herself to take tiny sips of her milk shake. What she really wanted was a second shake. But this one cost nearly four bucks, and she'd have to leave a buck tip, and that was five bucks that she hadn't budgeted on spending. Five bucks she really shouldn't spend.

She looked down at her cell phone, and for the tenth time that day, tried to force herself to call her sister. Willa had plenty of money. Arthur was rich, and Willa hadn't worked a day since she'd married. It was rotten of her to cancel at the last minute, and even rottener not to offer to pay her share anyway. Back when she'd invited herself to come along with the others, she'd even hinted to Dorie that she'd be happy to pay for both their shares. Of course, she'd never mentioned the offer again.

She shouldn't have come, Dorie thought glumly. When Willa had canceled, she should have stayed home too. She had no business spending all this money for a month at the beach. Especially now.

The waitress came over, and the woman next to her ordered a club sandwich and an iced tea. Dorie's stomach growled. Suddenly she felt she would *kill* for a club sandwich. Even though she'd had a grilled-cheese sandwich for lunch back at the house, not to mention a mound of potato chips.

Dorie turned back to her magazine and tried to concentrate on an article offering "Ten Tips to Save Money Now." The article was a joke, advising readers to cut corners by giving up their Starbucks and doing their own nails. Dorie didn't go to Starbucks. And she hadn't had a professional manicure in years.

A few moments later, the waitress was back with the woman's food. "Can I get you anything else?" she heard the waitress ask.

"Um, well," the blond woman said, her voice low. "I'm looking for a motel room around here. Nothing fancy. It doesn't have to be on the beach or anything. Just something clean and cheap, maybe with a little kitchenette. Would you have any suggestions?"

"Cheap?" the waitress laughed. "Honey, this is high season at Nags Head. I guess that would depend on what you call cheap. My cousin and her kids stayed at a little place over on the inlet. Joint didn't even have a pool. And they had to give close to two hundred bucks a night."

"Oh." The blonde's voice sounded tired, defeated even.

"You might want to drive on down the road, check someplace like Elizabeth City. I think they got a Motel 6 over there."

"Thanks," the blonde said. The waitress drifted away.

"Excuse me."

Dorie looked up from her magazine.

"Could you pass the pepper, please?" Maryn pointed at the pepper shaker directly in front of Dorie.

"Here you go," Dorie said, sliding the shaker over.

Maryn deconstructed her club sandwich, carefully removing each layer of bread, and with a knife, scraping off the excess mayonnaise before sprinkling the thin slices of bloodred tomato with an avalanche of pepper.

She caught Dorie watching her with interest. "I wish, just once, they'd ask before slathering mayo all over everything," she said.

"I know," Dorie agreed. "I'm the same way with mustard. A little goes a long way, if you ask me. But that sure is a pretty tomato."

"Um-hmm," the blonde said, restacking her sandwich. "We don't get tomatoes this nice until really late in the season back home. But there's nothing like a Jersey tomato."

Dorie laughed. "You haven't tasted one out of my daddy's garden. He grows these huge ones, he calls 'em Mortgage Lifters, I could eat 'em 'til I'm sick."

"Are you from around here?" the blonde asked.

"Nope," Dorie said. "I'm from Savannah, Georgia. How 'bout you?"

"Jersey," Maryn said, deliberately vague. She took a delicate bite of her sandwich and dabbed with her napkin at a bit of mayo on her lip.

"My friends and I are here for the whole month," Dorie volunteered.

"Oh?" the blonde put the sandwich down. "At a motel? Isn't that pretty expensive?"

"We've got a house," Dorie said proudly. "Right on the beach. There are three of us, and we share expenses, so it works out to be way cheaper than a motel. Of course," she added ruefully, "it's more expensive than we'd planned, because my sister canceled on us at the last minute."

"A house," Maryn said thoughtfully. "How do you go about finding something like that?"

Dorie laughed. "Ellis, one of my girlfriends? She's a planning freak. She put this whole trip together. I think she found it on VRBO. Or maybe Craigslist."

"VRBO?"

"Vacation Rentals by Owner. It's like an international website for rental houses all over the world."

"Never heard of that before," Maryn admitted. "Maybe I should check it out. I'm looking for a place to stay around here for a couple weeks."

"Good luck on that. I think things get booked up around here pretty early. Ellis booked our house months ago. Of course, that's when we were planning to have five people instead of only three."

"This was sort of a last-minute decision," Maryn said, shrugging. "Guess I'll maybe look for a place in Elizabeth City. Although the idea of a Motel 6, that's kinda grim. I was hoping to find something on the beach."

Maryn returned her attention to her sandwich.

And Dorie had an idea. Her bedroom—the one she and Stephen were to have shared on the top floor, was lonely. She'd felt isolated with Ellis and Julia on the second floor, so she'd moved down to the room that would have been Willa's.

She eyed the blonde warily. She was expensively dressed, well groomed. Was it crazy, this idea taking root? She'd been obsessed with money worries since arriving at Nags Head. Maybe, just maybe, it wasn't such a crazy idea.

Dorie cleared her throat. "Um, don't take this the wrong way, okay?"

The blonde turned and raised her sunglasses. Her eyes were a clear corn-flower blue. "Yes?"

"Look," Dorie said, blushing a little. "I had an idea. You're looking for a place to stay at the beach, and as it happens, we've got an extra bedroom and bath. . . ."

"Oh," the blonde said. "Well, I don't know. . . ."

"It's pretty private," Dorie went on. "You'd have the top floor of the house. My husband and I were going to stay there, but he couldn't come at the last minute, and then my sister canceled too, so we've got all this extra space."

The blonde stared at her, as though she were inspecting a head of cabbage at the supermarket. Dorie felt herself blushing again. What the hell was she doing? Inviting a total stranger to move in with them? The girls would think she'd gone nuts.

"I could use the kitchen?" the blonde asked.

"Uh, yeah. I mean, of course," Dorie stuttered. "You can have access to the whole house. We're pretty casual, it's just the three of us. I'm a schoolteacher, and my friend Julia is a model. And Ellis works at a bank. Or, actually, she used to work at a bank."

"How much?" Maryn asked.

Now it was Dorie's turn to stare back. The blonde's clothes looked expen-sive. And her jewelry looked even more expensive. She wore a huge diamond solitaire on her right ring finger and a diamond tennis bracelet on her left wrist. The handbag she balanced on her lap was white ostrich skin, the size of a small dog. The zipper pull bore a Prada nameplate. And the gold letters on the sleek tortoiseshell sunglasses perched on her head spelled out DIOR. Dorie was no expert, but the pocketbook and the sunglasses looked like the real thing to her.

She did the math in her head, adding an extra five hundred-dollar cushion, and named the price.

"Hmm," the blonde said. "I wasn't thinking anywhere near that much."

"It's the nicest bedroom in the house," Dorie pointed out. "With beach access. And off-street parking."

"Is there a garage?" Maryn asked eagerly.

"Yeees," Dorie said, though she had no idea if the garage guy would be willing to let somebody else park in it. Maybe if they offered to throw some of this woman's cash his way, he'd agree to share.

"Does it have a private entrance?"

Dorie bit her lip. There was an outside spiral staircase leading up to the third floor, but it was narrow and scary-looking, and none of the girls had even thought to try going up it. Still, it was technically a private entrance. And this woman was anxious to have a room with a garage and a private entrance. And she obviously had the money to pay for both.

"It has a private entrance," Dorie said, nodding for emphasis. "But if you want to park in the garage, that'll be an extra hundred bucks a week."

The blonde took a sip of her iced tea. She put her glass down on the counter, and twisted the diamond solitaire ring for a moment. Dorie found herself holding her breath.

"Fine," she said finally. "I'll take it."

Dorie grinned. "Great. But we'll want the rent in cash. In advance."

Maryn shook her head. "I'd prefer to pay half now, half at the end of the month. In case I have a change of plans."

"Deal," Dorie said, putting out her hand. "By the way, my name is Dorie Dunaway."

The blonde hesitated, and then took Dorie's hand. "I'm Madison. Madison Venable. When can I move in?"

Dorie looked down at her watch. "How's four o'clock? I'll want to let my friends know you're coming and make sure your space in the garage is empty."

"That'll work," Madison said. "I've got some things to take care of this afternoon, then I'll be over."

"The house is called Ebbtide," Dorie said, putting her money on the counter beside her empty glass. "It's three blocks north of here, on the beach road, which is Virginia Dare. There's a sign at the entrance to the driveway, and you'll see my red van."

12

Julia and Ellis were sitting on the front porch, painting each other's toenails a ridiculous shade of neon green. "There you are!" Ellis cried, as Dorie flopped down onto a rocking chair beside her. "Where'd you disappear to?"

"I woke up and you guys were gone," Dorie said accusingly.

"We went for ice cream," Julia said. "We didn't think you'd care."

Dorie laughed. "That's what I did too, only it was a milk shake." She licked her lips. "Yummy. I don't know when the last time was that I had a real milk shake made with real chocolate syrup and ice cream and the works. Not to mention whipped cream and a cherry."

"Sounds divine," Julia said. She held the bottle of nail polish aloft. "It's called Lime-a-Lishus. Want to be next?"

"No thanks," Dorie said. "I did my toes right before I left home."

"We were just talking about what to do about dinner," Ellis said. "It's your turn tonight. Got any thoughts?"

"Not yet," Dorie said, sitting on the edge of the rocking chair so that it leaned into the girls. "Listen, you guys, I just did something kinda crazy."

"What? You picked up a guy along with your milk shake?" Julia laughed. "Now that's our old Dorie!"

"Lord no!" Dorie said. "Here's the thing. I kinda rented out the top floor of this house to a woman I just met."

"Sure you did," Ellis said lazily, flexing her toes and admiring her daring new look.

"For reals," Dorie said, sitting up straight. "I totally did. Her name's Madison, she dresses like she's got plenty of bucks, and I overheard her asking the waitress about renting a motel room with a kitchenette. She was sitting next to me at the restaurant, and we kind of struck up a conversation. So I offered her the room that was going to be mine and Stephen's. And she took it. She's going to pay us six hundred dollars more than Willa would have. So what do you guys think?"

Julia put the bottle of nail polish on the floor. "I think," she said slowly, "that you have lost your freaking mind. You can't be serious, Dorie. Do you mean to tell me you just invited a total stranger to live with us for the next month? Don't you think that's something you might have run by Ellis and me?"

Dorie bit her lip. "Yeah, I guess. But the money will more than make up for what Willa would have paid. I just thought, I mean, it's sort of my fault Willa let us all down. She's my sister, and I'm the one who talked you guys into letting her come. I should have known she would pull a stunt like that. I just figured it was my responsibility to fix things. So I did."

Ellis took Dorie's hand. "You're really worried about the money part, I know. But honey, you're not responsible for what Willa did. And Julia and I aren't mad at you about it. That's just Willa."

"I am worried about the money," Dorie cried. "I mean, Ellis, you're out of work, and Julia's not working as much as she used to, so I think money's tight for all of us. . . ."

"Who says I'm not working?" Julia said, bristling. "What the hell is that supposed to mean?"

"Nothing," Dorie said, backpedaling.

"Julia!" Ellis said sharply. "Cut the crap. You just told me yourself that you're not working as much. And anyway, you know Dorie didn't mean it like that. The truth is, money is kinda tight for all of us. But Dorie, you really should have talked to us about this before you offered to rent out your room."

"I know," Dorie said, sniffling. "God, I'm such a screwup. But, it all happened so fast. And it just seemed like a good idea at the time."

"What do you even know about this girl?" Julia asked.

Dorie hesitated. "She's from New Jersey, and on vacation, sort of a spur-of-the-moment beach trip . . . and, oh yeah, she hates it when they put too much mayo on a sandwich."

"Oh, she's a mayo hater, is she? Say no more! That seals the deal for me." Julia rolled her eyes.

Dorie bit her lip. "I guess I could tell Madison we've changed our minds. . . ." Her voice trailed off. "She's coming over at four. I'll tell her then."

"Well. . . ." Ellis cleared her throat. "It is a lot of money."

"And the room's just sitting there, empty," Dorie reminded them. "It's not like she'd be rooming with us. Not even on the same floor as the rest of us."

"But she's a stranger, Dorie," Julia said. "You don't really know anything about her. Maybe she's a pathological liar. Maybe she's really from Arkansas. And maybe she actually adores mayo and can't stand ketchup. Who knows? She could walk down those stairs one night and murder us all in our beds, as we're sleeping."

"But, why would she do something like that?" Dorie asked, digging in her heels. Julia's bossiness was starting to wear thin with her. The more Julia protested Madison's coming, the more Dorie thought it was a good idea. "Anyway, if you're that worried about her, we could all get locks on the bedroom doors."

"Surely, that's not necessary," Ellis said, her voice trailing off.

Dorie studied Ellis, knowing she was the swing vote on the matter of Madison.

"Just meet her, please?" Dorie said, keeping her eyes on Ellis. "You'll see, she's perfectly nice. And the setup is perfect. Madison could come and go by that outside stairway around back. That's what she wanted, a separate entrance. And she wanted to make sure she could use the kitchen, and of course, I told her that would be fine. You guys, she seems like somebody we could trust. She agreed to pay cash—half up front, half at the end of the month. I watched her drive off. She's got a new-looking Volvo SUV. And she's got some major-league diamonds. And, I mean, she was wearing Dior sunglasses and carrying a Prada bag. I guess they were the real thing, I don't really know a lot about that kind of stuff. . . ."

"I do," Julia said quickly. "I can spot bootleg Prada from a mile away."

"Okay, when she comes over, you can totally check out all that stuff," Dorie said. "What do you say?"

"It couldn't hurt to meet her," Ellis said. "Right, Julia?"

"Whatever," Julia said, mustering a stern look. "But when this homicidal maniac slashes you to pieces with a butcher knife, don't say I didn't warn you."

"Then it's settled," Dorie said happily. "Unless you guys get just a really weird vibe, Madison is in. Now, I'll just run upstairs and leave some clean towels in the bathroom. It's the least I can do, since she's taking up Willa's slack."

"I'll give you a hand," Ellis volunteered.

"There's just one more thing," Dorie added. "Madison wants to be able to keep her car in the garage. I told her we'd have to charge her a hundred dollars more a week, and she didn't bat an eyelash."

"We don't have access to the garage," Ellis said. "Garage boy keeps his Bronco there."

"There's room for two cars," Dorie said. "Maybe Ty Bazemore wouldn't mind. Maybe you could ask Mr. Culpepper for permission."

"Maybe," Ellis said, sounding noncommittal. "I'll check and see."

13

Maryn watched Dorie's red van pull out of the parking lot. Had she done something totally crazy? She'd just agreed to rent a room in a house full of women—total strangers—sight unseen. Why? Something about this girl made her feel safe. Dorie seemed like somebody she could trust. And Maryn couldn't remember the last time she had trusted another woman she wasn't related to.

She told herself the new plan made perfect sense. This way her name wouldn't show up on any hotel or motel register. She wouldn't be using a credit card. She'd be hidden away in a private home, in a place he'd never look, her car parked in a garage, hidden from prying eyes.

Maryn pulled her cell phone from her handbag and checked for messages. Four missed calls from Don. She deleted them with a tap of her fingertip, wishing the task were as easy in the real world as it was in the digital one. She wondered idly if she should call Adam, tell him how right he'd been about Don. She wished she could tell him, wished they could talk. Adam was the only one she could trust. But it wasn't safe. Not for him, not for her.

Maryn nibbled nervously at her cuticle. What should she do? Call the police? Call the old man, R.G. Prescott himself? And tell him what? "I used to work for you, and my husband, Don Shackleford, is your accountant, and incidentally, he's ripped you off to the tune of a couple million dollars, have a nice day?"

No. She had no real proof. She hadn't worked for the insurance company in months. Shortly after their marriage, Don had insisted she quit—he had plenty of money, they didn't need her penny-ante salary, and anyway, she had plenty to do at home, the three-thousand-square-foot town house they were renting while the new house was under construction. She'd kept up the friendship with Adam after leaving the company, but she was careful not to mention Adam to Don, who thought Adam was a loser—and anyway, why couldn't she make friends with the wives of some of his golf buddies?

Adam had called on her cell phone last Friday, and it was obvious that something was wrong. "We need to talk," he'd said, his voice low, insisting they meet at a coffee shop miles away from Cherry Hill.

She'd laughed when he walked in fifteen minutes late, wearing oversized sunglasses and a baseball cap pulled low over his face. "What, you're incognito?"

"This is serious, Maryn," Adam had said. "Listen. We had outside auditors show up at the office today. They wouldn't tell anybody what they were looking for, but I know for a fact that something's funny with half a dozen of our accounts."

She shrugged. "What's that got to do with me? I haven't worked there in months. And anyway, I just handled claims processing."

"This isn't about you," Adam said. "It's about your husband."

"Don?" She still didn't get it.

Adam smirked. "How do you think he got so rich? How many other CPAs do you know who live like him? The houses, new cars, trips to Vegas, Palm Beach, Bermuda? How much do you think it costs to belong to a country club like yours?" He gestured towards Maryn's engagement ring. "Robby Prescott is old money, third generation, and his wife doesn't have a ring like that."

"That's crazy," Maryn said heatedly. She got up to leave. "Don doesn't have to steal. He owns investment property, an office building on the south side, some self-storage companies. Just because you don't like him doesn't mean he's a crook."

Adam grabbed her sleeve, and her coffee spilled all over the table, splashing on her favorite Armani skirt. "Listen to me," he insisted. "The guy is dirty. There's money missing, or at least unaccounted for. Like, two million dollars."

"You're talking about my husband," Maryn said, her voice cold. "Now let go. And don't call me again. Ever."

Her anger lasted all of a day. And then she started to wonder. Just where did all Don's money come from? Why was he so secretive about his business affairs? He was generous with her, but she had no checking account of her own, not even a debit card, only credit cards, and she never saw a bill or bank statement. Everything was sent directly to his office. If she needed cash, she asked, and Don gave. "I'm your own personal ATM," he told her more than once, graphically demonstrating just what he expected from her in return for his generosity.

And exactly twenty-four hours after her meeting with Adam, Maryn had started to look for answers. And what she found was much, much more than she bargained for. The truth hadn't set her free at all, she thought now. It had sent her running for her life.

She put the phone away and dismissed any thought of asking anybody for help. Who would believe her? For now, she had more pressing matters to attend to. Her designer clothes—big-city career pieces—made her stand out like a sore thumb in a beach town. And the few pieces of clothing she'd hurriedly thrown into her duffle were just as unsuited to her current situation.

There was an outlet mall just down the road. She'd pick up a new wardrobe for the new person she'd just invented on the spot, a few minutes ago. Madison would need some shorts and T-shirts, a pair of Levi's, some flip-flops. And her own clothes—Maryn's clothes, the ones with all those expensive designer tags that she'd once lusted over? There was a Goodwill donation bin

in the parking lot of the mall. That would be the end of Maryn. And the beginning of Madison.

"Here she comes," Dorie said, as the Volvo bumped along down the driveway.

"Nice car," Julia said, eyeing it. "Wonder where she stole it?"

"Be nice," Dorie warned, jumping up from the rocking chair she'd been
perched on.

She waited until Madison had parked the car in front of the driveway, and
then walked slowly down to meet her.

"Hi, Madison," Dorie said, smiling. "I'm so glad you're here. Did you have
any trouble finding us?"

"Not at all," Madison said, unloading her duffle bag and laptop case from
the trunk.

"Here," Dorie said, tugging at the strap of the duffle bag, "Let me help you
carry your stuff in."

"No!" Madison jerked the duffle bag away. "I mean, no thanks. I can manage by myself."

"All right," Dorie said. "Come on up to the porch. We're just having some
iced tea. The girls are dying to meet you."

"If it's all right with you," Madison said, "I've had a long day. I'd just as
soon see my room first, and get settled in. Maybe we could handle the intro-
ductions later?"

Dorie's cheeks flushed hot pink. "Actually, I was a little bit premature in
offering to rent the room without everybody having met you first. "

Madison's smile was tight. "They want to check me out, make sure I'm not
some kind of freak, right?"

"I'm so sorry. It's just that I did this all on my own, without consulting
anybody," Dorie said apologetically. "I'm not usually this impulsive. But I'm
sure it'll be fine, as soon as they meet you."

Madison let out a long sigh of annoyance. "Let's get it over with then."

"Girls," Dorie said, "this is Madison."

Ellis stood up and held out her hand. "Madison, hi. I'm Ellis Sullivan."

Julia stayed in her rocking chair. She looked Madison up and down and finally put down her glass of iced tea. "Hello," she said. "I'm Julia."

"Hi there," Madison said warily. She clutched her pocketbook and looked around the porch. "This looks very nice. Thanks for agreeing to let me horn in on your getaway."

"We're glad to have you," Ellis said. She gestured towards the rocking chair she'd just abandoned. "Join us, won't you? I just made a pitcher of iced tea."

"Thank you," Madison said. She put the duffle bag and laptop on the floor beside the rocking chair and took the glass of iced tea Ellis poured.

An uneasy silence fell over the porch, punctuated only by the rhythmic sound of Julia's chair, rocking back and forth on the worn wooden floorboards.

"I guess Dorie told you about all of us," Ellis said, anxious to break the ice.

"Not really," Madison said. "She just said you all were old friends. From Savannah?"

"Actually, I'm the only one still living in Savannah," Dorie said, jumping in. "I teach English at a Catholic girls' high school. Ellis lives in Philadelphia, and she's in banking."

"Was in banking," Ellis said. "I've just been downsized."

"And Julia lives in London. When she's not traveling. She's a model. You've probably seen her in magazines. Sumptuesse shampoo? That was Julia," Dorie said. "She was the face of Sumptuesse."

"But not lately," Julia said wryly. "What about you, Madison? What brings you to Nags Head?"

Madison had been waiting for it, and she was ready with an answer that was mostly true.

"I'm running away from home," she said glibly, with a toss of her head. "Man troubles."

"So sorry," Dorie said, reaching out and awkwardly patting Madison's hand.

"I'll get over it," Madison said, her smile tight.

"Where's home?" Julia said, pressing on.

"Good question," Madison said smoothly. "I've bounced around a lot. Jersey most recently. But that's about to change. I'm examining my options."

"I know what that's like," Ellis said, nodding her head in agreement. "Time for reinvention, right? I'm not even sure I'll go back into banking."

"What?" Dorie said, looking confused. "You never told us you're planning a career change. What would you do?"

Ellis shrugged. "Who knows? Maybe I'll take up skydiving. Or run away and join the circus."

"Right," Julia said. "And I'll take up brain surgery."

"Ellis is afraid of heights," Dorie said, seeing Madison's questioning look. "And Julia can't stand the sight of blood. She flunked high school biology because she refused to dissect her fetal pig."

Madison yawned and set down her iced tea glass. "Sorry," she said. "I hope I'm not being rude, but I really am tired after a day of driving." She glanced over at Dorie. "If that's all right?"

"Of course," Dorie exclaimed, looking over at the other two women. "Right?"

Julia shrugged. Ellis stood up again. "Welcome to Ebbtide," she said warmly.

"Come on, Madison," Dorie said. "I'll show you your room. Or would you like to see the rest of the house first?"

"I'll take the tour later, if you don't mind," Madison said.

"All right," Dorie said, trying not to look surprised. "Sure. Well, your entrance is around the back of the house. I'll show you the way."

"Thanks," Madison said.

Dorie picked her way carefully up the three flights of stairs, clinging tightly to the metal rail. The paint was rusted and peeling and stuck to the damp palms of her hand. Madison was only a few steps behind, and while Dorie could feel herself winded after just the first floor, the other woman's step was light, her breathing unaffected.

She and Ellis had made quick work of getting the room ready for their guest. The room, which had been empty, was stifling, so they switched on the air-conditioning unit to try and cool it down. Then, while Ellis made up the bed with clean linens, Dorie had dragged a small oak dresser, nightstand, and ancient green desk lamp from the attic storage space. They'd damp mopped the floor and swept the cobwebs from the windowsills. It had taken both of them to force open the warped door to the outside-stair landing. It obviously hadn't been used in quite a while.

Dorie opened the door and stepped aside to let Madison enter the room first, keeping her fingers crossed that the room would meet her approval.

It took Madison only a moment to look around. She set her duffle bag on the bed and stood her laptop case on the dresser. She walked over and looked out the front window. From here she had a clear view of the street. A double window faced the ocean.

"It's fine," she said briskly.

"I'm glad," Dorie said. She pointed through the bedroom door to the stair landing. "Your bathroom is right there. You have a set of clean towels. There's a laundry room off the kitchen."

"What about the key?" Madison asked.

"The key?"

"To the door," Madison said impatiently. "Doors, that is."

"Oh." Dorie looked at the exterior door they'd just come through. It had an old-fashioned keyhole. The bedroom door had a thumb-latch lock, but nothing else. "We don't have a key to the outside stairway," Dorie admitted. "I guess maybe we could ask Mr. Culpepper about getting one."

"Yes," Madison said. "I'll need a key."

"I don't think there is a lock for your bedroom door," Dorie said, gesturing towards it. "But you don't need to worry about that. Since you've got the whole top floor, nobody else will be coming up here."

"I'd feel better about having a lock," Madison said.

"Really? I mean, we do have locks on the downstairs doors," Dorie said, "and I'll get you a key made for those. But half the time we don't even remember to lock up. It's the beach, and I guess that's not something we worry about."

"I worry about it," Madison said firmly, her hand on the door to the inside-stair landing. "I'm used to living in the city. I won't sleep until I have a lock and a key—to both these doors. I'll be happy to pay to get a locksmith in."

Her eyes flickered to the hallway, a clear signal to Dorie that she was dismissed.

"All right," Dorie said finally, getting the hint. "I'll let you get some rest. And I'll get Ellis to ask Mr. Culpepper about the locks."

"Thank you," Madison said, giving Dorie a tight smile. "I'd appreciate that." She picked up the Prada bag, took out a thick, white envelope and handed it to Dorie. "My rent," she said. "I just assumed your friends wouldn't want to take a check."

Dorie's face colored. "Well, uh, we hadn't really discussed that. . . ."

Madison started to close the door.

"Oh!" Dorie said, poking her head back inside. "I nearly forgot. We take turns cooking, and tonight's my night. It's nothing fancy, just rotisserie chicken from Harris Teeter and Caesar salad. But we'd love it if you'd join us for dinner. We usually eat between seven and eight."

"That's very sweet," Madison said. "But I'll probably take a rain check. That club sandwich I had this afternoon will tide me over 'til morning."

"Well . . . if you change your mind, or want to join us in a glass of wine or something," Dorie said, heading down the stairs. "Just come on down."

"I'll do that." Madison closed the door, and Dorie heard the thumb latch click into place.

Julia and Ellis were sitting on the sofa in the living room when Dorie got downstairs.

"Well?" Ellis asked expectantly. "Did she like the room?"

"More importantly, did she pay the rent?" Julia asked.

Dorie sat down in one of the faded chintz armchairs by the fireplace. "She liked the room fine, as far as I could tell. Madison's just, well . . . reserved, I guess you'd say." She held up the envelope of cash. "And yes, she gave me the rent money. In cash." She stared accusingly at Julia. "She was sure you guys wouldn't take her check."

"Cash is king," Julia said lightly. "Is she coming downstairs for dinner?" Julia craned her neck in the direction of the stairs, as though Madison might be coming down at any moment.

"Not right now," Dorie said. "She said she's pretty tired. I get the feeling she might have just driven into town today."

"She's got New Jersey tags on that Volvo she's driving," Julia reported. "And I think you're right about her having money, Dorie. That is not a cheap car. Those XC70s run around forty-seven thousand dollars, and that's just for the basics. Hers is loaded, got the onboard nav screen and the works."

"How do you suddenly happen to know so much about cars?" Ellis asked. "You haven't owned one in years, right?"

"Oh, Booker's turned into a total gearhead," Julia said airily. "That's the car he's been lusting after for months now."

Dorie had opened the envelope and was silently counting the money. "You guys," she said, looking from Julia to Ellis. "There's three thousand dollars here. All in fifty-dollar bills."

Ellis peered over Dorie's shoulder at the cash. "Didn't you say she only wanted to pay half in advance and half at the end of the month?"

"Let me see that," Julia said, putting out her hand for the money. She fanned the bills out across her bare, tanned legs. "Holy mother," Julia said. "Dorie's right. And these are all brand-new bills. What do you make of that?"

"Maybe she knocked over a bank on the way over here?" Ellis said, giggling uneasily at her own joke.

"She did ask if we could get a new lock put on that door to the outside staircase. And get the key to her room," Dorie said reluctantly. "And she wants a key to the front door too. She said she was willing to pay to have a locksmith come in. Maybe that's why the extra money."

"What the hell?" Julia said angrily. "Does she think we're a bunch of thieves or something?"

"She said she's used to living in the city, and that she won't sleep at night until she feels secure," Dorie said. She looked over at Ellis. "Maybe you could ask Mr. Culpepper if it's all right to get the locks put on? Tell him we'll pay for it?"

"I can do that," Ellis said. "But I really don't want to let him know we're subletting that third floor room. He's already charging us an extra fifty dollars a week to use the garage. I'm afraid if he figures out what we're doing, he'll hit us up for even more money."

"You're right," Julia said. "Just don't even mention Madison. Just blame it on one of us. Tell him we're paranoid or something."

"That's not far from the truth," Ellis said. "I'm really not a scaredy-cat, but maybe when we get the locksmith in, should we ask him to put locks on our bedroom doors too?"

"Why would we do that?" Dorie asked. She took the bills from Julia, and stuffed them back into the cash envelope.

"Because," Julia said slowly. "We've just invited a stranger into our midst, and we actually know virtually nothing about her. Did you guys notice how evasive she was when I asked her about herself? If she's that interested in locking us out, maybe we need to start thinking about doing the same for ourselves."

"Oh, Julia," Dorie said, flushing. "That's not fair! I mean, I know you were pissed that I rented the room out, but honestly, I think I know a little bit about people. Madison seems perfectly nice. Perfectly normal. She's just a little shy. And she wants her privacy. What's so scary about that?"

"Nothing scary to me," Julia said. "But if she can drive a car that costs nearly fifty thousand dollars and carry a two-thousand-dollar pocketbook, which, by the way, is the real deal, doesn't it seem a little odd to you that she wants to rent a crappy bedroom in a fairly crappy house? And that she's willing to pay all this money to do it—sight unseen?"

"I'm sorry, but I've got to agree with Julia, it really does seem odd to me," Ellis said.

"And I for one intend to keep my eyes and ears open around the woman," Julia added. "There's a lot more I'd like to know about this Madison."

"I really don't care why she wants to live here," Dorie said. "All I care about is that now I don't have to call my sister and grovel and beg her to pay her share for the house. So you guys can go ahead and lock your doors and play detective all you want. Just don't chase her off. Okay?"

14

The cable was out. When they turned on the television after dinner, the screen was as gray and fuzzy as a discarded sweater.

Ellis reached for her iPhone. "I'm e-mailing Mr. Culpepper. Honestly, we get one thing fixed, and something else breaks down."

"Why don't you just call him?" Dorie asked.

"I don't have his phone number," Ellis said, typing away. "And he's pretty cagey about letting me know where he lives, or believe me, I'd be camped out on his doorstep until he got everything here squared away."

Julia poured herself another glass of wine and leaned back in her chair. "Don't get your panties in a wad on my account. I could care less about watching television. Especially in the summertime."

Ellis loaded up the dinner plates and silverware and dumped them into the deep sink she'd filled with soapy water before sitting down to dinner. This part of the summer, she noted happily, was going just as planned, especially now that they had Madison, and her money, contributing to their financial well-being. Madison had been there three days now, and turned down all their invitations to join them for dinner, explaining that she didn't really "do" dinner.

She was, as Dorie had said, shy around them, spending most of her time in her room, with an occasional walk on the beach. The day after she'd moved in, she'd brought a bike home, and now, when she left the house, it was usually on her bike. Despite Julia's dire predictions, nothing out of the ordinary had happened since Madison's arrival.

She was odd, a loner, evasive when asked for personal information. Ellis had suggested that Madison was suffering from a broken heart, and Dorie seconded the emotion. "That ring of hers," Julia had commented, "would go a long way towards healing my broken heart."

"Come on, Ellis," Dorie called now from the dining room. "Leave the dishes 'til later. I'm glad the television's on the fritz. Let's do something together. There's a bunch of jigsaw puzzles here. Let's work on one of those."

"Suits me," Ellis said.

"Ugh, jigsaw puzzles," Julia said, making a face. "Why don't we just put on our Supp-Hose and eat some stewed prunes while we're at it? Come on, you guys, we've got to figure out something livelier than that. We're not dead yet, are we?"

"I brought some DVDs," Ellis started. "Or we could play a board game. What's over there, Dorie?"

"Mmm, let's see. Uno, Monopoly, Trivial Pursuit. Oh, I know, cards. Let's play five hundred, like we used to do at the beach at home."

"Yeah," Ellis said, getting up from the table. "Five hundred. Shuffle the cards, Julia. And I'll make some popcorn."

"Open another bottle of wine, while you're at it," Julia ordered. "And not that cheap crap, either. I put a nice bottle of pinot grigio in the fridge before dinner."

Ty read the latest e-mail from Ellis Sullivan and laughed despite himself. Maybe she wasn't wrapped quite as tightly as he'd thought.

To: Mr.Culpepper@Ebbtide.com
From: EllisSullivan@hotmail.com
Subject: Cable's out
Dear Mr. Culpepper, Hate to pout, but our cable is out.—Ellis

Of course her cable was out. His cable was out too. He had a pile of past-due notices on his desk, and the disconnect warning was on the very top. He toyed with the idea of trying to bypass the cable box. A buddy had shown him how to do this back in his college days. But with his luck, he'd get caught and get his ass slammed in jail.

To: EllisSullivan@hotmail.com
From: Mr.Culpepper@Ebbtide.com
Subject: Cable
Dear Ellis: Please don't have a hissy. I've called Comcast, but the line is busy.

Pleased with himself for this small accomplishment, he pushed the send button. And then he forwarded her latest missive to the file where he had kept all the rest of her e-mails. It was getting to be quite a collection.

Without television and the Nationals game he'd planned to watch, the evening stretched out before him seemed as empty and depressing as the silent television screen perched on the plastic milk crate in the corner of his living room.

He went to the fridge, got a beer, and walked out onto the deck. He slumped down onto a chair and stared out at the water. Must have been a good sunset, he mused, looking at the orange-and-purple-streaked sky. He'd missed it, of course, because he'd been online, searching for a way out of his predicament. That's how he spent most of his time these days, looking for a way out of the hole he'd dug himself into. It was a hell of a note. He'd risked everything buying this place, desperately wanting to live on the ocean again. Now he had it—Ebbtide, perched right on the edge of the Outer Banks, and he might as well have been living in a cave for all the good it did him. He hadn't surfed, hadn't gone for a morning swim, hadn't even caught a decent sunset—not in weeks.

There had to be a way out. But how?

He took a long pull on the beer bottle. He heard laughter and music coming from the direction of Ebbtide. If he stood at the far end of the deck, he could see into the dining room, bathed in the golden yellow light of the chandelier.

The three women were sitting around the table, playing cards. There was a wine bottle on the table, and half-filled glasses. The tall one, Julia, was talking rapid-fire, waving her hands for emphasis. The cute little strawberry blonde was giggling helplessly, running her fingers through her hair. Ellis, he noticed, seemed to be the scorekeeper. She was arguing, and smiling, and writing something on a pad of paper. Suddenly she looked up. Ty ducked instinctively. Had she seen him watching him? Nah. One of the women said something, and Ellis pelted her with a piece of popcorn, and now they were having a full-on popcorn fight, and their shrieks of laughter floated over the dune and out to sea.

The cards and the golden light and the silvery peals of laughter reminded him of summers past. The whole family was staying at Ebbtide, and his mother and grandmother were having a meeting of what they called "the swill sisters." He'd been, what? Six? His father had to explain that these ladies were not really his mom's sisters, but just a few old friends his mom had known since she was a girl, nearly his age.

His grandmother had spent the day of the swill sisters meeting feverishly baking little cookies and making egg-salad, pimento-cheese, and chicken-salad sandwiches, all cut into tiny, crustless triangles. His mother had fluffed and fussed and swept and scrubbed the old pine floors to a fine, dull gleam. A flowery tablecloth had been spread across the battered dining room table, and from the big cedar chest that sat in the hall under the stairs, a set of gold-rimmed, rose-strewn dishes and delicate pink wineglasses he'd never seen before were produced.

At six o'clock, his grandmother had banished them. "No boys allowed," she'd said, laughingly pushing them out the door. So he and his dad had walked down the road to the pizza parlor, where they'd slowly eaten a large pie and watched the Braves game on the television mounted on the wall over the bar. His dad had beer, and he'd given Ty a sip, warning him not to tell "the womenfolk."

When they'd walked back home, the sandy driveway was still filled with cars, so he'd waited by the kitchen door, and his father had tiptoed into the house, emerging a moment later with a paper napkin filled with the little cookies and cakes, and a can of root beer for Ty.

"Contraband," his dad had called it in a conspiratorial whisper. They took their stolen treats and went to the garage apartment. Back then, they still called the apartment Tillie's house, because it was where his grandmother's maid, Tillie, and her three children lived every summer when they came down to the beach from his grandmother's big house in Edenton.

Ty had only a vague memory of Tillie, a slight, stoop-shouldered black lady who colored her hair bright red, chewed gum nonstop, and wore what looked to him like a white nurse's uniform. He did remember how Tillie put ice in her coffee in the morning, and how she liked to boss his mother around. But Tillie had quit coming to the beach in the '80s, because, as his father reported, she wanted to be paid a living wage, "and your grandmother, bless her heart, is tight as a tick."

So Tillie's house had become a place to store unused furniture and an overflow of houseguests. The night of the swill sisters meeting, his father dragged two rickety wooden chairs out to the deck, and they'd sat there and gorged on desserts. They could see his grandmother and his mother and a gaggle of women, arrayed around the gussied-up dining room table. Music was playing, and some of the ladies were playing a card game, and everybody was laughing and having a real party.

Ty had been mesmerized by the glimpse of his mother and his usually dignified grandmother, acting like the girls in his class at school. "What are they talking about?" he'd asked his father, who was leaning with his back against the deck railing. "What's so funny?"

"Who, them?" Ty's father glanced in the direction of the big house and shrugged. "Son, there ain't no telling what's on a woman's mind. You get a bunch of hens together like that, and all bets are off. They might be talking about shoes or clothes. Or they might be talking about whoever's not there tonight. Probably they're talking about how sorry somebody's husband is. Doesn't really matter. 'Cause even if you and me were right in there with 'em, we probably wouldn't understand what's so funny. Not in a million years."

. . .

"Rummy!" Ellis shouted jubilantly, slapping the cards faceup on the table.

"Oh no, not again," Dorie said. She fanned her own cards for the others to see. "You caught me holding a handful of aces and kings. Again." She ticked her fingertips across the cards. "That gives me, like, minus sixty."

"I'm at forty," Julia reported, laying down her own cards. "Where's that put us, Ellis?"

"Hmmm. I'm at 485. Julia, you're at 410. And Dorie, honey, you're at 220."

"I'm hopeless," Dorie said, yawning. "And tired. It's what, nearly midnight? I think I'm gonna take myself off to bed."

"Not yet," Ellis protested. "It's still early. And you could still have a comeback. Come on, Dorie, don't go to bed yet. Not when we're having so much fun. Hey, what about some ice cream? I've got Fudgsicles in the freezer."

"Chocolate?" Dorie raised an eyebrow. "Well, why didn't you say so? I may suck at cards, but I'm grrreeatttt at chocolate."

"You didn't always suck at cards," Julia observed. "You used to whip us all single-handed. I never saw anybody who could memorize cards like you, Dorie."

Dorie pushed her hair back from her face. "My mind's not in it," she said lightly. "I'm having a blonde spell. A strawberry-blonde spell."

"What *is* on your mind?" Julia asked. Ellis shot her a warning look, but Julia never took her own eyes from Dorie.

"Oh, you know," Dorie said. "Money. Work. The usual stuff. Never mind me. I'll be better once Ellis hands out those Fudgsicles she's bribing me with."

"Dorie?" Julia slid her chair over so that it was beside her friend's. "Come on, girlfriend. We know something is upsetting you."

"Julia!" Ellis said. "You promised."

Julia shrugged. "I lied. Now, come on, Dorie. Out with it."

Dorie's face paled. She swept all the cards on the table into a pile, and busied herself rebuilding the deck. "I'm that obvious?" she asked, looking from Julia to Ellis.

"No poker face at all," Ellis said, taking a seat on Dorie's other side. "But you don't have to talk about it if you don't want to."

"It's Stephen, isn't it?" Julia broke in, ignoring Ellis's glare.

"Oh God," Dorie whispered. "Yes. Stephen . . ." A single tear slid down her face. She bit her lip. "Stephen and I . . . God. I can't believe this is happening. I can't even make myself say it."

Julia filled a glass with the last of the pinot grigio and slid it in front of Dorie. "Here. Drink up."

"No," Dorie gently pushed the glass away. "I can do this. I can. I have to. Starting tonight." She took a deep breath, and suddenly the words came pouring out.

"I lied to you all. I did. And I'm sorry. The truth is, Stephen finished his thesis weeks ago. He didn't come to the beach with me . . . because . . . we're getting a divorce. And he moved out two weeks ago. And now I've got to sell the house. I couldn't tell you. I haven't told anybody. Especially Willa. Oh God, what will Willa say? And my mom? This will absolutely kill her. How am I going to tell her? And the school? I know one of us has to quit Our Lady of Angels. We can't both work there. Not now. But I don't know what to do. I can't think. Not even about the simplest stuff. I can't even decide what kind of cereal to eat for breakfast, or what to wear in the morning. It's like my brain is frozen. And I shouldn't have come to the beach. I should have stayed home and figured everything out, but I wanted to come. I wanted to get in my car and run away. Just keep driving. All I could think about was, 'I am going to the beach. And I am not going to deal with this. When I'm at the beach, none of this will matter.' So, I came."

The torrent of words stopped as suddenly as it had started. Dorie's shoulders slumped. She wiped ineffectively at the tears that were now streaming down her face. "Oh, God. What a mess."

"Oh, Dorie," Ellis said, throwing her arms around her friend. "I am so sorry." She was crying too. "Oh, sweetie, I don't know what to say." She felt utterly helpless in the face of Dorie's pain.

"I know, right?" Dorie said, her voice shaky. "Mr. and Mrs. Perfect are getting a divorce. How screwed up is this?"

Julia took a long sip of Dorie's untouched glass of wine. "I knew it. As soon as I laid eyes on you at the airport, I knew it was something like this. I kept hoping it wasn't, you know, this. But I just knew in my heart that it was."

"You're a witch," Dorie said, dabbing at her eyes with a paper napkin. "You always were."

"Not really," Julia said. "You're just so incredibly easy to read. You haven't called him, he hasn't called you. You've been weepy and mopey. And you can't play cards for shit."

"I'm sorry," Dorie said, sniffing. "I hate being Debbie Downer."

"Do you want to talk about it?" Ellis asked.

"No. I mean, yeah, I can talk about it. If you guys don't mind the popcorn getting all soggy. I don't even know where to start."

"Let me guess," Julia said. "I bet Mr. Perfect has himself a girlfriend. Am I right?"

"Julia," Ellis said, through gritted teeth. "Before this night is out, I am going to strangle you. I really am."

Dorie's laugh was shaky. "Let her alone, Ellis. Maybe she's not as witchy as I thought. You're only half right, Julia. Stephen does have somebody else. But it's not a girl. It's a guy."

"What?" Ellis cried.

"No way!" Julia said. "You're telling us Stephen is gay?"

Dorie was crying again, and the words were streaming as fast as the tears. "I'm such an idiot. How could I not have known? I mean, I knew *something* was wrong, but I never dreamed it was this. Easter break, we were supposed to go to Destin with another couple from school, and a day before we were supposed to leave, Stephen announced that he wasn't going. He said he didn't care if I went, in fact, he wanted me to go, but he said he'd had a rough semester, and he just wanted to go off hiking, by himself, up in the mountains. I told myself it was because he doesn't really like my girlfriend's husband, Brad. I mean, Brad can be hard to take sometimes. He's a marathoner, and he never shuts up about running and his times and all that. So I let Stephen go off hiking. And when he got back, I thought he'd be in a better mood. But he wasn't. He got moodier. And that's not Stephen. Not normally. Normally, he is Mr. Happy-Go-Lucky. Which is why I fell for him. And we had fights. Not a lot, and not about anything important, but you know, the whole two years we dated, we never, ever fought."

Julia guffawed. "Well, that should have been a warning signal right there. Booker and I fight every day of our lives."

"But we didn't," Dorie said. "My mom and my dad, you know, before they got divorced, they fought like cats and dogs. Willa and Nash and I, we were so glad when they finally split up. You never saw kids so happy about a divorce. And I told myself when I got married, I would never fight like they did. Because if two people are right for each other, and they love each other, they don't have to fight, you know?"

"My parents used to fight now and then," Julia said thoughtfully. "Not like Booker and me, but yeah, they'd get into it every once in a while. But then Daddy would buy Mama flowers and a piece of jewelry, or she'd make his favorite cannoli, and they'd make up like nothing happened. And they were married for like, forty years."

Ellis thought about her own parents. Lawrence Sullivan had been a patient, quiet man who doted on Ellis's mother. She couldn't remember him ever disagreeing with her mother, at least not in front of her and Baylor. Fighting would not have been his style.

"Your daddy and mama were pretty special," Ellis told Julia. "Like Ward and June Cleaver."

"Or Doris Day and Rock Hudson," Dorie said sadly. "Only Rock Hudson turned out to be gay. Just like Stephen."

Dorie looked up and saw Julia watching her. She sighed. "Now you're gonna ask me how the sex was, right?"

Julia grinned. "I was scheming a way to get you away from Ellis, 'cuz I knew Ellis would never let me ask."

"Who says?" Ellis retorted. "I'm not that big a prude. Am I? I mean, I know it's totally none of our business, but still. We are your best friends. . . ."

"C'mon, pretty please?" Julia pleaded. "You don't have to give me all the hot and steamy details. Just big picture, you know?"

Dorie rolled her eyes. "The sex was fine," she said, exasperated. "It was never even an issue. I got married at thirty-three, for God's sake! And while a lady doesn't like to get a reputation, I think you know I wasn't exactly celibate before I met Stephen. You think I would have married him if we weren't good together in bed?"

Julia considered this. "So . . . there was nothing kinky?"

"No," Dorie snapped. "And I didn't catch him dressing up in my panties, or hanging out at the men's room at the park, or trolling the squares in downtown Savannah after midnight. I'm telling you, and you can believe me or not, but up until two months ago, I thought I had a marriage that was rock solid."

She blinked furiously at the tears welling up in her eyes. "I loved Stephen. And I believed he loved me. And now, it's all gone to crap."

"Don't cry any more," Julia begged. "I'm sorry I brought it up. It's Ellis's fault for letting me, right? Let's all be pissed off at Ellis. And Stephen, too. May he rot in gay hell."

15

Ellis went out to the kitchen and got the box of Fudgsicles and a roll of paper towels, which she solemnly handed around to Dorie and Julia.

Dorie licked the ice cream bar in silence, while Julia attacked hers, biting off the top and demolishing it in minutes. Ellis licked and chewed and wiped frantically at the ice cream dripping down onto her hands.

"Better?" she asked Dorie.

"A little," Dorie said, sniffling.

"There's not enough chocolate in the world to fix this kind of thing," Julia said. "Dorie, Ellis is going to kill me for asking, but I can't help it. How . . . I mean . . . how did you find out about Stephen?"

"Jesus, Julia!" Ellis said. "Would you please let her alone?"

"It's all right, Ellis," Dorie said. "It's like a car wreck. You know it's terrible, but you just can't help looking, right? I didn't catch him with another man, if that's what you're wondering. It was just a bunch of little things. I thought he was stressed about getting his master's, so I didn't pay much attention. And then, he quit his soccer team. You guys met Stephen, right? He lived and died for soccer, not just coaching the girls at school, but playing. But he just quit the team. And the thing is, he didn't tell me he'd quit. He'd leave the house, and I just assumed he was going to practice, but it turns out he wasn't."

"He was going to meet his boyfriend?" Julia asked.

"No," Dorie said. "He swears he wasn't. He says now he just sort of drove around. He'd go to the mall and sit in his car, or drive out to Tybee and back."

"Why'd he quit soccer?" Ellis asked gently.

Dorie's face turned pink. "The guy . . . his name is Matt? He's on the team too. He's always been out. But not in a swishy, flamer kind of way. Stephen said . . ." She gulped and looked down at her hands. She'd twisted the paper ice cream wrapper into a cylinder, and now she was shredding it. "He said he realized months ago that he was, I guess, attracted to Matt. And it really scared him. And disgusted him."

"Oh, poor Dorie," Ellis said with a sigh.

"Stephen swears he never meant for anything to happen," Dorie went on. "That's why he quit the team. He thought if he didn't see Matt, didn't talk to him, it would be all right."

"But it wasn't, was it?" Julia asked.

"As soon as school was out in May, Stephen flew out to Omaha to be with his dad. Henry had a stroke while Stephen was there. He's alive, but he's on a ventilator, and now, they've told the family it's just a matter of time."

"God. On top of everything else," Julia muttered. "So, what happened?"

"When he came back home, he wouldn't talk about his dad," Dorie said. "He started drinking, you know, not a lot, but more than usual. Scotch, too. He never really drank hard liquor before. Neither of us did. And then, one night, right before the Fourth of July, he just . . . he just . . ." She faltered, and started crying again. This time Julia tore off a paper towel from the roll and handed it to Dorie.

"Blow," she ordered. Dorie nodded and did as she was told. Ellis took a paper towel and dabbed at her own eyes. "Gotta remember to add Kleenex to the grocery list this week," she said absent-mindedly.

Dorie took another deep breath and launched back into her story. "He just went for a drive, and he didn't come back. Not that night. I was going crazy! He wouldn't answer his cell phone, and I called everybody we knew asking if they'd seen him. I even called the emergency rooms at Saint Joe's and Memorial to see if he'd been in an accident."

"You must have been terrified," Ellis said. "I don't even know what I'd have done if I were you."

"I'd have been so pissed," Julia said.

"I was terrified, and then when he came home and he was all right, I was really pissed. We had the biggest fight ever. I was standing in the kitchen, in my nightgown, and, you guys, I was screaming. I mean screaming at him. And Stephen, he just broke down crying. And that's when he told me. That he'd gone to a bar, and Matt was there, and he was drinking, and ... he just ... went home with Matt. And he didn't call me because he didn't want to lie to me."

Dorie took another deep breath. Her eyes were red from crying, and her nose was running. Ellis and Julia were crying too.

"So that's it?" Ellis asked. "He's gay, and you're getting divorced? End of story?"

"End of story," Dorie agreed. "End of Mr. and Mrs. Perfect. End of every-friggin'-thing."

"Is that what you want? Have you thought about going to counseling?" Ellis asked.

"Counseling!" Julia hooted. "She just told you the man is gay. What good is marriage counseling when it comes to something like that?"

"I don't know," Ellis said helplessly. "Maybe, maybe Stephen really isn't totally gay. It was only one time, right? Maybe this is just ... like a phase. Dorie said he's been under a lot of stress, with finishing his thesis, and his dad being so sick. Maybe if they got counseling, if they could talk things out with a therapist ... I just think there has to be another way."

"Well, that's just dumb," Julia said, shaking her head. "What, you think this is like that column in your mom's *Ladies' Home Journal*—CAN THIS MARRIAGE BE SAVED?"

"I hate to say it, but Julia's right," Dorie said. "Don't you see? I'm screwed. Stephen says he loves me, and I believe him, I really do. But he's not *in* love with me. There's somebody else. How do I compete with that? If it were a woman, I'd do something. Cut my hair, dye it, lose weight, get a boob job. . . ."

"A boob job?" Julia exclaimed, slapping the tabletop for emphasis. "You're a friggin' 32D, Dorie. You've worn a D cup since, like, kindergarten." It was only a slight exaggeration. "You're so skinny everywhere else, if you got any bigger, you couldn't stand upright."

"I know," Ellis chimed in. "Remember, Dorie? In seventh grade, when we were just getting our training bras, you were already in an underwire."

"Double-D Dunaway," Julia crowed. "Nope, the only way you compete with this Matt guy, as far as I can see, is if you manage to grow a penis."

Dorie started to giggle. Ellis started too. In a moment, the three of them were all laughing so hard, tears were running down their faces. They laughed until they were crying and then laughing again.

"You guys, hush," Dorie said, waving her hands and pointing towards the ceiling. "You'll wake up Madison."

"What's she gonna do?" Julia demanded. "Call the cops on us?"

"I'm so sorry, Dorie," Ellis said, pressing her hand to her own chest. "It's not funny, not really."

"It's a friggin' tragedy," Julia agreed, snorting pinot out her nose.

That got them all started laughing again—the giggle fits from hell.

Until Dorie's green eyes widened. "Oh no," she said, gasping for air between guffaws.

"What?" Julia demanded.

"I think," Dorie said, haltingly. "I think I just peed my pants."

Which sent Ellis into peals of merry laughter. "You guys, do you remember Patti Shaffhausen from second grade at Blessed Sacrament? Miss Raterman's class? She used to wet her pants, like, every other day. And because I sat in back of her, Miss Raterman would make me go to the girls' bathroom and help her get cleaned up. Remember, we used to call her Pee-Pants Patti?"

"Oh my God," Dorie said. "Pee-Pants Patti Shaffhausen! You won't believe this, but Patti Shaffhausen is my dentist. She and her husband live on the same street in Ardsley Park as Willa. And he's a urologist."

"Stop!" Julia begged. Now it was her turn to clutch at her chest. "Stop, or I'm gonna pee my pants."

"Guys," Dorie said. "It's not just the laughing. I pee my pants—just a little—like, every day. I'm pregnant, guys."

16

"That's not funny, Dorie," Julia said.

"But it's true."

Ellis and Julia both chose that moment to take large gulps of wine.

"Is this what you call a pregnant pause?" Dorie said finally, her grin lop-sided.

"When?" Ellis asked, when she could catch her breath. "I mean, when are you due?"

"I'm three months pregnant. The baby's due in February. I'm hoping for Valentine's Day." Dorie turned to Julia, her green eyes flashing. "And before you ask, yes, I do intend to keep the baby. I don't know what else is going to happen in my life, but the one thing I do know is that I am going to have this baby."

Julia bristled. "I wasn't going to suggest..."

"Good," Dorie said, her voice becoming uncharacteristically firm. "I know you don't go to church anymore, Julia, but I do. I'm not one of those crazy bomb-flinging right-to-lifers, but for me, I just don't believe in abortion. End of discussion!"

"I can't believe you still buy into all that Catholic voodoo," Julia muttered.

"I do," Dorie said. "Well, most of it anyway. I guess I'm gonna have to figure out the divorce part, though."

Ellis flung her arms around Dorie. "Oh my God! A baby. This is amazing! I can't believe it. We're gonna have a baby, y'all." She looked over Dorie's head at Julia, who sat back in her chair, arms folded across her chest. "She's pregnant! Bet you didn't see that coming, Witch Julia."

"Nope," Julia agreed. "I totally didn't see that one coming."

"I can't believe you didn't guess, Julia," Dorie said. "I've been running into the bathroom every five minutes, it feels like, and feeding my face every minute of the day. I can hardly stay awake, I'm so sleepy all the time."

"But you've been drinking wine with the rest of us," Julia said accusingly.

"Nope," Dorie laughed. "You guys have been so busy sucking down the wine and margaritas, you didn't even notice me dumping my glass in the sink. I haven't had a drink since the dipstick turned blue back in June."

"What does Stephen think about all this?" Julia asked.

Dorie gazed down at her belly. Her voice, when she answered, was very small. "He doesn't know yet. You guys are the first ones I've told."

"I don't understand," Ellis said finally. "You found out you're pregnant in June. Way before you and Stephen split up. Why didn't you tell him about the baby when you found out?"

"I just . . . didn't," Dorie said. "We weren't trying to get pregnant. Not at all. This was all my fault. A slipup. We'd talked about a baby, and he said he wanted kids, eventually. But somehow, when I found out about the baby, right after Stephen's dad had a stroke, it just seemed like a terrible time to announce that I was pregnant. I knew he'd be worried about money, and I just didn't want to pile on another responsibility."

"For God's sake, Dorie," Julia said. "That is so like you. How can this be all your fault? Unless you impregnated yourself with a turkey baster when Stephen wasn't looking. You're the one who's got to carry this baby for nine months, along with everything else, and you're worried about poor old Stephen having too much responsibility. He doesn't deserve you, Dorie. He never did."

Dorie pressed her fingertips over her eyelids. "A month ago, I would have said you were all wrong about Stephen. Now? I just don't know what to think. One minute I hate his guts. I want to scream and rant and rave and kick him in the nuts and grab him and shake the crap out of him and ask him why on earth he ever married me if he thought there was even a remote possibility he was gay. I mean, how *could* he? How *dare* he? And then, I start thinking how painful all this must be for Stephen."

"Go with the kicking-in-the-nuts reaction," Julia said dryly.

"Damn," Dorie said, standing up abruptly. "Now I've gotta pee again. You see what I'm like? I'm a mess. Guess I'll run upstairs and change my shorts while I'm at it. I don't want you guys to start calling me Pee-Pants Dorie."

When Dorie was out of earshot, Julia poured herself another glass of wine, and after a moment's hesitation, topped off Ellis's glass too.

Ellis took a sip of the wine. She felt inexplicable tears welling up. Were they for what her best friend was facing, or were they, selfishly, for herself—unmarried and still childless at thirty-five, a state she'd never envisioned for herself?

Her brother Baylor was five years older, and as a child, Ellis had always longed for a baby sister to play with—even after her mother patiently explained that Ellis was "the caboose," as she called her. She'd been a funny little girl, the kind who still played with dolls when all her other friends had long since abandoned them. She'd always baby-sat as a teenager, and still did, occasionally, for friends back in Philly. All their children called her "Aunt Ellie." Was that all she'd ever be, Aunt Ellie?

"Wow," Ellis whispered, hoping Julia would assume her tears were for Dorie instead of herself. "I don't believe this. A baby."

"Me neither," Julia said. "What are we gonna do?"

"We're going to throw her a fabulous baby shower," Ellis declared. "Can't you just be happy for her? You heard Dorie. She wants this baby. She'll make a wonderful mother."

"A single mom," Julia said glumly. "I don't believe she ever envisioned doing it all by herself. And speaking of mothers, I do not want to be around when she drops this little bomb on her mom."

Ellis winced. "Ow. Yeah. I'm sure old Phyllis will have plenty to say on this topic."

"She'll figure out a way to make this all Dorie's fault," Julia predicted. "You wait and see. She'll blame Dorie for turning Stephen queer."

"Julia!" Ellis laughed ruefully. But she couldn't argue with what her friend said, because it was too true. Phyllis Dunaway had a talent for finding fault with her youngest daughter. She might have been a big-deal college English professor, but as a wife and mother, Dr. Dunaway was, to Ellis's way of thinking, a big dud. For years, she'd bullied Dorie's dad, Gabe, a sweet and slightly nebbishy college professor whose specialty was *Beowulf.* It had been Phyllis's idea to name all three Dunaway children after American writers—Willa for Willa Cather, Nash for Ogden Nash, and Dorie, the baby, who had been burdened with the unwieldy and unlikely name of Eudora, for Eudora Welty.

"What about Gabe?" Julia asked. "Does Dorie ever see her dad these days?"

Dorie and the girls had just started seventh grade at OLA when the Dunaways announced they were splitting up. Not long after, Gabe Dunaway moved an hour away, to Statesboro, to take a job teaching English at the college there.

Ellis shrugged. "I think he sends birthday cards and Christmas gifts. But he remarried a couple years ago, and you know how her mom is. Dorie doesn't dare mention his name, even after all these years. She couldn't even invite him to the wedding, since Phyllis was paying for it."

"What an evil shrew," Julia said. "It's amazing to me that Dorie turned out as well-adjusted as she did, especially considering all those years of verbal abuse Phyllis subjected her to. God, my mother hated her. Did you know, that time when we were sophomores and Phyllis threw Dorie out of the house because she found out Dorie was sneaking around dating that boy who got kicked out of Savannah High for selling weed, my mom actually tried to talk my dad into asking Phyllis to let Dorie live with us?"

"No!" Ellis said. "That's so funny. When that happened, I begged my mom to adopt Dorie. I was so clueless, I didn't understand you couldn't adopt somebody whose parents were still living. God bless Mama, she actually got up the nerve to call Phyllis and suggest that Dorie wasn't really the tramp of the town. Phyllis never spoke to my mom again. Mama and I have had our own moments, God knows, but I'll never forget how proud of her I was when she stuck up for Dorie that time."

"If Phyllis had been my mother, I think I would have taken an axe to her years ago," Julia said. "Like it was Dorie's fault that she was so pretty. I think Phyllis hated the fact that Dorie looked like her dad's side of the family. Remember how she used to call Dorie 'her pretty little flake'?"

"And Dorie wasn't dumb," Ellis agreed. "Maybe she didn't have a 4.0 GPA like Willa, but she made decent grades."

"Didn't matter," Julia said. "Willa was always the smart, successful one according to Phyllis. So Willa went to law school and made partner when she was only in her thirties? Whoopie-shit. And now she's not even practicing law. And what about good old Nash, the only son, the golden boy who could never do wrong? What's he doing these days? I'm almost afraid to ask Dorie."

"Nash," said Ellis succinctly, "is still Nash. Still writing poetry, although as far as I know, he's never had a word published. Last I heard, he was living rent-free in Dorie's grandma's old house on Forty-eighth Street. And you'll love this part: he drives a big ol' '70s hearse, and he gives these ghost tours of haunted houses downtown."

"You're kidding me," Julia said. "For real?"

Ellis slapped her right hand over her heart. "As God is my witness. Last time I was home, I saw him handing out flyers on Bay Street. You should have seen him," she said, giggling. "He was wearing this zip-front jumpsuit, and an army surplus gas mask, and he had what looked like an old vacuum cleaner canister strapped on his back. He gave me his business card. At first I thought maybe he was hitting on me, then I figured out he just wanted me to cough up eighty-five dollars for his stinkin' tour. Can you believe it? Julia, he's even got a website."

"Ghostdusters.com," Dorie said, padding barefoot into the dining room. She'd changed into a pair of drawstring cotton pajama pants and a Hello Kitty tank top, her hair caught in a ponytail on top of her head. She looked all of thirteen. "Could you die? All that fancy education, and he's squatting in

Granny's house and hustling tourists with these ridiculous stories about talking tombstones in Colonial Cemetery and headless duels in Monterey Square."

Ellis blushed guiltily. "It sounds like it could be a pretty successful business, though."

"Yeah, maybe if he wanted to work at it, it could be, but you know Nash. Work really is a four-letter word as far as he's concerned. Hey, is anybody else hungry? I'm thinking about fixing myself a grilled cheese sandwich."

"We just ate four hours ago," Julia reminded her. "Not to mention popcorn and Fudgsicles."

"I'm eating for two now," Dorie said. "At least now that you guys know, I can stop sneaking around and binging on cereal and scrambled eggs when you're not looking."

"If I ate like that I'd blow up like a balloon," Ellis said. "I still can't believe you're three months pregnant, walking around looking like a stick."

Dorie pulled up her tank top and pooched out her tummy. "A stick? Look at this gut! There's a baby in there, for real." She turned around and wiggled her butt at her friends. "And look at this ass. It's like, two axe handles wide, as my daddy would say."

Julia gave Dorie's butt an affectionate slap. "Who are you kidding? You've still got the tiniest hiney on the planet, Dorie. For now anyway. Come on. I'll fix you your grilled cheese, little mama."

The three of them trooped into the kitchen. Dorie and Ellis perched at the kitchen table while Julia melted butter in a frying pan and assembled Dorie's sandwich.

When the sandwich was golden brown, with melted cheddar cheese oozing out the sides, Julia flipped it onto a plate and slid it in front of Dorie, along with a glass of milk.

"Oh, bliss," Dorie said, taking a bite and rolling her eyes. "Stephen always says the best sandwich in the world is the one somebody else makes for you."

"About Stephen," Ellis said slowly. "Dorie, you really are going to have to tell him about the baby. Have you even talked to him since he moved out?"

Dorie chewed slowly. She took another bite of grilled cheese and then another. When the sandwich was half eaten, she pushed the plate away.

"I can't," she said. "I can't talk to him. I can't hear his voice. I can't see him. Not yet. He calls, but I don't answer. I know he drives past the house. I've seen his car cruise past half a dozen times. He doesn't have the balls to stop and ring the doorbell. Which is good, 'cuz I don't think I could answer the door if he did."

"Do you even know where he's living?" Julia asked.

"At Matt's, I suppose," Dorie said. "He's got a big old Victorian in Midtown. We went to a party there last fall."

"You're going to have to talk to Stephen, Dorie, and sooner would be better than later. You know what a small town Savannah is," Julia said. "You're gonna start showing sooner or later. And you know how people talk. You need to figure out the next step."

"I can't," Dorie wailed. "I don't know what to say to him. Anway, I don't know what the next step is. I don't know how to get a divorce."

"I do," Ellis said lightly. "It's not that hard, really. Look at me, I got mine at twenty-three. If this is really what you want, Dorie, I'll give you my lawyer's name. He was one of Baylor's fraternity brothers. He's still in Savannah, I know, because he sends me a Christmas card every year. Guess he thinks that now I'm in my thirties, I'll start throwing some divorce work his way."

Dorie tore off a chunk of the grilled cheese sandwich and nibbled at it. "I never, ever thought I would be thinking about getting a divorce. After my parents split up, I swore when I fell in love, it would be forever. You guys know how many men I went with over the years. I never even considered marrying any of them. Not until I met Stephen. That's why I waited so long to say yes. I wanted to be sure." She propped her feet up on the kitchen table. "The only thing I know for sure now is that nothing is for sure. And look at me—I'm barefoot and pregnant in the kitchen. And oh yeah, my baby daddy has a boyfriend." She sniffed loudly.

"How could you know?" Ellis said sympathetically. "I mean, you guys lived together for a year. We all thought it was the real deal."

"Yeah, he fooled even me," Julia agreed. "And you know I never liked any other guy you dated before. My gaydar is usually pretty accurate." She glanced over at Dorie. "I really am sorry, honey. Do you want to talk about something else?"

"It's okay," Dorie said, trying to smile through her tears. "Don't mind me. I'm just hormonal. I cry all the time. I cried this morning when I realized we were out of Frosted Flakes."

"I'll get another box," Julia said. "Promise."

"Are you sure you still feel like talking?" Ellis asked. "It's getting late, and I know you must be emotionally exhausted."

"No, I'm all right," Dorie said, brushing bread crumbs from her tank top. "It feels good to finally talk to somebody about all this. I've had all these secrets bottled up inside me. It just felt like I was going to explode if I didn't tell somebody about the baby."

"You didn't want to tell Willa?" Ellis asked. "I mean, she's your only sister."

Dorie shook her head. "Willa! I love her, but bless her heart, you guys know how she is. She's so bossy. She'd tell me I'd chosen the wrong obstetrician, the wrong hospital. The wrong man, for sure. She'd be dragging me to La Leche meetings and I don't know what all. And she'd for sure rat me out to Mama. And I can't handle any of that right now. I need time to process, to figure it all out." She sniffed. "I need this time at the beach with you guys, I really do. I need August like I never needed it before."

"You got it," Julia said. "We're here, and we got your back."

Ellis went to the sink and began rinsing out the wine glasses. "Listen, Dorie," she began, "when does school start back?"

Dorie grimaced. "Don't remind me. The week after Labor Day. Teachers report back the Thursday before, for preplanning."

"That's only a little over three weeks," Julia pointed out. "Are you sure you're up to going back to work at Our Lady of Angels? Especially with Stephen working there too?"

"I've got to," Dorie said dully. "I signed a contract. Anyway, I need the money, and I'm gonna need the medical benefits, at least until after the baby comes."

"Doesn't Stephen have the same medical benefits?" Ellis asked. "Wouldn't you be covered under his policy, assuming you didn't go back to OLA?"

"I don't know," Dorie admitted. "But it doesn't matter. I'm not quitting my job. I love teaching the girls, I really do. The money's not great, but that's not the point."

"It will be, if you're going to be a single mother," Julia said. "Don't forget, you'll have to pay for day care, and a hundred other things. And what about a place to live? What will you do about the house? Do you think Stephen will let you keep it?"

Dorie clapped her hands over her ears. She rocked back and forth in her chair. "I don't know, I don't know, I don't know," she singsonged. "I just freakin' don't know. I only know I hate Stephen. Hate. Hate. Hate."

"I hate him too," Ellis said, yawning.

"I hate him more than both of you," Julia declared. "I know. Let's fire up the van, drive over to his place, and key his car."

"No," Ellis said, taking up the challenge. "Let's egg his house and TP it."

"Or key the car, egg the car, and TP his house *and* his car," Dorie countered, getting into the spirit of things. "Remember when we did that to Amber Peek, senior year, after she started spreading rumors that Julia was pregnant right before Christmas break?"

"I just remember my daddy made me pay for a whole new paint job for that piece-of-crap Tercel of hers when we got caught," Ellis said.

"It was worth it though," Dorie said. "Amber Peek. That lying bitch."

They were both looking at Julia now, waiting for her to chime in with her own diatribe against her mortal enemy, Amber Peek.

"Good old Amber," Julia said. "She was a bitch, and a sneak, and I'm glad you guys screwed up her car. But she wasn't lying. Not that time. I really was pregnant, you know."

17

Ellis and Dorie sat back in their chairs, too stunned to speak.

"Don't look at me like that," Julia said shakily. "I wanted to tell you. But my mother was so mortified ... so ... ashamed. She made me swear I'd keep it a secret. I almost told you, that night after her funeral, back at the house, but I couldn't do it. Not in her house. Not after I promised."

Finally Ellis picked up the discarded deck of cards. She began laying out a hand of solitaire.

"Why tell us now?" she asked.

"I need to," Julia said. "I've needed to tell you for a long time. But I was afraid of what you'd think of me."

"Oh, Julia," Dorie said softly. "Julia."

Ellis wrinkled her brow. "But ... you didn't even have a boyfriend your senior year."

Julia grinned the old Julia grin. "Not one you guys knew about. You wouldn't have approved. He was an army Ranger, stationed at the air base at Hunter. We met at an oyster roast. He asked me out, I went. He was cute, even with those awful haircuts they made the guys get, and I could tell he was totally smitten."

"Did he have a name?" Ellis asked, annoyed, all these years later, that Julia had managed to conceal such a huge secret.

"Jack," Julia said. "His name was Jack, he was twenty years old, and the thing I liked best about him was that he was a good half-a-head taller than me—which sealed the deal. I mean, I was six feet tall, so there weren't a lot of guys out there that I could look up to. We went out exactly four times before we had sex."

"He forced you!" Dorie cried. "Raped you?"

"Nope," Julia said. "He was nice. Horny, but nice. I wanted to. I was eighteen years old, and I'd decided I didn't want to be a virgin anymore. After all," she said, nodding at Dorie, "you'd already done the deed, the summer before we were seniors. And as far as I knew, Ellis might never pop her cherry. So I just decided to go for it."

"And?" Ellis said, trying to decide how she felt about being regarded as a potential nun.

"He was sweet," Julia said, her face softening at the memory. "Although I don't think he had a hell of a lot more experience than I did. There were no fireworks—but then again, no nightmares, either. Anway, you know that crap we used to hear about how nobody ever gets knocked up the first time they do it? Turns out, it really is crap."

"You had unprotected sex, with an army Ranger?" Dorie said, her eyes widening. "You could have gotten AIDS. Or syphilis."

"It wasn't totally unprotected. He had a Trojan, although as it turned out, it must have been a really old Trojan. I didn't get an STD. I just got pregnant."

"Oh. My. God." Ellis swept the cards into a pile. "Julia, how did you manage to keep it secret? We never had a clue. Ever. Not even when Amber Peek started running her mouth."

"The baby?" Dorie guessed. "At Christmas, when you had your appendix out? That's what really happened?"

"It's not what you're thinking," Julia said. "When I missed my first period, I didn't think anything of it. You guys remember, I never had normal periods. But when I skipped my second one, I knew. But I just couldn't bring myself to tell my parents. It would have killed them. As it turned out, I didn't have to. The last day before Christmas break, right after my chemistry final, I'd gone to the bathroom. My stomach was killing me. I was so damned ignorant, I just thought that was part of being pregnant. I didn't tell you guys, I didn't tell anybody. I was bleeding. There was so much blood, I was terrified. I remember, I bought a Kotex from the vending machine in the bathroom, and I went straight home."

"You were hemorrhaging?" Ellis asked.

"The bleeding slowed down after a while, but I had these godawful cramps," Julia said. "I was curled up in bed and Mama just happened to walk by my bedroom door. She heard me moaning and crying, came in, and I was in so much pain, I couldn't even speak. But I had a fever, like 102 degrees, and then she saw the blood on my sheets, and she freaked out.

"Loaded me in her Cadillac and carried me straight to the emergency room at Saint Joseph's, where the doctor, who just happened to be a woman in Mama's Bunco club, had to break the news that her daughter, still dressed in her Catholic girl's school uniform, was not suffering from a ruptured appendix, as Mama insisted, but rather, that I had an ectopic pregnancy."

"You could have died," Dorie said solemnly.

"Right at that moment, I wished I had," Julia said. "If you'd seen the look on Mama's face when I had to admit that yes, I really was pregnant. It was like she'd been punched in the stomach."

"What . . . what did they do?" Dorie asked. "I'm sorry, I know this is hideous to ask, but I can't not."

"It's all right," Julia said, shrugging. "After all, I made you bare your soul, didn't I? Anyway, they did laparoscopic surgery. Right before they sent me home from the hospital, the doctor, Mama's friend, came in to see me. She told me the embryo had attached itself to the wall of my fallopian tube, which caused the tube to rupture, and that it never would have been a viable pregnancy. She also gave me a prescription for the pill, bless her heart."

"What about your parents?" Ellis asked. "How were they with it?"

"As far as Daddy knew, I really did have my appendix out," Julia said. "In the car on the way home from the hospital, Mama just told me she was disappointed in me. Jesus! Disappointed! Talk about a guilt trip. It was ten times worse than being screamed at or punished."

Dorie shuddered. "I don't want to think about how Phyllis would have handled that when I was eighteen. I don't even want to think about how she'll handle my pregnancy now, and I'm thirty-five and haven't lived at home in fifteen years."

"Mama said that it was Our Lady of Angels who intervened on my behalf and saved my life. I really could have bled out and died, probably would have if she hadn't barged into my room. Mama pointed out that she wasn't even supposed to be home that afternoon, she was supposed to go Christmas shopping, but something made her decide to cancel and stay home. Every year after that, right up until she got too sick to leave the house, she went to Mass in the chapel at OLA on December twelfth, the anniversary of the day I went to the hospital, to leave a wreath of flowers on the statue of Our Lady."

"Your mama was a saint," Dorie said, shaking her head. "I hope you know that."

"I do," Julia said, her lower lip trembling. "You don't know how much I miss her."

Ellis raised her wine glass in a toast. "To Catherine Capelli. God rest her soul. And to hell with Amber Peek!"

Julia raised her own glass, and Dorie, lacking one, raised her Fudgsicle stick.

Later, after they'd pushed a sleepy Dorie off to bed, Julia and Ellis went back to the kitchen to clean up. By unspoken agreement, Julia put away the dishes and Ellis swept the floors. "I'm turning in," Julia said finally, draping the dish towel over the back of the kitchen door. "All this emotional upheaval just wears me out."

"Can you stand one more question? I swear, after this, I won't bring it up again," Ellis said.

"I think I know what you're gonna ask. Jack, right?"

"Well, yeah," Ellis said. "Did you ever tell him? Or even see him again?"

"No, and no. He got shipped off to paratrooper school at the end of October, right around the time I missed my first period. He wrote me a couple times, and I wrote back once, but we were just kids. He wanted me to come see him, but I had school, and anyway, in my case, absence didn't make the heart grow fonder. As for telling him about the pregnancy—no, I never did. I couldn't even really admit it to myself, let alone him. I was all about denial."

Ellis touched Julia's shoulder lightly. "That was a hell of a secret to keep all these years. Does Booker even know?"

"No," Julia said sharply. "I told you, aside from my mother—and that bitch Amber Peek, who only found out because her cousin happened to be in the emergency room with a broken wrist the night I was there—nobody knew."

"Will you tell him now, since you've told us?"

Julia sighed. "Probably. He wouldn't care so much about the pregnancy thing, Booker's been around. The thing is, he wants kids. And I'm not even sure I can have a baby."

"Oh yeah," Ellis said, her eyes widening. "What does your gynecologist say?"

"I've never really asked," Julia admitted. "At the time, they told me lots of women get pregnant and have babies after having an ectopic pregnancy, even with only one good tube, like I have. All these years, it's never really been an issue. I had a great career, I'd seen my mother drowning in babies and diapers, and I told myself that was never gonna happen to me."

"But now?"

"Who knows?" Julia said lightly. "Anyway, I really am going to bed now. G'night, Ellie-Belly."

When Julia was gone, Ellis wandered aimlessly around the house. She put the deck of cards back in their box, pushed chairs under the dining room table, straightened sofa cushions. She tried the television again, but the cable was still out. She got out her phone for the first time in hours, checking to see if she had any e-mails or missed calls.

Nothing. She'd halfway been hoping for an e-mail from Mr. Culpepper. She smiled at the memory of his last message, and wondered again just how old Mr. Culpepper might be. Not that it mattered.

It was late, well past midnight, but she was oddly restless. The bookshelves by the fireplace were full of paperbacks. She trailed her fingertips across their spines—mostly romances, mysteries, and thrillers. She chose a battered Kathleen Woodiwiss paperback, *The Flame and the Flower,* smiling at the memory of how she and Julia had swiped Julia's mother's copy of the same book. They'd been what, thirteen? They'd taken the book out to the Capellis' boathouse and read it by flashlight, giggling over the smutty parts.

Ellis went upstairs and put on her pajamas. The air in the room was hot and still. She turned on the ceiling fan and dialed down the thermostat on the window air-conditioning unit. She climbed into bed, and switched on the old-fashioned white hobnail glass lamp on her bedside table. Its shade was yellowed and coated with dust, and the bulb threw off a tiny, tired glow of orangish light. Not that it mattered. She was too keyed up to settle down with a book. She turned off the light and willed herself to sleep.

Eventually, she closed her eyes and drifted into a dream. She was in a hospital nursery, full of dozens and dozens of beautiful, pink, pudgy babies. In her dream, she leaned over a pink bassinet and saw an infant with Dorie's strawberry blond hair, freckles, and green eyes. The next bassinet held a long, slender baby with Julia's perfect cheekbones and dark, almond eyes. And next to that was another infant—with familiar marble blue eyes, protruding ears, and the Greene thin upper lip. The little boy opened his mouth and screamed—well, yowled—as she leaned in closer to look. Ellis's dream self scurried away, and in the next bassinet, she saw the most beautiful baby of all: a little boy with a thick shock of dark hair like her mother's, and her father's calm, steady gaze. The baby was sucking his thumb, and when he saw dream-Ellis, he looked up and winked.

The wink startled Ellis awake. She sat straight up in bed, and for a moment, wondered if the dream meant anything. Eventually she decided maybe it just meant she shouldn't drink so much wine late at night. She yawned and wished she could sleep again, but the loud hum of the air conditioner and the responding rattle of the window glass now had her wide awake. And hungry.

She went downstairs and out to the kitchen, opening cupboards and the refrigerator, trying to decide what she was hungry for, and settling for a chunk of cheddar cheese. She ate half, and then pitched the rest into the trash. Not really hungry, not really sleepy. What a mood she was in. She turned off the kitchen light, intending to go back to bed, but when she glanced out the window, she saw the full moon and reconsidered. She was at the beach, wasn't she? Might as well enjoy it.

It was still hot out, but a breeze rustled the sea oats on the dunes, and she smelled a hint of beach rosemary mixed with the salt air. The worn boards of the walkway were cool to the soles of her bare feet. When she reached the landing at the top of the walk, she was startled. Somebody was sitting in one of the beach chairs. Suddenly remembering how she was dressed, she started to back away, but it was too late.

The garage guy turned around in his chair, a cigar clamped between his lips. The lit end glowed in the deep purple darkness. He looked her up and down, and then turned back towards the ocean.

It pissed Ellis off, him dismissing her like that. Did he think she'd turn tail and run, like the last time? She had as much right to be here as him. Pajamas or no.

"Hey," she said, defiantly sinking down into the chair next to his.

He grunted an acknowledgment and continued staring off at the twin moons, one hanging low in the summer sky, the other reflected in the ocean.

Ellis settled back into the beach chair. She wished she'd thrown a robe or something over the thin cotton tank top and baggy pink boxer shorts with their silly design of flying cupcakes. She crossed her arms over her chest, hoping Ty Bazemore hadn't noticed her bralessness. Or the cupcakes.

The beach below was totally deserted. It was high tide, and the waves rolled lazily in over the spot where the three women had earlier spread out their umbrella and chairs. Ellis stared up at the stars and tried to relax. This was August, damn it. The month she'd been planning for and anticipating ever since Julia's mother's funeral. She had earned this vacation.

But there was a lot to think about. Dorie and Stephen. Dorie and the baby. Julia's big secret. And what about her own life? She felt guilty worrying about herself when her best friend's life was in such turmoil, but the truth was inescapable. She felt stuck. A lifetime of planning and living by the rules had netted her a nest egg, a paid-off car and house—the safety net her father had always emphasized—and a life as dull and colorless as the sand beneath her toes. She was being strangled by that damned safety net. She would get another job, maybe move to another town if necessary, but would her life really be any different? She'd spoken glibly of reinvention to Madison, their odd new housemate, but that had just been talk, hadn't it?

She glanced over at Ty Bazemore. His eyes met hers.

"How's it going?" he asked.

"Not so good," she blurted, instantly regretting her own candor.

He raised an eyebrow.

"Can't sleep," she said lamely. "Those window units make a terrible racket. And," she rushed on, "I lost my job. And I don't know what I want to do next. I don't know if I should stay in Philly, or cut my losses and move on. But I don't know if I could sell my town house in this market. And anyway, where would I go? Back to Savannah? I love my mother, but she drives me nuts sometimes."

Ellis clamped both hands over her mouth. Had she really just dumped her whole life out in the open for this total stranger, the guy who lived in the garage and peed off the deck?

"Sorry," she said, feeling her face flush. "TMI."

"Huh?"

"You know. Too much information. Don't mind me. Guess I'm a little wired tonight."

"What do you do?" Ty asked.

"Huh?"

"Back in Philly," Ty said. "What kind of job did you get fired from?"

"Not fired," Ellis corrected. "Downsized. My bank got taken over by a bigger bank."

"But you don't work there anymore."

"True."

"And leaving wasn't your idea."

"No. I loved my job. Or so I thought."

"You thought?"

Ellis shrugged. "It's really a long story. But the bottom line is, it turns out bank marketing was not the stuff of fairy tales."

He laughed. "But you still got fired."

Ellis frowned. Who did this jerk think he was? "It was a downsizing," she repeated. "My department was redundant. It's really a very generous severance package. Anyway, what kind of work do you do?"

Ty considered a moment before answering. She already knew the answer to her own question, because Mr. Culpepper had told her. But he wasn't supposed to know that, was he?

"I do a little day trading," he said.

"How's that going?"

"It's up and down. Like the market. I do all right."

He really was infuriatingly smug.

"Got any good stock tips for me?" she asked.

"Buy low. Sell high."

"Gee, thanks," Ellis said sarcastically. "Let me write that one down."

"Sorry," Ty said. "I'm kinda in a mood myself. But that was unnecessary. No, I don't have any stock tips. You wouldn't want one of mine anyway." He tapped the cigar ash into the sand, and decided to change the subject.

"This your first time on the Outer Banks?"

"Yeah," she said. "I grew up in Savannah. Which is kinda on the beach. But it's totally different here. The dunes and all. It's beautiful, in a wild kind of way."

"You should have seen it when I was a kid," Ty said. "Most of these houses weren't here. It was mostly dunes and beach. You know, there are still wild ponies on the beach up in Corolla. It was an awesome place to grow up. Never put on a pair of shoes from the time school let out in June 'til the time we went back in September."

"You grew up here?"

He'd said too much. "Around here," Ty said vaguely. "I went to high school in Manteo. I practically lived on the beach. Got my first surfboard when I was ten."

"So," Ellis said, giving him a winning smile, "so, what's the deal with you? Are you hiding a wife and children in this little garage apartment?"

"Nothing like that," Ty said. "No kids, not married. Currently."

Ellis tucked away the word "currently" for further thought.

"And have you always been a day trader?"

"No, that's kind of a recent thing," he said. "I was in law school, but I dropped out. I've always been interested in real estate and investing, so I decided to give it a shot. Of course, I would pick the worst time since the Depression to dabble in the stock market."

"Tell me about it," Ellis said. "Banking's not so hot either. But you must do okay with the market, right?"

He flipped the lid on his cigar lighter and stared out at the water. "I've picked some winners, but seems like I've picked more dogs lately. To tell you the truth, I've been picking up some bartending shifts at a place down in Kitty Hawk to pay the bills. Cadillac Jack's. You ever hear of it?"

"No," she said. "We haven't really been going out at night much."

"You guys should come in and check it out. I'm actually working tomorrow night."

"Maybe we will," Ellis said, sounding uncertain.

"Been up to Jockey's Ridge yet?" Ty asked.

"Not yet," Ellis admitted. "We've been lazy bums, just kinda hanging around on the beach. But we've got the whole month, right?"

"Lucky you." Ty gave her a questioning glance. "So, seems like the three of you have been friends for a while, right?"

She grinned. "Only our whole lives. We met in grade school, in Savannah. I was the new kid, since I went to public school until third grade. Dorie and Julia have been friends since kindergarten. And we've just stayed close, even after all these years. Of course, we don't get to see each other that often. Dorie still lives in Savannah, but Julia lives in London. She's a model. And of course, I'm in Philly. Or I was." She frowned then. "Dorie's older sister, Willa, was supposed to come with us, but she blew us off at the last minute. Willa can be a real pain in the butt, so we didn't really mind that much."

"What about the new girl?" Ty asked. He'd seen her riding her bike up and down the beach road, but never with the other girls.

"Oh. Madison?" She gave Ty a furtive look. "Do me a favor, okay, don't mention her to Mr. Culpepper. We don't want him to jack up the rent any more."

"My lips are sealed," Ty said, clamping them together to keep them from twitching in amusement. "So, she's not one of your regular posse?"

"Not hardly," Ellis said. "Dorie met her in a restaurant, and they got talking, and Madison mentioned that she was looking for a motel room. Dorie's been pretty worried about money, and one thing led to another, and she offered to rent her a room at Ebbtide."

"Just like that?" Ty raised an eyebrow. "Seems kinda risky to me, inviting a stranger to live with you. What do y'all know about her?"

"She's been living in New Jersey, but she just broke up with her boyfriend. Or so we gathered. Madison says she's 'in transition.' She's sort of odd. She keeps strictly to herself, usually won't even eat with us. But she pays her share of the bills—with cash, so I guess it's working out okay."

"Yeah," Ty said cautiously. "It must be pretty expensive, taking that big house for a whole month. How much is old man Culpepper getting for the place, anyhow?"

"Too much," Ellis said. "The place could be nice, you know? It's a gorgeous old house, but the furniture's really ratty, and the house itself could use a lot of maintenance. I've had to really keep after Mr. Culpepper to take care of stuff like the stove and a leaking faucet. And don't even ask about the flea situation." She shuddered and held out an ankle. "Look—it looks like I've had the measles."

Ty considered her ankle. It was a pretty ankle. Ellis had nice ankles, and good legs, and the outfit she was wearing—a tight-fitting tank top and some kinda girly boxer shorts with ridiculous cupcakes printed all over them—was an excellent look for her. It didn't hurt that she was obviously braless, another look Ty was highly in favor of.

She caught him taking in more than her ankles, and quickly tucked her feet primly under her chair, all the while blushing furiously.

"Mind if I ask you something?" Ty said quickly, hoping she'd forgive his ogling.

"Depends on what it is."

"What is it about women? I mean, the three of you are scattered all over the place—but you still take the trouble to rent a house and spend a whole month together. What's up with that? I mean, I have buddies, old friends, but I can't imagine any of us spending a weekend away together, let alone a month."

Ellis shrugged. "Why wouldn't we want to spend time together? These are my best friends in the whole world. We've been through a lot together. You know, all that teenage drama, and then college, and family stuff. Dorie's parents had a nasty divorce when we were in middle school, and then I lost my dad a few years ago, and both Julia's parents are dead now. And don't get me started on the men stuff."

She hesitated, and then plunged ahead. "I don't know if I could have gotten through my divorce if it weren't for Dorie and Julia. It was an awful time for me, but they were totally there for me. Julia took the train down from a magazine shoot she'd been doing in New York and actually moved in with me for two weeks. I was a pathetic mess. I eventually took a leave of absence from work, but Julia refused to let me wallow in my misery. She made me eat, get my hair cut and colored, and go back to work. And Dorie—she's a schoolteacher, so she couldn't just drop everything, but she called me every night and every morning, for months, just to see how I was doing."

Ty raised an eyebrow. "You're divorced?"

She blushed again. She really was good at it, too.

"It was a long time ago. I got married right out of college. I was young and dumb. It lasted all of three months. Crazy, huh?"

"What happened?"

Ellis gave it some thought. "We worked at the same bank. He was different from the guys I'd dated back home. He was the same age as me, but he seemed older, you know, very sure of himself, and he gave me this big rush. I didn't really know him. He didn't really know me. I guess I was in love with the idea of being in love with him. And then, after the big wedding, when we were actually living together, away from our families and friends and everybody, it turned out he wasn't such a nice guy. In fact, it turned out he was a total shit."

Ty frowned. "What, he hit you or something?"

"Nothing as dramatic as that," Ellis said. "One night at dinner, he just announced the 'marriage thing' wasn't working, and that he'd discovered he didn't actually love me."

"That must have sucked."

She turned and leveled a gaze at him. "Why am I telling you all of this? I never, ever talk about my divorce, except to the girls. And here I am, spilling my guts to you."

"And you don't even like me," Ty said helpfully.

"You didn't make a very good first impression," she reminded him.

"Hey!" he protested. "I didn't know you were spying on me. You could have let me know you were standing there or something, you know."

"Do you always parade around in your drawers and pee in public?" Ellis asked. "What if somebody else had seen you? Like a child? You could get arrested for public indecency."

"It was early. Nobody ever gets to that part of the beach that time of day. And anyway, somebody would really have to work at seeing me from the beach, what with the dunes and the sea oats and everything."

"*We* see you from that part of the beach," she said pointedly.

"And I haven't hardly walked out on the deck in my boxers at all lately, either," Ty said. "Anyway, can I help it if you and your gorgeous friends choose to run around in your skimpy bathing suits right outside my deck? I mean, it would be un-American if I didn't appreciate the natural beauty right there on the beach."

"Humph," she humphed. But the corners of her lips twitched slightly. She concluded that up close like this, Ty Bazemore wasn't nearly as repulsive. In fact, he was alarmingly attractive, with his rumpled hair and cleft chin. She'd always been a sucker for a cleft chin.

"I'll just bet you do enjoy looking at Dorie and Julia," she said lightly. "I mean, Julia's a model, and as for Dorie, well, no matter what she does to try to hide it, she's always had the kind of looks that draws men like flies."

He raised an eyebrow. "Yeah, they're okay," he said. "Especially the curvy little redhead. But actually, since you mention it, you're pretty killer in a bathing suit yourself, Ellis Sullivan. Especially that black one-piece."

She gaped at him, blushing furiously.

He grinned innocently. "Hey, don't look at me like that. It's a simple observation. A compliment. No need to call the vice squad."

This conversation was taking a decidedly personal turn, Ellis decided. She fought the urge to cut and run. Ty Bazemore had just told her he liked her black bathing suit. She should stay and flirt. She remembered how to flirt, didn't she?

In the meantime, he was still looking at her, lazily taking in those stupid cupcake boxers and her flimsy tanktop. Panic set in again. She yawned widely and stood to go.

"Bedtime," she said. "Well, good night."

"So soon?" he said, standing up lazily. "What's your hurry?"

"No hurry," she said lightly, starting back up the boardwalk towards the house. "It's been a long day and I'm tired, that's all."

"I scared you with that compliment, didn't I?" he called. "Funny, you didn't strike me as a wussy."

That stopped her in her tracks. Wussy? Who was he calling a wussy?

She marched right back to the deck, stopping when she was inches away from him. "You take that back," she said, her fists clenched. "I killed a rattlesnake in my backyard with a shovel when I was ten. My daddy was standing right there but he was terrified of snakes. He barfed when he saw what I'd done. I was the only girl at our neighborhood pool who would backward dive off the high dive. I was the quarterback on my college coed flag-football team, and I broke my nose and played the next day anyway. I am *not* a wussy."

It was all true—all except for the high-dive part. But *he* didn't know that.

"You're scared of me though," Ty said, looking her right in the eyes.

"Am not."

"Prove it."

Her eyes narrowed. "How?"

"Like this," he said, pulling her towards him and sliding his arms around her waist. His mouth was an inch from hers, her eyes half closed. "You're afraid to kiss me," he taunted, his lips barely grazing hers.

"Am not," she said, her breath catching as she said it.

"Prove it."

She sighed impatiently, wrapped her arms around his neck, tilted her face to his and kissed him softly. Her lips were full and warm with promise. Gently, he pulled her closer, gathering the soft fabric of her shorts into his hands. With his tongue, he teased her lips apart. She melted into his chest. For a moment. And then, without warning, she wriggled out of his arms.

"Told ya I wasn't a wussy," she said, and then Ellis Sullivan, flying cupcake boxers and all, was scampering up the walkway in the bright moonlight. He slowly followed, pausing to take a last look at the water, and when he got to the deck of his own place, he looked over at Ebbtide, just in time to see the next-to-last light in the house blink off.

18

Julia was nearly asleep when she heard her cell phone vibrating on the rickety wooden nightstand. She fumbled for it in the dark, and sighed when she saw the screen.

"Hey," she said, sitting up in bed.

"Hey, baby," Booker said softly. "You missing me?"

"Yeahhh," she said slowly, smiling as she pictured him. He'd be sitting there in his favorite ratty gray high school gym shorts and a bleached-out T-shirt. His wiry gray-streaked hair would be standing on end, because he ran his fingers through it when he was bored, and the horn-rimmed glasses would have slid down on his nose. Most likely he'd be drinking his favorite late-night treat—Dr Pepper. "Come to think of it, I am."

Julia Capelli had been a nineteen-year-old college dropout, bumming around Europe for a year, picking up modeling assignments wherever she could, when she met Booker Calloway in a grotty pub in Brighton.

He was a fashion photographer, and she'd been hired for a low-budget teenybopper catalog shoot. She'd been drinking with a couple of the other girls, and he'd stopped at their table to buy them all drinks and hit on Geenie, the busty redhead in their bunch. He was already thirty then, sexy as hell with his long, dark hair, gold-flecked hazel eyes, and ever-present Nikons slung bandolier-style across his chest. He was a confirmed expatriate who'd grown up in California and who swore he'd never go back.

Booker completely ignored Julia that night, but the next day, after the shoot, he'd pulled her aside to offer her some advice—"get yourself to a tanning bed, for Chrissake"—and to offer to take some better head shots for her book. They'd done a couple more shoots together, and after that, Booker was acting as her de facto agent, and then one day, she'd realized that they were essentially working—and living—together, full time.

It seemed to Julia that their couplehood had just gradually evolved. And why not? He was smart, successful, a thoughtful and kind lover, a level-headed presence in the crazy world they both inhabited. Everybody loved Booker, even her mother, who'd been fully prepared to hate the totally inappropriate older man who'd seduced her daughter into staying in England instead of coming home to the States, college, her family, a normal life. Within five minutes of meeting him, Catherine Capelli was totally won over. The only thing her mother didn't like about Booker was that her headstrong daughter steadfastly refused to marry him.

Booker never let her forget that one of the last things her mother told her before her death was that she should "marry that nice man, Sugar, before he gets away."

"I could come down there Saturday morning," he was saying now. "My meetings in DC are over Friday night. It's not that long a drive, I could head back here Monday morning. What do you say?"

She sighed again. "Book, we've already been over this. This is a chick trip. No boys allowed. Anyway, it's barely been a week. I need some time to sort things out. We have an agreement, remember?"

"You have an agreement," he grumbled. "I didn't have much choice in the matter, did I?"

She chuckled ruefully. "Not much. Now, can we talk about something else? How's it going up there? Do you like the people you're working with?"

"They're all right, a pretty tight-knit bunch. I'd forgotten how bureaucratic a magazine can be. They've got policies and procedures for everything. And it's gonna take a while to get up to speed with their software."

"You can do it," she reassured him. "And anyway, they're making it worth your while, remember?"

"Damned straight they are. Hey, guess what? I think I found us a house today."

She flopped back down onto her back. "Oh, Book. I don't know. I told you . . ."

"Julia, just hear me out," he said, his voice pleading. "You'll love it. It's in Alexandria. Right on the metro line. Built in 1918, what's that style house you always talk about, the ones with all the built-in china cabinets and bookcases and stuff?"

"Craftsman?"

"Yeah, that's it. The real estate agent said it's the best example of Craftsman architecture in the whole neighborhood. It's got a big, wide porch across the front, and these great windows that give the most amazing light. And hardwood floors. Three fireplaces. Living room, den, and master bedroom. Four bedrooms. Only two baths, but there's this funny little trunk room just off the master that would make a great master bath. The kitchen needs a total redo, but the agent thinks we can get the house for way less than asking price, because the owner's already taken a job in LA, and he's desperate to unload the place. Hey, I took a bunch of shots with my cell phone. I'll send 'em right now. Wait until you see this place, Julia."

She squeezed her eyes shut. He was like a kid describing a new bike. And he hadn't heard a damned thing she'd been telling him for the past six weeks.

"Oh, Book," she said finally. "It sounds wonderful. Really. But I don't need a house. I don't need to live in DC. I don't need to get married. I love you. I do. But I can't do this."

Silence. "I just . . . I mean, I guess I don't get it. You say you love me. You know I love you. I thought the new job, moving back to the States, would be a good thing. I'll have real security for the first time. No more crazy freelancing, running all over the globe, running down assignments. We can have our own house. A real home. No more shitty flats in London."

"I love that shitty flat," Julia put in, picturing it in her mind's eye: the orange Arne Jacobsen Egg Chair she'd picked up at a car-boot sale in suburban London, the white leather Conran sofa she'd bought with her first earnings from a magazine job, the bits and bobs of silver and china picked up at the Bermondsey Market, all arranged against walls she'd painted and layered with pictures and photographs picked up at junk markets and antique stalls in every city she'd ever visited.

Now, faced with the possibility of giving up her home for the past ten years, she realized she'd been nesting without even realizing it.

"Ok, well, maybe we keep the flat for when you're over there for modeling gigs."

She cringed at the mention of her career. "Booker, denial is not just a river in Egypt. I'm not getting modeling gigs these days. Not the kind I used to get. I'm thirty-five. I'm not cover-girl material anymore, except for maybe *Modern Maturity*. Last month I did a catalog shoot for Lands' End, for God's sake. Next thing you know, I'll be the spokesmodel for Depends."

"What are you talking about?" he demanded. "Julia, that's nuts. You forget how many years I was in the business. You've got more work than you can handle. Yeah, I realize it's not *Elle* or *Vogue,* but you're also not exactly ready for the glue factory just yet. You are still a sensational-looking girl, and you can have a career in modeling for as long as you want."

"Maybe I don't want a career in modeling anymore," Julia said.

"All right," Booker said wearily. "Do something else. Nobody said you had to model. I just thought that's why you've been so mopey lately, because you hate the offers you're getting."

"That's just it," Julia said. "I don't know how to do anything else. I quit college after one semester, remember?"

"And now's your chance to go back to school, if that's what you want," Booker jumped in. "Or not. I don't give a damn. I just want you with me. I want us to get married, have a kid—if I've still got any swimmers—and get old together. Is that so awful?"

"No," Julia said. "Not awful. Sweet. You're sweet, and I'm a mixed-up bitch."

Now, she thought. Now was the time to tell him the truth. Maybe she couldn't even have a baby. Telling the girls was such a relief. How had she walked around with this secret for so many years? What had she been afraid of?

She walked over to the bedroom window and looked idly out at the beach. There was a full moon, and now she could see a couple standing at the end of the boardwalk, on the little deck there. It was a man and a woman, and they were standing close, and now they were embracing. The girl pasted herself to the man's chest, and the moment was so sensual, Julia almost turned away. Almost. A second later, the girl pulled away and began running back towards the house.

"Good Lord," she breathed. "Ellis!"

"What?" Booker demanded. "What's wrong?"

"Nothing," Julia chuckled. "I just saw our Ellis, outside in the moonlight, making out with a strange man."

"I thought you said this was a chick thing. No guys allowed."

"I did. They weren't," she said.

"Julia," Booker's voice was plaintive. "Have you heard a single word I've just said?"

She was staring down at Ellis, who was walking towards the house at a fast clip. She was in her pajamas, for God's sake. And even from where Julia stood, with the moonlight making things absurdly bright, she could see the bemused smile on Ellis's face. Well good for Ellis. But who on earth was the man? He stood for a long while on the deck, staring at the house. Julia hadn't turned the light on in her room, so she was sure he couldn't see her, but just in case, she took a few steps away from the window.

"I hear you, Booker," she said sofly. "But I can't talk about this any more. Love you. G'night."

He was still sputtering when she disconnected. Julia heard the downstairs screen door open and close, and then the sound of the front door closing. Ellis's bare feet trod lightly on the stairs.

Julia stayed at the window, peering out. Finally, the man walked slowly up the boardwalk towards the house. Julia held her breath. Delicious! Was he going to follow Ellis into the house, sneak into her bedroom for a secret tryst? Wait. He was heading towards the garage. What? When he stood for a moment under the garage light she saw his face clearly. It was the garage guy, Ty Bazemore. Ellis and Ty! What a lovely, unexpected development, Julia thought.

Maryn awoke with a start, and sat straight up in bed. For a moment, she struggled to remember where she was. The air in the room was hot and stagnant. Her sweat-soaked nightgown clung to her body. Then she heard the crunch of tires on the crushed shell driveway outside, and with a jolt, she knew exactly where she was.

She glanced at the cheap clock radio on the nightstand. It was 2 A.M. A car was rolling slowly down the driveway. Bile rose in her throat, and for a moment, she felt paralyzed. Then she got up, knelt down, clawing at the thin mattress, until her fingers closed over the pistol she'd hidden there. She ran to the window opposite her bed and peeked out between the faded cotton curtains. She exhaled slowly. It was the red Bronco, the one driven by the man who rented the garage apartment.

Maryn watched as he pulled into the garage. A moment later he walked out of the garage, illuminated by the motion-activated light at the edge of the porch. He was dressed in faded jeans and a white T-shirt, and wore a green baseball cap with the bill pointed backwards. His name was Ty, Dorie had said, and he was a day trader. He looked tired as he slowly climbed the wooden staircase on the exterior of the garage.

She stayed at the window, watching, until she saw the lights switch on in the garage apartment. She could see him through the uncurtained windows, walking around. He went to a table near the window and looked out. She backed away from her own window, not wanting to be seen. She looked down at the .32 still clenched in her right hand.

It was Don's pistol. He'd given it to her not long after they first started dating and she was living in that rat-hole apartment on Pinelawn. Her car had been broken into and her cell phone stolen, and he was insistent that the neighborhood wasn't safe. Which it wasn't.

The next night when he came over, he had a brown paper bag which he carefully set down on her kitchen table.

She gasped when he pulled the gun from the bag. She'd never been around guns. Her father never owned one.

"Don't be afraid, baby," Don had said gently. He showed her how to load it and unload it. Then they'd driven out to the country. He set a row of beer cans on a tree stump, and he showed her how to aim and fire.

"Don't I need a permit for this?" she asked, after he was satisfied that she knew how to use the thing.

"Nah," he'd said. "I've got a permit, and anyway, if you ever have to use the damned thing, you'll shoot first and ask questions later."

She'd thought it was sweet, that he wanted to protect her.

When he insisted that she move out of the apartment and into the condo in a complex he owned closer to town, it was so she'd be living someplace nicer. The rent was twice what she could afford on her salary at the insurance company, but since Don owned the condo and had no intention of letting her pay rent, that wasn't a problem. It hadn't dawned on her that it was more convenient for Don, her living there. He came by most nights, bringing takeout Chinese or a steak that they'd grill on the little enclosed patio off her living room.

They'd met at the office. Don had grown up with the Prescotts, and now he was the firm's accountant. She never would have met him at all, except that one day, two years ago, Marie, Robby Prescott's administrative assistant, had jury duty, and Maryn was drafted to answer the boss's phone. As luck would have it, that was the day Don Shackleford showed up to take Robby Prescott to lunch.

It was a chilly fall morning, and he wore an expensive-looking cashmere coat over his suit. She was on the phone when he entered the office, and he stood impatiently at her desk, tapping his fingers on the papers in Marie's in-box, glancing at his watch, which had annoyed her. Was he tapping to let her know what a big, important man he was? Too important to be kept waiting? So she let him wait, pretending to be listening long after her call had actually ended, just so he knew she was busy too.

"Yes?" she'd said coolly, looking up as though she were seeing him for the first time.

"I'm here for Robby," he said impatiently. "Where's the other girl?"

"Marie? She has jury duty."

"And you work here too? What's your name?"

"Maryn," she said. "I work in claims processing." She said it with the faintest hint of a smile. "I'll let Mr. Prescott know you're here." She got up from her desk, stuck her head in the boss's office, and quietly let him know he had a visitor. Prescott was on the phone, but mouthed he'd be out when he was done.

When she got back to her desk, Don had seated himself on a leather wing chair opposite her desk. "He's on a call, but he'll be out as soon as he can," she told the visitor. She went back to her computer, to the file she'd been working on, but she felt his eyes on her. He was checking her out, which was fine, because she was checking him out too.

And she liked what she saw. Don Shackleford was in his early forties, with thick white-blond hair, a deep tan, ice blue eyes above pronounced cheekbones, and a wide mouth and perfect teeth. He wasn't particularly tall, maybe five-eight, and he had a thick neck and athletic build. She noticed right off that he didn't wear a wedding ring.

Maryn wasn't surprised when Don was back the next week. This time, he hunted her down at her own desk, on some pretext that they both knew was absurd. He asked her to lunch, and she refused, saying she had plans. What about next week, he'd persisted.

"Next week when?" Maryn had asked, not caring.

"Any day next week," he'd said. "Or the week after that. Come on. You know you're going to go to lunch with me. Why not make it sooner than later?"

"Next Friday," Maryn told him. "But I only get an hour. Come by for me at one."

That next Friday, she'd worn her best outfit, a Marc Jacobs pantsuit she'd bought—the tags still on it—at an upscale consignment shop in Philly. The red jacket fit her like a glove, and she'd worn high-heeled black boots that made her only two inches shorter than him.

"You look good," Don said, holding the door of his silver Carrera. They'd gone to the Valley Brook Country Club for lunch, and they'd dined in the men's grill, where all the men sitting around in golf clothes greeted Don like they'd known him for years. He saw their questioning glances at Maryn, but he didn't bother to introduce her. "Horny old bastards," he said with a laugh.

He'd taken her to lunch again the next Friday, but the Friday after that, he'd driven directly to the condo, with no explanation. "Whose place is this?" she'd asked, once they were inside, and he was unzipping her skirt.

"Mine," he'd said, his mouth on hers. There were no more questions. He knew she only had an hour for lunch.

It hadn't taken Maryn by surprise, really. She was surprised he'd waited this long. Don Shackleford was a man who was used to taking what he wanted, and she'd known, the first time she met him, that he wanted her.

If she were honest with herself, Maryn would admit she'd been attracted to Don because of his single-minded pursuit of her. It was absurdly flattering to be so desired, so adored. Nobody had ever wanted to take care of her the way Don did. It didn't occur to her until many months later that he didn't want to just take care of her. He wanted to possess her.

Two months after their first date, she was living in Don's condo. Adam, not surprisingly, made it clear that he didn't approve of Don.

"He's using you," Adam would say when she'd come back after lunch, her hair still damp from her hurried shower.

"How do you know I'm not using him right back?" Maryn had asked. She didn't care who knew she was sleeping with Don. She was doing her job, wasn't she? So it was nobody's business.

Adam was Maryn's age. He'd gone to work at R.G. Prescott Insurers two years earlier, right out of the local community college. There were five other women in their office, but with the exception of that bitch Tara Powers, they were older, married, and clearly none of them, especially Tara, liked or approved of Maryn—or Adam, for that matter.

So it was Adam and Maryn, just hanging out as friends, although Adam clearly wanted more from her than that. She always insisted on paying her own way when she was with Adam. She saw lots of guys, but there was nobody special. Not until Don came along.

"He's way too old for you," Adam said. "I mean, come on, Maryn, what is he, forty?"

"He's forty-two," Maryn said. "Anyway, my mother always said I'm an old soul. I've always dated older guys. You're just jealous of Don, that's all."

"You're only sleeping with him because he's rich," Adam said accusingly.

"And he's amazing in bed," Maryn said, taunting him. When Adam's face flushed, she regretted what she'd said, knowing she'd hurt his feelings.

"I don't like him," Adam had said finally.

And Don didn't like Adam, either. He made that very clear when Maryn had suggested, once or twice, that Adam join them for drinks after work. "That loser?" he'd sneered. Eventually, she'd quit asking.

She got a twinge in her stomach thinking of Adam. She needed to talk to him so badly.

19

Raindrops tapped at the tin roof of the old house, and the thin cotton curtains billowed at the windows of Ellis's bedroom. She stretched and yawned and sank blissfully back into the pillows. She couldn't remember the last time she'd slept so soundly. The breeze and the rain had a narcotic effect, she decided.

But then she thought again about last night. The kiss. Her lips curved dreamily at the memory of it. When had she last been kissed like that? Wait. Had she *ever* been kissed the way Ty Bazemore kissed her on the beach the night before?

Definitely not.

She wondered what it could mean. Ty had chosen her. From his vantage point on that deck, he surveyed a vast buffet of beautiful women sunning themselves on the beach below. And he had the kind of looks that could make even a sane woman yowl at the moon. Julia and Dorie for sure had proclaimed him their instant summer crushes. He could probably have any woman he liked. But he liked her. He'd told her so himself, last night.

So what? the practical Ellis taunted. She'd been standing right there in the moonlight, only half dressed in those skimpy pjs. Easy pickings. And it didn't mean a thing. Not to him anyway.

She sat up and swung her legs out of bed. The rain sluiced down the windows, and now it was pooling on the scarred wooden floor. She went to the window and looked out at the sky. Heavy gray clouds covered the horizon. There would be no beach today. And no chance encounter with Ty Bazemore either. Reluctantly, she closed the window and headed for the shower.

Maryn slept badly. Unable to shake the sense of dread settling into her psyche, she'd tossed and turned the rest of the night, and not even the gentle rain beating on the roof just above her head could lull her back to sleep.

Finally, at six, she got up and fetched a paperback romance novel she'd bought on one of her bike rides around the island. But the plot—all dizzy, frothy nonsense about true love and undying devotion—bored her to tears.

Her thoughts kept turning to that terrifying scene back home, of Don, white-faced with fury, gripping her arm, his fingers digging into her flesh, his eyes burning into hers.

After the meeting with Adam, Maryn had to know the truth. Was she married to a thief? Where did all Don's wealth come from? She'd waited until the end of the week, a morning when she knew he had a standing golf date with a client who always wanted to play thirty-six holes. Taking his spare office keys from a tray he kept on his dresser, she drove to his office in a bland strip mall and let herself in.

It took most of the day, fumbling around in his computer files, before she'd finally blundered into a file with rows and rows of damning figures. She wasn't a CPA, but she'd taken enough accounting classes to get their meaning. As she read, she grew nauseous.

Everything Adam had said was true. Don had helped himself to, from what she could tell, at least two million dollars, writing checks to bogus companies controlled by him on five different Prescott accounts. Sick with fear, she'd locked up the office and left, so upset she never noticed Don's Escalade trailing her all the way home.

He'd stormed into the house moments later.

"What the hell are you up to?" he'd demanded, grabbing her by the shoulders and slamming her against the wall. "I saw you pulling out of the parking lot at my office."

"Nnnnothing," she stammered. "I went shopping and thought I'd stop by to see if you were back from golf."

"I saw you coming out of the office," he said quietly. "Watched you lock up and leave. What were you doing in my office, Maryn?"

She'd never seen him so angry before. Should she tell him what she knew? Confront him with the truth?

"Tell me," he said, grabbing her by the forearm, squeezing until she thought she could feel her bones crumble to dust.

"Don, for God's sake, stop. You're hurting me." For a moment, she wasn't even sure he knew what he was doing. But he knew. He always knew exactly what he was doing.

"I asked you a question, Maryn." He tightened his grip, and she thought she would pass out from the pain.

"I know," she said, nearly screaming. "I know you've been stealing from Prescott. Adam knows too. He told me."

Don let go of her arm, and she slumped to the floor, crying softly.

"Adam knows what?" he said, looking down at her. He prodded her with the toe of his golf shoe. "I asked you a question, Maryn."

"He knows there's something funny about the way you've handled Prescott's finances. The company has hired outside auditors! They know you've been stealing from them."

"Adam doesn't know dick," Don said calmly. "The auditors don't know dick." He jerked her up by the arm to a standing position. "And you don't know anything either. Do you hear me?"

"Don," Maryn said, her eyes riveted to his. Maybe there was a mistake. Maybe she'd misunderstood. "I saw the files in your office. It doesn't look right."

"Shut up," Don said. "And listen carefully. You didn't see anything in my files. You don't know anything."

"I hear," she mumbled.

"Understand me, Maryn," Don said, a strange light coming into his pale-blue eyes. "If you say anything to anybody, I will bury you. Someplace where you'll never be found. Nobody will even know you're missing until it's too late. Not Adam, not your mother, nobody will know what happened, where Maryn has gone." He'd smiled at the thought of that. A moment later, he'd released her, but not before bending his head to her forearm and tenderly kissing the angry red welts he'd left there.

He glanced at his watch. "I'm meeting Robby and a couple of the guys at the club for drinks, and I'm already late. The other wives are meeting us for drinks and an early dinner, and Robby made a point of letting me know he expects you to join us."

Maryn had stared at him wordlessly. Five minutes ago, he'd threatened to kill her. Now he was casually inviting her to dinner—with his client, who was also her former boss at R.G. Prescott Insurers, Robby Prescott, from whom, she was certain, he'd embezzled a couple of million dollars.

"I . . . I'll try," she'd stammered. "My mother called, and she's been begging me to come for a visit. . . ."

"No," Don said, shaking his head curtly. "Tell your mother you're busy. If Robby wants you to have dinner with us, that's what you're going to do. And you'll be just as relaxed and charming as you always used to be. Understood?"

"Well . . ." Maryn started, her mouth dry.

"Then I'll see you at six," Don said, heading for the front door, content that he'd given her the day's marching orders. His golf cleats clicked across the marble foyer. "And for Chrissake," he added, his look taking in her disheveled hair and tearstained face, "get yourself put together before you show up at the club tonight." He'd reached in his pocket, pulled out his money clip, and flung a wad of fifties at her.

After Don was gone, Biggie stood by the bedroom door, his liquid brown eyes bewildered. He knew a suitcase meant a trip, and every other time, if they went to the Jersey shore, or just away for the weekend, Biggie went too. Maryn knelt down beside him and cradled his graying muzzle in her hands. "Not this time, buddy," she said, stroking his soft fur.

There was no time for more. She'd been dressed for shopping, her cover story in case Don got home early, in a cream sleeveless silk-wrap blouse, black slacks, her favorite black patent leather slingbacks. She changed into a top that would hide the angry red welts on her arm and she threw clothes into a duffle bag she found on the closet floor, not wanting to take the time to drag her big suitcase out of the guest-room closet. She tossed in some toiletries, her makeup bag, a jumble of shoes, unsure of what she'd need or want since she had no destination in mind. Just away. Far away. She grabbed the cash hidden in her boots and her Rolex Oyster watch and threw them into her cream Prada bag. At the last minute, she remembered her laptop. She slung the strap of the black-leather carrying case over her shoulder and ran for the front door.

And there was Biggie, sitting by the door, ears pricked up, the red-leather leash in his mouth. "Oh, Big," she'd said, mourning the dog already. She stepped outside and closed the door quickly, but she could hear him scratching at it.

Maryn ran to the Volvo SUV and threw the duffle bag and laptop case on the passenger seat. She drove without purpose, intending only to put miles between her and the stranger she'd married.

And now, nearly a week had passed. This house was quiet. Too quiet. She had to know what was going on at home. Had the auditors discovered the extent of Don's embezzlement? And what about Don? He'd been leaving messages on her phone. She'd been too terrified to listen to any of them, deleting them as soon as they arrived.

She had to know something. She picked up her cell phone, intending to call Adam, or at least see if she had any other missed calls. Damn. The phone was dead. In her haste to flee the town house, she'd left the wall charger behind, and she'd been keeping the phone charged with her car charger. Which was, of course, out in the car. In the garage.

But there was still the laptop. She hadn't even bothered to look at it since she'd moved into Ebbtide, unsure of whether or not the house had wireless Internet.

Only one way to find out. She picked up the black-leather case and lifted it onto the bed. For the first time, she was struck by how heavy it was. Don was a nut for new gizmos, and he'd bought both of them the latest ultra-slim Mac-Books back in the springtime. She mostly used hers to play online games or to shop. Frowning, she unzipped the case and reached in to grab the computer. Instead, her hand closed over a thick rubber-band-bound bundle of paper.

Not just paper, though. Currency. She was holding an inch-thick stack of bills. With trembling hands, she rifled the stack. All hundred-dollar bills. Now she picked up the case and dumped the contents out onto the bed. The MacBook slid out, and so did nine more identical bundles of bills.

Maryn stared down at the money and the MacBook. Her laptop was hot pink. This one was white. In her frenzy, she'd grabbed Don's briefcase. And his computer. And his money.

So much money. Thousands. Hundreds of thousands, probably. Her hands shook as she picked up one of the bundles of bills. Where had this much money come from? Too much for Vegas winnings. What was Don doing with all this cash? And what would he do when he discovered it—and Maryn— were missing?

Suddenly, there was a soft tap at the bedroom door. Maryn's heart felt as though it would leap right out of her chest.

"Madison?" It was Dorie, the strawberry blonde who'd befriended her in the luncheonette.

"Yes?" she managed to croak.

"I hate to bother you, but since it's Sunday, and it's raining cats and dogs out, we decided to fix a big ol' brunch. Julia's making waffles and bacon, and I've got fruit salad, and we're having mimosas. Why don't you join us, Madison? We've hardly gotten to see you at all since you moved in."

The smell of bacon and coffee wafted all the way up to the third floor. Her stomach growled. She hadn't eaten since lunch yesterday. Maryn looked down at the pile of money on the bed, and then back at the door. All week, she'd managed to avoid the women except for a couple of brief, awkward encounters while she was coming and going from the house on her bike. Now, it was raining out, so she couldn't very well take off on her bike. Her stomach growled again. She'd been a hermit long enough. Maybe one meal wouldn't hurt. Hurriedly, she began scooping the money back into the briefcase. She would figure out what to do about it later.

"Brunch sounds nice," she called finally. "Just let me get myself presentable, and I'll be right down."

"She's coming down," Dorie reported to the others. "See, I told you we should ask her."

"Oh goodie," Julia said sarcastically, bowing and grandly waving her spatula like a scepter. "We finally get a real audience with the queen." She dipped a quick curtsy. "Hello, your majesty."

"Shh, she'll hear you," Dorie said. "You wait. She's not stuck-up. She's just . . . an introvert, I think."

Julia drummed her fingertips on the wooden tabletop. "I don't buy that bit about her being in 'transition' after a breakup with some man. What's she really doing here? Money obviously isn't a problem, so why hang out in a dinky little beach town like this? Why isn't she someplace glamorous? Why doesn't she have any friends or family? She keeps her bedroom door locked every second she's gone. I know, because I've checked. And she hasn't moved that car of hers since she parked it in the garage. I'm telling you, she's hiding from somebody or something, and I intend to figure it out."

"She's a mystery, all right," Ellis agreed. She popped the cork on the bottle of champagne and started filling the plastic flutes they'd picked up at the dollar store earlier in the week. Dorie put her hand across the top of her own flute. "No champagne for me, remember?"

"Of course," Ellis said. "But orange juice is good for you. No coffee, though, right?"

"Nope," Dorie said, shaking her head. "Caffeine's not good for the baby, sad to say. I'm missing that a lot more than the alcohol. And I'm already getting tired of drinking all that milk."

Julia glanced over her shoulder at Dorie. "Have you even gained any weight yet?"

"Actually, I've lost seven pounds," Dorie reported. "But that's just because I had hideous morning sickness the first two months. The nurse-midwife at my obstetrician's office says I'm doing just fine. She says some women don't really start gaining until they're in the middle of their second trimester."

Julia shook her head. "Only you, Dorie Dunaway, could get pregnant and actually lose weight."

"Is somebody pregnant?" Madison stood in the doorway, looking elegant even in white capris and an oversized pink-and-white striped shirt. Her blond hair was in a ponytail, and she wore pink Ferragamo ballet flats.

Dorie blushed and Julia looked chagrined.

"Well . . ." Ellis began.

"I am," Dorie said, smiling brightly. She sat down at the kitchen table and held up one of the champagne flutes. "Come sit and hear my tale of woe."

Madison sipped the mimosa cautiously as Dorie calmly repeated the story she'd told her friends just the night before.

"Wow," Madison said, when Dorie had finished. "So . . . your husband doesn't know yet?"

"No," Dorie said, nibbling on a piece of bacon she'd snagged from the platter in the middle of the table. "I'm such a coward, I just really haven't been able to face talking to him yet—let alone tell him about the baby."

"Well," Madison said, "I admire your courage. I don't know how I'd feel about being a single mother. My folks split up when I was thirteen. It was rough. I mean, raising a baby alone, that's a lot."

Julia slid a waffle onto Madison's plate. "So," she said, trying to sound casual. "What about you, Madison? Kids? Husband?"

"Neither," Madison said without looking up. "I guess I've been too busy concentrating on work to settle down and start a family."

Julia's eyes flickered meaningfully at Maryn's ring finger—the one with Don's diamond solitaire. "Oh, this?" Maryn said, fluttering the finger in question. "This is an old family piece."

"Some family," Julia said.

"Julia and I have already appointed ourselves Dorie's baby's godmothers," Ellis was saying.

"Fairy godmothers," Julia added. "Of course, she'll be the most beautiful child in the world. With Dorie's hair and eyes."

Madison glanced at Dorie. "Oh, you already know you're having a girl?"

"No," Dorie said. "I don't want to know the baby's sex ahead of time."

"Julia thinks she's a witch," Ellis explained. "She thinks she can just *will* Dorie to have a little girl so we can spoil her rotten."

"Naturally," Julia agreed. "An angelic little girl. With red-gold curls and green eyes. Her Aunt Julia will teach her how to dress and accessorize—skills her mommy, unfortunately, never learned."

"Hey!" Dorie said good-naturedly, smoothing the wrinkles in her faded Our Lady of Angels soccer tournament T-shirt. "I think I resent that."

"Her Auntie Ellis will teach her math, and how to swim, and of course, we'll read lots of books together. I'll take her to the zoo, and the beach. . . ."

"I'll take her to New York and Bergdorf's," Julia said.

"And if it's a boy?" Dorie asked, spreading the palms of her hands across her belly.

"We'll put him on a raft and gently shove him out to sea," Julia declared.

"Julia!" Ellis and Dorie exclaimed.

"Kidding," Julia assured them. "Mostly."

20

It was nearly three by the time Maryn managed to pry herself away from the other women. Brunch had been a leisurely affair, and truthfully, she'd been surprised to find how much she enjoyed their company. They hadn't made her feel like an outsider at all. It felt good to laugh, relax, let her guard down. And with women her own age. That was the big surprise. But she'd only allowed herself to relax a little. Ellis and Dorie seemed genuinely warm and friendly. But Julia was a different story. Julia listened intently to every little shred of information Maryn had reluctantly imparted about herself.

Lying about her marital status had been a mistake. When had she become such an accomplished liar, Maryn wondered. She should have just admitted that she'd left her husband. They would have been sympathetic. Instead, Julia was now even more suspicious. She wasn't overtly hostile, but Maryn could tell from long practice when another woman was sizing her up. Just as Maryn was accustomed to sizing up every woman she met, right from the start. Well, that was fine. Julia was watching her. And she was watching Julia.

Maryn knelt beside the bed and reached for the briefcase. She laid the stacks of bills out on the bed and counted the money, her heart pounding as the amount grew. Ten thousand dollars in each stack, a hundred thousand dollars in all. The stacks were bound with green rubber bands, not the neat paper bands a bank would use. And the bills weren't new; their numbers were nonsequential.

Her mouth felt dry. What was Don doing with this much cash? She looked warily at the laptop. Were the answers locked somewhere inside Don's computer?

She grabbed the power cord and plugged in the MacBook. It booted up right away. But she didn't have Don's password. For twenty minutes, she played around with different combinations of letters, words, and numbers. His birthday, her birthday. Their anniversary. That was a laugh!

She'd managed to lie to herself just as convincingly as Don had lied to her, right from the very start of their relationship. As it turned out, he already had a family. Of course, she hadn't known about his wife and teenaged children until they'd been practically living together for three months.

Adam had broken the news to her. Reluctantly, he claimed. It had been a terrible blow to Maryn. She'd never claimed to be an angel. She'd slept with her share of men, broken her share of hearts. But she had a rule. No married men. Ever. She'd never do to some other woman what another woman had done to Maryn's mother. She was a lot of things, but she wasn't a home wrecker. Or so she thought.

Another lie. There had been so many, she'd forgotten what was truth and what was not.

She'd confronted Don about his lies, and he'd laughed them off. "We've been living apart for years," he told her. "Abby doesn't care what I do or who I sleep with, as long as the money keeps flowing. She thinks I'm her personal ATM. So why do you care?"

"What about your kids?" she'd demanded. "Don't you care about them?"

"I see the kids," he'd said carelessly. "It's not like they're in first grade. Ashley's what, fourteen? Cash is sixteen. They have their own lives, their own interests. They're not interested in taking a trip to Disney World with Daddy, Maryn."

He'd left a copy of the divorce papers on the dresser, where she'd see them.

And three months later, on a Friday in early February, he'd come home and proposed. If she were brutally honest with herself, she had to admit that the diamond solitaire, twinkling from its white satin cushioned box, had blinded her. To everything. She'd wanted a real wedding, with at least her mother and Aunt Patsy—and Adam—present, but Don had flatly refused. In the end, they'd gotten married before a justice of the peace Don knew, and flown to Aruba for a five-day honeymoon.

Those five days had been the happiest of her life. Don was relaxed, he was tender, attentive, everything she'd dreamed a husband would be. He'd talked about their future together. He'd already bought a lot where they'd build their dream home: ten thousand square feet, five bedrooms, five baths, a three-car garage. And it was on a lake. Maryn would have a bathroom with a fireplace and a whirlpool tub, all marble. And a kitchen that would rival any in the best restaurants in town.

"And kids," Maryn said dreamily. "I know you've done that already, but I want kids of our own, Don. I'm thirty-two. My clock is ticking."

"Whatever," he'd said, brushing aside any specifics.

She tapped away now at the laptop keyboard, trying different passwords. His company name, his kids' names—Ash and Cash, he called them—the nickname his golfing buddies used for him, Shack. None of them worked.

Madison fetched her duffle bag from the armoire. She stacked the money in the bottom of it, and put a dirty T-shirt on top before placing the duffle under her bed. Her thoughts drifted back to Adam. She had to talk to him, let him know where she'd gone.

Rain pelted her as she stepped out onto the rusted iron spiral staircase. She locked the door behind her and, clutching the rail with both hands, picked her way down the steps, feeling the staircase sway with every step. When she got to the bottom, she ran to the garage and unlocked the car. She turned the key in the ignition, plugged in her phone, and sat waiting as the battery recharged.

When the phone's display window lit up, she saw that she had eleven missed calls. All from Don. He'd left voice-mail messages too. Now she forced herself to listen.

Don's voice was low. "Maryn. Where the hell are you? We need to talk. Look, I admit I lost my temper. But you know I never intended to hurt you. I love you, baby. Call me, okay? And let me know you're all right. You're starting to worry me."

She snorted. Oh yeah, he was worried all right. Maybe a little about her. What she'd seen, who she might tell. But mostly, she was sure, he was worried about that briefcase full of money. And his laptop computer and whatever secrets it might hold. She went down the phone log and tapped each of his messages, deleting without listening. She was done listening to Don Shackleford.

She called Adam's cell phone, and it went directly to voice mail.

"Adam, it's me," she said breathlessly. "I've . . . I've left Don. I'm down south. Look, a lot has happened. You were right. About everything. I really need to talk to you, okay? Call me as soon as you get this, no matter what time it is."

Madison considered calling her mother, but rejected the idea immediately. They hadn't talked in months, why call her now? She didn't think Don would have contacted her mother. He had no interest in her family, and she was fairly sure he didn't even have her mother's phone number.

Idly, she tapped the phone. A wallpaper screen came up, a photo she'd taken right after they'd returned from Aruba. Don, sitting on the porch of the town house, relaxed, smiling, his arm draped companionably across the shoulder of his one true friend. Biggie.

Biggie! Why hadn't she thought of that? Maryn jumped out of the car and ran, splashing through the rain, for the house. And Don's laptop.

21

Ellis found herself drawn to the window in her bedroom. She told herself it was the scenery, the dark blue-green waves crashing on the sand, the rain and wind blowing and bending the tufts of sea oats lining the dunes below. She pulled a wooden chair up to the window, and rested her forehead against the moisture-beaded glass. And if she leaned in just the right way, she could see the weather-beaten boards of the garage, and the apartment above, and the dull glow of one lit lamp within.

He was home. She could see his Bronco parked to the side of the driveway. What was he doing on this rainy Sunday afternoon? Probably working, planning his next trade. She decided he was definitely not doing what she was doing. No way he was reliving that moment on the beach last night. No way he was analyzing that kiss, that amazing, lingering kiss, or the feeling of dizzying heat when they'd embraced. No way Ty Bazemore was telling himself to get over himself. Which was what Ellis was doing.

She tried reading. She had a stack of book club books, the ones she'd been too busy to read over the past year, back when she had a career. They were all highly recommended books, literary masterpieces, food for the mind. Stacked on her nightstand, they gently reproved her. But right now what she craved was mind candy, the idle, delicious retelling of a love story—featuring a heroine who looked uncannily like Ellis Sullivan and a hero with sun-streaked hair who could only be Ty Bazemore.

At five o'clock, she watched as Ty came splashing down the wooden stairs from his apartment. He wore khaki cargo shorts, top-siders, and a black T-shirt with CADILLAC JACK'S in hot pink script across the back. He jumped in the Bronco and headed down the driveway. Ellis watched him go, and a plan took root.

At seven, Ellis wandered into the kitchen, where she found Julia, dressed in cut-offs and a faded black tank top, and Dorie, still dressed in cotton pajama pants and an oversized Braves T-shirt. They were studying a handful of takeout menus.

"Pizza or Chinese?" Julia asked, looking up.

"Neither," Ellis said. "We've been stuck inside all day and I've got a bad case of cabin fever. I say we get dressed up and head out and do the town. We could do girls' night out, like the old days."

"What town?" Julia asked. "Are you telling me there's a club scene in Nags Head?"

"Not really a club scene," Ellis said hesitantly. "But I've heard about a place—Cadillac Jack's. They've supposedly got a halfway decent menu, and a bar, and music. Sunday nights it's supposed to be the place to see and be seen."

Julia raised one eyebrow. "By who?"

"By whom, you mean," Dorie said, yawning. "You guys go on without me. Since I can't drink, I might as well stay home and eat leftovers. Anyway, I'm gonna turn in early tonight."

"That leaves us," Ellis told Julia. "Unless we want to include Madison?"

Dorie turned from the refrigerator with a bowl of leftover chicken salad. "She's not here. I saw her drive off about thirty minutes ago."

"Really?" Julia narrowed her eyes. "Wonder where she was headed?"

"Who cares?" Ellis said impatiently. "What do you say, are you in?"

"Why not?" Julia headed for the hallway. "Just give me fifteen minutes to get changed."

Twenty minutes later, Julia sat in the living room, thumbing through a magazine. She was dressed in faded denim capris and a tight black T-shirt that barely covered her tanned midriff. She wore brown leather gladiator-style sandals, and she'd done her hair in a loose braid that hung over one shoulder. Large gold hoops gleamed from her ears.

"Ellis!" she hollered, staring up at the ceiling. "Hurry up and get down here before I change my mind and decide to stay home with Dorie."

"Keep your shirt on," Ellis said, carefully taking one stair at a time.

Julia swung around to see her friend.

"Hey!" she said suspiciously. "You didn't say this place was dressy."

"This isn't dressy," Ellis said, walking into the living room.

"That's a dress you're wearing," Julia said, stating the obvious.

It was, in fact, a dress Ellis had never even worn before—a short, cotton Lilly Pulitzer sundress with a pattern of stylized hot-pink-and-yellow daisies. The dress's spaghetti straps were of a contrasting lime green, and the tight-fitting bodice showed a healthy stretch of Ellis's freckled cleavage. She wore lime green ballet skimmers, and a pair of dangly pink-pearl earrings nearly brushed her shoulder tops. Ellis had swept her hair into a French twist updo, with feathery bangs.

"No fair," Julia said, coming closer to examine her friend. "You look like the queen of the Junior League summer country club dance!"

"And you look like a gorgeous high-fashion model who happens to be slumming it in Nags Head," Ellis said. "I've gotta bring out the big guns if I'm going anywhere with you."

Julia studied Ellis carefully. "You're even wearing makeup."

"First time since we got here," Ellis agreed. "Are you going to stand there giving me the fish-eye, or can we go?"

"Waitin' on you," Julia said.

Cadillac Jack's was actually in Kitty Hawk, eight miles up the road. It was housed in a former Piggly Wiggly supermarket. The old neon sign with the jaunty winking pig still stood by the roadside, but the 1940s-era stucco build-ing had been painted charcoal gray, and the large plate glass windows were shaded by scalloped pink-and-black striped canvas awnings. Ellis joined the line of cars streaming into the parking lot, where a burly off-duty cop in jeans and a navy T-shirt with SECURITY stenciled on the back waved them into one of the few remaining spots, at the rear of the lot.

"This joint is jumping," Julia said as they walked towards the entrance. "How'd you hear about it?"

"I think I read something in a magazine," Ellis said vaguely.

"This is kinda cool," Julia said when her eyes had adjusted to the semi-darkness. The club's walls were still plastered with age-darkened signs advertising specials like CREAM OF WHEAT and COLLARDS and HAM HOCKS with Eisenhower-era prices, but now black leather-upholstered booths filled one wall of the cavernous room and round tables were scattered around the center, with a postcard-sized, slightly elevated wooden dance floor. Music thumped from speakers mounted around the ceiling. Ellis thought she recognized Lady Gaga's latest hit, but nobody was dancing. The crowd was an eclectic mix, with groups of couples and singles Ellis's age, but also lots of college kids, the girls in clingy tops and short skirts, guys in preppy polo shirts.

A bar took up the back wall of the room, with the grocery's retro neon MEAT MARKET sign flashing off and on, the light reflecting in the rows of bottles and glasses on the back bar.

"Are we the oldest ones in here?" Ellis asked anxiously, staring at the bobbing heads of girls who looked a generation younger than herself. She suddenly felt horribly, terrifyingly out of place in her childish pink-and-green getup.

"Who gives a shit?" Julia said, tugging at Ellis's hand. "Come on, let's get a drink and snag a table."

"Wait," Ellis said urgently. "It's so crowded. I didn't think there'd be so many people. Maybe we should just find a quiet restaurant...."

"Too late," Julia declared, plunging into the crowd, dragging Ellis by the hand towards the back of the room, and the bar.

People were stacked three deep at the bar, but Julia expertly managed to wedge herself into a spot at the corner, between a pair of middle-aged men who were nursing beers and eyeing the crowd.

"Get you somethin', darlin'?" The taller of the two men had horn-rimmed glasses and wore a pale blue ball cap with UNC embroidered on the bill. He grinned at Julia, and even seemed to include Ellis in his admiring glance.

"No thanks," Julia said, flashing him a smile that managed to turn him down without shutting him down. It was a uniquely Julia art, one Ellis had always coveted.

Now Julia was leaning over and across the bar, her long, tanned arm waving in the air. "Excuse me," she called loudly. The bartender, whose back had been to her, turned, and on seeing who was calling, put down the glass he'd been polishing.

"Hey there," Ty Bazemore said, walking towards them. "Ellis. Julia. This is a nice surprise." His easy grin took in both the women, but Ellis thought, just maybe, the warmth was directed at her.

"Wow, yeah," Julia said, half turning and shoving Ellis forward. "It sure is a surprise. I didn't know you worked here. Did you, Ellis?"

Ellis felt her face turn as pink as her dress. "Oh, well, yeah, I think maybe I did know that."

"Hmm," Julia said, enjoying her friend's discomfort for a moment.

"Can I get you something?" Ty asked.

"What have you got?" Julia asked.

"Well drinks are two for one for the next ten minutes," Ty said. "But you don't want any of that rotgut. I've got a decent pinot and a cab, or I could fix you something else. . . ."

"Tanqueray and tonic for me," Julia said decisively.

"Uh, well . . ." Ellis floundered.

"Give her a cosmo," Julia said. "You don't happen to have any food, do you? We actually didn't eat dinner."

He frowned. "The kitchen closes early on Sunday, but I'll see what I can do." He turned away, fixed their drinks, and was back a minute later. "I hope you like quesadillas. Go ahead and get a table, and I'll get somebody to bring them over."

"Thanks," Julia said, pushing a twenty-dollar bill across the bar. "I think you just saved our lives."

"Well," Julia said when they'd settled into a booth on the far side of the bar with a pair of two-for-one drinks for each of them, and a heaping plate of chicken quesadillas. "That was quite a coincidence, wasn't it? Running into garage boy at Cadillac Jack's of all places?"

"Umm-hmm," Ellis said, sipping her drink.

"I think he is totally hot," Julia said, looking past Ellis at Ty moving up and down the bar, slinging drinks and making small talk with fluid efficiency. "Don't you?"

Ellis shrugged nonchalantly. "I guess he could grow on you. It was nice of him to get us some food after the kitchen was closed."

"I think he likes you," Julia said, her tone lightly teasing. "I checked my watch. Happy hour ended half an hour ago, and he still gave us the special."

"Oh, no," Ellis said, busying herself by slathering the quesadilla with sour cream. "He was just being polite. But what makes you think he likes me?"

"I'm a witch, remember?" Julia said, resisting the impulse to admit that she'd seen Ellis and Ty in a moonlit clinch the night before. "I can read the future. And I definitely see a man in your future, Miss Ellis Sullivan."

"Hope so," Ellis said fervently.

"Since when are you looking for a man?" Julia challenged.

"You think I'm not interested in men?"

Julia shrugged. "Are you?"

"Well . . . why not? Look, I know we promised each other that this would be a chick trip. But to be honest with you, I haven't really dated in a while."

"How long a while?"

Ellis knew exactly how long it had been. Five years, give or take a month or two. She'd made a brief, disastrous stab at online dating. Nine dates with four different guys. She actually felt queasy thinking about it.

She toyed with a piece of lettuce on her plate. "Please don't make me talk about this," she said quietly.

"How bad could it be?" Julia asked.

"Awful," Ellis said, taking a large swallow of her cosmo. "Soul-searing."

"Which is exactly why you *should* talk about it," Julia coaxed. "Dorie and

I are your oldest, bestest friends. There's nothing you could say that would shock *me*, of all people, for God's sake."

It was true. If the game were truth or dare, Julia's confession of the night before had raised the stakes for all of them.

"If I tell you about it, will you swear never to tell another living soul?"

Julia leaned in until her forehead nearly grazed Ellis's. "Of course. But, you don't even want me to tell Dorie?"

"No. Dorie wouldn't understand. She's so gorgeous, she's never had to worry about meeting men. Not that you've ever had that problem either."

Julia cocked her head. "Hey, don't you remember what I looked like in junior high? That bad perm my mom gave me, the braces, the flat chest? And my God, my acne! I was the original pizza face. Not to mention I weighed, like, eighty-seven pounds and looked like a damned stork."

Ellis sighed. "Yeah, but by the time we were seventeen, the braces were off, the acne cleared up, and you grew boobs. It was like revenge of the ugly duckling."

"Turns out my mother was right," Julia agreed. "I really *was* a late bloomer."

"Not as late as me," Ellis said, her voice low. "I'm thirty-four, Julia. And I haven't really been with a man since . . ." She paused, and then forced herself to say it. "Since Ben."

Julia's eyes widened. "For real?"

Ellis took another sip of her drink and forced a smile. "Yeah. I'm a freak, right? Eleven years without sex. Not quite the forty-year-old virgin, but close."

"You are not a freak, Ellis Sullivan!" Julia said fiercely. She gestured at the couples on the dance floor, and in particular at a woman about their age who was grinding her hips into her dance partner, her arms locked around his neck, eyes closed, lips apart. "The freaks are these chicks who'll give a lap dance or a blow job to some asshole they just met at a bar while on vacation."

"You're just saying that," Ellis said. "Although I appreciate the sentiment."

"Okay, fine," Julia said. "I'm not going to make you tell me." She raised an eyebrow, as though daring Ellis.

Ellis slurped up the last of her cosmo and took the bait. "Oh well. I guess it won't hurt. I mean, lots of people do it. . . ."

"I knew it," Julia said triumphantly. "You were online dating, weren't you? Come on. Out with it. eHarmony or Match.com?"

Ellis buried her face in her hands. "Match.com. It was the year I turned thirty. I made this stupid New Year's resolution that I was going to really be out there, you know, in the marketplace. Never again. I'd rather die alone, the crazy lady living in a double-wide down by the river, with forty-seven cats and a houseful of hoarded tin cans and toilet paper, than try that again."

Julia rubbed her hands in delight. "Tell me everything. Don't leave out a single, grotesque detail."

"I only did it for three months," Ellis said. "Two different women I worked with met their husbands that way, and they were totally normal, average to above-average nice guys. But I think those women got the last two normal guys on the planet. Either that, or I'm just a major creep magnet."

"Details," Julia interrupted. "Gimme."

"Gawwwwd," Ellis moaned. "I've spent years trying to forget all this stuff. And now you want me to dredge up all the dirt again. Isn't it enough that I admit I made a major mistake?"

"No," Julia said. "Quit stalling."

"Okay," Ellis said, wincing at the memory. "The first guy—his name actually was Guy—seemed nice, at first. We e-mailed back and forth for a couple weeks, until I convinced myself he wasn't some kind of psycho axe murderer. We met at a coffee shop on a Saturday morning. He was wearing jeans, a polo shirt, well-groomed, nothing scary at all about him. Until he ordered."

"What? What did he order?"

"It wasn't what he ordered, it was *how* he did it. I mean, he made the waitress repeat our order back twice to him, and then when she brought the coffee and his danish, he made this big stink about how she'd screwed it up, and insisted he'd asked for decaf. And I heard him. He did not ask for decaf! And then he said the danish was stale, and it tasted fine. He harangued this poor girl for five minutes, until she was in tears, and when we finished, he left a penny for a tip."

Julia rolled her eyes. "I can't stand a waitress baiter. Or a stingy bastard. I'm guessing you never saw Guy again."

"Never," Ellis agreed. "But the next guy was worse." She shuddered. "I've blocked out his name."

"No you haven't."

"Okay. It was Bart. Or Barf, as I came to think of him afterwards."

"What was wrong with Bart?"

"He was maybe the best-looking guy I've ever gone out with. I mean, gorgeous. Tan, muscular, elegant manners. He took me to dinner at this really nice Italian restaurant. And of course, he ordered in Italian, which was a little bit of a turnoff. I mean, who gives an entire order in Italian?"

"You can't hate the guy just because he spoke Italian."

"He did kind of remind me of Kevin Kline in *A Fish Called Wanda,* but it wasn't the Italian that was the turnoff. It was the fact that he took me on a date—commando!"

Julia guffawed. "Seriously? How do you know? Maybe he was just wearing, like, you know, low riders."

Ellis blushed beet red and giggled. "I know, okay? He was totally commando."

"I don't believe it," Julia said, taking a long sip of her drink.

"No, Julia," Ellis said, leaning forward again. "The way his pants were cut, sort of loose, you know, I could tell he was, you know . . ." she whispered, "free balling. That's what Baylor used to call it. But Baylor only did it at the beach, when he was a teenager. Not on a first date at a nice Italian restaurant!"

Julia's face contorted, and she pressed a paper napkin to her face. "No fair! You made me snort gin out my nose. What did you do when you realized he wasn't wearing any underwear?"

"What could I do?" Ellis said. "I didn't realize it until he got up to go to the men's room, and he was walking back across the restaurant, and you know, his goods were kinda jiggling around as he walked."

"Oh no," Julia laughed. "Eeeeww. Poor Ellis."

"It wasn't that funny at the time," Ellis said, laughing now. "I just had to get out of there, but I'd already ordered dinner. So I scarfed down my entrée, then I faked a migraine, told him I was so nauseous I'd better leave immediately. I literally ran out of the restaurant, hailed a cab, and hightailed it home. And that was it for me and online dating."

"Oh my God," Julia giggled. "I've been with Booker so long, I had no idea things were that awful out there in the dating world."

"You don't know the half of it," Ellis agreed.

"So what changed your mind about dating again?" Julia asked.

"Nothing," Ellis said. "And everything. Losing my job—it's corny, but I think it's time to take stock. And I've decided it's now or never. If I meet a nice guy, who knows? Anyway, Ty's not really a bartender. He's a day trader. He's just moonlighting here because the stock market is so crappy right now."

"I'm no snob," Julia said. "I wouldn't care if he really was just a bartender. He seems like a nice guy. I think you should go for it, Ellis. Come on, a little summer fling would do you a world of good."

Ellis toyed with her second drink. "You think?"

The waitress was back with another round of drinks, and this time she didn't look happy. "Ty asked me to tell you ladies that he gets off in thirty minutes," she said. "He was wondering if you're going to stick around that long."

"Oh," Ellis said. "Well, sure. I mean, does that sound all right to you, Julia?"

Julia finished off her drink. "You stay, Ellis," she said casually. "If you don't mind, I'll take the car and go on back to the house. I think I feel a migraine coming on. Maybe Ty will give you a ride home."

"No!" Ellis said, feeling panicky. "You can't go already, Julia."

"You can stay," Julia said, reaching over and patting her friend's hand. "You're a big girl. You can do this."

The waitress cleared her throat to let them know she was waiting.

Ellis gulped. Her heart was racing. She looked up at the waitress. "Tell him I'll be here."

Julia stood up and put a twenty-dollar bill on the tabletop. "There's the tip," she said, nodding at the money. She dropped a kiss on the top of Ellis's head. "Have a good time," she whispered. "And don't worry. I've been watching Ty all night. He does a lot of bending and stretching, getting beers out of that cooler on the back bar. I'm a hundred percent sure he's wearing underpants."

22

"Strawberry Shortcake is staying, but her friend is outta here," the waitress told Ty.

"Nella!" Ty said reprovingly. "Don't be mean. It doesn't suit you."

"Can't help it," Nella Maxwell said, dumping her tray full of dirty glasses into the bar sink. "It's my nature. Who is she, anyway?"

"Her name is Ellis," Ty said, filling a shaker with ice and vodka. "She's a friend."

"Doesn't look like your usual variety of 'friend,'" Nella pointed out. "The hottie who left is more your type."

"Julia?" Ty frowned. "Not really. Anyway, I like Ellis. She's . . . different." He gazed over at Ellis, sitting alone at her table, chin propped up on her fists, watching the swirl of people around her. She was wearing a girlish pink-and-green sundress, and with her hair swept off her neck, he could see a sprinkling of freckles on her sunburnt shoulders and chest, and a surprising amount of cleavage, especially from a woman whose bathing suit looked like something you'd wear to a swim meet. Nella was right about one thing, Ty thought. Ellis looked just like a sweet, pink confection. Totally out of place in a bar like Cadillac Jack's, with its writhing mass of on-the-make college kids and black-clad hipsters. He wanted to sweep her up and out of there, maybe back to the beach, someplace quiet, someplace without the throb of music and din of shrill voices.

He'd been unaccountably thrilled to look up an hour ago and see Julia towing Ellis along in her wake, steaming towards the bar. He'd never expected Ellis would actually take him up on his invitation to drop by the club. She didn't seem like the type to go club hopping, but maybe it had been all Julia's idea. Not that he really cared. He was happy Ellis had come and even happier that Julia had bowed out.

Ty looked down at his watch and frowned. "It's after nine, and I'm supposed to be off. Angie told me Patricia was coming in to work the rest of the shift. You seen her?"

"Nope," Nella said. "But I need two frozen 'ritas and a Natty Lite for one of my tables five minutes ago."

"Patricia better get her butt in here," Ty said darkly, dumping ice and margarita mix into the blender jar. "I'm tired of covering for her. Do you have her cell number?"

"Patricia's?" Nella hooted. "Get serious. Even if I had her number, she wouldn't answer. She and Jason had a big fight last night, and he threw her out of the apartment. And you know that piece-of-crap car of hers quit running a week ago, so with Jason out of the picture she's either gotta ride her bike or thumb a ride to get here."

"Swell," Ty muttered, looking around the bar. It was a typical summer Sunday night at Cadillac Jack's. The place was jammed and people were still coming in. Patricia Altizer was a sweet kid, in her midtwenties, but she had terrible taste in men, and worse luck when it came to managing her own life. When she made it in on time for her shift, she was a hard worker, but Ty had already had to fill in for her the past couple of times she was supposed to work, and he had the sinking feeling that tonight would be another of those nights.

Sure enough, at 9:30, Angie, the club owner, slipped behind the bar, a look of chagrin on her face. "Patricia's a no-show, as I'm sure you already figured," she started. "Ty, honey, I hate to ask, but can you stay 'til closing?"

"You can't get anybody else?" he asked. "I've kinda got something to do tonight. And you swore you weren't going to keep asking me to close."

Angie turned and looked in the direction of the table she'd seen Ty gazing at as she approached the bar. Ellis had finished her drink and was fiddling with her cell phone. Ty had been so busy, he hadn't even had time to send over another drink—or an apology for keeping her waiting.

"Yeah, Nella told me you've got a new friend," Angie said, a note of sarcasm in her voice.

"Nella needs to mind her own business," Ty said.

"Look, Ty," Angie went on. "I'm desperate, okay? Patricia's definitely not coming in, and I've called all over, trying to round up somebody else to work, but you're it. If you'll stay 'til closing, I'll owe you big time. You name it, you got it. Just don't walk out of here and leave me without a bartender."

Ty thought about it. Angie really was in a jam. If he left now, with only Nella and one other girl waiting tables, there'd likely be a riot. Anyway, he was in a jam of his own, wasn't he? It was mid-August, and September was closing in. He needed to make some money, and he needed to make it fast. He looked over at Ellis, who returned his gaze. She smiled, raised her eyebrows, and gave a little wave.

He sighed. "You're gonna have to spell me for half an hour. Then I'll be back, and I'll stay and close. But this is the last time. And it's gonna cost you."

"Anything," she said fervently. "Name it."

"You're paying me twenty bucks an hour tonight," Ty said. "Plus tip out. And no skimming. Nella and I can tell what tips oughta be tonight, and if you try and short us, it'll be the last time I set foot in this place. Understand?"

"That's extortion."

"Yep," Ty said. "And you could always refuse to pay, and I could take a walk."

"Hey," Ty said, sliding into the booth across from Ellis.

"Hey yourself," Ellis said. "Pretty busy tonight, huh?"

"Yeah, and I've got bad news," Ty said. "The chick who was supposed to be coming in at nine isn't coming. Which means I've got to stay and close up—and I won't get out of here 'til at least 1 A.M."

"Oh," Ellis said, trying to hide her disappointment. "That's too bad."

"It's a pain in the ass," Ty said. "But they can't get anybody else this late, so it's all me. Look, I've got, like, a fifteen-minute break. I'll run you home, and if you'll give me a rain check, maybe we could hang out another night."

"Sure," Ellis said, trying to sound noncommittal. "But don't worry about me. I can get a cab or something. . . ."

"No way." He held out his hand. "C'mon. The quicker we get out of here, the more time I can spend with you."

"All fifteen minutes," Ellis said.

Ten minutes later they pulled into the driveway at Ebbtide. The porch light was on, and Madison's room on the top floor of the house was lit up, but the rest of the house was dark.

Ty left the Bronco's motor running. "This really sucks," he said fervently.

"It's all right," Ellis said. "It's not like we had a date or anything."

"We didn't really have a date, but that's not all right with me," Ty said. "What about another night this week? Most of the best restaurants are closed Mondays. Maybe Tuesday night?"

"Uh," Ellis said. Her brain was frozen. He was asking her out. For a real date. Suddenly, she was fifteen again, tongue-tied and paralyzed with shyness.

"Wednesday night, then?" Ty asked.

"No, I mean, yes, Tuesday night would be fine," Ellis finally managed.

"Great," Ty said, relieved.

Grateful that the awkward moment had ended, Ellis fumbled around, looking for the door handle. But before she could find it, Ty leapt out of the car, jogged around, and opened it for her.

He took her hand and helped her out of the car, pulling her to him in one fluid movement, just as naturally as if he had done it a million other star-filled summer nights. And to her amazement, her arms went around his neck, just as though she'd been doing this all her life too. He found a tendril of dark hair trailing on her shoulder blade, and tucked it behind her ear, kissing first her shoulder blade and then her ear. Finally, his lips found hers. He teased her lips open with his tongue. And then the front pocket of his jeans began to vibrate, and then ring.

"Damn it," he said, reluctantly letting her go. "That's Angie, screaming that I gotta get back. Which I do."

He kissed the tip of Ellis's nose. "To be continued, right?"

"Right," Ellis agreed. "Absolutely."

She made a concerted effort to march briskly up the steps to Ebbtide, turning at the door to watch Ty's car backing down the driveway. She hummed lightly as she swept through the ground floor of the house, checking the locks, corking a bottle of wine somebody had left on the kitchen counter, turning off the lights.

Ellis was halfway up the stairs when she recognized the tune she'd been humming. "Dancing in the Dark." In her bedroom, she hung up the pink sundress, slipped into her cupcake pjs, and climbed under the covers. She stretched and yawned contentedly, and clicked off the lamp on her bedside table. A summer fling! Ellis Sullivan was having herself a summer fling. As Julia had said, "It's about damned time."

23

Tuesday morning, Dorie rolled down the elastic waistband of her pajama bottoms so that they barely rested on her pubic bone. She lay flat on the worn chenille bedspread, lifted her chin, and stared down at the soft, pale roundness of her belly. Sometime in the past ten days, when she'd been preoccupied with the future, the present caught up with her.

She closed her eyes and rested the palms of her hands lightly on the bump. Her belly. Her baby. This was really happening. She'd dog-eared her second-hand copy of *What to Expect When You're Expecting*. And at fourteen weeks, she—and the baby—were right on track. Her boobs had grown at least a cup size, spilling out of all her bras and the last bathing suit that still fit. The nausea was gone, she was starting to regain her energy, and just the night before, she was sure—positive, really—that the flutter she'd felt was the baby stirring. Now, if only the rest of her life would get on track.

It was 10 A.M. She'd been watching the clock since waking shortly after seven. At every hour mark, she thought about Stephen. He'd always been an early riser. Should she call him at daybreak? Dorie couldn't bear to think about her husband waking up in Matt's bed. Or would he be alone? At eight, she forced herself to rehearse what she would say when she did call.

"Stephen? There's something I need to tell you. I'm sorry to do this on the phone, but I just couldn't see you before. And I didn't know how to tell you. But now I do. And the thing is . . . I'm pregnant."

She'd imagined a dozen different responses from him. Shock. Disbelief. Anger. Confusion. Happiness? Could this possibly be news he'd welcome? Could he possibly feel what she'd come to feel—deep, unalloyed joy?

The joy was something else that had taken her by surprise. Not that she wasn't still worried about the future—she was! But thinking about this baby gave her a feeling of peace, of such completeness, such absolute rightness, she was almost afraid to allow herself to dip her toe in such a fountain of happiness. The baby books said it was hormonal, but she didn't care. Whatever else happened next, nothing could change the fact of this baby.

At nine, Dorie told herself she should wait. Just a little longer. Let Stephen settle into the day. He would be at school now, she thought, putting together lesson plans for the coming year. Or maybe he'd be in meetings with the rest of the coaches, plotting the soccer team's upcoming season.

Thinking about school, about their colleagues there, made Dorie queasy, and not for the first time. Our Lady of Angels Academy was a small community. Six hundred girls, thirty teachers. It was a Catholic school with conservative values, ruled by the sixty-six-year-old Sister Mary Thomasine, who'd been running OLA with an iron will and a velvet voice since way before Dorie's own school days there. What would Sister Thomasine make of Dorie and Stephen's situation—of Stephen leaving his wife, and for another man? And what would she say about Dorie—and her pregnancy?

Stephen was such an introvert; he had friends on the faculty, but Dorie couldn't think of anybody he might have confided in about the demise of their marriage.

At ten o'clock, she could stand it no longer. She tapped the icon on her phone for Stephen's number, holding her breath, half afraid he would answer, half afraid he wouldn't.

On the third ring, he picked up.

"Dorie?" he was out of breath.

"Hey, Stephen," she said softly.

"Hi," he said. He took a deep breath. She did the same. "It's good to hear your voice."

"Yours too," she said, frowning. He could have called her. He hadn't even tried.

"So," he said finally. "You're still in Nags Head? With the girls?"

"Yes," she said. Stupid question. He knew perfectly well where she was.

"How's it going?" he asked. "Is it as hot there as it is here?"

"Maybe a little cooler," she said. "We had a big rain Sunday, and that cooled things off. How is it down there?"

This was ridiculous, Dorie thought. If she wanted a weather report, she could just look it up on the Internet. She had to quit stalling.

"You know," Stephen said wearily. "It's Savannah in August. Hot. Muggy. Buggy. Pretty much unbearable."

"How's your dad?" Dorie asked. "Any better?"

"Oh." His voice dropped. "Oh, God, Dorie. I . . . you didn't know?"

"Know what?"

"Dorie, I left you a message. On the house phone. I thought you knew. Dad . . . Oh Jesus. Dorie, we lost Dad. It's been, what? A week? I thought you knew."

"What?" she cried. "How would I know? I never check the house phone for messages, Stephen, you know that. Why didn't you call my cell?"

"It all happened so fast," Stephen said, his voice sounding defensive. "They put him in hospice care on a Thursday, and Mom thought, well, we'd still have some time. And the next morning, as soon as she got to his room, he just . . . his heart just stopped."

"Stephen!" She was weeping now. "I am so, so sorry." Sorry for the sweet man Henry had been. For Stephen's mother, a quiet, reserved Midwesterner whom Dorie had never quite felt comfortable calling "Mom." And yes, she was crying for Stephen, and for herself, and for this baby she was carrying, who would never know its grandfather Henry.

"Is your mom okay?"

"You know," he said. "She's sad, she misses him, but my mom isn't one to talk a lot about that kind of stuff. Stoic, I guess that's the word for her."

"Have they already had the funeral?" she asked, sitting up, dabbing at her eyes with the corner of her bedsheet.

"Well, yeah," Stephen said. "It was last week."

"And you didn't think to try to call me? To make sure I knew?" Dorie's face grew hot as her voice rose. "How could you?"

"I just . . . I don't know," he said, his voice drifting away. "I'm sorry, Dorie. After what's happened with us, I didn't know if you would, you know, care."

"So that's it?" she cried. "You sleep with somebody else, move out, and you think that's it, you just click your heels together and we're done? All our history, what we had together, all that's over because you've decided you don't love me anymore?"

"Dorie!" Stephen's voice cracked. "Don't. You know it's not like that."

"No, Stephen," she said. "I don't know that it's not like that. How would I? We haven't talked all summer."

"I tried to call you. I came by the house. You saw me. I know you did. I'm sorry I didn't let you know about Dad. Truly. He loved you, Dorie."

"And I loved him," Dorie said. "Which is why it hurts that you didn't let me know." She was being unbelievably bitchy, unfeeling, cruel even. She sounded just like her mother had, screaming at her father, back in the bad old days. And she just couldn't stop herself. "Let me ask you something, Stephen."

"What?"

"Did you tell *Matt* about your dad's death?"

"Stop it, Dorie," he said.

"Just tell me. Did you?"

"Of course. He was standing right there when I got the call."

"And did *Matt* go to your dad's funeral?"

"God. No. Just stop it, Dorie. I mean, what's the point of all this?"

"Did he go to Omaha with you? Did he?"

"I'm not discussing this with you."

"He did, didn't he?"

"Cut it out."

"No. I won't cut it out. I think I have a right to know who's taking my place. So, I think we've established that Matt went to Omaha. How did you introduce him to your mother? 'Hey Mom, Dorie's out of the picture, meet the little mister?' So now the next question is this: did the two of you sleep in your old room? The one with the *Star Wars* bedspreads and all your soccer trophies? In the same bed *we* slept in?"

"Fuck you, Dorie," he said. "I'm hanging up now."

She had never heard him use that kind of language before. But then, she'd never talked to him this way before either. "Don't you dare hang up," she said shakily. "Wait just a minute. There's a reason I called you today. And I'm so glad I did, since we seem to be sharing secrets."

"What? I've gotta go, Dorie. I don't have time for your crap."

She hesitated, feeling the bile rise in her throat. This was not how she wanted to share this news. Not this way. She did not want to float the baby news on this regrettable torrent of anger. But the toothpaste was out of the tube now, as her grandmother would say. And there was no going back.

"Congratulations, Stephen," she said finally. "You're going to be a father. I'm pregnant."

"What? What did you just say?"

Not the reaction she'd been expecting from him, this sudden deafness.

Dorie took a deep breath, enunciating each syllable with care. She didn't intend to repeat herself again. "I said . . . I'm pregnant."

There was a long silence. She could hear his breathing, rapid and ragged. Maybe he'd just gotten back from a run. Or maybe her news was giving him a heart attack.

"Stephen?"

"I'm here," he said. "Oh, God, Dorie. A baby? When?"

"February. I'm almost four months pregnant."

"Wow. Just . . . I don't know what to say, Dorie. I mean, you call me up and yell at me because I didn't tell you about my dad, and now you just casually blurt out the news about this baby?"

Dorie tried to laugh, but it wasn't funny. "Not so casual. I've been trying to figure out how to tell you for weeks and weeks. I even rehearsed what I'd say.

Somehow, it didn't go as well as I'd planned. I'm sorry I yelled at you. And I'm really so sorry about Henry. The sweetest, dearest man . . . I wish he could have known about the baby."

"A baby," Stephen repeated. "And you're four months already? You couldn't have told me sooner?"

"No," she said simply. "I found out right around the same time we found out about your dad's cancer. I felt guilty, giving you something else to worry about. So I kept waiting for the right time, when you weren't so upset about your dad. And then you were acting so weird and withdrawn, and then, well, Fourth of July happened."

"I see."

Her palms were sweaty. She switched the phone to her right hand, which was trembling. "Well, what do you think?"

"About the baby? I don't know. It hasn't sunk in yet. What do *you* think? I mean, it's not something we'd talked about. And now . . ."

"I'm happy," Dorie said simply. "Despite everything that's happened, I am so happy and excited about this baby. I've got a lot to figure out, but for right now, I am going to concentrate on this child I am carrying. And I am going to be a good mother. I swear, I won't be anything like Phyllis."

"You're nothing like your mother. But do I get any say in any of this?" Stephen asked.

"If you want," she said carefully. "But I think we both know the marriage is over."

"Is it?"

She shook her head. Was he really this dense?

"Yeah. It really is over," she said. "Stick a fork in us. We're done."

His breath slowed, and now she wondered if he was having a stroke instead of a heart attack. "I still love you, you know."

She put her right hand over her belly, and wondered if the baby could hear what he'd just told her. "Do you really?"

"Yeah," he said sadly. "It kinda sucks, doesn't it?"

"And what about Matt?"

He sighed. "What can I tell you? You want me to lie and say there's nothing there? That it was all a big mistake? I can't tell you that, Dorie. No more lies. When my dad got sick, when I flew out there to see him that last time, I knew I probably wouldn't see him again. And I realized it was time. Time to quit lying to myself about who I was and what I wanted."

"It would have been good if you could have told *me* who you were and what you wanted," she said quietly.

"I didn't know how," Stephen said. "I was scared. And ashamed. God help me."

"Oh, Stephen," Dorie said, reaching for the sheet to wipe her eyes again. By the time they were done talking, she'd have to change the bed. "What are we gonna do now?"

"I guess we better start figuring that out," he said. "What about school? Have you told Sister? About us? Or the baby?"

"No," she said. "I haven't told anybody else, besides you and the girls. But I've got a contract, and I intend to work just as long as I can. How about you? Have you told anybody . . . that we've split up?"

"No," Stephen said. "I thought we should talk first. Figure out the next step."

She rolled her eyes. This was how it was going to be. Stephen was never going to be the person to take the first step. He was going to avoid the reality just as long as possible.

"Ellis's brother Baylor has a friend who's a divorce lawyer," Dorie said briskly. "I'm going to talk to him about getting the paperwork started as soon as possible. We'll have to sell the house, I think."

"Why?" Stephen said. "You love that house."

"But I can't afford to live there on just my paycheck. And neither can you." She pointedly did not ask him where he intended to live.

"Dad left me a little money," he started.

"Enough to pay off the mortgage?"

"No, nothing like that," he said hurriedly.

"I rest my case," Dorie said. "Look. I'm going to talk to Baylor's friend. I think you'd better find a lawyer too. And a real estate agent, so we can get the house listed. I'll call you when I find out how we file the papers and everything."

"I don't want a lawyer," he said dully. "You can have everything, Dorie. I want our baby to have a home. And this is all my fault. I did this to you. I hate fighting with you. And I hate the idea of a divorce."

"I hate it too. But you don't want to be married to me anymore. It looks like you want to be with Matt," she reminded him. "You can't have it both ways, Stephen. I don't want to fight with you either, and I have no intention of taking you to the cleaners. I just want half the proceeds from the house. And I'll need child support, of course."

"Dorie?" Stephen sounded urgent. "About the baby. When do you think it happened? I mean, I thought you were taking precautions."

"May," she said, closing her eyes, trying to shut out the memory of that night. "The night before graduation. The end-of-the-year faculty party at Kristin and Bruce's house. We'd both had too much to drink, remember? So instead of driving home, we stayed in their guest room. And . . . you'd been so distant, but that night, you were so being so sweet and silly. It was like when we first met. So . . . we ended up making a baby."

"Yeah," he said softly. "I guess we did. And . . . I guess, despite the rotten timing, I'm glad too. Are you feeling okay? Taking care of yourself?"

"It was a little rocky at first, but the nausea's finally subsided and I'm feeling great now," Dorie said, smiling for the first time. "The girls are totally pampering me."

"Good," Stephen said. "Look, I really have to go now. Will you call me as soon as you get back to town? I really need to see you."

"I will," she promised. "But I'm warning you, I'll be a blimp. See you then."

24

It was the first hot, sunny day in nearly a week. Right after breakfast Julia had set up their camp—the quilt, the chairs, the cooler—on their favorite stretch of beach. Then she'd gone for a jog. Julia hated running, but with all the eating and drinking she'd indulged in since arriving in Nags Head, her inner disciplinarian had finally kicked in. Despite what she'd told Booker, eventually, when this month was over, she'd have to find work again. And nobody was going to hire her for a modeling assignment if she showed up looking like the Pillsbury Doughboy. She'd even reverted to her old regime: black coffee and a hard-boiled egg—without the yolk—for breakfast.

And now she was pounding down Virginia Dare Trail when she spotted a familiar figure on a silver beach cruiser pedaling along in front of her. Julia sped up until she came up beside the bicyclist.

"Madison, hi," she called.

Madison looked over, startled. The bike swerved off the pavement and onto the shoulder of the road, and the cool blonde tumbled headfirst over the handlebars.

"Oof." She was sprawled out on her back, in a patch of sandspurs.

"Oh my God," Julia cried. She ran over and squatted down beside the fallen woman. "Are you all right?"

Sand clung to Madison's arms and bare legs and the right side of her face. Blood oozed from a scrape on her elbow.

"Fine," she said, glaring at Julia. "You startled me."

"Sorry," Julia said, offering her a hand up and looking away from the blood, the sight of which was already making her feel light-headed.

Reluctantly, Madison took the hand and hauled herself to a standing position. She looked down at the bike, which had landed hard on the pavement. The front wheel rim was bent. "Damn it," she muttered.

She picked the bike up and grabbed the rim, grimacing as she tried, ineffectively, to straighten it out. Then she set the bike upright and tried to wheel it away, but it wobbled crazily.

"Well, that's all screwed up," Madison said, slamming the bike back onto the pavement.

"I really am sorry," Julia said, taken aback by Madison's burst of anger. "Look, I'll go get Dorie's van. We can load it in there and take it to the bicycle repair shop. There's one just up the road, I noticed it on my run."

"Whatever," Madison said, stony-faced.

Julia touched the other woman's elbow gingerly and looked away quickly. "You're bleeding. Come on, we're just a block from home. Ellis has a first aid kit. We'll get you cleaned up and then come back for the bike. Nobody's going to steal it while it looks like that."

Madison looked back at the bike and sighed. "All right."

Julia was soaked in sweat, her orange nylon running shorts and white tank top clung to her tanned body, and her hair was held back with a white visor. She looked over at Madison, dressed in cheap black capris, a pale blue T-shirt, and no-name sneakers, limping along beside her.

"Did you do something to your ankle?" she asked sympathetically.

"I think maybe I twisted it," Madison grimaced.

"I really am sorry," Julia repeated. "I'll pay to have the bike fixed."

"Don't worry about it," Madison snapped. "It's a piece of junk. Not a big deal." Despite her injured ankle, she sped up.

Julia sped up too, until she was alongside the other woman again. "Have I done something else to offend you?" she asked. "Have the rest of us—Dorie and Ellis—done something to piss you off?"

"No," Madison said. "What makes you think that?"

Julia shrugged. "Every time we see you, every time we ask you to come down and eat with us, or join us on the beach, you act like we want to poison you or something. Dorie says you're just shy, but I think there's something else. Maybe you just plain don't like us?"

Madison kept walking. "I don't have anything against any of you. You all seem like perfectly nice girls. It's just . . . I'm not one of you. Okay? And that's fine with me. I don't want to pledge your little sorority or be your BFF. I just want to pay for my room, and eat my meals, and ride my bike in peace."

"O kaaaay," Julia said, stung by the outburst, "Fair enough. I'll let the others know. We'll keep our distance, if that's what you want."

They walked on in silence. When they reached Ebbtide, Ellis was on the porch, sweeping off the night's sand deposit.

"What happened?" Ellis asked when she saw Madison, limp and bleeding.

"I fell," Madison said.

"Come on inside, and I'll get the first aid kit," Ellis said.

Dorie was sitting at the table finishing her breakfast when the two women walked in. "Good Lord," she said.

"I fell off my bike," Madison repeated. "It's no big thing."

Ellis got Madison to sit at the table while she gently washed the sand off her scraped elbow, dabbed the abrasion with antiseptic cream, and bandaged it. "What about your ankle?" she asked, lightly touching Madison's ankle, which was already swollen and discolored. "Do you think maybe it's sprained?"

Madison flinched. "It's just a twist," she said, determined to avoid further contact. "It'll be fine."

Dorie jumped up, went to the freezer, and scooped up a handful of ice cubes. "I'll put these in a ziploc bag and we'll fix you up an ice pack to get the swelling down." She looked over at Ellis. "Do you have some aspirin or ibuprofen in that kit?"

Ellis shook a couple of tablets from a bottle and handed them to Madison, who rolled her eyes but swallowed them without water.

Julia came into the kitchen then. "I'm going to take the van and go get your bike and take it to the repair shop," she announced, brushing aside Madison's protests. "You probably don't need to be walking on that ankle."

"She doesn't," Ellis agreed.

"I'm fine," Madison repeated. "I'm just going to go up to my room and wash off all this sand."

"You shouldn't be going up stairs on that ankle," Ellis said, but Madison grabbed the ice pack, pretended not to hear, and kept walking out of the room and up the stairs.

"Geez," Ellis said, watching her go. "What the hell did you do to her, Julia?"

"Nothing! I was jogging back towards the house, and she was in front of me on her bike, so I ran along beside her and said 'Hi!' and she just freaked out and fell off," Julia insisted. "I apologized, I offered to pay for the bike, I totally groveled, but she acts like I did it on purpose."

"She's so prickly," Ellis said, shaking her head. "I totally don't get her."

"I even asked her if we'd done something to offend her."

"What did she say?" Dorie asked.

"She basically told me she doesn't want to play in our sandbox," Julia said, laughing uneasily. "I'm telling you, Ellis, there's something going on with that woman. And I intend to find out what it is."

"Julia," Ellis said, a note of warning in her voice, "leave her alone. You are not Nancy Drew."

"That's what you think," Julia said. "Dorie, I'm gonna take the van and pick up her precious bike and take it to get it fixed. Be back in a few."

Julia pulled the minivan onto the shoulder of the road, directly beside Madison's mangled bike. It was nearly noon and the sun blazed white hot overhead. Her running shoes sank into the soft sand as she stood over the bike, and a bead of perspiration trickled down her cheek. Impatiently, she yanked her top over her head and tossed it inside the car. Dressed in her bright orange running shorts and hot pink sports bra, she bent over and grasped the bike's handlebars with one hand and the rear wheel with the other. As she was transferring the bike into the back of the van she heard a soft clunk. A cell phone had fallen from a purple-and-black foam cup holder bolted to the bike's handlebars.

She knew at a glance whose cell phone it was. The few times Madison had deigned to join the other girls, she had that cell phone clutched tightly in her hand, and Julia had never seen her without it.

She picked it up, and just as she did so, a car's horn blared, and there was a chorus of loud wolf whistles. A battered black Land Cruiser full of shirtless, sunburnt college boys pulled up alongside her. "Hey baby," the driver called. "You need a hand?"

She flashed them what Booker always called her "money smile," the one she'd perfected in her early days of modeling, after studying Farrah Fawcett's iconic red-bathing suit poster. Julia raised her chin, tilted her head slightly to the side, and shook her long hair back over her shoulders. "Fuck off," she said sweetly. She shoved the phone into the pocket of her running shorts, slammed down the van's hatch, and got back in the driver's seat.

The Land Cruiser's driver treated her to another blast of his horn, and then peeled away, leaving a trail of oily black exhaust. "Assholes," Julia muttered. But she was secretly pleased that at thirty-five she still had the looks—and the power—to stop a carload of randy college boys and drive them just a little bit nuts.

Bikes on the Beach occupied the end slot in a small strip mall on Croatan Highway. Every slot in the parking lot was full, so she double-parked and ran into the shop. A middle-aged woman with waist-length dyed black hair sat on a stool at a counter, leafing through a catalog of bicycle parts. "Help you?" the woman asked, looking up.

"I've got a bike in my van with a bent wheel," Julia said. "Is that something you can fix?"

"Sure thing," the woman said. She eased herself off the stool and followed Julia out to the van. The woman easily hefted the bike out of the van. Inside the shop, she gave Julia an index card to fill out, with her name, address, and cell phone number. "My husband does the estimating and repairs, and he just left to deliver some beach chairs down the road. I'll have him call you as soon as he gets a chance to look at it," the woman said.

"How long before it's fixed?" Julia asked, remembering Madison's annoyance at the prospect of being without her bike.

The woman shrugged. "If we've got a replacement wheel, it could be done this afternoon. But if he's got to get one sent over from a supplier, it could be a few days."

"Great," Julia said.

"We got plenty of rentals," the woman said, gesturing at the front of the shop, where a couple dozen bikes of all description were parked.

"I'll let her know," Julia said.

She was getting back into the van when she heard an unfamiliar noise. It sounded like a dog's urgent bark—but it was coming from her hip. Julia reached for her pocket and brought out the cell phone. Madison's phone. The display screen was lit up. UNKNOWN CALLER.

Julia hesitated, but then curiosity got the better of her. "Hello," she said. "Madison's phone."

"Maryn?" It was a man's voice and he didn't sound happy. "Come off it. I know it's you."

Julia frowned. "Who is this?"

"Who the hell is this?" the man demanded.

"This is Julia Capelli," Julia shot back.

"Put Maryn on."

Swiftly, Julia disconnected. "Maryn?" she said softly. "Who the hell is Maryn?"

The phone rang again, almost immediately, and again, the display screen said UNKNOWN CALLER. This time, Julia let it ring. A moment later, the phone dinged, and she saw that the caller had left a voice mail.

She glanced around to see if anyone was watching. The shopping center was nearly a mile from Ebbtide. There was no way Madison could have walked all this way with a sprained ankle, especially not in this heat. But Julia decided not to take any chances.

She pulled the van around to the back of the shopping center and parked behind a dumpster. She touched the icon for voice mail, and the screen showed eight voice mails. Four of them were from someone named Don. She touched the icon and listened to the call that had just come in.

"Maryn, damn it, call me back." It was the same man she'd hung up on. "Don't do this to me. I'm going crazy here. I know you're pissed about what happened, but I can explain. Call me back, okay? Just let me know where you are, and that you're all right. I'm sorry, you know? I didn't mean to hurt you. I would never deliberately hurt you."

It was easily ninety degrees inside the van, but Julia shivered despite the heat. She touched the icon for the next voice mail, and the next, each from someone named Don. In each message, Don addressed his caller as Maryn, and each time, implored her to call him, the urgency in his voice increasing with each message. It was clear to Julia, from the first time she heard Don, that he was also the unknown caller.

"Who the hell is Maryn?" Julia wondered aloud. One caller might have misdialed Madison's phone by accident. But this caller, this Don, had repeatedly called somebody he knew as Maryn.

With her index fingertip, Julia touched the icon that would play back the phone's voice mail message. "This is Maryn," she heard a familiar woman's voice say pleasantly. "Leave me a message and I'll get back to you as soon as I feel like it." The voice was indisputably Madison's.

"I knew it," Julia said. "I knew that chick was a phony."

She looked down at the phone with renewed interest. In just a few moments, she could check call history, she could check Madison's e-mail on that phone too. Just as she was about to do so, the phone began barking again, startling Julia so much that she dropped the phone to the floor of the car. Julia looked warily at the screen. To her amazement, it was Dorie calling.

"Hello?" she said hesitantly.

"Julia, is that you?" Madison's voice was brittle with anxiety. "So you found my phone? Thank God! Was it with my bike?"

"Uh, yeah," Julia said, guiltily. "It fell out of the cup holder. I was just bringing it back there to you."

"Great," Madison said. "See you in a few."

Julia held the phone in her right hand and considered what she'd been about to do. Madison, or Maryn, or whoever she really was, was back at Ebbtide, and she knew Julia had her cell phone. Julia was not somebody who was easily intimidated. But Madison, with her icy stare and aloof demeanor, was potentially a very scary person. As was this unknown man, Don, whoever he was, who had hurt her, and was now begging her to come back.

Gingerly, Julia set the phone down on the passenger seat and started the van's engine. The air conditioner came on, full blast, and Julia shivered again. This time, she didn't know if it was from the frigid air, or the realization of just exactly what she'd gotten herself into.

As soon as she pulled into the driveway at Ebbtide, Madison was out the front door, hobbling towards the van, her hand outstretched for the phone.

"Here ya go," Julia said, handing it over. "Uh, the lady at the bike shop said she'd call me and let me know when it's going to be ready."

"Thanks," Madison said. She looked at the phone, and then at Julia, who found herself going crimson with embarrassment.

"You had a couple of missed calls," Julia offered.

"Uh huh," Madison said. She turned without another word, and went back into the house.

Julia went inside too, and followed the sound of voices coming from the kitchen, where Ellis and Dorie were constructing bacon, lettuce, and tomato sandwiches.

"Want one?" Dorie asked, pointing to the platter of crisp bacon and tomato slices.

"Okay," Julia said. "Well, maybe just the bacon, lettuce, and tomato. No bread." She went out into the hallway and looked up the stairwell, and then came back in the kitchen.

"Did she go back to her room?" Julia asked, her voice soft.

"Who, Madison?" Dorie asked. "Yeah. She said she wasn't hungry. I swear, I don't know why she's so shy."

"Her name's not Madison," Julia said softly. "And she's not just shy. She's a phony."

"What?" Dorie said, putting down her butter knife with a frown. "What are you talking about?"

"Why are we whispering?" Ellis asked.

"I don't want her to hear me," Julia said urgently. "You guys! Her name is really Maryn. Or something like that."

"And how do you know that?" Dorie asked.

"Because while I was retrieving her bike down the road, her cell phone rang, and I just answered it. You know, sort of without thinking."

"Nuh-uh," Ellis said. "You did it on purpose. Don't even try to pretend otherwise. This is us you're talking to, Julia Capelli."

"Okay, fine. I answered it because I wanted to know who was calling her," Julia said readily. "It was a man, and when I answered, I said something like 'Madison's phone', and the guy said, 'Maryn, quit screwing around.' Then, when he realized it really wasn't Madison—or whatever the hell her real name is—he wanted to know who I was. So without thinking, I told him my name. And then I got scared and hung up."

"*You* got scared?" Dorie said, looking incredulous. "Since when does a man scare *you*?"

"This guy was really pissed," Julia said. "So I started messing around with the phone, and I saw she had a bunch of missed calls, and I listened, and they were all from the same guy. Don somebody. Each time, he called her 'Maryn'. He was begging her to call, to come home, telling her he didn't hurt her on purpose. You guys, it was really creepy."

"Maybe he had a wrong number," Ellis offered.

"Nope," Julia said. "I thought of that too. I listened to the message on her voice mail. It's Madison's voice, but she calls herself Maryn."

"Maybe she's in trouble," Dorie said, her brow wrinkled. "She did tell us she'd broken up with her guy. If he physically hurt her, and he's looking for her, maybe that's why she acts so skittish."

"Or maybe she's some kind of criminal on the lam," Julia suggested.

"Oh, Julia," Ellis said, "I'm sure there's a good explanation. Don't be such a drama queen."

"I'm not," Julia protested. And then she had an idea.

"Dorie," she said, holding out her hand. "Give me your cell phone."

"What do you want with it?" Dorie asked, handing it over.

Julia opened a kitchen drawer and found a pencil and pad of paper. She flipped Dorie's cell phone open and scrolled down the call history until she found the number she was looking for.

"What on earth do you think you are you doing?" Ellis asked.

"Just a little detecting," Julia said smugly, snapping the phone closed. She held up the piece of paper. "This is our friend's cell phone number."

"So?" Ellis said.

"So now that I've got it, I'm going to see what I can do to find out who that phone of hers is registered to."

"For Pete's sake," Dorie said. "Don't you have anything better to do with yourself?"

"Not really," Julia admitted, tucking the phone number in her pocket. "Anyway, let's hit the beach while the sun is still shining. I can look this up later."

25

An hour later, Julia, Ellis, and Dorie were stretched out on the beach.

"Dorie," Ellis said, tapping her friend's ankle. "Turn over. Your back is getting blistered already."

"I know," Dorie said, propping herself up on an elbow. "I think it must be all the hormones." She stood up and adjusted the beach umbrella, tilting it forward until the upper half of her body was now in its shade. She sat back down and fixed her chair's headrest so that she was propped up at a forty-five-degree angle. Finally, she slathered more sunscreen on her legs, and uncapped a bottle of water from the cooler.

"That's better," she said, after emptying half the bottle in one prolonged gulp. She settled back onto her chair and picked up her magazine again.

"Dorie?" Ellis began. "I'm not trying to be nosy, but did I hear you talking on your phone this morning?"

"Yep," Dorie said. "You guys will be proud of me. I called Stephen and I told him about the baby."

"You did?" Ellis squealed.

"What?" Julia asked, removing her iPod ear buds. "What's she saying?"

"She called Stephen and told him about the baby!" Ellis said excitedly.

"For real?" Julia asked. "Good for you. What'd he say?"

"He was . . . taken aback," Dorie said. "And even more so when I told him we're getting a divorce."

"This came as a shock to him?" Julia asked. "What planet is he living on?"

"The planet denial," Dorie said simply. "He claims he still loves me. But he's totally not ready to give up Matt."

"He told you that?" Ellis asked.

"In so many words," Dorie said. "God. He is just so screwed up, he doesn't know which way to turn."

"Not your problem anymore," Julia said. "You've got yourself and the baby to think about. He's just going to have to get over himself and act like a grown-up."

"You don't know him like I do," Dorie said. "I know I shouldn't but I feel so sorry for him. You guys, his father died. Like, a week ago! And he didn't even call. I yelled at him, and he just said he didn't think I would care. Can you believe that? Henry was my father-in-law! So then I really screamed at him, and I made him admit that he took Matt out to Omaha for the funeral. I was such a bitch! So he told me to fuck off. I don't think I have ever heard him use that kind of language before. God. You should have heard me. I totally sounded just like my mother. It was depressing."

"It was the hormones!" Julia said loyally. "Anyway, whatever you said to him, he totally had it coming."

"You said it yourself," Ellis said. "He's all screwed up. So what next?"

"Well, I'm going to have to do all the heavy lifting when it comes to the divorce," Dorie said. "He doesn't want anything. He says it's all his fault, and he says I can have everything, including the house."

"So take it," Julia advised. "He's the one who screwed around on you. You deserve it."

"No," Dorie said, shaking her head. "We bought the house together. I told him we'll sell the house and split the proceeds. Neither of us can afford to keep it on our own. Although Stephen doesn't know that. I always took care of all the finances. He doesn't have a clue about that kind of stuff."

"If you sell the house, where will you live?" Ellis asked.

"I've been thinking about that," Dorie said slowly. "I guess I could move in with my mom. . . ."

"Phyllis?" Julia said, "Are you nuts? Why would you subject yourself to that kind of torture?"

"She is my mother," Dorie said. "And her house is only five minutes away from school. It's in a much nicer neighborhood than I could afford on my own. I'm pretty sure she'd let me have Nash's old garage apartment, since he's basically living at Granny's house on East Forty-eighth. It's got a little studio kitchen and a bathroom. It's nothing fancy, but that way we wouldn't actually be under the same roof with Phyllis. She retired from teaching last year, so maybe, at first anyway, she'd be willing to help with the baby, just until I get day care figured out."

"Oh, Dorie," Ellis said sympathetically. "Is that really what you want to do?"

"No," Dorie admitted. "But I think it's what I have to do. At least for the short run. I know Phyllis can be pretty difficult sometimes, and I'm dreading telling her about . . . everything . . . but she really does love me. She'd never turn her back on me. Or her grandchild. She's devoted to Willa's kids."

"There has to be a better way," Julia said, flopping back down onto her chair.

"I'd be open to any suggestions," Dorie said. "But in the meantime, it is what it is."

"It sucks," Julia said.

"It really does," Ellis agreed. "But we'll think of something. In the meantime, take my advice and start buying lottery tickets. That's what I've been doing ever since I got downsized."

She took a deep breath. All morning she'd been trying to figure out how to tell Dorie and Julia about her date with Ty without making it seem like it was a big deal. Although it was a big deal for her. A huge deal.

"You guys," she said slowly. "I know we made a girls-only pact when we got down here. But I've got a confession to make."

"You, a confession?" Dorie said lazily. "What did you do? Steal from the grocery kitty?"

"I already know. Ellis has a boyfriend, Ellis has a boyfriend," Julia sing-songed.

Pink tinged Ellis's tanned face.

"Really?" Dorie lifted her sun visor. "Somebody you met here?"

"Right here," Julia said smugly. "On this very beach."

"You met a guy on the beach? Where was I?" Dorie said.

Julia could stand the suspense no longer. "It's garage boy," she said. "Ty Bazemore. Tell the truth, Ellis, you've got a date with Ty, right?"

"Reaallly?" Dorie sighed happily. "That's great, Ellie-Belly."

"Please don't call me that," Ellis said. "Especially within earshot of Ty."

"I wouldn't," Dorie assured her. "Although there's no telling what Julia might do."

"I would never do anything to screw up a romance for Ellis," Julia said loyally. "Just as long as she shares all the smutty bits with us."

Ellis rolled her eyes again. "It's just dinner. I swear, we are not planning to elope. He's . . . nicer than I knew. Really a sweet guy."

Dorie raised her right hand and made the gesture of a benediction. "Then you have our blessing. Anyway, the 'no boys' rule wasn't my idea in the first place. It was Julia's."

"I give," Julia said readily. "Now let's go get our little girl ready for her big night out. Did anybody bring any condoms?"

Dorie giggled. "Don't look at me. Apparently I flunked that lesson."

"Ditto," Julia said, rolling her eyes.

26

Ellis had just gotten out of the shower and was peering into the tiny, clouded mirror over her dresser when Julia burst into her room.

"What are you wearing for your big night tonight?" Julia asked, flouncing down onto the bed.

Ellis pointed at the yellow floral sundress hanging on the outside of her closet door. "That."

"Really?" Julia got up and walked over to the closet. She fingered the cotton fabric, rubbing it between her fingers. She glanced at the label sewn into the inside of the dress. "Meh."

"What's wrong?" Ellis asked anxiously. "Too low-cut? Too slutty?"

"Slutty?" Julia asked with a hoot. "My first communion dress showed more skin than this rag. Don't you have anything more . . . tantalizing?"

Ellis's bedroom door opened again and Dorie wandered in, dressed in her pajamas and eating a Popsicle. "What are we doing?" she asked, seating herself on the bed.

"Trying to find something for Ellis to wear out to dinner with Ty that won't make her look like June Cleaver," Julia said. She brandished the yellow sundress. "This is what she had in mind."

"Meh," Dorie said. And then, quickly, "Although Ellis does look nice in yellow."

"Nice is not how you want to look on a date with somebody like Ty Bazemore," Julia said.

"Well, no," Dorie said.

Ellis rolled her eyes. "How should I look, if not nice?"

"Hot," Julia said, without hesitation. "Mind-blowingly hot. Smoking hot. Right, Eudora?"

"Oh yeah," Dorie nodded vigorously. "What you said. Pardon the expression, sex on a stick."

"Easy for you two to say," Ellis retorted. "You wake up in the morning looking hot, and just get better through the day. I wake up looking like . . . me. And Ty's picking me up in an hour, and since we don't have time for a whole-body makeover, I'll settle for nice, if you don't mind. Now you two run along and find something else to do."

"Fine," Julia said, giving the sundress a dismissive flick with her index finger. "Suit yourself. Have a *nice* time tonight. Maybe you two kids can share a banana split after the putt-putt."

Dorie got up too. "Have a good time, sweetie," she said, blowing Ellis an air kiss.

The two friends were at the door when Ellis caved.

"Okay," she said. "I know I'm probably going to regret this, but what did you have in mind?"

Julia and Dorie exchanged high fives. Julia opened Ellis's door with an exaggerated flourish. "Follow me," she said.

Dorie uncapped a frosted jar of moisturizer and applied it to Ellis's face with feathery, practiced strokes.

"Mmm," Ellis said, her eyes closed. "What is this stuff?"

"Fluide d'Agneau," Julia said, tossing an armful of clothes onto the bed.

"It's supposed to be made out of the amniotic fluid of sheep raised by monks on shaded slopes of the Swiss Alps. Two hundred dollars an ounce. You believe that?"

Ellis's eyes flew open. "Good God!"

"Relax," Julia said. "The beauty editor at *Self* loaded me up with goodies from the sample closet the last time I was over there for a shoot." She held up a short zebra-print skirt. "This?"

"No animal prints," Ellis said firmly.

Julia nodded and tossed the skirt aside. She picked up a low-cut orange spandex tank dress that resembled a rubber band with shoulder straps. "Too short?"

"Ellis is five inches shorter than you," Dorie pointed out. "Tight is the issue here. That dress will only work if she wants him to jump her as soon as they get in the car."

Julia picked up and quickly discarded half a dozen more garments. Finally, she held up a flirty short skirt in black flower-sprigged chiffon. The hem of the skirt ended in a bias-cut ruffle. "Too girly?" she asked, holding the skirt at arm's length.

Ellis held her breath. She actually liked that skirt. A lot. But she knew if she made a fuss over it, Dorie and Julia would automatically nix it.

"Not bad," Dorie said. She took the skirt and held it up to Ellis. "It's normal length on her. Don't take this the wrong way, Julia, but you must look like a hoochie mama when you wear this thing."

"My legs are my best asset," Julia said. "And Booker loves me in short skirts."

"Hmm," Dorie said, peering at the skirt's waistband. "I don't see a label. Is this another magazine sample or something?"

"Nope," Julia said. "It's mine."

"You mean you actually bought it with your own money?" Ellis asked.

"No, I actually designed it and made it with my own hands," Julia said.

"No way!" Dorie said. "Really? I didn't know you could sew."

"I fool around with it a little bit," Julia said lightly. "Don't you remember, in eighth grade, when you guys took French II, I took home ec instead? Sister Marguerite made me rip out my zipper, like, two hundred times while you guys were conjugating verbs."

"We took French, but I can just barely order bouillabaisse," Ellis said. "And in the meantime, you're making your own clothes?"

"Not all the time," Julia said. "When I get bored, or I get an idea, if I have the time, I'll make something. I actually like the drawing part better than the sewing, because I can do that on planes or in a hotel room."

"Amazing," Ellis said, turning to Dorie. "Did you know she could sew?"

"She's pretty good at secrets," Dorie said. "It's part of that whole witch thing. What kind of a top?" she asked, turning back to the skirt.

"I have a cute white blouse," Ellis started to say, knowing immediately that this was a misstep.

Dorie wrinkled her nose. "No white. What do you wear that with, Julia?"

Julia's eyes lit up. "Wait. This will be genius." She went to the battered wooden dresser and pulled out what looked like a scrap of black lace. "Ta-da!"

"Okay," Ellis said, eyeing the lace warily. "What do I wear over the bra?"

"This is not a bra," Julia said. "It's a corset top. Just the hottest look this season. It's a knockoff of a Gaultier. I wore it for a shoot in the Bahamas this past winter." She held the top up against the skirt.

"Yum!" Dorie said enthusiastically.

"Nuh-uh," Ellis said, defiantly crossing her arms over her terry cloth–clad breasts. "I am not going out on a first date wearing a bra for a blouse. No how, no way."

"You're not listening, Ellis," Julia said, trying to stay patient. "This is not the bra."

She went back to the dresser and brought out a pink lace push-up bra. "*This* is your bra." She held it up in front of her own black tank top, and then placed the corset over it. "See? Two sets of straps. Very alluring."

"Oh yeah," Dorie chimed in. "Adorable. You gotta wear it, Ellis."

"I don't know," Ellis said. "I'm already jumpy as hell. You guys wouldn't understand. I haven't dated, uh, in a really long time. I need to wear something that's in my comfort zone. Maybe if this thing with Ty works out, I could wear this next time."

"Nuh-uh," Julia said, holding her ground. "We've seen your comfort zone. Granny panties and cotton schmatas. Come on, Ellis, just try it on, okay?"

"Yeah, Ellis," Dorie said. "If you really, really hate it, you don't have to wear it. Just try it on for me. Pretty please?"

"Oh, all right," Ellis said. She threw her robe onto the bed and grabbed for the bra. She glanced at the shell-pink satin label. "34C?" She looked over at Julia. "Since when are you a C cup?"

Julia gave them a sheepish grin. She cupped her hands under her breasts. "Since last year," she said. "Implants. The girls were starting to get a little droopy, so I had them hiked up and upsized."

"Really?" Dorie's eyes were big as saucers. "I hadn't even noticed. What was that like?"

"No big thing. I couldn't work for a couple weeks, 'til the swelling went down and they removed the drains."

"Drains?" Ellis made a face. "That doesn't sound like fun."

"It's not supposed to be fun," Julia said. "It's business, that's all. But the boob job wasn't nearly as bad as when I had my nose done. Now that was a major pain. You should have seen the bruising. I looked like I'd been worked over with a baseball bat."

"Julia!" Ellis said. "I had no idea you'd had your nose done. And I've known you all your life." She got up and stood inches away from Julia's face, gingerly touching her nose. "You can't even tell."

"That's because I had the best plastic surgeon money could buy," Julia said.

"What was wrong with your old nose?" Dorie asked. "I mean, it couldn't have been all that bad. You've been modeling since you were nineteen."

"Too ethnic," Julia said. "I had the Capelli schnoz. And I gotta tell you, the first time my daddy saw me after the surgery, and figured out what I'd done, he was brokenhearted. It really hurt his feelings. But I told him it's just business. When you're in this business, your body and your face are your equipment. And you gotta take care of your equipment."

Dorie sat back down on the bed and leaned against a stack of pillows. "Julia, you keep talking about how you're too old and your career is over. But I don't get it. You're more beautiful than ever. Your skin is great, your body is to die for. Who wouldn't hire you?"

Julia flashed Dorie a grateful smile. "You're sweet, Eudora. But you don't understand my world. I'm thirty-five. The girl on the cover of *Elle* this month is seventeen. She wears a size zero. If that. And don't talk to me about Heidi Klum, because she is not the norm. Anyway, I was never Heidi Klum. I was Julia Capelli, who had a couple of lucky breaks and knocked around Europe and did some editorial and runway work. And now, well, that's all winding down. I look good to you guys because you love me, and you don't know any better. But it's okay. Don't worry about me. I'll get it figured out. I always do, right?"

Ellis had been concentrating on lacing up the black satin ribbons crisscrossing the corset top. She sucked in her breath and tied the ribbon in a double knot.

"There is so much more to you than just your looks, Julia," Ellis said. "You're smart. Really smart. And don't give me that crap about never going to college. I'm not talking about degrees. You know real stuff. You've traveled everywhere, you know art and books and music. You've met people! Look at me, I've got a degree in finance, but I spent nearly fifteen years locked up in a bank vault—and what did it get me? Fifteen years of hanging out with pencil pushers and bean counters. And now I don't even have a job."

"And what about me?" Dorie put in. "I'm ten credit hours away from having a master's degree in secondary education. I spend my days trying to pound sentence structure into teenage girls who could give a crap. Don't get me wrong, I love my job, and I love the girls, but a sanitation worker in Savannah makes more money than I do."

"But you have careers," Julia said. "And you both have a piece of paper that *says* you're smart. And I don't. I'll tell you the truth: If it weren't for the money, which is very, very nice, I wouldn't care if I never got another modeling job. I even told Booker that the other night. I am so over all of that. But modeling is all I know."

"No, it's not," Ellis said. "You know a lot about lots of stuff." She picked up the black chiffon skirt and slipped it over her head, then turned with her back to Julia so that she'd zip it up. "What about this?" she said, turning and shaking her hips so that the flounce softly flared. "This skirt is amazing. I'd totally buy something like this, wouldn't you, Dorie?"

"If they made it in a maternity size," Dorie said. "What about it, Julia, have you ever thought about designing clothes instead of modeling them?"

Julia shrugged and waved her hand dismissively. "This is just something I like to mess with. Anyway, you don't know how the industry works. You don't just buy a bunch of sewing machines and call yourself a fashion designer."

"But you do know how it works," Ellis pointed out. "You've been around the business since you were a kid. Come on, Julia. Tell the truth, if you could do anything at all with your life, what would it be?"

"You mean when I grow up?" Julia snorted.

"Yes," Dorie said quietly. "Next week. Next year. What would you be?"

"Hold that thought," Ellis said, peering into the mirror on the back of Julia's closet door. She held her arms out. "I can't wear this, y'all. I'm sorry. But I feel naked in this rig."

"Here," Julia said, thrusting a filmy black jacket in her direction. "Put this on. And quit being such a baby."

Ellis slid her arms into the jacket. It was a nearly sheer, cobwebby fabric, with tight-fitting sleeves that flared gently at the wrists. At least it covered her shoulders. She did a little pirouette. "You think?"

"Absolutely," Dorie said, applauding. "Perfection. You look amazing." She turned to Julia. "And you, my friend, are a genius. So how are we going to put all that talent to work?"

Julia took a deep breath. "Well . . . actually, the job I want isn't in front of a camera. It's behind it."

"You want to be a photographer?" Ellis asked. "I've never even seen you with a camera."

"Not a photographer, a stylist," Julia said. "A photo stylist."

"Really?" Dorie asked, starting to apply makeup to Ellis. "What all does that entail?"

"The stylist is the one who's responsible for the look of a shoot," Julia said. "She shops for all the props and accessories, fluffs everything and makes it pretty—whether it's a modeling shoot, or a food or interiors piece. I've always loved to mess around with that kind of stuff."

Ellis lifted her face to allow Dorie to brush mascara onto her lashes. "So do it, already."

"I'd love to," Julia said. "But it's nearly impossible to break into. It's really competitive. And unfortunately, with print magazines going out of business right and left, the job market sucks right now."

"Could Booker help you get a job as a photo stylist?" Dorie asked. She was lightly fluffing powder over Ellis's cheeks.

"Probably."

Julia leaned in to assess Dorie's handiwork. She picked up a flat black compact and a long-handled brush and handed it to her. "Excellent. Now put some of this blusher across her cheekbones and contour it just along the edge of her jawline."

Dorie nodded and went to work. "Have you told Booker you want to be a photo stylist?"

"Noooo," Julia said, picking up a comb and going to work on Ellis's hair. "It's just something I've been thinking about. I'd probably have to get a job as a stylist's assistant first."

"What does a stylist's assistant do?" Ellis asked.

"Grunt work," Julia said. "You make the cappuccino runs, help load and unload the props and equipment, catalog and return the props to the stores where you bought or borrowed them. Nothing glamorous about it. And the pay is shit."

"And you told me Booker wants you to move back to the States and marry him," Ellis added. "So tell me something, Julia Capelli. What's your problem?"

"I don't know," Julia admitted. "I wish I did."

Julia gathered Ellis's thick straight hair in one hand and picked up a pair of scissors in the other. "Good Lord, Ellis," she complained. "You've been wearing your hair—parted straight down the middle, down to your shoulders—like this since sixth grade. Talk about a rut."

Ellis looked up in alarm. "You are not going to make me change my hair. I can't. I just can't."

Dorie and Julia exchanged a look.

"Ellie-Belly," Dorie said plaintively. "Don't you trust us?"

"No," Ellis said firmly, taking the scissors away from Julia. "I'll wear the corset-thingy. I'll wear the skirt. I'll even wear this damned pink push-up bra that is poking me in the ribs. But I am not letting her cut my hair. Not. Happening."

"All right," Julia said, her expression clearly saying it was not all right. "I'll do what I can. But at least let me try something new. Okay?"

"No cutting," Ellis said between her clenched teeth.

"Wimp," Julia muttered.

"Bitch," Ellis answered back. But she was grinning. And as Julia gathered her hair at the nape of her neck, twisted, and then expertly pinned it up, she blinked. Between the hair and the makeup, she looked like someone completely different. Like herself, but prettier.

There was a polite tap at Julia's bedroom door. The three of them turned to see Madison leaning into the room. Her face was pale beneath the bandage on her cheek, and ugly bruises had already blossomed on her elbow.

"Wow," Madison breathed. "Ellis, you look amazing."

"See?" Julia and Dorie cried in unison.

"Hey, Dorie," Maryn said. "I hate to bother you, but I'm wondering if I could borrow some more ibuprofen. My ankle's kinda starting to throb."

"You poor thing," Dorie said, getting up from the bed. "It's in my room. I'll get it and come right back." As she passed her in the doorway, Dorie bent down to get a better look at Madison's ankle. "It's really swollen now," she reported. "I've got an Ace bandage in my first aid kit. I'll bring that too." She gestured towards Julia's bed. "Sit over there," she ordered.

"Oh no," Madison demurred.

"Sit!" Ellis repeated.

Madison clearly looked uncomfortable perched on the edge of Julia's bed. She looked around the room, and then back at Ellis. "Special occasion?" she asked.

Ellis blushed. "Just a dinner date. But Julia and Dorie decided I needed an extreme makeover."

Madison nodded hesitantly at Julia. "Great job."

"Thank you," Julia said, reluctant to accept the compliment.

Ellis glanced at the clock on Julia's bedside table. "Okay, are we done here? Because he's picking me up in, like, ten minutes."

"What about shoes?" Julia asked. "I shudder to think what kind of shoes you'd planned to wear tonight."

"I didn't bring that many shoes," Ellis said. "Mostly just flip-flops and tennis shoes. The only thing I have that would go with this rig is my black ballet flats."

"God no," Julia said swiftly. She went back to the open closet, but stopped and frowned. "No good. My feet are like gunboats. I wear a ten, and you're like, what, a size six?"

"Six or seven," Ellis said. "The ballet flats will be fine."

"Ballet flats?" Dorie said, arriving with pill bottle and first aid kit in hand. "No, no, no. You need some strappy little sandals with heels with that skirt. I've got just the thing. Can you squeeze into my fives?"

"Not if I want to walk," Ellis said dryly. "Guys, it's fine. It's just a pair of shoes."

"It's never *just* a pair of shoes."

All three heads swiveled in Madison's direction. She stood, wincing. "Don't move. I'll be right back."

"Where are you going?" Dorie cried. "You really shouldn't walk until I get you taped up. . . ."

But Madison was already limping down the hall, towards the stairway.

Five minutes later, she was back, dangling a pair of wicked-looking sandals. They had a tangle of black grosgrain ribbon straps, three-inch spike heels, and the soles were an audacious red.

"Perfect!" Dorie said, clapping her hands in delight.

"Christian Louboutin?" Julia said, raising one eyebrow. "You bring Christian Louboutins to the beach?"

Madison handed the sandals to Ellis and sank down onto the bed. "So kill me. I have a thing for nice shoes. Anyway, I got them on end-of-the-season clearance last summer." She nodded at Ellis. "I'm a seven and a half, but Louboutins run small. Go ahead. Try 'em on."

Ellis examined the shoes carefully. "But these have hardly been worn," she said, tapping the bright crimson, unmarred shoe sole. "I can't wear your brand-new shoes."

"Sure you can," Madison said easily. "Look, in my old life, I had several pairs like this. But all that's gone. I don't even know why I packed 'em. Please, Ellis. I would love it if you'd wear them tonight."

"I don't know," Ellis said, but she slid her feet into the sandals and fastened the straps. She stood, wobbily, and did a slow pirouette.

Dorie and Ellis applauded and whistled. Even Madison gave a quick golf clap.

"Wait one minute," Julia said. She scrabbled around in a quilted satin box on her dresser before triumphantly holding up a pair of dangly chandelier earrings made from crystals and jet beads.

Ellis screwed the earring backs to the posts. "Done," she said. She blew kisses to her friends and tottered towards the door. "Gotta go. Thanks, guys. I mean it. You're the best."

"Run along," Dorie said. "Have fun. Okay? You do remember how to have fun, right?"

"And don't do anything I wouldn't do," Julia advised.

"I can't think of anything you wouldn't do," Ellis said.

Julia nodded approvingly. "That's my point."

27

The girl who answered the door at Ebbtide looked only vaguely like the Ellis Sullivan Ty had seen on the beach and on Sunday night at Cadillac Jack's.

Ty was no fashion expert, but it looked to him as though Ellis had been transformed. She was wearing some kind of lacy, low-cut black lingerie-looking top with a cobwebby jacket sort of thing over it. The hem of her skirt barely brushed the tops of her knees, and she was wearing some ridiculously high heels. Her hair was in some kind of sophisticated updo, with earrings that nearly brushed the tops of her nearly bare shoulders.

She opened the screen door and stepped onto the porch, giving him a shy smile. "Hey," she said.

He knew he was staring, but he couldn't help himself. "You're beautiful," he blurted. Mental headslap. Of course she was beautiful. Ellis Sullivan was beautiful in those goofy cupcake boxers, with her hair in a lopsided ponytail. But tonight, she was different. He'd have said she looked spectacular, if he were the kind of guy who ever used the word "spectacular."

Ellis blushed. "Julia and Dorie double-teamed me," she said. "I feel sorta like Cinderella. This is all borrowed finery. The only thing I'm wearing that's my own is my panties." She gasped and blushed even harder. "Sorry. TMI again. You seem to have that effect on me."

"Whatever you're wearing, it's working," Ty said. He gestured down at the khaki slacks he'd so laboriously pressed and the starched white button-down shirt, which he'd found still in the dry-cleaner's bag at the back of his closet, along with his navy blazer, which he hadn't worn since the time when, in one last desperate attempt to rein him into the family fold, Kendra had dragged him to a cocktail party at her father's country club. He'd even polished his best loafers until they shone like they hadn't since the day he bought them. No socks, though. He had to draw the line somewhere.

"Sorry, but this is all my own stuff," he joked. "Good thing Julia and Dorie aren't here to see me."

He took her hand and led her down the porch steps to the Bronco, which he'd washed and vacuumed earlier in the day. He'd even thrown away all the beer bottles and fast-food wrappers.

"Oh, they can see you, all right," Ellis said, nodding her chin just slightly north. "They're watching us from the window in Julia's room."

Ty glanced up, but all he saw was the slightest twitch of a curtain. "Let's give 'em something worth watching," he said, taking Ellis's hand and kissing the back of it before he opened the car door and helped her in. Then he turned and waved, and the curtain twitched again. As he pulled the Bronco out of the driveway, he saw Ellis, glancing nervously in the rearview mirror.

He'd chosen a seafood restaurant in Duck, twenty minutes north of Nags Head. It was a tiny place at the end of a gravel road, at a marina overlooking the sound. It had weathered cedar-plank walls, a rusted tin roof, and a buzzing neon sign out front that said FISH FOOD.

"Don't let the decor scare you," Ty said, parking the car. "This is the best food on the Outer Banks."

"This looks very nice," Ellis said with a look of surprise after they'd been shown to their table at a window overlooking a long row of docks. "You know, before we came down, I sent away for the chamber of commerce information packet, and I even bought the Mobil Outer Banks travel guide, and not one of them mentioned this place."

"You sent away for stuff?" Ty laughed. "Who does that?"

"I do," Ellis said. "I don't like surprises. And anyway, they usually have good coupons. You know, for, like, a free appetizer or dessert."

"I thought all women loved surprises," Ty said. "Anyway, you won't find Fish Food in a restaurant guide. And I'm pretty sure they don't give coupons. This is kind of a local place. Eddie, the chef, used to wait tables at a restaurant I worked at in high school. He's got kind of a squirrely sense of humor, but he knows his way around the kitchen."

The waitress came, and Ty asked Ellis if she wanted a drink. "I'll have a Blue Dawg—you've got that on draft, right? And she'll have . . ." He looked over at Ellis, trying to remember what she'd ordered Sunday night, at Cadillac Jack's. "A cosmo, right?"

They chatted aimlessly until the waitress was back with their drinks and the menus.

"What's good here?" Ellis asked, looking down at the grease-spattered photocopied sheet of paper.

She was sitting up very straight in her chair and was fiddling with the ribbon that seemed to tie her top together in the front. When she wasn't trying to hike the top up to keep her breasts from further spilling out, she was tugging at the hem of her short skirt, which was a lost cause anyway. The skirt barely brushed the tops of her thighs, which were lightly dusted with freckles, as was her nose, or what he could see of her nose underneath the layer of sparkly powder covering it. Ty's fingers itched to reach across the table and yank at both ends of the ribbons, just to see what would happen. Was that pink lace bra thing attached to the girdle-looking top she was wearing? He decided that would need further study.

"Ty? Oh my God, is that really you?"

He looked up. Kendra and Ryan were standing, waiting to be seated at the next table over. He felt the blood drain from his face. And now Kendra was actually coming over to their table, with Ryan, that fuckhead, trailing right behind.

Kill me now, Ty thought. Right here.

"It is you," Kendra said shrilly. "All dressed up in your Sunday best."

Ty Bazemore had been "raised right," at his mother's and grandmother's insistence. Two years of cotillion, relentless etiquette drilled into him. You addressed your elders as "sir" and "ma'am." You stood when a lady entered the room, and you greeted a gentleman by looking him in the eye, smilingly, with a firm handshake. Reluctantly, Ty stood. "Hi, Kendra," he said, his face expressionless. He nodded in Fuckface's direction. "Ryan." He would not shake Ryan's hand. If his mother had been alive, even she would have understood. If his grandmother had been alive, she would have applauded, or maybe smacked Fuckface across the face with her ever-present flyswatter.

"Hey, dude!" Ryan, clueless, held out his hand, but when Kendra shot him a withering glance, he dropped it back to his side.

"How *are* you?" Kendra gave him a hug, standing on her tiptoes, even in heels, to do it. He was enveloped in a toxic cloud of her signature scent, which, to him, smelled like overripe pineapples.

"Just fine," Ty said, extending only a wooden, one-handed half hug. When she finally released him, he took a step backwards, just in case Fuckface got any ideas. He would throw away this blazer and shirt when he got home. *If* he got out of here alive.

"Really?" Kendra said, frowning. "You're sure? I've been thinking about you a lot lately. Ever since we moved back. Did you know? Daddy finally talked me into joining the firm. Of course, I think he only did it because he knew he'd get Ryan as part of the package. A twofer, he calls it."

"Great," Ty said. "Congratulations." If there was a bigger, more pompous asshole than Boomer Wilcox on the Outer Banks, Ty had never met him. Ryan and Boomer deserved each other.

"We heard you're day trading," Kendra said, her voice oozing concern. "I know that's got to be tough in this economy, right?"

"It's all right," Ty said, managing to unclench his teeth. "You win some, you lose some." He looked desperately around the room, hoping that something, somehow, would make this horror show grind to a halt. A lightning bolt, maybe. But he'd settle for a minor grease fire.

And now he saw Ellis, still seated, looking up at him, smiling expectantly. In his mind's eye, he could see his grandmother's flyswatter hovering at the back of his neck, just waiting to deliver a smack, should he forget his upbringing.

"Kendra, Ryan, this is Ellis, my, uh, friend."

"Oh, hi," Kendra said, her voice going up a decibel. "Alice?"

"Actually, it's Ellis," Ellis said. "With an E."

"Hiya, Ellis," Ryan said, automatically extending his hand. Ellis, who had apparently also undergone some rigorous training—and who, after all, had no history with Kendra or Fuckface—stood, smiled radiantly, and shook both their hands.

"Ellis is such an unusual name," Kendra was saying. "I don't believe I've ever met a woman named Ellis before. Are you from around here?"

"No," Ellis said, "I'm originally from Savannah. My friends and I are visiting here for the whole month."

"How did you happen to pick the Outer Banks for vacation?" Kendra asked. "I mean, of course, we adore it, but then, I grew up here."

"It was sort of a compromise," Ellis explained.

"Wonderful!" Kendra trilled. "Where are you staying? Here at Duck?"

"We're staying down at Nags Head," Ellis said.

Ty felt his scalp prickle at the mention of Nags Head. A slow dread started to work its way south. He knew what was coming, and he was powerless to stop it.

"Oh!" Kendra said. "Nags Head. That's my old stomping grounds, you know. Mama and Daddy have Cedar Haven. Do you know it? It's that huge, rambling, old pile of junk on the Beach Road."

Ryan wrapped a proprietary arm around Kendra's waist. "She calls it a pile of junk," he said with a chuckle. "What she doesn't tell you is that Cedar Haven is one of the original houses on Nags Head. There's only about a dozen of 'em. The 'unpainted aristocracy,' they call them. It's a showplace. Five thousand square feet, and it sits on an ocean-side double lot. Her grandfather built the first swimming pool on Nags Head there."

"I think I know that house," Ellis said excitedly. "It's about a mile from where we're staying. On Virginia Dare, right?"

Don't say it, Ty pleaded silently. Do not go there.

"Where are you staying?" Kendra asked.

"The house we're renting is kind of a dump," Ellis confided. "I mean, it could be wonderful, but it hasn't really been maintained in a while."

Ty looked frantically around the dining room. The waitress was approaching with a basket of bread and a cruet of olive oil. Deliverance. He wanted to kiss her on the lips.

"Hey, listen," he said. "Here comes our bread. We don't want it to get cold. They have awesome yeast rolls here. Eddie makes them himself." He pulled Ellis's chair away from the table and practically shoved her into it. "Good to see you guys," he said, giving Kendra and Ryan a dismissive nod.

Kendra gave him an odd look, but she allowed herself to be herded back to her table.

"They seem nice," Ellis said, helping herself to one of the yeast rolls.

If you only knew, Ty thought.

Dinner was agony. He ordered for both of them, and he tried to act normal. But every time he looked at Ellis, he saw the table just behind her. Kendra and Fuckface, laughing, talking, their golden heads bowed together. Every once in a while, Kendra would see him looking, and she'd lean in closer, her hand hiding her mouth, whispering something in her husband's ear. They were talking about him, he knew. Mocking him in his yellowing dress shirt and frayed college graduation blazer with the sleeves just a quarter inch too short. His stomach burned.

Their entrées took a lifetime to arrive. He couldn't have said what he ordered. It was hot, and it was vaguely seafoodish looking. Somehow, he managed to choke it down. Ellis picked at her broiled swordfish, nibbling delicately at the steamed broccoli and the couscous on her plate.

At one point, the waitress appeared with a bottle of chilled wine. It was Moët & Chandon Nectar Imperial Rose; Ty knew the label well. Sixty bucks a bottle, and that was if you bought it at Harris Teeter. "We didn't order this," he said, pushing the wine bucket away.

"The lady and gentleman at that table there sent it over. With their compliments," the waitress said.

He looked up, and Kendra gave him a little finger wave. The Imperial Rose was her favorite, and it had triggered many a fight when they were practically penniless first-year law students at Carolina. Their friends were all in the same boat, living on ramen noodles and Hot Pockets. When they had parties, they were glad to swill whatever rotgut was on sale. But Kendra, who said life was too short to drink bad wine, would appear with a bottle of her Moët & Chandon, paid for with the money Boomer had transferred into their checking account every month.

"How nice," Ellis murmured. Ty couldn't send the bottle back, not without making a scene. So he allowed the waitress to pour Ellis a glass, but he'd be damned if he'd touch the stuff himself. Instead he asked for another draft Blue Dawg.

He emptied the glass in a couple of long swigs. Ellis sipped hers slowly.

A dead, awkward silence fell over the table. He thought he'd averted disaster, but he'd been wrong.

The waitress came back to their table. She was a local, with purple-streaked blond hair and too much black eyeliner and a tattoo of an octopus whose swirling tentacles slithered all the way across her chest and probably cost more than the girl made in a week working for Eddie. She looked down at their half-eaten meals and shrugged, although she didn't bother to pick them up. "Dessert?" she asked, putting a large black slate on a stand on the table. "Eddie's got fresh peach cobbler with homemade lemon-basil gelato, and the cheesecake tonight is turtle track, which means it's done with toasted pecans and butterscotch topping . . ."

Ty gave Ellis a questioning glance. "I don't know," she started to say.

"Just the check, please," Ty said brusquely.

And of course it took her forever to come back with the check. Ellis sipped her wine and Ty drummed the tabletop with his fingers, determined not to look over at Kendra's table.

Finally, the waitress brought the check. He was tucking the cash in the leather-bound check holder, his escape imminent, when out of the corner of his eye, he saw Ryan get up from his table and start to approach.

Ty tried to calm himself. Even Fuckface had a right to go to the men's room, and he couldn't get there without passing the table where Ty and Ellis had been seated.

But no, Ryan stopped right beside their table. Ty stood and pulled Ellis's chair out, his back to Ryan, determined to make his escape unscathed, even if it meant ignoring Fuckface.

"Hey Ty, buddy," Ryan said, putting his hand on Ty's sleeve, leaning in, talking low, confidentially. Like they were old pals. "Look, Kendra and I were just talking. We saw the notice about Ebbtide in the legal ads. Kendra was saying Ebbtide's been in your family as long as Cedar Haven's been in hers. Helluva note, losing it after all these years. Thing is, we're in the market for a place of our own. So maybe we could help each other out."

Ty froze. Could this really be happening?

Ryan reached into the inner pocket of his sport coat and came out with a sterling silver monogrammed card case. Somewhere, in the boxes he'd never unpacked after moving back to Nags Head, Ty had an identical card case, although with his own initials monogrammed on it. His had been a wedding gift from Kendra's mother, who was never noted for her originality.

Now Ryan was holding out a business card, casually, between his thumb and forefinger. "Gimme a call, will ya? No need to let the bank take Ebbtide."

Ty dropped the card onto Ellis's plate of half-eaten swordfish. He took Ellis's hand and pulled her not so gently away from the table. Away from a restaurant called Fish Food. And Kendra and her fuckface new husband and their sixty-dollar bottle of pink wine.

28

Ellis allowed herself to be rushed out of the restaurant and practically slung into Ty's Bronco. She managed to keep her temper tamped down for maybe five minutes. Then she exploded.

"*You* own Ebbtide?"

He winced, then nodded. "I do. For now, anyway."

"And Mr. Culpepper? Our crusty-but-kindly landlord?"

Ty sighed. "You're looking at him."

"This whole time? I've been e-mailing *you*? Asking Mr. Culpepper about *you*? Complaining about *you*?"

"Afraid so," Ty admitted.

"Cute," Ellis said, biting off the word. "I bet you think you're really cute, pulling one over on me like that. I bet you've been laughing your ass off at me, over there in that garage of yours."

"Look, it wasn't just about you," Ty said. "I never tell my tenants about Mr. Culpepper. If they knew the landlord lived just over the garage, I'd never get any peace. They'd be hammering on my door at midnight, bitching about the hot water heater, or the bugs, or any damned thing. Or they lose their key. And I'm supposed to drop what I'm doing because they can't keep track of something as simple as a key? You wouldn't believe what a pain in the ass people can be. This way, I'm just some anonymous slacker dude next door. If they want something from Culpepper, they have to e-mail him. And he takes care of it. Eventually."

"And I'm the biggest pain in the ass of all, right?" Ellis said. "Bitching night and day."

"Well, yeah, at first," Ty said truthfully. "I mean, I thought you were a pain in the ass at first, but then, when I met you, well, it was different. Hey, I got you a new stove, didn't I? And those dishes with the pink flowers? Those were my grandmother's dishes, you know. And I wanted to tell you about Mr. Culpepper, I really did."

"But you didn't," Ellis said, crossing her arms over her chest. Julia's underwire bra was cutting into her rib cage, and the corset thing was tied so tightly she couldn't breathe, but she didn't dare touch the ribbons lacing it together, for fear she'd explode out of the stinking thing. Why the hell had she let the girls talk her into this outfit? What was she doing with this loser, this liar?

"I was going to," Ty said. "Like, tonight. I was going to tell you. But I didn't get the chance."

"Unbelievable," Ellis said. She turned and stared out the window.

Eventually, they pulled into the crushed-shell driveway at Ebbtide. He parked the Bronco beside the garage, and before he could get out and come around to open her door, she opened it herself and was out of the car like a shot.

"Ellis," he started.

"Thanks for dinner . . . Mr. Culpepper," she said. It was all she could do to keep from running into the house. Anyway, she couldn't have run in those damned high-heeled sandals Madison had loaned her. She walked, head up, back straight, just as fast as she could, without as much as a backward glance at Ty Bazemore, aka Mr. Culpepper. And when she got to the screen door at the house, its slam echoed in the still, hot, summer air.

. . .

Dorie and Julia heard the screen door slam from the kitchen, where they'd been playing a desultory game of Hearts.

"What the hell?" Julia said, glancing at the kitchen clock. It was barely nine o'clock.

They heard the furious tapping of the stiletto heels on the worn wooden hall floors, then heard them ascending the stairs, and then the second slam, of a bedroom door.

"Uh-oh," Dorie said. "That can't be good."

"Damn," Julia nodded in agreement. "And I had such high hopes." She raised an eyebrow. "Do you think we should go up there and talk to her?"

"Ix-nay," Dorie said, yawning. "If she wanted to talk about it, she'd come looking for us. You know how Ellis is."

"I do," Julia agreed. She sighed loudly. "I really thought this guy might be it, you know? He's totally hot, and he's hot for her, and I thought she was kinda hot for him."

"You know something I don't?" Dorie asked suspiciously.

"I kinda saw them making out the other night," Julia said sheepishly.

"What?" Dorie slapped her cards down on the table. "And you held out on me? In my condition?"

"It was totally by accident," Julia said. "Not like I was spying on them or anything. It was late, and Booker called, and I was kinda pacing around the room talking to him. I just happened to look out my window, and I saw this couple—just, wrapped up in each other, out on that boardwalk over the dunes. And it was just so sweet, you know? Summer love, that whole thing. It wasn't until they pulled apart—reluctantly, I might add—and the girl was walking back towards the house, that I realized it was our Ellie-Belly. With garage guy."

"I'd never say this to Ellis, but Ty doesn't really seem like her type," Dorie mused. "I mean, don't get me wrong, I think he's adorable, but nothing like the guys she used to be attracted to."

"She is, though," Julia said. "Sunday night, when we were at Cadillac Jack's? That whole 'I've got cabin fever, let's us girls go out on the town?' All a ploy. She knew he was working there that night. She only dragged me along so it wouldn't look like she was stalking him. You should have seen Ty's face when he caught sight of her, Dorie. There were all these hoochie mamas and pretty young things hanging around the bar, hoping he'd give them a glance, but when he saw Ellis, it was like he'd just been handed the biggest lollipop in the store." She sighed. "So, so, sweet. And of course, Ellis was all nervous and tingly. Dorie, did you know she hasn't, like, been with anybody since whatsisname?"

"Doesn't surprise me," Dorie said. "After whatsisname, I didn't think she'd ever allow herself to fall for another man."

"She tried, though," Julia said. "She was doing online dating! Do you believe that?"

"I know a lot of girls who've met their husbands online," Dorie said. "But I am a little surprised that our Ellis got up the nerve to try it. And that she admitted it to you."

"I swore not to tell," Julia said. "But she had to know I'd tell you."

Dorie patted Julia's hand. "That's all right. You're great at keeping your own secrets, but everybody else's? Not so much." She yawned again. "God, I feel like I can never get enough sleep. I'm going to bed. Maybe by tomorrow, things won't look so bad to Ellis. Maybe this was just a little tiff. Or something. I want this for Ellis."

Julia cocked her head and studied Dorie. Her strawberry blond hair was gathered into pigtails, and her face was pink from the sun and just a little fuller than usual. It was hard to believe her old friend, who looked barely out of her teens, would be a mother in a few months.

"What do you want for Ellis?" Julia asked. "A good lay? God knows, she's due. It's been twelve years or something. Who knows, she might have forgotten how."

Dorie rolled her eyes. "No, not just a good lay. Stop being such a cynic. Ellis deserves everything. True love, a husband, children, all of it. I don't care what you say, Julia Capelli, I think that's what all of us really want. You just think it's not cool to admit it."

"I do?"

"Absolutely. You had a great career, and I know you say that's all over, but it still looks pretty fabulous from where I'm sitting. And you've got this great guy, Booker, who loves you and wants to marry you and give you whatever you want. And you're just too stinkin' cool to say yes."

Julia pushed her chair away from the table. "Thanks for the cut-rate analysis, Eudora. Now, let me ask you something. Are you telling me that after all you've been through with Stephen, who has essentially left you for another man—while you are carrying his child—that you still believe in that happy-ever-after fairy tale stuff? Can you tell me that, straight-faced, with your own screwed-up family history, you buy that crap?"

Dorie leaned forward, her green eyes glittering with intensity.

"Look at me, Julia. I am telling you, yes. Yes, with absolute sincerity, despite Stephen, despite my parents' shitty marital history, despite all evidence to the contrary, that yes, I do still buy what you call 'that crap'. I have to believe Stephen really did love me, and that I loved him, and that we will love this baby I'm carrying. I'm furious and sad about what happened with us, but that doesn't make me believe that what we had wasn't real. And it doesn't make me believe that I won't find something that real again. I may be looking at being a single mother, at having to move in with my mom again, at working my ass off teaching school for peanuts, but you're the one I feel sorry for, Julia. Because you do have it all, but you don't believe it, and you don't appreciate it. And that's the saddest thing of all."

Ellis kicked off the high-heeled sandals and peeled herself out of Julia's clothes. She climbed into her cupcake pajamas and went into the bathroom, where she brushed her teeth until they bled, and scrubbed off every trace of the face Dorie had so carefully painted on her only a few hours earlier.

"Idiot," she said, scowling into the mirror at the real Ellis Sullivan.

Back in her bedroom, she got out her cell phone, and erased each and every duplicitous e-mail she'd sent or received from Mr.Culpepper@Ebbtide.com.

When she was done, she padded back and forth in her bedroom, stopping every so often to glare out the window in the direction of the garage apartment. The lights were all on, but she couldn't see Ty. Wait. As she watched, he came down the stairs from the apartment and went over to the Bronco. A moment later, the headlights flashed on, and he was backing out and down the driveway. Well, it was only 9:30, after all. Maybe he had another date. Maybe he was heading over to Cadillac Jack's, to hook up with one of the willing women who'd flocked around him at the bar there. She didn't care, Ellis told herself.

Screw him.

But the thing was, she did care. She'd let down her guard, let herself believe somebody like Ty Bazemore could care about her, let herself believe that she could ever be with somebody like him. Which was a joke, right? And she was the punch line.

Eventually, she heard footsteps on the stairs, light ones that must have been Dorie, barefoot, going to bed early. Maybe half an hour later, she heard the soft flapping of leather-soled sandals—those would be Julia's. She heard their bedroom doors close, thankful that neither of her best friends had knocked on her own door to enquire about her "big date."

What a laugh.

She tried to read her paperback, but gave up after realizing she'd reread the same chapter three times. Ellis settled back into the pillows on her bed, staring up at the ceiling fan whirring overhead. She studied all the cracks in the plaster ceiling, the watermarks on the faded flowery wallpaper. The air conditioner wedged into the window by the bed wheezed and rattled the window glass in a futile attempt to cool temperatures that were probably in the eighties. The place really was a dump. She'd been so happy to finally be here with her friends, so full of anticipation of the month, she'd glossed over the truly deplorable condition of Ebbtide.

It had been a grand old house at one time, she could tell. Large, square, high-ceilinged rooms, generous windows with amazing views of the ocean and dunes. Ryan, that guy at the restaurant, had mentioned that the house had belonged to Ty's family. And that the house was about to be foreclosed on.

Served him right, Ellis tried to tell herself.

But it didn't wash. Ty had told her he was a day trader, trying to recoup his losses in the stock market. The reality was that he was trying desperately to keep from losing his family home. Which explained why he rented out the big house and lived in the garage apartment. But it still didn't explain why he couldn't have just told her, after their first encounter on the beach, that *he* was Mr. Culpepper.

Not that it mattered. He didn't owe her anything. She was just another pain-in-the-ass summer renter.

With only two weeks left at the beach.

Screw it, Ellis thought.

She jumped out of bed and padded barefoot down the stairs, and out through the kitchen. She wasn't worried about encountering Ty Bazemore again, as she had last time. He was out tomcatting around Nags Head.

Ellis found the deck of cards the girls had abandoned on the kitchen table. She dealt herself a hand of solitaire, but gave up on it after fifteen minutes. She couldn't even beat herself at cards, she thought, slapping the cards down in disgust. It was hot in the kitchen too—suffocating, really. She wet a paper towel and dabbed her forehead and wrists to cool herself down.

A walk on the beach, she decided, might be the only thing to calm herself down. Upstairs, she pulled on a pair of shorts and a T-shirt. She picked up the sandals Madison had loaned her only a few hours earlier, and tiptoed upstairs. She paused outside Madison's door. The light was on, but she heard no movement from inside. She was probably reading. Ellis thought about knocking, about blurting out the truth of her whole, awful evening to a pair of neutral ears, but decided against it. Madison wasn't the kind of girl who wanted to hear about somebody else's drama. Instead, Ellis set the shoes carefully on the floor and left.

She let herself out the kitchen door and sped over the boardwalk and down to the beach. A slight breeze ruffled the sea oats, but otherwise, it was quiet. She left her flip-flops on the soft sand at the base of the steps and hurried out to the water's edge, not stopping until her toes were licked by the cool wavelets. The moon was still near full, shining brightly on the gleaming silvery beach.

Better. She took a deep breath and started walking on the hard-packed wet sand. She wove her way up the beach, side stepping the incoming tide, although occasionally a wave caught her, slapping water up as high as her thigh. She kept walking. The farther south she went, the closer together houses were packed. Lights were on in some of the houses, and occasionally she heard a drift of music, or laughter, but the beach was otherwise deserted.

Ellis stopped occasionally, bent over and picked up a seashell, but dropped the ones that were crushed or broken. At one point, she found a perfect, white, palm-sized sand dollar at the water's edge. With her fingertip, she traced the indentations in the brittle surface of the shell, trying to remember what Sister Marguerite, her biology teacher back at Our Lady of Angels, had told her the indentations meant. Something about the cross, and the trials of Jesus. Carefully, Ellis tucked the sand dollar into the pocket of her shorts and kept walking.

At some point, the wind picked up, and the waves began crashing harder into the sand, the tide creeping up. Ellis stopped, turned around, and stared up at the cluster of unfamiliar buildings at the edge of the dunes. She shivered and crossed her arms over her chest. Just how far had she come?

Time to turn back. The encroaching tide had driven her closer to the dunes. She tried walking faster, struggling as her feet sank into the powdery soft sand. Each time she came to a set of stairs leading up and over the dunes, she looked up, trying to decide if it was her stairway, leading back to Ebbtide.

But now, in the dark, all the dunes and stairways looked alike. She felt her heart racing, and told herself this was silly. She wasn't lost. Couldn't be. After two weeks, she knew her own stretch of beach perfectly. There was a faded, pale yellow catamaran pushed into the beach rosemary and sea oats below Ebbtide. The battered red metal trash barrel bolted to a piling near their house was crisscrossed with painted-on graffiti: "TIGERS RULE, COCKS SUCK" and "RENE LOVES BUSTER."

And her shoes! Her lime green flip-flops. She'd left them right at the base of the steps. All she had to do was find those flip-flops. She powered onwards, squinting in the dark, looking for the catamaran and the red trash barrel. After another thirty minutes, her calf muscles burned, and she was nearly out of breath. The tide kept inching closer, until it was lapping right at the base of the dunes, and still there were no familiar signs.

Finally, exhausted, she stopped and sat on a worn wooden step. The water swirled around her ankles, and she realized it would have swept her flip-flops away. What should she do? She stepped into the water and craned her neck to look up. These steps led up to a boardwalk similar to the one at Ebbtide, and a house that looked nothing like Ebbtide. Should she climb up, cross the boardwalk, and find her way to the road?

And then what? Walk barefoot on the asphalt for who knows how far, with cars whizzing past and God-knows-who looking at her in her soggy shorts and windblown hair, not to mention the fact that she was braless?

No. She'd stick to the beach. She stood and started trudging. Ten minutes later, she heaved a sigh of relief when she spotted the yellow catamaran. Thank God! She almost felt like kissing the paint-spattered red trash barrel. Almost. Instead, she grabbed the handrail of the staircase and heaved herself up the steep first step.

It wasn't until she'd reached the top step that she smelled it. Cigar smoke. In the darkness, she saw the glowing red tip first, and then the outline of the beach chair. And Ty Bazemore, beer in hand.

29

He'd been sitting on the deck for at least an hour, smoking a cigar, nursing a Heineken. After the disastrous aborted date, he'd gone up to the garage, shed the jacket and khakis, and tried to forget about it and just get some work done. He'd been reading about a small agribiz company in Kentucky that had recently patented a new kind of grass seed with promising drought-tolerant qualities. But he was glassy-eyed from reading all the technical reports, not to mention the company's P&L statements.

Ty's heart wasn't in it, anyhow. He'd tried to shake off the depression that was settling over him like a thick woolen blanket, but didn't have much luck. And anyway, he was seriously starving. So he'd jumped in the Bronco and hit the drive-through at the burger joint up the road.

Sometimes, a good greasy cheeseburger and fries were the only antidote to misery. He'd eaten the burger and half the fries, and lit up the last of his good cigars, but he wasn't feeling that much better about life. He was, however, developing a bad case of heartburn.

The wind had picked up, and the surf was pounding away at the beach below. And suddenly, he looked up, and there she was, climbing up the last stair.

Cinderella was gone, and in her place the old Ellis Sullivan seemed to have washed ashore. The carefully arranged hairdo had been blown all to hell. She was barefoot, her baggy pink shorts were soggy, and her damp T-shirt clung to her body. It was apparent, even from where he sat in the darkness, that she'd been crying.

"Oh," she said when she spotted him. "It's you."

"I live here," Ty said. He stubbed out the last of his cigar on the top of the beer can. "Are you all right?"

She looked down at her sandy legs, wiped her nose with the sleeve of her T-shirt, and nodded. "I think the tide took my shoes. Other than that, I'm just peachy. I thought you were gone."

"I was," he said, gesturing to the paper sack with the remnants of cheeseburger and French fries. "I ran out for a little midnight snack. But now I'm back. What were you doing down there? Going for a midnight swim? Not to scare you or anything, but there are sharks out there."

"I went for a walk," Ellis said, leaning against the deck railing. "What time is it?"

He consulted his watch. "Nearly midnight. Must have been a hell of a stroll. I've been out here for over an hour."

She slumped down onto the deck, her legs suddenly rubbery with fatigue. "I guess I lost track of where I was going. God, I must have walked a couple of miles along the beach. And then the tide started coming in, and I sort of freaked out. At night, in the dark like this, all these stairways look alike."

"I'll give you a tip," Ty drawled. "Tomorrow, when you go out on the beach, look up at the stairways. Most of 'em have metal address numbers attached to 'em. Ours even says EBBTIDE, although you have to really get pretty close up to see it."

Ellis leaned her head back against the railing and stretched her legs out on the deck planks, which still retained some of the heat from the sun. She wanted to jump up and run down the walkway, back to her room, away from Ty Bazemore. But she was exhausted. Physically and mentally.

Ty sat back in his chair and looked at her expectantly. Waiting for her to blast him again.

"Maybe," she said, after a couple minutes of awkward silence, "maybe we could just pretend tonight never happened. You could go back to your garage and computer, and I could go back to . . . whatever."

He got up from his chair and sank down onto the deck beside her, sitting so close that they were brushing shoulders.

"Why would we want to do that?" he asked. "I mean, was there any part of tonight that you enjoyed?"

"Seriously?" she asked, shaking her head in disbelief. "Are you telling me you had a good time tonight?"

"You didn't?"

"I asked first," she pointed out.

"But I paid."

"Okay," she relented. "Are you sure you want me to go off on you again?"

"Why not? Everybody else does."

"As far as first dates go?" she said, brushing at the sand on her shorts and her legs. "This was pretty awful. Catastrophic, you might say."

He tilted his head and looked at her. "If you had to pinpoint it, where would you say it all started to go wrong? The jacket? I guess it has gotten a little short in the sleeves."

"The jacket was fine," Ellis said. "Except for the dry-cleaner's tag attached to your right sleeve."

"You coulda said something."

"You could have told me you own Ebbtide," Ellis said. "So we're even. Anyway, it was a first date. You don't tell that kind of stuff on a first date."

"Oh."

Ty went back over the evening in his mind again. "I did notice you didn't eat very much. So, you didn't like the restaurant? I considered a steak house, or Italian, but then I thought, seafood. Who doesn't like seafood at the beach?"

"I loved the restaurant," Ellis said, hesitating.

"But?"

She wrinkled her nose. "Swordfish. Ugh. Hate, hate, hate swordfish."

"Again, you could have said something."

"I was trying to be polite," Ellis said.

"Next time, just tell me what you want to eat," Ty said, exasperated.

"Next time maybe you could ask me what I want to eat. Wait," she said. "There's going to be a next time?"

"I only ordered the swordfish because it was the most expensive thing on the menu," he went on. "I was trying to impress you, in case you didn't notice."

"Really?" She tilted her head and considered him. "That's sweet."

"Okay. Aside from the swordfish, and the dry-cleaner tag, and the finding out about Mr. Culpepper thing, what else was bad?" Ty asked. "You know, so I can improve on my technique."

Ellis rolled her eyes. "It's not your fault, I suppose. But it's still pretty awkward running into your old girlfriend and her husband when we're on a date."

Ty made a choking sound. "That wasn't an old girlfriend."

"No? You could have fooled me. I definitely sensed some history there. Also hostility. Not so deeply repressed hostility, I might add."

"Oh, Kendra and I have history, all right," Ty said ruefully. "If you consider two years of marriage to be history."

"Marriage? You were married? To her? For two years?"

"It seemed a lot longer at the time," Ty said.

"Wow. Just . . . wow." Ellis said. "How long have you been divorced? If you don't mind my asking."

"It was a long time ago."

Ellis hugged her knees to her chest, to warm up a little. "She's beautiful."

"She certainly thinks so," Ty agreed. "And I guess most people would agree."

"You must have thought she was pretty at some point," Ellis said. "You did marry her."

"We dated in high school, got married after college," Ty said. "Everybody always said we were perfect for each other."

"And then?"

"Kendra is the kind of girl who always has a plan," Ty said. "I guess she gets that from her old man. Boomer used to be in politics, was in the state house, like that. Now he concentrates on running his law firm. And his daughter's life. And that's fine with Kendra, fits right in with her plans."

"But it didn't fit with yours?"

"It did at first," Ty admitted. "Law school seemed like a great idea. I made decent grades in high school and as an undergrad. We got out of college, worked for a couple years, mainly so I could save money to go back to grad school, but then Kendra got the bright idea we should go to law school together. I thought, why not? We both applied to law schools. Kendra got accepted a bunch of places. Me? Looking back on it, I think Boomer probably pulled some strings to get me in at Carolina. He was on the board of visitors."

"And then what? If you don't mind my asking?"

"Ancient history now," Ty said with a shrug. "It just wasn't a good fit for me. Kendra and I were doing okay. We lived in a ratty little apartment off Franklin Street, and we were starving law students, just like all our friends. Or at least, I was. Kendra had a separate bank account, and her daddy kept it filled up all the time. So we fought about that. And a lot of other stuff. And by the time I was halfway through my second year, I knew, absolutely, that law school was not the place for me. But I stuck it out, finished the year. Then, when I told Kendra I was dropping out, she announced that she was dropping me."

"Ow," Ellis said. "Ryan?"

"I prefer to think of him as Fuckface," Ty said. "They were on the law review together. According to Kendra, things just . . . happened."

"Where have I heard that before?" Ellis sympathized.

"She claimed they were 'just friends,'" Ty said. "Of course, when she moved out of the rat hole, she moved in with him. Just a coincidence, I'm sure."

"Again, ow. What did you do then?"

"I got a job working as a glorified office boy at a stock brokerage firm in Chapel Hill. Kept my eyes and ears open, started doing some trades, and figured out I kind of liked it. Turns out, I'm an information junkie. The guy I worked for taught me a lot, and I hit some lucky breaks. I stayed with his firm for a couple more years, then moved to Charlotte to work for another couple years. But I always missed being on the coast. I lived lean, saved my money, and eventually moved back here to Nags Head."

"To Ebbtide," Ellis said.

"Nah. I moved in with my dad," Ty said. "Ebbtide belonged to my mom's family. When my grandmother died, she left it to my mom's brother, my uncle Ralph. He lives out west and didn't really have much interest in the place. He was gonna sell it last year. By that time, real estate prices here were in the tank, and I'd managed to squirrel some money away, so I got the bright idea to buy it and keep it in the family."

"I think that's nice," Ellis said. "Has your family always owned it?"

"Always," Ty said. "And until I bought the place, virtually nothing had been done to it in all those years. Turns out, the joint is a money pit. It needs a new roof, new plumbing, new electrical. And you see the shape the kitchen and the bathrooms are in. I moved in right after I bought it and started working on it, but then the stock market did a nosedive, and I ran out of money."

"The economy sucks," Ellis said sympathetically. "I know, that's what happened to me at the bank I worked for in Philly. We got swallowed up by another bank, and everybody in my department got pink slips."

"Have you got another job lined up?"

"Not yet," Ellis admitted. "I've got résumés out, but . . ."

"Yeah," Ty said. "I feel your pain. When I first moved back here, I tried finding a job, but let's face it, Nags Head ain't Charlotte. It's all about tourism here. Anyway, I'm tired of working for other people. I'd rather figure it out on my own, even if I have to live on next to nothing while I do that. That's why I moved into the garage apartment and started renting out the big house. But it was too little, too late.'"

Ellis shivered and hugged her knees tighter.

"You're cold," Ty said. He slipped an arm around her shoulder and pulled her to him. "We could go inside," he offered.

"I'm all right," Ellis said. She looked up at him. "What Ryan said tonight, about Ebbtide? Is it really in foreclosure?"

"Prick," Ty muttered. "Yeah, that's right. I got in over my head, pure and simple. I don't want to sound too melodramatic, but if I don't figure out a way to raise some money, fast, by September fifteenth, I'll lose Ebbtide. That's why I've been moonlighting at Caddie's."

"It would be so sad to lose your family home," Ellis said. "Isn't there anything you can do? Have you talked to anybody at the bank? I mean, I was never in the mortgage side of things, but it seems to me the last thing a bank wants right now is to have to manage another foreclosed property. Maybe you could work something out with them?"

"I'm trying," Ty said, "but they're not local. The bank I got my mortgage from got taken over by another bank, in Virginia. I've called and written letters, but I can't ever seem to get in contact with a real human being. And in the meantime, the clock is ticking. The legal ads have started to run. And the vultures have started to circle."

"Like Ryan and Kendra," Ellis said.

Ty's face darkened. "I'll burn it to the ground before I let them get their hands on my house."

Ellis's eyes widened at the ferocity of his response.

"Not literally," Ty said. "I'll think of something. Anyway, could we change the subject?"

"What did you have in mind?" she asked.

Ty pulled Ellis closer. He nuzzled her hair and her neck. "I was hoping maybe we could discuss your giving me a do-over on this evening."

Ellis reached for the paper bag he'd left sitting beside his chair. "Only if you agree to share whatever's in this bag. I didn't have much dinner, remember?"

"Later," Ty said. He turned her face to his and found her lips in the dark.

30

There was a knock at Julia's bedroom door. When she opened it, Madison stood there, holding her cell phone in her hand. "We need to talk," Madison said, her dark-ringed eyes still and serious. Her unwashed hair hung from a center part, and her cheap brown T-shirt was wrinkled and shrunken from the wash. She limped into the room without being invited, and sat down on the edge of a rickety orange-painted wooden chair.

The chair was one Julia had found at a charity thrift shop on Croatan Highway over the weekend, and in a fit of boredom, painted a shade called Valencia.

"Hey," Julia started to say, but Madison held her hand up, palm outwards, stopping her before she could get started with any fake outrage.

Julia sank down onto her bed, which she'd just made up with a cheap cotton spread with bright pink, orange, and turquoise stripes, picked up at the Target store on her way back from the paint store.

"What's up, Madison?" Julia asked, smoothing out a nonexistent wrinkle in the spread.

"What did you say to him?" Madison asked.

"Who?"

"Him!" Madison said, thrusting the phone at Julia. "Look, I know you think you're smart, messing with my phone, checking my messages. But you have no idea who you are messing with here. So just cut the act and tell me exactly what he said. And what you told him." She crossed her legs and added, "Please."

Julia sighed. "Is Maryn your real name?"

"That's none of your business."

Julia leaned forward. "Oh, but it is my business. You're living under the same roof as me. I've got a right to know who you are and what you're doing here."

"Okay, fine. You got me. I lied. Now tell me what you told him."

"You mean Don? I didn't tell him anything. Who is he, anyway?"

Madison's face was taut. "He told you his name?"

Julia thought about that. "No. He asked for Maryn, I told him you weren't there. He asked who I was, and then he hung up."

"You're sure that's all that was said? Julia, this is really important. What did you say when he asked you who were?"

She shrugged. "I said I'm Julia Capelli. Who the hell are you? When the phone rang, the caller ID just said 'unknown caller.' After he hung up, I listened to some other messages on your phone from 'Don.' It was the same voice."

Madison crossed and uncrossed her legs. She nibbled on a ragged bit of cuticle. Julia noticed that she wasn't wearing the big diamond engagement ring. "You actually told him your name?"

"Why wouldn't I tell him my name?" Julia asked. "Madison, why don't you just tell me what's going on here and stop with the twenty questions? Who is this Don guy? And why are you running away from him? What's got you so scared?"

Madison shook her head violently. "You wouldn't understand. Anyway, it's not your problem."

"The hell it isn't! I told him my name!"

Madison looked down at the phone. "His name is Don Shackleford. He's my husband. I found out he's into some bad stuff. So I left. End of story."

"Nuh-uh," Julia said. "You didn't just leave. You ran. And you're traveling under an assumed name. I think you owe us an explanation."

"The only thing I owe you guys is the rent on that crappy room upstairs," Madison said. "Which I already paid. And if you hadn't been so damned nosy, messing with my phone and snooping in my private life, none of this would be an issue."

"What kind of bad stuff is he into?" Julia asked, her eyes glittering with excitement. "Drugs? Gun running?"

"You watch too much television," Madison said. "It's nothing that exciting. He's . . . dishonest, that's all. I should have known better. I did know better, once."

She stood up abruptly. "Look, my rent's paid up. I'll leave as soon as I figure out my next step. Probably by the weekend. In the meantime, could you please keep this to yourself? The less people who know my real name, the better. Don doesn't have any reason to think I'd come someplace like Nags Head. I didn't know I was coming here myself until I saw the sign on the interstate for the turnoff."

Julia followed her to the door. "I already told the girls I know Madison isn't your real name."

Madison rolled her eyes. "Another big surprise."

"You don't have to go, you know," Julia said. "Maybe we could help. You know, help get you out of whatever kind of jam you're in."

"No!" Madison said quickly. "I don't want any help. I'll be out of here by the weekend. Just do as I ask—don't be running off at the mouth about me, and stay out of my business."

She left the room as quickly as she'd come, leaving Julia with more questions than answers.

31

Maryn slammed her bedroom door and locked it. There was no getting around facts: she had to leave Ebbtide and Nags Head. What if Julia was lying about her conversation with Don? God knows what she might have told him.

Her mouth went dry at the prospect. But no, she sternly told herself. Julia might be a nosy little sneak, but she was well-meaning. And besides, she had no reason to lie once she'd been confronted. Not that it mattered now. No matter how innocuous Julia's comments to Don seemed, she couldn't risk staying.

She took the duffle bag out from beneath the bed, propped it on the wooden chair by the door, and started to pack. She was surprised and irritated at how sad the idea of leaving this place made her. This cruddy little room in this big, crumbling old house had become her refuge, a home in a way that the gaudy, nouveau riche town house where Don had installed her would never be a home. And these women—Ellis, Dorie, and even Julia— they weren't friends, not really. But they were decent, generous women who might have become her friends if she'd dared to let down her guard. But she couldn't. And now it was too late.

She had no idea where she would go next, but go she would. Maybe she'd head west? Mexico was too obvious—and anyway, she didn't speak a word of Spanish. And what about all that money? The stacks of cash terrified her. She was no Pollyanna, but she was sure Don hadn't earned that money legally. So far, except for her rent, she'd mostly resisted spending it. She'd need money to get as far away as possible.

The ring. Her engagement ring. She dug the black velvet box out of her dresser drawer and flipped the top open. The huge solitaire seemed to wink impishly at her. Don was a phony. Their marriage was phony. She only hoped that the diamond was real, because it was looking like her ticket away from both Don and the marriage.

Maryn was making a mental list of all she needed to do before leaving— gas up the car, find a decent road map, look up a jeweler who might buy, or at least appraise, the ring—when she realized that her cell phone, which she'd tossed onto the bed, was buzzing.

For a moment, she felt paralyzed. But then she grabbed the phone, and when she saw the caller ID on the readout, she could have cried with relief.

"Adam!" she said, fighting back tears. "Where are you? All you all right?"

"I'm fine," he said. "I'm in Philly. But where the hell are you? I've been worried sick about you."

"Don . . . he didn't hurt you?"

"No. Why would he?"

"He caught me, after I left his office. Oh God, you were right about him. I took his key and I went over there, and I found some of the Prescott files. He's been robbing them blind." The words tumbling out of Maryn in a torrent. "Don flew into a rage. He . . . hurt me. And I couldn't help it, I told him what you'd told me, about the auditors and everything. Of course, he denied everything. He even wanted me to go to dinner with him and Robby Prescott that night. As though nothing had happened. But he told me if I didn't do exactly as he said, he'd kill me, and hide my body where nobody would ever find me."

"So you ran?" Adam said. "Why didn't you call me?"

"I tried to call you," Maryn said accusingly. "I left messages, didn't you get any of them? I was frantic with worry, afraid he'd come after you next. Where were you?"

"Oh, Maryn," Adam said. "I am so sorry. I was on vacation. Don't you remember? I told you I was going hiking with my brother and some friends. I just got back and saw all the missed calls."

She had no such memory. Adam, hiking? But it didn't matter now.

"Listen," she said. "Has Don called, looking for me?"

"Yeah," he said, his voice dripping disdain. "I think he must think I'm hiding you or something. Prick."

"He's more than just a prick," Maryn said. "He's a lunatic. A dangerous lunatic. And what's worse is, I married him."

"So . . . what are you gonna do?" Adam asked. "Get a lawyer and divorce his ass?"

"Eventually," Maryn said. "But right now, I've got to get as far away from him as I can."

"Aren't you being a little overly dramatic?" Adam asked.

"You didn't see the look in his eyes when he was threatening me," Maryn said. "I did."

"Okay," Adam said quickly. "I get your point. What can I do to help? Where are you, anyway? You still haven't told me."

Maryn hesitated. But Adam was her best friend. He'd tried to warn her about Don, but she'd refused to listen. And look what had happened.

"I'm on the Outer Banks," she said. "Nags Head."

"That's in North Carolina?" Adam asked. "What made you go all the way down there?"

"Nothing in particular," she said. "After I ran, I'd been driving all night, and I was exhausted, and I saw a billboard, so I just headed east and ended up here."

"Here, where?" Adam wanted to know. "Are you in a hotel or something?"

She looked around the barren little room and laughed ruefully. "Not hardly. I'm renting a room in an old house, right on the beach. I'm sharing it with three other women. It's too long a story to go into right now. Doesn't matter, anyway, because I'm leaving here just as soon as I can."

"Why's that?"

"It's not safe," Maryn said. "One of the women happened to pick up my cell phone, and Don called, and she answered it. She swears she didn't tell him anything, but I just can't risk staying here."

"Just what is it that makes you so terrified of him?" Adam asked. "I'm not saying you shouldn't be afraid, but you just sound . . . so . . . unhinged. Why not just come back home, get yourself a good lawyer, and proceed to take him for every last dime?"

"You don't get it," Maryn said, her voice growing shrill. "Don is a criminal. And no, I am not overreacting. Adam, when I left the house, I was terrified. I threw some clothes into a suitcase, grabbed my laptop case, and got the hell out. When I got down here, I went to unpack my laptop, and that's when I discovered it—I'd grabbed Don's computer instead of mine."

"Did you find any secret documents or smoking guns?" Adam asked.

"Not really," Maryn said. "Don's too cagey for anything like that. I didn't find anything on the computer—it's what I found in the computer case that's got me nervous."

"Like what?"

"Like a hundred thousand dollars," Maryn said. "Neat little bundles of hundred-dollar bills."

"Holy shit," Adam breathed.

"Now do you get why I can't come back there?" Maryn asked. "That money is dirty. It has to be. And Don knows I have it. And his computer."

"So . . . give the money back," Adam said. "Tell him you don't want it, and you don't want him, either."

"You make it sound so easy, so rational," Maryn said. "But Don's not rational. And I don't think he'll just let me walk away—not from any of it. I don't know where I'm going next, but the one thing I do know is that I'm not coming back there, or anywhere near where Don can find me."

"Where will you go? And what'll you do?" Adam asked.

"I don't know," Maryn repeated. "I haven't thought that far ahead. Somewhere. I'll get a job again. Earn my own keep. I did it before I met Don Shackleford, and I'll do it again."

Adam laughed. "You're telling me you're going to go back to driving a ten-year-old Honda and wearing markdowns from Loehmann's? Living in some cruddy studio apartment like that dump you were in when you met him? All just to prove you don't need a sugar daddy?"

Maryn's eyes rested on her Louboutin sandals, which she'd found outside her bedroom door when she'd gotten up to use the bathroom in the middle of the night. They'd cost eight hundred dollars, and she'd bought them without a second thought after Don gave her the American Express Black Card. She wished now that she'd told Ellis to keep them.

"I damn well don't need somebody like Don!" Maryn cried. "I don't understand why you're talking to me like this, Adam. You're the one who always accused me of only dating Don because of his money. I thought you were my friend."

"I *am* your friend," Adam assured her. "But I just want you to stop and think things all the way through before you do anything else drastic. Why spend your life on the run if you don't have to?"

"I don't see any other way," Maryn said, rubbing her eyes. She was suddenly exhausted, physically and emotionally. And now, damn it, she was crying. And she'd never, ever been a crybaby.

"Look," Adam was saying, "I've still got a few days of vacation left. I'm not due back at work 'til Monday. Why don't I come down there? We'll have a couple of drinks, take a walk on the beach, and talk. We can figure it out together. Okay? What do you say?"

"I don't know," Maryn said, feeling her resolve weakening. "What if Don figures out where I am? He talked to Julia. She swears she didn't tell him anything, but now she knows my real name. It just doesn't feel safe anymore."

"You're giving Don too much credit," Adam said soothingly. "He's just not that smart, Maryn. You say you're not staying at a hotel, so you're not registered anywhere, right? How's he gonna find you?"

"He is that smart," Maryn retorted. "You don't know him like I do."

"Whatever," Adam said. "Will you do that for me? Just hang for another day or so. I can drive down there tomorrow. We can hang out, talk. And if you still feel like you've got to take off, fine. I can help you figure that out. I know you, Maryn. You put on that tough girl front all the time, but at some point, you've got to quit being a loner. You've got to trust somebody. Right?"

"I guess," Maryn said, relenting. Maybe Adam was right. Maybe it was time to lean on somebody else. At least for a little while.

"Okay," she said, sniffling. "I'll wait here. You'll leave tomorrow?"

"First thing," he assured her. "But you've got to tell me the address there."

"You know, I don't even know the address," Maryn said. "Just the name of the street. South Virginia Dare. Oh yeah, and the house name. All the beach houses down here have names. It's Ebbtide."

"Ebbtide," Adam repeated. "I'll leave here first thing in the morning, and I'll call you when I'm about an hour away. Get some sleep, okay?"

"I'll try," Maryn promised. "See you tomorrow."

32

When she got back from her morning run shortly after nine, Julia walked, breathless and sweat-drenched, into the kitchen, where she found Dorie and Ellis already dressed for the beach, loading ice and cold drinks into their cooler.

Julia helped herself to a bottle of water, gulping it down so fast it splashed onto her tank top. She sank down on a kitchen chair and rolled the icy bottle across her forehead and neck. "Cute suit," she said, eyeing Ellis's midriff-baring coral tankini. "Is that new?"

"Kinda," Ellis said, as she smeared sunscreen on her chest and arms. "I bought it in Rehoboth Beach last summer, but I never wore it because I wasn't sure I really liked it."

"You mean you were too shy to wear it out in public," Julia said bluntly. "Ellis, this is the perfect suit for you. The top's not too low cut, but it shows off your nice flat tummy and that cute little booty of yours. Now, promise me you'll throw out that hideous black one-piece you've been wearing. I mean, my nona had a suit just like that one."

"It is not an old-lady suit!" Ellis protested. "Is it, Dorie?"

Dorie wrinkled her nose and helped herself to the bottle of sunscreen, squiggling lines of lotion up and down her arms and legs.

"Really?" Ellis sighed. "Dorie, I thought you were on my side."

"I'm not on either side," she said. "I'm neutral. Like Switzerland. I will say, however, that I like this bathing suit a whole lot better than the other one."

"Yeah," Julia said. "That black suit looks like something out of the 1968 Miss USSR pageant."

"Fine," Ellis said, slipping a cover-up over the pink suit. "Go ahead, gang up on me. I'm a big girl, I can take it."

She picked up her beach towel and tote bag, and grabbed the handle of the rolling cooler, heading for the back door. "Are you coming down to the beach with us, Julia?"

"After I shower," Julia said. "Have you guys seen Madison this morning?"

"Nope," Dorie said. "And I've been up since seven. I went out to the store at eight, to pick up more cereal and orange juice, but her bike was already gone."

"Her car's still parked in the garage," Julia said. "So that's good." She walked to the front of the house and peered out the living room window, then came quickly back to the kitchen.

"Listen," she said, lowering her voice. "I'm going up to Madison's room to check things out. One of you go out front and watch for her. If you see her coming, give me a signal, okay?"

"Julia, no," Dorie said, her voice sharp. "You've got no right. . . ."

"Madison admitted to me last night that she's been lying to us," Julia said. "Her real name is Maryn. That guy who called her cell phone? Don? He's her husband. She's terrified of him, you guys. She told me last night that she found out he's into something bad, and she ran away. That's how she ended up here, on Nags Head."

"What?" Ellis said. "She just suddenly opened up and confessed? When did all this happen?"

"Last night, while you were out on your hot date with garage guy," Julia said smugly. "And don't think we don't expect a full report about last night, either, Ellis Sullivan. We want to know why you came home so early. And why you left again and were out past midnight."

"What are you, Harriet the Spy?" Ellis asked, blushing nonetheless. "It was a date, that's all. Nothing to tell."

"Hmmph," Julia said. "We'll get back to you later. So, yes, Madison, or rather, Maryn, did open up to me. She came into my room not long after you left, ready to bitch me out because she'd figured out I'd been snooping around her cell phone."

"She had a right to be pissed at you," Dorie pointed out. "We're your best friends, so we expect a certain amount of nosiness, but it's different for her."

"She was pissed," Julia admitted. "But she wanted to know what I'd told her husband, Don, when he called. Then she really grilled me, so I grilled her right back, or tried to. But she wouldn't tell me much. So now, I'm just going to take matters into my own hands. Watch the front door, okay?"

Julia pulled her cell phone from the plastic case clipped to the waist of her running shorts. "If you see Madison coming, give me a call, and then try to keep her occupied until I can get out of there."

"Absolutely not," Dorie said. "You can't just go rifling through her things. You've got no right."

"Don't sweat it, Dorie," Ellis said. "Julia can't get in there, anyway. Madison locks her bedroom door every time she leaves the room."

Julia gave a conspiratorial smile. "True that. But I don't necessarily need a key. Madison sleeps with the windows open. I noticed it when I was out on the beach the other day. There's an access door onto that widow's walk on the third floor from the attic. I'm just gonna go out the door, climb onto the widow's walk, and then crawl in her bedroom window. It's a teeny-tiny room, it won't take but a few minutes to check it out."

Dorie crossed her arms over her chest. "I can't stop you, but I'm not gonna help you, that's for damned sure. If Madison's in trouble, we need to help her, not turn on her."

"I *offered* to help," Julia said. "She just told me to mind my own business. She says she's leaving by the weekend, if not sooner. So it's now or never."

Julia turned to Ellis. "What about you? Are you in, or are you out?"

Ellis sighed. "Oh hell. I don't like it, but I don't like the idea of her lying to us, either. How do we know she's not the one who ran away because she's into something illegal?"

"My point exactly," Julia said triumphantly. "Okay. Cover me, Ellie-Belly. I'm going in."

Dorie snorted. "You two are crazy as bat-shit. And when Madison comes home, and figures out you've been messing with her stuff, I do not want to be around to pick up the pieces."

But Julia didn't bother to respond. She took the stairs to the second and third floor at a trot. When she got to the third floor, she twisted the doorknob of Madison's room, just to make sure. As Ellis had predicted, the door was locked.

Julia went down to the end of the hall and tugged at the door to the attic. But the summer's heat and humidity had caused the old wooden door to swell. She tugged harder, then braced one leg on the door frame, and yanked with all her might. The door swung open suddenly, throwing Julia backwards, landing on her butt on the splintery wooden floor.

"Damn," she muttered, picking herself up. She gasped as a wall of heat engulfed her when she stepped into the low-ceilinged attic. She pulled the door nearly shut, to ensure she could make a quick getaway once she'd finished searching Madison's room.

A single window high in the roof peak illuminated the room. Julia picked her way past piles of cardboard boxes and dust-shrouded furniture, sneezing as she headed for the door onto the widow's walk. It had to be close to a hundred degrees in the attic, she thought, as sweat poured down her face, back, and arms.

The access door had an old-fashioned slide lock as well as a dead bolt. Julia's hands, slick with sweat, couldn't budge the lock mechanism. In frustration, she yanked off her top and used it to grasp the lock and jerk it open. She took a step backwards and kicked the door as hard as she could with her running shoe. The brittle old wood splintered, and the door flew open.

Gasping for air, Julia stepped out onto the widow's walk, dressed only in her shorts and sports bra, the tank top tucked into the waistband of her shorts. The temperature outside was already in the mid-eighties, but the air was refreshingly cool compared to the blast-furnace atmosphere in the attic. And the view was spectacular. The beach spread out below, and Julia believed she could see all the way to Currituck, to the south, and Corolla, to the north. But there was no time for sightseeing. She had a job to do.

The wooden widow's walk was narrower than it looked from the beach, only four feet wide, with a wooden railing that stood not quite hip high. The railing was rotted in places, as was the decking of the walkway. She glanced down and gulped. If she fell, it was at least a fifty-foot drop.

But she wouldn't fall. She edged down the walk until she came to the window outside Madison's room. It was propped halfway open. Julia grasped the window sill and pushed upwards. Stuck. She gritted her teeth and pushed harder, and slowly, the stubborn window inched higher. When she'd raised it a full eighteen inches, Julia managed to wriggle into the room, feet first.

"Gaawwwd," she groaned, falling in a heap onto the floor.

She was struck, instantly, by the clinical neatness of Madison's room. In contrast to Julia's own room, with its unmade bed, discarded magazines, empty soda cans, and clothes strewn haphazardly over every surface, Madison's room reminded her of a nun's cell. Or an army barracks.

The worn cotton sheets were pulled taut on the narrow iron bed, two pillows were stacked atop each other, the faded chenille bedspread was folded in a crisp rectangle at the foot of the bed. The nightstand held a lamp and a dog-eared paperback romance novel. The top of the wooden dresser was bare, except for a black vinyl zippered cosmetic case.

But a wooden chair beside the door held an open duffle bag, filled with a stack of neatly folded clothing. Madison hadn't been lying about that, Julia thought. She really did intend to leave. And soon.

Julia opened the armoire door. A couple of inexpensive cotton sundresses and some blouses still hung there. Lined up on the floor were a pair of black canvas espadrilles, a pair of pink flip-flops, and the Louboutins. On the shelf sat a black leather laptop case. Julia tugged it down. She unzipped the case and lifted the computer out.

Julia stared down at the laptop. In the movies, the heroine always managed to power up the computer, figure out the passwords, and instantly uncover all the data locked within in a matter of seconds. But Julia's knowledge of computers was mostly limited to reading her e-mails and playing games of Freecell when she was bored. She had neither the time nor the necessary expertise to unlock Madison's secrets. Reluctantly, she slipped the computer back into the case and hefted it back onto the shelf. She tried sliding it all the way to the back of the shelf, but something was back there.

She grabbed the wooden chair and dragged it over to the armoire, climbing up to peer inside. She reached up to move aside whatever was at the back of the shelf. Her fingers closed on a stack of paper.

When she saw what she'd grabbed, Julia nearly fell off the chair. It was a stack of money. Hundred-dollar bills, bound by a paper bank wrapper. She took the laptop and set it down on the floor, and reaching in with both hands, grabbed an armload of similar money bundles. Thousands of dollars.

"Whoa," Julia breathed. "What the hell are you into, Madison?" Her fingers itched to take all the bundles down, to count it and examine it, but there was no time for that. Hurriedly, she shoved the money to the back of the shelf, then set the laptop in front of it.

She closed the armoire door and moved quickly to the dresser. The drawers were half empty, the clothing within neatly folded and stacked. As Julia rifled through the clothing she reflected that for a person with all that money stashed in her closet, Madison's clothes were appallingly cheap, most of them apparently purchased either at thrift or discount stores. So how did that jibe with the Prada pocketbook, the Louboutin sandals, and the honking big diamond ring?

Mildly disappointed that the dresser didn't hold any more money, Julia searched the nightstand's single drawer for more clues to the Madison puzzle, but all she found was a plastic bottle of aspirin.

Julia glanced around the room. There was nothing much else to search. She flopped down onto her belly and peered under the bed, halfway expecting to find another suitcase full of cash. But the only thing she found was a single white sock.

She scooted onto her knees, and as a last thought, did what they always do in the movies. She lifted the thin, worn mattress and ran her hand under the space between it and the box spring. When her fingertips closed on the cool, smooth, metal object there, her mouth went dry.

She pulled the object out and stared down at it. A gun! Julia knew a little bit about guns. Her father and brothers were hunters, stalking deer in the piney woods of Georgia and quail at a friend's South Carolina plantation. This was a revolver, a Smith & Wesson. Her hands trembled badly as she fumbled with the barrel.

Briiing! Briinng! Startled, she dropped the revolver onto the bed. Her cell phone vibrated in its plastic holder at her waist.

She fumbled again, trying to get it out of the holder. The screen told her Ellis was calling.

Julia flipped it open.

"She's coming!" Ellis whispered. "Madison just rode up on her bike. I made Dorie go out and stall her, but you know Madison isn't chummy. Get the hell out of there!"

"Shit!" Julia said. "Do something. Anything. Keep her downstairs. Ellis— Madison's got a gun under her mattress. And a shitload of money hidden in the back of her closet."

"Oh my God," Ellis breathed. "Oh shit. Shit. Shit. Shit. She's coming in the house. I think I'm gonna have a heart attack. Or pee my pants."

"Don't you dare!" Julia clicked the phone closed. She started to shove the revolver under the mattress, but then, thinking better of it, shoved it in the waistband of her shorts. She smoothed the rumpled bedcovers, then ran across the room, hoisted herself out the window, and closed the window back to its original position.

This time around, she didn't linger long enough to consider the view, or the possibility of falling to her death. She scurried back inside the attic door, pulled it shut, and a moment later was taking the stairs, two at a time, back to her own bedroom on the second floor.

33

It was Dorie who saved the day. It was Wednesday, trash-pickup day, and even though they'd theoretically discarded Ellis's chore chart, it was Dorie's turn to take out the trash. She was just wheeling the overflowing plastic bin down to the curb, muttering to herself about *certain people* who couldn't be bothered to separate recyclables from the real trash, when Madison came pedaling down the street towards the house.

And then, despite all her protestations to the contrary, she found herself an unindicted co-conspirator.

"Madison," Dorie called, her mouth going dry with fear. "Hey! You're up early today. How was the bike ride?"

Madison coasted up to where Dorie was standing and braked. "It was fine," she said briefly. "I like to get out before all the tourists wake up and start clogging the roads with traffic."

"How's the ankle?" Dorie asked, glancing at Madison's leg. It was neatly taped with the Ace bandage.

"It's fine," Madison said, wiping a bead of sweat from her brow. "Thanks to you and your ice and ibuprofen."

She started to wheel away.

Dorie swallowed, trying to think of something to say, a way to stall Madison and keep her from going up to the house where Julia was, right now, rifling through Madison's belongings.

"Do you like that bike?" Dorie asked. Dumb question. Really dumb question, but it was all she could think of. Could pregnancy really do this to a person? Could the baby growing inside her really be siphoning off all her normal intelligence? She remembered a couple of the teachers at school joking about the dumb stuff they'd done while they were pregnant. Mommy minds, they called it, and Dorie always thought they were exaggerating, but now she knew different. She was dumb, and she was pregnant, and yes, pregnant by her gay husband, which made her just too stupid to live.

"The bike's all right," Madison said. "It's cheap, but it rides pretty good."

"I've been thinking about buying myself a bike," Dorie babbled. "It's supposed to be such good exercise, everybody says. But God, I don't think I've ridden a bike since I got out of college. I bet I wouldn't even remember how."

"Sure you would," Madison said. "That's why they always say what they say about riding a bike."

"What do they say?" Dorie asked. She was blanking, she really was. This baby better be a friggin' rocket scientist, she told herself, because it had already sucked out every brain cell Dorie had ever possessed.

Madison shifted impatiently from one foot to the other. "People always say something easy is like riding a bike, because you supposedly never forget how to ride a bike." She leaned closer and peered into Dorie's eyes with something like concern.

"Dorie, are you all right? You seem kind of, uh, spacey this morning."

"The teachers at school say it's something to do with your elevated hormone levels," Dorie explained. "Sharon? She's teaches freshman English? She was pregnant last fall, and not once, not twice, but three different times she got me to give her a ride home from school, and then remembered that she'd actually driven to school that day. I had to turn right around and take her back to school to get her own car."

"Yeah, that's crazy," Madison said. "Well, anyway, it's just a temporary condition, right?"

"I certainly hope so," Dorie said fervently. Madison was starting to walk her bike down the crushed-shell driveway. Dorie caught up with her. "So, we were just getting ready to go down to the beach. Supposed to be a beautiful day today. Not too humid. Anyway, not as humid as it gets in Savannah, which is, like, a million percent humidity. Maybe you could come hang with us at the beach today."

"Maybe later," Madison said. She stopped and turned towards Dorie. "Look, I know Julia told you guys about me. I'm sorry I lied to you. But I had my reasons. Anyway, not that it matters, because I'm leaving tomorrow, but I just wanted to tell you, you know, thanks. For letting me stay here. And everything."

Impulsively, Dorie gave Madison a hug. "Thank you," she said. "That morning we met, at that restaurant, I was really feeling pretty desperate. My sister flaked out on us, and I was so depressed and worried about money. I guess you thought I was some kind of nut, a perfect stranger, trying to rent you a room."

"You were nice," Madison said shyly. "And I'm sure Ellis and Julia— especially Julia—gave you some crap about renting to me without consulting them."

"They were fine with it, once they got over the initial shock," Dorie insisted. "They're really not so bad, once you get to know them. I think they'd like you as much as I do if you'd let them, Madison. Or should I call you Maryn?"

"Doesn't matter now, but I've kind of gotten to like being Madison."

"What made you pick that name?" Dorie asked, again, trying desperately to stall.

"Remember that movie, *Splash*? Where Daryl Hannah plays the mermaid, and she rescues Tom Hanks from drowning and falls in love with him? And she names herself Madison, because she sees the street sign for Madison Avenue? That was my favorite movie as a kid," Maryn said. "I named all my dolls Madison. I even named my kitten Madison." She smiled wryly. "I guess I wasn't a very imaginative kid."

"I named my kitten Kitty," Dorie said. "So, what does that tell you about me?"

"Tells me I hope you do better with this baby you're having," Maryn said, and they both laughed.

But now Maryn was walking towards the house again, picking up the pace, and Julia—oh God, she only hoped Julia had chickened out. Unlikely, knowing Julia.

"I wish you wouldn't go," Dorie said, meaning it more than the other woman could know. "I wish you'd stay here, and let us help you with whatever kind of trouble you're having."

"You can't," Maryn called over her shoulder.

"Get out, Julia," Dorie thought. "Get the hell out. Now!" She turned around, walked back to the curb, and fetched the unwieldy trash bin, trundling it halfway back to the house when it struck her: "Mommy mind, my ass," she grumbled, run-walking the still-full bin back towards the street because she had to pee. Again.

Ellis made an elaborate show of setting herself up on the beach, tilting her beach chair at what she thought would be her most flattering angle, slipping out of the filmy cover-up, and reclining facing the water. She did not allow herself to glance in the direction of the garage apartment. That would be just too obvious. Instead, she busied herself with her book and the cooler of cold drinks.

Dorie flopped down into her own chair and took the bottle of water Ellis offered. "Is everything okay?" she asked. "Is Julia coming down?"

"In a minute," Ellis said. "And when she gets down here, I am going to read her the riot act. You were right, Dorie. She had absolutely no business breaking into Madison's room. I swear to God, when I saw her walking that bike down the driveway, I nearly had a myocardial infarction. I haven't been that scared since your mom came home early from work that time we were seniors in high school and almost caught you and Kevin Boylan doing it on your dad's Barcalounger."

Dorie took a sip of water. "That wasn't Kevin Boylan. It was Kieran, his older brother. And we weren't technically doing it. Just messing around, as Kieran liked to say."

"Yeah, well, I wasn't about to explain the technicalities to Phyllis," Ellis said. "It was bad enough that we'd cut school and I'd drunk half a bottle of Jägermeister and puked in the backseat of Willa's Camry. And then here comes Phyllis, and I'm trying to act sober and tell her you had cramps so Miss Deal gave me permission to drive you home from school early. And the whole time I'm praying to the Baby Jesus that Kevin will get his pants on and get the hell out of your den before Phyllis asks where you are."

"It was Kieran, not Kevin, wasn't it?"

Ellis and Dorie looked up as Julia unfolded a quilt and spread it out on the sand beside them.

"I was just explaining that to Ellis," Dorie said. "Kevin Boylan had terminal dandruff. I would never have let Kevin Boylan get to third base. I did have certain standards, you know."

"Oh, please," Julia said, dropping down onto the quilt. "Don't talk to us about standards. We were there, remember? You only let Kieran get into your pants because he drove a cool car and you thought he'd invite you to all his fraternity parties at Georgia."

"And you guys agreed to go along with our little party because you assumed I'd get you dates with his KA brothers," Dorie said serenely. "And, if I recall correctly, Julia Capelli, you were the one who shoplifted that Jägermeister from Johnnie Ganem's Liquor Store."

"The beginning of a life of crime," Ellis said somberly. She flicked her towel at Julia. "And you, you idiot, are never to pull a stunt like that again. Ever." Ellis fanned herself. "My nerves can't take the strain."

"Your nerves," Julia drawled. "What about mine? When I found all that loot stashed in the back of Madison's closet? Not to mention the gun under her mattress."

"What?" Dorie sat straight up on her lounge chair. "You are making that up." She turned to Ellis. "Phyllis was right about one thing, though. Julia Capelli was, and still is, a bad influence."

Julia did a cursory sign of the cross. "On my daddy's grave. I'm telling you the truth. Madison must have, I don't know, like, twenty thousand dollars in cash. Shoved to the back of the shelf in her armoire. But that's not the scariest thing." She plunged her hand into her beach bag and withdrew a menacing-looking black handgun.

"This," she said triumphantly, "is what she had under her mattress. Now tell me again about poor, unfortunate, innocent Madison-slash-Maryn."

Ellis and Dorie stared goggle-eyed at the gun, until Julia shoved it back into the bag.

"Is it real?" Dorie asked.

"Is it loaded?" Ellis demanded.

"Not anymore," Julia said.

"You actually stole her gun?" Dorie groaned and shook her head.

"I did it for you guys," Julia said. "Who knows what she planned to do with that gun?" She held out one hand. "Diet Coke, please. All this sleuthing has left me absolutely parched."

"Oh my God," Dorie said, still eyeing Julia's bag. "Madison must be in awful trouble. Y'all, we have got to try to help her."

When Julia had finished her Diet Coke, and they'd made her recount the search and seizure of the contents of Madison's room not once, but twice, the three women agreed that it was time to do something.

"She told me this morning, she's leaving tomorrow," Dorie pointed out. "So it'd be a waste of time to kick her out. Anyway, I don't want to kick her out. I want to figure out how to help her."

"Dorie," Ellis said, sounding calmer than she felt. "You don't help a woman who has a closet full of cash and a loaded weapon. You just keep out of her way."

"Not happening," Julia said, her voice low, as she nodded in the direction of the stairway from the dunes.

Madison, or Maryn, was steaming down the stairs, blood in her eyes.

She kicked her shoes off at the base of the steps and kept coming, until she was standing at the very edge of their little beach camp, a damp tank top clutched in her right hand.

"Hi, Madison," Dorie attempted.

"You bitches!" Madison spat the words. "I knew moving in here was a mistake. Knew you'd never trust me and that I could never trust any of you."

Madison stood, hands clenched on her hips, staring down at Julia. "You've got some goddamn nerve, breaking into my room," she said. "Did you think I wouldn't find out?"

Julia's complexion paled a little under her tan. She propped herself up on her elbows. "What are you talking about? Me? Why would I be interested in your room?"

"I don't know why," Madison snapped. "Maybe because you're a pathetic loser, with no life of your own, so you have to go snooping around in mine?"

"I resent that," Julia said.

"Fuck you," Madison said. She glanced over at Dorie and gave her an even more withering look. "And you. With all that phony bullshit compassion, telling me you want me to stay. All the while you're really just stalling me so I won't catch *that* one in the act of burglarizing my room."

"It wasn't phony!" Dorie blurted out. "I mean, yes, I was stalling you, because I didn't want you to catch Julia. But I meant what I said. And I mean it even more now. Julia told us about the money."

"So now what? You've concluded that I'm a bank robber? An embezzler? Or maybe just a madam for a high-class call girl outfit? I'm surprised there's not a patrol car parked up at the house. You did call the cops, right?"

"It was a lot of cash," Julia pointed out.

"I don't have to explain myself to you people," Madison said, shaking her head in disbelief.

"Let me ask you something," Julia piped up. "How did you figure out I'd been in your room? I mean, I was so careful. Did you set up some kind of booby trap or something, just in case somebody did go snooping around?"

"Some cat burglar," Madison sneered. She held up the garment in her hand, which turned out to be a still-damp, white nylon running shirt, and flung it in Julia's face. "You left this."

34

The three women watched as Madison/Maryn gave her best effort towards stomping off in the damp khaki-colored sand. When she'd abandoned the beach, they returned their attention to Julia, who'd slumped back onto her beach towel, her hands thrown across her eyes, blocking the sun and their inquisitive stares.

"Your top?" Ellis said finally, flicking the sweaty garment with a dismissive fingertip. "Really, Julia? You didn't notice you'd left your top behind?"

"I'm sorry," Julia cried, her voice so shrill that a nearby seagull squawked in answer, and a small child walking by scampered quickly away, towards the water and an incoming wave. "Don't look at me like that. Jesus! You saw how I was dressed. I'd just come back from my run. And that attic—the temperature must have been about two hundred degrees. I couldn't get the door latch to open—sweat was pouring off of me, my hands were slippery, so I took off my top—for God's sake—I was wearing a sports bra! And I used it to get the latch open. And then I climbed in the window, and I was rummaging around in her room. She didn't even have the air conditioner on up there.

Why am I explaining all of this to you? She's the one with the stash of cash and the gun under her mattress."

"This was just a really, really bad idea," Ellis said, her voice low. "Unforgivable. I should never have gone along with this. I knew it wasn't right, but I did it anyway. I feel awful."

"Me too," Dorie said. "And I'm just as bad as you guys. I could have stopped Julia, if I'd really tried."

But Julia was unrepenetant. "Okay, so maybe I shouldn't have ransacked her room. I'm sorry. Okay? It was all my idea, and you guys are off the hook. But can we just get back to the matter at hand—which, after all, is what do we do about Madison and her gun and her giant stack o' cash?"

Dorie looked uneasily at Ellis. "I think you should go talk to her."

"Me?" Ellis was indignant. "Why me? I'm not the one who invited her to live here. And I'm not the one who is chasing her off because I went prying into her private business."

"Who else?" Dorie asked. "She hates Julia. And she doesn't trust me anymore, that's for sure. You're the calm one. The smart one. You can talk to her. You can talk to anybody. Weren't you the one who persuaded Phyllis all those years ago that the moaning coming from our den was me, writhing with cramps, instead of Kieran Boylan, crying like a little girly man because he cut his knee crawling out the back window?"

"Just ask her where the money came from," Julia advised. "But don't say anything about the gun, okay? I mean, we don't want to piss her off, just in case she's got another one hidden in her car or something."

"No!" Ellis said, flinging the sweaty top at Julia. "I am putting my foot down." Despite her protests, Ellis knew it was no use arguing or stalling. They were all in their thirties now, but she, Ellis Sullivan, was still designated driver for life.

She took a deep breath and knocked lightly on Madison's door.

"Go away," came the muffled response.

"Madison," Ellis called. "Please let me in. I want to talk to you. I want to apologize . . . for all of us."

"Fine. Whatever," Madison called. "I'm leaving in the morning, so just let it be. Let me be."

"I can't," Ellis said plaintively. "You know Julia. She's not going to let up on any of us until I talk to you. Face-to-face."

The door opened abruptly. "Make it fast," Madison said, gesturing her inside. "But this is a complete waste of time."

Ellis crossed the threshold and looked around the room. The thin, white, cotton curtains ruffled listlessly in the faint breeze.

"May I sit down?" Ellis asked.

"It's your house," Madison said bitterly. "I'm just a boarder here. With no property rights."

"About that," Ellis said, clearing her throat and perching on the edge of the narrow bed. "We owe you an apology. All of us. Except maybe Dorie. She was totally against what Julia did, but we pressured her to act as lookout, and in the end, she caved."

"Nice to know," Madison said. She was emptying the drawers of the wooden dresser, folding clothes and placing them in a duffle bag.

"We really would like to help you," Ellis said. "If you'd let us."

Madison wheeled around, fire in her eyes. "Why should I let any of you near me? Why should I trust any of you?"

"I don't know," Ellis said truthfully. "Maybe you should trust us because we've trusted you. We rented you a room, based solely on what you told us, which turned out to be a lie. We know you're mixed up in something . . . complicated. And that you're afraid of your . . . is he your ex-husband?"

"Not yet," Madison said grimly.

"What did he do?" Ellis asked. "To make you run the way you did? You don't strike me as a scaredy-cat."

"If I tell you, will you just let me alone?" Madison asked. "Not try to meddle in my affairs?"

"I'll try," Ellis said. "I can't speak for Julia—nobody speaks for her. And nobody controls her."

"My husband . . ." Madison started. "He's an accountant, back in Jersey. He handled the books for the insurance company where I used to work.

That's where we met. He asked me to lunch, I went, and pretty soon, we were living together."

"And?" Ellis said gently.

"Don was married when I met him," Madison blurted. "Of course, I didn't know that, he didn't bother to tell me he still had a wife and two teenagers. They were separated, and he did get divorced, but he was definitely still married when we started dating."

"Would you have dated him if you knew he was married?" Ellis asked, raising one eyebrow.

"Hell, no!" Madison said. "But I should have figured it out. There was a lot about Don Shackleford I should have figured out before we moved in together."

"You told Julia he was into something really bad," Ellis prompted. "What did you mean by that?"

Madison bit her lip. "He's a thief and a con man. He's been stealing from his clients, at least two million just from the insurance company, that I know about. There's probably more, though."

"How do you know?" Ellis asked. "I mean, you didn't have anything to do with it, right?"

"Oh, because of the money, right?" Madison said bitterly. "You just assume I'm a thief too?"

"I don't know what to think about you," Ellis said, exasperated. "You keep everything such a freakin' secret, what am I supposed to think?"

"I may be a lot of things, but I'm not a thief," Madison said. "Swear to God. The money was Don's. Or whoever he was stealing it from."

"So how do you know your husband was stealing?"

"Adam—he's a friend from work—told me that a team of auditors had been in the office, looking at all the files. They were investigating Don. I didn't want to believe Adam. He's always been jealous of Don, he had kind of a crush on me. So I snuck into Don's office and checked, and Adam was right. Don had all these bogus companies set up, being paid from Prescott accounts."

"What did you do?" Ellis asked. "Did you confront your husband? Did he bother to deny it?"

Madison's laugh was mirthless. "You don't *confront* Don Shackleford. It was the other way around. He drove up to the office as I was leaving and followed me home. He knew I'd been up to something, and he . . . made me tell him what I found out."

"He hurt you?"

"Not in a way that would be visible to anybody else. He grabbed me, threw me up against the wall, and calmly informed me that if I told anybody about my suspicions that he'd kill me and hide the body where nobody would ever think to look."

Ellis studied Madison's face. "You think he's capable of something like that? Murder?"

"I do now," Madison said soberly. "He's capable of that and worse."

"So you ran?"

"I didn't know what else to do," Madison said. "I was terrified. I'd begun to understand a little bit about Don—about his coldness, his dishonesty, but I truly didn't know he was capable of something like that. Not until I saw it with my own eyes. As soon as he drove off, I knew I had to get out."

"You couldn't call somebody? A relative?"

Maryn's voice was colorless. "You wouldn't understand. I don't have a lot of family, just my mom and my aunt, and we're not close. Emotionally or geographically."

"What about a girlfriend? Somebody from your office?"

"Don made me quit my job right after we got married. And anyway, I wasn't exactly chummy with the women in my office. Adam was my only friend there. He's coming here tomorrow. Him I can trust."

"Like you can't trust us?"

Maryn shrugged. "Breaking into my room, that was a really shitty thing to do. Friends wouldn't do something like that."

"You made it very clear that you didn't need any friends," Ellis reminded her. "But you're right, it really was shitty. At some point, when she starts to really think about it, Julia will realize that too."

"Doesn't matter now," Madison said.

"You still haven't told me about the money," Ellis reminded her. "You've got to admit, it's kind of shady, having all that money hidden in your closet."

"It's a long story," Madison said. "Just go, okay? Tell the others they don't have to worry about me any more."

"I'd still like to hear it, if you don't mind," Ellis said.

"Whatever," Madison said. She'd stopped folding clothes and was leaning against the wall opposite the bed where Ellis sat.

"After he threatened me, Don just left," Madison said. "It never would have occurred to him that I might disobey him. Or leave.

"But as soon as he was gone, I knew I was outta there. I threw some clothes and stuff into that," she said, gesturing towards the duffle bag. "I didn't have a plan. I mean, I had some money squirreled away." She laughed again. "My mother used to call that 'get outta town money', and how right she was. It came to a little over six thousand dollars. I grabbed that, and on the way out the door, I remembered my computer. My laptop. Don bought us new computers a few months ago. They came with matching cases, too. So I grabbed my laptop and threw it in the back of the car. And I left."

"And drove until you got to Nags Head," Ellis said. "What made you come here?"

A ghost of a smile flitted across Madison's lips. "I told myself it was a co-incidence. I was driving south, saw a billboard for Nags Head, and headed in this direction. But on all those long bike rides I've been taking, I've done some soul-searching. Nags Head was no accident."

"You'd been here before?"

"As a kid, with my parents. It was the only vacation they ever took me on. We stayed in a little motel, swam in the pool, went on the bumper cars, ate ice cream—all the stuff normal happy families do. I'd saved my allowance, and I bought a little shell-covered jewelry box with NAGS HEAD, NC, written on the lid; the first thing I ever bought with my own money."

"I think I had a jewelry box just like that," Ellis volunteered. "Except mine said TYBEE ISLAND, GA. I still have it, come to think of it."

"Mine's long gone," Madison said dully. "My parents split up when I was thirteen. We'd been living in Fayetteville, North Carolina. As soon as school was out that year, my mom loaded me in the car and we moved to New Jersey to live with my Aunt Patsy. We just drove off, with our clothes in some cardboard boxes from the liquor store. Left everything else in the house."

"Oh Lord," Ellis said. "What about your dad?"

"He got remarried," Madison said. "To a woman who'd been my mom's best friend."

Ellis looked down at her right hand, at the narrow gold band lined with tiny diamond chips that her father had given her for her thirtieth birthday. It was the last of a long line of gifts her father had given her over the years.

"Did you ever see him again?"

"Who? Oh, my dad? Not much. They moved to Daytona."

"I'm sorry," Ellis said.

"It is what it is," Madison said, practiced at not caring.

Ellis wanted to change the subject. "Your ring. The one you said was an old family piece. I noticed you stopped wearing it."

"My engagement ring. Don bought it for me, right before we got married. I'm thinking of pawning it. Wanna make me an offer?"

Ellis glanced at Madison's now-bare hands. "Why do you need to pawn it? With all that money?"

"I'm not touching that money," Madison said. "I didn't even know it was there, not until I went to unpack my laptop and realized I'd actually grabbed Don's by mistake."

"And the money was in his laptop case? Do you mind if I ask how much?"

Madison shrugged. "Close to a hundred thousand dollars."

"For real?" Ellis's eyes widened.

"I've got Don's money. And I know he's stolen millions more. He probably thinks I meant to take the cash. Now do you see why I was in such a panic when I found out Julia talked to him? What if he finds me?"

"You think he'd hurt you? To get at the money?"

"A few months ago I'd have said no. Now, for sure. With Don, it's not just about the money. It's about control. Ownership."

Ellis looked down at her hands, then out the window, thinking about her own brief marriage, and its sudden, emotionless ending. It had been so painful at the time, but maybe, in comparison to what Madison was going through, Ben's way was preferable.

"So . . . you and Don were already having problems before this?" Ellis asked.

"Yeah," Madison said sourly. "If by problems you mean he was sleeping with somebody else and I'd moved into the guest bedroom."

"Oh," Ellis said weakly.

"Don't know why I was surprised," Madison said, tossing her head, as though she didn't really care. "He cheated on his ex-wife with me, why wouldn't he cheat on me with somebody else?"

"Any idea who she is?"

Madison reached in an open dresser drawer, balled up some shirts, and tossed them at the duffle bag. "I've got a very good idea who."

Now that she'd starting talking to Ellis, it was as though she'd turned on a spigot and was powerless to turn it off. The words just kept spewing.

"Tara Powers! We worked together at the insurance company. We weren't friends or anything—but she knew Don was married to me."

Ellis kept thinking about all that money. "A hundred thousand dollars. Do you think he meant to give it to his girlfriend?"

"No way," Madison said quickly. "Not his style. Don keeps his women on a tight leash."

"So, what was he doing with all that money?" Ellis persisted.

"I don't care anymore," Madison said. "After tomorrow, I'm out of here. I'm only sticking around today because Adam begged me to. He thinks there's something he can do to get me out of this."

"Adam? That's your friend you used to work with?" Ellis asked, her curiosity aroused. "He's coming here? To Nags Head?"

"He should be about halfway here," Madison said. "He's kind of a nerd, but in a really sweet way."

"You two worked together?"

"Yep. And he's still there. He's taking a vacation day to come down here."

"You told him everything that happened?" Ellis asked, surprised.

"Most of it," Madison said. "He was on vacation when I took off. I kept try-ing to text him, but he never got back to me until last night. You won't believe this—he actually thinks I should go back to Jersey and calmly start divorce proceedings against Don. As if!"

"Let me ask you this," Ellis said. "You say you're not going back. What about the insurance company, the one you used to work for, that he ripped off? Don't you care about any of them?"

"I care!" Madison said. "But I don't have any proof. Those files I saw at his office? All gone now, I guarantee."

"What about his laptop? You've got that, right? Maybe there are incrimi-nating files on that."

"I don't have the password."

And you have no idea if the auditors found anything about the embezzle-ment to tie it to Don, or whether or not the insurance company has brought charges against your husband?"

"No," Madison said. "I rode my bike over to the library, thinking I could get online on their computers, see if there's been anything in the news up there," Madison admitted. "But they won't let you use the Internet unless you've got a library card. And I wasn't about to apply for one and start giving out personal information."

"Hmm," Ellis said, looking out the window. She could just see the edge of the deck of Ty's garage apartment. She could access the Internet with her iPhone, but she had an ulterior motive—seeing Ty.

"I know somebody who's got Internet access," Ellis said. "And I think maybe he'd be willing to let us use his computer, too. That is, if you want our help."

Madison hesitated. "No, never mind."

"Suit yourself," Ellis said, shaking her head. "I did my best, but you really just don't let anybody get close, do you?"

She got off the bed and went to the door. "I'll tell the girls . . . what? You're leaving tomorrow, or the day after, when your friend gets here? Dorie will be sad. She really thought she could reach out to you."

Madison let her get down the hallway before she called after her.

"Ellis?"

She turned and walked back, poking her head inside Madison's bedroom.

"What the hell," Madison said. "I've been wondering what that garage apartment looked like inside."

"Me too," Ellis said.

35

Ellis came flying down the stairway, with Madison trailing reluctantly behind. Julia and Dorie sat at the table in the dining room, pretending to play cards.

"We're going over to Ty's, to look up some stuff on the Internet," Ellis started.

"We know," Julia interrupted.

"What?" Madison said, stopping short, her eyes narrowed. "You bugged my room while you were ransacking it?"

"Sorry," Dorie said meekly. "We really didn't mean to eavesdrop. We were up in my room, and as it turns out, the airshaft from Madison's room runs right through my closet. We kinda heard everything you guys were saying."

Ty answered the door before they could knock. His hair was still wet from the shower, and he was dressed in khaki cargo shorts and the black Cadillac Jack's T-shirt.

"Hey!" he said, his face lighting up when he saw Ellis. He leaned forward and kissed her cheek lightly, as though they'd been doing this forever.

"You're Madison, right?" he said, holding out his hand. "The new girl. Nice to meet you."

"And you," she said stiffly.

Still swooning from the scent of Ty's soap and shampoo, Ellis blushed happily. "Are you on your way out?"

"Yeah," Ty said. "They're short a bartender again, and God knows I can use the money, so I agreed to come in and cover lunch, then hang around 'til closing. Hey, maybe you and the girls could all come over later. They're having a special drink promotion for some new citrus vodka. It probably tastes like crap, but the drinks are cheap."

"Maybe," Ellis said. "But we were wondering if we could use your computer. For research."

"Sure," Ty said, looking puzzled. "Come on in."

The apartment was even smaller than it looked from the outside. The walls were knotty pine, the varnish blackened with age, and worn green-and-white checkerboard linoleum covered the floor of what was essentially an all-in-one living room, dining room, and kitchen. The kitchen consisted of an old white-painted Hoosier cupboard stocked with a mismatched assortment of plastic dishes; a two-burner stove; and a small, rust-spotted refrigerator.

"Welcome to my office," Ty said, gesturing towards a stout oak kitchen table. A PC was set up on the table, and a metal, rolling office chair with cracked leatherette upholstery was pulled up to the makeshift desk. Nearby a rickety blue-painted bookshelf held an assortment of business books, magazines, and stacks of folders.

He leaned over, pressed a button on the computer's monitor, and the screen lit up. "The printer's right there," he said, pointing to a small table doing double duty as end table and printer stand beside the lumpy two-seater sofa. "Anything else you need, just help yourself."

"Thank you," Madison said, pulling out the desk chair and seating herself. Ellis walked out onto the deck with Ty.

"Wait," he said, ducking back inside. When he came back, he held out a single key.

"Just lock up when you leave," he said. "And keep it, if you want."

Ellis raised an eyebrow.

"I already have a key to your place," he said, with that slow grin. "Not that I'd use it without your permission, though." He glanced back towards the apartment. "What's going on with you guys? I thought you said Madison was pretty standoffish."

"She was," Ellis said. "But Madison is in real trouble. Her husband, back in Jersey, is some kind of criminal, and . . . well it's too complicated to go into right now. But she's trying to figure some stuff out, and I want to try to help her."

"That's nice," Ty said absentmindedly. "So . . . listen. When can I see you again? Tonight? Any chance you might wait up for me after I get off work?"

"There's a chance," Ellis said lightly. "Text me when you're leaving. And maybe I'll see you at Caddie's, depending on what we figure out about Madison's situation."

"We're good now, right?" he asked, catching her hand in his.

"Very good," she said. "Talk to you later."

Madison was staring quizzically at the computer screen when Ellis rejoined her. "I figured out how to open his Internet browser, but now what?" she asked.

She saw Ellis's look of surprise.

"I'm not really a computer person. I mean, I used one at work, but they had all kind of rules about using the computers for personal use. And as for my laptop at home? All I really use it for is to play online blackjack."

"Okay, well, let's go to the website for the *Philadelphia Inquirer,*" Ellis suggested. She leaned over Madison's shoulder and started typing into the browser bar.

Madison quickly got up and yielded the chair to Ellis. She leaned eagerly over Ellis's shoulder and watched as she navigated around the *Inquirer's* website. "How do you spell your husband's last name?"

"S-H-I-T," Madison said, snickering, and then quickly supplying the correct spelling. Ellis typed the name into the site's search bar, and waited for a moment.

"Here it is," she said, tapping the screen.

"CHERRY HILL BUSINESSMAN WANTED FOR QUESTIONING IN EMBEZZLEMENT SCHEME," the headline read.

"Oh my God," Madison whispered as she read.

The story was over a week old.

Sources close to an investigation by local police have revealed that prominent Cherry Hill financial wiz Donald Shackleford has been implicated in an embezzlement scheme that may have drained millions of dollars from several of his client companies, including R.G. Prescott Insurers, also of Cherry Hill.

"So, you were right. The insurance company wasn't the only client he ripped off," Ellis said.

Attempts to contact Shackleford for comment have been unsuccessful, although neighbors in the upscale town house development where Shackleford lived with his second wife, Maryn, say neither he nor his wife has been seen in recent days. According to Shackleford's company website, D. Shackleford & Assoc. provides accounting and investment services to a range of firms throughout the state. Investigators have begun contacting other companies that were clients of Shackleford in an effort to determine how widespread the alleged fraud may have been.

The rest of the newspaper story detailed Don Shackleford's ties in the community and ended with a statement from his attorney saying he was confident any investigation would prove that the complaints against his client were baseless and not worthy of further comment.

Madison ran her hands through her hair and stared at the computer screen. "Can you find out if there have been any more recent stories?"

Ellis began typing into the search bar on the newspaper's website, and a moment later, links to two stories appeared.

She clicked and started reading. "Here's a piece that ran last Sunday," she said.

"EMBEZZLEMENT SUSPECT HAD TIES TO VICTIMIZED INSURANCE COMPANY," the headline read.

As forensic accountants try to piece together what local investigators characterize as an ever-widening probe into embezzlement claims against Cherry Hill financial wiz Donald Shackleford, investigators say they have also begun looking into the possibility that Shackleford's wife, Maryn Vance Shackleford, 32, and her close associate, Adam Kuykendall, 33, of Camden, may also be involved in Shackleford's alleged scheme to embezzle and defraud local firm R.G. Prescott Insurers of millions of dollars. Maryn Shackleford and Kuykendall were employed in "sensitive positions" at Prescott for the past two years, and investigators believe they may have aided Don Shackleford's criminal activities.

"What?" Madison shrieked. "They think I had something to do with this shit? Sensitive position? I was a claims processor, for God's sake. Adam worked in accounting, but there's no way he had anything to do with this mess. 'Close associate'? Are these people freakin' nuts? We're not the thieves, Don is."

"Calm down," Ellis said, glancing at Madison. "It's just a newspaper story. And you'll notice none of the information has any kind of real attribution. 'Sources said'? I'm sure these reporters are just fishing for a real story without knowing any of the facts."

"Look at this!" Madison cried, flicking the computer screen. "Can you believe this?"

At least one R.G. Prescott employee, Tara Powers, 28, an account executive at the firm, characterized her former coworkers Maryn Shackleford and Adam Kuykendall as "shadowy types" who rarely mixed with others at the insurance company. Powers pointed out that Maryn Shackleford met her future husband while acting as personal assistant to the company's president, R.G. "Robby" Prescott III, a position that gave her unlimited access to the company's financial records.

"That bitch," Madison screeched. "Shadowy types? Personal assistant? I filled in for Robby's secretary one freakin' day! That's all. One freakin' day. It happened to be the day I met Don, but what's that got to do with anything? I had access to nothing—except Robby's phone and an old copy of *People* magazine his real assistant left on top of her desk. And as for Tara being an account executive? Don't make me laugh. She works in the file room. If I ever get my hands on the little slut . . ."

"What about this?" Ellis asked, pointing to the next paragraph in the story.

Sources say Maryn Shackleford left the company several months ago, and that Kuykendall abruptly resigned from his position yesterday. Investigators questioned Kuykendall the day he resigned from R.G. Prescott, but they have been unable to contact Maryn Shackleford, who they say abruptly disappeared from the area within the past ten days. The insurance company is offering a $10,000 reward for information leading to the whereabouts of Maryn Shackleford.

Madison pounded the desktop. "God! They've put out an APB on me. And a ten-thousand-dollar reward. For what? I didn't do anything. I don't know anything."

"But this is your friend Adam, right? The one who tipped you off that auditors were looking at Don's records?" Ellis asked.

"Yeahhh," she said, looking perplexed. "But when we talked yesterday, he didn't tell me he'd quit his job. In fact, he told me he's been on vacation."

"Why would the cops question Adam about Don's embezzlement scheme?" Ellis asked.

"Maybe because he worked in the accounting department?" Madison said, looking perplexed. "I guess I'll ask him that when he gets here tomorrow."

Ellis's stomach lurched. "Madison, um, did you tell him about the money you found in Don's briefcase?"

"Yeah," she said quietly. "Sure? Why wouldn't I tell him?"

"You don't think he had anything to do with any of this, do you?"

"No!" she said. "Adam is, like, my best friend. He was my *only* friend in that office. All those backstabbing bitches I worked with treated me like a pariah. You know, they didn't even have a going-away lunch for me when I quit? Adam was different. I trusted him. My last day of work, he took me out to lunch, and we got hammered on tequila shooters. I never even went back to the office after lunch. I mean, what was the point?"

"Did you tell him where you're staying?" Ellis inquired.

"He knows I'm in Nags Head. I didn't give him the exact address, because to tell you the truth, I don't even know it."

"That might be just as well," Ellis said. "I mean, I'm not saying anything against him, but maybe, just to be cautious . . . I mean, for one thing, there's that ten-thousand-dollar reward. Adam knows what kind of car you drive, right?"

"Of course," Madison said, getting impatient. "He also kinda knows where I've been staying. I told him it's on South Virginia Dare. I told him the name of the house. Ebbtide. But I'm telling you, I know him. Adam wouldn't hurt a fly." She held up her cell phone. "I'll call him right now, get this straightened out."

Madison scrolled through her phone's recent call log, punched in a number and waited.

"Adam? It's me. Look, we need to talk. Call me right back, okay? This is really important."

She closed the phone and looked at Ellis. "I know this guy, okay? He's not like Don. He wants to help me."

Ellis wasn't totally convinced. But she didn't want to make Madison any more anxious than she already was. "Okay," she said finally. "We'll just wait and see what happens, right?"

36

hat did you find out?" Julia demanded as soon as Ellis and Madison got back to Ebbtide. "Is there an APB out for Maryn?"

"Madison," Dorie gently corrected her. "Remember, she likes Madison better."

"Whatever," Julia said, slapping the dining room tabletop with the palm of her hand. "Come on. Give."

Ellis glanced at Madison, and she nodded.

"So . . ." Ellis began. "We may have a problem."

She filled Dorie and Julia in on what they'd discovered from the newspaper stories.

"They're offering a ten-thousand-dollar reward for me!" Madison blurted out. "Like I'm the criminal! Like I had anything to do with stealing that money."

Ellis took a deep breath. "And there's some question about her friend Adam. He told Maryn he's on vacation, but the paper said he quit his job."

Madison shook her head and frowned. "Adam can't afford to quit. He just bought a brand-new Camaro, back in the spring. And I know for a fact his credit cards are always maxed out. Bill collectors were always calling the office looking for him."

Dorie looked horrified. "You think he'd turn you in for that ten-thousand-dollar reward?"

"No!" Madison exclaimed. "He's my friend. He wouldn't do that to me. There's gotta be an explanation for all this. Look, probably the newspaper got it wrong about him quitting his job. There's a woman at the office, Tara, I'm pretty sure she's sleeping with Don. She's the one telling the paper all these lies about me and Adam."

Dorie and Julia exchanged a look.

"I think," Ellis said, "maybe we should call the police. Just in case."

"And tell them what?" Madison said heatedly. "Here's the woman they're looking for up in Jersey? The one who maybe helped her husband steal a couple million dollars?"

"If I was a cop, I'd lock your ass up in a heartbeat," Julia said matter-of-factly. "And that's before I knew you had a hundred grand hidden on the top shelf of your armoire."

"Maybe we don't call the police right away," Dorie murmured.

"Okay," Ellis said. "What do we do—to keep Madison safe until she can go home and clear her name?"

"Look," Madison said, sounding braver than she looked. "Adam Kuykendall isn't exactly Al Capone. He's not even six feet tall, weighs maybe 160 pounds, soaking wet. He wears Coke-bottle glasses, and I happen to know he flunked out of community college. Twice. He's not that scary and he's really not that smart."

"But from what you say, he's in debt up to his eyeballs, and he's definitely motivated," Ellis reminded her. "That sounds like a scary combination to me. Plus, he knows where you're staying."

"I could leave," Madison replied heatedly. "I will leave. As soon as I let Adam know what's going on, I'm outta here."

"That's not necessary," Dorie said. "If you say your friend can be trusted, we believe you. We want you to stay. Right?" she said, glaring first at Julia, and then at Ellis.

"Right," Ellis mumbled.

"I never said she should go in the first place," Julia muttered.

37

Dinnertime. Julia stared into the refrigerator, studying its contents with a mixture of disdain and outright disgust. "Leftovers. A jar of marinara sauce. A package of chicken thighs. Since it's my night to cook, I move that we go out for dinner tonight. My treat. All in favor?"

Madison's hand shot up in the air. Dorie glanced apologetically at Ellis, and then raised her hand too.

"Oh, all right," Ellis grumbled. "I'm sick of chicken too. What did you have in mind? Do we have any coupons?"

"Pizza!" Dorie crowed. "I have been craving pizza all day. Thick, gooey, triple-cheese pizza."

"Pizza? Here?" Madison said. "What do southerners know about pizza? Have you people ever tasted real pizza? There's a place at home. Carmine's. The owner is right off the boat from Italy. The crust is so thin, it's like paper. The cheese is real fresh-shaven parmigiano-reggiano, not that crap from the green can, and they make the tomato sauce themselves, smoke and cure their own pepperoni, and they bake it in a real wood-fired pizza oven."

"Oh, God," Julia moaned. "Not a pizza snob. Spare me, please. I really don't care where we go, I just need to get out of this house tonight. I'm getting cabin fever."

"I know," Ellis said meaningfully. "It's been a long day."

"I've got a better idea than pizza anyway," Julia announced. "What about that place up the road, Tortuga something? The menu is in that notebook of yours, Ellis, and it looks pretty good. But more to the point, did you know they've got a beach-volleyball court in the back of that place?"

"Since when do you play beach volleyball?" Ellis asked.

"I don't, but guys do," Julia replied, waggling her eyebrows. "Hot, sweaty, tanned, ripped, buff guys. And did I mention shirtless? Yes, shirtless. Mmmm. How does that sound?"

"I'm in," Dorie said breathlessly.

"Dorie!" Ellis exclaimed.

"What? Look, I'm pregnant, not dead. This all-girl stuff is fine as far as it goes, but my hormones are friggin' raging out of control right now. I just want to engage in a little harmless spectator leering. Is that so wrong?"

"I wouldn't mind staring at some man-candy myself," Madison admitted. "Take my mind off my worries."

Ellis was leafing through her notebook. "Here it is," she cried triumphantly. "Tortugas' Lie! Two-for-one weeknight appetizers. But we've got to get there before seven."

"It's twenty 'til," Julia announced, getting up from the table. "Let's roll!"

They ordered steamed shrimp and crab, conch fritters, and Baja fish tacos, and ate all of it from paper plates, sitting on the wooden bleachers overlooking the restaurant's sand volleyball court, where a dozen shirtless men, as promised, jumped and spiked and dove and joked and hollered.

"Ah," Julia said, sniffing the air appreciatively. "The sweet smell of testosterone." She took a long swig from her lime-spiked Corona and tilted up the brim of the straw cowboy hat she'd grabbed on her way out the door.

"Y'all, I have a confession to make."

"This'll be good," Ellis told Madison under her breath.

"I folded. I called Booker this morning and invited him down for the weekend."

"Yay!" Dorie clapped her hands. "When's he coming?"

"He's driving down after work tomorrow. I hope nobody minds."

"Not me," Ellis said. "Does this mean you're considering his offer?"

"Offer?" Madison said.

"Booker has been begging Julia to marry him for the past year. He's taken a job as art director for a magazine in DC," Dorie explained. "He wants to buy a house and get married."

"And knock me up," Julia said dryly. "And no, this does not mean you guys should start shopping for bridesmaids' dresses. It just means that we haven't seen each other in over a month. A girl has needs, you know."

"When the trailer is a-rockin', don't come a-knockin'," Dorie quipped happily.

"Actually," Julia added, "I think he's just as interested in seeing the house as he is me."

"Which house?" Madison asked.

"Our house. The one we're staying in. Ebbtide. I've been e-mailing him the pictures I've been taking of all of us with my cell phone, and for some reason, he's fascinated with the place. I'd suggested maybe we'd want to get a hotel room, just for the weekend, you know, but Booker says he's dying to see the house. If you guys don't mind him staying with us."

"I think we might all feel a little safer with a guy around," Dorie said, and Madison nodded her agreement.

"He'd better get a good look at the house while he's here," Ellis said glumly. "Ebbtide is in foreclosure. If Ty doesn't find a way to catch up on his payments by September fifteenth, the bank will auction it off on the courthouse steps."

"What's Ty got to do with Ebbtide?" Julia asked.

Ellis smiled enigmatically. "Turns out Ty Bazemore is actually Mr. Culpepper. He owns the place! His mother's family built the house in the thirties, and Ty bought it last year from his uncle, who'd inherited it. He's been living in the garage apartment, renting out the big house, trying to raise enough money to fix it up and keep it. But then the economy went to hell, and now, if he doesn't figure something out, he'll lose it."

"Garage boy is actually Mr. Culpepper?" Dorie repeated. "Why didn't he just tell you that from the beginning?"

Ellis shrugged. "He says he never tells the tenants that he lives on the property, because then they'd be pestering him night and day. He does all the rentals, all the communication by e-mail, like he did with me. That way, he can concentrate on doing his stock research and trading."

"Hey," Julia said. "You never did tell us how your date went last night. Come on, give. And don't you dare leave out the sexy bits."

Eventually, the sun went down, and the volleyball players, sweaty and covered in sand, retreated into the bar to be joined by hordes of girlfriends and thirsty college kids.

"Where to now?" Julia asked, shouting to be heard over the din.

Ellis hesitated. "Ty mentioned that they're having some kind of special promotion at Cadillac Jack's tonight, for a new citrus-flavored vodka. Cheap drinks and karaoke. You, know, if anybody's interested."

"Karaoke? Hmm," Julia said. "So corny."

"So fun!" Dorie insisted. "Come on, you guys. Let's go. I'm finally starting to get some energy again. And I love karaoke. You guys can party and not worry. I'll be the designated driver."

Twenty minutes later, they were pulling into the parking lot at Caddie's. A huge hot-pink canvas banner fluttered from the front of the building. PUCKER-UPPER NITE, it proclaimed. PUCKERADE COCKTAILS, $2.

"I can't wait to see what goes into a Puckerade cocktail," Julia said as they elbowed their way into the crowded bar.

"There's Ty," Dorie said, pointing towards the bar. "Come on, let's get a table." She gave Ellis a gentle push in that direction. "Let him know we're here, and order us some drinks, okay? See if they can make me something without any booze, will you?"

"Well, hello," Ty said, when Ellis finally managed to slither through the three-deep row of women pressed up against the bar. "How about a Pucker-Upper? Tastes like shit, if you ask me, but these women seem to be lapping them up."

And it was true, it seemed that each woman in the crowd was clutching, or sucking from, a yellow, vaguely lemon-shaped plastic orb with a straw sticking out of the top.

"Okay," Ellis said. "Three Pucker-Uppers, and something nonalcoholic for Dorie."

Ty handed her one of the lemon cups, and Ellis, feeling suddenly overcome with shyness, took a long drink. And then another.

"Not so bad," she pronounced.

"The others came too?" Ty asked, obviously pleased. "Even Madison?"

"Even Madison," Ellis nodded. "Hey, thanks for letting us use your computer. It looks like Madison may be in more trouble than we knew. According to the Philly paper, it looks like the police back in Jersey want to talk to her about the money her husband embezzled from the insurance company where she worked. There's sort of a reward out for her."

"You really think somebody might come looking for her? Is it safe?"

"I'm not sure," Ellis admitted. "Madison's friend from work, a guy named Adam, is somehow mixed up in all this stuff, and he's supposedly on his way here to see her. I'm a little worried because he knows she's staying at Ebbtide. Not the address, exactly, but he does know the street name and the name of the house. So yeah, I don't want to sound too paranoid, but I'm actually a little worried."

Ty frowned. "I've got a friend who's a sheriff's deputy, Connor Terry. In fact, he's working the door tonight. I could ask him to roll past the house in his county cruiser, keep an eye out."

"Could you?" Ellis said gratefully. "That would make me feel a lot better."

"Sure, no problem," Ty said. "Where you sitting? I'll send Nella over with the drinks as soon as she comes back."

Ellis reached for her pocketbook to pay, but Ty shook his head. "On the house," he said.

Julia took a cautious sip of her drink. "Not bad," she admitted.

Madison sipped, but made a face, pushing the souvenir cup away. "Kinda tastes like lemon Pledge, if you ask me."

"It's okay," Ellis said, working on her second drink of the night. "Anyway, the price is right."

"Ooh, free drinks," Julia drawled. "Aren't you clever, shagging the bartender?"

"I am not . . ." Ellis started, and then dissolved into a fit of Pucker-Upper fueled giggles.

"Yet," Dorie said, hopefully.

"Yet," voted Madison, suddenly realizing how much she enjoyed the company of these women, how much fun it was to tease Ellis, and yes, even to bait Julia.

An hour later, their tabletop was littered with yellow plastic Pucker-Upper cups. Karaoke had started, and three sunburnt chicks wearing UNC-Greensboro T-shirts stood on the postage-stamp-sized stage, arms locked around each other's shoulders, swaying as they shrieked a drunken, tuneless version of "Lady Marmalade."

"Sounds like a cat got skinned," Madison complained. "Voulez vous shut the fuck up?"

"Think you can do better?" Julia retorted.

"Not a chance," Madison said. "I'm a wanted woman, remember?"

"Ellis!" Dorie cried. "You have to. Please?"

"Who, me?" Ellis laughed. "You know me better than that. As far as I'm concerned, karaoke is strictly a spectator sport."

"Don't look at me," Julia warned. "This was your idea, not mine."

"Spoilsports," Dorie said, pretending to pout. "Y'all are no fun anymore."

So they stayed, and drank, and danced as a pack, even persuading Madison, once, to join them in the Electric Slide, and Ty kept sending drinks over, and Ellis kept glancing over her shoulder to watch him in action behind the bar. He was so fine, she thought. So fine. And mine.

In the end, it was Dorie's bladder, not exhaustion, that did them in. "Y'all," she complained, hopping from one foot to another. "The line to the ladies room is like twenty people long."

"Oh, just go in the men's room," Julia grumbled. "There aren't hardly any men here tonight. No *straight* men, that is."

"There's twice as many girls in the men's room line," Dorie said. "Come on, y'all, if I don't get out of here right this minute, I'm gonna pop."

"Might as well," Ellis said, getting somewhat unsteadily to her feet. "They close at two. C'mon, Julia, let's get little mama home."

She tried to catch Ty's eye as they were leaving the club, but there was still a crowd standing at the bar, and Dorie was tugging at her, urging her to hurry.

When they got back to Ebbtide, Dorie pulled the red van almost to the edge of the porch, put the car in park, and jumped out and raced for the front door, fumbling for her keys as she went.

Madison hesitated, getting out of the backseat of the van. She looked up at the silent house, and the dull, yellow glow of the porch light they'd left burning, and then back again at the end of the driveway, bathed in a pool of pale white from the street lamp. No cars drove past. It was eerily quiet, except for the thrum of cicadas.

For the tenth time, she pulled her cell phone from her purse to check for missed calls. Nothing. She frowned.

Ellis climbed out of the van in time to see Madison tuck her phone away.

"Maybe Adam changed his mind," she offered.

"He should have been here by now," Madison fretted. "Something's wrong. I just know it. It's not safe. If Don figures out I'm here . . ."

"He won't," Ellis assured her. "Anyway, Ty is friends with a sheriff's deputy here. He was actually working the door at Caddie's tonight. Ty promised he'd get the guy to drive past the house tonight and tomorrow in his sheriff's cruiser. You know, just in case."

"A sheriff's deputy?" Madison shrugged. "I guess it couldn't hurt."

"Anybody hungry?" Dorie asked hopefully, standing in the kitchen doorway.

"After all that stuff we ate tonight?" Madison shook her head. "I guess you really are eating for two now."

"She's always been like that," Julia said. "Ever since she was a kid. Eats like a little piggy and never gains an ounce."

"What did you have in mind?" Ellis asked. "Have we got any dessert?"

"Fudgsicles and some store-bought pound cake and some strawberries," Dorie reported.

"Okay, you talked me into it," Julia relented. "All that dancing we did tonight has to have burned off a boatload of calories. And I'll run off the rest in the morning."

"I'm in," Ellis said. "Madison?"

"Not me," Madison said. "I'm turning in." She turned and headed for the stairway, but then stopped, and came back into the kitchen.

"Hey, ladies," she said shyly. "Thanks. I had a good time tonight. So thanks . . . for everything. Really. In case I forget to tell you tomorrow."

Julia managed a crooked smile. "And Madison? I really am sorry about the, you know, uh . . ."

"Break-in?" Madison shrugged. "What break-in?"

Julia groaned and pushed away the half-eaten bowl of strawberries and cake. "Gawwd. Why did I let y'all talk me into eating this mess? I'm going to bed. Booker will be here tomorrow, and I've got to get my beauty sleep."

"I'm coming too," Dorie said, stacking the bowls in the sink. "You, Ellis?"

"I'll be along," Ellis said casually. "I think I'll just tidy up in here a little bit." It was after two, and she'd promised Ty she'd wait up for him. She had her cell phone on the counter, and kept eyeing it, waiting for his text.

"You don't fool me, Ellis Sullivan," Julia said, yawning again. "You're waiting for a call from garage guy."

"Actually," Ellis admitted, "he said he'd text me when he was leaving the club."

Julia gave Dorie an elaborate wink. "She's gonna have to pay for all those free drinks one way or another."

"You're such a romantic, Julia," Dorie said. She grabbed Julia's hand and tugged. "C'mon. I'll race you for the bathroom."

38

Alone in the kitchen, Ellis washed, dried, and put away the dishes. She smiled as she traced the faded pattern of green leaves and pink rose-buds on the delicate gold-edged china. Such a sweet gesture on Ty's part, giving them his grandmother's dishes.

It was nearly 2:30 in the morning. To kill time, she got a bottle of spray cleaner and spritzed all the counters. Then she swept the floor, and finally, took the damp dish towel out to the back porch to dry on the makeshift clothesline the girls had rigged up between the weathered gray porch posts.

It was still unbelievably hot and humid outside. She glanced at the rusted Sunbeam Bread thermometer tacked to the wall beside the kitchen door. Eighty-six degrees! Still, she thought, glancing up at the deep, velvet sky, the stars were so plentiful and bright this time of night. Maybe she'd take a walk on the beach while she waited for Ty. She'd read a magazine article about how summertime was the season when sea turtles lumbered ashore all along the East Coast to lay eggs, and had even seen signs on the beach warning people not to disturb the turtle nests. Wouldn't it be amazing if she came across a nest of sea turtle eggs? She ducked back into the house, grabbed her cell phone, and strolled down the boardwalk over the dunes.

Leaving her shoes at the bottom of the beach staircase, Ellis let her feet sink into the cool, damp sand. The tide was out. She walked to the water's edge, letting the incoming waves tickle her ankles. She inhaled deeply, taking in the scent of salt and sun-baked sand, and started walking north, confident that she would not get lost or panicked this time.

She walked for fifteen minutes, zigzagging between the waterline and the dunes, before she saw it: two wavy, parallel lines in the sand, which crossed in a X shape, leading up to a sort of crater shape in the soft sand at the edge of a dune.

Ellis tiptoed over to the crater. The sand here had clearly been disturbed. Had she found a turtle nest? She looked back towards the water, wondering about the odd X-shaped lines, until it occurred to her that if she had indeed discovered a nest, maybe one track was from the turtle, making its way up to the dune line, and the other was the turtle's return track to the ocean.

She knelt in the soft sand and peered down at the impression in the sand, holding her breath, as though even the softest sound might disturb what was under the sand. Should she touch it if it was a nest? And if it was a nest, and she did touch it, would that deter the mother sea turtle from returning to tend to its eggs? She frowned, wishing she knew more. She really wanted to feather the sand aside, to see if, by some miracle, there could be eggs there. She straightened and looked around, but the beach was deserted. As she looked up, she felt a drop of water on the back of her neck.

It had started to rain. Reluctantly, she stood up, brushing sand from her knees. She looked around for something to mark the nest, so that she could find it again in the morning. Finding a piece of a windbreak, she managed to wrench off a weathered wooden stake, and poked it into the sand a few inches from the nest.

"Okay, turtle babies," she whispered, as the rain began to fall harder. "I'll check back with you little guys later, okay?"

As she trotted back through the rain, she heard her cell phone ping, and looked down at the text message there.

I'M HERE. WHERE ARE U?

Ellis smiled, tucked the phone back into her pocket to keep it dry, and picked up her pace.

She was soaking wet and out of breath as she climbed the last step to the garage apartment deck. The light was on inside, and she tapped on the door. Ty opened it and laughed when he saw her bedraggled condition.

"Get lost again?" he asked, pulling her inside and out of the rain.

"No," she said excitedly. "I was walking on the beach, and I saw these tracks in the sand. Ty, I think maybe I found a sea turtle nest!"

"Really? Cool. This is definitely nesting season. Were there any eggs in it?" He disappeared into another room and came back with a dry towel.

"Thanks." She started toweling off her arms and her hair. "I was afraid to disturb it. I mean, I know sea turtles are endangered, and I didn't know if it was against the law to tamper with a nest, so I just found a piece of wood and stuck it down in the sand to mark it. If it really is a nest, maybe I can find it in the morning and check it out."

"You did the right thing," Ty said approvingly. "Did you notice what mile marker the nest was near?"

"It was at number seventeen," she said proudly.

"I'm sure it'll be fine," Ty said. "I'll call the Sea Turtle Patrol hotline and let them know you found it, and they'll cordon it off and monitor it. Sometimes, if they find a nest in a high-traffic area, they'll even move it to a safer place, where it won't get disturbed."

Ellis's face glowed with excitement. "We could go back now, couldn't we? And just shift the sand a little, to see if there are any eggs?"

He gestured towards the deck. "In this rain?"

She looked out the window and saw that the rain was coming down in sheets now.

"Oh," she said, sounding deflated. "I guess maybe not."

She looked down at the floor, where a small puddle of rainwater had formed beneath her feet, and shivered.

"You're cold," he said, and he ducked into the next room. When he came back, he was holding a faded, navy blue terry cloth bathrobe.

"Here," he said, handing it to her. "You're soaked. Get out of those clothes, and I'll put the kettle on. And," he said, sternly, "don't give me that look. I'm not gonna jump you, for God's sake. I'm not that kinda guy."

Ellis laughed despite herself. "How do you know I'm not that kind of girl?"

"Some things you just know," Ty said.

She went into the adjoining room, his bedroom, and closed the door. She looked around with interest. The walls here were the same bleached-out cedar as the exterior of the apartment. The wooden floors were painted battleship gray, covered with a faded red-and-white-striped rag rug. The bed was a double with a lumpy mattress, but it was tidily made up with a quilt of blue-and-red patchwork stars. A standing fan in the corner stirred the air in a desultory way.

Ellis stripped off her wet clothes. She went into the adjoining bathroom, found another towel, and finished drying herself off before folding herself into the oversized bathrobe, inhaling its perfume of aftershave. The bathroom was tiny, with a scarred linoleum floor, a miniscule wall-hung sink, and a commode. She gazed into the cloudy mirror and fluffed her damp hair, finger combing it away from her face. She squeezed a dollop of Ty's toothpaste onto her index finger, and scrubbed her teeth as best she could.

Tonight, she thought, shivering in anticipation. She placed her wet clothes on the towel rack, belted the robe snugly, and padded barefoot out into the living room.

"Here," Ty said, handing her a heavy china mug. "I don't have any milk or anything. How about some honey?"

"Honey would be good," Ellis said. She watched as he pulled a plastic bear-shaped bottle from the shelf of the Hoosier cupboard and drizzled honey into the cup. And before she could stop him, he added a healthy slug of Jack Daniel's from a bottle he had standing on the counter.

"Hot toddy," he said, handing the cup back. He picked up his own mug, and steered her towards the sofa.

She sat down and took a sip of the steaming tea, enjoying the sweet burn of the whiskey. Ty sat beside her. She propped her bare feet up on a coffee table made from a battered ship's hatch, and snuggled into his arms. The robe slipped open at the hem, but Ellis decided she didn't care. Tonight.

"Long night," Ty said, as he yawned.

"Long day. All that drama with Julia burglarizing Madison's room. I really thought she was gonna tear Julia limb from limb," Ellis said. "I think maybe we're okay now, though."

"Good," Ty said, yawning elaborately again. "I saw you guys dancing together. It looked like you were having fun with the Electric Slide."

Ellis blushed. "It was all those Pucker-Uppers you kept sending over."

"Just trying to keep the ladies happy," Ty said nonchalantly.

She turned and looked at him. "You did." After a moment she said, "Ty?"

"Hmm?" He kissed the top of her head, and they yawned in unison.

"This is kinda nice," Ellis said, after a long, companionable silence. His hand found its way inside the neckline of the robe, and he was stroking her bare collarbone. She closed her eyes, savoring the warmth of his skin on hers. This, this was what she'd been missing all these years. She felt warm and safe and . . . cared for.

"Mmm-hmmm," Ty said. "Ellis?"

"Mm-hmm?"

"Do you think this could be our do-over date?"

"Kind of a weird date, don't you think?"

"Yeah, but it's nicer than our first one."

"That's true." She put her head on his shoulder and yawned sleepily.

"So, that would make this, like, our third date, if you count the first do-over."

"Whatever."

Her eyelids drooped, and he gently removed the mug from her hand.

A lifetime later, she stirred, and turned her head because the sun was shining in her eyes. She stretched luxuriously, and then, startled, sat up. She was stretched out on the sofa, with the blue-and-red patchwork quilt tucked around her, and sunlight was streaming in through the slats of the wooden blinds.

She walked to the bathroom, washed her face, and squeezed another line of toothpaste onto her finger and applied it to her teeth. The clothes she'd peeled out of the night before were laid out on a wooden bench at the foot of the empty bed, still damp. She shrugged. So much for her big plans for last night. What a dud she was. Tightening the belt of the bathrobe, she went back to the living room. The computer was on, and there was a stack of papers and books beside it.

Ellis opened the screen door to the deck. Ty was looking out at the ocean, his back to her, with the wind blowing his sun-streaked blond hair. His baggy white boxers rode low on his lean, tanned hips, and his bare shoulders gleamed in the sunlight, muscles rippling just beneath the skin as he lazily raised his arms and did a full stretch. Oh God, he was so gorgeous. She could see the outline of his butt through the thin white cotton of his boxers, and she was so aroused, and so surprised by how aroused she was, it took her breath away. And then he turned, caught her watching him, and his lips did that slow, secret-smile thing. Just for her.

"Mr. Culpepper?" Ellis said.

"That's me," Ty said, opening his arms. "What can I do for you?"

"I'm sorry about last night," she said, snuggling up to his bare chest. "Please don't take it personally. It was all that booze. I can't believe I just passed out on you like that."

"Entirely my fault," Ty told her. "But I think I know how you can make it up to me."

He took her hand and led her into the bedroom. "I'm gonna need that robe back," he said, stretching out on the bed.

"Right now?"

He nodded solemnly. "Afraid so."

Her fingers fumbled as she tried to unknot the belt. Damn it! She could do this. She'd been ready to do it last night. Why was she so nervous now—in the daylight? She had done it before, hadn't she? Ty tugged at the belt and pulled her down till she was sitting on the edge of the bed beside him. "Allow me," he said. "I have some experience with this type of thing."

"I bet you do."

He had the grace to blush. "I meant, it's my robe. That's all. It was a high school graduation present."

"From Kendra?" She regretted it the minute the words were out of her mouth.

But Ty seemed unfazed. "No, from my nana. Mrs. Culpepper."

"Ohhh," Ellis said.

Ty unknotted the robe and slipped it from her shoulders, running his hands down her shoulders, to her bare hips, pulling her closer. He cupped her breast in one hand, lowered his head and kissed it delicately. Ellis shivered, and he gathered the other breast and did the same. Was this really happening, at last?

He looked down at her and smiled. "You're beautiful, you know that, Ellis Sullivan?"

She shivered again, and felt suddenly shy. "You're just saying that."

"No," he shook his head. "I've thought it since the first time I spotted you the day you moved in here. You're gorgeous. Especially now. Especially naked. Naked, you're a goddess."

She laughed, and then his face grew serious. He pulled her down beside him, and his lips found hers. But then his hand inched lower, touching her between her legs with feather-soft stokes, and she grew dizzy as her body remembered long-forgotten pleasures. He touched her, and she arched up to meet him, and her body throbbed in a way she was sure it had never done before.

Ty flicked his tongue across her nipple, and she heard herself gasp. She trailed her fingers down his chest, lightly, lightly, until they rested just below the waistband of his boxers. She felt him shudder, and she slid her hands down his hips and effortlessly rolled the boxers down to his ankles. He kicked them free of the bed, rolled to one side, and fumbled for something in the nightstand beside the bed.

He held the foil-wrapped package so she could see it. "Ellis Sullivan, are you usually the kind of girl who does this on a fourth date?" he asked, his gray-blue eyes twinkling.

"Not usually," she told him truthfully, taking the condom from him and ripping the foil. "But in your case, I'm willing to make an exception."

39

Ellis was relieved to see that the red van was gone. She unlocked the front door and tiptoed into the house. She'd almost made it to her bedroom when Julia's bedroom door opened and she popped her head out.

Julia's glance took in Ellis's disheveled appearance, the borrowed bathrobe, and the armful of Ellis's own, damp clothing. "So," she grinned approvingly. "It finally happens. Ellis Sullivan does the walk of shame. Wish Dorie were here to enjoy it with me."

"Shut up," Ellis said happily. "Where is Dorie?"

"You won't believe it," Julia said. "Remember that bouncer at Caddie's last night? Ty's friend Connor?"

"Ty mentioned him, but I didn't get to meet him," Ellis said.

"No, but Dorie apparently did get to meet him at some point last night, and make a favorable impression," Julia said. "He 'dropped by' a little while ago, allegedly to check on our security, but actually to check out Dorie. You should see this dude! Six-four, and bald as a billiard ball."

"Allegedly?"

Julia's lips pressed together with barely suppressed mirth. "I realize that you've been a little, ahem, *preoccupied* today, but yes, if you'd seen the way he looked at her, you'd know he's definitely interested in Dorie."

"Oh, come on, Julia," Ellis said, leaning on the bathroom doorjamb. "Does everything always have to be about men with you?"

"Me!" Julia said with a wicked cackle. "I'm not the one who snuck out after midnight and came strolling home at noon wearing nothing but a smile and her boyfriend's bathrobe."

"Ty's not my . . ." Ellis stopped in midsentence. If Ty wasn't her boyfriend, what was he, and what did that make her, since she had just spent the whole delicious morning in his bed?

"You still haven't told me where Dorie is," she said, changing tack.

Julia rolled her eyes. "You haven't been listening. She's gone off with Connor Terry. He was driving his county unit, and even though he's off duty, there's some kind of rule against civilians riding in a cop car. Unless they're under arrest. So she was following him in the van. Of course, they left here three hours ago, so God knows where they've gone now. Or what they're up to," she added hopefully.

"You have a one-track mind, Julia Capelli," Ellis said primly. "A smutty one-track mind. And I, for one, am headed for the shower."

"What?" Julia said mockingly. "You and Ty didn't shower off together?"

Ty had, in fact, strongly suggested a communal shower. But since the garage apartment's shower consisted of a tiny wooden stall on the deck overlooking the beach, with only a slatted wooden door separating a bather from the beach, and said beach was already teaming with summer sun-seekers, Ellis had firmly assured him that she would just as soon shower at Ebbtide, thank you very much.

"Next time," Ty had said, reluctantly, his hand just barely brushing her breast as he handed her the robe. "It's got hot water and everything."

Ellis shivered with delight at the thought of the next time. And the next. How had she gone this long without sex? And how could she have mistaken what she had with Ben for what she had with Ty? And when could she have it again?

. . .

Ellis was slipping a clean T-shirt over her head when her cell phone rang.

"Hey," she said, feeling unaccountably shy.

"Hey," Ty said. "Listen, I completely forgot we were supposed to go check on that sea turtle nest you found last night."

"Oh, my gosh, you're right," Ellis said. "I guess, uh, with everything else . . ." Looking in the mirror over her dresser she saw that her face was in flames.

"Yeah, I guess you could say something came up," Ty laughed. "And now, damn it, I've got to go in to Caddie's. I can't afford to turn down a shift right now. So, if I give you the Turtle Patrol number, can you call them and tell 'em where to find it?"

"Absolutely," Ellis said, scrabbling around in the drawer of her nightstand for a pencil and paper.

"Great," Ty said. "I'll call you later, okay?"

"Okay," Ellis said.

"You doing anything tonight?" he asked.

"Only if you want to," Ellis said.

"I want."

Julia and Ellis were sitting on the porch when Madison came pedaling down the driveway towards Ebbtide.

"We're gonna go grab some lunch," Julia said casually. "Wanna come?"

"No thanks," Madison said, mostly out of habit. And then, "Oh, hell. Who am I kidding? I'm starved. Where did you have in mind?"

"Let's just cruise down the main drag and see what looks good," Ellis suggested.

"That place," Madison said, when they'd driven a couple miles north on Croatan Highway. She was pointing at a roadside diner. BOB'S GRILL, the sign said in large letters, and in even larger letters, EAT AND GET THE HELL OUT.

"I've been riding my bike past that joint for two weeks, laughing my ass off every time," Madison said. "Breakfast all day. Let's check it out."

They ordered Diet Cokes and perused the menus. Ellis decided on the

Southwestern omelet, with sour cream, extra salsa, and bacon, Madison ordered a club sandwich, and Julia, reluctantly, asked for scrambled eggs, one slice of dry whole wheat toast, and a bowl of melon. "I got an e-mail from my agent, and he's booked me for a JCPenney catalog shoot the first week of September," she said gloomily. "Holiday and midpriced resort wear. Week after next."

Ellis felt a pang of panic. Only one more week of August. One more week of Ebbtide. One more week with Ty.

"You don't sound too excited," Madison observed.

Julia shrugged and sipped her Diet Coke. "It's work. I've got to make a living. It's as simple as that."

"Not really," Ellis said. "You hate modeling. You told us yourself. Booker wants to marry you. He makes a good living, and he'd support you no matter what you decide to do next."

Julia looked over at Madison, who was busy shredding her paper napkin. "Would you tell her, please? Tell her what happens when you get married to somebody just to keep a roof over your head? What happens when you sell yourself?"

"Julia!" Ellis said sharply, her face burning with embarrassment for Madison.

But Madison didn't look angry or embarrassed. "Is that what you think I did?" she asked, rubbing her bare arms absentmindedly.

"Didn't you? That was the impression you gave us when you talked about Don Shackleford," Julia said.

"My mistake wasn't in marrying Don," Madison said. "It was in falling in love with him. My mistake was lying to myself about what he was, and then, when it became painfully clear what he was, in telling myself that I could change him. My timing really sucked," she said, laughing ruefully. "I didn't decide to leave him until the minute he decided he would never let me leave."

Julia sat back in the diner booth and looked blankly at the woman opposite her. The woman who'd been living in their third-floor bedroom for the past three weeks, an enigma personified, was suddenly baring her soul as casually as she'd just ordered lunch.

"Deep down, I knew Don for what he was," Madison went on. "And if I'm being brutally honest, I probably suspected he was married when we met. Even though I always talked the talk about not dating a married man. The signs were there. I just chose to ignore them."

"That doesn't make you a bad person," Ellis said, feeling suddenly loyal.

"Nope, just an incredibly stupid one," Madison agreed. "I think Amy Shackleford was probably ecstatic I took Don off her hands. She got the money, and she didn't have to live with him. Smart lady."

Madison stopped fiddling with her paper napkin. She leaned across the table and stared directly at Julia. "You're a smart lady too, Julia. If you love this guy, if you want to be with him, and make a life with him, do that. Stop worrying about your mother's marriage, or mine, or anybody else's. Life is too damned short. . . ."

"I'm only thirty-five," Julia protested. "I've got plenty of time."

Madison raised one eyebrow. "And how old is Booker?"

The waitress arrived with a tray full of food. She set their meals down. Julia took one look at the scrambled eggs and dry toast and handed it back to the waitress.

"Sorry, but I changed my mind," she said. "I'll have the breakfast burrito with cream cheese and crabmeat, a side order of country sausage. And a biscuit. A big ol' biscuit. With butter and jelly."

She looked at Ellis and Madison.

"I decided you two might be right," she said simply. "Life's too short to eat dry toast. I'm still working on the rest."

Ellis waited as long as she could, and then took a bite of her omelet. "I'm sorry," she said. "It's terrible, with all that's happened. But I can't help it. I am truly about to faint from hunger."

"Go ahead," Madison said, waving airily. "I'm hungry myself." She lifted the edge of the top layer of toast, and delicately salted the deep red tomato.

"Not as hungry as Ellis," Julia said mischeviously. "I think she probably skipped breakfast, but I'm not certain, since she never came back home last night."

Madison picked up a piece of bacon and nibbled. "Why, Ellis!" she said. "Congratulations."

40

"Well, hello," Ellis said, propping herself on her elbows and shading her eyes from the low-lying sun. "Where on earth have you been all day?"

Dorie giggled as she spread out a blanket on the sand beside her friend. "I've been . . . everywhere." She unloaded a *People* magazine, a tube of sunscreen, and a bottle of water from her tote bag.

"Alone?"

"Nope," Dorie said, "I've been with Connor. All day."

Ellis lowered her sunglasses and peered over them at Dorie. Her hair was windblown and her nose and cheeks were sunburnt. Over her bathing suit she wore an oversized T-shirt with the Dare County Sheriff's Department logo emblazoned on the front, and she had a black DCSD baseball cap jammed on her head.

"Is that so?"

"Yes, it is," Dorie said. She rolled up a beach towel, propped it under her head, opened her magazine, and began humming.

"Is that . . ." Ellis strained to catch the melody.

"Don't bother," Dorie said airily. "I guarantee you don't know it."

"Hum some more," Ellis ordered. It was an old game she and Baylor played as children on long family car rides. Their own version of *Name That Tune*, even though they were decades too young to have ever seen the old television show.

Dorie hummed another bar. "Give up?"

"Oh, all right," Ellis said. "What's the song?"

"'Crazy Ex-Girlfriend.' Miranda Lambert."

"Country music?" Ellis said in mock horror. "Since when?"

"Since today," Dorie said. "Connor loves country music. We went for a ride in his boat after lunch, and we listened to a country radio station. But not that old twangy 'my dawg died and my mama's in prison' crap. We listened to Miranda Lambert and Lady Antebellum and Big & Rich...."

"Hmmm," Ellis said.

Dorie looked up from her magazine. "What's that supposed to mean?"

"Nothing. Just hmmm. I mean, you just met this guy when he came roaring up in his police cruiser this morning, then you spend the entire day with him, and suddenly you're a country music expert. The next thing we know, you'll be picking out china patterns."

"Not funny," Dorie said, snapping the pages of her magazine. "He's a nice guy, that's all. And for your information, I'd met him earlier."

"How much earlier?"

"At the club," Dorie said, sniffing. "Ty introduced us when I was coming back from my ninth or tenth trip to the bathroom. He said he loved my Electric Slide, and he wanted to know if he could buy me a drink."

"And you said ... ?"

"I said, 'Hi, my name's Dorie. I'm not currently drinking alcohol because I'm four months pregnant, but I'm getting divorced. Are you a Virgo?"

"Hmm."

"Kidding!" Dorie said. "I didn't even give him my phone number. Anyway, you're the one who asked Ty to have his bouncer-slash-cop friend drive by the house, so this is really all your doing."

"Not my business," Ellis said.

"Look," Dorie said, slapping the magazine down on the blanket. "I'm not like you or Julia. Okay? I like guys. Always have. I like talking to them, hanging out with 'em. And I like sex. Always have. That doesn't exactly make me a dirty girl, you know."

"I know," Ellis said hastily. "I'm really not judging you. . . ."

"Good," Dorie said. "Connor is a decent guy. He makes me laugh. He's so different from Stephen. He's . . . uncomplicated. He says what he thinks. He loves country music, and riding around in his boat. He's got a Harley too. He likes his job. Loves his job, actually. I told him I'm gonna be living alone when I get back home, and he's offered to take me to the firing range and show me how to fire a gun. And I'm going to do it, damn it."

"You're sure this is not about being on the rebound from Stephen?" Ellis asked.

"Maybe, but I don't think so. Look, this sounds conceited, but you've known me my whole life. Guys come on to me. All the time. They just do. And you know I'm not doing anything to encourage them. Just since I've been up here, I've been hit on by the seafood manager at Food Lion, the pimply gross guy at the pizza place, even the pharmacist at Walgreens, for God's sake, when I was picking up my prenatal vitamins!"

Ellis sighed. "It's a fact. You're a man magnet."

"And I have totally blown off each and every one of those guys," Dorie said. "Just not interested. Until Connor. He really is different from those other guys. I'm not saying I want to marry him. But I would like to spend time with him, and see what comes of it."

"Did you tell him . . . ?"

"Yes," Dorie said, sounding exasperated. She pulled up the tank top and pooched out her tummy. "I really can't hide it in this bathing suit. And I didn't want to. I told him the short version. That I'm pregnant, and I'll be getting a divorce as soon as I get home."

"What was his reaction?"

"He was so sweet," Dorie exclaimed. "He's got a sister who's exactly the same number of weeks pregnant as me. It didn't seem to faze him a bit, Ellis. He's a little bit younger than us, but I swear, he's way more mature than Stephen could ever hope to be. So that's where we stand."

"Are you gonna see him again?"

"As a matter of fact, we're supposed to have dinner tomorrow night," Dorie said. "I know it all seems like this is happening pretty fast, but I'm only here for another week. I want to see how this plays out. And so does he. And there's just one more thing I've been thinking about."

"What's that?" Ellis asked warily.

"Well," Dorie said, giving her an exaggerated wink, "I can pretty much do whatever I want right now. You know, romance-wise."

"How's that?" Ellis asked.

"'Cuz I'm already knocked up!"

"Incorrigible," Ellis laughed. "Eudora the incorrigible. Anyway, I really, really hope this thing with Connor will work out."

"Because?" Dorie gave her a fishy look.

"Because I would just love to see the look on Phyllis's face the day you introduce her to your gun-totin', Harley-riding, country-music-loving, bald-headed cop boyfriend. I bet she'd blow a gasket."

"Definitely," Dorie agreed. "Plus I forgot to mention he only went to college for two years. And," she crowed. "Get this: Connor is Baptist."

"Oh yeah," Ellis said. "That'd put her in the grave for sure."

At some point, Ellis dozed off. When she awoke, it was nearly six, and Dorie was also, apparently, rousing herself from a catnap. The tide was coming in, and the languorous waves were lapping perilously close to their base camp.

Ellis stood and began to gather her belongings.

"Where you headed?" Dorie asked.

"Up to the house," Ellis said. "I've had enough beach for one day."

Dorie reached for her cell phone and checked the time. "Might want to give it another thirty minutes or so."

"Why's that?" Ellis asked, stowing her book and towel in her bag.

"I was up at the house for a potty break, around four o'clock, and Booker had just gotten in," Dorie said. "I think Julia was hoping for some 'quiet time.' "

"Gotcha," Ellis said. "I haven't seen Booker in ages. How is he?"

"He's okay. Still not what I expected for Julia. But nice. Kinda quiet. I guess I knew he was older, but maybe I forgot. His hair is totally gray, which I personally think is sexy as hell. Julia, for all her blasé attitude, was really, really excited that he was coming. After you guys got back from lunch she even went to that day spa down the street and got a pedicure and a Brazilian wax."

"Ow," Ellis said.

"Ditto," Dorie said. "Makes me glad I'm a natural redhead." She swung her head around and studied Ellis. "You ever get one of those?"

"Hell, no," Ellis said emphatically. "I don't even like to get my eyebrows waxed. I am definitely not letting some strange Vietnamese chick pour boiling wax on my girlie parts. Anyway," she added, "I really haven't needed to worry about landscaping that area of the territory until recently, if you get my drift."

Dorie grinned. "Until very recently, from what I understand."

"No comment," Ellis said. "I suppose Julia already spilled the beans?"

"Absolutely. What did you expect? Anyway," Dorie said primly, "I don't judge."

"Ha!"

But when Ellis and Dorie came trudging up the boardwalk towards the house, they were met by the sight of Booker, laying flat on his stomach on the deck, with a long-lensed camera, snapping photographs of the house, with Julia standing beside him, another camera lens in hand.

"Hey, Booker," Ellis said.

"Hey there," Booker said, looking up from the camera and giving her a brief smile before turning back to his camera.

"He's trying to shoot the back of the house before he loses the light," Julia explained.

"Okay," Ellis said. "We're going to head for the house, will we be in the way?"

"Not at all," Booker said. "In fact, it'd be good to have somebody in a few of the shots. When you get up to the porch, stand at the rail and look back towards me, if you would, please. But not at me, right?"

Dorie and Ellis got up to the porch and stood self-consciously for a moment, looking out at the dunes and the deepening twilight. A slight breeze bent the sea oats, and large dragonflies skimmed just over the waving fronds.

"It's so beautiful this time of day," Dorie said, pushing a strand of hair from her face. "I'm really gonna miss this place."

"Yeah, me too," Ellis said, feeling the now-familiar pang in her chest.

"I'm gonna miss you guys even more, when I get home," Dorie said. "I'd forgotten how much fun we always have. I've got friends at home, but it's different with you guys."

"Same here," Ellis said. "I really hate to see this month end."

"You could move back to Savannah," Dorie said impulsively. "We've got tons of banks in Savannah. And Willa's husband knows everybody in town."

Ellis smiled, and glanced over at the garage apartment. Ty's Bronco was gone, but he'd sent her a text telling her he was working at Caddie's again tonight.

"I think I'm done with banks, Dorie."

"Really? What are you gonna do for a job, then?"

"Haven't a clue," Ellis said. And for the first time in a long time, she realized that it had been many days since she'd clenched her teeth in panic about her future.

The smell of charcoal wafted from the back of the house. Ellis, her hair still wet from the shower, found Booker and Julia in the kitchen. Julia was shucking ears of corn from the farm stand down the beach road, and Booker was shooting pictures of Julia in the unlikely role of domestic goddess.

Ellis helped herself to a slice of tomato from a platter at Julia's elbow. "Are we shooting some kind of documentary?"

"Better," Julia said, her eyes shining with excitement. "Booker, the brilliant, brilliant love of my life, has a brilliant, brilliant scheme."

Booker chuckled. "You heard that, didn't you? I'm the love of her life? Not to mention brilliant?"

"I'm your witness," Ellis agreed, sitting at the kitchen table. "So what's the scheme?"

"What scheme?" Dorie said, wandering into the kitchen. She was dressed in a jade green tank top and matching loose-fitting drawstring pants, and her damp hair fell in a braid down her back. With her sun-speckled breasts spilling from the low-cut top, she looked like a modern mermaid.

Julia finished up the corn and wiped her hand on a dish towel. "You tell 'em, Booker."

"It's not really all that brilliant," he said modestly. "You know that Julia's been snapping photos of everything, the house, the three of you at the beach, everything she sees, really, since you got here. And she's been e-mailing them to me. Right?"

"Riiight," Ellis said.

"She's really a pretty talented amateur photographer," Booker said. "Of course, it makes sense, since she learned from the master. I know she's always had a fabulous eye, but those photos she sent were especially evocative."

"And I was only shooting with my cell phone," Julia interjected. "You know, just messing around, trying to show Booker where we were staying."

"Anyway, I forwarded some of her photos to a friend of mine, who works out in California."

"He's a location scout for the movies!" Julia said. "And Booker never told me a thing about him."

"I hadn't seen the guy in a couple of years," Booker said mildly. "We used to do some work together, when I was doing fashion shoots. Anyway, he was intrigued with Julia's photos."

"Especially the ones of Ebbtide," Julia said. "You guys, he thinks this house would be perfect for this movie he's working on. It's a chick flick, and I'm not allowed to say who all is in it, but let's just say *Legally Blonde, Pretty Woman, Miss Congeniality!*"

"Julia," Booker lowered his camera and gave her a reproving look. "They haven't actually all signed on yet, remember."

"I didn't mention any names," Julia said coyly.

"Anyway, Simon, my friend the location scout, has actually hired me to take scouting shots of the house, and the beach, and some of the nearby houses and businesses and things," Booker said. "I've already e-mailed the shots I did this afternoon, because he's meeting with the producers tomorrow. They're on a very tight production schedule because all these, um, unnamed actresses only have a brief window of availability. They were going to shoot at a beach house on the West Coast, but the art director hated all the houses they showed him. Too contemporary, too glitzy."

"But he loves how shabby and worn-out Ebbtide looks," Julia interrupted. "Of course, he hasn't seen the bathrooms."

"The movie is supposed to be set on Cape Cod, in the summer," Booker explained. "But all the houses they scouted there looked too elegant and old-money. Which brings us to Nags Head, and Ebbtide. If the producer likes what he sees, Simon will want to talk to your friend, Ellis, about the possibility of renting it for three or four months."

"For real?" Ellis asked. "When would they want it?"

"Right away, I imagine. Production is supposed to start September fifteenth. They want to wait until after Labor Day, when tourist season is over and crowd control won't be such an issue."

"Isn't that awesome?" Julia asked. "Won't Ty just flip over the idea?"

"Awesome," Ellis repeated. "If he can hang on to the house until then."

41

The dinner dishes had been cleared away, the last of the wine drunk. Booker had graciously accepted all the women's compliments for the dinner he'd masterminded: tuna steaks on the grill; chipotle-pepper-roasted corn on the cob; and risotto with green peas, asparagus, shallots, and basil. Dorie and Ellis spilled a five-hundred-piece jigsaw puzzle depicting the Cape Hatteras lighthouse onto the dining room table and declared their intentions of finishing it by midnight. Madison, who'd finally given in to their pleas, joined them for dinner, but declared herself hopeless at puzzles. For the first time since she'd been living in the house, she seemed at ease with the group.

"Come on, Book," Julia said, flipping him lightly with her dish towel. "I can't stand all this excitement. Let's take a walk on the beach."

She led him down the beach stairs and onto the sand. They left their shoes in the pillowy sand at the base of the steps and walked hand-in-hand out to the water's edge.

"Which way?" Booker asked.

"Hmm, north, I think," Julia said. "Cottage Row is just up ahead."

"What's that?"

"What's left of the original old houses built in Nags Head at the turn of the century," Julia said. "There were originally, like, a dozen or so houses. All of 'em wooden, like Ebbtide. They call them the 'unpainted aristocracy.' Ebbtide's not one of them. Ty told us his family had the house built in the 1930s."

They walked slowly, stopping to gaze at the stars, or just stand in the moonlight, looking up at the rows of houses, lit up with summertime occupants. Voices and the sound of a radio playing drifted down from the houses beyond the dunes.

"These are the oldest houses," Julia said, when they'd walked a little further. The houses were further apart here, sprawling wooden structures with outward-canted porches, their wooden walls gleaming a dull brownish-silver in the moonlight.

"Not very fancy," Booker said approvingly.

"Nope," Julia agreed. "From what Ty tells us, the old-time Nags Headers consider it crude to flaunt your money by fixing up your house or adding on a wing. Nothing at all had been done at Ebbtide in decades, until Ty bought it from an uncle and started trying to fix it up."

"You like it here," Booker said, sounding surprised.

"It has a certain charm that grows on you," Julia admitted. "At first, I was pretty grossed out by the place. I mean, I didn't want to hurt Ellis's feelings, since she did all the research and work of tracking down the house and getting it lined up and everything, but it was seriously skanky when we moved in."

"Not exactly the kind of beach house you're used to." Booker laughed, nudging her gently.

"We had a little bit of a rocky start," Julia said. "Ellis was being so... bossy. She even made up a chore chart for the kitchen, if you can believe it."

"And we all know how Julia Capelli deals with authority, now, don't we?" Booker said.

"We worked things out," Julia said. "Pretty much. It's been an interesting month, that's for sure."

"And what about you?" Booker asked. "What's been going on with you? Aside from the pictures and a couple phone calls, you've been surprisingly quiet for the past month, Julia."

"I know," she said, squeezing his hand. "You've given me a lot to think about."

"Come to any conclusions?"

"Some."

"Such as?"

Julia brushed her long hair back from her face. "I'm done modeling."

Booker nodded. "Have you told the agency?"

"Not yet. They've booked me for a JCPenney catalog shoot when I leave here. I guess I'll have to go ahead and do it, because I don't want to leave Jessica in the lurch. But that's it. No more."

"Sounds reasonable," Booker said.

"The girls think . . ." she started. "No, I think I'd like to try doing photo styling."

"You'd be a natural," Booker said. "You've been doing it on your own for years, anyway. I've always said you have the best eye in the business, Julia."

"I'd need your help," Julia said, giving him a sidelong glance. "You know everybody. The magazine people, the photographers, art directors."

"Not everybody," Booker said. "But I do have some resources."

"I know I'd have to start off as an assistant," Julia went on. "Doing the grunt work. Cataloging props, making coffee runs, ironing shirts and pillowcases."

"Not very glamorous," Booker said.

"I was thinking of asking Annette Joseph if she'd take me on," Julia said.

"Do I know her?"

"I met her at a catalog shoot in Miami last year," Julia said. "She works out of Atlanta, but she does a lot of work for shelter magazines, so she gets assignments all over the East Coast."

"Atlanta," Booker said, his face impassive.

"It makes sense because of the airport," Julia said.

"We have two airports in DC, you know."

"Hear me out," Julia said, taking a deep breath. "We could sell the flat in London."

Booker stopped walking. "You'd consider it?"

Julia swallowed hard. "If I'm not working in Europe, it doesn't make sense to keep it. I know the real estate market is crap right now, but Mayfair is so trendy, even in a down market we should be able to make a killing when we sell it."

"Or lease it, long-term," Booker said. "In case you change your mind."

"I won't," Julia promised. "I've been in a holding pattern for too long, avoiding the inevitable. London was wonderful, my work was exciting, but it isn't anymore. Hasn't been in a long time. You're here in the States. I want to be with you. It's that simple. I *have* missed you, Booker."

"Have you?" He put his arms around her waist and pulled her to him.

She wound her arms around his neck and kissed him fiercely. "I do love you, you know," she said, resting her forehead on his chest. "This month, at the beach, with everything the girls have been through, sort of forced me to stop and take stock of things. Dorie basically told me off the other day."

"Dorie? Sweet little Dorie?"

"Not so sweet if you really get to know her," Julia said ruefully. "And then, Madison, who barely knows me at all, said something at lunch today that kind of tipped the scale for me."

"And what was that?" Booker inquired, running his hands up the back of the thin cotton peasant top Julia was wearing, and kissing her neck.

"She kind of called me out," Julia said. "She said I couldn't keep making chickenshit assumptions about marriage based on other people's mistakes."

"Smart girl," Booker said, holding her closer.

"I guess . . ." Julia stopped and pulled away, but Booker had no intention of letting her go.

"You guess what?"

She turned, so that her back was to him. "I guess I don't think I deserve somebody like you. Somebody as good as you. Maybe that's why I keep trying to push you away."

"What?" He put his hands on her shoulder and wheeled her around. "What kind of crap is that?"

Julia shrugged and swallowed hard. She took a deep breath. "There are things about me . . . things you don't know."

He chortled. "We've lived together for nearly ten years. Tell me one thing about you that I don't know. Come on. I dare you."

She bit her lip. "The thing is . . . I got pregnant when I was eighteen. It was an ectopic pregnancy, Book. I only have one good fallopian tube. I don't know if I can have children." A tear rolled down her cheek. "I'm sorry. I should have told you years ago."

He traced the tear with the tip of his thumb. "And you think this is some kind of deal breaker for me? Julia, love. Is this the thing that's been eating at you all this time?"

She nodded sadly, the tears flowing nonstop now. "People think I'm this perfect model *thing*. But I'm not! It's all plastic! I've had my nose fixed, and my boobs done, and for all I know, I'm infertile, too."

"Stop that," Booker said sternly. "And listen to me. The only person who thinks you're plastic is you. You are the warmest, realest woman I have ever met. I don't give a damn about your nose or your fallopian tube, or your hammertoes or whatever. I fell in love with you, Julia Capelli. The whole package. And as far as I'm concerned, you are perfect. Hell, look at me. I'm pushing fifty. Maybe I'm infertile too. Yeah, I want kids. But only if you do too. So maybe we do this the modern way. Test tubes, petri dishes, adoption, I don't care. I just want you. Have you got that?"

Julia sniffed and nodded, slowly. She rested her cheek on Booker's shoulder, and surreptitiously rubbed her runny nose on his shirt. He rubbed her back reassuringly.

"Madison said I should just quit worrying about other people's lives, and get on with ours."

"I think I like that girl," Booker said, slowly working his thumbs under the edge of Julia's bra.

"And she reminded me that life is short, and nothing is guaranteed. Carpe diem, baby, you know?"

"Latin?" Booker said, with an exaggerated groan. "You know how turned on I get when you talk foreign."

"Grow up," Julia said. But she'd slipped her hands into the waistband of his shorts and was fully aware of how turned on Booker had gotten.

"I think," Booker said solemnly, "we had better turn back to Ebbtide so you can take advantage of me. I mean, how will we ever know if we can make babies unless we actually try?"

"Mmm," Julia said. "You're probably right. The house would be much more civilized than the beach. Wouldn't want to scare the seagulls."

They made it all the way back to the stairway at Ebbtide and sat on the bottom step to brush the sand off their feet.

"I hate to break this golden moment," Booker said finally. "But I can't help wonder how you're going to be with me in DC, and at the same time work in Atlanta."

Julia kissed his nose. "With the money we'll make from selling the London flat, I can rent something tiny and convenient in Atlanta. A pied-à-terre, if you will. I'll live full time in this amazing house you've bought us in Alexandria, and travel to shoots wherever I'm needed. Of course, this is all predicated on a couple of things. First off, I'll have to persuade Annette to give me a shot at learning the business."

"Not a problem. You're a very persuasive girl, in my experience."

"And then," Julia said, dusting the sand off her shorts and climbing onto Booker's lap, "I'll have to figure out how to plan a wedding before Dorie gets as big as an elephant and Ellis takes a new job God knows where. And since you've just started a new job, when will you be able to take some vacation time?"

"A wedding?" Booker mused. "Is somebody having a wedding?"

"We are, if you'll have me," Julia whispered. "Just name the date."

"Oh, I'll have you, my love," Booker said. "You'll just have to let me consult my calendar. It's upstairs. In your room."

42

Saturday morning, Ellis raced over to the garage apartment, bursting with the news about Booker's friend Simon, the movie location scout. But the Bronco was already gone.

She considered calling his cell, but decided against it. He could be anyplace, and she wanted to tell him the news in person. She fished the key Ty had given her out of the pocket of her shorts, and climbed the stairs to the apartment.

He'd obviously come in late the night before. A Styrofoam takeout tray sat on the table Ty used as a desk, along with an empty Corona bottle and a crumpled newspaper. A cereal bowl with a film of milk sat in the sink, along with a spoon and an empty juice glass. The counter was cluttered with a cereal box, empty orange juice carton, and a sugar bowl with a spoon stuck in it. A single fly buzzed lazily around, batting against the wire window screen.

Ellis walked into the bedroom. The quilt and bedcovers lay in a rumpled heap at the foot of the bed, and Ty's T-shirt and shorts were thrown on the floor, along with a still-damp towel.

She sighed happily and started to put the tiny apartment to rights. She washed and rinsed the dishes, putting them away in the Hoosier cupboard, and wiped off the gummy kitchen counter. She opened the door to the deck and swept what seemed like a pound of sand out the door and through the cracks in the deck boards, just as she remembered her mother sweeping out the houses they rented at the beach at Tybee during her childhood summers.

Ellis smiled contentedly as she stripped Ty's bed, gathering the sheets and discarded clothing into a bundle. She would wash them in the laundry room at Ebbtide, she decided, and surprise Ty when he got back from his errands.

As she was stepping out of the apartment onto the deck, a car came bumping down the Ebbtide driveway. It was a sleek dark gray Mercedes convertible, with a man at the wheel and a woman with long blond hair sitting beside him, her eyes shaded by a pale blue sun visor. The driver pulled the car directly up to the garage, as though he knew exactly where he was going.

Were these prospective renters for Ebbtide? Ellis wondered. Ty hadn't said anything about showing the house while she and the others were still in residence, but she assumed he'd want to rent the house out again as soon as they vacated the place next Saturday.

There was that stabbing feeling in her chest again. Vacate. Saturday was only a week away.

The woman got out of the convertible and looked up at Ellis in curiosity.

The blonde was Kendra. Ty's ex-wife. And the driver was Ryan, or as Ty referred to him, Fuckface.

"Hey there," the blonde called, waving. "Is Ty around?"

"Nope," Ellis said. "Haven't seen him this morning." She turned and went back inside the apartment. What should she do? Call Ty?

Before she had a chance to decide, she heard footsteps pounding up the wooden staircase, and a brisk knock at the door.

She opened it, and Kendra gave her a breezy smile. "Oh! It's you." She knit her brow, searching for the name. "Hi there, Ellen, right?"

"It's Ellis."

"Oh, right. So, I'm Kendra, and I guess you remember we met at Fish Food the other night. Kinda awkward, right, bumping into the ex like that?"

Ellis shrugged. "Ty's not here," she repeated. "I'm not sure when he'll be back."

Kendra's full red lips pouted. "I've been calling and calling, leaving messages. He never returns any of them. That's why we finally decided to run over here this morning, to see if we can talk to him about Ebbtide. You know, before next month."

"I don't know what to tell you," Ellis said. "He stays pretty busy. But I can let him know you dropped by." She gathered up the bundle of laundry and stepped outside onto the deck, locking the door behind her.

Ellis hurried down the stairs. Ryan had gotten out of the Mercedes and was walking around the outside of the garage, leaning down, poking at the boards, walking around inside the garage itself, staring up at the old rafters with the assortment of junk hanging from the beams: rusted lawn chairs, rotting hanks of rope, what looked like an old sail.

"Can I help you?" she called sharply. Fuckface had some nerve wandering around the place like he already owned it.

"Nope," Ryan said, immune to her tone. "Say, you have any idea how many square feet are in that apartment up there?"

"No," Ellis said woodenly.

"But it's got a kitchen, right, like an efficiency? And a bathroom? Is it a full or half bath? We're trying to figure out if the apartment would work out as income property. It's hell to get new bathrooms approved, is why I ask, so if there's an existing full bath up there, that would be awesome."

"Honey, I think I remember that it's got a sink and a toilet, with the shower out on the deck," Kendra called down.

Ellis whirled around. Kendra was not only still on the deck, she was actually peering in the glass insert in the door, her hands cupped to shut out the glare of the sunlight. "The kitchen's small, but it's got everything you'd need. We'd want to replace the appliances, and the linoleum would have to go right away too. New cupboards and countertops, of course. It might be worth a trip to IKEA for that stuff."

"Hey!" Ellis called. "I don't think Ty would appreciate having you poking around his apartment while he's gone."

"Okay," Kendra said. She came bopping down the stairs and joined her husband, who'd finished inspecting the garage. Ellis noticed that Kendra's sun visor was the exact same shade of Carolina blue as her sleek sleeveless top and running shorts. And, of course, her Carolina blue running shoes matched everything else she wore, including the scrunchy that held her long blond hair in a ponytail.

"Say, Alice . . ." Kendra started.

"It's Ellis. E-L-L-I-S."

"Right, sorry. Listen, you don't happen to know who's renting Ebbtide right now, do you?"

"No," Ellis lied.

"Hmm," Kendra said, turning to stare up at the house. A trio of damp bathing suits clipped to the clothesline stretched between the porch posts flapped in the breeze. As she watched, Booker emerged from the house with a camera slung around his neck.

"I really, really need to get a look inside the house, hon," Kendra told her husband. "Ty's nana was sweet, but she was really *not* much of a house-keeper, and God knows, Ty never cared about that kind of stuff. As long as the fish were biting or the surf was up, he didn't care what the house looked like."

She pursed her lips, still looking up at the house, thoughtfully. "Window air conditioners. And I'm sure there's no insulation, or even a furnace. Guess I'm not surprised. I don't think the Culpeppers ever did winterize the house." She gave Ellis a sad smile. "Ty's grandparents were the salt of the earth, but there was never much money there."

"Roof looks pretty bad too, sweetness," Ryan added. "We'd have to gut the place."

Ellis's stomach twinged at the word "gut." She wanted to grab the broom she'd recently abandoned and chase these two opportunists down the drive-way and off the Ebbtide property. Even though it wasn't her place, she felt strongly that Ty would approve of such a course of action.

Before she could suggest that Kendra and Fuckface vacate the premises, she was saved by the cheery chirping of Kendra's cell phone.

"Hi-i-i," Kendra said, her face brightening. "No, nope. He's not here. His *friend* says she doesn't know where he's gone, or when he'll be back. What's new about that, right? Probably off surfing with some of those lowlife buddies of his."

Kendra's caller talked for a while, and she listened intently. "No, we won't give up. I'll leave him another message, and if that doesn't work, we'll just check back later. I promise you, Daddy, when we hand him a check, he'll be happy to take it and walk away. Okay? See you at lunch, then."

She clicked disconnect and pocketed the phone. "So," she said brightly. "You'll be sure and tell Ty we came by?"

"As soon as I see him," Ellis promised.

Kendra turned to her husband. "Daddy wants us to meet them at the club for lunch. That leaves us a couple hours to kill. We could run up to Duck in the meantime. Bailey and Ferris have been pestering me to drop by and see what they've done to their place, and then we'd have an excuse to leave."

Ryan nodded enthusiastically, and without another word to Ellis, they jumped in the Mercedes and sped off.

Ellis watched them go, her fists clenched in rage. She marched herself back to Ebbtide, dumped her load of laundry into the washing machine, spun the dial, and punched the start button.

Late afternoon, and the house was eerily quiet. Booker had insisted on treating all of them, including Madison, who'd tried without success to beg off, to a late lunch at the Beach Grill.

When they were seated at a table overlooking the dunes, Booker gave Julia an ill-concealed wink. She produced a bottle of champagne from her big straw beach tote, and Booker stood up and tapped his water glass with a spoon.

The other diners in the restaurant turned, gave them a look of mild interest, and then turned back to the Braves baseball game they were watching on the big-screen television mounted over the bar.

Booker pulled Julia to her feet, and for the first time any of the girls could remember, Julia was actually blushing.

"I have an announcement to make," Booker said, wrapping an arm around Julia's waist and struggling to look serious.

"Yessss!" Ellis squealed.

"Oh, hell yeah!" Dorie squealed in unison.

"Quiet!" Julia demanded. "Have you no sense of decorum?"

The waitress returned to their table, bearing a tray of cloudy, water-spotted champagne glasses and a basket of individually wrapped saltine crackers. "Thank you," Booker said, dismissing her with a nod.

"Now, as I was saying," Booker continued. "As you may know, I have been pursuing this flower of southern womanhood, Julia Elizabeth Capelli, for well over a decade. And as you also know, your friend Julia has, thus far, refused—nay, scorned—my entreaties to allow me to make of her an honest woman."

"Boo!" Dorie booed.

"Hiss," Ellis hissed. "Get to the good part, would you?"

Julia rolled her eyes. "Now you know what I've been dealing with for all these years."

"Be that as it may," Booker went on, gesturing grandly. "Last night, under the influence of a full moon, not to mention nearly two bottles of very good French pinot gris, your friend, and my beloved, did me the great honor of agreeing to, at a date to be announced, make me the happiest man on earth. May I introduce to you all my fiancée, the future Mrs. Julia Capelli-hyphen-Calloway."

With that, Booker grabbed the champagne bottle and popped the cork, and with the champagne spewing over his hands, he clasped Julia and planted a huge, noisy kiss directly on her laughing lips, while Dorie, Ellis, and Madison cheered wildly.

The lunch that followed was the happiest, craziest, loudest meal Ellis could remember attending in recent memory.

Julia had finally, after much baiting and begging, agreed that the wedding would take place sometime in the fall. "Before you get too fat," she told Dorie, "and he," she said, turning fondly to Booker, "has time to change his mind and find another girl."

But Booker had more than one surprise up his sleeve, they soon discov-

ered. When their appetizers arrived, Julia stared down at her plate of cala-
mari, and finally, with a fork, picked up a vinaigrette-drenched ring—platinum,
with a band of small diamond chips surrounding an enormous, glittering
cushion-cut diamond.

"Booker!" Julia sputtered. "What the hell?"

Booker lifted the ring from the tines of Julia's fork and slid it, dressing and
all, onto her left hand. He kissed the ring, and then Julia's palm, and finally,
her lips.

When she'd recovered from the shock, Julia held her hand up and twisted
it back and forth, admiring the glint of sunlight on the diamond. "It's perfect," she declared. "If I'd designed it myself, it could not have been more perfect. It looks so much like my grandmother's engagement ring. How did you
know? And where on earth . . . ?"

Instead of answering her, Booker stood, picked up the camera he'd slung
over the back of his chair, aimed, and started shooting photos of the group
around the table.

"It *is* your grandmother's," he told her.

"But . . ." Julia sputtered. "Mama left it to my brother Joe."

"And your sister-in-law decided it was hideously old-fashioned," Booker
said, planting yet another kiss on Julia's cheek. "I'd e-mailed to ask if there
was a piece of family jewelry he might be willing to part with, in the remote
event that you would ever agree to get married, and he was only too happy to
let me take this off his hands."

"You!" Julia squealed. She got up, backed him into a chair and then planted
herself on his lap, kissing him passionately.

"Get a room," Dorie called.

After lunch, as the group was filing out of the restaurant, Booker pulled
Ellis aside.

"Great news," he said. "Simon texted me just as we were getting in the car
to drive over here. The producers loved the scouting shots. He's flying in with
them first thing Monday to work on lining up the rest of the locations. Have
you told Ty about any of this?"

"That's so great," Ellis said, trying to refrain from squealing. "I haven't talked to Ty, he's been gone all day. But I'll call him right away and let him know you need to talk to him."

"Good, because Simon says the whole production schedule's been sped up. It's supposed to be top secret, but one of the leading ladies just disclosed that she's pregnant."

"I wonder which one," Ellis said, watching Dorie climb into the driver's seat of the red van. "Um, Booker, do you have any idea how much the movie people will pay to use the house?"

"Nope," Booker said. "That's something Ty will need to negotiate."

It was close to six when Ellis saw the Bronco pull into the garage. A few minutes later, her phone dinged, announcing the arrival of a text message.

COCKTAILS ON MY VERANDA? MR. CULPEPPER.

She grinned and texted back:

B RITE OVER.

Ellis pulled on a pair of white shorts and a scoop-necked lime green top that made her tan look golden. After slicking on some lip gloss and spritzing on some perfume, she strolled over to the garage apartment.

Ty was just emerging from the shower, a beach towel wrapped around his waist, when she got to the top of the deck stairs.

"Oh," she said, blushing. "Uh, guess I'm early."

He laughed at her modesty and pulled her to him. He was still damp from the shower, but she didn't mind at all that her top and spotless white shorts were getting equally damp.

"There's some beer and a bottle of white wine in the fridge," he told her. "And I think I've got some chips and salsa, if you're hungry. I'll get dressed and be out in a minute."

Ellis set out the chips and salsa, poured herself a glass of wine, and took it out to the deck. She stood at the rail, looking out at the beach, which was mostly deserted now, with the exception of two adolescent boys riding skim-boards at the water's edge.

She'd noticed the boys earlier in the morning and realized they'd spent the whole day lounging on the beach, playing Frisbee, and now skimboarding. It was probably their last free weekend before school started, Ellis realized, feeling that prickle of sadness again. She couldn't remember when she'd been so sad to see the end of summer.

Ty was behind her now, his arms around her waist, kissing her neck. "You smell good," he said, breathing in her scent. "Is that for me?"

"All for you," she said, turning to return his kiss.

They sat companionably in the teak Adirondack chairs, sipping their drinks and catching up.

"I know you hate swordfish, but how do you feel about grouper?" Ty asked. "A buddy of mine called me early this morning and asked if I wanted to crew on his charter. That's where I've been all day. We caught the hell out of the grouper and snapper."

"I love grouper," Ellis said. "Are we having dinner?"

"Thought I'd try to impress you with my culinary skills," he said. "You're not one of those girly girls who won't eat fried fish, are you?"

"Not me," Ellis said.

He nodded approvingly. "Okay. Fried grouper sandwiches and coleslaw for dinner. You're in charge of the coleslaw."

"I can do that," Ellis said, following him into the kitchen. "But first, I've got a proposition for you."

43

"S ummer Fling could be the thing that saves Ebbtide," Ellis said, outlining what Booker had told her about his friend Simon. "A big Hollywood movie. If they use your house for filming, they'd probably pay enough in rent to get you out of the hole."

Ty gazed out the kitchen window at the big house. "But Ebbtide's a wreck. You said so yourself. Who would want to shoot a movie here?"

"Apparently they like what they've seen," Ellis insisted. "Starting with the crummy pictures Julia took with her cell phone, and including the professional-quality photos Booker's been taking for the past couple of days. Maybe the movie's about an old house. They make movies like that all the time, and they can't all be filmed from specially built sets."

"I guess," Ty said, placing the flour-coated grouper into a cast-iron skillet full of bubbling oil. "I never go see movies anymore. Probably the last one I saw was *Die Hard 2.*"

Ellis buttered the hamburger buns and put them in the tiny oven to brown. "Well, I see lots and lots of chick-type movies, and I can tell you that my favorite ones are the ones where the houses are as much a character in the plot as the actors. And," she added, "with the actresses that have supposedly already been signed for *Summer Fling*, it sounds like a really big-budget flick."

With a long-handled fork, Ty flipped over each of the fish fillets. "You like tartar sauce, or do you wanna try my super-secret sauce?"

"What's your super-secret sauce?"

"If I tell you that, it won't be a super secret, now will it?"

"What if I swear not to tell?" Ellis asked. "Pinky swear?"

"I've got a better idea," Ty said, wrapping his arms around her waist and kissing her.

"And the secret?" Ellis asked, stepping away from his reach.

"Bottled chili sauce, lemon juice, horseradish, and Duke's mayo," Ty said.

He laid out the grouper on a brown paper grocery store sack to drain, deftly mixed up his sauce, and five minutes later, they'd pushed aside the papers on the tiny dining table/desk to eat.

"Mmm," Ellis said, biting into her sandwich. "I am officially impressed. This might be the best grouper sandwich I've ever had. And growing up in Savannah, I've had a lot."

Ty lifted a forkful of coleslaw. "This slaw's not too shabby either. How'd you make the dressing? It's not mayonnaisey, which I like."

"It's my mama's recipe, and my daddy taught her how to make it," Ellis confided. "You just sprinkle sugar and salt on the shredded cabbage, and you crunch it together with your hands 'til the cabbage kinda 'weeps.' Then you heat up some apple cider vinegar on the stove, and put in some more sugar and some celery seed. You just pour that over the cabbage while it's still warm, mash it around with a wooden spoon, and put it in the fridge. It's even better if you let it sit a day or so."

"We make a decent team," Ty said, resting his elbows on the table. He looked around the room. "Apparently, somebody broke in here today and cleaned the joint up. They even did my laundry. You ever hear of a burglar doing that?"

"It was me," Ellis admitted. "Don't know what came over me. I was so excited about this movie thing, I ran over here this morning to tell you about it.

I let myself in, and I kinda got carried away." She flashed him an apologetic grin. "Sorry. It won't happen again."

"Why not? I mean, who am I to tamper with your domestic urges?"

"Oh my gosh," Ellis said, setting her fork down. "I completely forgot! You had a visitor while I was here cleaning up. So much has happened today— what with Julia and Booker getting engaged, and the movie stuff—it totally slipped my mind."

"Who came by?" Ty said, his mouth twisted sardonically. "Another bill collector?"

"Your ex," Ellis said. "And her husband."

"I hope you ran 'em off with a pitchfork," Ty said. "What the hell did they want?"

"To get a better look at this apartment, and the house, of course," Ellis said. "They actually wanted me to let them inside so they could figure out if this apartment would make a good income property."

"That's Kendra," Ty said bitterly. "Never lets any dust settle under her feet once she's on a mission."

"She said she's been calling you and leaving messages that you never return."

"Hmm," Ty said. "Guess I must have forgotten."

"I couldn't believe how nervy they were," Ellis said. "She was up here peering in the windows, trying to scope out the kitchen, while he was down in the garage with a measuring tape! And then, she had the gall to ask me if I thought your tenants in Ebbtide would let them in to look around."

"Amazing," Ty said, shaking his head in disbelief. "What did you tell her?"

"That I had no idea who the tenants were," Ellis said, pleased with her subterfuge.

"Good," Ty said sharply. He got up from the table and began to clear their plates. "Now, can we think of something else to talk about? Anything else?"

The mood in the room had subtly shifted. Before, they were just messing around, flirting, having fun, getting comfortable together. But now, Ellis sensed, Ty was moody, withdrawn. She was sorry she'd mentioned Kendra. She wouldn't make that mistake again.

She helped him wash the dishes, and while he was drying and putting them away, she picked up the broom from the corner and started to sweep the kitchen floor, needing a way to work out her nervous energy.

"You don't have to do that," Ty said, taking the broom from her hands. He looked around the room for a diversion. "Can't watch television."

"Maybe you should call the cable company," Ellis suggested.

"And lie and tell them I promise to pay them next month?"

"Oh." She'd put her foot in it again, reminding Ty of his financial situation.

"I'm sorry," Ty said, catching her hand in his. "None of this is your fault. It's just . . . One minute I think I'm digging myself out of the hole I've gotten myself into, and the next minute, Kendra and Fuckface are knocking at my door, looking to buy my house out from under me."

"I understand," Ellis said softly. And she truly did. "Look," she said. "It's been a nice evening. Dinner was great. But I think maybe you could use your space tonight."

"No," he protested. "Stay. It's early yet. I thought we'd take a walk on the beach. . . ."

"Another night," Ellis promised. "I want to go back to the house and make sure we've got everything tidy. Remember, the movie people are flying in tomorrow."

"There's no way they'll want Ebbtide," Ty said. "It's just an ugly, falling-down old dump. Look around. These days, places like Ebbtide are a dime a dozen."

"They'll love it!" Ellis insisted. "Please don't talk like that, Ty. I know it's discouraging, but I honestly believe this could work out and be the break you've been waiting for."

"Break?" Ty looked dubious. "People like me don't get breaks. I'll just have to figure something else out. My dad offered to loan me the money, but I can't let him touch his retirement." He gestured towards his computer, which Ellis had jokingly covered with a dish towel during dinner. "There's a stock I'm watching. I've been reading the reports on this company, and I think it's radically undervalued. They're working on a new software application, and if they get it patented before anybody else, *that* actually could be the break I need."

"Okay," Ellis said, feeling herself being dismissed, literally and emotionally. "Thanks for dinner, Ty. I'm going to give your cell phone number to Booker so he can give it to Simon, and you can talk to him directly, instead of having me be the go-between."

"What? Now you're mad at me? Did we just have a fight?"

"Nope," she said, trying to make her voice sound lighter than she felt. "I just don't happen to agree with you. No fight. We'll talk tomorrow."

She was climbing the first step to Ebbtide's porch when she heard her cell phone ding in her pocket. She took it out and saw that she had a text. And it was from Ty.

I'M AN ASS. I'M AN ASS. I'M AN ASS.

"You certainly are," she muttered to herself. She put the phone back in her pocket and went into the now-dark house.

She found Madison stretched out on the sofa in the living room, reading a moldy-looking paperback detective novel.

"Where is everybody?" Ellis asked.

"Dorie had a dinner date with her new cop friend, and I think Julia and Booker decided to go catch a movie," Madison said.

Ellis flung herself into an armchair opposite the sofa, kicking her legs over the arms. "What's that you're reading?" she asked, squinting to get a look at the lurid cover illustration.

"John D. MacDonald, *The Turquoise Lament*," Madison said. "There's a whole shelf full of them here. My grandfather always used to read John D. MacDonald, and he used to talk about Travis McGee as though he were a real person."

"Never heard of him," Ellis said. She got up and roamed idly around the room, leafing through books and putting them down, picking up magazines only to discard them.

Her cell phone dinged and she looked at the screen.

PLEASE COME BACK.

Ellis snorted and with the press of a button, cleared the screen of its latest text. "Men are idiots, you know that?"

Madison looked up from her book. "Who me? You're talking to me?"

"Of course," Ellis said.

Madison put the book facedown on her chest and sighed. "Having man problems, are we?"

"It's Ty," Ellis blurted. "He doesn't even want to help himself. I told him about Booker's friend, the movie scout, and no matter what I say, he just seems to think this is some big fantasy of mine. And now he's got his panties in a wad because I told him his ex-wife and her new husband came around the house while he was gone today, sizing it up to buy it out of foreclosure. Like any of this is my fault."

"You said it yourself," Madison said. "Men are idiots. And take it from me, on that I *am* an authority. The problem is, there really aren't a lot of good alternatives. So you just have to decide if you want to deal with a whole gender of people who are intrinsically flawed."

"I have been doing without men for years. A decade, actually," Ellis said gloomily, slumping down in her chair. "I finally thought I'd found a guy who was different, who was smart and funny. . . ."

"And sexy as hell," Madison said meaningfully. "Ty Bazemore is all that."

"And he's got a chip on his shoulder the size of Texas," Ellis added. "I don't need that."

"Of course not," Madison said. "You can just go right back to Philly and your old life there, and leave his stupid foreclosed self right here in Nags Head. Let him figure out how to save his house on his own."

"I will," Ellis said. "That's just what I'm going to do."

"Good for you," Madison said. She picked the book up again.

"Have you heard anything from Adam?" Ellis asked, determined to forget her own problems.

"Not a word," Madison said. "He still hasn't returned any of my calls. I'm definitely getting bad vibes now."

Ellis's cell dinged again. Madison raised one eyebrow, but otherwise remained motionless.

Ellis got up and walked into the kitchen. She could see the yellow light burning in the window at the apartment above the garage. *I miss you,* Ty's text said. She looked up and could see him now, standing in the window, looking directly at her; she was perfectly silhouetted in the dim kitchen light. The phone dinged again.

DEAR ELLIS SULLIVAN. I CAN'T DO WITHOUT YOU. PLEASE GIVE ME ANOTHER CHANCE. PLEASE? MR. CULPEPPER.

"Madison," she called, heading for the kitchen door. "I'm going out for a while."

"Tell Ty I said not to mess it up this time," Madison called back.

At dawn, they sat in the Adirondack chairs, drinking coffee made in Ty's grandmother's battered aluminum percolator, watching the sunrise. A lone pair of fishermen stood ankle deep in the water, surf casting, but the beach was otherwise deserted.

"Nice morning," Ellis said with a yawn, feeling completely at peace.

"Nicer night," Ty said, putting down his coffee cup.

"Mmm, hmm," Ellis said.

"Know what would be really, really nice?" Ty asked, pulling her to her feet.

"Again?" Ellis clutched the blue terry cloth bathrobe a little tighter.

"Oh. Well, maybe later. For now, I was thinking that I really, really need a shower," Ty said. "And if I just had somebody to help wash my back ..." He had the bathrobe belt nearly unknotted. He was a very fast worker, Ellis thought.

"I don't know," Ellis said uneasily. "Those guys out there ..." She nodded towards the fishermen.

"They've pulled in two bluefish, just while we've been sitting out here," Ty pointed out. "Those guys are in the zone. They're oblivious to us."

He was tugging her towards the wooden shower enclosure, pulling his own T-shirt over his head. He turned on the faucet, opened the door, and stepped out of his boxers. "Come on," he grinned, pulling at her belt. "You'll love it." The bathrobe fell open, and she was just as naked as Ty.

"Oh well," Ellis said. She let the robe fall to the deck and stepped into the shower.

"One minute," Ty said, picking up the fallen robe. He put his hand in the pocket and brought out a foil-wrapped condom, holding it up for Ellis's approval. "Be prepared," he said solemnly.

Warm water sluiced down on her head. Ty had a bottle of baby shampoo. He squirted some into his hands and rubbed it into her hair, massaging her scalp expertly with long, tapered fingers. She took the bottle from him and returned the favor, running her fingers through his thick, soapy, sun-bleached hair.

They stood under the water, blinking and giggling. Ty took the shampoo bottle and traced a line of amber liquid from her shoulder to her right breast, and then her left. He put the bottle back on the little wooden shelf, and turned his attentions to Ellis. He worked the shampoo into a fine white foam, caressing her breasts, soaping her belly, slowly tracing a line in the soap lower, and lower, finally sliding into her.

They moved together, and Ellis forgot to be self-conscious, forgot to be inhibited, forgot all the rules. "Splinters," she whispered at one point, as her soapy butt rubbed up against the rough-hewn cedar planks, but that too was quickly forgotten.

They were on their second lather, and the water was just beginning to get noticeably cooler, when Ellis heard footsteps on the wooden stairs.

"Ty!" she whispered.

"Hmm?" He was behind her, soaping her back.

"Somebody's here."

"Hmm?" He turned her around and nuzzled her neck.

"Hellooo!"

Ellis froze. She knew that voice.

"Shiiiit," he whispered. He knew it too. All too well.

"Oh my God," Ellis breathed. "Hide me."

"Why?" he whispered back. "What do you care?"

"Ty?" her voice came closer. They could tell Kendra was almost at the top step.

"Do something," Ellis pleaded. "I'll die of embarrassment if she sees me like this."

"Stay here," Ty whispered. "I'll get rid of her and be right back."

Ellis looked down and realized that if Kendra got any closer she'd surely notice two sets of legs inside the wooden shower stall. She sat on the narrow wooden bench and drew her legs up to her knees.

Ty shut off the water, snatched up his boxers, and pulled them on. The next minute, he was wrapping the bathrobe around himself and stepping out, firmly pushing the shower door shut.

"Kendra," Ellis heard him say. "What the hell do you want?"

Ellis looked down at the water streaming off her body. She shivered and saw the fine goose bumps prickling her bare skin. *Hurry,* she thought. *Hurry!*

44

"Tyyyy," Kendra's voice was shrill, teasing. "Did I catch you at a bad time?"

"You always manage to catch me at a bad time, Kendra," Ty snapped. "It's barely 7 A.M. What the hell do you want?"

"If you'd return my phone calls, you'd know what I want," Kendra said, totally unfazed by Ty's rudeness. "Ryan and I want to talk to you about buying Ebbtide."

"Talk to the bank, not me," Ty said. "It's out of my hands, as you well know."

"We could help each other," Kendra said sweetly. "You need to get out of debt, and Ryan and I are looking for a beach house. A beach house with age and character, just like Ebbtide. But we'd like to just take a look around the place before we make an offer. I'm thinking it's gonna need an awful lot of work, and we'd like to ballpark it before we get to auction."

"Nothing doing," Ty said flatly. "Go away."

"You don't have to give me attitude," Kendra said. "I'm not the bad guy, you know."

Ellis hugged her knees tightly to her chest. The sun hadn't fully risen yet, and the morning air was still chilly. As chilly as Ty's voice.

"Sure you are," Ty said. "You and your asshole husband are a couple of vultures, circling around my house, looking to swoop in and snatch it away from me. And if you think I'm gonna actually help you do that, you're dumber than I thought."

"I'm dumb? I'm not the one who dropped out of law school and threw away a brilliant career as a lawyer. I'm not the one who walked away from a marriage the first time it hit a bump in the road, because my fragile little ego couldn't take a dose of reality. And I'm certainly not the one who's fixing to lose his house, and everything else, because I refused to face facts and cut a deal with somebody who could save my bacon."

"You've got an interesting take on history, Kendra," Ty drawled. "I wonder if ol' Fuckface knows you regard him as 'a bump in the road.' "

"Stop calling him that," Kendra snapped.

"Stop showing up at my house, uninvited and unannounced. Stop calling me, and stop leaving me messages," Ty said. "And now, get the hell off my property, before I call the cops."

"I'll go," Kendra said, and Ellis heard her feet moving across the deck. She breathed a sigh of relief.

"But throwing me out doesn't change anything, Ty," she taunted. "*Ryan* and I will still be on the Dare County Courthouse steps on the fifteenth, and we'll have our checkbook out. And there's not a damned thing you can do to stop us. We're gonna buy Ebbtide, Ty. And when we do, the first thing we'll do is kick your white trash ass right to the curb."

"Beat it," Ty said. "Now."

The footsteps were rapidly retreating. Evidently, Ty looked as menacing as he sounded. Ellis heard an engine roar to life, heard the accelerator being floored, and then, the eminently rewarding sound of Kendra's tires, spinning ineffectively in the crushed shell driveway.

Ty chuckled. He walked over to the shower stall and poked his head inside.

Ellis was curled in a ball on the bench, her knees pressed to her chest. She managed to smile up at him through lips turned blue. "Y-y-you d-d-da m-m-man. Now, could I please have a t-t-towel?"

45

Ellis heard the thrum of the vacuum cleaner as soon as she opened the front door. Dorie was running it across the worn rug in the living room. She waved at Dorie, and walked into the kitchen to find Madison waxing the floors. Upstairs, Ellis found Julia flitting about among the bedrooms, her arms full of new linens, pillows, quilts, and throw rugs.

"What's going on?" she asked, catching Julia coming out of her own room. "What's all that stuff?"

Julia pushed a strand of hair behind her ear. "Getting the house styled up for its big moment. And this," she said, pointing with her chin at the stack of linens in her arms, "is lots of stuff to girly up the bedrooms. Booker and I did a little shopping at HomeGoods last night. A lot of shopping, actually."

"But, who's gonna pay for all of it?" Ellis asked. "Ty's broke."

"Don't worry," Julia assured her. "The price tags are all intact. As soon as these guys leave, I'll take it all back for a refund."

"Can you do that? Is it legal?"

"It's not like anybody actually slept on the stuff, Ellis," Julia said, rolling her eyes.

"Where's Booker?" Ellis asked.

"If you were coming from Ty's, you probably walked right past him," Julia said, ducking into the hall bathroom. She began folding and arranging a stack of fluffy, white bath towels. "He's out in the garage, trying to get the lawn mower started. Which I can't wait to see—Booker using a lawn mower."

"And all of this is for the movie people?" Ellis asked. "I was gonna just make sure all the beds were made, but Julia, this is above and beyond the call."

"It's nothing," Julia said. She opened a shopping bag and lifted out a clear-glass apothecary jar, which she began filling with sun-bleached seashells from another shopping bag. She placed the jar on the back of the toilet tank, then stepped back to critique her handiwork.

"What do you think?" she asked. "Too fussy?"

"Very pretty," Ellis said. "But is all of this necessary?"

Julia shrugged. "It couldn't hurt, right? And anyway, we're kind of having fun. It's like getting ready for a big, important party. Besides, this is not all self-less. If Simon's people use the house for the movie, Booker gets a nice finder's fee. And if they make a movie here, maybe I can snag a job working for the set dressers. Wouldn't that be awesome?"

"If, if, if," Ellis said worriedly. "So much riding on this."

"The house is going to look fabulous," Julia assured her, steering her to-wards her own room. When Ellis opened the door, she almost didn't recognize the space that had been hers for nearly a month. The yellowing sheers at the windows had been replaced with simple, white-cotton curtains with ball fringe, caught back on the sides with lengths of rope. The threadbare bed-spread was gone too, and in its place was a quilt in soft sea-glass shades of blue, green, and aqua. Three fat pillows were plumped at the head of the bed. The cheesy art in the room, blurry prints of lighthouses and ducks, had been replaced with large, atmospheric, black-and-white photographs of Ebbtide, the dunes, and the beach right outside their back door.

"Booker?" Ellis asked, touching one of the frames.

"Yup. We had some of his shots printed at Kinko's, and then we stuck 'em in frames from Kmart," Julia said. "He does nice work, doesn't he?"

"They're gorgeous," Ellis agreed. "Do you think he'd sell me copies of some of these? They'd be a great souvenir to remind me of Nags Head and Ebbtide."

Julia gave her a curious look. "Do you need a souvenir?"

"Too soon to tell," Ellis said. "Now, give me a job."

"Easy. Booker says the thing that will sell the producers on the house is the amazing light, and the location, of course. So we need to wash all the windows, which it doesn't look like has happened since the Reagan administration."

"I'll hit the inside windows, but I'll have to get Ty for anything requiring ladders," Ellis said.

She went down to the kitchen and filled a bucket with ammonia and water, and found a stack of old newspapers to wipe the windows. While she was texting Ty, Dorie walked into the kitchen and sat down at the table, her cell phone in hand, a stunned look on her face.

"Anything wrong?" Ellis asked, her heart racing. "The baby's okay, right?"

"Huh? Oh, yeah. The baby's fine. I'm just . . . shell-shocked, I guess. Stephen just called."

Ellis sat down in the chair opposite Dorie's. "What did he want?"

Dorie had both hands resting lightly on her tummy. "He said he was just checking in, he wanted to see how I'm doing. He asked about the baby, you know—if I'm showing yet, if it's kicking yet, et cetera."

"That's kinda sweet," Ellis said, waiting for the other shoe to drop.

"He's hired a divorce lawyer and started proceedings," Dorie said, her lower lip trembling. "And . . . he wants to buy out my share of the house."

"Really? That's good, right? Isn't that what you wanted?"

Dorie's eyes filled with tears. "I guess. It's just sort of sudden, you know? I thought I was going to have to be the one to get the ball rolling, because Stephen is such a procrastinator, but all of a sudden, he's in a big hurry to get all these papers signed and get shed of me."

"You were the one who was insisting on the divorce, Dorie," Ellis reminded her. "And you just told me yesterday that it's time for you to get on with your life. You're even dating. Sorta."

"Connor and I aren't really dating," Dorie protested. "I didn't even let him buy me dinner last night. I paid for my own."

"Have you kissed him?"

Dorie blushed.

"Maybe Stephen wants to get on with his life too," Ellis said.

"Oh sure, he gets to have his life all neat and perfect," Dorie said. She looked up at Ellis. "He's leaving Our Lady of Angels. He's been offered a job at Savannah College of Art and Design, in the development office. He says it's a big pay raise, and something he's always been interested in. I guess that's how he can afford to buy me out."

"That and the fact that he has a rich boyfriend," Ellis reminded her. "Anyway, a raise means he won't be making the same crappy salary you make. If he's working at SCAD, it'll mean he can afford to pay a decent amount of child support."

"It doesn't seem fair," Dorie said bitterly. "He's the one who screwed up our lives. He got me pregnant, and he cheated, and he walked out. Now, he gets the house, he gets a great new job . . . and what do I get?"

"You get to be a mom," Ellis said softly. "That's more important than a house, or a job, or money. Right? You get what you've always wanted: a child. None of that other stuff matters. You will be a fabulous mother, and Stephen will always have to know that he walked away from sharing a life with you and his child."

"You make it sound like a Hallmark card," Dorie said, sniffing. "What if I screw this up? I know I made a lot of noise about wanting this baby, but Ellis, I'm terrified. I don't know if I can do this all by myself."

"You won't screw up," Ellis said. "And you won't be by yourself. For better or worse, you have to let Stephen be a father to this baby. And you've got Willa, and Nash, and the rest of your crazy, screwed-up family. And Connor, it sounds like. And us. You've got us, Dorie. You know that, right? We've got your back. Always have. Always will."

"Willa!" Dorie said. "I almost forgot. Willa knows about the baby. Stephen ran into her this morning, and he just assumed I'd told her, and so he said something about her being an aunt. He said she nearly dropped dead of a heart attack."

"If only," Ellis said. "Oops."

"So now I've got to call her and tell her the whole sordid story," Dorie said, slumping in her chair. "And then she'll tell Phyllis, and there'll be this big shitstorm."

"You could just do an end run and call your mother yourself," Ellis suggested. "Sort of a preemptive strike."

"Nuh-uh," Dorie said glumly. "I'll face Phyllis when I get home. And not until."

Dorie propped her elbows on the table and rested her chin on her fists. "I am *not* looking forward to having this conversation with my sister."

"I'm surprised she hasn't called you," Ellis said.

"Oh, she has," Dorie said. "Repeatedly. I just haven't chosen to call her back."

"Coward," Ellis said.

"Yup, that's me."

"He's here," Julia announced at six that evening, walking into the kitchen where the girls were congregated. Dorie was making guacamole and Ellis was squeezing limes for margaritas. Madison was coating the rims of newly purchased glasses with a mixture of lime juice and salt. "Booker just pulled into the driveway. He and Simon are walking around outside, talking."

"Look," Ellis said, dropping a halved lime onto the countertop. "My hands are shaking. I can't believe how nervous I am."

"Relax," Julia said, tossing her hair. "He'll love the place. Hell, I love it, now that we've got it all pimped out like this."

"You did a great job, Julia," Dorie told her, tossing the diced avocados with some of the juice from Ellis's limes. "I never thought this house could look so good."

"I'd make a movie here," Madison added. "Hell, I'd live here, now that you've fixed it up like this."

"It's no biggie," Julia said lightly. "Any idiot could do what I did. Clean windows, waxed floors, some potted geraniums and ferns on the porch. . . ."

"All the furniture rearranged, new curtains in all the windows, new rugs, new art, flowers in every room, the deck pressure washed, the whole yard landscaped, porch rails repaired," Ellis said, ticking off the day's accomplishments on her hands. "I'm exhausted just talking about it. And I think Ty's totally overwhelmed by the change. I think he's actually starting to think this movie thing just might happen."

"It will happen," Julia vowed. "You wait and see. Booker says Simon is not easily impressed. So if he's here, the deal is almost certainly going to happen. Where is Ty, by the way?"

"Showering," Ellis said. "Or more likely, asleep standing up in the shower, after all the work you had him doing today."

"It's all going to pay off," Julia said. "I guarantee."

"I believe you," Ellis said. "The trick now is to make Ty believe."

The dining room table was littered with glasses, empty Corona bottles, shards of chips, and globs of salsa and guacamole—not to mention Dorie's empty caffeine-free Diet Coke cans. It was ten o'clock. The women, worn out from trying to make a good impression, had all scattered to their rooms. Simon had been wined and dined, plied with shrimp and grits and fried green tomatoes, all served up by Julia, Ellis, Madison, and Dorie, turned out in low-cut sundresses that showed their gleaming summer tans and welcoming Southern smiles.

Simon was in his late forties, balding, the remainder of his white-blond hair gathered into a tight little braid at the back of his head. He wore a snug-fitting black T-shirt with the word FAÇADE in white letters across the front; black linen shorts, which Julia cuttingly referred to as "manpris" behind his back; and high-top black sneakers worn unlaced.

He'd toured the house for two hours, looking in every nook and cranny, not saying much. Following that, he'd been driven up and down Croatan Highway by Ty and Booker. He'd stood on the bay side, watching the sunset with a practiced eye, and taken a cursory look at two other old houses Ty had found that might work for other locations for the movie. Now he leaned back in his chair and looked across the table at Ty, who was still sipping his first and only beer of the night.

"It'll work," he said succinctly. "Not perfect, but we can make it work. When can you be out?"

"Out?" Ty said blankly.

"Move out," Simon said. "We'll need access immediately. Didn't Booker tell you?"

Ty rubbed his eyes and yawned. "He said you wanted to start shooting in September?"

"Shooting, yes," Simon said impatiently. "But we've got to get our crews in here right away. This place, if you don't mind my saying so, needs a lot of work."

"I thought you wanted an old house," Ty protested. "Booker said . . ."

"We need to make it look even older than it is," Simon said. "The art director wants the house to be weathered blue shingles. Like on Cape Cod."

"But this house doesn't have shingles," Ty said.

"It will when we're done," Simon said. "Also, Joe wants awnings. Striped awnings, for Chrissakes. We need a gazebo on that deck of yours, overlooking the water, and that piece-of-crap garage? That's going to be a barn. A faded-red barn."

"It's a garage," Ty pointed out. "It doesn't look anything like a barn."

"It will," Simon said. "When we're done, you'll wonder where the cows went."

"Oo-kay," Ty said slowly.

"So you can move immediately?"

Ty blinked. "Why can't I stay in the garage apartment?"

"Because it's going to be a barn," Simon said, speaking slowly, as though he were dealing with someone with a marked learning disability. "We're going to make a movie in it, remember?"

"Let's back up," Ty suggested. "First off, my tenants, you remember my tenants? Julia, Ellis, Dorie, Madison? They have this place rented for another week yet. I can't just kick them out."

"Fifty thousand dollars," Simon said pleasantly. "For three months. We'll throw in a housing allowance for you, as long as you don't try to gouge us. How does that sound?"

Ty swallowed and tried to look uninterested, although his pulse was racing, his throat was dry, and his heart was hammering so hard he was afraid to look down at his shirtfront. He took another sip of the warm beer as a stalling tactic.

"The girls stay 'til the end of next week, as planned," he said finally. "They have a rental agreement, and I won't break it. Your people can work around them, can't they?"

Simon shook his head. "They'll stay out of the way?"

"Of course," Ty said. "Who'll be doing the work on the house, the construction and painting and all that?"

"A crew," Simon said. "Maybe you can help us line up some decent locals? Union, of course."

"Maybe I can be the general contractor," Ty said easily. "I've done all the work on the house up to now, but I've got buildings with are carpenters, painters, electricians.

"About the money," Ty said. "I'm gonna need a big deposit."

"How big?"

Ty felt a vein in his neck bulge, but chose to ignore it. "Half up front."

Simon shook his head vehemently. "Not happening."

"Okay," Ty said, taking another swig of beer. "No hard feelings. Maybe you can find another house on the water with somebody willing to turn a garage into a barn in, like, a week."

Simon eyed him. "Are you dicking around with me?"

"Yeah," Ty said. "But I need twenty-five thousand dollars up front, along with a signed agreement, and all the usual stuff I'm sure you people do with insurance and bonds and all. Or it's no deal."

Simon pushed his chair back from the table and stood up. "I'll get back to you in the morning. You wanna give me a ride to my motel, or are you gonna charge me extra for that too?"

"No charge," Ty said smoothly. "It's my pleasure."

"One more thing," Simon said. "What do you know about that lot next door? The one with the burnt-out house? That might work for us too."

"I'll get back to you on that," Ty said.

46

The trucks came rumbling down Ebbtide's driveway around two o'clock on Tuesday. Ellis had just come up from the beach, and now she stood on the front porch, with a red Solo Cup of iced tea, watching the parade approach. The first one was a lumber company tractor-trailer, piled high with pallets of wooden shingles, plywood, rolls of roofing, and lumber of every description. Right behind it came a big box van with RELIANCE AIR stenciled on the doors. It was followed by two beat-up cargo vans, which were followed by a red pickup truck, which was followed by Ty, in his weatherbeaten Bronco, minus the surfboard.

Ty parked the Bronco close to the street and jogged down to the house, directing the drivers where to park. Finally, he walked up to the porch, greeting Ellis with a brief kiss.

"What's all this?" she asked. "It looks like invasion of the house snatchers."

"Close," Ty said. "They're just going to do a little 'fixing up,' as Simon puts it. But I made 'em promise you girls won't be bothered too much. They're going to start on the garage first."

"You mean the barn?"

"Right."

Ellis pointed to the Reliance Air truck. "And that would be?"

Ty grinned. "Just a brand-spanking-new heat pump and two two-and-a-half-ton central air units. Hollywood likes the illusion of old, but talent as expensive as they've hired can't shoot a movie without air."

"Really? Do you get to keep it after the movie's done?"

"Absolutely. All the 'improvements' stay with the house afterwards, including the new cedar shake roof, the gazebo, and the barn. Although I still can't believe they can make that garage look like a New England barn."

"Yippee!" Ellis said, clapping her hands. "Air! How long will it take them to hook it up? I mean, I hate to complain, but the unit in Dorie's room is dead, and the one in my room is close to it. Madison gave up on hers as soon as she moved in."

Ty frowned. "Maybe you guys should consider moving over to a hotel. I told Simon I wouldn't let him run you off, but if the air's not working, that's not good. I'll make them pay for your rooms. I really didn't think they were gonna get everything going this fast. It's crazy, isn't it?"

"It makes my head spin," Ellis admitted. "You never told me if you were able to work things out with the bank. Did it go okay?"

"It did," Ty said. "I finally got a face-to-face with an actual human being. I showed him my contract with the movie people and wrote them a check for twenty thousand dollars, with the understanding that there'd be another payment as soon as shooting is completed and I get the rest of my money. For now, the foreclosure sale has been canceled."

"That's great," Ellis said. "You only gave them twenty thousand dollars? But you said Simon gave you twenty-five thousand."

"Right," Ty said. "I used the other five thousand to put an option on some land."

"I don't understand," Ellis said. "I'm not trying to second-guess you, but Ty, don't you need to put every penny back into saving Ebbtide?"

"Not every penny," Ty said. "The land I optioned is right over there." He pointed to the sandy lot next to Ebbtide, the one with the burnt-out foundation.

Ellis still looked puzzled. "You want to build a house right next to the house you already own?"

"Nope," Ty said. "Not right now, anyway. I'm going to rent it out to Simon and his buddies for the movie. They need an old-timey country store because one of the characters in the movie runs one. They've been looking all over the Outer Banks, but everything here is too shiny and new. So Joe and his people are going to build a store." He gestured with his chin. "Right over there."

"How did you know?"

"Simon asked me Sunday night, when we were negotiating, in a casual kind of way, about that lot. I figured they wanted it, and I told him I'd look into it."

"You knew who owned the lot?"

"Of course. Ruthann Sargent owns it. Her mother was my grandmother's best friend. Ruthann hasn't been to Nags Head since before Miss Penny passed away, four or five years ago. Not long after Miss Penny died, the house was struck by lightning and burned to the ground."

"How awful," Ellis said.

"Not so very awful," Ty said cheerfully. "The house was falling to pieces before the fire. Ruthann was more than happy to sell me a six-month option on it. If the movie people rent it, I'll give her half of what they give me. She's a nice gal, took care of my grandmother after her heart attack."

"I'm impressed," Ellis said. "You really are more than just a pretty face."

"You're just saying that because you want to get into my pants," Ty countered. "Now, what about the motel? Do you think you wanna move over there?"

"It's only for five more days," Ellis said, trying to sound lighthearted. "Four really, because our rental agreement clearly states that checkout time for Ebbtide is 10 A.M. Saturday."

"Yeah, well, I happen to know the landlord," Ty said. "Culpepper's a crusty old sumbitch, but I think we can probably get him to cut you some slack on that. But are you sure you want to stay with all this going on?"

"I don't know about the girls, but I don't mind. It's actually pretty exciting. I've never seen a movie being made."

"Don't know about the exciting part," Ty said. "It's going to get noisy and crowded, I guarantee, once all the subs start piling in here."

"Maybe we'd be in your way," Ellis said.

"Never," Ty said. He touched her chin with the tip of his finger. "Seriously, Ellis, I know it's selfish, but I want you here. Look, I need to talk to you about that. I mean, I don't want you to leave. Not just Ebbtide. I don't want you to leave Nags Head. I don't want you to leave. . . ."

A gleaming black Land Cruiser came bouncing down the drive, sand and crushed shells spinning from beneath its wheels, its horn honking madly. A man's arm was waving from the driver's side window.

"Oh shit," Ty said, distracted. "That's gonna be Joe, the art director. He's called me, like, twenty times already today. I better go deal with him. Can we talk about this later? Tonight?

"Sure," Ellis said. "I'm not going anywhere. Yet."

As promised, carpenters and electricians and movie-type people started crawling all over Ebbtide. When Joe, the art director, set up an office on the kitchen table, the girls decided it was time to have dinner at Barnacle Betty's.

Their appetizers had just arrived at the table. "I think," Julia announced, spearing a fried shrimp with a fork, "I may have snagged myself a job with the movie folks."

"Really?" Dorie crowed. "That's fantastic. What would you do? When would you start?"

"I'll be a gofer," Julia said, dipping the shrimp in a plastic cup of cocktail sauce. "And I won't start for another week or two, which'll give me time to go up to DC and take a look at this house Booker is so hot to buy."

"Is there any chance they'll let you do something more artistic than just running errands?" Madison asked.

"Maybe," Julia said. "They're not making me any promises, but I figure, I'll hang around, schmooze, and worm my way into their hearts. It's kind of my specialty."

"It really is," Dorie told Madison. "Julia, when she's not being a bitchy diva, can really be totally charming."

"Hard to believe," Madison cracked, and they all burst out laughing.

"I've got news too," Madison said, choosing her words carefully. "I'm going to take off in the morning."

"Madison, no!" Dorie said. "Why? We've got the house 'til Saturday, and things are just starting to get interesting. I'm hoping maybe Cameron or Reese will show up later in the week. Don't you want to be able to say you met them?"

"Not really," Madison said. "It's just . . . time to go. You guys have been great, and I truly appreciate all you've done, but . . . I don't have a good feeling about Adam. I still haven't heard from him. And Don has stopped calling too. It's . . . eerie."

"Where'll you go?" Ellis asked.

Madison grimaced. "Believe it or not, I've decided to go back to New Jersey. I'll hire a lawyer, contact the authorities, and tell them what I know about Don's embezzlement. I've got the cash, or most of it, and that should make them sit up and listen. I hope."

"Ballsy move," Julia nodded approvingly.

"I'm tired of running," Madison said. "It's time for me to figure out what I'm going to do with the rest of my life. So, tomorrow's just as good a day as any to get started."

"No it's not," Julia said. "You've got to stay 'til Friday night. Please?"

"What's so important about Friday night?" Madison asked warily.

"My birthday," Julia said.

Dorie clapped her hand over her mouth. "Oh my gosh, Julia, I'd forgotten."

"Me too," Ellis said guiltily. "And you guys know I never forget a birthday."

"I'll be thirty-six," Julia said. "I never thought I'd get that old. But this year, thirty-six doesn't seem so ancient."

"We're having a party?" Ellis asked. "You went and planned your own party?"

"Karaoke," Julia said. "At Cadillac Jack's. Friday night. Our last night. Who's in?"

"Me," Dorie said.

"Me too," Ellis added.

They all looked expectantly at Madison.

"Oh, all right," she said, caving. "A couple more days won't make that much difference. I guess I can just as easily leave Saturday as tomorrow. One more thing," she said, glaring at all of them in turn. "I *do not* karaoke."

"Karaoke is not a verb, Madison," Dorie said sweetly. "Anyway, we'll see about that."

Ellis was climbing into Dorie's van for the ride back to Ebbtide when she heard her cell phone ding. She dug through the contents of her purse, eager to see if the text was from Ty.

"Oh Lord, y'all," Julia announced. "Ellis has gone boy crazy on us. She and Ty are texting each other day and night. He's probably wanting to know when she's due back at the love nest."

"Shut up, Julia," Ellis said, laughing. "We're not that bad."

"Yeah, you are," Dorie said, turning around from the driver's seat. "But I think it's cute."

Ellis finally found her phone and touched the message icon. She had to squint to read in the faint light.

"What's he say?" Julia asked, peering over her shoulder. "Oooh, is he sexting you?"

"Noooo," Ellis said, blinking, and rereading the message to be sure she hadn't misunderstood. "This isn't from Ty. It's from a woman I used to work with at the bank." Ellis looked up. "You guys, she's offering me a job!"

47

"It's my last night in the apartment," Ty told Ellis when she got back from dinner with the girls. "They're going to start tearing it down tomorrow, putting up the barn."

"Kind of sad, huh?" Ellis said.

He shrugged. "It's just a crappy garage apartment, I know. My grandfather built it with lumber from another house up the road that was blown down in a big storm. And later, my grandmother's maid used to live here with her kids. And the garage is literally so eaten up with termites, it could fall down before they tear it down. But I've kinda gotten used to living here."

They were sitting in the Adirondack chairs, out on the deck, staring out at the stars. The construction crews had finally packed up for the night and gone off to their motels, but they could hear the hum of the gas-powered generators set up to run the work lights.

"I think your place is adorable," Ellis said. "I love everything about it, except maybe the outdoor shower, and even that I wouldn't mind so much if it weren't so, uh, exposed."

That gave them both a laugh.

"I'd love to have seen the look on Kendra's face when she found out she wasn't going to get the chance to kick your white-trash ass to the curb," Ellis said.

"She's still trying to figure out where I got the money to stop the foreclosure proceedings," Ty said. "I've seen her drive past half a dozen times in the past two days, craning her neck, trying to see what's going on here."

"Ty," Ellis said, after a while. "What's going to happen when the movie people are gone and the money runs out? Do you think you'll still be able to hang on to Ebbtide?"

"Good question," Ty said, crossing and uncrossing his legs. "The movie money will buy me some time. And now that I'm paid up with the bank again, I'm going to see about getting the mortgage refinanced. Interest rates have dropped nearly three hundred basic points since my uncle sold it to me, so I'll save a bundle that way. After that, I honestly don't know."

Ellis was quiet. Suddenly, the generators shut down. Now they could hear the waves rolling in on the beach below. Fireflies blinked amongst the tall strands of beach grass, and a few yards down the beach, a group of college kids huddled around a bonfire. Ty and Ellis heard drifts of music from their iPods, saw two of the kids wandering away from the others, into the dunes, hand in hand.

"School starts back up pretty soon," Ellis said, watching them go. "I'll bet this is their last big party before everybody heads back to their real lives."

Ty's fingertips brushed against Ellis's.

"I don't want you to go," he said, staring straight ahead.

She smiled to herself. "I was hoping you'd ask me to stay tonight. The last night of the old crib. Maybe we'll even have one last shower out here for old time's sake—as long as it's before daylight."

"Not just tonight," Ty said. "I don't want you to go. Period. I don't want to stand here and watch you drive away on Saturday."

"Ty . . ." Ellis started.

He caught her hand in his. "Stay. Please?"

She sighed. "I wish I could. I've thought about it all week. Before that, even. Who wouldn't want to live at the beach year round and play house? With you?"

Ty kissed the back of her hand. "Good. Then it's settled."

"Ty, I've had a job offer." She blurted it out.

He dropped her hand. "What? When did this happen?"

"Just a little while ago. It was totally out of the blue. Dana, this woman I used to work with at the bank, texted me the offer, like, fifteen minutes ago. The thing is, it's my dream job. Dana's been hired to head up this new project at Pacific Trust, and she wants me to come with her. The money is fabulous, great benefits, they've even got a relocation package. They'll sell my town house! Nobody does that anymore."

"Pacific Bank? What? You'd be in their East Coast office?"

"No. The job's in Seattle."

He turned to look at her. "You're not seriously considering taking it, right?"

"I'd be an idiot not to. In this economy? Nobody's hiring. I haven't had a single response to any of the résumés I sent out last month. Not one! But this—this is amazing. Dana says I'd come onboard as an assistant veep. And I'd report direct to her. It'd be a huge promotion for me."

Ty hunched forward, his head in his hands.

"Say something, please?" Ellis whispered.

"Like what? Congratulations?"

"That would be a nice start."

He turned and stared at Ellis. "Have you heard anything I've been telling you tonight? I want you to stay. Right here, with me. In Nags Head."

"And do what?" the old, practical Ellis asked. "How would I make a living?"

"We could live on love," Ty said, trying to sound like he meant to be funny, but she could tell he was serious.

"And do what when it comes time to pay the bills?" Ellis asked. She swung her legs around and pressed her knees up against Ty's. "Your life here is a beautiful dream. You know how to make it work. You live by your wits, day trading, picking up shifts as a bartender, renting out the house in the season. And that works great for you. But it's not me, Ty. I've always had a nine-to-five job. Not the most exciting or glamorous life, but it works for me. I'm a list-maker, a rule-follower."

"You could find a job here," Ty said, but he knew as soon as the words were out of his mouth that it was a lie. "Maybe not making as much money, but you could find one."

"Or you could move to Seattle with me and find a job." Ellis gave him a crooked smile. "It's a different ocean, but it's still the coast. Kinda."

"I could give it a try," Ty said. "If you wanted me to."

"What was that you told me on that first awful dinner date? About never having another job in an office?"

"Yeah, well, I was just blowing off steam. I could do it, Ellis, if I had to."

"That's the point, Ty. I don't want you to think you have to. You'd be miserable in an office job. And then I'd be miserable. Did you ever see any of those old Tarzan movies when you were a kid?"

"Huh? How many drinks did you guys have at dinner?"

"No, listen. When I was a little girl, my brother Baylor was obsessed with Tarzan. He read all the Edgar Rice Burroughs books, got my dad to go buy him the videos of the movies—these old black-and-white films from the early forties. We'd watch them Friday nights, which was my parent's date night. Baylor's favorite Tarzan was Buster Crabbe, he was a silent movie star. But I loved Johnny Weissmuller. Oh my God, he had a body, running around in that loincloth. I think he'd been an Olympic swimmer. And Jane was Maureen O'Sullivan, so glamorous. My favorite one of those movies was called *Tarzan's New York Adventure*. I don't remember all the details, but Boy gets kidnapped and taken to New York, and Tarzan and Jane get on a plane and go after him. And Jane has to civilize Tarzan, you know, to get him prepared for the big city. They go to a tailor and have him fitted for a suit, and he has to ride in a cab, and all this other stuff. And Tarzan, who is this action hero, is just so sad, so out of place in the city. . . ."

"And you're saying if I were to move to Seattle to be with you, that I'd be like Tarzan—lost in New York? Ellis, this is Nags Head, North Carolina, not deepest, darkest Africa. And I'm no jungle savage. I have a college degree, two years of law school. I may not enjoy wearing a coat and tie, but I do wear shoes on a semiregular basis . . ."

Ellis pushed a strand of hair from her forehead. "You know that's not what I'm getting at. I'm just saying you've figured out how you want to live your life, and you're doing that. And me dragging you off to Seattle, making you wear a tie . . ."

"Instead of a loincloth?"

She laughed in spite of herself. "I wouldn't mind seeing you in a loincloth, now that you mention it. But I just don't see how we could make it work. I've tried it before, with a man who was totally different. It was a disaster. You and I don't even want the same things."

"How do you know it would be a disaster this time?" Ty asked. "How do you know what I want? Or what you really want? Are you telling me you want to go back to a job in banking, like you had before?"

"No," Ellis said. "Not exactly."

"And Seattle? That's the city of your dreams?"

"No!" Ellis said. "I've never even been to Seattle. But I've got to be practical. This job offer means something to me, Ty. It means I haven't been wasting the last fifteen years of my life. It means somebody values what I do. I'll have a profession, and a title at the bank. And yes, a paycheck and benefits and all those boring middle-class trappings you hate. So yes, I admit, I might have to compromise, move to a new city, go back into banking."

"You'll compromise for a crappy job you don't even really want, but not on taking a chance that we could make things work together?" Ty pushed his chair back and away from hers.

"I've known you for less than a month," Ellis said, her voice pleading. He stood at the deck railing, staring off at the water.

"A month is enough for me to know how I feel about you," Ty said, his back to her. "A week was enough. You were such a pain in the ass with those e-mails of yours, pestering me to get into this house. And then I saw you come bopping up the driveway, in your little pink shorts . . . I knew I was a goner."

She got up and stood beside him. The wind had picked up, and it was whipping her hair into her face. "I could come back out here, weekends, like that. Banks have lots of holidays. Columbus Day is what, six weeks away? You could come out there and visit. A long-distance relationship isn't ideal, but lots of people do it. Look at Booker and Julia."

"Booker and Julia are getting married. She's moving to DC to be with him, isn't that what you told me?"

Ellis bit her lip and wished she hadn't brought it up. "They've been together for years and years. It's different with us, Ty. You know it is."

He looked at her steadily, at her dark hair blowing in the wind. She kept trying to brush it away from her face, control it. Maybe she was right, maybe he didn't have any right to ask her to believe in him, to believe in them. But shouldn't she believe in them too?

"Time's got nothing to do with it," he said finally. "Kendra and me? We'd known each other since grade school. Started dating in eighth grade. I thought I knew everything about her. She sure as hell knew everything about me, or so she thought."

The wind had picked up more, he turned his back to the railing, and now he was looking at the apartment, thinking about his last night here, and how he wanted it to be. Through the kitchen window, he could see the bottle of wine he'd bought, sitting on the counter. And he was thinking about how he'd been planning this evening ever since Joe broke the news that they'd tear the place down come morning. Things were not going according to plan.

"Kendra and I were together, from the time we were, like, fourteen, 'til we split up in law school," Ty said. "This apartment? I shouldn't tell you this, but for some reason, I feel like I have to. We'd sneak over here in high school, you know, late at night. It was never locked."

He saw the look of mild shock on Ellis's face. "We were kids, still in high school. Kendra loved breaking the rules, loved the idea of pushing her daddy's buttons. He'd have had me arrested if he knew what we were up to over here."

"I don't want to hear this," Ellis said, stony faced. "I realize it was a long time ago, but I don't want to hear about you sleeping with your girlfriend in the same place where we've been sleeping."

"Not the same bed," Ty said hastily. "God no. There wasn't even a bed here, back then. Just an air mattress."

"Why are you telling me this?" Ellis demanded. "You want to hurt me, because I'm being realistic? Because I won't just throw my life away and move in down here with you? Move in where? You won't even have a place to live after tomorrow."

"I've got a little cottage rented less than half a mile down the Beach Road," Ty said. "Pelican Cottage. It sits right on the dunes. It's rustic, but you'd love it. And then, when the movie people are gone, we could come right back to Ebbtide."

"Not the point," Ellis said.

"I'm telling you all this," Ty said, "because I have a point to make. And that point is, it doesn't matter how long you've known somebody. People change. Or you don't really know them as well as you thought you did in the first place. You told me you made a huge mistake marrying a man you'd only known a short time. Well, I made a huge mistake too. Only I'd known Kendra most of my life. And it didn't make any difference, because we ended up just as miserable as you were. We were kids back then, young and dumb. Not like now."

Ellis was looking at the apartment too. It was tiny, cramped, barely two rooms. She'd fantasized about staying here with Ty, waking up with him, about moonlight showers and beach walks at sunrise. But it wasn't until this moment that she realized all her fantasies were based on the one sun-splashed idyllic summer month they'd spent together. Summer.

September was a handful of days away. And then summer would be gone.

"You're right," she told Ty. "We're not kids anymore. We're old enough to recognize that some things are just . . . of the moment. Ephemeral. Like the shells you pick up at the beach. They're so shiny and perfect and pearlescent when you pick them up, and then when you get them back home, they're all bleached out and lifeless. I'm afraid that's what we'd be like. Three months from now, six months from now, wondering what we saw in each other . . ."

Ty's expression darkened. "Really, Ellis? That's what I am to you? Just some hot guy you picked up at the beach? A fling?"

"No!" Ellis cried. "You know that's not what I meant."

"Sure you did," Ty said quietly.

"You're making this harder than it has to be," Ellis pleaded.

He looked at her calmly. "Do you love me?"

"Yes! But that's not the point."

"Do you want to be with me?"

"You know I do. But it's just not that simple."

"It's not that hard," Ty said. "Not to me. I want to be with you, so I'll do whatever it takes to make that happen. Apparently you don't feel the same way."

Ellis took a step backwards. Ty's face was cold, impassive. If he could be that calm, so could she. She took a deep breath, and then another, willing herself not to cry or slobber or, God forbid, beg. "Where does that leave us?" she asked finally.

"I think it leaves me living here and you on your way to Seattle," Ty said. "Alone."

48

Ellis stared moodily down at her coffee cup. No truths there. Just inky, lukewarm, bitter blackness.

For once, she was glad to have the kitchen all to herself. If she were truthful, she'd have to admit that after a month together, much as she and Dorie and Julia loved one another, they were all probably getting on each other's nerves.

Madison was wiser than any of them. It was time, Ellis thought, to go home. She was already devising a game plan for packing up: stripping all the beds, running a last load of laundry, disposing of the refrigerator's contents, loading the car. What she would not think about, under any circumstances, was what she would be leaving behind.

She heard the low rumble of a diesel motor coming from the front of the house and ran to see what it was. A flatbed trailer was parked in the driveway, and a handful of men were waving and directing as a bright yellow bulldozer inched its way down a steel loading ramp.

When the operator had maneuvered the dozer off the ramp, a man in an orange safety vest and a hard hat ran over, jumped into the cab, and conferred with the driver. A moment later, the hard hat guy was back in the driveway, waving and pointing at the garage—and Ty's apartment. But there was no sign of Ty. His Bronco was gone, and the garage was empty.

Now Ellis noticed a huge jumble of stuff piled off to the side of the garage—its former contents: a three-legged ping-pong table; a stack of bald tires; a rusty barbecue grill; the skeletons of aluminum lawn chairs; even a small, wooden skiff with a rotted-out hull. And a surfboard. A faded yellow surfboard.

As she watched, the bulldozer lumbered purposefully towards the garage, aiming at the support beam that separated the two parking bays. She closed her eyes, and a moment later, she heard the sickening sound of boards snapping, beams tumbling to the ground, the garage sliding easily, effortlessly to the ground, with a thud she felt as well as heard.

She heard whistles and applause, and when she opened her eyes, a cloud of dust and sand still swirled in the air around the demolished garage.

Ellis felt a hand on her shoulder. She turned and saw Madison standing beside her.

"I saw the trucks coming from my bedroom window," Madison said. "I came down because I had half an idea you might still be up there," she jerked her head in the direction of where the apartment had stood, "with Ty."

They heard the screen door open and slap shut behind them. Julia and Dorie joined them on the porch, barefoot, in their pajamas.

"Jesus, Mary, and Joseph!" Julia exclaimed, gaping at the remains of the garage. "I heard that crash and I thought somebody'd dropped a bomb on the place."

"Wow," Dorie said. "That didn't take long."

"Where's Ty?" Julia asked. "How was your last night together in the love shack?"

Ellis stuck her hands in the pockets of her shorts. "I don't know where Ty's gone. I didn't spend the night. We . . . had a fight. Not a fight, per se, but . . ."

"Oh Jesus," Julia groaned. "Don't tell me you guys broke up. Don't tell me you actually want to take that stupid job at that stupid bank in Seattle."

"I told Dana I'd get back to her Monday," Ellis said. "You wouldn't understand, but this is just too good an offer to pass up. Ty doesn't understand either. So probably we just weren't meant to be."

Dorie gave her a hug. "Oh, Ellie-Belly. I'm so sorry. What happened?"

"Nothing," Ellis said. "He wants me to stay here, to live on love and peanut-butter-and-jelly sandwiches. It's sweet, but it won't work. One of us has to have a job, and benefits . . . and common sense."

"Let me guess," Julia drawled. "That someone would be you."

"Don't start," Ellis warned. "I am not in the mood for relationship advice."

By noon, the remains of the old garage had been scraped up and loaded onto a dump truck headed for the landfill. More lumber trucks and pickup trucks arrived, and even from the beach, the women could hear the whine of power saws and the sharp bursts of nail guns.

"One more day," Julia said under her breath, glancing over at Ellis, who'd deliberately set up her beach chair and umbrella several yards away from Dorie, Julia, and Madison. "Our last full day at the beach, and she manages to screw it up for all of us."

"I can't believe she's just going to walk away and leave Ty," Dorie said, keeping her voice low. "He's the best thing that's ever happened to her, and tomorrow she's just going to get in her car and drive back to Philly—and then pick up and move across the country?"

Madison sat cross-legged on her blanket, sipping from a cold bottle of water. "Maybe she's just not ready for a relationship. To commit."

"Hah!" Julia chortled. "You don't know Ellis. Nobody was ever more ready for a relationship than Ellis. Before Ty, she hadn't been with a man in, like, dog years."

"Ellis got married right out of college to this totally inappropriate guy," Dorie said, filling Madison in.

"The marriage was over before she got the wedding dress back from the dry cleaner's," Julia added. "Literally. Right, Dorie?"

"She was devastated," Dorie agreed. "It stunted her emotionally. For years."

"She buried herself in work at that damned bank, never took a vacation, and then, poof! They go and downsize her. She wakes up and realizes she's thirty-five, single, with no prospects in sight. And then garage guy walks in, and sweeps her right out of those damned sensible shoes of hers. But because Ty doesn't have a 401(k) and he doesn't fit into her game plan, she refuses to consider how right they are for each other," Julia said, glancing furtively at Ellis to make sure she couldn't hear her life being dissected.

"Look at her, poor thing," Dorie whispered, nodding towards Ellis, who had dozed off, facedown on her chair. "She was probably up all night crying after their big fight."

"It's sad," Madison observed.

"Ellis never talks about it, but I know she's always wanted a family," Dorie said. "That's what's so heartbreaking. She could have that with Ty. I mean, he's perfect for her."

"And hot. Smokin' hot," Julia pointed out.

"They did seem pretty sweet together," Madison said. "But she's a grown-up, right? And she knows what will and won't work for her."

"Not this time," Dorie said. She looked at Julia. "We've got to do something. And quick."

Julia jumped to her feet, tiptoed over to the sleeping Ellis, grabbed her beach tote, and brought it over to her own chair. She rummaged around inside the bag, setting aside sunblock, lipblock, paperback novel, and a notepad containing Ellis's to-do list. Finally, jubilantly, she held up Ellis's cell phone. "Don't worry," she told the others. "I'm on it."

The tiny print on the computer screen seemed to swim before his eyes. The agribusiness start-up he'd been following was announcing its IPO. He glanced over at the notes he'd made. The research was more than promising. The opening stock price was ridiculously low—four dollars a share? Two months ago, he'd have taken the plunge, gone all in. He had a little cushion now, with the cash from the movie people, so why couldn't he make himself place the stock order?

Ty shook his head, got up from the wooden table he'd moved over to his new cottage, and walked out to the screened porch. The sky was crystal blue, cloudless, a slight breeze coming off the beach. He stretched and rotated his shoulders. He'd been at the computer most of the morning, deliberately avoiding Ebbtide.

He hadn't actually planned to move over to Pelican until later in the day, but after the breakup with Ellis the night before, he hadn't seen any point in staying in the apartment another night. He'd sat at the kitchen table, drinking half the bottle of wine, then dumping the rest down the sink before he loaded his stuff in the Bronco and moved it over to Pelican Cottage sometime after midnight.

Instead of making him sleepy, the wine had made him annoyingly hyper. So he'd spent the early morning hours burying himself in the minutiae of day trading.

It was nearly eleven now, and he knew the garage was gone, because Joe had e-mailed him a photo taken at the precise moment the rotted wooden structure collapsed into the sand. Ty had glanced at the photo and deleted it. Not a moment he wanted to celebrate.

He should have been at the house by now. He'd hired the frame carpenters and laborers needed to start the barn raising, but somehow, he just couldn't make himself take the half-mile trip down the road to Ebbtide. He wondered if Ellis had watched the garage being torn down. She'd probably applauded its demise. Why the hell had he told her about his idiotic teenage trysts there with Kendra?

Ty went back inside the cottage and began shutting down his computer. His cell phone dinged, signaling he had a text message.

DEAR MR. CULPEPPER: WE NEED 2 TALK. MEET ME @ BEACH, MIDNIGHT, 2NITE. YR. FRIEND, ELLIS SULLIVAN.

He stared down at the text block. She wanted to talk? About what? As far as he was concerned, she'd done all the talking that was necessary the night before.

The hell with her, he told himself, typing rapidly.

NOTHING LEFT 2 SAY.

. . .

"Shit!" Julia exclaimed, staring down at Ty's text. "He's as stubborn as she is."

"Now what?" Dorie asked, keeping an eye on the slumbering Ellis.

Julia flexed her fingers and looked towards the sky for inspiration, but found only a flock of seagulls circling overhead.

"We just have to get them together," she muttered. "He's crazy about her. She's crazy about him. What's so hard about this?"

"Talk about crazy, you two are insane if you think this is going to work," Madison said. "We're talking about two adults here, not a couple of sitcom characters."

"Let's analyze," Dorie said. "What is it that's keeping them apart?"

"Money," Madison said quickly. "Lack of it."

"Not really," Dorie said.

"Ellis is the least materialistic person I know," Julia agreed. "But she's so friggin' practical."

"And rigid," Dorie threw in. "If she can't list it, chart it, or graph it, Ellis doesn't get it. She craves security."

"Security," Madison with a snort. "I thought I was getting that when I married Don, and look where it got me."

"If she knew Ty had some kind of a job, and if she had a job—one that would allow her to live here with him—I think Ellis would stay," Julia said.

"Well, let's get them jobs," Dorie said, as though it were the simplest thing in the world.

"Doing what?" Madison asked, flopping back down to the sand. "This is hopeless."

Julia scowled at Madison. "We can do this. I know we can. We just need to think outside the box."

"You said she worked at a bank," Madison said, trying to regain favor. "What kind of work did she do there?"

"Marketing," Julia said.

"Couldn't she do that down here?"

"If there were any really big banks here, sure, but Ellis did corporate marketing," Dorie said kindly. "And those jobs are in big cities, like Philly or Charlotte, where she worked before, or Seattle, where she's going to move if we don't stop her."

"Couldn't she telecommute?" Madison asked. "I mean, these days, if you have a computer, a BlackBerry, and a headset, you can do just about any kind of work, anywhere."

"No," Julia said peevishly. "It doesn't work like that."

Dorie looked quizzically at Julia. "Why couldn't it work that way? One of our math teachers at school, her husband does IT work for a company out of Boston. He flies up there one week out of every month, but the rest of the time he works from home, right there in Savannah."

"See?" Madison said smugly. "Telecommuting. That's the answer."

"It could be," Julia said slowly. "But Ellis has a job offer. You heard her. It's the total package: pay, promotion, benefits. You know how the economy is. There just aren't that many jobs out there."

"Because she's really only applied for jobs in bank marketing and on the East Coast," Dorie pointed out. "Maybe if she sorta branched out, you know, widened her target, with the idea of telecommuting, she'd have a better shot."

"Maybe," Julia said. "It's worth thinking about. Ellis is terrific at what she does, nobody's harder working, or more creative or talented, that's for sure."

"And what about Ty?" Dorie said. "That's a tough one. Ellis told us Ty said he never wants another office job, never wants to have to put on a tie or sit in a cubicle again."

"I don't know, I don't know," Julia moaned. "This is hurting my head."

Dorie was still watching Ellis, who'd stirred, just the slightest bit, throwing an arm over her eyes to block out the sun. "Let's get back to business," she whispered. "Before Ellis wakes up and catches us with her phone. What are we going to say to Ty to get him to meet her on the beach at midnight?"

"Even if you get *him* here, how are you going to get Ellis here?" Madison asked.

"First things first," Julia said, typing again.

. . .

Ty read the text once, and then again, to make sure he'd read it right.

IF YOU LOVE ME, YOU'LL COME.

He typed rapidly, without thinking.

SEE YOU @ MIDNIGHT.

As soon as the "sent" icon lit up, he closed the phone and slipped it in the pocket of his shorts. He opened his computer, rebooted, and went to his account page. The IPO offer for the agribiz seemed to be going well. Share prices were up to $4.25. He hit the "buy" button, nodded, and shut the computer down again.

He went outside, unlocked his beach cruiser, and pedaled quickly up the road to Ebbtide. It was going to be an interesting day, no matter what.

"Oh my God!" Dorie squealed, when Julia handed her Ellis's phone. "It worked. It totally worked. He's coming." She held her hand over her heart and sighed deeply. "This is so romantic, I could die."

"You *will* die, because Ellis will probably kill you two when she finds out what you've been up to," Madison said. "Now, tell me, geniuses, how are you going to get Ellis down to the beach at midnight?"

"We'll get her there," Julia said, "doing what we do best: lying and trickery. All we have to do now is keep Ellis away from Ty until their midnight meeting. Just in case he happens to mention getting those texts."

"That won't be hard," Dorie predicted. "Ellis hates confrontation. If she even sees Ty, I bet she'll run the other way."

"Even so, I don't want to take any chances," Julia said. She took the cell phone back from Dorie, and carefully cleared the texts to Ty from the memory. Then she tucked it back in the beach bag, and tiptoed over to where Ellis was just beginning to stir.

Julia plopped down onto the sand beside Ellis, at the same time dropping the bag casually beside her chair.

"Hey," Ellis said, shading her eyes from the sun's glare. "What are you up to?"

"Nothing," Julia said innocently. "Just wanted to tell you to turn over. Your face is getting too much sun."

"Thanks," Ellis said, yawning. "You're the best."

"You don't even know," Julia said, handing Ellis a bottle of sunblock. "Listen, Booker left this morning, and I still need to return all that stuff I bought to HomeGoods. Dorie's got a farewell lunch date with Connor, and Madison . . . well, you know Madison. Anyway, I was wondering if you'd go with me to help load and unload the stuff. Dorie says we can take the van."

Ellis frowned. "I was kinda thinking I'd start cleaning out the fridge and packing this afternoon."

"Madison volunteered to clean the fridge," Julia lied. "And you'll have plenty of time to pack this afternoon, before we head out for karaoke tonight."

"Yeah," Ellis said slowly. "About karaoke. I know it's your birthday and all, but I really don't think I'm gonna be up for a lot of partying tonight. I'll go to dinner, but after that, I think I'll just have a last quiet night at Ebbtide. I want to get an early start in the morning."

"Nuh-uh," Julia said. "You're not weaseling out of karaoke. It's our last night together, not to mention my birthday. Don't make me play the guilt card, Ellis. Either we all go, or nobody goes." She crossed her arms and glared defiantly at her friend.

"Does it have to be karaoke at Caddie's?"

"Yes, it does," Julia said. "Anyway, it's Friday. Even if Ty is working tonight, he'll be too busy slinging margaritas to see what you're up to."

"This isn't about Ty," Ellis started.

"Sure it is," Julia said. She stood up and offered a hand to Ellis. "Now let's get moving. I'm pretty sure you've drawn up a new Kaper chart back at the house, telling all of us what we've got to do before checkout tomorrow."

49

"Ty," Angie said, "I'm at my wit's end here. Patricia's a no-show again. It's our last college night of the summer, and the place is already packed to the rafters. I'm begging you. Just come in 'til midnight. I'll get Nella to close, but if I don't get somebody behind the bar, like, right now, I may have to kill myself."

Ty pushed his chair away from the computer. He walked out of the cottage and stared out at the sky. It was past eight and the last orange streaks of sunset were barely visible over the dunes that separated Pelican Cottage from the beach. The view wasn't nearly as good as his own view back at the garage apartment at Ebbtide had been. He was going to miss that view, but there would be other sunsets, and in ninety days, give or take a few, he would be back home at the old house, this time for good.

"Sorry, Angie, can't do it," Ty said. "I've got something else tonight."

"What?" she demanded. "Look, I told you I'm desperate. Just tell me what it'll take to get you here, right now, and I'll pay it."

He considered Angie's offer. She was over a barrel, and he knew it.

"A hundred bucks an hour," he said promptly. "Cash. Plus tip out."

"Shit!" Angie groaned. "I could get five bartenders for that."

"So get 'em."

"No, damn it. I need you and you know it. Get over here now."

"Sure," he said. "But there's just one more thing. I can't stay 'til midnight. I gotta be out of there by eleven thirty. Sharp."

"Okay, fine, whatever," she said.

"I mean it, Angie. I don't care if every damn college kid on the Outer Banks is in there tonight. I'm walking at eleven thirty. No matter what. Understand?"

"Just get here," Angie snapped.

Julia sauntered into Ellis's room just as she was zipping herself into the pink Lilly Pulitzer sundress.

"Don't start," Ellis warned, when she saw Julia's disapproving frown. "I've already packed everything else except what I'm wearing in the morning. And I am not borrowing any more of your clothes tonight. This is who I am. I'm not Julia Capelli. I don't wear spike heels or black lace bras as tops. I am Ellis Sullivan. Boring, predictable, safe Ellis Sullivan. So deal with it!"

"I was just gonna ask if I could borrow your silver hoop earrings," Julia said, seating herself on the edge of the bed. "But if you're gonna go all postal on me, never mind."

"Earrings? That's all you want?"

"Yeah. What did you think I wanted?"

Ellis reached into the pink satin jewelry roll that sat on top of her dresser and fished out the silver hoops. "You didn't come in here to try and get me all skanked up tonight before we go to Caddie's?"

"Nope," Julia said.

"And you're not gonna try and talk me out of leaving tomorrow? Instead of staying here, with Ty?"

"Nope," Julia said. She held out her hand. "Just a pair of earrings. That's all I need. Oh yeah, Dorie asked me to come up here and tell you she needs you down in the laundry room. She can't figure out which towels are yours and which ones stay in the house."

"The fugly gray and maroon towels stay here," Ellis said, turning back to the mirror.

"Yeah, but she said there's some other laundry, she can't figure out who it belongs to. Extra sheets and pillowcases. You know Dorie, she gets flustered by the least little thing."

"Oh all right," Ellis said, running a brush through her dark hair. "I'll go."

"Great."

Julia followed Ellis to the stairway. She waited until Ellis was halfway down the stairs before she darted back to her room. She picked up Ellis's purse, fished out her cell phone and car keys and pocketed them quickly, before heading back to her own bedroom.

He had his back to the bar while he poured tequila from the blender, but Ellis knew that muscled back. She knew those wide shoulders, the narrow hips. She caught her breath and took a step backwards, but Dorie grabbed her arm.

"Come on, Ellis," Dorie said. "You don't even have to talk to him. We'll find a table in the far corner."

"You guys," Ellis pleaded. "Don't make me do this."

"Do what?" Madison said, hooking her hand through Ellis's elbow. "Come on, Ellis. It's ladies' night. Our last night. You don't want to spoil Julia's birthday, do you?"

"Anyway, this place is jammed," Julia pointed out as they maneuvered through the crowd. "He'll never even know you're here."

"I'll know," Ellis said darkly, but she allowed herself to be towed to a table near the tiny stage, and then, reluctantly, to be talked into a lemontini. And then another. The music got louder, and then the karaoke mistress stood up and began taking requests.

First up were a pair of leather-clad biker dudes, one short and round, the other a foot taller, with an impressive beer belly and an even more impressive handlebar mustache.

"'Hotel California,'" Julia predicted. "I guarantee." And when the two launched into the Eagles classic, the women shared high-fives all around.

A pudgy brunette in too-tight white jeans, her breasts spilling out of a white tube top, clambered to the stage next, and shocked the crowd by singing a rendition of "Crazy" so pitch perfect, the women all swore she was Patsy Cline come back to life.

While they all stood, giving the Patsy wannabe a standing ovation, Ellis glanced over at the bar. Ty was clapping, whistling. In a split second, his eyes caught hers. He nodded, smiled, as though nothing had happened. Ellis felt her face flush, and she looked away.

Two songs later, Dorie stood and announced, "I'm taking a potty break. Anybody need anything?"

"Potty break and a Connor break, right?" Julia teased. "You think we didn't see you watching the door to see if he was working tonight?"

"I have to pee every thirty minutes," Dorie said. "Can I help it if the ladies' room is right by the bouncer's booth?"

Twenty minutes later, she was back, a tray of drinks in hand, with the karaoke catalog tucked under her arm.

"Ty sent these over," she announced, distributing the cups. "He saw me talking to Connor, and insisted that he wanted to buy us all a round of drinks since tomorrow's our last day. He says we're the best tenants he's ever had. Isn't that so sweet?"

"Adorable!" Julia said, staring at Ellis, who nodded mutely, and then knocked her drink back in one long guzzle.

Dorie and Julia exchanged a worried glance.

"Hey, slow it down," Julia said. "You don't wanna be driving with a hangover tomorrow, do you?"

Ellis tossed her hair. "I think I know what I'm doing."

"So. What are we gonna sing?" Dorie asked, flipping the catalog open.

"We? There is no we," Madison said.

"I thought we'd do a group number," Dorie said, looking around at the others. "What'll it be?"

"How 'bout 'It's Raining Men'?" Julia asked.

"Or what about 'Love Shack,' you know, since the B-52s are from Georgia, like us," Dorie suggested. "What do you think, Madison?"

Madison glanced down at the book, turned the page. "I don't do karaoke, as I think I mentioned previously," she said. "But if I did, I'd have to say we should do 'I Will Survive.'"

"Oooh, good one," Ellis had to admit. "I think that could be the theme song for all of us, right?"

Dorie nodded absentmindedly, still turning the pages of the book. "No. I got it. This is it. The one." She pointed at Julia, Ellis, and Madison. "And we are all gonna sing it. Together. Every single one of us. Because it's Julia's birthday. Right, Julia?"

Julia craned her neck to see what song Dorie had chosen. "Right. I'm the birthday princess and you all have to do what I say. So, what are we singing?"

"You'll see," Dorie said, slamming the book shut. "When it's our turn."

He'd found the house with little difficulty, thanks to the faded EBBTIDE sign by the mailbox. He'd cruised past half a dozen times during the day, but there was a surprising amount of activity, some kind of construction project going on, with cars and trucks coming and going. At one point, he'd even ventured down the driveway, simply following a caravan of pickup trucks full of workers. He'd spotted Maryn's Volvo, parked off to the side of the house, and smiled to himself. She was still here.

After six, when the workers left for the day, it was easy to pull into the lot next door, and hide his vehicle behind the foundation of a burnt-out old house.

It had been ungodly hot, waiting, but finally, darkness fell, and he could see silhouettes of the women moving around inside the house. So far, he hadn't spotted Maryn, but it didn't matter. She was there, he knew that. And he could afford to be patient.

Finally, close to nine o'clock, he saw the lights in the house being switched off, one by one. He got out of his vehicle, crept to the edge of the stack of lumber that had been unloaded only hours earlier, and watched while the women filed out of the decrepit old house and piled into a red van. The other three women were dressed stylishly, as if for a night out, but not her. He smiled, seeing Maryn dressed incongruously in cheap jeans and an oversized T-shirt, with her hair tucked up beneath a long-billed baseball cap. As though that would make her unrecognizable to anybody who knew the real Maryn.

Ebbtide was a ramshackle old wreck of a house, with thick beams, walls of cedar planks, and solid wooden doors. The locks, however, were a different matter. He'd easily jimmied the rusted lock on the kitchen door at the back of the house. Once inside, he'd quickly moved through all the bedrooms to ascertain which one was Maryn's. He'd cursed silently when he discovered that she, alone among the women, had locked her bedroom door. Not that it had slowed him down much. He'd seen the open window from the beach side of the house, and the old-fashioned catwalk that led to it from another third-floor door. It had been easy enough to find the door to the attic, and the corresponding window. And somebody, it appeared, had recently taken that same route to Maryn's room, judging by the fresh-looking splinters on the attic access door.

And how convenient, he marveled, that he'd been provided such a neat and convenient escape route—the steel spiral staircase leading directly from Maryn's room to the ground floor, and the burnt-out skeleton of the house next to Ebbtide, where his vehicle awaited, behind a clump of shrubbery.

From the looks of things, his timing was impeccable. Their departure was imminent. Maryn's duffle bag was packed. It took him only a moment to find the laptop case, shoved to the back of the shelf in the closet. He sat down on the room's only chair to wait. He had all the time in the world.

Eleven o'clock came and went. Julia caught Dorie's eye and glanced meaningfully at her watch. "Hey, Dorie," she said. "How much longer before our number comes up?"

"Oh," Dorie said, catching the meaning. "Uh, well, there were a bunch of requests in front of mine."

Ellis picked up Julia's drink and took a sip. "What's the hurry? The party's just getting started."

Julia reached over and put her hand to Ellis's forehead. "Are you hallucinating? I can't believe you're not champing at the bit to get home and finish packing. You didn't even want to come tonight."

Ellis pushed her hand away. "I changed my mind. Is that a crime?" She turned to Dorie. "Hey, pass me that karaoke thing."

Dorie rolled her eyes. "Really? You? You're going to do karaoke? By yourself?"

But Ellis was flipping through the pages of the catalog, pausing only when she came to the next to the last page. She looked up and glanced over at the bar, and she was sure Ty looked away.

"Yep, this is the one," she said, getting to her feet. She grabbed a wad of bills from her pocketbook and pushed her way through the crowd towards the karaoke mistress.

"Is she drunk?" Madison asked, looking from Dorie to Julia.

"Drunk or in love. Either way, this ain't the Ellis we know," Julia said grimly, and Dorie nodded in agreement.

When Ellis got back to the table, she had another drink. As soon as she wasn't looking, Julia dumped most of the contents of Ellis's cup into her own.

Two songs later, the emcee called out, "Ellis. Ellis, baby, where you at?"

A moment later, an Ellis they'd never seen before was prancing around the vest-pocket-sized stage, doing her best to channel Cyndi Lauper singing the anthem that had been theirs in parochial school, when they'd prance around Julia's princess pink bedroom in their Our Lady of Angels Peter Pan blouses and blue-plaid jumpers, pretend microphones in hand, warbling about how "Girls Just Wanna Have Fun."

Despite dissolving into a fit of nervous hysterical laughter halfway through the first verse when she forgot the words, Ellis's enthusiasm and confidence grew with every beat, so that by the end of the song, seemingly every woman in the club was on her feet, snaking around the dance floor in an impromptu conga line, chanting over and over, "they just wanna, they just wanna-uh-uh-uh . . ."

Stuck behind the bar, Ty had to scramble on top of an empty bar stool to catch a glimpse of her. When he did, the slow grin spread across his face again. "Attagirl," he said softly, to nobody in particular.

When Ellis made it back to their table, pink faced and sweat drenched, the three women stood and applauded. Ellis collapsed into her chair. "I did it!"

"You sure did," Julia agreed, glancing at her watch. "Now we really probably need to get you home."

"No!" Dorie cried. "We are not leaving here tonight until we all do our group number." She gave Julia an accusatory look. "You promised."

"Fine," Julia said. She plucked a ten-dollar bill from her pocketbook and strode towards the karaoke mistress.

"Think you could move Dorie and friends in the lineup?" she asked, cupping her hands to the woman's ear. "One of the girls is pregnant, and we need to get her home pretty soon. And it's our last night at the beach. Our swan song, you might say."

The karaoke mistress palmed the bill. "No problem," she said. "One more song, and you guys are on."

Julia nodded her thanks and went back to the table, nonchalantly glancing in the direction of the bar. To her satisfaction, she saw Ty, deep in conversation with an older, blond woman. He was gesturing angrily at his watch. She was shaking her head, but a moment later, Julia saw Ty head for the front door.

"We're next," Julia announced.

But Ellis wasn't listening. She'd been surreptitiously watching the bar, wondering if Ty would approach the table, maybe try to catch her attention, or even draw her outside to talk. Now though, she saw him scurrying for the front door, and her heart sank. He hadn't come anywhere near the house all day. As far as Ty was concerned, she thought bitterly, they'd already said their good-byes.

She picked up her neglected drink and knocked back half its watery contents, then turned her attention back to the stage, where a gaggle of drunken chicks were inexpertly grinding away at The Pussycat Dolls' "Don't Cha."

And then the karaoke mistress was calling. "Dorie and friends! All the way from Savannah, Georgia. Come on up here, girls, and show 'em how it's done!"

Madison crossed her arms defiantly over her chest. But Julia Capelli was having none of it.

"Let's go," she said, jerking Madison's chair backwards. "Showtime!"

Ellis looked at Madison and shrugged. "Come on," she said. "It's our last night. Might as well get it over with."

Dorie herded them all onstage, and they heard the distinctive introductory bass thumps. "Okay," she said, taking charge. "Julia and I will do the Travolta part. Ellis, you and Madison do Olivia Newton-John."

And the next moment, the four of them were sashaying across the stage, warbling "Summer Nights" from *Grease*. And when it came to the part about how summer flings don't mean a thing, Ellis Sullivan sang that verse with newfound wisdom.

50

That was awesome!" Dorie cried, throwing her arms around her friends at the end of the song.

"Yeah, we totally rocked it," Julia agreed, herding the women in the direction of the table. "But you guys, I think the birthday princess needs to go home now, before she turns into a pumpkin."

"Sounds good to me," Madison said readily.

They piled into the red van, with Dorie behind the wheel, and were almost home when Julia, trying to sound casual, pulled out her cell phone and groaned.

"Oh, no. My battery's dead. And I promised Booker I'd call him before midnight. Damn!"

"I'd let you use mine," Dorie offered, "but I've used up all my minutes for the month."

"Here," Ellis said, rummaging in her purse. "Just call him on mine."

"Okay," Julia said, holding out her hand.

"Well, hell," Ellis said, sounding puzzled. "It's not in here." She dumped the contents of the purse onto her lap, and pawed through the lipsticks, pens, billfold, Kleenex packets, and a notebook of lists.

Julia turned around from the front passenger seat. "Are you sure it's not there?"

"Positive," Ellis said. "And my keys are missing too. Dorie," she cried, "turn around. We've got to go back to Caddie's. I think maybe my phone and keys fell out of my purse back there."

"What?" Julia said, sounding panicky. It was ten minutes before midnight. "I didn't see your phone and keys on the table. And I was sitting right beside you all night."

"They've gotta be there," Ellis insisted. "Dorie, please go back. You guys can stay in the van, I'll just run inside and check the table and be right back."

"It can't be there," Julia countered. "Right, Dorie?"

"When was the last time you remember seeing your phone?" Dorie asked. "Think back."

"I don't know," Ellis said. "I've been running around all day, between the house and the beach, and packing, and cleaning, and starting to load the car."

"The beach!" Dorie cried. "Oh my God, of course. Ellis, it completely slipped my mind. When I was picking up my chair and towel this afternoon, I noticed your phone and keys on your beach chair. I meant to say something, but I just figured you were planning to go back down there later in the afternoon."

"Dorie!" Ellis said, annoyed. "Why didn't you say something sooner? Or just pick it up and bring it to me?"

"I'm an idiot," Dorie wailed. "It was so hot out there today, and then Willa called me on my cell to yell at me some more, and I just forgot."

"For Pete's sake," Ellis grumped. "That means my phone and keys have been out on the beach for hours. Somebody probably already walked off with them."

"Maybe not," Madison said helpfully.

"Look," Julia said, "we're almost home. You can just hop out of the van as soon as we get back to Ebbtide, and go check. I'm sure they're still there."

"Not likely," Ellis said gloomily.

. . .

Ty's hair was still wet, but he'd managed to shower and change out of his work clothes in ten minutes flat and walk down the beach from his new cottage to the stretch in front of Ebbtide. Now, at exactly five minutes 'til midnight, he stood on the beach, wondering if coming back here tonight was a mistake.

He glanced up at the spot where the garage, and his apartment, had been only twenty-four hours earlier, and looked quickly away. He'd done the right thing, what needed to be done, but he'd miss the old rattrap.

Somebody had left a folding beach chair in the middle of the spot where the Ebbtide girls had pitched their camp for the past month. A pink-and-orange striped beach towel was tossed across the back of the chair, and as he looked closer, he saw a cell phone and set of keys under the edge of the towel. He picked up the phone, pushed the on button, and seeing the call log, realized it belonged to Ellis.

Ty sat down on the chair to wait.

He was waiting, sitting quietly in the dark, on the chair by the window—the same window Madison looked out countless times, every morning and night, searching for any sign of trouble. A bead of sweat trickled down his back as he sat in the stifling closet-sized room. He'd considered turning on the rusty air conditioner stuck halfway into the window by the bed, but then decided to do so would alert her that somebody had been in the room.

He glanced down at the LED display of his wristwatch. Nearly midnight. Had she met another man? His eye twitched at the thought of Maryn with somebody else. Then he shook his head. Impossible. He'd seen the red van roll away from the house hours ago with the four women inside. Girls' night out. Completely harmless.

Not that it mattered. He patted the laptop case on the floor, its sides bulging with the cash he'd easily discovered hidden on the top shelf of the armoire. His cash. He'd earned it. He meant to have it, and he would have it, just as soon as he dealt with Maryn. He'd had time to count it, waiting for her, stacking the bills in rows that completely covered the bed. And it was all there, save for one hundred dollars. That surprised him, that Maryn hadn't spent the money, hadn't fled the country as soon as she figured out what she had. Maryn had never struck him as a particularly noble type. She was a hard-edged realist, just like he was. Which was why he'd been attracted to her.

He saw the play of lights on the opposite wall of the darkened room and stood up to look out the window. The red van was bumping down the driveway at a fast clip. It didn't stop until it was directly in front of the porch. Then the engine switched off, and a petite redhead jumped from the driver's seat and raced for the front porch. A moment later, the back doors of the van opened, and he watched, his pulse quickening, as Maryn climbed out, stretched, and said something to the lanky blonde who got out the other side of the car. The two of them looked up at the house, and he stepped back, quickly, even knowing that there was no way she could see him up here, in the dark. Still . . .

Getting up and walking softly to the door, he opened it just far enough to hear the front door opening below. Lights clicked on, and there were more voices. This time he was certain he heard Maryn, and one of the other women, giggling conspiratorially. He closed the door and took up a position just to the side of it.

Minutes passed. He heard steps coming up the stairs. "G'night, y'all," an unfamiliar woman's voice called gaily. The steps stopped at the second floor, and he heard a door close, water running, and then the flush of a toilet, the sound of the bathroom door opening, and moments later, another door closing.

He resumed his wait, slumped against the wall, listening to his own even breathing. He heard more footsteps on the stairs, and tensed. His hands were slick with sweat. He dried them on his jeans, stood, moving towards the door, his hand on the pistol shoved into his waistband. The footsteps paused at the second-floor landing. Maybe it was one of the other women, Maryn's housemates? But then the footsteps resumed, slowly climbing the stairs to the third floor.

It was serendipity, really, that she'd chosen this room, isolated on the top floor of the house. Not a surprise though. Maryn didn't trust anybody, especially other women. The big surprise was that she'd moved in with these strangers at all. Didn't matter why she'd choosen this room, all that mattered was that it was perfect for his needs.

The footsteps were coming closer now. And she was humming. What was it? "They just wanna," she crooned, "they just wanna-uh-uh." Cyndi Lauper? Maryn? He'd never known her to hum, let alone sing. Was she drunk or high? The footsteps paused in front of the door, and he held his breath as she fumbled to fit the key into the lock.

The door opened slowly. "They just wanna, they just wanna-uh-uh." She stepped inside, her hand searching for the light switch.

He waited until the light was on, then he stepped forward, throwing his forearm across her throat, dragging her into the room, closing the door quietly behind them.

Her eyes widened in terror, and before she could scream he clamped his hand over her mouth. "Welcome home," he whispered in her ear.

Ellis grabbed a flashlight from beneath the kitchen sink and hurried out the door towards the walkway over the dunes. How on earth, she wondered, had she managed to leave her phone and keys at the beach? She could have sworn she'd seen them in her beach bag once she'd gotten back to the house, but the day had been so busy, maybe she'd just imagined it.

She kicked her sandals off at the landing on top of the dunes, and pointing the flashlight at the steps, gingerly climbed down, holding tight to the railing. It seemed especially dark tonight, she thought. Glancing up, she saw that dense banks of purple-edged clouds obscured the moon. The temperature had dropped, and the wind had picked up. Heat lightning crackled over the water, and she heard the low rumble of thunder. She prayed it wouldn't start raining until after she'd found her phone.

When she reached the beach, she played the flashlight back and forth until she spotted the forgotten beach chair, with her towel still draped over it. And Ty Bazemore seated in it. She inhaled sharply and grabbed the stair rail, her instincts telling her to turn and run back towards the house.

But before she could move, Ty was standing up, and he was looking at her, and, wait . . . Was he smiling? At her? Anyway, it was too late to run now.

She made herself walk towards him, like it was the most natural thing in the world. But her mind could not form a sentence that wouldn't sound idiotic. In the end she settled for, "I think I left my phone and keys down here today."

Ty held up the phone. "You did," he said. "They were right here on the chair." But he made no move to give them to her.

"I wasn't sure you'd really come tonight," he said. "Hell, I wasn't sure I'd come. But I'm glad you asked me to. I don't want things to end like this, Ellis."

"What are you talking about?" she asked, coming to a dead stop inches from the chair. "Asked you to do what?"

"Come on, Ellis," Ty said, feeling his face grow hot. "This was your idea, not mine. Don't do this."

"Ty," Ellis said. "I really have no idea what you are talking about. What are you doing here? Why did you come out here tonight?"

He reached out and brushed a strand of her hair, tucking it behind her ear. "I came because you texted me and asked me to. I came because you said if I loved you, I would come. I do love you. I'm here. I'll meet you more than half-way, if you'll just give me a chance."

"I texted you?"

He frowned. "What is this? Some kind of sick joke?"

She took her phone from him, checked the log of text messages. It was empty. She held it up for him to see. "I did not text you today. I swear."

"You did, by God," Ty said. He pulled his own phone from the pocket of his cargo shorts, pulled up the screen, and showed her. "See! Why would I make up something like that?"

Ellis read the messages, glancing up at Ty, whose face had gone stony. Her own face was beet red.

Suddenly, she knew. "Julia!" she cried. "And Dorie! They did this. They stole my phone while I was asleep on the beach this afternoon, and they sent these texts to you. I woke up, and Julia was fiddling with my beach bag. I thought she was getting my sunblock out, but she must have just been putting the phone back. And then sometime later, she must have stolen it again, and planted it out here."

"And why would they pull a juvenile stunt like that?" Ty demanded. "They're your friends. Why would they punk you like that? Or me?"

Ellis wanted to die. She wanted to sink into the sand and disappear from the humiliation.

"Because," she said, biting back tears, "my idiot, deranged, meddling friends have this stupid idea that we belong together. They feel sorry for me, because they know I'm a loser, that I have no life outside my job. They know you're the first man I've been with in eleven years, and they probably have this stupid idea that we're in love. . . ."

"Hey," Ty said softly, catching her hand in his. "That's not so stupid."

She looked up at him, tears streaming down her face. "It's not stupid for them to send you fake texts from my phone to lure you down here?"

He chuckled. "That part was totally stupid. But it worked, didn't it? Here I am. And here you are."

She sniffed loudly. "Because they stole my phone and my car keys. I thought I'd left them back at Caddie's, but Julia forbid Dorie to drive back there so I could look. Dorie had this lame-ass story about how she'd seen them down here when she was leaving the beach this afternoon. I should have known. She's the world's worst liar."

"They wanted you here at midnight," Ty pointed out. "Because they knew that I'd damn sure be here, especially after that last text of yours."

Ellis blinked back a fresh set of tears. "Which one was that?"

He put his arms around her waist and pulled her close. "The one that said 'If you love me, you'll come.' I do. I did. So what should we do now?"

It started to rain. Fat, seemingly random drops full of August heat. Ellis rested her cheek against Ty's chest. Right here, in this moment, safe in the arms of a man who would do anything to make her happy. She had the answer. And all she had to do, she realized, was let him love her. Let go and let love happen. She felt the sand swirling around their ankles, the wind tearing at their clothes, the rain, coming down harder now, and above it all, she heard the crash of the surf.

She leaned her head back to look up at him, and his hair was already plastered to his head. "I think we better run for it," she said.

Ty grabbed her hand, and the two of them raced up the steps over the dunes. Ellis stopped at the top of the stairs to catch her breath, and her eyes drifted past the boardwalk, to Ebbtide, a shadowy gray hulk. The lights were on in the top-floor bedroom, Madison's room, and silhouetted there, she realized, were two figures. And one was a man.

"Ty," she said, pointing. "Up at the house. That's Madison's room. There's a man in there with her."

"Good for her," Ty said, tugging at her hand, pulling her towards the house.

"No," she said, stopping dead in her tracks. "It's got to be Adam. The man she worked with in New Jersey. She was expecting him a couple of days ago, but he never showed. We all thought there was something fishy about him, but Madison insisted he's harmless."

"I still don't see a problem," Ty said. "Look, can we have this discussion inside?"

"How did he get in the house? We lock the place up tight every time we leave. Madison locks her bedroom door, even if she's just going to the bathroom. Ty, he knows she has all that money. A hundred thousand dollars. She told him. He must have broken in while we were gone tonight."

51

"You still haven't asked me why I came down here," Don said, leaning back in the chair to enjoy the sight of the usually cool and composed Maryn fighting the panic he knew she must be feeling. Her face was pale and beaded with sweat.

"I know why you're here," she said, jerking her head in the direction of the briefcase. "You came to get your money back. It's all there. So take it and get out, why don't you?"

"What?" he said in mock disbelief. "My adoring wife doesn't enjoy spending time with her adoring husband?"

"Adoring?" Maryn hooted. "You never adored *me*. You adored owning me, bossing me around, showing me off to your friends. But I was just a thing to you. Nothing more, nothing less."

"And you didn't adore spending my money, living in the home I gave you, flashing that big diamond engagement ring, honeymooning in Bermuda?"

"Believe it or not, Don," Maryn said, grimacing, "I fell in love with you. The nice things were . . . nice, but for a while there—until I figured out who you were, and what you'd made me—I did love you."

"About that ring," Don said. He lifted one hip and reached for his pocket.

Maryn flinched. He's got a gun, she thought. He's got a gun, and he's going to shoot me.

Instead, Don brought out the black velvet ring box. He opened it, and thrust it towards Maryn.

"It hurts my feelings that you're not wearing your engagement ring," he said. "Put it on, why don't you? As a token of your affection."

"Fuck you," Maryn said, batting his hand and the ring box away. "It hurts *my* feelings that you've been screwing around with Tara Powers. Did you think I wouldn't find out? Taking her to the same restaurants you took me when we were dating? The same freakin' motels, afterwards? You've got the ring. Give it to your little whore Tara. Let her wear it."

Ty and Ellis stood, riveted, watching the shadow man reach out and slap the woman in the top-floor bedroom. "We've got to do something," Ellis said.

"First we've got to get out of this rain," Ty said, and hand-in-hand, they went splashing up the boardwalk towards the back porch. When they were safely under the shelter of the porch roof, Ellis remembered the cell phone she'd stuck in the pocket of her dress only a few minutes earlier.

"I'm calling the cops," she said. "Dorie and Julia are inside the house. What if he tries to hurt them?"

"Nine-one-one," a recorded woman's voice said. "You've reached Dare County Emergency Services. This line is to be used exclusively for life-threatening situations. If you are calling to report a nonemergency or inquire about county services, hang up and dial the number listed in your telephone directory. If you have a bona fide emergency, please stay on the line until an operator can assist you."

A faint hum came on the line.

"I'm on hold!" Ellis said, listening to a series of beeps. "Damn it, I have a real emergency. Come on, come on."

Ty pulled his own phone from his pocket and started punching numbers. "I'm calling Connor," he said. "He's still at the bar, but if he picks up, he's only ten minutes away." He waited, listened, and frowned. "It went to voice mail," he reported. "He probably can't even hear the damn thing ringing." He waited a moment. "Con, it's Ty. Look, we've got an intruder at Ebbtide, and I think he's holding one of these women hostage, in the top-floor bedroom. We've tried calling 911, but we're on hold. If you get this, haul your ass over here, right now."

"We can't wait," Ellis said. "The girls are alone inside the house. I've gotta get them out of there." She started for the kitchen door. "I'm gonna sneak upstairs and let them know what's going on, and get them out as quietly as I can."

"Fine," Ty nodded. "I'll stay here and watch the back staircase, in case he tries to take Madison out of there. Stay on the line for the cops. And be careful, okay?"

"Okay." Ellis eased the kitchen door open just far enough to slip inside.

Ellis tiptoed up the stairs, praying her bare feet would avoid the creaking boards, that she'd make it to the second floor undetected.

She heard water running in the bathroom, saw a flash of light from under Julia's bedroom door. She pushed into the room without knocking, finding Julia pulling a pink sleep camisole over her head.

"Julia!" Ellis whispered. "He's here."

"Who?" Julia said, stepping into her yoga pants. "Ty?"

"Not Ty! I mean, yes, Ty's downstairs, watching the back staircase. It's that Adam guy. He's upstairs, in Madison's room."

"How do you know?" Julia asked, alarmed.

"We were coming in off the beach because it started raining, and I happened to look up at the window. There are two people in Madison's room, and one of them is a man. It's got to be Adam!"

"How the hell . . . ?" Julia exclaimed. "How did he get in here? How'd he find the house?"

"I don't know, but he did," Ellis said. "We've got to do something."

"What?"

"I don't know," Ellis said. "I'm on hold for 911, and Ty left a message for Connor, asking him to get over here right away. But in the meantime, he's up there with Madison. We saw him slap her!"

"Where's Dorie?" Julia asked. "It would be just like her to go tripping upstairs to have one last gabfest with Madison."

They heard the sound of running water coming from down the hall. They tiptoed towards the bathroom. Julia tapped lightly, but there was no answer.

"Dorie," she whispered. "Open up."

"I'm not done yet," Dorie called, her voice echoing on the tile walls. "For God's sake, if you have to go that bad, use the downstairs bathroom."

"Let me in, damn it," Julia whispered hoarsely. "And shut the hell up."

Dorie opened the door looking peeved. Her hair was gathered in a purple scrunchy on top of her head, and she was wrapped in a damp towel. "What do you want?"

"Shut up!" Julia exclaimed. "You'll get us all killed." She grabbed Dorie's arm and yanked her out of the bathroom, herding her down the hall to her own bedroom. When they were inside the room, with the door locked, Ellis pointed upwards with her index finger.

"He's here!" she said. "Adam! In Madison's bedroom. He must have broken into the house while we were at karaoke. Ty and I were coming in off the beach, and we saw him."

"Call the cops, for God's sake," Dorie said.

"I have," Ellis exclaimed. "I've been on hold for, like, forever."

"Are you really on hold?" Julia asked. "Can they do that, put you on hold for 911?"

"I'm waiting for the next operator," Ellis said. "What should we do?"

"I know what I'm gonna do," Dorie said, heading for the door. "I'm gonna go put on some underwear. I can't handle an emergency naked."

"Wait for me," Julia said. "Come on, Ellis. We need to stay together."

Don Shackleford crossed his legs and sat back in the chair, regarding Maryn with a sardonic smile.

"You see," he said, shaking his head. "When you go nosing around in other people's business, you might find out stuff you regret. You shouldn't worry about Tara. She was just . . . convenient."

"The same way I was convenient when you met me?" Maryn asked. She let her right arm drift casually to the side of the bed, inching it down until her right hand rested loosely on the edge of the box spring.

"Not the same thing at all," Don said. "I married you, didn't I?"

"Eventually," Maryn agreed. "Although you conveniently forgot to mention that you were already married when we met."

"Separated, technically," Don said. "But you never asked if I was married, did you?"

"You also conveniently forgot to mention your vasectomy," Maryn said bitterly. "When were you going to tell me about that, Don?"

He sighed. "You've been speaking to Amy, I guess. Such a vindictive bitch. You'd think the fact that I never miss a child-support payment would soften her attitude, wouldn't you? Anyway, you don't really want to have a baby, Maryn. You're too self-involved to be a good mother. And God knows, I've been a less than stellar parent to the two brats I did father. No, I won't be reversing the vasectomy."

Maryn inched her fingertips between the mattress and the box spring, silently praying that she'd feel the comfort of the cool, blue steel at any moment.

"Look, Don," she said. "You've got your money. That's what you came down here for, right? Take it and go. I'm not going back to Jersey. As soon as I get settled and get a job, I'll hire a lawyer and we'll get a nice quiet divorce. You and Tara can sail happily off into the sunset. Just leave me the hell alone."

"A divorce?" Don tsk-tsked, mockingly placing a hand over the breast pocket of his crisply pressed, pale yellow dress shirt. "Why would I want a divorce? Why can't we just happy-ever-after?"

"I'm done," Maryn said, her fingers searching between the layers of foam and batting. She felt crumbs, and was that a dead fly? Where the hell was the revolver? "I'm not going back. I don't care what you did back there. The money, whatever went on with Prescott's? None of my business. I don't want to know it. I don't know anything. Not really."

Don sighed. "Oh, Maryn, I'm really disappointed in you. Never bullshit a bullshitter, okay?"

. . .

Voices wafted from beneath the door of Dorie's closet.

"The air shaft!" she whispered, pointing to the door. She tiptoed over and opened the closet door while Ellis closed and locked the bedroom door.

They heard Madison's voice.

"What happened to Adam?" she asked. "He's coming down here, you know. He knows I'm here. And he knows you threatened me. If anything happens to me, he'll go to the police."

"Don?" Julia whispered. "She's talking to Don? The husband?" She turned to Ellis. "I thought you said it was Adam up there with her."

"It was a guy, that's all I could tell," Ellis said, cupping her hand over the cell phone. "We were worried about Adam. How the hell did the husband figure out where she is?"

"Oh, bad news," Don said. "Adam won't be able to make it, I'm afraid. But he sends his regrets."

Maryn felt the hairs on her neck prickle. "I talked to him on the phone. What did you do to him?"

"Me? What about what he did to me? Blackmail is a crime, you know. Did you realize your boyfriend was a filthy little blackmailer?"

"Adam is not my boyfriend," Maryn said through gritted teeth. "I know somebody as promiscuous as you might not believe it, but I never cheated on you. Not with Adam, or anybody else."

"So you say. But he was under the impression that you were going to cheat on me. And that you were going to run off with him, just as soon as he got this money." Don patted the briefcase.

"Adam didn't know about the money," Maryn lied. "I deliberately didn't tell him about it."

"He knew all about it," Don corrected her. "It was supposed to be his. Do you mean you hadn't figured that out?"

"I don't believe you," Maryn said, but a sickening feeling in the pit of her stomach told her Don was telling the truth.

"It was only supposed to be twenty-five thousand dollars, in the beginning," Don said. "Adam isn't nearly as smart as he thinks he is, but he was just smart enough to go poking his nose where it didn't belong. He came to me with his suspicions, and although I didn't admit anything, I did agree to a payoff. It was supposed to be twenty-five thousand dollars. He was supposed to keep his mouth shut, but the greedy little bastard just couldn't do it. He had to keep pushing. And then . . . well, you know what happened then."

"Adam called in the auditors?" Maryn asked, confused. "Why would he do that?"

Don shrugged. "He was squeezing me for more money, and I really didn't believe his threats. I guess he decided to show me who had the upper hand. Rookie move."

"But why tell me?" Maryn asked.

"He probably thought you'd leave me and run away with him," Don said, chuckling. "Not that it matters now. I've got five million dollars stashed away. And Adam? Well, poor Adam won't be making any more idle threats."

Dorie looked wide-eyed at Ellis, who still had the cell phone pressed to her ear. "Are you still on hold?"

Ellis nodded.

"We've got to do something," Dorie said. She grabbed a pair of shorts and a T-shirt and started dressing. "This guy is a maniac. Do you hear how calm he is? Discussing bribery and embezzlement? And murder? He'll kill Madison, I know he will. What can we do?"

"What are you saying?" Maryn asked, horrified. "What have you done to Adam?"

She kept fumbling around with the mattress, trying to keep her expression calm, impassive. Had Don found the pistol and confiscated it? He had to remember he'd given it to her, even showed her how to fire it.

"Adam wanted another hundred thousand dollars after he called the auditors. And you. He said if I didn't come up with the money, he'd make an anonymous phone call to the state attorney general's office. They were already sniffing around by then, and so I agreed to the little bastard's demands. And that," Don said, patting the briefcase, "is how the hundred thousand dollars came to be in my laptop case."

"Adam was blackmailing you? I don't believe it," Maryn said, stalling, because now, actually, she really could believe Adam was capable of blackmail.

"I don't give a rat's ass what you believe," Don said. "But since we're having this chat, you should know that I was going to meet *him* that morning, the morning you made the unfortunate decision to go snooping around my office."

"Why? Why would he do that?" Maryn had her hand completely under the mattress, but the pistol definitely was not where she'd put it. Don? No, wouldn't he have shown her the gun first thing? Slowly, it dawned on her. Julia! She was the only other person who'd been alone in this room. She'd found the money easily enough. Had she found the gun and swiped it? Damn her!

"You can imagine how desperate Adam got when he realized his plan backfired," Don said. "And that you'd absconded with all his money. Not that I ever really intended to give him a cent," Don added.

He looked at Maryn with interest. "What are you fiddling with over there?" He stood abruptly and jerked Maryn off the bed.

She cried out in pain as her head hit the sharp edge of the nightstand, and the lamp fell to the floor, its glass base smashing to bits.

Maryn was sobbing softly.

One floor down, Dorie, Ellis, and Julia were riveted to the spot.

"He's hurting her," Dorie exclaimed. "Ellis, are you still on hold? Hang up and redial, for God's sake."

"What?" they heard Don say, with a low chuckle. "Were you looking for that pistol I gave you? I already looked. It's not there, is it?"

"The pistol," Julia whispered. "My God, I forgot to put it back under her mattress." She sprinted from the room and came back with her beach tote, holding the gun out with a look of horror and fascination.

"What should we do?" Dorie asked. "Y'all, we can't wait for the cops."

Ellis clicked the disconnect button. "I'm calling Ty," she whispered. "He's out back. He needs to know things are getting hairy in here."

"Where'd you put the gun, Maryn?" they heard Don ask, and when she kept crying, they heard the sickening sound of a slap, and then Maryn crying harder.

"Do something," Dorie implored. "He'll kill her."

Ellis's fingers were shaking as she tapped his name on her cell phone. The phone rang twice, three times, no answer. "Come on, Ty," Ellis breathed. "Pick up. Please, please, pick up." A moment later, she got his voice mail. "Hi, it's Ty," his voice said. "Leave a number and I'll hit you back."

"Ty, it's me," she said, cupping her hand over the phone, her lips close to the receiver. "The man in Madison's room is her husband. He's beating the crap out of her. I still can't get through to 911. Get your friend, get the cops, get somebody over here now. And hurry."

"Maryn?" Don's voice was threatening.

"The gun's not here," she cried. "It was stolen from my car the first week I was here. I haven't had time to get another one. That's why I put the locks on the door."

"You're sure it's not in your purse?" Don asked, and they heard the clink of change and metal on the wooden floor.

"I told you it was stolen," Maryn whimpered. "Why would I lie?"

"All right," he relented. "Maybe you're telling the truth. Doesn't matter, does it? Come on, get up. And be quiet." He slung the briefcase over his shoulder.

Maryn was crying again.

"I said get up, damn it," Don growled, pulling his own pistol from his waistband.

Maryn gave another cry of pain, and they heard footsteps on the wooden floor.

"Where are you taking me?" she asked, her voice quivering.

"You wanted to see Adam Kuykendall, I'm taking you to see him," Don said. "Let's go."

"I'm not alone here, Don," Maryn said. "My friends—they've probably already figured out you're here. They'll call the cops. They won't let you . . ."

He slapped her so hard her ears rang.

"Friends?" he sneered. "You don't have friends, Maryn. Those women let you live here—why? Because you paid them? Nobody's coming to save you, Maryn. It's just you and me. That's the way it's always been. The way it always will be. Now move, God damn it."

When they heard the sound of the heavy door opening, the slide of the dead bolt, all three of the women knew what was happening.

"Come on," Ellis said, racing for Dorie's door. "He's taking her down the back staircase. Ty's down there, somewhere. Julia, is that thing loaded? Do you know how to shoot it?"

"It's loaded now," Julia said, her voice grim. "I haven't fired a gun since Daddy showed me how when I was fourteen, but it'll come back to me."

"Wait for me," Dorie said, sliding her feet into a pair of flip-flops.

"Stay here," Julia ordered.

"The hell I will," Dorie said fiercely, and the three of them sprinted down the stairs as fast as they could go.

When they reached the living room, Ellis made a detour towards the fireplace. "What are you doing?" Julia whispered.

Ellis raised aloft the heavy wrought-iron poker, and Julia nodded approval.

"Wait a sec," Dorie ordered, peeling off towards the kitchen. When she came back, she was brandishing a meat cleaver and a butcher knife. "Now we're set," she said.

Crouched under the rear stairwell, Ty heard the rusty door hinges squeak, and finally heard the heavy old door swing open. Shit! He felt the vibration of footsteps on the old steel stairway.

Madison was crying. "Don, no. Please, no. I won't tell anybody. Please . . ."

"Shut up!" The man's voice was hoarse, and Ty heard the sickening sound of a slap, flesh against flesh, and Madison cried out again. "Go on, move," the man ordered. "Move or I'll, by God, throw you down these stairs."

Ty looked around for something, anything, to use as a weapon, but the only thing handy was a scrap two-by-four left behind by the construction crew. He looked longingly at the shovels and rakes lying around by the construction site, but that was thirty yards away in the open, and it was too late now to risk making a run. He'd be seen for sure if he tried to move. The staircase shuddered under the weight of the footsteps descending it.

"Move, God damn it," came Shackleford's hoarse whisper.

52

The women crept onto the front porch, huddling together in a knot. "I wonder where Ty is?" Ellis worried. She peered out at the driveway. The rain had gotten steadier, and mist rose eerily from the construction equipment and debris scattered around Ebbtide's weedy yard. "How'd Don get here?" she whispered. "There's no car in the driveway."

"Maybe he parked somewhere down the block," Dorie suggested.

"No good, because then he'd have to drag, or carry, Madison to his car," Julia said.

"Wait," Ellis said. She ran across the driveway, veering around the remains of the old garage, towards the lot next door, the one where she'd parked what seemed like months ago to get her first sneak peek at Ebbtide. A moment later she was back, panting and out of breath.

"There's a black Escalade parked over there, behind that burnt-out foundation," she told them. "That's got to be Don's. Dorie, do you think you can make it over there to the car, like, fast?"

"Of course," Dorie snorted indignantly. "I'm not a cripple, for God's sake."

"Okay," Ellis said, gesturing to the knives Dorie wielded in each hand.

"Get over there and slash his tires. If he does manage to get Madison past all of us, that should slow him down. And then get the hell away from there."

"Be right back," Dorie promised. "Don't do anything without me."

When she was gone, Ellis and Julia crouched down and crab walked towards the edge of the front porch.

"What's the plan?" Julia asked, her voice unaccustomedly shaky. "Ellis, even if I could pull this trigger, I've only ever shot at hay bales, in broad daylight, with Daddy right beside me. I've got no idea whether or not I could actually hit anything, especially in the dark like this."

Ty felt the footsteps coming closer. He crouched into a fetal position, willing himself to fade into invisibility. Rain trickled down his head and into his ears, it dripped off the tip of his nose. He blinked and shook his head just slightly, with sudden understanding of the efficiency of Chinese water torture.

"God damn it, move your ass," Shackleford rasped. "Or I swear I'll kill you right here."

"My ankle," Madison moaned. "I think I twisted it."

Ty looked up and saw Shackleford shove Madison down the last few steps of the staircase. He saw the gun, too. She cried out, landing in a heap on the matted grass. The man stepped over her and jerked her to her feet. He had a briefcase on his shoulder.

"This way," he growled hoarsely, shoving her in the direction of the driveway.

Now or never, Ty thought grimly. He stood and launched himself into a flying tackle, fueled more with testosterone than skill, remembering his high school coach's mantra: "Square up and drive, son." Ty slammed into the back of Shackleford's thighs, sending him sprawling headfirst onto the ground. *BOOM!*

The gunshot was so close and so loud, for a fleeting moment, Ty wondered if he'd been shot. Madison fell too, and now the three of them were flopping around in the rain and the mud, arms and legs hopelessly entangled.

"What the . . . ?" Shackleford rolled onto his back. Ty slapped awkwardly at Shackleford's gun hand, managing only a grazing blow, and Shackleford retaliated with a vicious backward kick to Ty's gut. Now he was pointing the gun directly at Ty, who was scuttling backwards in the mud, trying desperately to get out of firing range.

Madison somehow managed to scramble to her feet. "No!" she screeched. "No!" She darted forward and managed to land one good kick in her husband's ribs before he caught her foot and jerked her off balance. She screamed in pain, screamed in fear, screamed until she thought her lungs would catch fire. Senseless with rage, she kicked out at Shackleford, who grabbed her ankle with his left hand and flipped her to the ground.

Seizing the moment, Ty spied a piece of scrap two-by-four, grabbed it, and was advancing on Shackleford. But the other man saw him coming, raised up on his elbows, aimed, and fired.

BOOM!

This time he didn't have to wonder. Ty felt a searing pain in this thigh.

Ellis and Julia startled at the screams coming from the back of Ebbtide. "He's killing her!" Julia whispered, peering around the corner of the garage. "We've gotta do something."

"Wait!" Ellis said, clutching the hem of Julia's shirt. But the gunshots coming from the back of the house canceled the women's sense of caution.

"My God," Ellis gasped. "He's got a gun. And Ty's back there. He'll kill them both!"

Before Julia could stop her, or argue for a reasonable plan of action, Ellis was sprinting towards the rear of the house, with Julia close behind. Ellis's legs felt like concrete. Her lungs, calves, and thighs burned as though she'd set fire to them. But Ty was back there, and that bastard Don Shackleford had a gun. For once in her life, she didn't have a plan. All she had was adrenaline.

Rounding the corner of the house, in the dim yellow of a single porch light, Ellis saw Madison, her face streaked with blood, flailing around on the ground, screeching and kicking out at the man Ellis knew must be her husband.

Standing over Don Shackleford was a mud-covered Ty Bazemore, with a crazed look in his eye and what appeared to be a two-by-four raised menacingly above Don Shackleford's head.

In the moonlight, they saw the gun clutched in Shackleford's hand, pointed directly at Ty's chest. For a nanosecond, time seemed to stand still. And then Ellis heard her own voice, at a decibel level she didn't know she possessed. She burst out of the shadows, with Julia right beside her, the two of them screaming like banshees.

Instinctively, the friends split up, with Julia running in one direction towards Shackleford, and Ellis in another.

Julia stopped five yards away, held the pistol out, elbows locked, the gun clutched in both hands, the way she'd seen Clint Eastwood do in all those *Dirty Harry* movies Booker loved so much. "Stop, or I'll shoot!" Unlike Clint Eastwood, her voice cracked and the words came out more of a squeak than a roar. Also unlike Clint, her hands shook like a drunk with a bad case of the DTs.

Shackleford's expression was more of bemusement than terror. He shoved Madison aside and stood easily.

"I'll shoot your ass," Julia screeched, planting her feet and assuming the position.

"Sure you will," Shackleford said, laughing. He raised his own pistol and pointed it at Julia, but at just that moment, they heard an earsplitting burst of siren: *Whee-OO, whee-OO, whee-OO.* Startled, Shackleford turned his head, just for a second.

Whee-OO, whee-OO.

It was all the distraction Ty needed. He slammed the two-by-four across the top of Don Shackleford's skull, at precisely the same moment that Ellis, crouched behind Shackleford, circled around, leapt into the air, and with an unearthly howl which Julia later described as "half Karate Kid, half feral dog," made a direct hit to Shackleford's groin with the fireplace poker.

At which point, the bad guy, Julia said in subsequent retellings, "folded like a Kmart lawn chair."

53

Ty dropped the two-by-four and limped over to Ellis, gathering her into his arms, deliberately turning her away from the sight of Don Shackleford crumpled on the ground with a gaping gouge across the top of his head.

Julia stared down at Shackleford, who was motionless. Wordlessly, she dropped the pistol, and went to comfort Madison, who had retreated to the cover of the back porch, and was now weeping softly, clinging to the handrail of the iron staircase.

"It's all right," Julia said, hugging Madison. "You're all right. He can't hurt you anymore. Not anymore. Not ever." Her voice was soothing, singsongy. Madison shuddered, and Julia petted her, as she would a frightened kitten. "I swear, he'll never touch you again."

"You guys!" they heard a voice call. Looking up, Ellis and Julia saw Dorie loping towards them, through the mist. "I heard gunshots. Are you all right?"

"Dorie!" Ellis cried. "We're okay. We're all okay. Ty . . ." Her voice was as shaky as her legs, which now felt like they might collapse under the weight of her. "Ty saved us."

"You saved yourselves," Ty corrected her, wincing. Now Ellis saw the blood oozing from his left thigh. "You're hurt," she exclaimed. "Oh my God, he shot you." She looked wildly around. "Ty's been shot. We've got to get an ambulance."

"I'm fine," Ty said wanly, clamping his hand over his thigh. "Just a flesh wound. Like on TV."

Ellis fumbled in her pocket for her cell phone, but now they heard a different set of sirens, and looking up, saw a procession of blue and red flashing lights: three Dare County sheriff's cruisers, a K-9 drug enforcement unit, and an ambulance.

"Thank God," Ellis murmured.

Everything happened at once then. Cops with dogs swarmed out of the cruisers, weapons drawn. Connor Terry pulled up in his Jeep a moment later, and rushed to Dorie's side. The EMTs strapped Shackleford to a gurney and shoved him into the ambulance.

"Come on, buddy," said another technician, trying to herd Ty towards the same ambulance.

"Nothin' doin'," Ty said through gritted teeth. "I'm not getting in the same buggy as the asshole who just tried to kill us all."

Madison, despite her own vehement protests, was told that her head injury, and a shoulder that was likely dislocated, meant a direct ticket to the emergency room. Red lights flashing, the ambulance left, bearing both Madison and her unconscious husband to the emergency room.

Ty was still arguing with the EMTs when the pretty black paramedic who'd just finished applying a butterfly bandage to Madison's forehead came walking up. "Aw, Bazemore, don't be such a hardhead," she called.

"Kalilah, you know this guy?"

"Sure," she replied. "You know him too. He works the bar at Caddie's."

"Hey, Kalilah," Ty said. "I'm was just trying to tell your friend here it's no big thing."

"Lemme see," Kalilah said, pushing him gently onto the bumper of the nearest cruiser. Donning a fresh pair of latex gloves, and illuminated by the headlights of another cruiser, she gently probed the wound. "You are one charmed sumbitch," she told him, swabbing the wound with disinfectant. "Looks like that bullet only grazed you. Couple inches to the right, and it would've hit your femoral artery. You would've bled out before we got here."

"Yeah," added the first EMT, "and another inch to the right of that and you'd be singing soprano."

"My lucky day," Ty said, wincing.

Kalilah was an efficient worker, and a moment later she had his thigh cleaned and dressed. "Now," she ordered with a grin. "I need you to drop those pants so I can hit you with some antibiotics. Which one of those cheeks is the prettiest?"

Ty shrugged, and unflinchingly dropped his rain-sodden shorts to offer up his left buttock. Before he could stop her, she jabbed him with a second needle. "A lil' something for the pain," she said. "You're gonna sleep good tonight, my friend."

Thunder growled in the distance, and a streak of lightning tore through the night. But the rain had slacked off to a gentle drizzle, and finally, after what seemed like an eternity, after all the witnesses had been questioned and statements taken, the police cruisers made their bumpy exit down the Ebbtide driveway. The group stood, huddled under a green-and-white striped golf umbrella, watching them go.

"Hey," Ellis said suddenly. "It just struck me. That first siren we heard. Right when Don Shackleford was going to shoot Ty. Where the hell did that come from?"

Dorie laughed. "My bad." She reached in the pocket of Connor Terry's borrowed, bright yellow Dare County Sheriff rain slicker and brandished her weapon of choice. "You ever try to slash a steel-belted radial Michelin with the equivalent of a butter knife?" She gave Ty a reproachful head shake. "Dude, you gotta get some decent equipment in that kitchen of yours. I was still sawing away on that first tire when the Escalade's car alarm went off. I thought for sure he'd kill all of y'all."

"Actually, that car alarm probably saved my life," Ty told her. "Shackleford had a dead bead drawn on me. He'd have shot me for sure. So it looks like you're the real hero here."

"She did great," Ellis said, looking around at all their haggard, mud-splattered faces. "But I think we all did pretty good. We make a decent team, don't you think?"

"Awesome," Julia said. "But I'd just as soon not ever go through anything like that again. Ever."

Ty nodded his agreement, but his eyelids were drooping, and it was clear he was in pain. "Come on," Ellis said finally, draping Ty's arm around her shoulder. "I'm taking you home."

He looked off at the spot where his garage and apartment had been, and yawned. "Got no home anymore," he said drowsily.

"Sure you do," Ellis told him, nudging him gently towards the weather-beaten gray house. "Ebbtide's still here. It's not going anywhere. And neither am I."

Epilogue

Julia burst through the kitchen door. "Ellis," she exclaimed. "I just got back from my run and noticed that Madison's car is gone! I called the hospital and they told me she got herself discharged early this morning, AMA—that means 'against medical advice.'"

Ellis finished wrapping the last pink-and-green-flowered dinner plate with a sheet of newspaper and nestled it tenderly in a box with the other dishes from the now-empty cupboard. "Madison's gone," she said calmly.

Julia opened the refrigerator door and stood there, letting the chill spread over her sweat-soaked body. "You don't sound too surprised."

Ellis gestured towards the kitchen table, where the high-heeled Christian Louboutin sandals rested atop a scap of paper. "I was originally. But I guess it's not really all that shocking that she would leave like this. Not when you think about it."

"Okay if I read it?" Julia asked, craning her neck to look over at the note.

"Of course," Ellis said. "It's addressed to all of us."

Dorie came wandering into the kitchen then, barefoot and dressed in a navy blue Dare County Police Academy T-shirt over her shorty-pajama bottoms. She yawned and ran her fingers through her tousled strawberry blond locks. "What's addressed to us?"

"This," Julia said, holding the note. "It's from Madison."

"Madison?" Dorie scrunched up her face in confusion. "Isn't Madison in the hospital?"

"Not anymore," Ellis said. "Read the note, Julia."

Dear Ellis, Dorie, and Julia: I'm no good at good-byes, so this will have to do. The ER docs say I don't have a concussion, and they managed to stitch up my head and pop my shoulder back in place, so aside from some cuts and bruises, I'm good as new. Which means it's time to hit the road. I want to thank the three of you for giving me something I've never had before—friends. Real, true girlfriends. I know I'm not easy to warm up to—hah!—understatement, right, Julia? The three of you—and Ty— saved my life this summer, not to mention last night, literally. Now it's time for me to start over. Not sure where I'll end up, or what I'll do next, but I do know I'll try hard not to screw up this time around. You guys take care. Your friend, Madison.

P.S. The nurses at the hospital tell me Don has a fractured skull— and something they call "blunt force trauma" to the testicles. Bravo, Ellis! P.P.S. Dorie, your friend Connor is a nice guy. He called the police in Jersey and found out that the cops in Camden discovered Adam's body Friday morning. It was stuffed in the trunk of his car, parked in a mall. I would have been in that trunk too, if it hadn't been for you guys. So, thanks again. -M-

"Aww," Dorie said, sniffing and blotting her eyes with the tail of her T-shirt. "Where'd you find this, Ellis?"

"On the front porch," Ellis said. "I woke up around six thirty, because I thought I heard a car door. After everything else that happened last night, I guess I was still on edge. I ran downstairs and looked out the living room window, just in time to see a taxi pulling away. Madison's Volvo was right behind it. She left the note and those shoes."

"Wow," Dorie said, sinking down into a chair. "Poor Madison. First she finds out the only person she trusted betrayed her, and then she finds out he's dead. That's a lot to handle."

Julia plucked a peach from a bowl on the kitchen counter, and sank her teeth into it. For a moment, she chewed busily, letting the pink juice dribble down her chin. "I know it's awful, but I'm not gonna waste any time feeling bad for that guy. I'm guessing Adam's the one who told Don where he could find Madison. He sold her out!"

"I don't guess we'll ever know the truth about that," Ellis said. "I suppose there'll be a trial, either here or up in New Jersey. Wonder if Madison will show up to testify? Or if she'll just disappear all over again."

"I bet she'll testify," Dorie said loyally. "She cared about Adam, even after she was pretty sure he'd turned on her. She's a good person at heart. I mean, she could have taken off with all that money, if she'd been a crook. But she didn't, did she?"

"About that money," Julia said slowly. "What happens with that? A hundred thousand dollars is nothing to sneeze at."

"I saw one of the cops putting the laptop bag in the back of his cruiser," Dorie volunteered. "Maybe they'll give it back to the company Shackleford stole it from? I'll ask Connor."

"And when are you seeing your new *boyfriend* again?" Julia teased.

"He's coming over this morning to pick up the rain slicker I borrowed last night, and to help me pack the van," Dorie admitted. "But you've got to stop calling him my boyfriend. He's just a friend. . . ."

"Who happens to be a boy, who has a major crush on you," Ellis pointed out. "What's he think about you heading home to Savannah today?"

Dorie sighed. "He wanted to help me drive home, since Julia's not coming back with me, but I told him I didn't think that was a good idea. I've got so much to do when I get home, getting the house packed up, meetings at school, and classes start next week. Not to mention, I've got to have a long talk with my mother. Oh yeah, and meet with my divorce lawyer! Connor's got a week of vacation in October, and he wants to visit then."

"Have you decided where you're going to live?" Ellis asked.

Dorie's face brightened. "Willa—bless her interfering heart—managed to work that out for me. I think she must have laid a major guilt trip on Phyllis. Can you believe it? Mama called this morning and told me she wants me to move into my nana's house in Ardsley Park! Rent-free! She says my brother is fine with it."

"Of course Nash is fine with it," Julia said. "He's probably thrilled at the idea of you living there and cooking and cleaning for him."

Dorie shook her head. "Nuh-uh. Nash will have another think coming if he thinks I'm gonna be his personal housekeeper. I am done being Dorie the Doormat," she declared.

"What do you hear from Stephen?" Julia asked.

"He wants to see me as soon as I get home," Dorie said. "And he asked if he can come to my next OB appointment. He wants to be there for the ultrasound I've got scheduled."

"So, give him a printout," Julia snapped.

"I told him I'm fine with him coming," Dorie said. "He's the baby's father. I've seen Phyllis struggle with being a single mom. And I've been the kid whose dad never came to back-to-school night. I don't want that for this baby. No matter how I feel about the decisions Stephen's made, he's not a monster. He's a good man. And I want him in my child's life."

"You are such an adult," Julia said, shaking her head in admiration. "Really, Dorie. You amaze me."

Dorie dipped a curtsy. "Thanks. Sometimes I amaze me too. We'll see. How 'bout you, Julia? What time are you expecting Booker?"

"With Booker, you never know," Julia laughed. "He's driving down in the new car he bought me. I haven't owned my own car in years, but Book insists I'll need one, working here and living part-time in Atlanta. Thank God I kept up my Georgia driver's license." Julia glanced at her watch. "Which reminds me, I've got a production meeting at Joe's hotel in fifteen minutes. I know you need to get your car loaded, Ellis, but do you think Ty would mind loaning me his Bronco? Just for an hour or so?"

"What's this about taking my car?" The three women turned their heads in unison as Ty walked, stiff legged, into the kitchen. He was unshaven, and dressed in a threadbare blue terry cloth bathrobe, but otherwise looked remarkably fit for a man who'd been shot only hours before.

"Well," Julia started, "I just need to run up to Kitty Hawk for our production meeting, and I know Ellis probably wants to get on the road, so I thought maybe . . ."

Ellis and Ty's eyes met. Ty raised one eyebrow, and Ellis gave a barely perceptible nod. "Ellis," he said succinctly, "isn't going anywhere." He wound an arm around Ellis's waist, and dropped a kiss on her cheek. "Right? You wanna tell them, or should I?"

Ellis rubbed her face against Ty's day-old beard, reveling in the casual intimacy.

"That's not exactly accurate," she corrected. She turned to Julia and said apologetically, "Actually, I do need to get my car loaded this morning. But I'm sure you can borrow Ty's Bronco."

"What?" Ty looked taken aback. "We agreed. You said last night . . ."

Ellis shrugged. "I changed my mind."

Ty's eyes darkened. "Ellis, don't do this . . ."

She caught him by the belt of his robe and drew him back towards her, as though she were reeling in a particularly cooperative fish. "You," she pointed out, "took a bullet in your thigh last night. You can hardly walk. You don't need to be going up and down these stairs all morning. I can easily load my stuff myself, and move it down to Pelican Cottage. I loaded it in here by myself, and I can load it out by myself."

"Now wait," Ty started.

"You mean it?" Dorie squealed. "You're not going back to Philly? At all? You're gonna stay here? With Ty?"

"Well, not here at Ebbtide," Ellis said, trying hard to suppress a smile. "We'll be shacked up in that little hovel he rented just down the beach. For at least the next three months. Give or take."

"Give or take?" Julia said with a hoot. "Who are you, Ellis Sullivan? And what about that cushy job in Seattle? I thought you couldn't live without a job and a 401(k) and a parking pass. And a Kaper chart. What's the plan, Ellis?"

"There is no plan," Ellis said blissfully. "I guess I finally figured that out . . . last night. There's nothing I need or want in Seattle." She glanced at Ty, whose arm was around her shoulder. "I've got what I want. Right here."

"Happy ever after, that's the plan," Ty said. "I'm going to teach her how to surf."

"And I'm going to teach him how to read a spreadsheet."

"If you need us, we'll be at Pelican Cottage," Ty broke in. "And it's not a hovel. It's oceanfront, and it's quaint. . . ."

"It's a dump," Ellis said, shushing him. "Just like Ebbtide is. Was. But we can fix that. Fortunately for you, *Mister Culpepper*, I happen to have a weird fondness for dumps. And their landlords."

"Ellis Sullivan," Ty retorted, determined to have the last word. "You are a major pain in my ass. Promise me you'll be a pain in my ass forever and ever." He gathered her into his arms as Dorie and Julia danced around them, providing loud, inappropriate, immature smacking, smooching sound effects.

Ellis nodded, and allowed herself to be kissed, right on the lips, and right in front of her best friends. "Yes," she said solemnly. "I promise. I do. I will."

1. Each of the four characters comes to Ebbtide with a major problem. How would you characterize each problem?

2. Which of the characters' dilemmas did you find the easiest to relate to? Which one felt the least identifiable to you, and why?

3. There is a famous saying that "money is only something you need in case you don't die tomorrow." Do you feel that money could have solved each one of these characters' problems, including Ty Bazemore? Why or why not?

4. Maryn Shackleford leaves her life behind to create a new identity. If you were in her position would you have done the same? Would it be easy to leave your life behind? Have you ever been tempted to do so?

5. Does the idea of a monthlong rental with a group of girl-friends appeal to you? Where would be your dream place to go? What problems could you foresee occurring?

6. Do you think it's possible to be married to someone and not realize he's gay? If Dorie's situation happened to you, what would you do?

7. For someone who has devoted her entire life to her career, being fired is the ultimate devastation. Can you relate to Ellis's situation? Do you understand why this threw her so much? Do you think being fired can actually end up being the best thing that ever happened to you?

8. Julia fights against the physical realities of growing old. What do you really think she's worried about? Do you embrace the concept of aging with humor, acceptance, or dread?

9. Ty and Ellis could not be more opposite. But did you see any ways in which they are similar? Can you see their relationship working in the long term?

10. What is your go-to karaoke song?

11. If you were to create a sound track to go along with this book, what would be on the playlist?

For more reading group suggestions,
visit www.readinggroupgold.com

St. Martin's
Griffin

Spring
Fever

For Griffin, the new kid on the block, with a heart full of love

Acknowledgments

The author wishes to thank:

Thomas Norris for explaining tricky legal stuff. If I got it wrong, it's not his fault.

The Ritchie family of Salisbury, North Carolina, and the fine folks at Cheerwine for explaining how you make and market a delicious regional soft drink. If I got it wrong, it's not their fault.

Jack Reimer and Sharon Stokes and Beth Fleishman and Richard Boyette, who let me run away to their mountain cabins to work on the book, and who helped with some more stuff. I don't know what happened to all the good wine you guys thought you'd hidden, but it could be my fault.

Meg Walker, of Tandem Literary, who told me about marketing stuff, and who, in fact, is a genius at what she does.

The aptly named Grace Quinn, who keeps the wheels from falling off the bus on a weekly basis.

The Women of Weymouth: Alexandra Sokoloff, Bren Witchger, Diane Chamberlain, Katy Munger, Margaret Maron, and Sarah Shaber—and honorary chair Nancy Olson—who are absolutely essential to the writing process, and who beat me at Scrabble every time.

The divine Jennifer Enderlin, who somehow managed to slap me and my manuscript into some kind of shape. Again. Huge thanks also to the whole team at St. Martin's Press. If the book works, it's definitely your fault.

Stuart Krichevsky, the best damn agent in the business. Here's to more ice cream and roses.

My family, listed last, but first in my heart. Tom, Katie, Mark, and Andy. Nothing works without you.

1

From her seat in the sanctuary of the Church of the Good Shepherd, Anna-jane Hudgens wondered if there had ever been a more flawless day for a wedding.

Spring had arrived spectacularly early in Passcoe, North Carolina. Only the first week in April, yet the dogwoods and azaleas were already burst into bloom, and the weeping cherry trees lining the walkway to the church trailed fingertips of pale pink onto a blue and white carpet of violets and alyssum.

It was as if the bride, the equally flawless Celia Wakefield, had somehow managed to *will* perfect weather. Or perhaps she'd specified blue skies and color-coordinated bursts of blooms in one of her famously precise memos. If anybody could do that, Annajane mused, it would be Celia.

Could there be a more beautiful setting? Baylesses had been getting married at the Church of the Good Shepherd for nearly two hundred years. Not in this grand sanctuary, of course. The original church was a quaint, stoop-shouldered gray granite affair, with uneven oak floors, a single Gothic-arched leaded-glass window above the altar, and two rows of ten primitively wrought pine pews built by black laborers from the casket factory in Moore County, twenty minutes down the road.

Annajane could remember sitting beside her best friend, Pokey, in the Bayless family pew after countless Saturday-night sleepovers, back when they were both still in pigtails. By then, Pokey's grandmother had already started her slow descent into senility, although Annajane had not known that. Miss Pauline, for whom Pokey had been named, seldom spoke, but she was content to sit in church on Sunday mornings and smile and nod to the hymns, dabbing at her cataract-clouded blue eyes with her ever-present handkerchief and patting Annajane's hand. "She thinks you're me," Pokey would whisper, giggling at her grandmother's confusion and grimacing and holding her nose when Miss Pauline passed gas, which she did frequently.

When the "new" Church of the Good Shepherd was built in the early '90s, with reproduction Tiffany stained-glass windows, solid cherry pews, and a custom-built German pipe organ, the old church was renamed the Woodrow Memorial Chapel in memory of Pauline Woodrow, who died in her sleep the year Pokey and Annajane turned fourteen.

Annajane's own wedding had been held in the chapel, the one concession her new in-laws made to what they considered Annajane's "quaint" ideas. Since she'd paid for the wedding herself, she'd insisted on having an intimate affair, just family and close friends, fewer than forty people, with Pokey as her only attendant. It had rained the November evening of her nuptials, and at the time she'd considered it wildly romantic that the loud thrum of the rain on the church's tin roof threatened to drown out the wedding march played on the chapel's original wheezy pump organ.

Had it been only seven years ago? Sometimes she wasn't sure any of it had really happened at all, that it wasn't something she'd just remembered from a long-ago dream.

Today's affair was nothing like Annajane's modest wedding. The sanctuary was at capacity—beyond capacity, if you went by the county fire code, which said the church could hold five hundred people. It seemed to Annajane that every living person who had ever known or done business with the Bayless family, or even just sipped a bottle of their Quixie cherry soft drink, had crammed themselves into one of the polished wooden pews beneath the soaring exposed rafters of the imposing Episcopal church.

Annajane felt her eyelids droop now. It was too warm in the church, and the scent of the lilies and roses banking everything that didn't move was overpowering. She'd had almost no sleep the night before, and not much more sleep the night before that. And, yes, she'd had herself a good stiff drink, Quixie and bourbon on the rocks, back at the house, after she'd finished dressing and before she'd left for the church. She closed her eyes, just for a moment, felt her chin droop to her chest, and the next moment, she felt a sharp elbow dig into her ribs.

Pokey had managed to wedge herself into the pew. "Wake up and slide over!" she ordered.

Annajane's eyes flew open, and she looked up, just in time to see Sallie Bayless, seated in the front row, two pews ahead of them, turn and shoot Pokey a stern look of warning. Sallie's gleaming auburn hair shone in the candlelit church. She was sixty-four, but still had the dewy complexion, sparkling brown eyes, and slender figure of a woman twenty years younger. Now, those eyes narrowed as they took in Pokey's tardy and disheveled appearance.

Pokey gave her mother a grin and a finger wave, and Sallie's head swiveled back around, eyes front, head held high, the Bayless pearls, a double strand, clasped firmly around her neck.

Annajane offered an apologetic smile to the elderly woman to her right. The woman frowned, but begrudgingly inched aside to allow the new arrival to be seated.

As usual, Pokey Bayless Riggs took no notice of the stir she'd caused. She'd been causing a stir nearly every day of her thirty-five years, and today, her brother's wedding day, was no different.

The boatneck collar of Pokey's expensive new red silk jacket had slipped off her right shoulder, exposing a leopard-print bra strap and an unseemly amount of cleavage. Little Clayton was two years old, but Pokey was still struggling to lose her baby weight. She'd managed to pop one of the jacket's rhinestone buttons, and the tight silk skirt had somehow twisted around so that the zipper was now in the front, rather than on the side. She was bare-legged, which was a scandal in and of itself, but now Annajane noticed that her best friend had ditched the Sallie-mandated sedate dyed-silk slingback pumps in favor of a pair of blinged-out silver flip flops.

Pokey's thin, poker-straight blond hair had already lost its beauty-salon bounce, and now hung limply on either side of her full pink cheeks. Her lipstick was smeared. But her eyes, her amazing cornflower-blue eyes, glinted with mischief.

"Busted!" Annajane whispered, not daring to look at her best friend.

"Christ!" Pokey muttered. "This is so not my fault. I couldn't find a parking spot! The church lot's full and the whole block is lined with cars on both sides of the street. I had to leave the Land Rover clear down the block in front of the gas station and run all the way here."

"Aren't you supposed to be up there with your mom and everybody else in the family?" Annajane asked. "I mean, you *are* the groom's only sister."

"Screw that," Pokey said swiftly. "I refuse to make nice with that woman. Mason knows I don't like her. Mama knows it too. I'm taking a moral stand here."

"Who the hell are all these people anyway?" she asked, glancing around at the packed church and zeroing in on the bride's side of the aisle. "Not family, right? Since poor lil' Celia is an orphan, and the only family she could produce is that elderly great aunt staying over at Mama's house. Did Celia charter a bus or something?"

Annajane shrugged. "You're apparently the only person in Passcoe who *doesn't* think that Celia Wakefield is the best thing since flush toilets and sliced store-bought bread."

"Don't give me that. You hate her as much as I do," Pokey said under her breath.

"Not at all," Annajane replied. "I'm happy for them."

"Yippy-fuckin'-skippy," Pokey drawled. "Happy, happy, happy. It's fine for you. In less than a week, you'll pack up your U-Haul and head for Atlanta and your nice new life without even a glance in the rearview mirror. New man, new job, new address. But where does that leave me? Stuck here in stinkin' Passcoe, with my mama, my evil brother Davis, and good ole Mason and his new bride, Cruella de Vil."

"Poor, poor Pokey," Annajane mocked her right back. "Richest girl in town, married to the second richest man in town."

"Third richest," Pokey corrected. "Or maybe fourth. Davis and Mason have way more money than Pete, especially since people quit buying furniture made in America."

"Speaking of, where is Pete?" Annajane asked, craning her neck to look for him. Instead of spotting Pokey's tall redheaded husband, Pete, her eyes rested on another tardy couple, Bonnie and Matthew Kelsey, hurrying up the right-side aisle of the church.

Bonnie Kelsey's eyes met Annajane's. She blushed, and looked away quickly, clutching Matthew's arm and steering him into a pew as far away from Anna-jane's as she could manage in the overcrowded church.

Pokey saw the maneuver for what it was. "Bitch," she said.

"It's all right," Annajane said smoothly. "I mean, what do you expect? Matt and Mason play golf every week. From what I hear, Bonnie and Celia get along like a house afire. Best friends forever! Anyway, Bonnie's not the only one to sign up for Team Celia. Every woman in this room has been staring daggers at me since I walked into this church. I knew when I agreed to come today that it would be awkward."

"Awkward?" Pokey laughed bitterly. "It's freakish, is what it is. Who else but you would agree to show up at her ex-husband's wedding?"

2

O ut of the corner of her eye, Annajane saw more people eyeing her with undisguised curiosity. She gave a tight smile and looked away.

"I had to come today," Annajane reminded Pokey. "For Sophie. She made me promise. In fact, it's the only way she'd agree to be in the wedding. It's also my last official company function."

"I still can't believe you're leaving Quixie," Pokey said. "After how many years?"

"Too many," Annajane murmured. "I never should have stayed after the divorce. I just didn't have the gumption to get out and start a new life for myself. And then there was Sophie, of course."

"You spoil that child rotten," Pokey said, tsk-tsking. "And Mason is even worse."

But before she could launch into her lecture about the kind of strict parenting her niece really needed, the soft strains of organ music that had been playing as guests drifted into the church segued into harp music.

"A harp?" Pokey turned and craned her neck to look in the direction of the choir loft. "Where the hell did she find a harp in Passcoe?"

Annajane gave a little shrug. "The harp made its first appearance at the rehearsal dinner last night. Which you somehow managed to miss?"

"I had one of my migraines," Pokey said quickly. "I was all dressed and everything when it hit me. Pete gave me one of my pills and put me to bed at eight o'clock."

"Migraine or not, you are officially on your mother's list today, as if you didn't already know that," Annajane told her.

"I do not understand why Mama and my brothers have suddenly allowed Celia free reign with the company bank accounts," Pokey said. "If Daddy were alive, he would be shittin' kittens at the way they're throwing money around. Pete doesn't like it either. He says . . ."

Suddenly, the harpist was joined by a violin and a flute, the tempo of the music quickening.

"Shh," Annajane said. "It's starting."

A door beside the altar opened, and three men in dark tuxes emerged following the pastor, a personable young priest from Boston, Father Jolly, who'd only been at the church for a few months. He even looked the part, Annajane reflected bitterly, short and stout, with a fringe of dark bangs and a beaming choir-boy countenance. Perfect, perfect, perfect.

But it wasn't the priest Annajane was staring at. She involuntarily held her breath at the sight of Mason Bayless, in his flawlessly cut charcoal-gray Armani tuxedo. At thirty-nine, he still had the build of an athlete, broad shoulders, narrow hips, long, muscled neck. He looked like the baseball player he'd been in his college years. His dark blond hair had been carefully combed back from his high forehead, slicked into place with some kind of hair goo, a style he'd adopted only recently, since Celia came into his life. He was paler than usual, and those cornflower-blue eyes and ridiculously long curly lashes seemed focused on the floor, and not on the congregation eagerly awaiting the upcoming ceremony.

As Mason took his place to the right of Father Jolly, his younger brother, Davis, slid easily to his side. Pokey might have been the youngest of the three Bayless progeny, but Davis was now, and always, the baby of the family.

Twenty months younger than Mason, Davis was half a head shorter and easily weighed forty pounds more than his older brother. While Mason and

Pokey had the Bayless blue eyes and dark blond hair coloring, Davis, alone among the children, took after his mother Sallie's people. He had the Woodrow snapping dark eyes; thick, wavy dark hair; and the high cheekbones Miss Pauline always claimed came from their long-ago Cherokee ancestors. Davis looked eagerly around the room, tugging at the collar of his starched white tux shirt, nodding at friends and acquaintances, exchanging a sly wink with somebody, a woman, no doubt, seated on the far left side of the church.

Pokey caught the wink, too, and clucked her tongue in disapproval. "I did not think she would have the nerve to show up here today. Obviously, I have once again underestimated the low moral fiber of another of Davis's women."

"Who is she?" Annajane asked eagerly, studying the left side of the church.

"Name is Dreama, if you can believe it. Works at the bottling plant in Fayetteville. Not but twenty-two. Married, of course."

"Of course," Annajane agreed. "Does your mama know?"

"Does Sallie ever miss anything? She knows, but she's choosing to act like it's not happening. Denial is mama's religion. She made Davis ask Linda Balez as his 'official date' for the weekend. You remember Linda, right? She was in my deb group, went to Sweetbriar? She's living over in Pinehurst, does some kind of tax planning or something."

"Tall brunette? Little bit of an overbite? I think I met her last night."

"That's the one," Pokey said, nodding. "Sweet girl, really. Mama insisted that she stay in the guest room at Cherry Hill, but of course Davis has got little old Dreama stashed in the Davis Bayless Honeymoon Suite over at the Pinecone Motor Lodge."

"So that's why he left the party so early last night," Annajane said. "I was walking out to my car at nine thirty, when he went whizzing past me in the Boxster. I did see a woman in the front seat, but it was dark, and I just assumed it was his date."

"Doubtful," Pokey said. "I saw Linda at the brunch up at the house this morning, and Davis was nowhere to be found, the little shit. I don't know why any of us put up with his crap, do you?"

"We just do," Annajane said quietly.

Annajane returned her attention to the groomsmen. Pokey's husband, Pete, had taken his place to the left of Father Jolly. His bright red hair had just started showing gray at the temples, and his beard was neatly clipped. His tux fit him like it had been custom tailored, and his broad, toothy smile seemed to take in everybody in the packed sanctuary.

"Gawwd," Pokey moaned, gesturing at her husband. "Would you look at that man? Could you not eat him up with a spoon? It's just not fair. After all these years, even after everything he's put me through, I swear to goodness, if he asked me to, I would take his hand, leave this church right this minute, follow him out to the car, and drop my panties in a New York minute."

The blue-haired matron sitting beside Annajane gasped, clutched her yellowing pearls, and scooted over another six inches to the right.

"Nice visual," Annajane whispered, putting her lips to Pokey's ears. "But could you keep it down? I think you just gave one of your mother's bridge partners heart palpitations."

"Serves her right for eavesdropping," Pokey said. She leaned back and studied Annajane for the first time since she'd arrived at the church.

"You look amazing," Pokey said. She touched the cap sleeve of Annajane's dress. "Is this new?"

Annajane looked down at her cocktail dress. The fabric was a thick satin, the color of new ferns, cut close to the body, with a deep squared-off scoop neck and dressmaker details like tiny covered buttons, an inset waist, and a wide, shell-pink satin belt with a large rhinestone and pearl-encrusted buckle.

"This old thing?" she laughed. "It's vintage. Although I don't think it had ever been worn. I found it last year at the Junior League Thriftique. It still has the original satin Bonwit Teller label sewn in."

"Love that bracelet, too," Pokey commented. "Don't tell me you found that around Passcoe."

Annajane flexed her hands for her friend's inspection. She wore a wide antique cuff bracelet of rhinestones and pearls. "Sallie actually gave me this bracelet for Christmas the first year Mason and I were married. I think it was your grandmother's."

"I don't remember ever seeing it before," Pokey said.

Annajane's brow furrowed. "Oh. Damn." She fumbled with the bracelet clasp. "Bad form, wearing the Bayless family jewels to his wedding, right? I swear, it didn't dawn on me until just now. Just give it back to Sallie later, after I'm gone."

"Stop," Pokey said, closing her hand around Annajane's. "If Mama gave you this bracelet, I'm sure she wants you to keep it. Besides, she probably only gave it to you because it's costume jewelry."

"In the back of her mind, Sallie was probably saving back the good stuff for her *next* daughter-in-law," Annajane said. "Oh. Sorry. Didn't mean to sound bitter."

Pokey tapped the thick twist of silver on Annajane's left ring finger and then twisted her own two-carat diamond engagement band. "I still can't believe you gave back Grandmama Bayless's ring."

"I love *this* ring," Annajane said, lifting her chin. "Shane designed it himself."

"Sweet," Pokey said, with a dismissive sniff. "Although I never heard of an engagement ring without some kind of precious stone. And I still think you should have kept Mason's ring. You could just wear it on your right hand."

"It was a family heirloom," Annajane said quietly. "I'm not a Bayless anymore. I'm not sure I ever was one. It should go to you, or one of your boys. Or Sophie."

"Daddy would have wanted you to keep it," Pokey said. "He's the one who insisted Mason give you that instead of a new ring. He said you'd earned it. And you have. No matter what Mama or anybody else thinks."

Pokey held up her hand, left pinky extended. Annajane sighed, and linked her own pinky through her best friend's, just as they always had, since they were six years old.

"I notice Celia didn't get Grandma Bayless's ring," Pokey said.

"No, but she got one with a waaay bigger diamond, which I understand she picked out herself," Annajane said. "I don't imagine somebody like Celia Wakefield would want anything as old-fashioned as your grandmother's engagement ring."

"Hope she chokes on it," Pokey said pleasantly.

Without warning, Annajane suddenly began tearing up.

"Are you okay?" Pokey asked, digging in her evening bag for a tissue. "Honey, I really, really think it is not a good thing for you to watch this whole charade."

"I'm fine," Annajane insisted, refusing the tissue. "Really. Pinky swear. This is a good thing. For Mason, for Sophie, for the family. This is closure for me.

Honestly. Step one, Mason marries Celia. Step two, Annajane marries Shane. End of story. Everybody lives happily ever after."

"You're nuts," Pokey said. She jerked her head in the direction of the altar, where her big brother Mason stood, hands clasped behind his back, legs slightly apart, rocking back and forth slightly on his heels.

"He's nuts, too," Pokey continued. "And he is *so* not over you."

"Wrong," Annajane snapped. "He's been over me for years. And I am over him. Finally. Totally. Completely. Over. Him."

3

Getting over Mason Bayless was easier said than done. How do you stop caring for somebody you've loved your whole life? Five years ago, right after their breakup, when she'd cried herself to sleep every night for months and months, Annajane decided loving Mason might be like having some insidious virus. She could go for days, not allowing herself to think of him, ignoring his phone calls and e-mails, or speaking to him coolly, with complete detachment, her emotional firewall firmly intact. And then, one day, for no reason at all, she would have what she came to think of as a flare-up.

He'd swing through the office, with his rolling, loping gait, maybe flash that grin of his to one of the other girls in the office. Oh, that grin. When he gave the slow "hey-howyadoin" smile that exposed the chipped left incisor he'd broken during a teenage wrestling match with Davis, Annajane would come completely unglued. She'd have to get up from her desk, run to the lady's room, lock herself in, and bawl like a baby.

Sometimes the flare-ups happened in the car. She'd be driving along, and she'd hear their song. "Don't Stop Believin'" . . . Journey. Once she nearly ran a motorcyclist off the road, when she was driving home from the plant late at night when the song came on the radio. She'd had to pull off the highway, roll down the windows, and force herself to let the cold damp February air roll over her flaming cheeks and snap her back to reality before she could drive on.

She'd even tried her own version of an exorcism to get over Mason. Three years ago, on the two-year anniversary of their divorce, she'd snuck back to the lake cottage that held so much of their history.

A light winter rain was falling as she navigated the rutted gravel road that led through thick woods back to the lake. Officially the lake's name was Lake Wesley Forlines Jr., after a local decorated World War I hero. But everybody around Passcoe always just called it Hideaway Lake, because county budget cuts had long ago closed the only public beach and boat ramp. Now the only access to the lake was through the Bayless's property. Private property.

Weeds and sapling trees had sprung up in the narrow lane, and it struck Annajane that since she and Mason had moved out, the rest of the family had very likely forgotten the place even existed. Maybe, she thought, in one panicky moment, the house had finally succumbed to the inevitable, and simply tumbled all the way to the ground.

But the little stone cottage was still there, nestled beneath the leafless limbs of a huge old water oak. Acorns crunched under her tires as she rolled to a stop a few yards away from the house, and, as she stepped out of the car, she glimpsed the gray-green glimmer of the lake through a raggedy hedge of privet that had replaced the lawn Mason had so carefully cultivated.

Briars caught at the legs of her jeans as she pushed open the rickety cedar gate. Annajane plucked a dried bud from the canes of the New Dawn roses that twined through the pickets of the fence. The rosebushes, two of them, had been a wedding gift from her stepfather, who'd planted them himself, promising that the fast-growing climbers would blanket the fence with carefree pink blossoms within a year. And they had. The rosebushes had survived, even if the marriage had withered.

Annajane frowned when she got to the front door of the cottage. The periwinkle-blue paint she'd coated the old door with only three years earlier was already cracked and peeling. Worse, a rusting iron hasp and shiny new padlock had been fastened to the door. They'd never even had a key to the house when they'd lived there. But now that it was abandoned, somebody had seen fit to lock the house up tight. She tried to peer in through the front windows, but the inexpensive bamboo blinds were drawn, and anyway the windows were caked with dirt.

She walked around to the rear of the house and tried the back door, which led onto a small utility room. The wooden door was spongy with rot, but it had apparently been latched from the inside, and she was afraid if she tugged too hard the whole door would collapse on top of her. Which wouldn't do. Annajane didn't want to advertise her visit to the cottage.

So she moved over to the left, to the wide set of triple windows that looked out over the lake. Or at least, they'd looked out on the lake when it was their master bedroom. Now those windows mostly looked out on the tops of dead weeds. A lanky camellia bush partially blocked the center window, but she managed to slither behind it, praying as she did so that no snakes were hidden in the thick carpet of dead leaves underfoot. She grasped the window sill with both hands, grunted and shoved the window upward. She climbed inside.

Instantly she wished she hadn't. Her muddy shoes left footprints in the thick carpet of dust on the worn wooden floor, and cobwebs festooned the ceiling fan overhead. The furniture in the room, an old wooden dresser, matching mahogany four-poster bed, and chest of drawers of no particular vintage or value, had come from Cherry Hill's attic. But Mason hadn't bothered to remove any of it when he moved out. Now a pale green mist of mold dotted the dark varnished wood surfaces. Some kind of animal had been chewing at the bare mattress.

Annajane walked around the room, her shoulders sagging, fingers trailing across the walls she'd repainted three times in one crazy, Quixie-fueled weekend, before arriving at the exact right shade, Benjamin Moore Morning Sky Blue, cut to half-strength.

She shouldn't have come. She opened the closet, so small they'd once joked that it wouldn't hold even one of the Bayless family secrets. Not much left there. Some rusty wire coat hangers, a folded green wool blanket on the one shelf. On a hook on the back of the door she found a faded plaid flannel shirt of Mason's, which he'd worn for yard work. On the floor she spied his mud-spattered laceless work boots lined up companionably next to a pair of her own grungy tennis shoes. Without thinking, Annajane pulled the flannel shirt on over her own denim shirt. She burrowed her nose into the collar, seeking some sense memory of her former husband, of those happy times they'd spent making this cottage their own. Instead, she sneezed violently, expelling a tiny dried-up spider into the mildew-scented air.

Her footsteps echoed in the closed-up house as she walked from room to room. To be precise, the house only had three rooms, the bedroom, an L-shaped living-dining room, the kitchen, and of course a bathroom, which was not much bigger than their bedroom closet.

One by one, she opened and closed the kitchen cupboards. The cabinet beside the stove held a yellowing box of pancake mix and an opened carton of baking soda. Kernels of rice trailed from a sack of Mahatma, where a mouse had nibbled a hole in the plastic bag. The cupboard by the refrigerator held two mismatched coffee mugs and a stack of green-tinted Quixie promotional glasses. Rust spots freckled the fridge.

Annajane stood in front of the window over the sink and looked out at the lake. From here, she could see the weather-beaten dock that stretched out into the water. They'd sunned themselves on that dock, dove naked into the surprisingly cool water on moonlit summer nights, paddled out into the middle of the lake on another night to make a drunken attempt at lovemaking in the bottom of the old wooden rowboat, an attempt that had ended up dunking them both into the lake.

They'd had big plans once: to build a double-decker boathouse at the end of the dock, one with a deck and a screened porch and a stone fireplace up top, for cookouts and parties, with davits below to hold the *Sallieforth,* a derelict 1967 seventeen-foot Chris-Craft ski boat that Mason hoped to eventually restore to working condition.

So many plans. Once that lake had been a clear blue-green, lapping wavelets against a shore lined with the blue hydrangeas, red geraniums, and drifts of Shasta daisies planted by the original caretaker's wife. Now weeds and water lilies choked the shoreline and obstructed the water views. She felt a melancholy, as cold and gray as the winter lake, seep into her soul.

Turning away from the window, she wandered into the living room, where the only furniture that remained was a lumpy brown sofabed, handed down from one of Mason's college roommates. The sofa faced the fireplace, where a stack of half-burned logs perched atop a small mound of coals. The old copper tub on the hearth had once held pieces of kindling, matches, and twists of newspaper. She reached in, found a couple sizable twigs, a long wooden kitchen match, and some yellowing newspaper.

Annajane placed the newspaper and the kindling on top of one of the half-burned logs, lit the match, and held it to the paper until it caught fire. In a moment, the dry sticks were burning merrily. She sat on the edge of the sofa, watching, waiting for the fire to build. When it threatened to die down, she searched around the house until she found an old phone book. She ripped out the pages, wadded them up, and tossed them onto the fire, crouching in front of the fireplace, ready to feed the fire more paper, lest the blaze die down again.

Finally, the logs caught, too. She could feel fingers of warmth creeping into the chill, stale air. She sat back on the sofa, watched and waited. Waited for what, she asked herself? Some catharsis? A cleansing? A healing? Coming here had been a mistake. She stood, stripped off the flannel shirt, and tossed it onto the flames, which claimed it with a whoosh of orange and red flames.

She let herself out the window, closed it, and drove off without a backward glance.

Three years later, Annajane forced herself to study her ex-husband, standing there on the altar, waiting for his new bride. Marrying Mason off to Celia was the final step in her self-prescribed cure. It was the only solution. And once it was done, once she heard Father Jolly pronounce the happy couple Mr. and Mrs. Mason Sheppard Bayless, Annajane could move on with her own life. Away from Passcoe, the Bayless family, and, yes, even dear old Quixie, the Quicker Quencher.

Everybody in town said that if you were born in Passcoe, North Carolina, the home of Quixie and the Quixie Beverage Company since 1922, you were born with the cherry-flavored cola running through your blood. It wasn't quite true of Annajane Hudgens.

Ruth, her mother, always claimed she couldn't stand the taste of the stuff, but Annajane knew the truth of the matter was that it was the Bayless family who left a bad taste in Ruth Hudgens's mouth.

Annajane always secretly wondered if Ruth hated the Baylesses because her daddy, Ruth's first husband, Bobby Mayes, had been killed by a drunk driver while driving a Quixie truck, when Annajane was barely two years old. Ruth had married Leonard Hudgens a year later, and Leonard quietly adopted the little girl when she was four. Even though Leonard worked at the plant, Ruth wouldn't allow Quixie in her house, and she certainly wouldn't allow her only child to drink the stuff. No, it was milk or apple juice or lemonade for Annajane, never Quixie.

Annajane could still remember the first time she tasted Quixie. It was in kindergarten, when she was invited to Pokey Bayless's fifth birthday party.

Her mama had thrown the pink engraved invitation right into the trash. "Think they're better than us and everybody else in town," she'd overheard Ruth tell Leonard. "Probably only asked Annajane because they want to lord it over us."

"Ruth, for Pete's sake, the girls go to kindergarten together. They're friends," Leonard had protested. "Just 'cuz you can't stand the parents, that don't mean those little girls can't play together." In the end, Annajane cried and begged, until, finally, Leonard had persuaded Mama to let her go to Pokey's party.

It was a tea party, and for the event a caterer set up a big round table draped in pink tulle on the front porch at Cherry Hill, the Baylesses' rambling old Greek Revival estate.

The table was set with a child-sized bone china tea set that had been one of Pokey's birthday presents, and there were real sterling silver forks and spoons and cloth napkins. Each of the six guests—all girls—was presented with her own silver sequined tiara and a pink feather boa. And at every place setting on the table stood a perfectly chilled chubby little bottle of Quixie soda with a pink and white striped straw sticking out of the neck.

Annajane could still remember that first icy sip. She'd never tasted a carbonated beverage before, and the bubbles tickled her nose and gave her the hiccups.

To her, Quixie didn't taste like cherry Kool-Aid or cherry Life Savers, or even cherry Popsicles. The fruit flavoring was bold and spicy and tart and sweet all at the same time, like a sour cherry exploding on her tongue with sparkly after-notes, and Annajane had never tasted anything as delicious in her entire life.

Besides the bottles of Quixie, the party refreshments included trays of tiny little crustless tea sandwiches and cookies and petit fours and a three-tiered Care Bears birthday cake that Mrs. Bayless had ordered from a bakery in Pinehurst, but for Annajane, nothing could match that first taste of Quixie.

Pokey's daddy, who'd played butler and head waiter at the party, had been delighted at Annajane's enthusiasm for the family product, and he had gladly replaced that first empty soda bottle with two more bottles in quick succession.

When the party was over, each girl in attendance was given a huge goodie bag containing a full-sized Cabbage Patch doll, a monogrammed grosgrain ribbon hair bow, and yet another bottle of Quixie cola, this one with a special commemorative label that said: IN CELEBRATION OF POKEY BAYLESS'S FIFTH BIRTHDAY. A VERY SPECIAL DAY.

Even at five, Annajane knew better than to share all the details of the party menu with her mama. She hid the commemorative bottle of Quixie at the bottom of her toy box, and two hours after she got home from the party, still wearing her treasured silver tiara and feather boa, she found herself crouched over the commode, silently retching up the contraband soft drink.

But the upset stomach did nothing to dim Annajane's enthusiasm for Quixie, or for her new best friend, Pokey, who'd earned the nickname because she'd been born nearly two weeks after Sallie's due date.

Pokey was as blond and fair-skinned and round as Annajane was dark and skinny. To Ruth Hudgens's consternation, the girls became inseparable, alternating sleepovers at each other's house nearly every weekend. Ruth never said a word to Annajane against Pokey—how could she? Silly, sunny-natured, fairhaired Pokey was the golden child everybody—even Ruth, against her will, loved.

As for Sallie Bayless, she was always cordial to Pokey's best friend, but as Annajane grew older, she came to realize that she would never measure up to Sallie's standards. Not as a friend, and certainly never as a daughter-in-law.

At the Bayless house, Pokey's brother Davis was an annoying constant in the girl's lives, bossing, teasing, and tormenting the girls until they would retreat, in tears, to Annajane's house, out of his reach. Annajane heard a lot about Mason, the adored oldest brother, who was four years older than Pokey, but she saw him rarely. Mason went to boarding school in Virginia and spent summer vacations sailing and water-skiing at Camp Seagull on the coast. According to Pokey, Mason was very near to a saint. He was the hero who stood up for her against Davis, whipped everybody at every sport, and, during summer vacations, when the family spent a month at their house at Wrightsville Beach, took her fishing and taught her to play spades.

On the handful of occasions when she'd been around Mason as a kid, Annajane had been so tongue-tied in his presence that she was sure they'd never even exchanged more than a "hey-howyadoin?"

Every summer, the Baylesses would invite Annajane to join them for their August trip to the beach, and every summer, Ruth would refuse to let her go. Sallie Bayless would write Ruth Hudgens a polite note on her pale blue engraved stationery, and when that didn't work, Pokey's father, Mr. Glenn Bayless, would seek out Annajane's stepfather, Leonard, at the plant, clap him on the back, and declare loudly, "Now, Leonard, my daughter Pokey is fussin' and fumin' at me because y'all won't let your little Annajane come to the beach with us. It'd sure give me some rest if you could do without her for a week or so."

But Leonard had his orders. "I'm sorry, Mr. Bayless," he'd say firmly. "But August is when we get together up in the mountains with Annajane's grandma and aunts and uncles. I'd have the whole family down on my neck if I messed with the family reunion."

So every summer, Annajane obediently joined her mother's relatives in a crowded, damp mountain cabin on a dirt road, where the relatives played cards and listened to gospel music and the cousins slept on pallets on the porch, played endless games of Clue, and griped about the lack of television.

Finally, miraculously, the summer when Annajane was fifteen, Ruth announced that they would not be going to the mountains. Her sister and brother-in-law had sold the cabin and were moving to Florida and taking Annajane's grandma with them.

Annajane was on the phone with Pokey moments later. "Guess what?" she said breathlessly. "No more stinkin' mountains for me! I've got the whole summer to do whatever I want!"

"Guess what else?" Pokey countered. "Daddy says he'll give us jobs at the plant this summer, if we want. Real jobs! With name badges and paychecks and everything."

"No way!" Annajane squealed with delight. "Our own money. No more babysitting for me."

The Monday after school was out found Annajane reporting to the Quixie front office, where Voncile, Glenn Bayless's assistant, seemed surprised to see her.

"Mr. Bayless has a job for me," Annajane said quietly. "Pokey said so."

"Of course," Voncile had said, smiling and leafing through some papers on her desktop. Growing up, Annajane and Pokey had always had the run of the Quixie plant. Voncile looked up at Annajane, standing there in the neatly pressed plaid dress Ruth had sewn just for this occasion. "Where is Miss Pokey this morning?"

"Oh. I thought she'd be here already," Annajane said, her spirits sinking. Pokey had promised to meet her at the plant at nine sharp.

"Well. Do you know how to type?"

"Yes ma'am," Annajane said proudly. "Forty-five words a minute."

"Wonderful," Voncile said. She ushered Annajane into a tiny windowless office not far from the reception room. A long table and two folding metal chairs were in the center of the room, and an enormous canvas mail bin sat beside the table, where a computer had been set up. A large plastic tub held boxes of business-sized white envelopes, and a smaller one held glossy Quixie coupons.

"Here we go," Voncile said. She gestured at the mail bin. "Are you familiar with our Quixie Quickie summer promotion?"

"I don't think so," Annajane replied, trying not to giggle.

Voncile picked up a bulky padded envelope and ripped it open. Five distinctive red and green Quixie screwtop bottle caps tumbled out. Voncile swept them into the trash with one hand, and extracted a piece of paper from the envelope.

"This," she said, waving the slip of paper, "is what we're after. We've asked Quixie lovers to mail in five bottle caps, along with their name and mailing address, for a chance to win one of those." She gestured to a row of gleaming red Coleman coolers against the far wall. Each of the coolers was printed with the oval Quixie logo, the one with the Quixie Pixie, leaning against a Quixie bottle, smiling and winking impishly.

Annajane counted two dozen coolers.

"So," Voncile said briskly, handing the slip to Annajane. "You'll type the name and address into our database. Right?" She leaned over the computer, tapped a few keys, and brought up a blank spreadsheet. "Just type on each line, and hit tab when you come to the end of the address. You can do that, can't you?"

"Yes ma'am," Annajane said.

"Then," Voncile said, "Come to my office and let me know when you've typed in all these addresses. I'll print them out onto labels, and then you'll put the labels on those envelopes." She plucked an envelope from a box and showed it to Annajane. The Quixie logo was printed in the upper-left-hand corner of each one. "You'll put one coupon for a free twelve-ounce bottle of Quixie in each envelope, seal up the envelope, and put it in that other bin. How does that sound?"

"Fine," was all Annajane could think of to say.

"Good," Voncile said, glancing at her watch. "I've got a meeting right now, but you just sit right down here and get started, and I'll come back afterwards to see how you're doing. All right?"

"Yes ma'am," Annajane said. She sat down at the computer, flexed her fingertips, and got started. It was slow going at first, ripping open the envelopes, sorting out the addresses, and then counting out the bottle caps. She was shocked to discover some envelopes didn't actually contain five bottle caps. Others might contain three or four Quixie caps, but with a non-Quixie cap thrown in to fill out the mix. Annajane counted Coke caps, Pepsi caps, Dr Pepper caps, even a few Hires and Barq root beer bottle caps. These she indignantly threw in the trash, along with the sender's entry blank. Who did these people think they were fooling?

After an hour or so, she got a system going, opening twenty-five envelopes at a time, scanning the caps, and then typing the names into the computer. Every once in a while, she'd get up, walk around the room, and peek out the door, wondering what was taking Pokey so long. Hadn't they agreed they would start their careers today?

At noon, her stomach started to growl. Her shoulders ached, and she was getting a headache from staring at the flickering computer screen. She wished she'd thought to bring along a lunch. At one, she walked over to Voncile's office, to inquire about taking a break. But the office was empty, and Mr. Bayless's office door was closed, too.

Finally, she remembered the break room, where she and Pokey had played restaurant as little girls, serving paper cups of Quixie from the fountain machine to the plant workers and being treated to packages of Tom's salted peanuts or Cheetos from the vending machines.

She was back at her computer, sipping from a cup of Quixie and nibbling a Mr. Goodbar when the door flew open.

"Come on, you little brat," a man's deep voice called. "Mama sent me to take you to lunch." He stepped into the room, and Annajane was so flustered by an in-the-flesh glimpse of Mason Bayless that she knocked over her drink.

Speechless, she watched a bright red river of soda splashing onto the stack of contest entry blanks she'd just stacked beside the computer.

"Oh no," she cried, jumping up. She reached into the trash bin and grabbed a discarded envelope and started madly dabbing at the mess. But it was too late. She'd greedily poured herself a huge cup of Quixie, and now everything on the tabletop was soaked.

"Damn," she wailed, mopping and breathing hard, and trying not to look up at her best friend's big brother. When she realized that she'd cursed out loud, she blushed harder and mopped faster.

Mason Bayless was sunburned, which made his blue eyes look bluer, and his dark blond hair needed cutting because it brushed down his high forehead and across his thick dark eyebrows. His prominent nose had a bump across the bridge, but he had perfect white teeth, except for one chipped incisor. He was dressed in faded blue jeans and well-worn high-top leather work boots and a green Quixie Beverage Company uniform shirt with red pinstripes and an embroidered patch over his breast that said MASON.

Not that he needed a name patch. Not much. Every one of the three hundred employees at Quixie Beverage Company knew Mr. Glenn Bayless's oldest boy, as did just about everybody in the community. Passcoe was a company town, and Quixie and Passcoe had been inextricably linked for more than seventy years.

Mason's uniform shirt was untucked and the top three buttons unfastened. After a moment, he grabbed another envelope and began sweeping the ruined papers into the trash.

"Sorry," he drawled. "Didn't mean to scare you like that. I was looking for my sister."

"Oh, wait," Annajane said, grabbing for the trash can. "I can't, I mean, those are contest entries. And I've got to type them into the computer. Maybe I can get them dried out . . ."

"Forget it," Mason said. "Those are toast."

"But I'm supposed to type them all in. It's a contest, and the winner gets a cooler, and it's not fair . . ." she sighed. "I'll have to tell Voncile, I guess. I don't know what she'll say."

"Voncile won't give a rat's ass," Mason said. He smiled. "I'll just tell her I did it. Which is kinda true. It was my fault."

He cocked his head and considered her. "Hey. You've got stuff on your dress." He reached out and his fingertip brushed the sleeve.

She jumped several inches.

He laughed. "Sorry. You're kinda jumpy, aren't you?" He held out her hand. "I'm Mason Bayless. I don't think I've seen you around the plant before. Are you new?"

"I know," Annajane said, "I mean, I know you're Mason." Idiot! He'd think she was stalking him. She blushed and tried to start over. "Well, I mean, we've met, but it's been a long time. I'm Pokey's friend, Annajane Hudgens." She smiled nervously, glancing down at the large red stain blossoming across the front of her new dress.

"Pokey's friend," he said. "The one who disappears every August. Hell yeah. So you're working here?"

"Just for the summer," Annajane said. "Your dad gave us jobs. It's my first day."

"And where's my bratty sister?" Mason asked. "Did she bail on you already?"

"Um," Annajane stalled, not wanting to rat out her best friend.

Mason rolled his eyes. "That's what I thought. She never even showed today, did she?"

"She might have had summer school this morning," Annajane lied. "She's trying to get her Spanish grade up to a B."

"Riiight," Mason said. "What do you wanna bet her lazy behind is lying right beside the pool at the club, while you're stuck here at the plant, counting bottle caps?"

"Summer school could have run late," Annajane said, loyal to the end.

"If you do see Pokey, tell her I came by," Mason said. "I'll stop by Voncile's desk and let her know I kinda messed things up in here."

"Thanks," Annajane breathed.

"And don't worry," he added. "I won't blow Pokey's cover story. Not this time, anyway."

4

Annajane never told Mason she'd fallen in love with him that first day at the plant. She'd never told anybody. Not even Pokey. After all, she'd been fifteen, he was nineteen, working in the warehouse for the first time that summer after his freshman year of college, at his father's insistence. As far as Mason Bayless was concerned, Annajane was just some goofy girl who hung out with his baby sister.

He hadn't given her a second thought, or a second glance. It would be another four years before they exchanged their first kiss.

Her cheeks burned now at the thought of that first time. She shook her head violently, trying to dislodge the memory.

"You okay?" Pokey whispered. "It's not too late to make your escape."

But it *was* too late. The music swelled again, and the violins and flutes and organ began the fluttering notes of the Pachelbel's Canon in D. Every head turned toward the back of the church.

"Ahh." Annajane heard the chorus of approving sighs, and in a moment she spotted Sophie.

The five-year-old tiptoed slowly up the aisle. Somebody had attempted to tame the wild mane of blond curls, but the circlet of baby's breath and pink rosebuds rested at a crooked tilt, listing slightly over her right ear. She was angelic in the ankle-length pink organza dress with its delicate pin-tucked bodice and bell-shaped sleeves. Annajane held her breath as Sophie made her way up the aisle, flinging fists full of rosebuds from the satin basket dangling from her skinny wrist. Her sparkly pink cat-eye glasses slid down her nose, and she paused once, to push them back into place.

The sight of Mason's daughter caused Annajane unexpected tears. Sophie was not her child, although she should have been. Mason had fathered her during a brief one-night stand not long after their separation and had legally adopted her after the mother couldn't care for the baby.

People in Passcoe expected that Annajane would be outraged by the child's birth, so soon after her split from Mason, but Sophie had stolen her heart the first time she held her in her arms. How could anybody resent bossy, enchanting, Disney-princess-loving Sophie? Her Aunt Pokey's house was Sophie's second home, and since Pokey's best friend, Annajane, was there nearly as often as the child, Sophie considered her family. Which she was. Sort of. Leaving Sophie, losing her to Celia—the prospect of it felt like the unkindest cut of all to Annajane.

As always, Sophie seemed to move to her own inner soundtrack, which was unfortunately nowhere in sync to Canon in D. The little girl was anxiously scanning the aisles as she walked, looking, Annajane knew, for familiar faces. Finally, she spotted Annajane and her aunt Pokey and nodded solemnly. But behind the thick lenses of her glasses, her usually impish gray eyes were dark-rimmed and heavy-lidded. Her cheeks were hot pink in contrast to her alabaster skin.

Pokey leaned into the aisle. "You're doin' great, baby," she whispered encouragingly, and Annajane nodded silent agreement and blew her a kiss. Finally, the child gave a tremulous smile and pressed a wad of rosebuds into Pokey's outstretched hand. As she moved past, Annajane noticed that the streamers of the long satin sash were lopsided, and wet, which surely meant that the sash had somehow gotten dunked during a prewedding potty stop.

Why, Annajane wondered, hadn't somebody spotted the wet sash? Perhaps, somebody like Sophie's about-to-be stepmother? The dress was Celia's own design, and no matter what Pokey or Annajane thought of her as a person, it was no secret that Celia's successful children's clothing business, Gingerpeachy, had recently sold to a national chain, netting Celia and her backers a rumored ten million dollars.

A few steps past their pew, two-thirds of the way to the altar, Sophie came to a dead stop. She was looking uncertainly, right to left. The music kept playing, but Sophie was not moving. Annajane held her breath.

She looked up at the altar. Father Jolly seemed oblivious, but Davis and Pete were frowning, exchanging worried asides. Mason had taken a couple steps forward. He was half-kneeling, smiling, his arms extended to his little girl, encouraging her to finish her triumphant voyage up the aisle.

Annajane could read his lips, even from this far way. "Come on, sweetheart," he was telling her. "You can do it."

She could not see the child's face, only the slightest nod of her head, and then Sophie began to tiptoe forward again.

Only a few steps behind Sophie came a willowy redhead in an ankle-length cerise organza gown, cut so tightly through the skirt, she was forced to take tiny, mincing geisha-girl steps. The woman was in her late twenties and looked as though she'd just stepped off a Paris runway.

"Who's that?" Annajane asked.

Pokey shrugged. "Never laid eyes on her before. Just another of Celia's legions of best girlfriends, probably."

Six more women in silk gowns of the same hue followed the maid of honor. Annajane knew most of the women, some of them only slightly. But when she saw a familiar brunette with long, wavy, blond highlighted hair, Annajane felt a stab of jealousy. McKenna Murphey Kelleher was *her* friend. They'd known each other since junior high, and Annajane had introduced McKenna to Jimmy Kelleher, the man she'd ended up marrying. When had McKenna defected to Team Celia?

There was no time for further discussion. The processional music faded, and the heavy wooden doors at the rear of the church opened with a theatrical boom. The congregation stirred and stood, and in the brief silence the rustle of satin, silk, and good wool filled the church.

Annajane's eyes were riveted on the bride, the future Mrs. Mason Bayless.

Celia Wakefield was teacup-sized, with short, silvery hair and huge doelike liquid-dark eyes that were today emphasized with the most extravagant false eyelashes Annajane had ever seen. She seemed even smaller than usual, standing back there, poised and alone, framed by the twelve-foot oak door.

Mason, on the other hand, was at least eighteen inches taller than his new bride. He was solidly built, not heavy, but she estimated he weighed close to a hundred pounds more than Celia.

What, Annjane wondered idly, was sex like between the two of them? She squeezed her eyes shut, trying to dislodge the image of Mason and Celia, naked. After all, she was in church, not exactly the same church where she and Mason had been married, but it was still church, and the eyes of God and all of Passcoe were watching. *Must stop thinking about sex in church*, Annajane vowed.

Strings and woodwinds warbled, a lovely classical piece that seemed hauntingly familiar. "What's that song?" Annajane asked, craning her neck to get a better look at the bride.

Must not think of sex in church. Must not think of sex in church. Must not think of Mason naked.

Instead, she tried to think of Shane, naked. Her fiancé had a perfectly nice body, tall and rangy, and he had long, artistic fingers, but he was just the slightest bit self-conscious, even in bed, which she thought must be unusual. Weren't musicians supposed to be wildly uninhibited? Oh, but Mason, naked! Annajane felt herself shiver at the memory.

Fortunately, her best friend didn't notice. She was humming the processional under her breath. Pokey had taken piano for years at Sallie's insistence, and was actually a credible musician, when she cared to be. She gave a sniff of disapproval. "Handel. *Arrival of the Queen of Sheba.* As if."

The bride took her first step down the aisle.

Celia was tiny, dainty, exquisite, a queen of Sheba in miniature, Annajane thought. Her gown, another of her own designs, was a severe architectural strapless column of lustrous ivory satin, its only ornament a series of stiff fabric folds forming an accordion-pleat fan at the alarmingly low-cut bodice.

Seeing the regal bride, Annajane felt instantly five sizes larger, dowdy in her fussy vintage dress with its prissy row of buttons and old-fashioned buckle. She'd dressed with such care only a few hours earlier, and dulled her inhibitions with bourbon, but now, she decided, she'd seriously overdressed and under-medicated herself. What the hell had she been thinking?

"Geezus H!" Pokey chortled, elbowing Annajane in the ribs again. "That's some dress. I think I can actually see her nipples."

"Hush," Annajane said halfheartedly, looking around in panic for an escape route. But her pew was packed butt to butt. It was standing room only in the church, with latecomers lolling against the walls on the side aisles, and the bride about to process down the center aisle. No, not even Houdini could have extri-cated himself from such a tight prison. She would have to stay and see the cure all the way through to the bitter end.

The bride paused for a moment, basking in this, her moment of glory. She adjusted her train, raised her chin, and began to glide down the white-carpeted aisle. Celia's ensemble was simplicity itself. She wore no jewelry other than her engagement ring, except a pair of shoulder-brushing diamond drop earrings, and in the now-darkened church, the diamonds spun kaleidoscopic reflections on the ceiling. She clutched a single immense calla lily—the size of a majorette's baton—in her elbow-length gloved hands.

Halfway up the aisle, Celia's cloak of poise slipped, just a bit. She frowned and slowed her gait.

The music was still playing. Annajane turned toward the altar, to see what was holding things up. Father Jolly, Pete, and Davis stood expectantly, watch-ing the proceedings with detached solemnity.

Mason's back was ramrod straight. His lips were curved in a slight, frozen smile, but the rest of his face seemed a mask, his eyes flickering rapidly, side to side.

Sophie had stopped again, this time only a few yards from the altar. She was looking around, studying the flowers, her grandmother and cousins in the front pew, waving shyly at her adored nanny, Letha, in the row directly behind Sallie Bayless and family.

Letha leaned out into the aisle. "Go on, baby," she whispered. "You're doing great."

So what if the groom was nervous? Annajane thought. This meant nothing. It was perfectly natural. Mason had been single for five years. Since their di-vorce, he'd certainly played the field, dated his share of women, most of them wildly inappropriate, and one of those flings had resulted in Sophie, whose appearance, literally on the Bayless family doorstep, had at first been a shock and then what they'd all come to unanimously regard as a blessing.

She had to give Mason credit. Faced with a six-month-old baby and apparently irrefutable proof of the child's paternity, he had done the right thing. The Baylesses did not shirk responsibility. He had been forced to, as Davis so cynically put it, "man up." Letha had been hired as a nanny, and a nursery was established in Mason's house, just down the street from the Bayless compound.

Sophie, who'd been a spindly, colicky infant when she came to them, had slowly begun to blossom. Mason's responsibilities for Quixie had formerly kept him on the road four days out of every week, but after Sophie arrived, he'd reshuffled his responsibilities to allow him to spend most evenings with her. And he had fallen head over heels in love with his little girl.

Mason had a lot on his plate, Annajane thought. He had a first wife who still worked for the company, right under his nose, at least for the time being; a faltering business to run; and a crazy family to try to ride herd over. And any moment now, she thought, he would be adding a second wife and stepmother to that mix.

He seemed to be holding up reasonably well under the pressure, Annajane decided, studying him again. He rocked back slightly on his heels, and his lips tried, but failed, to form a smile as Celia began moving closer.

Annajane stared, her face growing hot again. A muscle twitched in Mason's jaw. He worked to erase it with his right index finger, but it twitched again. For a second, only a second, she felt Mason's eyes meet her own. And then his jaw muscle twitched six times in rapid succession, and he looked away.

Not soon enough. Annajane's pulse quickened and her throat caught. She felt dizzy and grabbed Pokey's arm for support.

It was a tell! How many times had she seen that involuntary signal? Across the room at a boring dinner party, in the middle of a contentious meeting with his mother or his brother? And yes, during the worst moments of their doomed marriage. When Mason was feeling trapped, desperate to flee, he would rock back on his heels, and his jaw muscle would twitch like a frightened rabbit's ears.

He wants out, Annajane thought. He does not want to marry this woman.

As she watched, she felt the past come rushing back with a ferocity that nearly knocked her down. And it struck her, this was not just a flare-up she was experiencing, not just a bout of spring fever. This was full-blown passion.

This can't happen. She can't have him. I want him back.

Her fingers gripped Pokey's arm in a death lock.

"Heey," Pokey whispered, giving her a worried look. "What's up? Are you okay?"

Annajane couldn't speak.

The music kept playing. Celia floated past them in a cloud of perfume. Annajane took a half step to the left, sending Pokey half-sprawling into the aisle, but Celia never noticed.

Stop that woman! Annajane wanted to scream. But the words wouldn't come out. And Celia was nearly at the altar. Father Jolly was beaming. Mason's jaw was twitching so violently now, even Davis was looking at him oddly.

No, no, no! Annajane cleared her throat. She was going to do it. She had to do it.

But suddenly, a forlorn, high-pitched wail rose above the violins and the piccolos.

It was Sophie. Just a few feet from the altar, she crumpled to the carpet in a pink tulle heap. She was writhing and clutching her tummy. She howled. "It hurts! Daddy, it hurts!"

5

For a moment, nobody moved. An instant later, Mason was kneeling at Sophie's side. He gently scooped her into his arms, and she twisted like a caged animal. Worse than screaming, she was only whimpering now, words Annajane couldn't quite make out.

The music kept playing. Father Jolly held a whispered conference with Pete and Davis, who were helplessly shaking their heads, looking around for some kind of direction. Celia reached the altar, but there was nobody there to meet her, because her groom was rushing toward the side exit. She stood, momentarily stunned, tightly gripping her oversized calla lily.

"Oh my God," Pokey whispered. "What on earth?" People were murmuring, heads turning, but mostly they were frozen in place.

Annajane didn't wait to hear any more. She managed to slide past Pokey, and now she was sprinting for the front of the church. She had to get to Sophie.

As she reached the door to the robing room, she heard Father Jolly's voice from the lectern. "Uh, folks," he said tentatively. "We've got a sick little girl on our hands here. If you would, I'd like to ask you all to bow your heads and pray for God's blessing."

. . .

She found Mason seated on a brocade loveseat in the robing room, cradling Sophie across his lap. She was moaning, and her face was gray and beaded with perspiration. Mason was smoothing her hair with one hand, and fumbling with a phone on a table with the other.

"Here," Annajane said, sliding onto the sofa beside him and extending her arms to the child. "Let me take her. Have you called for an ambulance?"

Sophie whimpered a little, but settled quickly into Annajane's arms. The child's body was hot to the touch, and as Annajane stroked her face, Sophie's face contorted. She shuddered, coughed, and vomited. And vomited again.

"Oh my God," Mason said, dropping the phone. "What . . . what should I do?"

Annajane grabbed for a box of tissue beside the phone and began mopping Sophie's face. "I'm sorry," the little girl sobbed. "I'm sorry." She vomited again.

"It's okay, baby," Annajane said. "It's okay." She wiped Sophie's face clean again, and poised her hand over the little girl's abdomen. "Can I touch your tummy? Just for a minute?"

The child nodded. Annajane placed the palm of her hand flat against Sophie's stomach, but even the lightest touch resulted in a yowl of pain.

"Jesus," Mason said, shakily. "What do you think's wrong?"

The robing-room door opened, and Celia rushed in. "Is she all right?" Celia started to ask. When she saw the vomit spattered across Sophie and Annajane, she took a step backward. Then she swallowed hard, bent down, and took Sophie's hand.

"Where does it hurt, honey?" she asked softly. "Tell Celia."

Sophie moaned and pressed her feverish face against Annajane's chest.

Celia patted Sophie's damp curls. "Poor baby."

She gave Mason an exasperated shake of the head. "She ate a lot of junk at lunch today. I personally saw your brother sneaking her at least two bowls of that damned Quixie ice cream. It's probably just a combination of an upset tummy and all the excitement."

"You think?" Mason asked hopefully, his hand hovering over the phone.

Celia looked over at Annajane, treating her to a conspiratorial smile. "Maybe you could be an angel and go get Letha and ask her to take Sophie home and put her to bed?"

"I don't think so," Annajane said. "This isn't just a bellyache. I'm sorry, Celia, but we need to get her to the hospital. Right now. She's burning up with fever."

"Excuse me?" Celia tilted her head, as though she hadn't heard correctly. "We've got five hundred people sitting in that church out there. We've got a soloist from the North Carolina Symphony, and over at the country club, we've got lobster thermidor and a steamship of roast beef. My great-aunt Eleanor flew in this morning from Kansas City. With an *oxygen* tank."

There was a quick knock at the door, and Father Jolly poked his head inside. "How's the patient?" he inquired. "I hate to intrude, but people are concerned." He shrugged apologetically. "Mason, your mother and sister wanted me to see how the little girl is doing. Mrs. Bayless doesn't want anybody to panic."

Celia stood and hiked up the sagging bodice of her dress. "Tell Sallie everything is fine." She gave Annajane a pointed look. "There is no need to overreact. We just need *somebody* to fetch Letha, and then, I think, we can go ahead with the ceremony. Right, darling?" She rested her hand lightly on Mason's broad tuxedo-clad shoulder, letting her fingertips drift down the lapel of his jacket. It was a clear signal of ownership, to Father Jolly, Mason, and most important, Annajane.

He is mine. I am in charge. The show must go on.

Mason glanced from his ex-wife to his next. He cleared his throat. "Well . . . uh . . ."

As if to settle the matter, Sophie moaned, coughed, and barfed again.

Annajane struggled unsteadily to her feet, clutching Sophie to her. She had had enough.

"Fine. You two do what you need to do. But in the meantime, Mason, I think you'd better call 911." She was making a deliberate effort to keep her voice calm. "Tell them we've got a five-year-old with abdominal pain and a high fever. Her belly seems rigid and tender to the touch. And tell them to please hurry."

"Excuse me?" Celia said. "What medical school did you say you attended?"

"My mother was a nurse for thirty years, and I was a candy striper all through high school," Annajane said calmly. "Anyway, it's just a matter of common sense. Feel her tummy, if you don't believe me."

Mason was dialing and reaching for Celia's hand. "I'm sorry," he said pleadingly. "But you understand. Right?"

Celia took only a moment to reevaluate the situation, shift tactics, and choose the proper response. "Of course," she cried. "Absolutely. Do you think it would be better to load her into my car and take her over to the hospital ourselves?"

"Just a minute," Mason said, turning his attention back to the phone. "Right. This is Mason Bayless. I'm at the Church of the Good Shepherd in Passcoe. There's something wrong with my little girl. What? No, I don't know the address. It's on Fairhaven, about a block from downtown. It's the only Episcopal church in town, for God's sake. Don't you people have a computer or something?"

He listened impatiently. "Yes, that's it. Okay. She's five years old, and she just . . . suddenly collapsed. She's in a lot of pain. It's her stomach. She's got a high fever, and she's throwing up . . . No, she doesn't have any allergies that I know of. No! She hasn't gotten into poison. Who the hell do you think you're dealing with here?"

Annajane took the phone from him. "Listen, you need to send an ambulance. Now. I'm no nurse, but I think maybe it's her appendix. Fine. We'll meet you out front of the church."

The robing-room door opened and Pokey stepped in. "What's the news?" she started, and then wrinkled her nose. "Oh no. Stomach bug?"

"Annajane thinks it might be her appendix," Mason said gloomily. "They're sending an ambulance."

"What do you need me to do?" She was addressing her brother, ignoring his fiancée, not something Celia was used to.

"Pokey, could you please ask Father Jolly to announce that the ceremony has been postponed?" Celia said, reasserting her authority. "Ask everybody to go ahead on over to the country club for the reception. Just say we're doing things backward. Reception, then ceremony. We've got all that food and champagne chilled down, and it'd be a shame to waste it. We'll try to get over there after we get Sophie taken care of at the hospital. But she's the first priority."

"We'll have to get all those cars cleared out of the driveway and the street outside, before an ambulance can get here," Pokey said. "And Mama's going to want to go to the hospital, too, I can tell you right now."

"Fine," Celia said impatiently. "You and Pete can take her, or Davis or somebody, but in the meantime, could you please get those cars moved?"

"Sure," Pokey said, bristling at being ordered around. She looked over at Annajane, who was pacing around the small room, softly humming to the whimpering Sophie. "I'll be right back after the announcement, and we'll get you some kind of clean clothes. You can't leave looking like that."

"I don't mind," Annajane protested. "Just do whatever you need to do, Pokey. I'm going to ride in the ambulance with Sophie." She glanced at Mason. "If that's okay with you?"

"Now, wait a minute," Celia snapped, not about to let Annajane usurp her authority. "Her father and I will ride in the ambulance. He's going to have to sign authorization for her to be treated. And I'm her, uh, I'm his wife."

Pokey turned to go. "Not yet, you're not." She said it under her breath, just loud enough for Celia to hear.

"Daddy," Sophie whimpered, reaching out an arm for her father.

"Right here, sugar," Mason said, stepping to Annajane's side and squeezing the little girl's hand. "We're going to get you to see a doctor right this minute. And guess what? You're gonna get to ride in an ambulance. What do you think about that?"

"Will it hurt?" Sophie asked, huge tears rolling down her pale cheeks.

"Not at all," Celia said brightly. "It'll be fun! I'll get them to blast the siren so everybody knows you're coming."

"It might hurt a little bit," Annajane said, shooting Celia a look. "But we'll be right there with you, the whole time. We need to get the doctors at the hospital to see what's wrong with your tummy. I think they'll give you something to make you sleep, and then they'll take a look and figure things out."

"Okay," Sophie said wearily. "Only, don't let me go, Annajane. Okay?" Her eyelids fluttered, and she dozed off, her forehead nestled against Annajane's ruined dress.

"I won't, baby," Annajane whispered. "I promise."

Mason reached over and gently removed the little girl's glasses, which had slid off the end of her nose, tucking them into the pocket of his tux jacket.

The door flew open again, and Sallie Bayless bustled in with Davis in her wake. "Pokey says there's some talk that it might be her appendix? And an ambulance is on the way? I just called Max Kaufman. He was on the third tee at the golf club when I reached him," she told her son. "He's going to meet you at the emergency room."

"Max Kaufman?" Celia asked.

"Chief of surgery at the hospital," Sallie said. "A very old family friend. He should have been sitting right out front in one of those pews, but Max is a hopeless philistine. Says he never goes to weddings or funerals. But he's a wonderful doctor, isn't he, Mason? He'll take very good care of the child."

"Mason and Annajane are going to the hospital, and I'll follow in my car. Maybe you could ride with me," Celia said.

Sallie shook her head. "Celia, dear, I think it would be better if you and I went on over to the club to greet our guests. Mason has his cell, and I have mine, and he can keep us posted."

"I don't know," Celia said, her brow furrowed prettily. "I think I need to be with Sophie . . ."

"Look, y'all, we don't all need to go to the hospital," Davis spoke up. "Mama, I'll take you and Celia over to the club for the reception. If there's nothin' seriously wrong with Sophie, Pokey can bring Mason back over there once Doc Kaufman gets it figured out. Hell, maybe it's nothing. It'd be a shame to cancel the party if it's only a bellyache."

He glanced toward the doorway, where Celia's sultry maid of honor leaned against the doorjamb, looking bored.

"Good idea," Mason nodded in agreement. He grasped Celia's arm and gently steered her toward the door.

"Well," Celia said hesitantly, "If you really think you can do without me . . ."

Mason walked her to the door. His hand rested lightly on the small of her back, and he brushed a kiss on Celia's forehead. "I knew you'd understand. Look, I'll call you the minute we know something. Maybe it's not really anything serious. In which case, I'll be at the club in an hour or so. Okay?"

Celia responded by wrapping her arms tightly around Mason's neck, molding herself to him, and kissing him deeply and passionately.

Sallie Bayless looked away politely. Finally, she cleared her throat. "Celia, dear, I think we'd better go. Your great-aunt is out there, and she's beside herself with worry . . ."

In the distance, they heard the approaching keen of a siren.

Mason peeled himself off the front of his bride's low-cut gown. "Better go," he said.

"Call me," Celia repeated, reluctantly allowing herself to be towed away.

When they were alone again, Mason went back to the settee, where Annajane was still holding Sophie in her arms.

"Let me take her," he whispered, holding out his arms.

"You'll ruin your tux," Annajane protested, but Mason was already sliding his arms under the child's limp torso. He straightened up and cradled Sophie against his chest.

"You really think it's her appendix?" he asked.

Annajane shrugged. "My cousin Nadine had appendicitis one summer when we were up at the cabin. Thank God Mama was there, because my aunt really thought Nadine was just constipated. Mama insisted they go to the emergency room, and, sure enough, that's what it was."

Mason blanched. "Maybe we should take her to Raleigh. Max Kaufman is a good enough country doc, from what I know, but Passcoe Memorial is just a little old podunk hospital with, what, fifty beds? Maybe she should see a pediatric specialist . . ."

The siren was getting closer now.

"Mason, Passcoe Memorial is a fine facility," Annajane said. "It's small, but they have a state-of-the-art surgical wing, thanks to your father's Rotary Club, and Mama always said Dr. Kaufman was the best surgeon, the best diagnostician, she'd ever seen. If it really is her appendix, there's probably no time to take Sophie to Raleigh. If it's something else, something more serious, Dr. Kaufman can refer us to a specialist, but in the meantime, let's just take one thing at a time, please?"

Pokey rushed into the room, pink-faced and breathless.

"Okay, the cars are moved, and the ambulance is pulling around front," she said. She put one hand to Sophie's cheek. "Oh wow, she really does have a fever," she said. "How long has she been asleep?"

"Just a few minutes," Mason said.

"Where's the bride?" Pokey asked, looking around the room. "Checking her makeup?"

"Not funny," Mason snapped. "Mama persuaded her to go on over to the country club. Maybe you should join them."

"Not a chance," Pokey said. "Pete's taking the boys over there, but I'm going to the hospital."

6

Geographically, the distance from the church to the hospital, which was located on the bypass just outside the Passcoe city limits, was only seventeen miles.

To Annajane and Mason, the ride seemed to take a lifetime. Jammed into the back of the ambulance, perched on either side, with Sophie's tiny form on a gurney between them, they could only watch helplessly as she writhed in pain.

"She's hurting! Can't you give her something?" Mason growled at the emergency medical technician riding in the passenger seat.

"Sorry, Mr. Bayless, but with kids this young, we just make sure their pulse and breathing are stable," the EMT said. "We'll be at the hospital in fifteen minutes, and they'll probably give her something then."

"Daddy," Sophie whimpered. "Annajane. It hurts."

She was awake again, and she looked terrified. Annajane squeezed the child's hot, clammy hand and brushed back a strand of hair from her forehead.

"We're taking a ride to the hospital, sweetpea," Annajane said. "Can you tell how fast we're going? This old ambulance goes even faster than your daddy's fun car."

Mason laughed despite himself. The "fun car" was what Sophie called his restored candy-apple red 1972 Chevelle convertible. It had been Glenn Bayless's favorite big boy toy, handed down to Mason as a twenty-first-birthday gift.

The convertible was currently garaged in a truck bay at the bottling plant, brought out only occasionally, for Sunday drives to the coast, or as a special treat for Sophie, because there wasn't room for it in the two-car garage at the house, what with his own Yukon and Celia's Saab. And also because Celia had taken an instant disliking to—and distrust of—what she called his "middle-aged crazy car," or, worse, "your pimp-mobile."

"Why can't you buy a nice Porsche, like your brother's?" Celia had asked. "Or something with say, air-conditioning? Or satellite radio?"

The Chevelle's air probably hadn't worked all that well when it was new, and as for a radio, Mason preferred its tape deck, on which he listened to his stash of '80s hair bands.

He'd had some times in that Chevelle, for sure. In his youth, he'd ripped up and down the East Coast in it, ridden the length of the Outer Banks, the one summer of his youth when he hadn't worked at Quixie, his summer of rebellion, when he'd gotten a job working at a convenience store at Nags Head. He'd even driven to California and back, following the old Route 66, the summer he'd graduated from Penn.

Sophie's tear-swollen eyes widened. "Can you make the top of the amb'lance go down so I can see out?"

"I can't do that, sugar," Mason said soothingly, "but just as soon as we get your tummy better, I'm gonna take you all the way to the beach in the fun car. Just you and me."

"And Annajane," Sophie added. "Annajane loves the fun car, too."

Mason exchanged a look with his ex. Her cheeks colored and she looked away. He wondered if she remembered.

He'd been driving the Chevelle the second time he remembered an important encounter with Annajane Hudgens. She was what? Maybe nineteen? Which would have made him twenty-three.

It was summertime, and he'd somehow allowed himself to be roped into driving the convertible in the Passcoe Fourth of July parade, chauffeuring a local beauty queen, Tamelah Dorman, who'd actually been crowned Miss Passcoe, although it should have been Miss Spray-Tan, because she was surely the most artificially overbronzed girl he'd ever encountered.

Anyway, he and Tamelah were having a pretty good time that day. She, perched on the back of the Chevelle, decked out in a short, low-cut spangly firecracker-red dress that definitely showed off her best assets, and he in shorts and a white Quixie Soda polo shirt. He'd filled a flask full of crushed ice, Captain Morgan rum, and Quixie, and he and good old Tamelah had emptied and refilled it before they got a quarter of the way down the Main Street parade route that morning.

The Fourth of July parade was always a major deal in Passcoe, and that year, the hundredth anniversary of the town's incorporation, made it an even bigger deal than usual. Thousands of people lined Main Street, seated on lawn chairs, standing in the shade of storefronts, or crouched on the curbs.

He'd hoped for a spot either at the very beginning or the very end of the parade lineup, but no such luck. They'd slotted him slap in the middle, between Patti-Jean's Twirling Tykes—three dozen tap-dancing, baton-twirling pre-schoolers, and the El-Shazaam Masonic Lodge's Shriner Klown Korps, which consisted of ten middle-aged men in white face, baggy pants, and red fright wigs, perched atop souped-up lawn-mower chassis.

Their progress was agonizingly slow. The Tykes' twirling routines were limited to two songs—playing over and over again—which blared out from a huge boom box mounted on a wagon pulled by Patti-Jean herself, a Sousa march and *I'm a Yankee Doodle Dandy*. Behind him, the Klown Korps guys zigzagged crazily across the pavement, popping wheelies and running a dizzying series of figure eights that left an acrid cloud of gasoline fumes hanging overhead.

The sun was blazing down, and Mason worried that their snail's pace would cause the Chevelle's supercharged engine to overheat.

What with the heat and all, he and Tamelah had slain one whole bottle of the Captain and were shaking hands with another, and they still had half a mile to go before they would reach Memorial Park, where the parade ended and a huge citywide picnic and carnival was set up. If his memory served,

Tamelah was so trashed that she'd given up her regal, queenly wave, and begun flipping off the good citizens of Passcoe seated on folding chairs along Main Street. Twice, when male admirers ran up alongside the car to snap photos of her, Tamelah had obliged by flashing them her boobs. She and Mason had already discussed a postparade meet-up back at his apartment later that evening.

At some point along the route, he'd glanced to the right and noticed that his wasn't the only Quixie soft drink unit participating in the parade.

There, pushing a hand cart and handing out complimentary cans of Quixie and fifty-cent coupons, was the company mascot, Dixie, the Quixie Pixie herself.

Somehow, somebody in the company had conned some poor sap into climbing into the pixie costume. Whoever it was, he thought, was probably ready to spontaneously combust in the outfit, which consisted of a long-sleeved green felt tunic, bright red tights, oversized green booties with curled-up toes, and a huge foam-rubber Pixie head, topped off with a pointy green and red elf cap.

Hell, he was roasting in the ninety-five-degree heat, and he was just dressed in shorts, flip flops, and a polo.

He slowed the Chevelle to a roll, waiting until the company mascot was right beside it. "Hey Dixie," he called over. "How's it goin'?"

The mascot head turned, and then the pixie made an exaggerated shrug and marched away at an accelerated pace. He studied the pixie's shape, trying to figure out who might be wearing the costume. The tunic was loose-fitting, but it was short, ending midthigh, and from the looks of the tights, he was pretty sure there was a girl under there. A girl with awesome legs.

"Whoossh that?" Tamelah demanded, whipping her head around to see what Mason was staring at.

"Why darlin', that's just our company mascot," Mason said, grinning.

"Zat a damned leprechaun?" Tamelah asked bleerily.

"Close. It's a pixie."

"What z'actly is a damned pixie?"

Mason gave it some thought. "A mischevious elf. Plus, it was the only word my grandmother could think of that rhymed with Quixie."

"Hmmpph," Tamelah hmmpphed. "Pass me that flask, will ya?"

Mason handed the flask back to Tamelah and rolled up alongside the pixie again.

"Hey Dixie," he called. "Wanna ride?"

This time the pixie did not bother to turn around. She tossed three cans of sodas to a trio of cat-calling teenage boys in rapid succession, and then took off again, the brass bells stitched to her curly toes jingling merrily with every step.

Mason chuckled under his breath, and accelerated the Chevelle.

"C'mon," he called, sliding easily alongside Dixie again. "Who is that under there? We're almost at the park. You can tell me."

But now the pixie was very nearly trotting, the cart bumping along on the street's uneven asphalt pavement, spewing chunks of ice in its wake. She managed to sidestep the baton twirlers, and then, suddenly, she disappeared into the crowd.

"That damned pixie just shut you down, Mason baby," Tamelah giggled. Mason turned his head, to tell her to pipe down, but he needn't have bothered, because right about then, Tamelah's eyelids fluttered, her head slumped to one side, and she rather inelegantly slid down onto the backseat of the Chevelle. Passed out cold. Or hot, in Tamelah's case, with her spangly dress hiked up nearly to her waist.

Shit. He hoped none of the Twirling Tykes had seen that little performance. Mason turned and yanked the hem of the dress down.

Thank God, he was within half a block of the park. He would have left the parade right then, but he was hemmed in tight.

Fifteen minutes later, he finally pulled the Chevelle into the shade of a towering oak in the parking lot at Memorial Park. He got out of the car and walked around to check on Tamelah. She'd slumped into a prone position on the convertible's white leatherette bench seat, her rhinestone tiara had fallen to the floor, and she was now snoring in a very unqueenly manner. Mason shrugged, again readjusted the hem of her dress for modesty's sake, and looked around.

It was nearly one o'clock, he was hungry, and the irresistible aroma of kettle corn and charcoal-grilled hotdogs was wafting through the treetops from the area of the food concession tents. He pocketed his car keys and set out to find himself some lunch.

The park was already mobbed with people. He had to bob and weave his way through the chest-high banks of shrubbery and flowers, and he was finally making a beeline for the Kiwanis Club's barbecue stand when he happened to see a flash of red out of the corner of his eye. He stopped short and grinned.

The slight figure of a girl in a green tunic and red tights was seated on a park bench a hundred yards away. The foam-rubber pixie head sat beside her on the bench.

Mason ducked behind an overgrown azalea bush, circled around, and came up to the bench from behind. He still couldn't guess the girl's identity. Without a word, he picked up the pixie head and sat himself down on the bench in its place.

"Well, hey there, Dixie," he drawled.

The girl turned and looked at him. It was her, his little sister Pokey's best friend, Annajane. She'd been a cute little kid when he'd seen her last, and he'd glimpsed her around the plant over the past two summers but had somehow never really run into her again.

He'd been right about the heat inside that pixie suit. Her hair was wet and plastered to her head, and her face was beet-red and slicked with perspiration. She'd taken off the oversized green booties, and was so busy rubbing her stocking feet that she hadn't seen his approach. Also, she appeared to be crying.

"Oh no," she said quietly, covering her face with her hands.

"No good," Mason told her. "I can still see you, even if you can't see me. It's Annajane, right?"

"No," she said, sniffing, and still not moving her hands. "I don't know any Annajanes. Go away, please."

He looked around. "Where's your cart?"

"G-g-gone," she wailed. "I was almost at the park, and this bunch of little thugs snuck up behind me. I could only see straight in front of me with that darned pixie head on. Two of the boys grabbed me by the arms and held me, and the others took off with the cart. I tried to chase after 'em, but I couldn't run in these stinkin' shoes. I tried, but I tripped and fell. I tripped and fell, and I've ripped these doggoned tights." She stuck her right leg out, and Mason could indeed see the stocking was torn and stained with blood.

"You're hurt," he exclaimed, bending over to get a closer look. He could see now that the sleeve of her tunic was also ripped and spotted with more blood.

"Just scrapes," Annajane cried. "But I've ruined the costume! And that cart—it was probably really expensive."

"Well, hey," Mason said. "It's not like it's your fault. Nobody's going to blame you. You were mugged!"

Annajane drew her knees up to her chest and clutched them tightly. "God! I just want to go home and take a cold shower and forget about today."

"Do you need a ride?" Mason asked. "How were you supposed to get the cart back to the plant today?"

She sobbed again. "I was supposed to call Voncile, and she'd have one of the route drivers pick me up once I got here to the park! I had my billfold and my car keys in the cart. And now it's gone! And I'd just cashed my paycheck yesterday, and I had a hundred and fifty dollars in it, and now it's all gone!" She buried her head and wept more bitter tears.

Mason looked around uneasily. He wasn't really good with girls who cried, but Annajane was about to break his heart.

He patted her back gingerly. "Hey, it's not the end of the world, you know."

She raised her head and looked at him, rivers of tears and rivulets of snot dripping down her crimson cheeks. "It is to me. I can't afford to lose a hundred and fifty dollars."

Mason felt like a heel. "I know. I'm sorry. I shouldn't have said that. Look, sitting here crying isn't doing you any good. We should find a cop, and fill out a report. Did you see what the kids looked like?"

"Not really. Just teenaged boys. Maybe thirteen or fourteen. I didn't recognize any of them from around here."

"Okay," Mason said with a sigh. "I'll go see if I can find a cop. Listen, are you hungry? Have you eaten today?"

"No," she said, her voice wobbly. "I mean, no, I haven't eaten, and yeah, I'm starved. But I don't have any money."

He stood up quickly. "All right. I'll be right back. Hotdog or barbecue?"

"Hotdog."

"Ketchup or mustard?"

"Both."

"French fries or potato chips?"

"Chips," she said, and then, managing a wan smile, "please."

He found a cop lounging against the cotton candy stand and told him how the gang of adolescent boys had made off with the Quixie cart with Annajane's billfold and car keys.

"I'll put out a watch for the cart," the cop promised. "They probably just wanted the drinks, and with any luck, they'll dump it somewhere. Have your girlfriend come by the station later and fill out a report."

Mason was about to tell him Annajane wasn't his girlfriend, but something made him hesitate.

Fifteen minutes later, he was back at the bench with a grease-spattered paper sack containing three mustard-and-ketchup-soaked dogs, a bag of potato chips and a package of french fries, not to mention two huge Styrofoam cups of sweet iced tea.

He handed her one of the cups. "I figured you'd probably already had your fill of Quixie today."

She nodded gratefully and gulped a mouthful of icy tea. "Oh God, this tastes good," she said.

He sat down beside her again and parceled out their food. She gobbled down the hotdog and potato chips as though she hadn't eaten in a week.

Finally, she sat back and sighed.

"Feel any better?" Mason asked.

"Fuller, maybe," Annajane said. "Thank you for lunch." She craned her neck and looked past him.

"What happened to Miss Passcoe?"

"She, uh, was a little tired out after the parade," Mason said. "She was catching a catnap in the car."

"Stone-cold drunk, right?" Annajane guessed. "Tamelah was a year behind Pokey and me in high school. She could drink the whole football team under the table, no problem."

"It was pretty hot out there today," Mason said, always the gentleman. "And we mighta had a little Captain Morgan's with our Quixie."

"A little?" Annajane raised one eyebrow. She'd somehow managed to clean herself up while he was on his food run. Her face had returned to its normal color, she'd fluffed her dark hair, and for the first time, he noticed her remarkable eyes, which were a light sea green in contrast to her thick, sooty eyelashes. She wasn't somebody you'd call beautiful. Her nose was kind of stubby, and her mouth was probably too wide for her face. But her eyes made you forget those inconsequential details.

"I should probably go check on Tamelah," Mason said reluctantly, balling up the paper sack. "What about you? Can I give you a lift back to your car?"

"You could," Annajane agreed, "but since I don't have my car keys, it won't do me much good."

"Riiight," Mason said thoughtfully. "Look. Come with me. We'll get Tamelah sorted out, and then I'll take you home. All right?"

She hesitated. "Actually, I was supposed to go over to your house this afternoon. My folks are gone for the weekend, and I'm spending the night with Pokey."

"Even better," Mason said, feeling his spirits unaccountably lifted. He stood and picked up the foam-rubber pixie head. "After you," he told her.

When they arrived back at the Chevelle, Tamelah was gone, tiara and all.

"Guess she had a better offer," Mason said, secretly relieved. He tossed the pixie head in the backseat and opened the passenger door for Annajane.

"Shouldn't we wait around, to see if she comes back? Maybe she just went to find the bathroom or get something to eat," Annajane suggested.

Mason checked his watch. "I'll give her ten minutes, and if she's not back by then, she's on her own."

Fifteen minutes later, he and Annajane were riding down the highway, listening to the radio and singing along at the top of their lungs. An hour later, they were headed for the lake house, which was nothing more than a run-down caretaker's cottage perched at the edge of the spring-fed lake they called Hideaway, on the Bayless estate. Pokey was nowhere to be found. But Annajane showered and changed into a bathing suit, and pretty soon they were cooling off in the lake, floating in a couple of old inner tubes Mason retrieved from the boathouse. Mason had been right about Annajane's legs. They were spectacular. And the rest of her wasn't bad either.

But the thing that did him in were her eyes. Those solemn, amazing green eyes. When she looked up at him through those lowered dark lashes, when she laughed, when she was surprised, or, later, as she dozed on a lounge chair, he couldn't quit thinking about those eyes.

He was stretched out on the chaise next to hers, on the dock, his head propped up on one elbow, staring at her when she woke up.

Her sunburned cheeks flushed a deeper pink. "What are you looking at?"

"You," Mason said. He leaned across and kissed her lightly on the lips. "Where have you been all my life, Annajane Hudgens?"

She blushed even deeper. "I've been right here. Pokey and I have been best friends since we were five. And I bet I've spent more nights at Cherry Hill these past five years than you have. You're the one who's never been around."

"That's about to change," Mason vowed. "Starting today." And for the next six weeks, they'd been inseparable. Knowing her mother's low opinon of the Baylesses, they deliberately kept their families in the dark about their relationship. Mason could never understand why Annajane wanted to keep him a secret. "Your mom doesn't even know me," he'd protested. "How do you know she wouldn't like me?"

"If your last name wasn't Bayless, she'd probably love you," Annajane finally admitted. "But Mama's funny. She's got some kind of bug up her rear about your family. She never has admitted she likes Pokey, even though we've been best friends our whole lives. Mama thinks your mother's stuck-up, that she looks down on anybody who doesn't belong to the country club."

"Well hell, she's right about that," Mason said with a laugh. "Mama is a big snob. But that doesn't make me one."

In the end, though, they both came to enjoy the illicit nature of the romance. Only Pokey was in on the secret. She'd meet Mason at the lake, or stay late after work, and they'd head over to Southern Pines for dinner and a movie. And on the last summer weekend before she had to go back to school at State, she fabricated a story about an all-day shopping trip to Charlotte with Pokey.

Instead, she and Mason snuck out to the lake house, where she gladly gave up her virginity on a creaky army-surplus cot.

The following Monday, Annajane went off to Raleigh for her sophomore year at NC State and Mason went off to grad school. It would be two years before she would see Mason Bayless again.

Her first few weeks back at school, Annajane told herself Mason hadn't called or e-mailed because he was busy with classes. Getting a master's in finance was no joke, she knew. The weeks stretched out, and he still didn't call or e-mail, and she was too proud to call him. She went home at Thanksgiving, but Mason didn't. When Christmas rolled around, she was sure she'd see him. The Baylesses made a big deal of Christmas, with a huge open house on Christmas Eve and an elaborate family dinner. But Mason, Pokey told her, had been invited to spend the holiday with a classmate, at his family's vacation home in Cuernavaca.

When Christmas morning came and went without so much as an e-mail from him, Annajane tore the card off the antique sterling silver cufflinks she'd bought for Mason and instead gave them to her stepfather, Leonard, who only wore short-sleeved dress shirts.

Stung by being so unceremoniously dumped, Annajane returned to school and threw herself into classwork and a rigorous social life. She dated with a vengeance, told herself she was in love with a cute but slightly dim-witted guy in her marketing class, slept with him once, and then swore off men who used more hair products than she did.

She found herself deliberately staying away from Passcoe, instead spending holidays with classmates, even taking a part-time job as nanny for one of her professor's bratty nine-year-old twins, so that she'd have an excuse to stay in Raleigh year-round instead of going home—and facing the possibility of seeing Mason riding around town in that shiny red car with a new girlfriend.

The summer before her senior year, she got an internship with a New York advertising agency and shared a roach-infested six-hundred-square-foot apartment in Brooklyn with two other girls from NC State. Annajane had herself a very large summer; got invited to house parties at the shore, and dated another intern, Nouri, who introduced her to Pakistani food and who promptly fell in love with her and begged her to transfer to Columbia and move in with him.

Instead, Annajane returned to Raleigh in late September, with highlighted blond hair, a discreet butterfly tattoo on her right hip, and a tiny silver nose ring, which she quickly discarded after the shock value wore off.

Somehow, she managed to avoid seeing Mason Bayless for nearly two years. Right up until the day Pokey got married. But that was another story.

7

True to his word, Max Kaufman was standing at the emergency room entryway when the ambulance pulled up the ramp at Passcoe Memorial Hospital. In his late fifties, with a close-shaven shock of graying hair and large, soulful brown eyes, Dr. Kaufman was already dressed in rumpled green surgical scrubs.

After Sophie had been moved to a gurney and brought inside, Dr. Kaufman nodded a brisk greeting to Mason and Annajane, and then was all business, feeling the listless child's forehead and gently probing her abdomen.

Sophie cried feebly at his touch. "It's okay, sugar," Mason said, clutching her hand. "Dr. Max is going to make you feel better." He leaned down, smoothed her hair from her face, and kissed both cheeks.

"We're going to take this little lady back and get her blood drawn right away, do a CT scan, and make her comfortable, but from what you've told me, I suspect it is her appendix, in which case, we'll just get that bugger out of there," Dr. Kaufman said. He nodded at the nurse hovering at his elbow, and she began to wheel Sophie away.

"Well, Miss Sophie," they heard the nurse say. "My name is Molly. And I've got a little girl just your age at home, and her name is Sophie, too. What do you think about that? I sure do love that pretty pink dress you're wearing. Did you have a birthday party today?"

"No," Sophie said. "We were getting my daddy married, but then I throwed up."

Dr. Kaufman chuckled, looking from Mason to Annajane, raising one bushy eyebrow at the groom's vomit-spattered tuxedo and his ex-wife's ruined dress. "Everybody good now? Fine. Fill out the paperwork, get yourself some of our world-famous crappy coffee, and I should be able to let you know something about the surgery in a few minutes."

"Is this really necessary?" Mason asked anxiously.

"What, an appendix?" Dr. Kaufman said, irritably. "Mason, nobody really needs an appendix, as far as we know. It's not terribly common for a five-year-old to have appendicitis, but it's not a rarity either. That said, if she does have a hot appendix, we need to remove it, or things will get really ugly really fast. So you need to let me go find out, all right?" Without waiting for an answer, he turned and disappeared behind the swinging door to the examining rooms.

"Thank you," Annajane called after him.

"Prick," Mason muttered. He turned without a word and went to the intake desk to start filling out the paperwork.

Annajane found herself alone in the emergency room waiting area, a cheerless room with beige linoleum floors, beige painted walls, and a row of army-green straight-backed leatherette chairs that faced a wall-mounted television showing a video of proper hand-washing techniques. The only other entertainment option in the room was a beige metal magazine rack holding a handful of well-thumbed copies of *Highlights for Children* and *Modern Maturity*.

Choosing *Modern Maturity* only because all the brain-teaser puzzles in *Highlights* had already been worked, she was idly scanning an article about prostate health when Mason returned, slumping into a chair once removed from her own. He sighed loudly and buried his head in his hands.

Annajane looked at the clock. "It's barely been fifteen minutes," she pointed out.

He didn't respond.

"She's a perfectly healthy little girl," Annajane added. "And Dr. Kaufman really does know what he's doing."

"I know that," Mason said, his voice muffled. "It's just...this place." He raised his head. His voice was strained and full of despair. "This place. You know?"

"I do know," Annajane said softly. She hesitated, but after a moment, she reached over and squeezed his upper arm. His hand found hers, and he patted it briefly before letting go. They both knew this room all too well.

A little over five years ago, she'd rushed into this same emergency room and found Mason sitting in almost the same place, slumped over, despondent, waiting for news from this same doctor, Max Kaufman. Only that time, the patient had been Mason's father, Glenn, and the news, when it did come, had been devastating.

Funny. That day was the beginning of the end of their marriage.

There had been other fights. Annajane wouldn't have called them fights, really. Quarrels, or tiffs, if anybody ever really used that word.

They'd been married less than two years, when the little fissures in their happiness began to appear.

Mason and Annajane were living in the caretaker's cottage at the lake. It was only a temporary address, Mason assured her, a rent-free solution until they saved enough money for a down payment on a house of their own.

The cottage had been abandoned for years. As children, she and Pokey had appropriated it for a playhouse, furnishing it with cast-off furniture from the big house, a wobbly kitchen table, a pair of rickety wooden chairs, and an army cot for campouts. They played at cooking with a battered saucepan, once nearly burning the place down after attempting to heat up a can of SpaghettiOs on Davis's Boy Scout camp stove.

And yes, she and Mason had snuck away to the caretaker's house for stolen hours in the first few months after they'd started dating.

At first, Annajane had been enchanted with the quaint honeymoon cottage, with its deeply pitched slate roof, leaded-glass windows looking out onto the lake, and stacked stone fireplace.

But living there was a different matter. The kitchen's warped wooden cabinets didn't close, the refrigerator barely cooled, and that adorable roof had a spot that leaked—directly over their bed. It was drafty in the winter and hot in the summertime, and damp and mildew from the lake seemed to creep in year-round. Also, there were mice. There was no washer or dryer, which meant they had to either troop into town to the coin Laundromat or drag their basket of dirty clothes up to the big house, like a couple of college students.

All that Annajane might have cheerfully accepted. She hadn't grown up in a mansion, as Mason had. Her family's two-bedroom brick ranch had one window air-conditioning unit—in Ruth and Leonard's bedroom—and just one bathroom. The real problem with the cottage was its location—directly in the looming shadow of Sallie Bayless, a constant presence in their lives, who was prone to dropping over uninvited to offer Annajane unsolicited advice on everything from housekeeping: "Annajane dear, you really must use lemon oil every week on Mason's grandmother's walnut dresser, to keep the wood from drying out"; to cooking, "Annajane dear, we never, ever use dark meat in chicken salad"; to marriage itself, "Annajane dear, no man wants to see his wife in the morning before she's fixed her hair and her makeup—and his breakfast."

Her mother-in-law never came right out and criticized the new bride in front of Mason. That wasn't Sallie's style, but the slow drip-drip-drip of her constant nitpicking had the effect of sand in Annajane's newlywed sheets.

Annajane knew it was no good trying to extricate their life from Mason's family, or his family's business. They were too tightly woven together now.

And it was all Pokey's fault.

She'd shown up, unannounced, at Annajane's studio apartment in Raleigh, on a freezing weeknight in February.

"Guess what?" she'd demanded, as soon as she'd stepped into the room. "I'm pregnant!" And next came, "You're gonna be my maid of honor. And I won't take no for an answer."

Pokey had been in no hurry to finish college. She'd declared herself on the six-year plan, until she met Pete Riggs at a fraternity party in Chapel Hill. He was from a wealthy Charleston family who owned a chain of fine furniture stores. He was tall and redheaded and had earned a full four-year golf scholarship to Wake Forest. Fun-loving Pokey called Annajane that night, dead serious, to announce that she'd met her future husband. And as always, what Pokey wanted, Pokey got.

Before Annajane knew it, she was being dragged to bridal boutiques for fittings and, yes, back to Passcoe, for a seemingly endless round of brunches, teas, dinners, and showers.

Mason was a no-show for all of the prenuptial hoopla. He was working as a regional manager for Dr Pepper, in Memphis, with his father's blessing, to gain experience outside his own family's business. He was, Pokey confided, being a major pill about the whole thing. "Mason doesn't approve of Pete, and he doesn't approve of me getting married and dropping out just a semester short of graduation, and he most definitely doesn't approve of me having a baby. He threatened to put a beat-down on Pete for knocking me up, until I admitted I actually got myself knocked up on purpose. But if you ever tell that to Sallie, I'll never speak to you again," Pokey said.

"Too bad," Annajane had murmured, trying to sound unconcerned about Mason's opinions. She was desperate to see him again, and desperate to pretend he'd never entered her life. It wasn't until she had to walk up the aisle on his arm, the day of Pokey's wedding, that Annajane allowed herself to remember how she felt when Mason Bayless touched her. It wasn't Mason, she told herself, it was just spring fever.

Still, she tried to avoid him at the reception, dancing with every man in the room who was under the age of seventy and hiding out on the veranda of the country club, behind a huge potted palm, between dances.

That's where he found her, leaning against the veranda railing, sipping a glass of lukewarm champagne toward the end of the evening.

"Shoes hurt that bad?" he'd asked, gesturing toward the high-heeled silver slingback sandals she'd slipped out of.

"They're killing me," Annajane said, taking a large sip of champagne, hoping he wouldn't notice her suddenly flushed face in the darkness.

He picked up the sandals and flung them high into the air and out over the women's practice green.

"Great," she said glumly. "Two hundred dollar shoes. Gone."

"I'll buy you another pair," Mason offered. "Maybe a pair you can actually walk in?"

She didn't smile. "What do you want, Mason?"

He sighed. "I really screwed up, didn't I?"

"Did you?"

"I was a shit heel," he said, resting his back against the railing.

"A deflowerer of virgins," she said, nodding her head in agreement.

He winced. "If I told you I never stopped thinking about you, all this time, would you believe me?"

"No," Annajane said, unsmiling. "Because if you'd thought about me, even once, I'm pretty sure you could have figured out how to get in touch with me over the past two years."

"You're not easy, are you?" Mason said, with an exaggerated sigh.

"Not anymore, no."

"Listen." He touched her elbow lightly, and she jerked it away, but he took it again. "Will you please listen?"

"No," Annajane said. But she didn't move.

"I fell hard for you that summer," Mason said.

She gave a snort of disbelief.

"I did. Honestly. But it wouldn't have worked out. Your mother made me realize that."

She whirled to face him. "My *mother*? What are you talking about?"

He raised one eyebrow. "She never told you she called me, did she?"

"No," Annajane said. "Why would Mama have called you? She didn't even know we were seeing each other."

"Your mother is not a stupid person, Annajane. She figured it out."

Annajane's jaw dropped, and she felt a shiver go down her spine. "All of it?"

"Yep," Mason drawled.

"Oh, God. And she never said a word to me. Never let on she knew." She grabbed Mason's arm. "What did she say?"

"Enough. She called me on my cell phone. From yours. I guess you'd left it lying around the house, and she took a look at the call history. Listened to some of the voicemails I'd left you . . . about meeting me out at the lake house."

Annajane remembered those voice mails. Her face burned with the memory of those sexy messages Mason loved to leave.

"Long story short, she told me to stay away from you. I tried to point out that you were nineteen, and legally of the age of consent, but that didn't cut much ice with your mother. She was very clear that I should get the hell out of your life and stay out. And she made some threats that weren't very nice."

"My mother? Threatened you? And you believed her? My mother wouldn't hurt a fly."

"Your mother said she would call the sheriff and have me arrested for statutory rape. And even if the charges didn't stick, it would ruin my life and ruin my family's reputation. And she meant every word of it."

"But it's not true," Annajane said. "You didn't rape me. Nobody would have believed a story like that."

Mason shrugged. "Doesn't matter. She was so intent on getting you away from me, she would have eventually cooked up something that would work. Anyway, you had to go back to State, and I was headed off to Penn. I decided maybe we should just cool it."

"Nice of you to let me know," Annajane said. "Coward."

"You're right," Mason agreed. "I suck. And the longer I went without talking to you, to try to explain things, the easier it got to just avoid Passcoe, and you. Pokey gave me reports of what you were up to, though."

"She did?"

"I heard about the guy in your marketing class. An SAE, right?"

"He was an ATO actually," Annajane said. "And dumber than a box of rocks."

"And wasn't there some mysterious Asian guy you went with in New York? Pokey said you got his name tattooed on your ass."

"His name was Nouri," Annajane said. "And he was Pakistani. And no, I did not get his name tattooed on my ass. It's a very small butterfly and it's on my hip."

"I'd like to see that," Mason said. "I'm very interested in entomology, you know."

"Fat chance."

"Pokey says you're currently unattached," Mason said.

"Pokey has a big mouth," Annajane said.

"You haven't asked me if I'm seeing anybody," he said.

She turned toward him and raised one eyebrow, almost afraid to ask. "Are you?"

"No," he said, drawing the tip of his finger up her forearm. "I've been saving myself for you."

Annajane gave him her sweetest smile. She plucked his hand from her arm and dropped it. "What a waste. Nice try, Mason."

She hopped off the flagstone veranda and set out onto the golf course in her bare feet.

"Hey! Where you going?" Mason called after her.

"To get my damned shoes," she muttered.

With a newly minted marketing degree in hand, Annajane took a job in Raleigh, working for a start-up fast food chain called PoBoyz. She set up PoBoyz promotions at high school football games, stock car racetracks, and minor league baseball games. She worked eleven-hour days and got promoted twice within eighteen months. And then her supervisor called her in for a face-to-face on a Friday at four o'clock.

Phoebe, the department's administrative assistant, gave Annajane a dark look.

"What?" Annajane asked. "It might be good news. I totally killed with that football game promotion. The franchisees said they'd never had so many buy-one get-one coupons fulfilled."

"It won't be good," Phoebe warned. "She never hands out attaboys on Fridays. Mondays are for attaboys. Fridays are for . . . well, I hope I'm wrong."

Eileen, her supervisor, got up and closed the door as soon as Annajane walked into her office. One look at her boss's face and she knew Phoebe had been right.

"I'm sorry," Eileen said, without preamble. "This is awful. I hate this. But I have to let you go."

"Why?" Annajane knew it was bad form to ask, but she'd never been fired before.

Eileen stared down at her desktop. "Howard Dewberry's nephew just graduated from college."

"So?" But Annajane knew what was coming next. Howard Dewberry was one of the company founders.

"The kid needs a job, and he thinks marketing would be 'fun,'" Eileen said. "And you know the kind of budget we're working with. I can't afford two marketing assistants. Anyway, Annajane, the truth is, you're too good for this job. You're smart and hardworking, and you've outgrown PoBoyz. I'm doing you a favor, really."

Annajane got up with a sigh. "Funny, it doesn't feel like a favor."

She kicked around Raleigh for another six months, sending out résumés and doing temp work, but when her savings ran out, she faced the inevitable and moved back to Passcoe.

But not to her mother's house. Not after the blowout they'd had after Annajane confronted her about making threats to Mason.

Instead, she got a crappy job selling ads for the town's only radio station, and she rented a crappy half of a duplex on a crappy street on the outskirts of town.

It didn't take long for Pokey to start matchmaking once Annajane moved home.

"What did you say to Mason at my wedding?" she demanded one day while they were sitting at her kitchen table. Pokey was spooning cereal into Denning's mouth, and he was spitting it out just as fast as she shoveled it in.

"Nothing," Annajane said. "I just let him know I wasn't interested in getting together."

"That's a big fat lie," Pokey said. "I saw you watching him at the wedding. And he was watching you. For God's sake, why don't you just sleep with him and be done with all the cat-and-mouse games?"

"I did sleep with him, and then he dropped me like a bad habit," Annajane said. "Remember?"

"You were just kids," Pokey said. "Anyway, you can't keep avoiding him forever. He's moving back to town, you know."

Annajane's pulse gave a blip. "When? Why?"

"Daddy finally talked him into giving up the job at Dr Pepper," Pokey said. "He's coming to work at Quixie." She looked over at the kitchen clock. "And I'd say he should be getting into town right about now."

She gave Annajane an innocent look. "He hasn't seen the baby in months. I made him promise to stop by as soon as he gets in."

Annajane stood up abruptly. "Pokey! This isn't funny. You should have told me you were expecting Mason. I don't appreciate..."

The kitchen door swung open, and Mason stepped inside. He stopped in his tracks when he saw that his sister had company.

He looked from Pokey to Annajane and sighed. "She tricked you into coming here, didn't she?"

Annajane nodded. "She tricked you, too, didn't she?"

"Yup." They both turned to confront Pokey, who'd scooped the baby out of his highchair and was beating a fast retreat out of the kitchen.

"Traitor!" Annajane yelled.

Mason sighed. "Did she tell you I'm moving back?"

Annajane nodded.

Mason stared at her intently. "It's a small town, Annajane. You can't hide from me for the rest of your life."

"I haven't been hiding from you," she lied.

"Sure looks like it from where I stand," Mason said. "Maybe let the past be past? At least agree to be friends again?"

She bit her lip and looked out the window. Because she knew if she looked at him, she would cave. Wasn't there some cure for the way she felt every time she was with him? Wasn't it about time she outgrew this adolescent obsession with Mason Bayless?

He reached out and tucked a lock of her hair behind her ear. "Please? Gimme another chance?"

She did. Two months later, she signed on as assistant VP of marketing at Quixie, working for Davis Bayless. Six months later she and Mason were engaged.

While Annajane figured out how to work for her charming, hyper, demanding future brother-in-law, Mason was busy climbing the corporate ladder.

Within six months, he'd been named divisional sales manager. For the first time, he was working for, and with, Glenn.

Father and son were on the road constantly, meeting with supermarket chains and convenience stores, trying to gain a foothold for Quixie in new markets.

Which meant that Annajane was back at home in Passcoe, working long hours, and trying hard to prove her own worth as a professional to Davis, who still tended to treat her like an annoying little sister. Which might not have been so bad, except for the fact that she could hardly complain about her job to her husband or her best friend—since Davis was their brother.

Two short weeks before the wedding, Ruth abruptly announced that she and Leonard were selling their house to move to Holden Beach.

"Now?" a bewildered Annajane had said, looking around at the boxes her mother had seemingly packed overnight. Leonard smiled wanly from his reclining chair, then looked away.

"It's his heart," Ruth had said. "The doctor says he's got congestive heart failure. From working at that damned plant . . ."

"He said no such thing," Leonard objected. "My heart trouble ain't got a damned thing to do with Quixie or the Baylesses. Thirty years of smoking and that chronic obstructive whatever you call it, that's what's done a number on my heart."

"But why the coast?" Annajane had asked. "You don't know anybody there. Why not stay here, where your family and friends are?"

"Because it's high time we got out of Passcoe," Ruth declared. "We've always wanted to live at the beach. Watch the sunsets, play golf, eat seafood whenever we want. Enjoy our lives while we've still got time."

"Your mother's allergic to shrimp," Leonard put in. "And I don't know a putter from a driver. We'll be bored to death. But I can't do nothin' to change her mind."

A month later, Leonard suffered the first of two heart attacks, and the emotional tug-of-war began in earnest.

Annajane made the long drive to Holden whenever she could, but when she couldn't, Ruth's sniping was relentless.

"I guess you got better things to do with your fancy new family than come all the way down here," her mother would say, with a martyred sigh. "Probably there's something going on at the country club."

Whenever she did spend the weekend with her parents, she felt guilty for not spending the time with Mason. Although Mason, she noticed, seemed to have no problems keeping busy when she was away, and even some weekends when she was home. He'd always been a huge fan of college football and basketball, but after their marriage, it seemed to her, he spent an inordinate amount of time either watching UNC games on television or in person.

"You didn't even go to Chapel Hill," she fumed the Saturday after Thanksgiving as he waited for his father and Davis and some other buddies to pick him up for the big UNC-Duke game, only a few hours after he'd gotten home from a weeklong business trip. "I don't see why this is such a big deal for you."

The words sounded bitchy and whiny, even to her, but she couldn't help it. She hadn't seen Mason alone in nearly two weeks. As it stood now, he would get back from Chapel Hill around noon Sunday, then turn right back around and hit the road with his father again on Monday.

He'd looked incredulous, and then annoyed. "Are you serious? This is just the biggest game of the year in this state. I've been going to this game since I was five years old. My grandfather took me to my first Carolina-Duke game. And his grandfather took him. If you really wanted to go, I could get you a ticket."

"And spoil all your fun by making you be the only guy who has to drag his wife along? No thanks," she'd said quickly.

Home alone most weeknights, Annajane, in turn, felt resentment seeping into her usually cheerful demeanor. Pokey was busy chasing her toddler son, so they didn't see each other that much. Her other friends, young and living the single life, occasionally invited her to join them for drinks or dinner, but she no longer enjoyed staying out til two in the morning, only to stumble to work half-awake and half-sober. She made up excuses not to go. She stayed home and dined alone on canned soup and a vague, simmering sense of dissolution.

And when Mason made his nightly long distance phone call, reporting on the dinners he'd just shared with important accounts at four-star restaurants in Atlanta, Charlotte, Nashville, or Charleston, Annajane would silently contemplate the shabby little cottage and her lonely bed. This was not what she'd thought marriage would be.

If Mason noticed her misery, he never mentioned it. He and Glenn were engaged in a high-stakes battle, trying to place Quixie in Maxi-Mart, a huge regional discount supermarket chain with nearly three hundred outlets around the South, many of them in new markets for Quixie. The deal was potentially worth millions for the company.

Among the Maxi-Mart executives father and son were wooing was a woman named Eva. Mason referred to her frequently in those late-night phone calls. "Eva wants us to meet with the guys down in Orlando," he'd say. Or, "Sorry, babe, we won't be home tomorrow after all. Maxi-Mart is the sponsor of a charity golf tournament in Richmond, and Dad and I are gonna play in a foursome Eva put together. You understand, right?"

She wasn't the jealous type. She and Mason were still practically newlyweds. And after all, this was company business. He was doing this for the company, and for them. Just six more months, Mason promised, "Maxi-Mart will be signed and sealed and we'll start house hunting. Hell, you can start looking now. All I ask is that you find something with a den for my big-screen, and a master bedroom big enough for a king-size bed. And no leaks overhead!"

"And a nursery?" Annajane asked.

"And a nursery," Mason assured her.

Still, she heard whispers around the office about this Eva woman. Whispers she chose to ignore. She'd asked Mason about Eva once, on one of their rare weekends together. "Yeah," he said, "I guess she's all-right looking, if you like that type."

"What type is that?" Annajane wanted to know. "Sexy? Flirty?"

Mason shrugged. "I guess some guys might find her sexy. You know, high heels, expensive business suits. She's pretty buttoned-up."

"Not your type?"

Mason laughed and reached around and began to tug at the zipper on Annajane's dress. "Nah, I'm more a zipper man my ownself."

And then Christmas rolled around.

Annjane had volunteered to plan the company Christmas party. She'd wangled a sizable budget out of Davis and spent weeks planning every detail, from hiring the perfect Santa Claus for the visit with the employees' children in the afternoon, down to the oyster appetizers and prime rib at the seated dinner at the country club. For the after-dinner, she'd rented a full-scale disc-jockey setup, with Mason spinning records for the first hour of dancing.

Mason and Glenn were scheduled to drive back from a four-day business trip to Atlanta that Friday, the day of the party.

With Mason out of town so much lately, their love life had definitely taken a backseat to business. But not that night, Annajane decided. She had a post-party seduction carefully planned out for her husband. She'd splurged on a new dress, a short, tight-fitting emerald green velvet sheath with a plunging neckline—cut as low as she dared to go in conservative Passcoe—to be worn with a pair of wickedly sexy five-inch-high stiletto heels. And underneath? She had a black-lace push-up bra and the merest suggestion of filmy black-lace panties. It was going to be, she vowed, an evening Mason would not soon forget.

At six o'clock that night, when she'd run home to change after the children's party, Annajane was chagrined by the fact that Mason's car was missing from the driveway. He'd promised to be back from Atlanta by 5:00 P.M., in time to shower and dress for the party. As she zipped herself into the green dress, she tried to ignore the fact that Mason's tux was still laid out on the bed, where she'd placed it earlier that morning.

She'd called his cell phone twice as she drove back to the country club, but both times her message went directly to voice mail.

By seven, when she stood at the door to the ballroom welcoming their guests, cell phone clutched in one hand in case he called, she was doing a slow burn.

Sallie, of course, noticed everything.

"What a lovely dress," she'd said, her eyes flickering on Annajane's daring décolletage. "But won't you be cold without a jacket or something?" Later, during dinner, Sallie walked past and noticed her constantly checking the phone and texting Mason. "Annajane, dear," she whispered, gently closing her hand over the phone. "This is business. Glenn and Mason are closing a deal. Sometimes things get complicated."

"But he promised to get here for the party!" Annajane whispered back. "And he hasn't called. Maybe something has happened."

Sallie had given her a tight, knowing smile. "It's just business, Annajane. Get used to it. I have."

All that night, she'd endured the embarrassment of having her husband a no-show. She sweet-talked Pokey's husband, Pete, into stepping in as deejay; table-hopped and chatted with every employee in the room; and, in between, picked at her dinner and glowered at the empty chair beside hers. All that night, her phone did not ring. Finally, at nine o'clock, she tucked her phone into her evening bag, resigned to the fact that it probably wasn't going to ring.

At eleven, she said her good-byes and drove home alone. The temperature had begun to drop at sundown, and now snowflakes were softly falling. White Christmases were a rarity in North Carolina. Any other night, she might have stood at the bay window, watching with wide-eyed glee at the snow sifting onto the lake and accumulating on the shaggy green evergreens ringing the little cottage. But on that night, she shut off the twinkling white lights on the Christmas tree she'd decorated by herself. In the bedroom, she hung up the party dress and changed out of the black lingerie and into a frowsy flannel nightie.

Their room was freezing, and the window panes rattled as the wind howled outside. Part of her worried about Mason driving home on treacherously icy roads; another part of her burned with anger and disappointment.

Finally, she drifted off to sleep, only to awaken at the sound of a car driving up to the house. She checked the clock on the nightstand. It was nearly two. She heard the front door open, heard heavy footsteps on the floors, heard their bedroom door open.

In the half-light from the hallway, she saw Mason drop his suitcase. He walked over to their bed, leaned down, and kissed her cheek.

Annajane pretended to be asleep. She made a show of yawning and half-opening her eyes.

"Sorry to miss the party, babe," Mason whispered.

She wanted to sit up in bed and throw something at him. She wanted to scream her rage about broken promises and ruined evenings. Instead, she rolled over and faced the wall closest to her side of the bed, her body rigid with suppressed fury.

Mason sat on the edge of the bed and took off his shoes. She heard water running in the bathroom, and a moment later he slid into bed beside her. Surely, she thought, now he will apologize. Now he will explain why he didn't call, why he came home so late. Surely, now, he will make it all right.

Her husband curled up beside her in the bed. He yawned and coughed.

Despite herself, Annajane whispered. "Everything all right?"

"Great," Mason said wearily. "We closed the deal! Three hundred new stores. But I'm beat."

Instead of an apology, he draped a proprietary arm over her shoulder, cupping one hand under her flannel-clad breast. A moment later, she heard his slow, deep, even breathing. And then, soft snoring.

8

Mason was still asleep. Annajane stared down at him, sprawled facedown across their bed. The covers had slipped, exposing his bare back and the waist of his pajama bottoms. It was nearly nine, and she had to go back to the country club to supervise cleanup after the party and to pack up the disc-jockey equipment for return to the rental company.

She'd halfway expected Mason to awaken early, maybe fix their coffee and bring it back to bed for her, the way he'd done the first few months of their marriage. Saturday mornings then were their sacred time. Mason liked—no, loved—sex in the morning. Later, he'd fix her cinnamon toast, and they'd lounge around the house for hours, laughing and talking and making plans for the weekend, eventually tumbling back into bed for another round of love-making.

Two years later, she couldn't remember the last time they'd had Saturday morning sex.

Her face hardened as she remembered the previous evening. If Mason didn't wake up soon and start apologizing, she told herself, they might never have sex again! Not that she meant it. She loved her husband, and loved their lovemaking. But, really, something had to change. They could not go on this way.

With a sigh, she headed for the front door, vowing to have this conversation when she got back home from the country club.

She sighed again, noticing, with annoyance, that Mason's company car, a big white Yukon with the Quixie logo on the door, had her own Acura blocked into the driveway. For a second, she entertained malicious thoughts of waking him up and making him move the car. But she could just as easily take the SUV. It was a bitterly cold morning, with at least an inch of snow on the ground. Mason wouldn't be going anywhere this morning, and if he did have plans, he could just take the Acura.

Annajane eased herself into the Yukon. She fumbled with the control buttons and adjusted the seat for her own frame, which was four inches shorter than Mason's. She backed the big car carefully down the driveway and was soon driving past the ornate wrought-iron Cherry Hill gates.

As she went through her mental checklist of everything she needed to accomplish at the club, Annajane absentmindedly punched the radio button on the Yukon's console. She wanted to hear the day's weather report, and then maybe some Christmas music might put her back into the holiday spirit.

Instead of the weather, though, she heard a sultry woman's voice singing "At Last." Etta James? Since when did Mason listen to the likes of Etta James? She'd have bet money Mason had never heard of the woman. With one gloved finger, she tapped the tracking button. The next song was even odder: "Let's Get It On," by Marvin Gaye. She punched the eject button and grabbed the CD as it slid out of the player.

It was a homemade mix, and written on the silvery disc in purple Sharpie, in a woman's handwriting, was, "Merry Christmas, baby. Think of me, cuz I'm thinking of you."

Annajane felt the blood drain from her face. Her hands were shaking so hard she had to pull the SUV onto the shoulder of the road. She sat there for five minutes, staring at the CD, considering the implications.

Think of me? Who was the me? The owner of the purple Sharpie? Eva? The Maxi-Mart exec? Was it Eva who'd made the mix of love songs? She bit her lip so hard it drew blood. Was this inevitable? After all, Mason was a competitor. He had to win, at any cost. And if it took sleeping with a sexy woman like Eva in order to close the deal, would he say no?

Would he?

Somehow, she pulled herself together and drove on to the country club. She managed to direct the workers who were loading up the sound equipment onto a truck for return to the rental company. She stayed until she was satisfied that the club's ballroom had been restored to its formerly pristine condition. Annajane was walking out the front door of the club when her mother-in-law arrived with her two best friends, Martha and Corinne.

"Oh good, Annajane dear," Sallie exclaimed, clutching her arm. "You're just the girl we need. We can have a nice lunch, and then, since Gaynelle has a cold, you can make up our fourth for bridge."

Annajane couldn't remember Sallie ever inviting her to join her foursome before, and she could not think of anything she'd rather do less. "I can't," she blurted. "I'm awful at bridge. And . . . Mason is expecting me back at the house."

But Sallie had insisted she stay for lunch with her friends, refusing to take no for an answer. Annajane managed to choke down just enough of the green salad and crab bisque to persuade her mother-in-law that she was all right. Finally, after an agonizing hour, she'd begged to be excused.

When she got back to the cottage, her Acura was parked in the same spot it had been that morning. Mason was sitting in the living room, dressed in faded jeans and his favorite raggedy Penn sweatshirt, watching a football game.

Without a word, she tossed the CD at him, bouncing it off his chest.

"Ow," he'd said, more surprised than angry. "What the hell is this?"

"You tell me," Annajane said, planting herself directly in front of the television. "It was in your car this morning. Interesting song selection."

Mason turned the CD from one side to the other. "It's not mine," he said. He tossed it aside. "Do you mind? Carolina is driving the ball."

Annajane picked the CD up and held it up. "Oh really? Not yours? But it looks like it's got a message for you. 'Merry Christmas, Baby. Think of me, cuz I'm thinking of you?' In a woman's handwriting? Purple Sharpie? Sound familiar?"

Mason shook his head. "Still not mine. Have we got anything to eat?"

"So you're telling me an alien broke into your car and planted a CD of love songs there?" Annajane repeated.

Finally, she had his attention. He looked up at her, his blue eyes narrowed. "What I am telling you is I'm hungry. Also, that is not my CD."

She thrust the CD into his hands. "Whose handwriting is this? Are you telling me it's not that Eva woman's?"

He took the CD and examined it. "I suppose it could be hers. I don't really know. Or care. And I don't get why you're getting so worked up about this."

"I'm worked up because you came home nine hours late last night," Annajane said. "And when I got in your car this morning, I found this CD. Are you trying to tell me you weren't with that woman?"

"Hell, yeah, I was with her," Mason said, standing now. "I told you, we finalized the Maxi-Mart deal last night. Dad and I took Eva and the others to dinner at the Ritz-Carlton around eight to celebrate. It was business, Annajane. That's what I do. I sell cherry soda. We ran into some people she knew at the restaurant, and we had to invite them to join us at the table, and by the time we got the check and got out of there, it was after ten, and there was a truck overturned on I-85. You know what the weather was like last night. We're lucky we got home when we did."

"It was two in the morning! Are you sure you and Eva didn't slip upstairs to her room while you were at the Ritz?" She hurled the words at him, blind with anger.

He stared. "Did you really just say that? Did you accuse me of having an affair?"

"Aren't you?'

"Have I ever lied to you, Annajane?" Mason's voice was level, which was infuriating. "Have I ever given you a reason to doubt me?"

"What about last night?" she ignored his first question. "It was the company Christmas party. You were supposed to be there! Everybody was expecting you. I was expecting you. Do you know how humiliated I was? I worked my ass off putting that party together. For you. And your family and the company. But you didn't even call. If you went to dinner at eight, you knew there was no way you'd be back in Passcoe. But you didn't even call to let me know?"

He shrugged. "Okay, my bad. I should have called. But Dad was with me. And we had Eva and the Maxi-Mart folks with us, and everybody wanted to head out and celebrate. I would have looked like a wuss if I'd begged off. What was I gonna say? 'Hey y'all, I can't go to dinner. I gotta call my wife.' "

"And that's worse?" Annajane asked. "Than letting me down? Breaking a promise to your wife?"

Mason was still holding the remote control. He tossed it onto the chair where he'd been sitting. "Okay. This is ridiculous. I was late last night. I missed the Christmas party. I should have called. For that, I am guilty, and I apologize." He turned and stomped toward the front door.

"Wait a minute," Annajane cried. "We're not through here." She shook the CD. "Just tell me how this got in your car."

Mason had his hand on the doorknob. " "I'm through. I am not talking about this anymore. Either you believe me or you don't."

"Where are you going?"

The door was open and he didn't look back. "I'm going over to Mama's. She's always got something to eat. Unlike here." He didn't slam the door. In fact, he didn't even bother to close it all the way.

Half an hour later, Annajane did slam the door. And she didn't bother to lock it as she left. Nobody locked doors in Passcoe, especially at Cherry Hill. She tossed a hastily packed overnight bag in the backseat of her Acura, backed out of the driveway, and headed for the main gate. The snow had already begun to melt, and the ancient oak trees lining both sides of the drive looked menacing, with their twisted gray limbs blocking out the weak winter sunlight. A carpet of acorns crunched beneath her tires. A rusted-out pickup truck with an enormous Fraser fir poking out of the bed rolled past her, headed toward the big house. She gave a dispirited wave to Nate, the Bayless's yard man. At the end of the drive, she picked up the remote from the passenger seat, mashed the button, and waited impatiently while the wrought-iron gates slowly creaked open.

Ten minutes later, she was on the bypass. At some point, she realized she didn't really have a destination in mind. All she knew was that she had to get out of Passcoe and away from the Bayless compound.

An hour later, her cell phone rang. She picked it up, and, seeing the screen, tossed it back onto the passenger seat without answering. Mason. She blinked back tears, and a moment later heard the phone buzz, letting her know he'd left a voice mail.

Five minutes later, it rang again. Annajane's hand hovered over the phone. She even picked it up, but then changed her mind. Let him call.

Two hours later, when she pulled into the driveway of the modest little frame house at Holden Beach, she paused before turning off the ignition. Had she really just done this? Picked a fight with Mason? Accused him of cheating, and then run home to Mama? This was crazy. She should turn around, go home, and talk things out calmly with Mason. Make him understand how badly he'd hurt her.

It was full dark. Multicolored lights were strung all across the eaves of her parents' house. A silly plastic light-up snowman was posed on the front steps. Annajane and her mother hated that snowman and tried to persuade Leonard how tacky it was, but her stepfather delighted in hauling it out of storage every Christmas. She could see the glow of the artificial tree through the drapes. Somehow, she felt reassured. Maybe things weren't as bad as they seemed.

Before she could change her mind and turn around to head home, Ruth was opening the aluminum storm door, but instead of surprise or pleasure at seeing her only daughter, Annajane recognized something else in her mother's face.

She jumped out of the car and ran to the door. "Mom? What is it? Is it Leonard? Is he okay?"

Ruth's face was pale. "Leonard's fine. Have you talked to Mason?"

"No," Annajane said bitterly. "Don't tell me he called you."

Ruth held out her own phone. "Here. You need to call him."

Annajane shook her head stubbornly. "Let him stew. Did he tell you what he did to me? He missed the Christmas party? Stood me up? Mama, I think maybe..."

Ruth shook the phone in her daughter's face. "You are not listening. Honey, you need to call Mason right this minute. It's Glenn. He's...Just call Mason. All right?"

Her mind was a blank. Her hands were trembling. Ruth dialed and handed her the phone.

"Mason? I just got to Mama's. She said..."

"It's Dad," Mason said. He sounded calm, detached even. "It's bad. They think he's had a heart attack. We're at Passcoe Memorial."

"Oh my God," Annajane breathed. "When? How long ago?"

"We're not sure. Mom found him on the floor of the bedroom when she got home this afternoon. They're working on him, but . . . we just don't know anything. Dr. Kaufman is in with him."

"I'm so sorry," Annajane said. "Mason, I am so, so sorry. I'm coming back. Right now."

"All right," he said. "I've gotta go. The nurse is coming out to talk to us."

"Call me," Annajane said. "Let me know what they say. I'm on the way."

She found Mason alone in the waiting room at the hospital, slumped forward in one of those hard-backed green chairs. Even with the harsh fluorescent overhead lights the beige room was wreathed in shadows. He didn't look up when she sat down and called his name.

"Where's Sallie?" she asked, looking around the room. "And Pokey?"

"Pokey had to go home," Mason said, his voice a monotone. "To nurse the baby. Mama's in the room with Dad. They tried to make her leave, but she raised holy hell and threatened to sue everybody, so they finally let her stay."

"What about Davis?"

Mason shrugged. "He went up to Boone early this morning, to go skiing. Phone reception is lousy up there."

"Is there . . . any change?"

"No," Mason said. He sat up and stared at the television. "It's not good," he said bleakly. "Dr. Kaufman says his brain had likely been without oxygen for at least an hour or more by the time Mama found him. The EMTs managed to get his heart started in the ambulance, but Dr. Kaufman told us, even if he does make it, he won't be the same. You know."

Annajane nodded mutely. "I prayed the whole way back," she said finally. "For your daddy. I don't think I've ever prayed so hard in my life."

"Okay," Mason said. "That's nice. Mama will appreciate it."

They sat like that, not talking for another hour. Finally, she could stand the silence no more. "I'm gonna get some coffee," she said, standing and stretching. "I'll get some for you, too."

"No thanks," Mason said.

She got up and walked over to the coffee station in the corner, taking her time with sugar packets and instant creamer. She was about to sit down again when Sallie Bayless appeared in the doorway.

She was still dressed in the elegant black cashmere sweater and slacks she'd been wearing hours and hours ago, when Annajane had sat through that awful luncheon. But Sallie's usually perfectly arranged hair was a tangled mess. Her face was pale, her lipstick chewed off, her eyes red-rimmed.

"Mama?" Mason stood.

She nodded. "He's gone. They did everything they could, but your daddy is gone, son." She burst into tears, and threw herself into her oldest child's arms, while Annajane stood by, mute and heartbroken.

The next few days and weeks after the funeral were a blur.

Glenn Bayless's sudden death shook his family, and the company, to its core. Sallie, his widow, wept constantly and seemed unable to cope with even the simplest detail of day-to-day life. The first few nights after Glenn's death, she declared herself afraid to stay alone in the rambling old house. It fell to Mason, the oldest son, to move into his old bedroom down the hall to keep her company.

After two weeks, Sallie's doctor prescribed sleeping pills, and Mason came home. To the lumpy pullout sofa.

He plunged into the work of settling his father's estate and came home exhausted and ashen-faced from endless meetings with the lawyers. If Annajane inquired, he brusquely replied that everything was "fine."

But things were not fine. Without confiding in his son, Glenn had quietly begun acquiring expensive parcels of land for a new bottling plant in the southern part of the state, anticipating increased demand for Quixie. But the owner of the key parcel, the only acreage with the direct rail access a plant would require, had suddenly backed out of the sale. The company was stuck with the land, bought at a top-of-the-market price, with a correspondingly high interest rate.

At the same time, Quixie's sales had taken a worrisome dip. Vitamin waters, energy drinks, and flavored bottled iced teas were eroding their share of the soft drink market.

And Annajane and Mason hadn't had sex since before the ill-fated Quixie

Christmas party. They lived in the same house and worked for the same company, their offices only feet apart, but the chasm between them seemed to widen every day. When Leonard Hudgens fell and broke his hip and died of pneumonia a month after the death of Glenn Bayless, Annajane spent two weeks in Holden Beach with her mother. By the time she got back to Passcoe, Mason had moved out of the caretaker's cottage. And the marriage was over.

9

The nurse who'd wheeled Sophie back to the exam room beckoned. "Dr. Kaufman wanted me to tell you that he's gonna go ahead and take out her appendix," she said hurriedly. "They're prepping her now. You can go back, but only for a minute."

They found Sophie clutching a teddy bear, with an IV-drip tube connected to her arm. Nurse Molly patted the child's hand. "She's been such a good girl," she told Mason. "Didn't even cry when we stuck her for blood or put in the IV needle."

Mason laid his cheek against Sophie's. "Hey kiddo," he said softly. "Dr. Max is gonna fix up your tummy now."

Her eyelashes fluttered. "Daddy?" she said woozily. "I got a new bear."

"I see that," Mason said.

Annajane took Sophie's hand. "What have you got there?"

Clenched in the palm of her hand was an empty glass vial, probably from some drug that had been injected into her IV tube. Sophie was a magpie. From the moment she'd first started to crawl, she had a habit of picking up random small items. A misplaced earring, paper clip, discarded gum wrapper, all of these were treasures to Sophie, who would carefully tuck them in a pocket or hide them under her pillow. Or more often than not lately, in her treasured pink plastic pocketbook.

"It's a baby bottle. For my new bear," Sophie said.

"I'll keep it for you," Annajane promised, carefully placing the vial on the table out of Sophie's reach. "Does the bear have a name?"

"Mittens," Sophie said. "I'm sooo sleepy."

"You rest," Mason told her. "And when you wake up, I'll be right here."

"Annajane, too?"

"Me, too," Annajane said. "I'm not going anywhere."

And then they were wheeling her into surgery.

When they got back to the waiting area, Pokey was there. She'd changed out of her wedding attire and was wearing jeans, tennis shoes, and a T-shirt. "The nurse told me they're gonna operate?"

Mason nodded tersely. "Did you go by the club? How's Celia?"

"Fine, I guess," Pokey reported. "Pete took Letha to help out with the boys. She made me promise to call her as soon as we know something. I talked to him a little while ago. He said people were a little shocked at first, just kinda standing around, staring at each other, but then Mama took charge, got the waiters passing appetizers and the bar up and running, and the band warmed up. Everybody's dancing and having a high old time."

She pulled her cell phone from her back pocket. "Mama has ordered me to make sure you call her with an update on Sophie."

He exhaled loudly. "I can't deal with her right now." He looked at Annajane. "Could you?"

Annajane was in no mood for a long conversation with Sallie Bayless either, but she took the phone, made the call, and reassured her former mother-in-law that Dr. Kaufman had things firmly in hand. She heard the sound of music in the background, the clink of glasses and ice, and voices.

"Thank you for calling, Annajane dear," Sallie said finally. "I know this can't be easy for you."

"Sophie is a little trouper," Annajane said. "But yes, I'll feel better once she's out of surgery."

"I meant the wedding," Sallie said.

Annajane allowed herself a wry smile. "I'm happy for Mason. And Celia," she added.

"Of course," Sallie said. Her tone said otherwise.

When she rejoined the others, Mason was thumbing through e-mails on his BlackBerry, and his sister was staring at the television with a blank expression on her face.

"Hey," Pokey said, standing up quickly. "C'mon, let's go raid the vending machines. I'm starved. Mase? Can we bring you anything?"

"Nothing," he said without looking up.

Annajane trailed along after Pokey. They found a bank of vending machines outside the hospital's cafeteria, which was closed.

Pokey dug in the pocket of her jeans and came up with a handful of coins. She studied the candy machine. "Hmm. Almond Joy or Butterfinger?"

"Nothing for me," Annajane said. "Maybe a bottle of water or something." She looked at the other machines. "Although I could use some aspirin or ibuprofen or something for this headache."

"Hangover?" Pokey gave her a surprised look. Annajane was almost never sick, and almost never drank to excess.

Her friend sighed. "I dosed myself with bourbon before leaving for the church this afternoon. Should have known it would come back later and bite me in the butt."

Pokey fed coins into the soda machine and bought bottled water for both of them, then, moving over to the next machine, bought a packet of Aleve for Annajane.

"Let's sit in here," she said, gesturing to the half-darkened cafeteria.

They found a table near the door, and Annajane gratefully swallowed the pain medicine with a swig of water.

"Something I need to ask you," Pokey said, leaning across the table. "And don't bullshit me, okay? We've known each other too long for that."

"Oh God," Annajane said warily. "What is it now?"

"I saw the look on your face in church today, when Celia came down the aisle. I saw the look on Mason's face, too. And I know him just as well as I know you."

"And?" Annajane wished she had not followed her friend out of the waiting room. She'd walked right into Pokey's trap.

"And I got the distinct feeling, right before Sophie got sick, that you were about to make a big move."

"That's crazy," Annajane said, laughing uneasily. "I don't know what you're talking about."

"Sure you do," Pokey said. "You shoved me into the aisle. I don't care what you say. I know you, Annajane Hudgens. And I know you are not over him. You are still in love with my brother."

"Absolutely not," Annajane said automatically. "I'm in love with Shane. I've moved on."

"You are *so* not over Mason. And I've got a news flash for you. He's not over you, either."

"You're delusional," Annajane said, taking another swig of water. "Either that, or smoking crack. Hey. What were *you* drinking before the wedding?"

"Skim milk. Straight up. Iron supplement chaser." Pokey said. "I'm pregnant."

Annajane nearly spit out her water. "Again! Oh my God, Pokey, are you sure?"

Pokey took a big bite of her Butterfinger and chewed for a moment. "The fourth time around, you tend to know these things. And the EPT test I took Monday confirmed it. Yup. Just call me Fertile Myrtle. Knocked up again."

Annajane grasped both her friend's hands in hers. "Oh honey, that's great. I mean, I know Clayton isn't even two, but you really were born for motherhood. Are you okay with it? What does Pete say?"

Pokey laughed. "I'm fine with popping 'em out one, two, three. And four. As for Pete, he did allow that he wouldn't *mind* having a girl this time around. I pointed out to him that he's the one shooting all the blue bullets so far. Anyway, don't try to change the subject. We were talking about how you and my brother are still stupid in love with each other."

Annajane sighed. "I'll admit it was hard today, being in church, facing the reality of, well, everything. Mason truly was my first love. Yeah, I dated around in college, but nobody else ever came close. I guess I just had the world's biggest, longest crush on him. But marriage is different. It's real life, not a fairy tale. You can't sustain a crush when bad things happen, when people hurt each other. When they *cheat* on each other and won't even be honest enough to admit what they've done. If Mason had just apologized, if he'd just acknowledged what had happened, maybe things would have been different. But I'm not going to dwell on that anymore. I've found a man I can love as well as trust. Shane would never cheat on me. He just wouldn't."

"Stop!" Pokey exclaimed. "I will *never* believe Mason ever loved anybody but you. So maybe he screwed up, maybe he slipped up. He's a man, and gawd knows none of 'em are perfect. Especially the *Bayless* men."

"What's that supposed to mean?" Annajane asked.

Pokey shrugged. "What it sounds like. Look at Davis. What a man whore! He sleeps with any and every girl that comes along, single or married, and he gets away with it because he's Davis. He behaves like a goat in rut and we all just roll our eyes and laugh. And my daddy? Annajane, you know there was never a bigger daddy's girl than me. I loved my daddy and I miss him every day, but I'm not dumb, and I'm not blind. I know he . . . fooled around on Mama."

Annajane had heard rumors about her former father-in-law's conquests over the years. After all, even in his sixties, Glenn Bayless was a startlingly handsome man, with a full head of hair that had turned silver in his early forties, piercing blue eyes, and a lean athlete's build honed from hours in the gym he'd set up in the basement of Cherry Hill, not to mention twice-weekly games of cutthroat tennis with partners half his age.

Still, this was not a topic she had ever discussed with anybody in the family. "You really believe all those old stories?"

"I just know, okay?" Pokey said. "The crazy thing is, I don't think it affected their marriage. Daddy worshipped the ground Mama walked on. I think he just, you know, liked the ladies. And they liked him back. But I am here to tell you that Mason isn't like that."

"And what makes Mason so different?" Annajane said flippantly.

"Because he knew Daddy screwed around on Mama," Pokey said flatly. "And it wasn't just a rumor. If you must know, Mason and I caught him at it. Red-handed. And Mason never forgave him for it."

Caught off guard, Annajane sat back in her chair and regarded Pokey, who was calmly finishing off the last bite of her candy bar.

"Mason never said a word," Annajane said.

"We swore to keep it a secret," Pokey said. "We didn't even tell Davis. It was awful. For both of us. You remember that summer Mason moved away? Right after graduation? The only summer he didn't work at the plant?"

Annajane nodded. What she remembered most was the way her heart beat faster the first time she saw Mason Bayless roaring through town in the red convertible, headed for a summer job at the Outer Banks, and how her sixteen-year-old self pined for a man who barely knew she existed.

"Daddy said he was giving Mason the Chevelle as a birthday present. But really? It was a bribe. Or maybe a peace offering. Mason wasn't even speaking to Daddy at that point. I don't think he spoke to him that whole summer."

"But Mason came back home in the fall. And he went back to work for Quixie," Annajane pointed out. "And I never heard him say a single bad thing about your dad. I always thought it was so sweet, the way they worked together."

"They patched things up," Pokey agreed. "But they were never as close again as they were before that summer. Mason loved Daddy, but he didn't respect him."

Annajane shook her head. "I don't even know why we are having this conversation. The past is past." She held up her left hand, and wiggled her ring finger pointedly. "I've got a new life; Mason has a new life. It's time, all right?"

Pokey rolled her eyes.

"I know you don't like Celia," Annajane went on. "And no, she's not who I would have picked for Mason, but the important thing is, he picked her, and he apparently loves her, and I honestly think she'll be good for him and for the company."

"The company!" Pokey exclaimed. "Who gives a rat's ass about Quixie? We are talking about my brother's happiness. And yours. Celia is totally wrong for him. Did you notice he only asked the bitch to marry him *after* you announced your engagement? And don't get me started on the topic of Celia as mommy material."

"Sophie seems okay with Celia," Annajane broke in.

"Sophie doesn't know her like we do. But I don't care what kind of show she puts on; Celia just barely tolerates Sophie. I mean, Sophie is another woman's baby, not hers. Celia doesn't have a maternal bone in her body. The woman is an ice queen. And as for her company—so what if she made money selling kids' clothes? That doesn't mean she can keep Quixie from going down the tubes.

Soft drinks are an entirely different ball game. I don't care if she is Miss Congeniality. I don't like her and I don't trust her. What do we really know about this woman, aside from what she's told us?"

"We know Mason wants to marry her," Annajane said softly. "Anyway, much as I love you and the rest of your crazy clan, Pokey, the company is no longer my problem. In case you forgot, I'm moving to Atlanta in five days. I have a new job, and I'm starting a new life. Going to the wedding was about closure. I'm engaged to Shane, remember?"

"Closure?" Pokey scoffed. "And you really intend to marry a guy named Shane? Really? Shane? What kind of name is that for a grown man? Is he a cowboy or something?"

It was Annajane's turn for an eyeroll. "Hello, Pokey? May I remind you that you named your own sons Glenndenning, Peterson, and Clayton? And that you have brothers named Mason and Davis?"

"Those are family names, and you know it," Pokey said.

"Fine. I think Shane is a perfectly nice name. And he's a nice guy, and he loves me and I love him."

A wicked, familiar glint shone in Pokey's eyes. "How's the sex?"

"None of your business."

"I knew it," Pokey crowed. "You've been dating, what, six months, and you haven't fucked him?"

"I hate that word," Annajane said irritably. "And our sex life is perfectly normal. Divine, if you must know. Although, remember, we do live four hours apart. And up until this week, I still had my job here."

"If you were really attracted to him, you'd be screwing like a pair of jackrabbits," Pokey said, "instead of hanging around here in Passcoe. You think I don't know how you and Mason used to be when you were engaged? Jesus! We never once had Sunday dinner on time in the old days, because you two were always off over at the lake, getting it on."

Despite herself, Annajane blushed. "You knew?"

"*Everybody* knew. Mama, Daddy, hell, I think even Nate the yard man knew what you two were up to, and he's nearly senile. Those windows didn't get steamed up by themselves. My point is, if you are really this hot for this Shane guy, nothing could keep you apart. Hey!" she said, brightening, "maybe he's gay."

Annajane stood up abruptly. "I think we're done here. Nice talking to you."

"You still can't admit it, can you?" Pokey taunted.

"Admit what?"

"You can't admit that you were wrong to end your marriage to Mason. That the divorce was a huge mistake. That you loved him then and you love him now, and you would take him back in a minute if you could."

"But I can't," Annajane pointed out, gripping her water bottle so tightly she heard the plastic crumple. "I'm engaged to another man. To Shane. And Mason's wedding was postponed, not called off. And as soon as Sophie is well again, this wedding is going to happen."

"*Fuck* the wedding," Pokey said fiercely. "You're still not being honest with me. You're still bullshitting me. Come off it, Annajane. We have been best friends since we were five years old. Just be straight with me. Will you?"

Annajane walked over to a trash bin and tossed in the water bottle.

"All right," she said finally. "Okay, maybe there is still something there. It's probably just jealousy, wanting what I can't have. But yes, I had a twinge when I saw Mason standing there at the altar."

She allowed herself a sad, lopsided smile. "Happy now?"

"Yesss!" Pokey said, fist-pumping.

"I don't know what to do," Annajane heard herself admitting. "I can't believe I am saying this out loud."

"Tell him," Pokey advised. "It's not too late. Just be straight with him. If not for yourself, then at least for Sophie's sake."

"I can't," Annajane said. "I am engaged to another man. He is engaged to Celia. This is hopeless. And pointless."

"Then I will," Pokey vowed.

"No!" Annajane clutched Pokey's arm. "Don't you dare. If you say a word about this to Mason, I swear, Pokey, I will never speak to you again. I mean it. Just stay out of it, please?"

"This is so stupid," Pokey said stubbornly. "He will ruin his life, and Sophie's if he goes through with this charade and marries Celia."

"But it's his life," Annajane said. "Not yours."

. . .

They heard the voice as they were rounding the corridor back to the waiting room.

"Now, darlin', you've got to eat something," Celia cooed. "I fixed up this basket just for you. Maybe just a ham biscuit, or some of the tenderloin. I had the waiter slice it from the rare end, just like you like it."

Annajane felt her spine stiffen. Beside her, Pokey made a soft gagging noise.

She wanted to turn around and run out the door. Instead, she forced herself to keep walking back to the waiting room.

Celia had changed out of her wedding gown and was wearing an aqua velour tracksuit, with the jacket unzipped far enough to reveal a tantalizing amount of cleavage. A huge picnic basket sat by her feet, and she'd dragged a table over to the seating area, where she was unwrapping foil packages and plastic cartons.

"Hey there!" she said, as she saw the two women approaching. "I hope you're still hungry, because Sallie had the catering people pack enough food for the Russian army."

"I've eaten," Pokey said bluntly.

"Annajane?" Celia held out a petite yeast roll stuffed with blood-red prime beef and a leaf of arugula.

"Oh, nothing for me," Annajane said, as her stomach grumbled the message that she hadn't eaten since breakfast. She looked at Mason, who'd removed his tux jacket and rolled up the sleeves of his dress shirt. "Any news about the patient?" she asked.

"The nurse just came out and said Sophie's doing fine," Celia volunteered. "So I was hoping maybe I could lure this crazy man of mine into finally relaxing and eating something." She reached over and gave Mason's knee an affectionate squeeze.

"And I was just trying to tell her that this hospital gives me the creeps, and I really don't want to eat anything here," Mason said, looking up at Annajane with an expression she couldn't quite fathom.

"Well," Annajane said brightly, looking from Mason to Celia to Pokey. "It's been a long day. And if the nurse says Sophie's all right, that's a huge relief. Maybe I'll go on home and check back here in the morning. I'll get here early, hopefully before she wakes up."

"I think that's a very sensible idea," Celia agreed, nodding her head vigorously. "There's really nothing you can do here tonight, Annajane. The nurse said they'll only let *family* back, once she's in the recovery room. Mason and I will keep a vigil, won't we, darlin'?"

Mason frowned slightly. "Annajane is family."

Celia laughed a silvery, hollow little laugh. "Of course. But she probably wants to go home and shower and get out of that stinky dress, don't you think?" She studied Annajane's face dispassionately. "Don't take this the wrong way, but you do look pretty beat."

Annajane looked down at herself. Her shoes were spattered with something unspeakable, her stockings had runs in both legs, and the dress was history. She felt her shoulders slump. She was no match for Celia's effortless perfection. She should go.

"I'll call you if there's any change," Mason said as he stood.

Clearly, Annajane thought, he wants to be alone with his bride.

"I'd better get home to make sure Pete puts the little heathens to bed," Pokey announced.

"I'll walk you both to your cars," Mason offered.

10

I'm right there," Pokey said, pointing to the Range Rover she'd parked in the ambulance loading zone.

Mason and Annajane watched Pokey scramble into the driver's seat and zoom off into the darkness.

It wasn't until she saw her friend's taillights disappear that Annajane remembered that she'd arrived at the hospital in the ambulance—and that her own car was parked back at the church.

"Oh hell," she told Mason. "I don't have a car here, and neither do you."

"That's right." Mason scratched his neck absentmindedly.

"I'll call her and get her to come back for me," Annajane said, reaching in her purse for her cell phone. A moment later she disconnected. "She must still have her phone turned off," she said.

Mason reached in his pocket and brought out a set of keys. "I'll give you a ride," he said. "We can take Celia's Saab." He pointed in the direction of the parking lot and started walking. "It's right over there."

"Shouldn't you check with her?" Annajane said uneasily.

"I don't have to ask Celia's permission to give you a ride, Annajane," Mason snapped. "She's my fiancée, not my supervisor. And she trusts me."

That last sentence hung in the air. Trust. Celia trusted him. Annajane hadn't. And here they were, many years later. Some things hadn't changed.

"Suit yourself," Annajane said finally. "I just meant maybe you should let her know you'll be gone for thirty minutes. So she won't think you've disappeared."

He scowled. "Be right back."

Fifteen minutes passed. It was getting dark, and the temperature had started to dip as the sun dropped. Annajane hugged herself and rubbed her arms, shifting from one foot to the other in an attempt to keep warm. But she would not go back inside the waiting room. Obviously Mason had underestimated his need for Celia's approval for this little outing.

She grinned and wished Pokey were around to enjoy the drama.

Finally, Mason strode through the emergency room doors. "Let's go," he said brusquely.

An uneasy silence fell between them as Mason expertly shifted the Saab into gear.

"Everything okay?" Annajane asked.

"It's all good," he said, keeping his eyes on the road. "Thank you for insisting we get Sophie to the hospital. I guess . . . I guess I was kidding myself thinking the wedding could go on."

"I'm sorry about your wedding. Celia was a beautiful bride. But I'm glad things turned out all right with Sophie," Annajane murmured.

"Celia really adores Sophie," he blurted out a moment later.

"I'm sure she does," Annajane said, although she was certain of no such thing.

"It's a lot for anybody to deal with," Mason went on. "Not just being a stepmother, but, you know, taking on my, uh, daughter by a woman she's never met."

As far as Annajane knew, nobody in the family had ever met Sophie's mother.

One day, while they were still legally separated, but before the divorce was final, Mason knocked on her office door and stepped in and closed it carefully.

The visit took Annajane by surprise. Since their split, Mason had gone out of his way never to be alone with her.

He sat stiffly on the edge of the chair facing hers and cleared his throat.

"Look," he said finally. "I've got something I need to tell you. I was seeing this woman..."

Annajane held up her hand. "Stop right there, Mason. You're single now, and who you see, or what you do, no longer affects me on a personal level."

He scowled. "Will you just listen? This is important. The thing is, we're not really together now, this woman and I. We were only together for a short time, actually, and then she got pregnant. But I only recently found out about the baby."

Annajane heard herself gasp out loud.

Mason cleared his throat and plunged ahead. "Sophie is three months old now. Her mother, Kristy, is single, divorced, actually. And she and the baby had been living with Kristy's mom, down in Jacksonville. But Kristy's mom just died of breast cancer. And Kristy—she's not a bad person, but she's probably not mother material. She could handle the baby, while her mom was living there and helping out. Now, though... she's pretty overwhelmed. She wants to go back to her job, and Sophie is kind of cranky, I guess you'd say, right now. So, uh, here's the deal. Sophie's coming to live with me."

Annajane laughed despite herself. "Right. You're gonna be raising a baby. Three men and a baby. Only not."

"Yes," he said, glaring at her. "I am. Is this somehow funny to you?"

At that moment, it dawned on her that Mason was perfectly serious.

"Are you telling me that you're an unwed father?" she said finally.

He shook his head in disgust. "If that's what you want to call it." He stood. "Okay, I can see this was a mistake. I just thought I owed you an explanation, because I realize, as soon as it gets out that I've adopted Sophie, some people are going to just assume I was having an affair with Kristy while I was married to you."

Annajane swallowed. "Were you?"

"No," Mason said quietly, getting up from his chair. "I never met Kristy until after we were separated. You can take my word for it or not, but as God is my witness, that's the truth, Annajane."

Sophie's arrival had, as Mason predicted, stirred up a lot of gossip in Passcoe. And although the knowledge that Mason fathered a child with another woman had come as yet another searing blow to Annajane's already-battered ego, she found herself curiously drawn to the motherless infant.

"Is she not the yummiest little thing you've ever seen?" Pokey crooned, the first time she held the sleeping child in her arms. "No denying she's a Bayless, either. Look at those eyebrows! And that high forehead. She is Mason made over."

"Actually, she looks enough like you that she could be yours," Annajane pointed out.

"She is just perfect," Annajane said, gazing down into Sophie's familiar blue eyes. She touched a fingertip to the baby's hand, and Sophie's fingers instinctively curled around her own. Annajane was enchanted.

She found herself dropping by Pokey's whenever she knew Sophie was in residence. Annajane had always adored Pete and Pokey's three boisterous sons, but her attachment to Mason's daughter was somehow deeper, and mutual.

As soon as Sophie was walking, she would run immediately to Annajane. When she could speak, Annajane's was one of the first names she said, right after Daddy and Pokey. If she was fussy, as she often was until she was almost two, Annajane was often the only one who could soothe her or rock her to sleep.

And if Mason was uncomfortable with his daughter's obvious preference for his ex-wife, he never showed it. He might be stiff or distant with Annajane when they were alone together, but he seemed genuinely grateful for her relationship with Sophie, and he made it a point to include Annajane in any family function centered on the child, to his mother's obvious annoyance.

When Annajane mentioned Sallie's pointed coolness toward her after Sophie's third birthday party, Pokey laughed it off. "Mama's just jealous," she said. "Sophie won't even look at her if you're in the room."

As she sat beside Mason now, on his ruined wedding day, Annajane wondered, once again, if Celia would attempt to discourage Sophie's relationship with her. And she had no intention of sharing her reservations about Celia's parenting skills or maternal temperament.

"Celia is an extremely competent person," Annajane said guardedly. "I'll bet she's never failed at anything. She'll handle this, too."

"What do you mean, handle?" Mason asked, frowning.

"Nothing," Annajane said.

"Pokey hates Celia," Mason said. "I wish she'd lighten up a little. I think she'd like Celia, if she gave her half a chance."

"Maybe," Annajane said, wishing he would change the subject. "You know Pokey. Nothing if not opinionated."

Mason tapped his fingertips on the steering wheel. "So," he said, after a long silence. "How's it feel to be moving away after all these years in Passcoe?"

Annajane exhaled slowly. "Good." She hesitated, looking out the window. Wildflowers bloomed in roadside ditches, and she caught a glimpse of a bluebird, perched on a power line. "Scary."

"Change is good," Mason said, nodding for emphasis. "I mean, don't get me wrong, you'll be missed. You've done a damned good job for us. I don't think Davis is gonna know what to do without you."

She wished, fleetingly, that Mason had said *he* didn't know what he'd do without her. "Davis will figure it out. And Tracey, the new girl, she's a fast learner."

"Farnham-Capheart is lucky to be getting you," Mason said. "I told Joe Farnham that when he called to make sure I didn't have any problem with his hiring you."

"He checked with you? Before offering me the job?" Annajane couldn't believe it. Farnham-Capheart had been Quixie's advertising agency for years, and Annajane had worked closely with Lacey Parini, the account exec assigned to Quixie. When Lacey decided to become a stay-at-home mom after the birth of her second child, she'd encouraged Annajane to apply for her old job.

Annajane had had lots of job offers over the years, but it wasn't until Celia Wakefield joined Quixie that she'd ever considered a career change.

"He called me as a professional courtesy," Mason assured her. "You know how Joe is. I guess we're probably his biggest account, and he didn't want to rock the boat."

She didn't know what to say, didn't know why she hated the idea that Joe Farnham thought he had to get Mason's approval before offering her a job. Suddenly, a thought occurred to her. Maybe Mason had actually asked Farnham to find a job for her. Maybe he thought it would be just too awkward to have his ex-wife working with his new wife.

Or maybe it had all been Celia's idea. Annajane clenched her teeth, thinking of the indignity of it. Never mind. It didn't matter how her new job came about. She'd wanted a change; she'd gotten a change.

Mason obviously knew he'd somehow strayed into dangerous territory. He cleared his throat.

"So," he said, casually. "Have you, and uh, your fiancé set a date?"

"Shane," Annajane said. "His name is Shane. We're thinking fall, probably."

"Not til then, huh?" Mason sounded surprised. "Any reason for waiting?"

"Shane's a musician, you know," Annajane said. "He plays Dobro in a blue-grass band, and spring and summer is their busiest time, with all the outdoor music festivals. I want to get settled into my new job before I have to worry about planning a wedding. Not that we're planning anything elaborate."

"Gotcha," Mason said, nodding his head. "Bluegrass? What's the name of his band, if you don't mind my asking?"

"I don't mind at all," Annajane said proudly. "It's called Dandelion Wine. They have a CD coming out in September. Shane wrote most of the songs himself."

"Have to look into that," Mason said.

Annajane laughed. "Oh please. You always hated bluegrass. And country."

"No!" Mason exclaimed. "You've got me all wrong. I love Alison Krauss."

"Okay, whatever," Annajane said, unconvinced. "I'll send you one when it comes out."

"Sweet."

He made the turn onto Main Street, where Annajane rented a loft above the old K&J Drygoods Store. "What's Ruth think about all this?"

"She's happy for me," Annajane said briefly. "Although I'll be a lot farther away in Atlanta. With Leonard gone, I hate to think about her living alone down there on the coast. I'm trying to talk her into moving. My aunt Nancy's a widow now, too, and she'd like Mama to come live with her down in Florida. But you know Mama. She's pretty set in her ways."

"What's she think about you getting remarried?"

"She *loves* Shane," Annajane said. "They've gotten really close. His own mother died when he was twenty, and I think Mama always wanted a son."

"Good for him," Mason said. "I'm glad she approves of the new guy, since she never cared for me."

Annajane sighed. They both knew that was putting it mildly. Ruth Hudgens didn't like Mason any better than she liked his parents. The night Annajane came home with Mason's engagement ring on her finger, mother and daughter had the biggest fight of their lives. Annajane had fled the house and moved in briefly with Pokey and Pete. Leonard, always the peace maker, had brokered an uneasy truce between mother and daughter, but the damage had been done.

Ruth adamantly refused to take any part in the planning of Annajane's wedding, and Annajane had just as adamantly refused to let Leonard pay for any of it.

Mason pulled the car to the curb in front of her second-floor loft. "Okay," he said, obviously still uneasy at being alone with her. "Here you go."

"Thanks for the ride," she said. It was so weird, so awkward, having him drop her off like this. She flashed back to all those nights years ago, when he would park his car down the block from her parents' house, so they could exchange their urgent, passionate good nights without Ruth's knowing who she'd been out with. There would be no kisses, no desperate groping, no disheveled clothes to rearrange tonight.

"G'night," she said, jumping from the car.

11

Mason woke with a start. He sat up in bed and listened intently. For a moment, he thought maybe he'd heard Sophie, oak floorboards creaking gently underfoot as she crept down the hallway to his bedroom, as she used to do before Celia moved in and put a firm but loving stop to that.

And then he remembered, Sophie was in the hospital. It was his wedding night, and he was alone.

He swung his legs over the side of the bed and rubbed his eyes. He needed sleep, and yet he couldn't sleep. It was 3:00 A.M. Too early to call the hospital to check on Sophie. He'd wanted to stay in the waiting room last night, in case she awakened and asked for him, but the nurses chased him off, telling him that Sophie would be just fine without him and promising to call if she did awaken.

Celia had decided to stay with her great-aunt in one of the guest rooms at Cherry Hill. The old lady was overwrought from all the excitement of the day, and Sallie had hinted broadly that she herself was in no condition to play nursemaid.

Just as well, Mason thought. He was in the damnedest mood. Jumpy and irritable. Well, the day had been a disaster, hadn't it?

He'd left Celia in tears, back at Cherry Hill.

"Our beautiful day," she'd said, peeling off the false eyelashes and depositing them in the ashtray of the Saab. "All our plans, everything. Ruined."

"I know," he'd said, kissing her, trying to soothe her. "And I'm so sorry. But it wasn't really ruined, was it? I mean, you looked amazing, and everything was just the way you planned it."

She pulled away and stared at him. "Are you out of your mind? Your daughter collapsed at the altar and had to be rushed to the hospital. All of our guests were just sitting there . . . stunned. And don't forget, we never did actually get married. There's a $3,500 wedding cake at the country club, getting stale even as we speak."

"The cake? Can't we just, freeze it or . . ."

"No," she cut him off. "We can't."

"Oh-kaaay, Mason said, trying to tread lightly. "But we will get married, I promise. We'll do it all over again. We'll get another cake. Just as soon as we get Sophie home and recovered from surgery."

"It won't be the same," Celia said sorrowfully. "You're a man, and you've already had one wedding. I guess I can't really expect you to understand. A girl dreams of her wedding day her whole life. She has just one shot at one perfect moment. No matter how hard you try, you don't get that moment back again."

"I'm sorry." It was all he could say. As she'd pointed out, he couldn't fix it, no matter how hard he tried.

He got up to go to the bathroom and stubbed his toe hard on the foot of a damned chair. Christ! Since Celia had redecorated the house, or decorated it, since, as she aptly pointed out, it had never been decorated at all before she moved in, he was always bumping into things, knocking things over, breaking things.

Mason limped downstairs and into the kitchen. He stood in front of the open refrigerator door, not really hungry, but wanting . . . what?

Celia's nonfat yogurt containers were lined up in neat rows, as were the bottles of mineral water. Half a roast chicken nested on a plate under a tinfoil wrapping. There were containers of strawberries and blueberries and raspberries, packages of cheeses he'd never heard of, a crisper drawer full of things like scallions and leeks and arugula, carrots and baby spinach and celery sticks. Everything looked healthy and wholesome and totally uninteresting. At the very back of the top shelf, he spied the comforting sight of a tall-necked brown bottle.

He took the beer and a chunk of the least stinky cheese he could find and went into the room Celia called his study.

It was a handsome room, he had to admit. Celia had taste to spare, even Pokey grudgingly gave her that. She'd had the builder-beige Sheetrock walls covered with weather-beaten boards taken out of an old barn out at the farm, had bookshelves built to line two walls, and had conjured up rows and rows of old leather and vellum-bound books to line the shelves. He'd opened one once, just to see what she thought he should be reading. But it was in German. He didn't know German. The rug underfoot was some kind of rope-textured thing, sisal maybe—and it felt sandpaper-rough under his bare feet. He'd asked about keeping the old red and blue oriental rug he'd originally brought over from the attic at Cherry Hill when he'd bought the house, but Celia had just laughed and promised she'd find a better place for it when she finished redecorating.

He sat down at his desk and thrummed his fingers on the leather top. The desk was one of the very few things he'd insisted on keeping from his short-lived bachelor years. It had come out of his grandfather's old office at the bottling plant. It was beat-up mahogany, with two banks of drawers that stuck and a deep knee-hole recess, where he could remember playing with his army action figures as a little kid, pretending that he was in a bunker. The chair had been his grandfather's, too; it was high-backed, with cracked and peeling green leather upholstery that creaked loudly when he reclined in it.

Mason switched on his computer and idly glanced at his e-mails. Nothing that wouldn't keep. He'd inherited Voncile as his assistant after his father's death, and she was ruthless about weeding out e-mails he didn't need to deal with—especially since he was supposed to be on his honeymoon right this minute.

His honeymoon! A week in Aruba, their own villa overlooking the ocean. He shrugged. Knowing Voncile, he was sure she'd gone straight to the office from the church, and begun canceling flights and arranging for refunds.

Thinking of the office reminded him of Annajane, and he frowned. Stuffed in the back of that ambulance, and then later, in the waiting room at the hospital, he'd seen glimpses of the old Annajane. She was as terrified as he, but they were together again, if only briefly, as a team. And then, in the car, she'd been so prickly, hostile almost.

She really thought she was something, getting remarried, telling him all about this Shane guy.

As though he hadn't already thoroughly checked him out.

Mason clicked a few keys and opened up the file he'd started on this Shane Drummond clown the day Annajane returned from a trip to Atlanta—and announced her engagement.

From what Pokey told him, Annajane had only been seeing the guy since early fall. And three months later they were engaged? Fast work.

Voncile had been only too happy to conspire on this little research project. She'd nosed around the Internet for a few days, made some discreet calls to a security firm recommended by a business associate in Atlanta, and put together a fascinating dossier.

He was looking at that dossier now. Voncile had even managed to scrounge up photographs. Mason studied the largest of these, a color publicity still she'd found on Drummond's agent's Web site. So *this* was the kind of guy Annajane was attracted to?

In the photo, Drummond was dressed in a plaid lumberjack-type jacket and scruffy jeans. His curly hair looked unkempt, and he had those dark, brooding, soulful-looking eyes women like Annajane probably found irresistible. And was that a tiny gold hoop earring in his left ear? What the hell was it with women and musicians? Why did chicks always fall for the bad boys?

He shook his head and returned to the document Voncile had assembled.

Hmm. Matthew Shane Drummond, thirty-two. Hah! A younger man. Annajane had resorted to robbing the cradle. Born in Gastonia, he'd received a bachelor's degree in English at Middle Tennessee State University. He'd knocked around the country for the past few years, working as a bartender and a short-haul truck driver, but mostly earning a living playing in country music dives.

From what Mason could tell, Annajane's fiancé had formed his current group, Dandelion Wine, in 2008. He found a brief mention of the group in an obscure music magazine, about a recording contract with a Nashville label he'd actually heard of. So what? Did that mean this guy was the next Rascal Flatts? Mason highly doubted it.

Drummond owned a car, a 1999 Dodge Aerostar van, and a house, located in what looked like a rural area outside Atlanta, and valued, for tax purposes, at $82,700.

End of report. Mason scratched his chin and thought. Nothing sinister here. The guy was no tycoon, but he apparently also wasn't a destitute bum. He owned an old vehicle—a van he probably used for gigs for his band. He owned his own house. It wasn't a mansion, but it probably wasn't a chicken shed either.

He scowled and closed the file. Nothing of interest here. Annajane was her own woman. If she wanted to marry an itinerant musician and spend the rest of her life living in a log cabin on a dirt road, driving around in a beat-up Aerostar van with him, that was her right.

The question that had been nagging at him ever since he'd left her earlier that evening was, Why? Why Shane Drummond? Why Atlanta? Why now?

And more important, why did he care so much?

12

Annajane sighed as she opened the door to the loft. She hated living in chaos. Half-packed boxes littered the floor and covered every surface in the living room. She knew without looking that her sink was piled with unwashed dishes and her bedroom floor covered with clothing. This was not like her. Not at all. She had let things get away from her. She picked her way through the boxes and went into the bathroom, where she stripped and tossed everything, except her bracelet, into the trash.

When she emerged from the shower wrapped only in an oversized towel, she pushed aside a stack of unfolded laundry and collapsed onto the bed. Her head still hurt. She was tired, and worried about Sophie. But mostly, she was worried about her own screwed-up emotions.

How could this happen? How could she possibly be falling for Mason Bayless again? And what could she do about it?

Forget it. Forget him, she vowed. Think of Shane. Of her new life. And get the hell out of Passcoe.

She could still make a clean break. By the end of the week, she would, by God, finish packing and get everything loaded in the rental van. By next Saturday, she'd be moving into her own studio apartment in a close-in Atlanta neighborhood.

She would be with Shane, who was good and true and loved her without reservation.

And I love Shane, too, she thought fiercely. *I do. I really do. Shane is my future.*

And the Monday after the move, she would start her first day of work at the ad agency. She'd be so busy, there'd be no time to think about everything she'd left behind in Passcoe.

She found a clean T-shirt and pair of jeans among the jumble of clothes on her bed, got dressed, and got busy.

For three hours, she worked feverishly, packing up a lifetime's worth of belongings. The quicker she got it done, the sooner she could see Passcoe—and the Bayless family—in her rearview mirror.

Annajane abandoned any semblance of order or organization in her packing. Emptying kitchen cupboards, she dumped spice containers in with dishes, cookware in with cookbooks.

She took grim satisfaction in assembling the flattened cardboard boxes, filling them, and then snapping a length of shipping tape across the intersecting flaps to seal them shut.

From the kitchen she moved into the living/dining room. She positioned a box in front of the bookcases and began unloading the shelves with a long sweep of her arm. A slip of paper escaped from one of the books and fluttered to the floor.

Stooping to pick it up, Annajane froze. It was a picture, an old snapshot of her and Mason, arms wrapped around each other, sitting on the front steps of the lake cottage.

She sank to the floor and studied the photo. They looked so young! Her hair was in a ponytail, and she wore a pink polka-dot halter top and white shorts and was sunburned, with a bad case of raccoon eyes from her sunglasses, and her mouth was wide open, in midlaugh. Mason was tanned and shirtless, his sunglasses obscuring his eyes, but his smile was wide and matched her own. The picture was undated, but she knew it had to be from their first summer together, when she was only nineteen. Funny, she remembered that top, bought on sale at the Gap for six bucks, but she couldn't remember the circumstances surrounding that picture. Most likely it had been taken by Pokey.

There were no other photos of them together. Annajane had burned them all, the day her divorce was final. They'd made a nice blaze in a rusty old grill in her mother's backyard at Holden Beach. How, she wondered idly, had this picture survived the fire?

Not that it mattered. She stood up and tucked the photo back into the book, but instead of dumping the book back in the box with the others, she walked into her bedroom and placed it on her nightstand. Thinking better of it, she put it under her pillow.

Then she picked up the phone and called Shane. His voice, when he answered, was husky.

"Oh no," Annajane said softly. "You were asleep. I thought you'd just be getting in from your gig. I'm sorry. Go back to bed. I'll call you in the morning."

"No, no," Shane said. "Don't hang up, baby. It's fine. I wasn't even in bed. Must've just dozed off in front of the television. What time is it?"

"Past three," Annajane said.

"What are you doing up so late?" Shane asked. "Something wrong?"

"Nothing's wrong," she said quickly.

Liar. Liar. Liar. Her subconscious taunted her even as she spoke the words.

"I just needed to hear your voice," she said, and that part was true.

It was his voice, deep, honeyed, and southern as sorghum syrup that had melted her heart the first time they met.

She'd gone down to visit her mother at Holden Beach back in September. After two lo-o-o-n-g evenings of watching *Wheel of Fortune* and *Golden Girls* reruns, in desperation one night, after Ruth went to bed at nine, she went out for a drive. She'd seen the Holiday Inn sign and noticed they had a lounge, and since her mother was a teetotaler and didn't keep any liquor in the house, she decided to go in and get a drink on the spur of the moment.

The Sandpiper Lounge, as it turned out, was the happening nightspot for locals. A band called Dandelion Wine was playing to a packed house that night. Annajane sat at a table near the bar, slowly sipping a glass of wine. The band played mostly bluegrass, with a little country and rockabilly, which she was surprised to discover she enjoyed. There were two long tables close to the stage, both of them packed with women, maybe two dozen, who all seemed to know each other and the band. The women seemed to range in age from early twenties to early sixties, but they were drinking and having a great time, singing along to every song, whooping and clapping at their favorites. The lead singer and Dobro player seemed to be their favorite.

And why not? He was tall and lanky, with a mop of satiny deep brown curls and the dark, gorgeous eyes of a poet. He had dimples, and just a hint of five-o'clock shadow, and he wore a faded plaid flannel shirt and jeans with worn-out knees.

When he'd start in on a song, the women whooped and called his name, "Shane! Shane!" He'd look up, smile shyly, and maybe treat them to a playful wink, but mostly he sat on a battered wooden barstool and played and sang.

Annajane had never believed any of that stuff she'd always heard about women falling for musicians. Until she met Shane Drummond.

She supposed she must have heard the song before, probably at those long-ago family reunions at her aunt's cabin. "On the Other Hand" was an old country standard, he told her much later, and it had been covered by greats like George Jones, Keith Whitley, and George Strait. But she'd never heard the song about a married man tempted to cheat like she heard Shane sing it that night.

His voice was deep and true and fine, and he managed to wring emotion from every word, and as his long slender fingers plucked at the Dobro, she wondered if he was singing to her and for her.

"I called you twice, earlier," he said now, sounding puzzled. "Didn't you get my messages?"

She had gotten his messages, of course. But she didn't want to tell him she'd been at her ex-husband's wedding when he called.

"My phone is kinda messed up," Annajane said. "What message did you leave?"

"I said I love you, and I miss you," Shane said. That was how he'd been right from the start. So open and loving.

That first night, at the bar, she kept thinking it was late and she needed to leave, but she couldn't. At the break, the rest of the band went to the bar, where the women mobbed them, buying them drinks, laughing and flirting. Annajane, bored, was scrolling through e-mails on her phone when she heard the scrape of a chair. She looked up and it was the Dobro player.

He had a glass of white wine in his hand. "The bartender thought this was what you're drinking," he said.

She took the wine and asked him to sit down, and the smile that spread across his face was liquid and sweet, and his dimples deepened. And for a moment, the insane thought occurred to her—*Wouldn't this man make beautiful babies?*

He glanced toward the bar, where his bandmates were engaged in slamming back shooters and flirting with the women flocked around them. She looked, too, and saw a couple of the women staring daggers at her. He started to say something, stopped, started again, and then just grinned.

"What is it?" she asked.

"I can't think of a single thing to say to you that doesn't sound like a pickup line."

"Oh." She thought about it.

"You've probably heard every pickup line in the book, I bet," he said.

"Not really." She wasn't being coy. She'd never been much for the bar scene, even in college. And she honestly couldn't ever remember anybody even approaching her with a pickup line in a bar. She was pretty enough, she thought, but she just didn't attract that kind of attention.

"I find that hard to believe," he said. "My name's Shane, by the way."

"So I gathered, from your fan club," she said with a laugh. "I'm Annajane."

"That's a pretty name, Annajane," he said. "Kind of quaint, a little old-fashioned. Are you an old-fashioned girl?"

"I was named for my grandmothers," she said. "But no, I'm probably not all that old-fashioned."

"Are you a bluegrass fan?"

"Not really," she said. "But I like your music. You've got a beautiful voice."

"Thanks." When he smiled, the dimples were so deep she was tempted to see if she could poke a finger in one.

"I really do like your name," he said thoughtfully. "I guess I'm a sucker for double names. Good for songwriting."

"Do you write music?"

He shrugged. "I tinker with it. Bars like this, though, the audience wants the familiar. You know, 'Rocky Top' and crap like that. How about you, what do you do for a living?"

She sipped her wine. "I work in marketing for a soft drink company."

"Coke?"

She laughed. "I wish. Nope. Quixie—you know it?"

"The quicker quencher, sure, practically mother's milk," he said. "Don't they make that somewhere around here?"

"Our headquarters are in Passcoe," she said. "So . . . if you know Quixie, you must be from the Carolinas, right?

"Gastonia," he said. "Went to Middle Tennessee, got an English degree, but decided I liked music better."

They heard chords of music coming from the stage, and when they looked up, saw that the band was getting ready to start playing again.

"Gotta go," he said, pushing his chair back. "Any chance you might stay for the next set?"

She looked at her watch, but it was a pretense. She knew she intended to stay.

Shane kept his eyes riveted to hers throughout the night. After the last song, as the last stragglers drifted out of the lounge, he came bounding up to her table, his Dobro case in hand, clearly delighted to still find her sitting there.

"How 'bout I buy us something to eat?" he asked.

They took her car and found a Waffle House out by the interchange, and Shane wolfed down a steak and eggs, with hashbrowns, covered and smothered. She nibbled at a grilled cheese sandwich. At three o'clock, they were the only customers in the place. He'd told her his story; she'd given him a brief version of hers.

Annajane drove him back to the Holiday Inn. She parked by the door of the lounge. He made small talk, clearly not wanting to get out of the car. "It's late," she said finally. "If my mama wakes up, she'll think I've been kidnapped by aliens."

"I know." He had the Dobro case across his knees. He leaned in and brushed his lips across hers. "Will it sound like the worst pickup line in the world if I tell you I don't want you to go?"

"Try it," she suggested.

He took her face in his hands and kissed her, this time, a long, slow, deep kiss. He rested his forehead against hers. "I don't want you to go."

She felt her toes curl. "Hmm. Maybe try it again?"

He kissed her again. Even better. She gave into temptation and lightly touched one of the dimples with her fingertip. He caught it and kissed her hand, and drew him to her.

The next time she looked up, she giggled.

"What?" Shane was distracted.

She gestured at the Acura's windows. "We've fogged 'em up," she said happily. She hadn't been with a man since her divorce. She hadn't realized how long it had been until just that moment. And she hadn't realized how much she missed being touched, either.

He pulled her toward him again. "You know, we don't have to stay down here in this car. I've got a room here. Deluxe king, nonsmoking. Free Internet. Free cable. Free coffee. And there are a lot of windows there that we could be fogging up ..."

Annajane sighed. "That sounds   nice. But remember how you asked me if I were an old-fashioned girl?"

"Yeah?"

"I guess I kinda am. I guess I'm not the kind of girl who picks up a musician at the Holiday Inn lounge and then goes to bed with him later that same night."

"Oh." He didn't bother to hide the disappointment in his voice. "You probably think I do this all the time. I swear, I don't. Maybe I did the first year the band was out on the road ... but not anymore."

"I believe you," she said. She let her fingertips trail down her arm. "Tomorrow's Saturday. Well, okay, I guess today is Saturday. I go home to Passcoe on Sunday."

"We're only here one more night before we head up to Roanoke for a gig," Shane said. "Can you come back tomorrow, I mean, tonight?"

"Probably," she said lightly. "Maybe I could bring a toothbrush."

He grinned, and his dimples were deep enough to dive into. "I'll buy you one my ownself."

The weekend after that, she'd driven up to Roanoke, and two weeks after that, they'd met in Nashville, and then, when the band had a week off right after Christmas, she met him down in Jupiter Beach at his cousin's condo. At some point, she was startled to realize how different he was from any other man she'd known. Being with him was so easy, so effortless. He was the exact opposite of the driven, intense Mason Bayless. And that was a good thing, she was sure.

On their last morning at the beach condo, she woke up and found Shane, his head propped on an elbow, gazing down at her.

"What's up?" she asked sleepily.

"I'm just thinking about how cool it's gonna be years and years from now when we tell our kids the story of how we met when I picked you up in a bar and I spent the next night at the Holden Beach Holiday Inn rollin' in my sweet baby's arms."

Kids? She'd deliberately told herself she was not getting that serious about Shane, that they were just two adults enjoying getting to know each other. But all along she knew she was falling for him.

"When and if we have kids, as far as they will be concerned, we met at a church picnic," she informed him.

Two weeks later, the band was playing at a tiny club in Durham. She was sitting in the audience, sipping the glass of wine he'd sent over to her table, when the band swung into "Could I Have This Dance?" She'd been a little surprised, because it wasn't on their usual set list, but mild surprise had turned to shock and numbness when Shane stepped off the bandstand, made his way to her table, and slipped the sterling silver band on her left ring finger.

"Okay?" he'd whispered in her ear, with everybody in the whole club watching. She'd started to cry, and eventually, she'd nodded her head yes. And so they were engaged. Just like that.

It wasn't until she'd gotten back to Passcoe and unpacked her suitcase that Sunday night that the enormity of the situation struck her. She'd just agreed to spend the rest of her life with a man she'd only met three months earlier.

Every time she started to have reservations about the engagement, though, Shane managed to persuade her that she was doing the right thing. Even when she called him at three in the morning and woke him out of a sound sleep, he was ready to whisper sweet nothings.

"Why don't you come on down here and let me show you how much I'm missing you?" His laugh was low and provocative.

"Can't," she said, hoping she sounded regret she didn't quite feel. "I've got a million things to get wrapped up here. I'm not even packed yet."

"I could come up there and help," he offered. "You really don't have to do this all by yourself, you know."

He was amazing. So thoughtful. He loved her. She loved him, too. Didn't she?

"No way," she said quickly. "If you got a good look at how disorganized my life really is, you'd run the other way."

"Never," Shane said. "I'll take you any way I can get you, not that I believe there's anything disorganized about you. You're the most together person I've ever met."

"Not lately," Annajane said, rifling through the pages of the book she'd put on her nightstand. "Lately, I feel like my life is all falling apart at the seams. And no matter how hard I try, I can't seem to hold it together."

There was a silence at the other end of the line.

"Okay, I'm coming up there," Shane said. "So don't tell me not to. I can tell you're upset. You're stressed about the move and the new job, and you're not sleeping. You're not yourself."

She found the photo again. As she stared at it, the image blurred through her tears.

Who was that girl?

"I'm fine," she told Shane. "Really, I am. Guess I was just feeling overwhelmed. I packed a bunch of boxes tonight, before I called you. The kitchen's almost done, and I've started on the bedroom and my clothes. I'm warning you Shane, we might have to add on to the cabin before the wedding, just to make room for all my shoes."

"Done," he said. "I've already moved all my stuff into the closet in the guest bedroom."

"Shane! You know I've rented my own place. I've got a six-month lease."

"I still think it's ridiculous," he groused. "A waste of good money, when you could just as easily move in here right away."

Why didn't she just move in with Shane? Why was it so important to have her own place? Didn't she want to live with the man she loved?

"It's only six months," she said softly. "Just til the wedding."

"And that's another thing. I don't get why we can't just get married as soon as you get down here. Yeah, I'll be on the road some this summer, but so what? You can come with me. It'll be fun. An adventure."

She laughed. "I'm starting a new job! Anyway, you forget I've seen how you live on the road. It's fine for you guys; you're used to piling four to a room, or sleeping in the van and living on warm beer and stale pretzels. But that's not me, Shane."

"We'll get our own hotel room," Shane said. "Like at Holden Beach. I don't care. Let's just get married. Right now. That's all I'm saying."

"We've already talked about this," she reminded him. "Remember? I want to be with you, I really do. But I need a little time, and a little space. Just six months. To transition. That's not so long, is it?"

"It's forever," he groused.

"How did the gig go?" she asked, wanting to change the subject. Shane loved to talk about his work. It was one of the things she admired about him, his unstinting enthusiasm for whatever went on in his life.

"It was awesome," he said. "This club has only been open a couple months. It was packed tonight, babe. They had to quit letting people in the door at ten, an hour before we went on! The energy was amazing. They want us to come back in June, and we'll be the headline act!"

"That's great," Annajane said.

"I've got an idea for a new song, too," Shane said. "About a girl with green eyes. And long legs."

"Anybody I know?"

"Only you," Shane said. "All my songs are about you now. Why can't you get down here tomorrow?"

"Hush," she said. "Go back to sleep."

He let out a long, extended yawn. "I'll call you tomorrow. Love you."

"Love you too," Annajane said.

Liar. Liar. Liar.

13

On Sunday morning, Annajane walked briskly down Main Street, turning three blocks down from her loft, onto Church Street. She passed Passcoe First United Methodist, Passcoe First Presbyterian, and the biggest church in town, First Baptist of Passcoe, with its imposing white columns and three-story marble-lined sanctuary.

It was early yet, not even eight o'clock, so the town's worshipers were still presumably at home, polishing off their bacon, grits, and eggs; pressing their dress shirts; or dabbing on a final bit of makeup. Because that's the kind of town Passcoe was, a nice southern town where nice southern men and women still wore suits and dresses to church on Sundays.

Two blocks past First Baptist, she finally came to the Quixie Beverage Company, which, in its own way, was just as much of a temple of worship as the real churches in town. The sprawling red brick complex even looked like a church from the front, with two-story columns and a peaked roofline. The building had been added onto so many times since Mason's great granddaddy founded the company in the 1920s, it now took up an entire block, fronting on Church Street and backing up to the railroad tracks.

Annajane skirted the front of the building, where a perky red-and-green-striped awning shaded a set of big plate-glass entry doors to the reception area. Instead, she walked around to the east side of the building, to the loading dock. A pair of boxy Quixie delivery trucks were parked at the dock, nose out, and she could hear the rattle of hand trucks and the soft murmur of voices as she climbed the worn wooden steps up to the dock.

"Hey, Annajane," called out a husky middle-aged man in a Quixie driver's uniform. He had a hand cart loaded with cases of Quixie poised at the open doors at the back of one of the trucks. "Thought you'd done moved off to Atlanta. What are you doin' round here on a Sunday?"

She'd known Troy Meeks since she and Pokey were kids playing hide-and-go-seek around the plant. He'd given them rides on his hand truck, bought their Girl Scout cookies, and turned a blind eye when they pilfered dented cans of Quixie to sell for a quarter apiece at school.

"Hey Troy," she said, giving the older man a hug. She reached out and gave his stubbly gray crew cut an affectionate rub. "I'm not gone just yet. I've still got a bunch of stuff to tie up in the office. That's why I came in this morning. I can never get anything done with Davis popping in and out all day long, giving me orders and trying to boss me around. I just need a few hours of peace and quiet."

"It's a sure bet you won't catch Davis Bayless in here on a Sunday morning," Troy agreed. "Especially not the day after his brother got married." He gave her a knowing wink. "That musta been some party."

"Well, that's a funny story," Annajane said. "The wedding didn't exactly go off as planned."

His mouth gaped. "You're kidding me. What'd you do—trip the bride as she went up the aisle?"

She shook a mock finger at him. "Careful. Celia's management now, you know."

He grinned. "Are you serious? The wedding really didn't happen?"

"Nope," she said. "Sophie got sick—right as Celia was walking up the aisle. They had to call the wedding off and rush her to the hospital. She had an emergency appendectomy."

He shook his head. "Appendectomy! Poor little thing. Bet old Mason was fit to be tied."

"He was. We were all pretty worried about Sophie. But Dr. Kaufman says she'll be right as rain. I talked to the nurse at the hospital this morning, and she's awake and demanding ice cream, so that's a good sign."

"Called off the wedding," Troy repeated under his breath. "Ain't that something." He gave Annajane a cockeyed smile. "Maybe there's still time for you to snag the boss. Again."

Annajane blushed. "Sorry, Troy. That ship has sailed." She held up her left hand so he could see her ring. "Anyway, I'm engaged."

"Damn shame, too," he muttered.

The thick, sweet smell of cherry syrup hung heavy in the air of the quiet plant. Annajane passed only two more workers, which was worrisome. At one time not so long ago, the plant would have been humming, even on a springlike Sunday morning.

But times had changed. The economy had soured. People were fickle. Their tastes and preferences in soft drinks and soft drink flavorings had changed. Quixie had lost market share to the spate of "energy drinks" flooding the market. Even their demographic had changed, from young and upbeat to, well . . . not.

When she'd been in college, Quixie had been the mixer of choice at parties. She and her friends had drunk Quixie and Captain Morgan rum, Quixie and vodka, Quixie and Southern Comfort, even—she shuddered to think of it now—Quixie and natty lite.

Somehow, though, the Quixie brand had gotten stodgy. Davis had commissioned market studies and focus groups to seek the root of the problem, but the answers hadn't been encouraging. Quixie just wasn't cool. Not that they hadn't tried.

The company had spent millions on surveys and focus groups and ill-fated ad campaigns. They'd overhauled everything, from the original flavoring formula to the size, shape, and color of the bottles, cans, and packaging, to the look of the brand itself. But nothing worked.

Annajane pushed open the heavy metal double doors leading from the plant into the office building. She followed a narrow corridor past a slew of closed office doors before pausing in front of her own. ANNAJANE HUDGENS, ASST. V.P.

MARKETING, said the plaque on her door. She slid the plaque out of the slot and dropped it an empty trash basket. By the end of the week, it would be Tracey's office, not hers.

She drew a spare key to her office from her pocket and unlocked the door. She flipped on the light and sighed at what she saw.

More cardboard boxes were scattered around the office. Stacks of books were piled on top of her desk, and even more stacks—of boxes, files, and miscellaneous papers—stood piled at precarious angles. There was a coatrack in the corner, and from it hung a couple of her old, threadbare sweaters, a Quixie Beverage Company red-and-green-striped driver's uniform shirt with her name embroidered on the breast pocket, and, yes, shrouded in an age-clouded plastic dry cleaners bag hung the dreaded Dixie the Pixie costume.

Annajane lifted a corner of the plastic bag and inspected the green felt tunic and red tights. Somebody—her mother, maybe?—had done a neat job of mending the rips from her Fourth of July fall all those years ago. She had a corresponding scar on her knee. You couldn't even tell—unless you looked really closely.

She smiled wryly and let the plastic drop. Old wounds. They faded, but they never really went away, did they?

No good worrying about that now, she decided, clearing a path to her desk. She sat down in front of her computer and plunged herself into her work.

Two hours later, she sat back in her chair and paused for a moment. The end-of-quarter sales figures she'd been scanning were depressing. Fountain sales, canned sales, liter bottle sales—all were down.

Her department was gearing up to work with supermarket chains around the region for an important summer promotion. The ad agency's art department had worked up sketches for the supermarket displays, but to Annajane they were uninspired and, worse, downright ugly.

She sighed and kneaded her forehead with her fingertips. Davis had already approved the sketches with an enthusiastic "looks great" scrawled in the margins. Annajane was only the second in command in marketing. The final okay was up to Davis—and Mason, to some extent. She had one foot out the door, so why should this matter to her?

It just did. She hated the idea of stores all over the region flooded with the tacky cardboard displays featuring a likeness of Quixie's new spokesman—a second-rate Nascar driver—holding the Quixie bottle. The colors were garish, the production quality mediocre, and the driver, Donnell Boggs, whom Anna-jane had met on his one and only stop in Passcoe for promotional purposes, was a skeezy drunk who'd instantly become Davis's new best friend.

She jotted some quick notes on a Post-it and attached it to the sketches be-fore returning her attention to her e-mail.

A woman's voice echoed down the hallway, and Annajane looked up, star-tled.

Celia Wakefield's slightly nasal Midwestern accent was impossible to miss. "No," she was saying to somebody. "No, we haven't discussed a new date yet. It just happened last night, for heaven's sake!"

Annajane felt the hair on the back of her neck prickle. Her office door was closed, but she found herself slumping down in her chair, just in case.

Celia's heels clicked on the linoleum hallway floor. She was coming closer, and apparently she was having a discussion on her cell phone. "No, Jerry," she said sharply. "You don't understand how things are done down here. It's not just a business to these people. We have to finesse this. It's a courtship, you know?"

"These people?" Was she referring to the Baylesses? And was Quixie the business under discussion?

Celia started to say something, but then she was quiet, probably listening to the unseen Jerry on the other end of the line.

"Mmm, actually, I think the younger brother is amenable. He's the middle child, and you know how they are. Starved for approval. I get the feeling he's interested in exploring his options."

Annajane sat up straight now. *Davis? Exploring his options? What the hell was going on here?*

Celia had passed Annajane's door now, and her voice was starting to fade. Annajane got up and pressed her ear to the door, feeling guilty even as she did so.

"Well, the sister is definitely *not* president of my fan club," Celia was saying.

You got that right, Annajane thought.

"Mmm-hmm, no, she doesn't participate directly, kids and all that. But yes, I think it's likely she does have a stake in the business. No, unfortunately, that's a bit tricky since she's best friends with Mason's ex."

Annajane bristled.

Celia laughed at something her caller said. "You don't even know the half of it," she drawled.

The footsteps receded, as did Celia's voice.

What the hell is she up to? Annajane wondered again.

She went back to her computer and tried to concentrate on the memo she was writing for Tracey, but her mind kept drifting back to the conversation she'd just overheard.

Ten months. That's how long it had taken Celia Wakefield to get her claws into first Quixie and then Mason Bayless. Knowing Celia as she did now, Annajane was only surprised that she hadn't managed it any faster.

Like everybody else in Passcoe, as well as at the company, Annajane had been thoroughly charmed by her first meeting with Celia.

Davis had been singing the praises of the hotshot management consultant he'd met on a business trip to Chicago for months.

"Mama actually met her first, if you can believe it," he'd told Annajane at a meeting the day after he returned.

Sallie often tagged along with both her sons on business trips after Glenn's death. Not that she had much to do with the day-to-day operations of Quixie, but she'd made friends over the years with people in the soft drink business, and Annajane suspected she was eager to go along on the trips because it gave her a chance to get out of Passcoe, stay in the best hotels, catch up with old pals, and shop. Sallie Bayless was a world-class shopper.

"Mama was sitting in our suite, leafing through the program for the marketing meeting, and she got all excited when she saw that Celia Wakefield was on a panel about brand building," Davis said. "Turns out, she'd just bought a little dress for Sophie from a company called Gingerpeachy at some ritzy boutique up there and went crazy over them," Davis said. "Of course, Gingerpeachy is Celia's company. Or was, until she sold it. Sallie insisted on sitting in on Celia's panel, and she was so impressed, afterwards she invited Celia to meet us for dinner. I had drinks with her in the bar first, you know, just to see if she checked out."

Davis rolled his eyes dramatically. "Of course, I took all of this with a grain of salt. I mean, come on, what does Sallie know about brand building, or marketing? I tried to get out of it gracefully, but you know Sallie. Damned if she didn't force me to go to dinner, and damned if she wasn't right. Wait until you meet this gal, Annajane. She's the real deal!"

"This is a woman who really understands branding," he told Annajane. "She built her own company from scratch—kids' clothing, starting from the time she was twenty-one years old, working as a sales clerk at a little boutique in the middle of nowhere. She was the designer, the manufacturer, the marketer—everything. Last year, she sold the company to a big retailer. Believe that? Ten million dollars! Guess she's gotten bored with the good life, because she's doing consulting work these days."

A few weeks later, Davis called her into his office and introduced her to Celia.

Annajane's first impression had been that this was the most exquisite creature she'd ever met. The chair she was sitting in seemed to swallow her whole. Even with five-inch stiletto heels on her lime-green pumps, she was barely a notch above five feet tall. Her blond hair was silvery against a deep tennis-player's tan, and her pale lavender suit and low-cut lime-green silk shell should have been too girly for business. But on Celia, it was perfection. She reminded Annajane of a hummingbird. The only thing missing was a tiny pair of wings.

"Annajane!" Celia had said, leaping up to shake her hand. "Davis has told me so much about you. He says you're the heart and soul of the company. How can I lure you into going to lunch with me and sharing your insights on Quixie?"

Of course, Annajane had been flattered. Flattery was one of Celia's many talents. She was warm and bubbly, so easy to talk to. They'd had a hilarious lunch, laughing and talking about the quirks of working for a small-town family-owned company. Celia had seemed surprised to learn that Mason was Annajane's ex-husband.

"Really? And you still work for the company after all that? How do you stand it?"

Annajane winced now at how easily it had been for Celia to draw her into her confidences. For a few weeks, they'd been best buddies, sharing drinks, lunches, even a shopping trip to Charlotte.

Everybody, it seemed, loved Celia. Everybody except Pokey.

"She's a phony," Pokey said, after the first and only lunch date with Annajane and Celia. "If she's so rich from selling her own company, why is she piddling around with contract consulting work for Quixie?"

Secretly, Annajane wondered if Pokey's dislike of Celia wasn't just a case of good old-fashioned jealousy. With three small children to ride herd over, Pokey was out of the loop on lots of things. And Annajane and Celia were seeing a lot of each other. But she kept that to herself.

Instead, she repeated what Celia told her about herself. "She's only thirty-two. I think the payout is probably over a number of years, and some of it's actually in stock she can't touch for a few years. She's too young to retire, and, anyway, she's one of these people who always have to be doing something. She loves a challenge. And you've got to admit, with the way things are going, we've got a big challenge on our hands at Quixie."

"She wants more than a job," Pokey warned. "You wait and see."

But before Annajane could come up with a good defense for Celia, the memos started.

Like Celia herself, they were charming and disarming initially, couched as questions at first, then as suggestions, and then, within a very short period of time, as directives and missives. Celia's range was broad—she was interested in anything and everything that happened at Quixie, and no detail was too small for her laserlike focus.

But it wasn't until she was on the receiving end of one of those memos—this one a coolly worded e-mail she received after filing an expense report following an out-of-town marketing association meeting—that Annajane realized just how lethal Celia's influence could be.

> *AJ: Don't you think it's excessive to bill the company for airfare, meals and a night at an expensive New York hotel when we both know these conferences are really more about gossip and personal networking than they are about Quixie business?—CW*

Stunned, Annajane had fired back with a memo of her own, detailing the subject matter of each meeting she'd attended and its value to the company, and adding the fact that she'd spent the other two nights of the conference in an old friend's apartment, which cost the company nothing. And she'd ended her memo with one last observation.

CW: Obviously, I disagree with you about the value of these conferences. And by the way, didn't you meet Davis and Sallie at a conference just like this one?—Annajane.

After that, there were no more lunches or shopping trips. She had, she admitted to Pokey, finally seen Celia's true colors. And they weren't pretty.

But to everybody else at Quixie, especially Mason, Celia Wakefield was regarded as the second coming. The one time Annajane had dared complain to Mason about one of Celia's pointed memos to her, Mason worked himself into a righteous indignation.

She'd entered his office meekly and couched her objection as tactfully as possible, but he'd issued her a stinging and immediate rebuke. "Frankly, criticism of Celia, coming from you, seems kind of petty. She sees the big picture, Annajane, something we desperately need right now. She's done a great job of analyzing these types of things, and I have no intention of reversing her."

Annajane could see the matter was closed. She and Mason had managed to keep their relationship at the office on an even-keeled, professional level after their divorce, but during that brief meeting, she realized things had changed. Celia was making sure of that.

Not long after that, she noticed that Celia had been given her own parking space, with her name stenciled on the pavement, situated between Mason's and Davis's in the company lot. And not long after that, she'd seen Celia and Mason leaving for long lunches together. Soon, they were arriving at the office together on Monday mornings.

"He brought her to Sunday dinner at Mama's," Pokey reported. "You know how many women he's dated since you two split up—and he's never brought any of those women around the family. Hell, we never even met Sophie's mother. I've got a bad, bad feeling about this chick."

It wasn't long before Annajane came to realize just how astute Pokey's assessment of Celia was.

The day Celia and Davis presented her with plans for the upcoming summer promotion with the Donnell Boggs tie-in, a promotion she'd had no hand in at all, Annajane realized that Celia had quickly and stealthily cut her out of the decision-making loop in the marketing department. Before that day was out, Annajane had begun updating her résumé and quietly putting out feelers to find a new job. Her days at Quixie, she knew then, were numbered.

Still, the engagement announcement, just six weeks after her own engagement, had taken Annajane totally by surprise. And not, she would admit now, in a good way.

Celia Wakefield was not a woman to be trusted.

Annajane's cell phone rang, startling her badly. She groped on her desk to find and answer it.

"Hello," she whispered.

"Hey, Annajane," it was Mason, sounding . . . awkward.

"Hi," she said, already feeling guilty about eavesdropping on Celia.

"I'm over at the hospital, and Sophie's awake, and asking for you," Mason said. "I told her you're pretty busy what with the move and all, but . . ."

"I was just wrapping up some work, and then I'll be over," Annajane said hurriedly. "How's she feeling?"

"She's kinda pitiful," Mason admitted. "She's trying to be brave, poor kid, but she can't understand why it still hurts. I thought maybe you could take her mind off it."

"I'll stop on the way over and pick up a video we can watch together," Annajane said. "I've got her copy of *Milo and Otis* at my place. She never gets tired of seeing that."

"Great idea," Mason said, sounding relieved. "Should have thought of that myself."

Yes, Annajane thought to herself. *You should have. Or your fiancée should have—if she weren't so busy plotting something nefarious.*

Annajane got up from her desk and looked around the room with a sigh. She really should make a start on clearing out some of this old junk before leaving for the hospital. That wooden bookshelf nearest the door, for example. The bottom shelf held a row of dusty cardboard filing boxes that had been sitting there since she'd moved into the office eight years ago. As far as she knew, the boxes hadn't been touched for decades before that.

She grabbed the hand truck she'd borrowed from the plant and stacked three of the boxes on it. The cartons were unexpectedly heavy. A plume of dust arose as she lifted the lid of the carton on top, and she sneezed repeatedly. Inside the carton were stacks of age-browned file folders with fading but neatly typed labels. The top file was labeled CORRESPONDENCE, 1972. Clearly, the boxes contained nothing anybody had needed or wanted in the past forty or so years.

Annajane maneuvered the unwieldy load of file cartons through the plant and out to the loading dock, where a large Dumpster was located. She grunted as she hefted the first box into the empty Dumpster. But when she bent to unload the second box, which had been somewhat crushed from the weight of the top box, its sides collapsed, spilling the contents onto the concrete surface of the loading dock.

"Dammit," she muttered, scooping up a load of papers.

Her mood changed when she saw the contents of the box. They were slick, full-color mechanicals of vintage Quixie advertisements.

The top ad had a vividly rendered illustration of Dixie, the Quixie Pixie, perched on the top of a Christmas tree, winking impishly and offering a bottle of Quixie to two pajama-clad children peeking around the corner of a living room that could have come straight out of a 1950s movie.

GO AHEAD, the ad's headline urged. SANTA WON'T MIND.

CELEBRATE CHRISTMAS WITH QUIXIE CHERRY COLA!

"Oh, wow," she breathed, looking closer. A notation on the bottom of the mechanical indicated that the ad had run in the December 1957 issue of *Look* magazine. The illustration was signed, in the corner, with familiar block lettering. She blinked and looked again, but the signature was still there. Norman Rockwell.

She had no idea the company had once hired the country's most famous illustrator for its ad campaigns.

Annajane looked at another mechanical. This one was for the June 1961 issue of *Saturday Evening Post* and showed Dixie again. The illustration had the mascot water-skiing behind a sleek speedboat driven by a pair of windswept but gorgeous bathing-suit-clad teenage girls. Both the girls held bottles of Quixie in their raised hands.

THE WATER'S FINE, the ad's headline said. *BUT QUIXIE IS EVEN BETTER*.

She fanned through the rest of the files. There were more mechanicals for Quixie ads over the ages, artists' sketches, and even memos about upcoming promotions.

One of the promotional pieces was a recipe booklet titled *Entertaining Ideas with Delicious and Nutritious Quixie*.

Delicious, yes, Annajane thought, but what demented marketer had dared to suggest that Quixie was actually healthy?

And yet, the booklet, which Annajane surmised was '60s-era, offered more than a dozen recipes with accompanying color photographs for Quixie-inspired dishes, ranging from a Quixie-glazed Easter ham to an elaborate three-layer molded Quixie JELL-O "salad" to a Quixie-based fruit punch featuring a festive cherry and lime sherbet-accented frozen ice ring.

The recipe for Quixie baked beans was illustrated with a color photo of an immaculately coiffed housewife offering the gooey-looking brown concoction to a trio of eager children. The woman in the photo was definitely a dewy-eyed, probably not more than nineteen-year-old Sallie Bayless, although the children were young models, since Sallie's own children weren't even born yet.

"Mrs. Glendenning M. Bayless proudly serves her family healthful dishes from her personal recipe files," the photo's caption proclaimed.

That one gave Annajane a laugh. She'd eaten countless meals at her former mother-in-law's house, and never once had Sallie served anything as pedestrian as baked beans. Sallie Bayless would have slit her own throat before following a recipe that called for combining canned baked beans, bacon, Vienna sausages, pineapple tidbits, and, yes, a twelve-ounce bottle of Quixie.

Still, the box was a miniature treasure trove of the company's marketing history. She shuddered now to think how close she'd come to trashing all of it.

Annajane slid the ruined box off the hand truck and lifted the lid on the bottom box. So this was why her load had been so heavy! Inside she found a dozen old glass Quixie soda bottles, each of them different. Of course she'd glimpsed some of the same bottles in the glass display case in the company foyer, but they'd been there so long, she'd really never taken the time to examine them.

Most of the old bottles were either clear or the same pale green tint that was used in the current Quixie bottle. But the shape and silhouette and labels varied. One in particular drew her attention. She lifted it out and held it up to the sunlight.

The bottle was short and squat, an eight-ounce size, and its base bore concentric rings. On the label, the winking face of Dixie leaned out from the Q in the company name.

"Adorable," Annajane breathed, turning the bottle this way and that. At the same time she was admiring it, she realized that she was thirsty, parched, dying, actually, for an icy-cold glass of delicious, even *nutritious* Quixie cherry cola. Talk about a subliminal message.

Suddenly, she heard the loading dock door open behind her and the familiar tap of heels and that overly loud voice.

"Well, hey," she heard Celia say. "What on earth are you doing, Annajane?"

Reflexively, Annajane shoved the top on the file box.

"Just cleaning out my office," she said, struggling to her feet.

"I'm so glad you're doing that!" Celia exclaimed. "I promised Tracey we'd get the office spiffed up before she moves in, but the last time I peeked in there, I realized we'll have a lot of work to do before the painters can come." She favored Annajane with one of her twinkly smiles. "I realize you've still got another week to work, but that's really just a technicality. I was hoping you'd get the place emptied out a little early. I know Davis wouldn't mind if you quit a few days earlier."

In other words, Annajane thought, *"Here's your hat, what's your hurry?"*

Annajane forced herself to return something like a smile, without Celia's phony wattage. "That's very sweet of you, but I wouldn't dream of taking off work until I get every last loose end tied up. And I've still got lots I need to accomplish, especially with the summer sales promotion."

In other words, back off, bitch. I'll leave when I'm good and ready.

"Well," Celia said reluctantly. "I guess you've got a better grasp of those kind of nitty-gritty details than me. Mason and Davis really want me focused more on the big-picture stuff."

Like selling off the company? Annajane wondered.

Annajane pointed at the cartons on the loading dock. "While I was emptying boxes I did find some interesting old files and old bottles I think Mason might want to keep."

Celia looked as fresh as a daisy. She wore a pale gray-blue sleeveless sheath that showed off her tanned arms, a chunky silver chain necklace, matching earrings, and gray-blue kitten-heel mules that brought her up to just about chin level with Annajane.

"Throw it all out," Celia said, waving a hand in the direction of the Dumpster. "I swear, this place has mountains of old crap that these people have been hanging onto since God knows when. And don't even get me started with Cherry Hill. Do you know that Sallie told me she actually still has all of Pokey's old baby dresses? What is it with you Southerners? Doesn't anybody ever throw anything away down here? Don't even bother Mason with that junk, please. He's got enough to worry about these days."

He sure as hell does, Annajane thought.

Instead, she gave Celia a pleasant smile. "I've thrown out most of it, but if it's all the same to you, I think I'll just box up some of the stuff and take it home myself. Sort of a memento from my time with Quixie, you know?"

"Really?" Celia said, cocking her head and crossing her arms. She looked Annajane up and down and shook her head. "I wouldn't have thought you'd be sentimental about something like your ex-husband's family's business. But then, I can't pretend to understand much about your arrangement, which even you have to admit is pretty unusual."

So now the claws come out, Annajane thought. *Mee-owwww.*

"I was born in Passcoe, and my daddy and my stepfather both worked for the company. And Mason and I had a life together," Annajane said finally. "Quixie was an important part of that, even after the marriage was over. Some of our times were good, some of 'em not so good. Just because I'm moving away doesn't mean I want to forget all of it."

"Help yourself, then," Celia said. She stepped daintily over the pile of advertisements.

14

Look who I brought!" Annajane announced when she walked into Sophie's hospital room. She held up the DVD so Sophie could see it.

"*Milo and Otis!*" the little girl cried.

Annajane brushed a kiss on Sophie's forehead and looked over at Mason, who was sitting in a chair at his daughter's bedside. "Is she being a good patient?"

"She's an awesome patient," Mason said, standing. "She's letting the nurses take her temperature and pulse and check her incision, and she just had a little Jell-O for lunch. Here," he said, gesturing toward the chair he'd just vacated. "Have a seat and I'll put in the movie."

As he was fiddling with the controls for the DVD player, the hospital room door opened.

"Aunt Pokey!" Sophie said. "We're gonna watch *Milo and Otis*."

"Thank Gawwwd," Pokey said dramatically, dropping a large pink beribboned gift bag on Sophie's bed tray. "I haven't seen *Milo and Otis* for hours and hours."

Sophie was tearing the tissue and ribbon from the gift bag. She held up the slightly dingy pink plastic purse that was her most treasured possession. "My pocketbook!" she exclaimed. She unsnapped the catch and took a quick peek at the contents.

"You left it in my car," Pokey volunteered. "I threw out the chicken nuggets because they were getting a little, um, stinky. But you can keep everything else."

Pokey looked over her niece's head to Mason. "She had one of my lipsticks, the baby's silver teething ring, some beer-can pop tabs, a key that I don't recognize, and an empty Altoids tin."

"Treasures," Sophie said, tucking the pocketbook under her blanket. She dove back into the gift bag, exploring the rest of her loot. "New crayons!" she exclaimed, holding up a box of sixty-four Crayolas.

"And some coloring books. Pocahontas, Little Mermaid, Sleeping Beauty."

Mason picked up one of the books and laughed. "How did Spider Man get in here with all these Disney princesses?"

"That's a gift from those brutish boy cousins of hers," Pokey said. "They seem to feel that Little Mermaid is strictly sissy stuff."

"Can you stay for a while?" Mason asked his sister quietly. "Letha's insisting on spending the night in the room with Sophie, but I sent her home to get a shower and some rest. I've got some stuff I need to do at the office. I'll be back in an hour."

"Why not?" Pokey said. "Pete took the boys out to ride around on the ATV around the lake. They won't be home for hours and hours. With any luck," she added, with a wink to her niece.

"Now it's just us girls," Pokey said, perching on the side of the hospital bed. "I love movie night with the girls. Think the nurses would make us popcorn if we ring that buzzer of yours, Sophie?"

"I can only have Jell-O. And apple juice," Sophie reported sadly.

"Never mind," Annajane said. "We'll have popcorn and Milk Duds next time for girls' movie night. And Quixie, of course."

"When?" Sophie asked, not missing a beat.

Pokey looked at her best friend and raised one eyebrow. "Yes. When, Annajane? Soon?"

"Pretty soon," Annajane amended. "Maybe Aunt Pokey will bring you to Atlanta to visit me after I move, Sophie. And we can have a whole girls' movie weekend."

"I don't want you to move to Atlanta," Sophie said plaintively.

"Me neither," Pokey added.

"Thanks," Annajane said, rolling her eyes. "Let's just watch the movie now, okay? We'll worry about coming attractions later on."

Ninety minutes later, with Otis and Milo trotting bravely across country, while Sophie snored softly, Pokey eased off the bed, stood, and stretched.

She glanced at her watch. "Ugh. This is what I hate about being pregnant. I'm always hungry. Have you had lunch?"

"I could eat," Annajane admitted. She moved over to the bed and smoothed a strand of Sophie's hair behind her ear. "Do you think we should leave her like this?"

"Mason should be back soon," Pokey said. "Anyway, she'll probably sleep for at least another hour after that last dose of pain meds."

They were getting ready to slip out of the room when the door swung open and Celia stepped inside. She held a huge stuffed pink rabbit under one arm and a plastic-wrapped slab of wedding cake in one hand, with a bobbing bouquet of balloons in the other.

"Oh," Celia said, taking a half step backward when she saw Annajane and Pokey. "Oh. Hi."

"We were just leaving," Pokey said, taking Annajane by the elbow and steering her toward the doorway.

"Where's Mason?" Celia called.

"Isn't he with you?" Pokey asked innocently. "He left here nearly two hours ago."

Celia frowned and put the bunny, cake, and balloons on the table by Sophie's bed. "He was supposed to meet me here."

"You know Mason," Pokey said with a shrug.

Outside, in the hallway, Annajane gave Pokey a stern look. "You know he's just out running errands. Are you trying to start trouble between Mason and Celia?"

"Yes," Pokey said. "I am. It was only by an act of God that they didn't get married yesterday. So now, I aim to do everything I can to get this wedding completely called off. Forever."

"You're crazy," Annajane said, walking as fast as she could through the hospital corridor. "And it won't do any good. By now you know Celia. She's unstoppable. She gets what she wants. And she wants Mason."

"Tough shit," Pokey said, trotting along beside Annajane. "How long have you known me?"

"Too long," Annajane muttered.

"How long?"

"Going on thirty years, God help me," Annajane said.

"Do you remember Toni? With an I?"

Annajane wrinkled her brow, trying to remember anybody from their shared past named Toni.

"I give up. Who was Toni?"

"Toni the Pony," Pokey prompted. "When we were ten?"

"Ohhhh, that Toni," Annajane said. "Poor old thing. How old did she live to be?"

"She was seventeen when she just laid down in the pasture and went to sleep," Pokey said proudly.

"And how does Toni the Pony have anything to do for your loathing of your future sister-in-law?" Annajane asked.

They'd left the hospital and were in the parking lot, headed, by unspoken mutual agreement, for Pokey's Land Rover.

"Do you remember how Toni came to live at Cherry Hill?" Pokey asked, sliding into the front seat of the unlocked car.

"You wanted a pony. Your daddy bought you a pony. That's how things usually worked in the life of Pokey Bayless," Annajane said.

"Not just any pony. I wanted Toni. I guess you've forgotten. Mama hired some company that had pony rides to come out to Cherry Hill for my tenth birthday. Remember, we had the cowgirl theme?"

Annajane laughed. "I just found my monogrammed cowboy hat and personalized cap pistol when I was packing stuff last week. And I still didn't throw them out, for some reason that escapes me right now. Your mama did throw some amazing birthday parties, that's for sure."

"The company brought four ponies to my party. And Toni was just . . . pathetic. She was so skinny, I wouldn't let anybody get on to ride her. She had sores on her neck, and her eyes were all runny. I begged Mama to get Daddy to buy her for me, but Mama wouldn't even consider it. She pointed out that Toni was about half-dead."

"So you went to your daddy."

"Exactly," Pokey said, nodding. "Daddy agreed with Mama. Said I already had a dog and a cat and a lizard, and we didn't even have a place to keep a pony, which was ridiculous, because we totally had a fenced-in pasture and the old dairy barn out at Granddad's farm."

"It's coming back to me now," Annajane said. "You pitched a fit and didn't quit."

"Toni would have died!" Pokey said. "She was sick, and those awful people treated their animals like crap. I begged and I pleaded. I got that woman's phone number and called her up and told her I was gonna report her to the police for being mean to animals."

"You were ten," Annajane said, marveling at the memory. "How on earth?"

"I just knew I was the only person who could save Toni. I told Mama I would never ask for anything else the rest of my life. I prayed every night that they would buy Toni for me. I went on a hunger strike, refusing to eat."

"Of course you ate when they weren't looking," Annajane reminded her.

"But not dinner," Pokey said. "I kept it up for a whole week, pestering and whining and carrying on, until I finally wore Daddy out and he bought Toni just to shut me up."

"You got your way," Annajane agreed. "So that's the moral of this story?"

"Toni came to live in a stall I fixed up for her at the farm. We got the vet to see her, and she got healthy and fat and happy, and I rode her every day until I got too tall to ride her without my feet dragging on the ground. So Toni lived out a long and happy life. And that, my friend, is the moral of this story. Never underestimate the power of Pokey Bayless Riggs, especially when it involves something or somebody she loves."

"Hmm," Annajane said. "You know I am your biggest fan and best friend for life, right? But you may have met your match with Celia."

Pokey whipped the Land Rover into the parking lot at the only restaurant in Passcoe that was open on Sunday. The Smokey Pig. She put the car in park and turned to give Annajane an appraising look. "You know something you're not telling me?"

Annajane shrugged. "I was in my office this morning. At Quixie. Trying to get some last-minute memos and reports out. I had my door closed, but I could hear her as she was walking down the hallway. You know how loud her voice is."

"Celia?"

"Yeah. She was talking to somebody on her cell."

"About?"

"I only heard one side of the conversation," Annajane admitted. "She was telling somebody named Jerry that they had to go slow—because these people's business was their life."

"People—as in us?"

"That's what I assumed," Annajane said. "Look, I don't really know what they were discussing."

"But you have an idea. Let's hear it."

"She talked about Davis—and how since he's the middle child, he always thinks he has something to prove to the world."

"Ain't that the truth," Pokey said under her breath.

"And that he was in favor of whatever Celia and her pal were discussing— because he wants to spread his wings, because he has bigger plans for himself. And she said she thought Davis was the key to the deal."

"Good old Davis," Pokey said. "Always scheming something. What else?"

Annajane laughed. "She said it might be tricky because the younger sister— you—didn't really like her very much, but that you probably have a substantial ownership interest in the company."

"Quixie!" Pokey exclaimed. "You think she was talking to this guy about trying to sell Quixie?"

"I don't know," Annajane said. "Maybe?"

"Son of a bitch," Pokey said slowly. "What else did you hear?"

"Nothing. She walked on past my office, and then my phone rang, and it was Mason asking if I was going to come to the hospital because Sophie was asking for me."

It was another beautiful spring day, so they found a wooden picnic table on the patio and placed orders for two Smokey specials—sliced pork, cole slaw, and potato salad. The waitress brought them jelly jars full of sweet iced tea, and they waved and greeted neighbors and acquaintances.

"We have got to stop Celia," Pokey said, leaning across the table to keep from being overheard.

"Stop her from what? We don't even know that she's up to anything," Annajane pointed out.

"First, we stop her from marrying my brother. Then, we stop her from whatever nefarious other plot she's scheming in that adorable little blond head of hers," Pokey said with a scowl. "This is war."

"We don't even know what she's up to."

"So we'll figure it out," Pokey said. "You're smart and I'm conniving. Are you in, or are you out?"

Annajane took a long sip of her iced tea. She plucked a package of Town House crackers from the basket on the table and picked nervously at the cellophane wrapper.

"I care about Quixie," she said finally. "And I care about you and the family, really I do. Especially Sophie. But let's be honest here. I don't actually have a dog in this hunt."

"You admitted to me yesterday that you still have feelings for Mason," Pokey protested.

Annajane sighed loudly. "I should have kept my big fat mouth shut."

"But you didn't. Anyway, you didn't have to tell me. It's written all over your face. You're still in love with Mason. And you still work for Quixie."

"Only until Friday. Although Celia suggested earlier I should get the hell out right away because she's having my office painted for my successor."

"And you said?"

Annajane gave her a conspiratorial grin. "That I couldn't possibly vacate the premises that early."

"Good for you," Pokey said. "Until Friday, you're still on the company payroll, so you actually do have a dog in this hunt. If Celia is plotting to take over the company or sell it off to the highest bidder, or whatever, this is an emergency. You have to help."

"You're being overly dramatic," Annajane said. "Maybe Celia was talking about something else entirely. I only heard a few sentence fragments, and we can't be sure . . ."

"Hey!" Pokey said, interrupting. "Oh my God." She held her hand over her heart, as though she were having palpitations. "I just realized we've both over-looked one incredibly important fact."

"That you can save a pony's life by nagging your parents?"

"No," Pokey said, a slow smile spreading across her round pink face. "I think we're both forgetting how much my daddy loved you."

"I'm not forgetting that," Annajane said. "Your daddy was always wonder-ful to me. Treated me like I was his own daughter."

"He sure did," Pokey agreed, nodding her head for emphasis. "He loved you so much he gave you your own stock in the company as a wedding gift, didn't he?"

Annajane's mouth fell open. "You're right. I had forgotten. Five hundred shares. He drove over to my mama's house the morning of the wedding. He wouldn't come inside, but I went out on the porch and he handed me an enve-lope, and kissed me on the cheek and told me I'd made him a very happy man. I didn't even know what a stock certificate looked like before that."

"You never gave the stock back, right? Not in the divorce or anything, right?"

"I still have it," Annajane said, sitting back in her chair. "I hadn't thought about it in ages. And I bet Mason hasn't either."

"So there's a chance Celia doesn't know you own stock in Quixie," Pokey said.

"It's just five hundred shares," Annajane pointed out. "A drop in the bucket compared to what you all own."

"True," Pokey said. "Still, down the line, that could be important. We won't know until Mr. Thomas meets with us about that stupid trust agreement. Right now, we've got to figure out what Celia is up to. And then we have to get Mason to open his eyes and see her for the scheming, manipulative little bitch that she is. And get him to realize he still loves you."

"In a week," Annajane said. "No problem. Easy. Peasy. We should be able to get that done by Monday lunchtime."

"We need to do some research on Celia," Pokey went on, ignoring Annajane. She reached into her pocketbook and brought out a pen. "What was the name of her company?"

"Gingerpeachy," Annajane said.

Pokey was making notes on the back of her paper placemat. "And it sold to who?"

"I think the company is called Baby Brands," Annajane said. "I guess I could look up the announcement of the deal on the Internet."

"Do that," Pokey said, scribbling. She put down her pen. "Who do we know that might know something we can use against Celia?"

"I don't know anybody," Annajane said. "She's not from around here, didn't go to school in the South. This is impossible. Celia's from a whole different world from us."

"Don't be such a defeatist," Pokey scolded. "Come on, think, Annajane, dammit."

"I think Celia is from Nebraska," Annajane said. "Do we know anybody in Nebraska?"

"We don't know anybody who even knows where Nebraska is, probably," Pokey said. "But I'll google Celia's name, just in case. Who knows? Maybe she's a wanted murderess. In the meantime, one of my sorority sisters is a buyer for Belk's. Maybe she'd know somebody who knows somebody. I'll give her a call."

"It's too bad we can't ask Davis what he knows about all this," Annajane said.

"Ha! He's the one we have to thank for bringing that pit viper into the family bosom in the first place," Pokey said. "Davis thinks Celia is 'awesome.'" She made finger quote marks.

"And you can't really ask Mason any questions about Celia," Annajane said. "What about your mama?"

Pokey toyed with a forkful of coleslaw. "Are you kidding? Celia's the daughter Sallie never had! Let's see. She's beautiful and skinny, plays tennis and golf, always looks perfect, and she's got an adding machine instead of a soul. Yup, Celia's everything I'm not. Mama's even giving her bridge lessons. Plus, she sucks up to Sallie every chance she gets. It's revolting."

"Hey," Annajane said sharply. "You're beautiful. Inside and out. You're a great wife, friend, mother, sister. You're what Celia will never be."

Pokey blew her a kiss. "Back atya."

"How do you think Sallie would feel about the company being sold, or moved, or whatever?"

"Good question," Pokey said. "If Daddy were still alive, the answer would be a big 'hell no!'"

"But he's not."

"I know," Pokey said. "She's always talked about Quixie being our family legacy. But if this were something Mason wanted, or if Davis convinced her it was a good idea, she might just go along with it."

"But it's not something you'd agree to, right?"

Pokey stared at her best friend. "Not in a million years. Not for a billion dollars. My brothers may think the grass is greener someplace else, but I don't. Passcoe is home. We were raised here. I intend to raise my own children here. And I don't intend to let anybody change that. Not without putting up a hell of a fight."

"That's what I thought," Annajane said, smiling.

"And what about you?" Pokey asked. "You're supposed to be leaving town Friday. That's what you keep telling me."

"I'd hate to see anything happen to Quixie," Annajane said, trying to choose her words carefully. "If the company got sold, or moved, or swallowed up by a bigger company, it could be devastating to Passcoe. I'm like you. No matter where I go or what I do, this is my hometown. And Quixie is a huge part of that. It's a part of me and who I am and what I've been doing for the past eight years. Yeah, I know it's just cherry soda. But I don't want to see Quixie get swallowed up or closed down. I can't promise anything, but I can make some phone calls, and ask around. I want to find out what Celia's up to."

"And if she's up to what we suspect?"

"I don't know," Annajane said.

"Have you talked to Shane? Did you tell him about Mason's wedding?"

"We talked late last night," Annajane said. "I didn't mention the wedding. Didn't think it was important. Not to Shane, anyway."

"I see," Pokey said.

"No you don't," Annajane said with a moan. "This is all just a big mess. And I don't know how to fix it. He wants me to move in with him, Pokey. As soon as I get to Atlanta. And he doesn't see why we should wait til fall to get married. I tried to explain to him, everything is all happening so fast. I love him, but I want it to slow down. Just a little."

"Are you sure that's all it is?" Pokey asked.

"Yes. No. I can't explain how I feel. Something's just . . . making me want to hold back. Maybe I'm just gun-shy about marriage, after what happened with Mason."

"No," Pokey insisted. "You are gun-shy because you don't really love Shane. You're still in love with Mason. And you're scared to death to admit that Shane is rebound guy."

"Oh Gawwwd," Annajane said, burying her head in her hands. "You can't be right."

"But what if I am?" Pokey asked.

15

Sophie's eyelids fluttered. She yawned widely and looked around the room.

"You're awake," Celia said brightly. "Did you have a nice rest?"

"Where did Annajane and Aunt Pokey go?" Sophie demanded. "We were watching *Milo and Otis*."

"You were sleeping, and they had to leave," Celia said. "But look what I brought you!" She propped the huge stuffed bunny on the pillow next to Sophie.

"Thank you very much," Sophie said politely, clutching the teddy bear the nurse had given her the night before and ignoring the bunny.

"You're welcome," Celia said. She whisked the plastic off the plate of wedding cake she'd placed on Sophie's dinner tray. "And look at this beautiful cake I brought you. It's our wedding cake!"

"It's pretty," Sophie said.

"Shall I get you a fork?" Celia asked. "We can ring the nurse and get her to bring one. And maybe some nice cold milk."

"No," Sophie said, shaking her head. "I'm only 'lowed to have Jell-O. And apple juice."

Celia laughed. "Who told you that?"

"Daddy."

"Oh, well, daddies don't know everything," Sophie winced as Celia's tinkly laugh filled the room. Mason pushed through the door. "What's this?" he said, trying to sound stern. "Since when don't daddies know everything?"

"I was just about to tell Sophie it wouldn't hurt for her to have a little piece of our wedding cake and some milk," Celia explained, snaking her arm around Mason's waist.

"She actually isn't allowed to have something like that," Mason said.

"See!" Sophie smirked.

"Sophie . . ." Mason said, trying to look stern. "That's not nice. Celia didn't know the doctor doesn't want you having much in the way of real food just yet—this soon after surgery."

"Oh," Celia said. "Well, of course. In that case, we'll just freeze some cake for her, and she can have it later, after she comes home from the hospital."

"I don't like wedding cake," Sophie said stubbornly.

Celia cocked her head and considered the little girl. "How do you know? I'll bet you've never even tasted wedding cake."

"Have too!" Sophie shouted vehemently. "Have too, have too, have too."

"All right," Celia said with a note of resignation. "If you say so, that's fine."

"She was a flower girl at my cousin's wedding last summer," Mason said. He gave Sophie another stern look. "But that is no way to talk to Celia. I'd like you to tell her you're sorry for being rude."

"I'm sorry for being rude," Sophie said. She pulled the sheet up until it completely covered her head. Her voice was muffled. "Now go away."

Celia shrugged and reached for her pocketbook. She patted Sophie's sheet-covered knee. "All right, lamb-chop. I'm going now. Feel better fast so we can bring you home!"

Mason shook his head. "I'll talk to her," he said in a low voice. "She's not herself."

Celia arched one eyebrow. "If you say so."

"I'll call you later," Mason said, kissing her cheek.

"Tell Celia good-bye, Sophie," Mason said.

"Good-bye, Sophie," the little girl singsonged.

. . .

Mason was sitting in the living room, reviewing a memo about maintenance costs for the Quixie truck fleet when he heard a key turn in the front door.

Celia bumped the door open with her hip. She was carrying a large sack of groceries and had an overnight bag slung over her shoulder.

"Let me get that," Mason said, jumping up to take the packages from her. He kissed her cheek and glanced at the contents of the sack. "What's all this?"

"Dinner for two," Celia said, heading for the kitchen. "You haven't eaten already, have you?"

"Uh, no," he said, following her into the kitchen and hoping she wouldn't find the greasy brown paper takeout bag from the Smokey Pig. "I was waiting to see what you wanted to do."

He put the groceries down on the kitchen counter. Celia wound her arms around his neck. "I just want to spend a quiet evening all alone with my man tonight. I want to cook him a gorgeous dinner, and drink some gorgeous wine, and later on, maybe show him just what he missed out on last night."

"You mean like a wedding? Hey, it's gonna happen. We just have to get Sophie . . ."

Celia gave him a coy smile. She unzipped the overnight bag and presented, with a flourish, a filmy black scrap of fabric, only slightly larger than a handkerchief. She held it up to her torso.

"I mean like a wedding night. I thought since you didn't get to see this last night, maybe we'd have a showing tonight."

Celia kissed him, and he kissed her back, and she pressed herself tightly against him, and his body responded in a predictable way.

"Mmm," Celia purred. But she pulled away. "Now don't try to distract me," she said, wagging a finger at him, as though he'd been a naughty schoolboy. "I have to get this dinner going."

Mason leaned back against the counter. "Need me to do anything?"

"Not really," Celia said. "I thought we'd just have a big, juicy pan-seared steak and some baked potatoes and garlic-creamed spinach. I looked up the recipe from that steak house in Charleston that you love. Oh, and a salad."

Celia removed a head of romaine from a plastic bag and rinsed it under the faucet.

"Mase?"

"Hmm?" He was staring out the kitchen window at a robin hopping around on the grass outside. He'd talked about putting in a garden out there. It was nice and sunny, but Celia didn't want the lawn disturbed, and, anyway, she'd informed him that tomato cages and pepper plants looked "trashy."

She hesitated. "I had a call from an old friend last week. I think maybe you might have met him around? Jerry Kelso?"

Maybe if he put the tomato plants in some nice wooden planter boxes or something? That wouldn't look trashy, right?

"Kelso?" He frowned. "The president of Jax Snax? You know him?"

"Davis introduced us at a marketing thing in Houston a few months ago."

Jerry Kelso was a name that had been on Mason's mind for weeks. Ever since Kelso requested a confidential meeting six weeks earlier. He hadn't said anything to anybody about the meeting, and was hoping that might be the end of the issue. But apparently, it wasn't going to be.

"Oh, yeah," Mason said. "Now I remember the name. What's up with Kelso? He trying to recruit you away from Quixie?"

She laughed the tinkly laugh, and it sent a shiver down his spine, as though someone had walked over Mason's grave. What was up with that?

"As if I'd leave Quixie. Or you."

"As if," Mason agreed.

"Did you know Jax Snax is the second largest packaged chip and cookie baker in the Eastern U.S.?" Celia asked.

"I knew they were big, but not that big," Mason said, wondering why they were having this discussion.

"They just bought out Cousin Ruth's Old-Tyme Chips and Pretzels, that company out of Knoxville," Celia informed him. "You've seen their stores; they're in all the malls."

"Yeah, maybe I read about that somewhere in one of the trade magazines," Mason said, trying to sound noncommital. "Didn't they buy another company at around the same time?"

Pole beans would be good. He could make tepees from bamboo for them to climb on. Pole beans weren't trashy looking, were they?

"Monster Cookie," Celia said. "They sell those enormous chocolate chip and peanut butter cookies you see in those jars at the convenience stores."

"That's the one," Mason agreed. "Looks like Jax is on a buying binge, huh?" He was mentally surveying that scraggly patch of lawn outside the kitchen window. Maybe he'd take a ride over to the garden center next weekend; if the weather stayed decent, he could put in a garden by Good Friday, which was when his granddaddy always planted.

Just how well did Celia know Jerry Kelso?

"A huge Dutch grocery conglomerate just bought a big chunk of Jax," Celia said. "They're pretty flush with cash right now. Jerry was saying they'd really love to add a soft drink company to their business mix. You know—Pepsi and Frito-Lay are the same company, so it makes sense."

That got his attention. "You've been discussing selling Quixie with Jerry Kelso?"

"No," Celia said hurriedly. "Of course not. Jerry just mentioned it. So I thought it would be worth mentioning to you. I mean, with Jax's saturation of the chip market—especially in convenience stores, where we're trying to grow Quixie, I thought it was an interesting idea. There's the potential for amazing synchronicity. That's all."

"Synchronicity, my ass," Mason said, his tone sour. "They'd like to gobble us up, spit us out."

"It's just something to think about. Don't get yourself all worked up," Celia said, wrapping her arms around his waist. "I don't want us to talk about business tonight. It's our wedding night, remember? Forget I even mentioned it."

"I will," he assured her. "Quixie is not for sale."

She changed the subject in a hurry. "I saved some of your chocolate groom cake from the wedding. It seemed like such a shame to throw it out. I thought we'd have it for dessert."

"Fine," Mason said, leaning back against the counter. "Sorry I jumped on you. Need me to do anything?"

"Not a thing," Celia said, unwrapping the steaks. "I have everything completely under control."

"As always," Mason said. He regretted it the minute the words were out of his mouth.

She wheeled around to face him with a mock pout. "What exactly is that supposed to mean?"

"Nothing," Mason said. "It's a compliment. You're the most organized, efficient woman I've ever met."

She frowned, and a deep crease appeared between her eyebrows. "Honey, it doesn't exactly sound like a compliment to me. You make it sound like I'm some kind of control freak or something."

"Not at all," Mason said. "Look, let's not fight, okay?"

Celia centered the romaine on a cutting board and began whacking at it with a large sharp knife. "This isn't a fight," she said, slamming the knife's edge against the hapless romaine. "It's a constructive conversation. If we're going to make this marriage work, we have to get things out in the open, Mason. So, I need you to know that it hurts me when you make derogatory comments about me." She took another whack at the lettuce, sending bits of it flying.

"I'm sorry," Mason said, picking a piece of romaine from his eyebrow. "I don't want to hurt you."

"See?" she said brightly. "Communication. It's the key to everything."

"Right," he said, feeling his jaw muscle twitch.

She sighed dramatically. "Sweetheart, while we're on the topic, I really think we need to talk about Sophie, and the way she spoke to me today, at the hospital. She treats me as though I'm the wicked stepmother—and you know I've gone out of my way to treat her like my own child."

Mason winced, and his jaw twitched again. Twice. "She's just a little girl, Celia. And remember, she just had surgery."

"I know, poor little angel. I just think you need to be a little stricter with her. Or let me deal with her, when it's an issue that affects me." She gave that little laugh again. "Honestly, I know everybody means well, but between you and Pokey and Annajane, you've all managed to spoil the child rotten."

"Spoiled?" One of his dark eyebrows shot upward. "Sophie's a nice, normal little kid. Somedays she acts out, cuts up. But that doesn't make her spoiled."

Celia began scooping the lettuce into a wooden bowl. "Look. I get that she feels threatened by me. I mean, Sophie's been daddy's girl her whole life, and she's had you all to herself. Until I came along and changed everything. I totally understand that. But I need you to back me up when it comes to disciplining her."

"Let me get this straight," Mason said, his fists clamped tight on the countertop. "You're calling Sophie spoiled and me spineless? Is this your idea of a constructive conversation?"

"No!" Celia cried. "Oh, I'm just no good at this. You know I adore Sophie. But I think she'd be happier with some guidelines. I want her to see me as an equal in her parenting. Mason, I'm sorry. I shouldn't have said anything at all. Never mind. I don't want our nice evening spoiled."

Celia gathered up the discarded steak wrappings and lettuce bits. She flipped the trash can lid to dump them in and spied the large Smokey Pig take-out bag. She held the bag up for Mason to see. "What's this?"

"Lunch?"

"Mason!" She dropped the bag back into the trash and put her hands on her hips. "You've already eaten dinner, haven't you? Why didn't you say something?"

"More like a late lunch," Mason protested. "But it was hardly anything. I'm still starved."

"You're just trying to humor me," Celia said. She dumped the bag and food scraps into the trash with a huge, martyred sigh. "Never mind. I'll just fix myself a salad. Will you still want dessert?"

"I had lunch hours and hours ago," Mason said. "Besides, you haven't eaten, have you? Come on, let's fix dinner together." He picked up the steaks. "You want me to grill these?"

"No," Celia said petulantly. "It'll take too long for the coals to get ready. I'll just pan sauté them." She grabbed a skillet from the pot rack hanging over the kitchen island and dropped it onto the range.

Mason took a step backward. "I'll open some wine. White, right?"

"Never mind the wine." Celia drizzled olive oil into the pan and turned on the burner. "I'm getting one of my stress headaches. The last thing I need now is wine."

But wine was what he really, really needed right now, especially if she was getting one of her headaches. He opened a bottle of burgundy and poured a hefty serving into one of the fancy ultrathin Riedel wineglasses they'd gotten as a wedding gift. At the last moment, the lip of the wine bottle clinked against the goblet. *Ching.* A wedge-shaped chunk of glass fell neatly onto the countertop.

"Damn," Mason said. He opened the cupboard and reached for his favorite cut-glass old-fashioned tumbler and transferred the burgundy out of the ruined Riedel.

Before he could stop her, Celia swept the wine glass into the trash. "It's all right," she said. "I can always order more from the store in Charlotte."

"Sorry," Mason said under his breath. "I'm gonna get out of your hair now. Call me if you need me to do something." He picked up his wineglass and retreated to the study.

But not a lot of studying got done. He made notes on the margins of the reports, began working on a draft of a memo to Davis, and read more e-mails, but from the clatter of pots and pans and the slam of cupboard doors coming from the kitchen, he could tell things were not going well.

He googled Jax Snax on his computer and was amazed by the number of hits his search brought up. Jax had been on a shopping binge for sure. Just within the past year, in addition to the cookie company and potato chip outfit Celia told him about, Jaz had bought up a family-owned soft-pretzel baker out of Pennsylvania called Dutch Uncle and a popcorn outfit from Iowa called Poppinz'. As he scrolled down the list of stories mentioning Jax Snax, he spied a reference from *Beverage World* that was only two months old. He clicked on the citation and read with alarm.

Jax Snax CEO Jerry Kelso confirmed that his company is on the hunt for a small-to-average-sized regional soft drink bottler to add to their mix of businesses. "We've got the expertise, the distribution channels and the proven success story in the convenience food business," he said in a recent interview. "We're looking at several options right now, including one novelty soft drink bottler in the Carolinas that we think could be ripe for the picking."

Mason slapped the cover of his laptop.

"Celia," he hollered.

She didn't answer. She was still out in the kitchen banging pots and pans around. He didn't get the big deal about dinner. He didn't get her compulsion to prove to him that she could cook. There were restaurants in Passcoe, not a lot, but enough that they'd never starve. They belonged to the country club and could eat there any night except Mondays, when the club was closed, and, anyway, he was a pretty decent cook himself. He'd fended for himself all those years after he and Annajane broke up, hadn't he?

"Damn!"

He looked up to see Celia standing in the doorway, holding her cell phone and looking supremely pissed off.

"Something wrong?"

"Your mother just called," Celia said. "It's my aunt Eleanor. She was napping in her room, and Sallie went to check on her, and according to your mother, there's something wrong with Aunt Eleanor's breathing."

Mason stood up abruptly. "Do we need to get a doctor? Take her to the hospital?"

"Who knows?" Celia said. "She's in her nineties. I don't know why she insisted on coming down here all alone for the wedding if her health is this precarious. I could just strangle my cousin Mallery for putting her on the plane."

Mason reached for his car keys. "Come on. I'll drive you over to Cherry Hill. We can call Max Kaufman, and if need be, he can come over and check out the old girl."

"I don't want to bother you," Celia said. She had her pocketbook over her shoulder and her car keys in hand. "It's probably nothing. I'll call you if I need you."

"What about your dinner?" Mason asked. "Can I just put it in foil or something for later?"

She glanced in the direction of the kitchen, her lips pursed. "I'm sorry, darling. Just pitch it out."

16

Mason exhaled slowly. Was Celia upset with him? She was usually so sweet and accommodating. What had gotten into her lately? She'd left in a huff. If she'd stayed, he would have had it out with her over this Jax Snax thing. She knew more about the subject than she'd told him. This was no casual bit of gossip. Celia didn't do casual. Maybe she just thought it best to alert him to the fact that they were being checked out by another company. No harm, no foul, right?

He should feel bad about their dinner, he knew. After all, her wedding had been spoiled, and her prospective stepdaughter was being a little bit of a pill, and now her great-aunt might be sick. Really sick.

Upon reflection, he realized he didn't actually feel bad at all. Probably this made him a terrible person, certainly a terrible husband-to-be. He should call and apologize, at least drive over to his mother's house and insist on helping her take care of her aunt, or *something*. But right now he really just wanted to do what he wanted to do. And hadn't she just called him spineless and his daughter spoiled, in a roundabout kind of way?

So he strolled out to the garage, found his golf clubs and some whiffle balls, and went out to the side yard, to that scruffy future garden plot. For an hour or so, he practiced putting because his short game sucked. He didn't think about postponed weddings, or pissed-off brides, or why he seemed to take such perverted pleasure in pissing off his bride to be. But he did feel something, unease, maybe, about the fact that he was actually feeling relieved that Celia's big night with him was probably not going to happen. He was a totally shitty husband-to-be, for sure.

After he'd worked on his putting, it was still daylight, and there was still at least another hour of warm, buttery sunshine left. Without giving it much thought, he got in his car and drove over to the bottling plant. He let himself into the garage, found a clean rag, and dusted a film of thick yellow pollen off the red Chevelle. Had it been that long since he'd driven the fun car? He got in and fired her up, doing a silent fist-pump when the engine throbbed to life. He put the top down and carefully backed it out of the garage.

Ten minutes later, he was tooling around Passcoe, seeing the sights, tooting his horn at anybody and everybody he recognized. He felt really, really good. But, and this surprised him, maybe a little lonely.

What he needed was a passenger. Somebody who could share his appreciation for just how cool it was to drive around on a beautiful spring evening with the top down. He reached for his phone, and without giving it much thought, tapped the icon for Annajane's cell.

Wrong. He disconnected before her phone could even ring. He drove another block and reconsidered. Why the hell not? It was just a car ride, for God's sake. He tapped the icon again, and at the next block, swung the Chevelle back in the direction of her loft. All she could say was no, right?

Annajane's cellphone rang once. The screen lit up, and she saw that it was Mason calling, but he'd disconnected before she answered.

She held the phone in her hand and stared at it. Should she call him back? Act as though she didn't know he'd called? She felt like a stupid teenager. She started remembering all the Friday nights she'd spent, staring at the phone, fantasizing about picking up the phone and hearing Mason's voice on the other end of the line. She remembered the sleepovers at Pokey's house and how she'd sneak into his empty room when the rest of the household was asleep, studying his books, his bed, the football and baseball trophies casually lined up on the shelves. She remembered the notebooks she'd filled in high school, practicing her signature: Mrs. Mason Bayless, written in stupid, girly flourishes. While she was remembering all the things she missed about being a stupid teenager, the phone rang. Mason, again. She let it ring three times and then answered.

"Hey, Annajane," he said.

"Hey, Mason." She felt herself blushing with pleasure. "How's Sophie?"

"She's good. Sleeping. So, there's something I was wondering about. We're okay, right?"

"Okay?"

"You know. As friends. We've been through some stuff together. Good and bad."

Annajane laughed ruefully. "That's the understatement of the year. But yeah. I'd say we're okay now. Mind if I ask why you're asking?"

There was a long pause at the other end of the line. "I don't know. This is just so weird. I guess I'm sad that you're leaving town. Leaving the company."

"That's sweet. But you've known for months that I was leaving the company and moving to Atlanta. And getting remarried," she reminded him.

"Yeah, but none of that seemed real until today. I went by your office at the plant, and I saw all the moving boxes and stuff."

"It's real. I've sold the loft. I'm finishing up packing right now," she lied. "Friday's my last day."

"I wish you'd stay," he blurted out.

Annajane held up the phone and stared at it. *Who was this guy? Were they really having this conversation? Mason had never once expressed any regrets about her leaving—not him, and not the company. No regrets, that's what he'd always told her in the past.*

"Staying is not a good idea," Annajane said. "Not for me. It probably wasn't a good idea for me to stay in town after we split."

"I don't know why you say that. I mean, yeah, it was a little awkward at times, but I think we managed to keep things on a pretty professional level. You don't think we could keep that going?"

No, she wanted to scream. *We cannot keep things going while you're married to Celia, because I want to throw up whenever I see you two together. We cannot keep things professional because I cannot keep telling myself I'm over you when I'm pretty sure I'm not over you.*

"This isn't about any of that," she said finally. "It's not about you and me, Mason. That's over. This is about me getting a great job offer and really challenging myself. It's about me starting a new life with Shane. Maybe even starting a family. I think it's time, and I think I deserve some happiness. You should be happy for me. I'm happy for you."

Liar, liar, pants on fire.

She heard him inhale and then exhale. "Hey," Mason said. "You're not doing this because you're pregnant, right?"

That's when she disconnected the phone and tossed it onto the sofa. Annajane stomped into the sleek galley kitchen and, spying the bottle of Maker's Mark she'd left on the counter Saturday morning, poured herself two fingers of bourbon, which she drank, straight up. She heard her phone buzzing from its resting place among the sofa cushions. It stopped buzzing. She poured a little more bourbon in the glass and, not wanting to become a sloppy drunk, thoughtfully added some ice cubes to the glass, forcing herself to sip slowly while the phone buzzed softly in the other room.

17

Mason banged his head on the Chevelle's steering wheel. Once, twice, three times. He needed to knock some sense into his own skull. What the hell was wrong with him? Had he really just suggested that Annajane was only getting married because she was knocked up? He massaged his forehead and tried to call her again. Of course she wasn't answering. He looked up at the second floor of her building. The lights were on. He redialed. Nothing.

He should go home, he knew, but he didn't feel like being alone, and he couldn't leave things with Annajane like this. He got out of the Chevelle, squared his shoulders and approached the inset entranceway to her loft apartment. The real estate listing sign had a cheery SOLD! placard attached. He scowled at it and pressed the intercom buzzer. Once, twice, three times.

He looked up and down the street. It was deserted. Sunday night in Passcoe. You could have fired a cannon down the middle of the street and not hit anybody. He put his finger on the intercom buzzer and left it there.

"What?" Her voice sounded tinny, but unmistakably pissed.

"I'm sorry," he said. "Really. Can I come up? I really need to talk to you in person. To apologize."

"No. Go away."

"Annajane?"

Silence.

He leaned his back against the faded gray brick wall and considered his next move. He was feeling desperate, not an emotion he was used to, especially when it came to women. Come to think of it, the last time he'd felt this shitty, this desperate, was when Annajane left him for good.

Mason rang the intercom buzzer again.

Her voice came on. "What?"

"Please let me come up," he said, enunciating each word. "Just let me apologize in person, and then I promise not to bother you again."

"All right," she said finally. "Let's get this over with."

She heard his footsteps echoing in the stairwell. He knocked once. Annajane unlocked the door and looked Mason straight in the eye. "You're a pig," she said stonily. "And for your information, no, I am not pregnant. Asshole."

"You're right, I am a pig," he agreed. "A swine."

He stepped inside the loft and looked around. "This is really nice," he said, sounding surprised. "I've never been in one of these places."

"Walk around. Enjoy the view. Because I'm outta here come Friday," she said, trying her best to sound mean. Why was it so difficult to be mean to Mason, even when he was being such a monumental jerk?

"You told me you were all packed," he said pointedly, gesturing around the decidedly not-packed-up room.

"I lied," she said. "So sue me."

"Can I sit down?"

"Whatever."

"Here?" He pointed at the sofa, which was covered with stuff.

She moved a stack of books from the sofa and gestured for him to sit, but she stayed standing, arms crossed defiantly. What she needed now was a position of power. "You were saying?"

"I needed to tell you face-to-face. What I said to you was inexcusable," Mason said, sounding miserable. "I'm sorry, Annajane. I don't know why I'm being such an asshole, when all I really wanted to do was say I'm gonna miss you.

And not just because you're great at your job and I'm worried about what's gonna happen at Quixie without you. Sophie and I are gonna miss you, Anna-jane."

He looked up and gave her that dopey sad-dog look of his.

She returned his look with steely resolve not to get sucked into the charm that somehow managed to ooze from every pore of his body with absolutely no effort on his part.

"Thank you," she said tartly. "I'm sure the company will survive without me. I hate the idea of not being around Sophie, but Pokey has promised to send me lots of pictures. Was there anything else?"

"Well, I did have an idea. But probably you don't want to hear it now. Because I'm such a major dickhead and everything."

Momentarily putting aside the need for power, she perched on the edge of the armchair opposite his. "I'm listening."

"It's a gorgeous evening," Mason said. "I actually came over here to ask you to come out and go for a spin in the Chevelle with me. Would you even consider that? For old time's sake?"

She felt her heart thudding in her chest. The memories came rolling over her like a tidal wave. The two of them, riding through the night in the fun car, top down, headed for the beach, back to their lake cottage, or even just to the Dairy Dog for soft-serve ice cream. Anywhere at all. Against her will, she felt the corners of her lips tilting into something like a smile.

"Annajane? Is that a yes?"

She sighed, and tried to force herself to think about reality. Those golden memories of hers were just that. Memories. Tricky and totally unreliable. They should be packed away like all the books and old clothes she'd bagged up for giveaway to the Goodwill. From now on, she was going to live in the here and the now. Right?

"I don't know if that's such a good idea."

"Why not?"

"What would Celia think?" She deliberately avoided the question of what Shane might think.

He shrugged. "I don't know. Maybe I don't care."

She raised one eyebrow. "Really?"

He stood up and walked over to look out the window onto the street. It was dusk, and the street lights were just winking to life.

"What is this about, exactly?" she asked, afraid to hear his answer.

"Does it have to be about anything? It's a gorgeous night. We're old, old friends. Can't you just come out and go for a ride with me? Just for the hell of it. I swear I'll be nice."

Annajane felt herself caving. What would be the harm in going for a ride on a beautiful spring night with an old friend? Old lover. Old husband. Whatever. She looked down at herself. She was dressed in tattered jeans with the knees ripped out, an old oversized Atlanta Braves jersey, and a pair of red Chuck Taylor high-tops. Her hair was pulled back in a headband. "I'm not really dressed to go out."

He turned and smiled. "You look fine. Great, actually. Do I recognize that jersey?"

She blushed. Why had she hung onto this ratty old shirt? In fact, it was his jersey, as he well knew. His lucky jersey, he'd called it.

The first spring after they'd gotten engaged they'd driven down to Atlanta for the Braves home opener. Mason bought her a sun visor and himself a jersey at the game, but their team had lost steam early, and by the seventh-inning stretch, with the Braves losing eight to zip, they'd left, returning to their cheap hotel not far from the stadium, telling themselves they'd watch the end of the game back in their room. It never happened. At his request, she'd modeled his jersey for him, doing a slow striptease while Mason did his own X-rated play by play of her performance. For the rest of that summer, she'd worn the jersey for him every time they made love. His lucky jersey had nothing to do with baseball and everything to do with sex.

She should burn the jersey.

Yeah. Right.

Mason obviously sensed her indecision.

He held up the car keys and jingled them tantalizingly. "I'm parked outside. C'mon, Annajane, for once, don't overthink things. Let's just go for a ride, can we?"

"What the hell," she said finally. She had all week to pack. It was, as Mason had said, a gorgeous night out. She shoved her phone in her pocket, grabbed her keys, and walked right out the door, with Mason following closely on her heels. She closed and locked the door in a hurry, before she could, as he'd put it, overthink things.

Annajane swept a film of cobwebs from the dashboard. "Wow," she said. "When was the last time you drove this thing?"

Mason turned off Main Street and onto Seventh, rolling past Willard's Feed and Seed, the Family Dollar Store, and a couple of boarded-up storefronts.

Seeing the vacant buildings made him sad. He could remember the name of every single business on that street. His father traded at Passcoe Hardware, and his mother always bought their school shoes at Fashion Shoe Shop, which she'd said was a joke, because the owners had zero sense of fashion. Cline Drugs was still hanging in there, but the soda fountain at the back was closed, and the last time he'd been in the store, the shelves looked more like a museum than a functioning store. His family had made a point of doing business at those stores because the owners were neighbors and friends. Passcoe was hurting, just the way Quixie was hurting. He hated to think about what would happen if Quixie left town.

"Mason?" Annajane snapped her fingers in front of his face. "Anybody home?"

"Sorry," he said, returning to the here and now. "I haven't driven the old girl for a few months," he admitted. "I've been pretty busy at work. And Celia hates this car. She refuses to ride in it. So I've been keeping it in the garage at the plant."

"But you used to love this car," Annajane said. "What's to hate about a classic convertible?"

"She says it's a pimp car," Mason said. "And as she points out, it doesn't even have air-conditioning."

"Hmm," Annajane said. She slung an arm on the open window and leaned back into the headrest. "So, where are we headed?"

"I thought we'd ride out to the farm," Mason said.

Cherry Hill Farms wasn't a real farm anymore, and hadn't been since Sallie's father, Sam Woodrow, passed away in the 1980s and the family had sold off the last of his cattle and horses. The last Annajane had heard, the old farm-house was being used as hay storage for the tenant farmer's cows.

"That sounds nice," she said.

Mason slid a cassette into the tape deck and "Walk This Way" blasted out of the speakers.

"Mötley Crüe?" Annajane rolled her eyes.

"Aerosmith!" Mason said, chastising her for her rock ignorance. "Root around under the seat there and find something else if you don't like it," Mason said, secretly disappointed in her musical taste.

"I like Aerosmith sometimes. Just not tonight. Have you got anything . . . mellower?"

Mason reached over the backseat and found a battered leather box that he plopped in her lap. "Here. Pick your own damn music."

Annajane opened the box gingerly. "Okay, let's see what you've got. Wow, this is like a for-real time machine. Led Zeppelin, Santana, Blue Öyster Cult. Were you even born when these guys started playing?"

"Those bands, madam, are rock classics," he said. "Ageless and timeless."

She held up a tape with a bright purple case. "John Denver. Really?"

He snatched the tape out of her hand and stowed it safely under his seat. "That's Sophie's. I think she saw him on an old *Sesame Street* rerun."

Annajane laughed. "I can't hate her for that. C'mon, give it back. Tonight's perfect for John Denver cheese. A little 'Sunshine on My Shoulder' maybe. Or some 'Rocky Mountain High'?"

"Nope," he shook his head. "You've hurt my feelings. I'm afraid you'll have to find your own mood music."

She leafed idly through the tapes, pausing to look out at the deep green countryside flashing by.

"Maybe later," she said. She threw her head back and enjoyed the feel of the wind whipping through her hair.

But she couldn't shake the need to know what had brought about Mason's unexpected visit. And she desperately wanted to know what had happened between the happy couple. She stole a sideways glance at Mason. He looked as happy and relaxed, as unguarded, as she'd seen him in years. And years.

"What's going on between you and Celia? Not that it's any of my business."

Mason shrugged. "Nothing really. She was annoyed that I ate a late lunch, and then she was annoyed because I broke one of our wedding-present wine-glasses. I think I kinda wrecked her plans for our big evening together."

"Where is she now?"

He laughed. "At my mom's. Her aunt had some kind of spell, and you know Sallie. She's not exactly Nurse Nancy. She called and issued a summons, and of course Celia went."

"Nobody, not even Celia, ignores a summons from Sallie Bayless," Anna-jane agreed.

Mason laughed. He'd forgotten how easy Annajane was to be around. Effort-less. With Annajane there was no subterfuge, no hidden messages. She was as open and real as . . . well, he didn't know. Just easy, that's all.

How the hell had things gotten so complicated, so quickly, with Celia? He felt like he was treading on broken glass every time they were together lately.

"Let me ask you something," he said. "Do you think I spoil Sophie?"

Wow, Annajane wondered. *Where was this coming from?*

"Spoil?" She repeated the question, stalling for time. "I don't know. I don't think so, but I'm probably biased. Sophie's . . . she's special, you know? She was so tiny, and so needy, when you first brought her home. I guess maybe some people might say you went a little overboard. But she's your daughter! And she is the sweetest, smartest, most loving little girl in the world. She doesn't ask for a lot. And it's not like she really plays you or manipulates you."

Mason was nodding thoughtfully as she spoke, so Annajane took a deep breath and asked a question of her own.

"Does Celia think Sophie's spoiled?"

"She thinks I should be firmer with her," Mason said. "Sophie was kind of rude to Celia today at the hospital. You know, pulling her covers over her head, not talking to her, that kind of thing. Kid stuff, really. But it really got under Celia's skin."

Annajane was tempted to fire off something clever or flippant about evil stepmothers. But something made her hold back.

Sophie's only five, but she's no dummy. She could tell Celia was trying to buy her off. And she can spot a phony, even if her clueless daddy can't. Tread cautiously here. Think before you open your mouth.

"Well," Annajane said finally. "Discipline and rules and politeness, those are things every child needs. It's not like Sophie to be rude. Maybe that's something you and Celia are going to have to work on together."

Mason nodded. "Yeah, probably you're right. Guess I shouldn't be so touchy, huh? Anyway, it's too nice a night to get into all this heavy stuff. We'll work it out. Eventually."

Hope not, Annajane thought.

18

When they got to the turnoff for the farm, Mason swung the car easily into the graveled drive. Lights glowed from within the old white-painted farmhouse, and a battered pickup was parked in the shade of the tin-roofed shed that had once sheltered tractors.

"Somebody's living here?" Annajane asked.

"You remember Grady Witherspoon? Maybe not. He was a little older than me. Went in the navy right out of high school, and I guess they've lived all over the world. He and his wife moved back last year. They're renting the place. He's planted one of the old cornfields, gonna be selling organic vegetables to some of the fancy restaurants over at Pinehurst. At least that's the plan."

The Chevelle bumped along over the rutted dirt road that skirted an old pasture gone to weeds. Waist-high pine-tree saplings lined the rusty barbed wire fence. More than once, the high-beam headlights caught a deer bounding gracefully across the path, and junebugs and moths seemed to float in the still, cool air. Finally, Mason pulled the car alongside a weathered outbuilding.

"What is this place?" Annajane asked, half-rising from the seat to get a better look. It had been years and years since she'd visited the farm.

"It's the old corncrib," Mason said. "It's about to fall in, along with the rest of the buildings out here. Davis and I used to bring sleeping bags and camp out here back in the days when we deer hunted together. We thought we were Daniel Boone and Davy Crockett."

He cut the engine and they let the quiet settle over them. It was a country kind of quiet, lush and deep and green, Annajane thought, with cicadas sawing away and the hooting of an owl echoing from a nearby treetop.

"Do you and Davis still hunt together?" Annajane asked, shivering involuntarily at the sound of the owl.

"No," he said, and she thought she detected a note of regret in his voice. "The only deer he's chasing these days are the kind spelled d-e-a-r. We actually don't do much of anything together anymore, except bicker."

"About the company?"

"That, and other stuff," Mason said. "Lately, I look at him and have to wonder how we could be so completely different and yet come from the same set of parents."

"Davis definitely marches to his own tune," Annajane said, trying to be diplomatic.

"That's part of the problem," Mason said darkly. "We're supposed to be running a family business. I keep trying to remind him of that, but it doesn't do much good. If he had his way, Quixie would be a division of some giant chemical company, and he'd be sitting in a penthouse office in Manhattan. But that wasn't my grandfather's vision for the company, and it sure wasn't Dad's. Nor mine. Jax Snax, my ass."

"Jax Snax?" she asked. "The potato chip company?"

"You won't say anything to anybody, right?"

"Of course not."

He cleared his throat. "They're making noises about buying a controlling interest in Quixie. Nothing formal yet, just talk. But some numbers have been floated. The people I've talked to say it's a decent offer. Not great, but decent, considering our recent sales slide."

She wondered if she should disclose the conversation she'd overheard Celia having earlier at the plant. Did Mason know his bride to be was in cahoots with his baby brother?

"Would you sell?" Annajane asked.

"It's kind of a moot point right now," Mason said. "You know Dad's biggest fear was that after his death the company might get broken up or sold off. He'd seen it happen to other family-owned companies, seen the kinds of feuds that erupted between siblings, and he was bound and determined it wouldn't happen to Quixie. Or to us. Which is why he put the company ownership in an irrevocable trust that would prohibit any discussion of a sale until after he'd been gone for five years."

Annajane raised an eyebrow. "I didn't know that."

"The rest of the estate was settled after Dad died," Mason said. "That part was pretty cut and dried. He left Cherry Hill to Mama, and Davis and Pokey and I got what we got. But none of us realized, until we met with Norris Thomas, Dad's lawyer, that he'd left it so that Quixie couldn't be sold. Not only that, he instructed Norris that the exact details of the trust couldn't be disclosed for five years."

"It's been more than five years now," Annajane pointed out.

"The clock on the trust didn't start ticking until April fifteenth, which was when the will was probated," Mason said.

"What's that mean for Quixie?" Annajane asked.

"In the short term, it means no sale," Mason said. "After that, we don't really know. Norris told me himself that Davis has been pestering him about the trust for a couple months now—probably ever since the Jax Snax people started talking about a deal. Davis even threatened to sue to get the trust arrangement revealed early, but Norris is a stubborn old bastard. He's sitting tight. He says he'll meet with all of us next week—on the fifteenth, and not a day before."

"Why all the secrecy?" Annajane asked, studying Mason's face for any clues. "I mean, your dad always said he was leaving the company to you kids, right? So I don't understand why he'd make y'all wait five years to find out exactly how everything would play out."

"You knew Dad. He was a poker player his entire life. He always liked to play his cards close to his chest. And to tell you the truth, I think he probably liked the idea of controlling us from beyond the grave."

"And your mama doesn't know what's in the trust agreement either?" Annajane asked.

"Nope. She swears she can't get Norris to tell her a thing. And believe me, she's tried everything up to and including bribery and death threats."

Annajane grinned. "How's that sitting with Sallie?"

"She's been pissed about it for five years," Mason admitted. "But there's not a damned thing any of us can do about it."

"I guess selling the company would mean a lot of money," Annajane said.

"That's why Davis is so fired up. A sale would make us all rich."

She coughed politely. "Pardon me for stating the obvious, but you're already rich."

"Moderately wealthy," Mason corrected her, laughing at himself. "On paper, anyway. Don't forget, Dad took on a lot of debt when he bought that land in Fayetteville. That's what Mama would prefer we be called. But Davis definitely would prefer to be rich. Filthy, stinking rich."

"What *does* Sallie think of all this?" Annajane asked.

"She's playing it cool. She says she'll listen to any offer. But she's gonna have to hop off the fence pretty soon. The Jax offer is looking like a reality, and if our costs keep rising and our sales keep sinking the way they have been, they may cut their price, or just go away for good."

"Would that be a bad thing?"

"We can't keep going the way we have been," Mason said. "We've been in a holding pattern since Dad died. Maybe it's my fault. I'll admit I've been reluctant to make any drastic changes."

He lowered his voice. "Not long before he died, Dad hired a food chemist to come up with some new flavors of Quixie. To extend the brand. He'd tasted and liked the key lime and pomegranate, but hated the peach soda. He'd pretty much made up his mind to do it—roll out one new flavor a year. But then he had the heart attack and died."

"So you put the plans on hold," Annajane said. "Probably wise, given the economy."

"Maybe," Mason said, sounding dubious. "Or maybe I'm just chicken. I keep worrying, what if I screw it up? And then I start second-guessing myself. That's no kind of leadership. Something has to give. That's all I know for sure."

He turned and gave her a half smile. "But none of this is your problem. In a way, I envy you. You can just walk away and start over. Do your job, cash your paycheck, clock out on Friday, and forget about it until Monday."

"Theoretically," Annajane said.

"Yeah," he agreed. "I guess maybe you'll never be a wage slave. You care too much about stuff."

"Way too much."

He yawned and stretched and slipped his arm easily along the back of the seat.

"Sophie is gonna miss you like crazy when you move," he said, deliberately changing the subject.

Annajane felt a sharp stab of sadness. "Leaving her is the hardest thing about making this move," she said. "God, I'm going to miss her. More than you know. Do you think Celia would let her come and visit me in Atlanta? Maybe with Pokey? I really can't stand the idea of not having her in my life."

"I don't think she'd have a problem with that," Mason said. "More importantly, I wouldn't have a problem with it. You're family to her. Always will be, if I have any say in the matter. Which I will."

"Thank you for that," she said earnestly. "I mean it. I guess it's weird to fall in love with your ex-husband's child. I didn't mean to, but not loving Sophie? That would be impossible."

They heard the owl hooting again, and Mason craned his neck to try to figure out where the bird might be perched.

"What about Shane?" he said, trying to sound casual. "How do you think he'd be with having your ex's kid hanging around?"

"I've told him how much Sophie means to me," Annajane said. "Shane loves children. And he doesn't have a jealous bone in his body. Anyway, he'll be traveling most of the summer."

"So . . ." Mason strung the word into two syllables. "You've set the wedding date?"

"Not exactly," Annajane said. "Shane wants to get married right away, but I'd really like to get settled in first. You know, new apartment, new job, new town. It's a lot, you know?"

"You're not moving in with him?" Mason sounded surprised.

"Why do people keep asking me that?" Annajane snapped. "Why do I have to live with him? Just because we're engaged? Do I have something to prove?"

"Not to me," Mason said quickly. "Seems to me you just met the guy. Why rush? In fact, I'd say you definitely should not live together."

"You and Celia have been living together for months," she pointed out.

"That's different."

"How?"

"I don't know," he sounded impatient. "It's not like I planned for Celia to move in with me. It just sort of happened. She left some clothes at my house, and then the place she was renting at first was so far from the office . . . Are you going to get mad at me if I tell you I don't think you're that kind of girl?"

Annajane smiled to herself in the dark, turning away from Mason so he couldn't see her reaction.

"I won't get mad if you mean that as some kind of twisted compliment."

"I do!" Mason said. "Of course it's a compliment. You act like I never say anything nice to you."

"Do you?" She swiveled around on the leather seat to face him.

He sighed. "Don't I?"

"No," she said decisively. "You haven't said anything, well, nice to me, in a personal way, in a really long time. You say things at work like, 'good job' or 'great idea.' Sometimes you copy me on an e-mail with a thumbs-up emoticon. But that's not really a compliment, Mason."

He nodded slowly and took a deep breath. "Okay. Maybe I'm just *thinking* the compliments. And I got out of the habit of saying them out loud." He paused. "Or maybe I got worried about what other people would say if I, you know, paid you special attention."

"People? Or Celia?"

"Celia," he said.

"Why would Celia care if you're nice to me? I'm certainly no threat to her."

Mason rolled his eyes. "That's not what she thinks."

Annajane had to think about that for a minute.

"Jeez," Mason said. "This is getting pretty heavy here. I think I could use a drink." He pointed at the dashboard in front of her. "See if my flask is still in there, would you?"

How like him, she thought, to want to distract her once things got uncomfortably personal. She thumbed the latch of the glove box, and its contents slid onto the floorboard. She rooted around in the heap: some gas station receipts, a messily folded map, some old cassette tapes, and, finally, a handsome chased-silver flask with its characteristic inverted shape molded to fit in a gentleman's hip pocket.

"Here it is," she said, holding it up. She unscrewed the cap and sniffed.

"You still drink Maker's Mark?" she asked, referring to the brand of whiskey he'd favored during their marriage.

"It's Blanton's these days," Mason said. "Celia introduced me to it. Try it out."

She took a deep drink of the warm whiskey, letting it glide slowly down her throat.

"Pretty good," she said reluctantly, before handing it over.

Mason sipped, nodded, and then drank deeply, wiping his mouth with the back of his hand.

"You and Celia were thick as thieves when she first came to Passcoe. But something happened. You really just don't like her now, do you?"

Instead of answering, Annajane took the flask and helped herself to another gulp of the amber liquid.

"Not much," she said, grateful for the courage the whiskey afforded. "But be fair. What do you think she thinks of me?"

"Pass that back," Mason instructed. He drank again.

"She thinks it's pretty weird that you'd hang around and work for me, for Quixie, that is, after we split up."

Annajane laid her head back against the cool leather of the headrest. "I guess a lot of people would agree with her. It certainly has inspired a lot of discussion around Passcoe."

"Who cares?" Mason asked. "Why can't people mind their own business? You're great at what you do. You're a huge asset to the company. In fact, I still can't quite figure out why you're leaving. You know, aside from the Shane thing."

She reached over and took the flask and drained it in one long swallow. She put the empty flask on the floor and picked up one of the cassette tapes, squinting to see what it was. In the moonlight, she thought the handwriting on the white plastic case looked familiar. It was her own.

Surprised, Annajane held it up for him to see. "Is this what I think it is?"

"What? It's just an old tape. I forgot it was in there."

But you don't keep it with the other tapes. You keep it hidden in the glove box.

Silently, she reached past him and turned the key in the ignition. The headlights winked on, and she slotted the cassette into the tape deck. He switched the headlights off.

Journey's "Faithfully" floated out of the speakers.

She turned to him in surprise. "This is the mix tape I made you all those years ago."

He shrugged it off. "It was a good tape."

She listened to the song and felt the whiskey warm in her belly, and she was aware of a sort of bittersweet longing, only dimly remembered, but now, achingly awful in its power.

Annajane turned up the volume. The song drowned out the cicadas, and the chorus of spring peepers coming from a nearby farm pond, and even the bass line of the invisible barn owl, floating from the treetop.

"You really can't figure out why I'm leaving, Mason? Are you that dense?" She turned in the seat to face him, to see if she could tell what he was thinking.

He bristled. "You're leaving because of Celia? Look, I know you've been unhappy with some of her decisions. And maybe Davis did let her undercut your position in marketing. You know Davis. He can be a bulldozer. But if you'd just come to me, and told me you were unhappy with the way things were going ..."

His voice trailed off. His arm slid down, and his fingertips rested rightly on her shoulder.

She felt her breath catch. Just the barest brush of a touch and she was already dizzy with the sensation.

"I didn't think it would make a difference," Annajane said quietly. "Clearly, you two were getting ... involved."

"Were we?"

"You came about five minutes away from getting married to her yesterday," Annajane pointed out.

"Yeah," his voice trailed off and he looked out into the darkness. "I'm really not sure exactly how that happened, to tell you the truth."

"You're telling me it was all Celia's idea—to get married?"

"No," Mason said. "I wouldn't exactly say that."

"What would you say? Exactly. Come on, Mason. Tell me what's going on here. Give me a clue, can you?"

His hand brushed her cheek. "I'd say I must have been out of my friggin' mind to let things get that far. Yesterday? It all seems so surreal now. I was standing there on the altar, and I saw Sophie walking towards me, and it was like I was in some kind of fog. Then that harp music started to play, and all of a sudden, here comes Celia in that damned white dress. I knew I should have been thinking about her, and how great she looked, and how glad I was. All that stuff. But then I saw you sitting in the pew, right beside Pokey. In your green dress. All I could think was—how did Annajane get in that pew? Why isn't she walking up the aisle, toward me? What happened? What the *hell* happened to us?"

Mason cupped his hand around her chin and stroked her cheek with his thumb.

She was barely aware of the small voice in her head, like an insistent, blinking red warning signal. *Turn back. Turn back.*

But she couldn't have turned back if she wanted to. She was as drawn to Mason Bayless now as she had been as a teenager all those years ago. The red blinking faded in the dark and she was only aware of his nearness and her need.

"My God, Annajane," he whispered. "What's going on? Why can't I let go of you?"

He didn't wait for an answer, which was good, because there was no answer. He leaned in. His whiskey-scented breath tickled her ear. His lips brushed her cheek.

What was she doing? She didn't care. *Don't overthink. It all feels right.*

Just like that, they kissed. So sweet, so slow. Her body had never forgotten his. Her arms went around his neck, his fingers twined naturally through her hair, and she felt a roaring in her ears. Mason pulled her closer, and she willingly went.

His kisses were hot, urgent, relentless. His hands slid down her back, and beneath the fabric of the baseball jersey. His lucky jersey. Effortlessly, he worked his fingers under the band of her bra, finding her breasts, caressing them. His head bent, and he effortlessly pulled the shirt over her head.

The night air came as a thrilling shock to her bare skin. Mason pulled her onto his lap, and she started to giggle at the sense memory of the steering wheel pressing against her back, but the giggle was supplanted by a gasp when his lips found her right nipple.

"Hey!" It was a man's voice, coming from only inches away. Next came the sound of heavy metal clinking against the driver's side door.

Annajane jumped. A beam of bright yellow light blinded her momentarily.

"What the hell?"

She dove off Mason's lap, scrambled onto her side of the front seat, grabbed desperately for the shirt, which seemed to have been swallowed up in the bowels of the Chevelle's floorboard. The glare was unblinking, unforgiving. She squeezed her eyes shut.

"Mason? Mason Bayless? Is that you? How the heck are you?"

The tape was abruptly shut off. The sudden quiet was deafening.

"It's me, Grady," Mason drawled. "How 'bout turning off that flashlight, and giving the lady here a little privacy, huh, buddy?"

Annajane did not dare lift her head. Mercifully, the light was snapped off, and she somehow managed to pull the shirt over her head with trembling hands.

In her mind, the red blinking light had transformed itself into neon foot-high letters flashing out *Damn. Damn. Damn.* And then the words morphed into something worse. *Cheater. Cheater. Cheater.*

"Maybe you could put the shotgun away now too, huh?" Mason said.

Shotgun? Why not kill me now? Annajane thought. *Put me out of my misery.*

She inched as far away from Mason as she could get, keeping her face averted from their clueless interloper.

"Sorry about that, Mason," Grady Witherspoon said with a chuckle. "Gail heard music coming from down here, so I came out to investigate. Since the weather turned warm, we've had kids coming out here, drinking, smoking dope, raising hell. I wouldn't care that much, but last week somebody went ripping through my patch of spring greens, mashed everything flat. Kale, radicchio, arugula. Total loss. You believe that? The gun ain't even loaded. I just wanna scare the little pissants off before they do any more damage."

"Totally understandable," Mason said easily. "I apologize for the disturbance. My bad. We'll just be going now."

But before he could start the Chevelle's engine, Grady Witherspoon craned his neck, walking all the way around the car until he stood just inches from Annajane.

"Don't I know you?" he asked, studying her face with interest. He snapped his fingers. "I got it! Annajane. Annajane Hudgens, right? My little sister used to babysit you when you were just a kid."

She thought her head would explode from shame.

"Hello," she said weakly, wishing the earth would open and swallow her whole.

Finally, Mason started the car. Grady Witherspoon gave them a friendly wave. "Bye now. Tell your mama I said hey, Mason, will you?"

Mason threw the car in reverse. "I'll sure do that."

19

Mason finally glanced over at her once they were back on the paved road. "You okay?"

Annajane buried her face in her hands. "No."

"Hey," he said softly, reaching for her hand. "It was just a kiss. Kinda embarrassing that Grady walked up and surprised us like that. But it was a long, long time coming. I'm not sorry it happened. Only sorry that we had to stop."

Annajane jerked her hand away from his. "We *do* have to stop! What we just did was not okay. It's called cheating. And I won't do it. I can't. You're engaged to another woman. I'm engaged to Shane."

"Allll right," Mason said slowly. "Take it easy. Don't get so worked up. You're getting way ahead of yourself here. Look, Annajane, maybe this, what just happened back there, it was inevitable. Maybe it's time we stopped avoiding each other and start thinking about us. Like we used to be."

Annajane felt her phone vibrating in her pocket. She took it out and glanced at the readout. It was Shane. Talk about timing. She let the call roll over to her voice mail and tried to think rationally about her situation.

She was suffused with shame and guilt and, yes, desperate happiness. Ten minutes ago, she'd been weak and willful. If Grady Witherspoon hadn't arrived when he had, she would have willingly climbed into the backseat with Mason. Her hormones had betrayed her, and she'd betrayed Shane. How could she hurt Shane the way Mason hurt her all those years ago?

"There is no us," Annajane said.

Mason looked at her incredulously. "You're telling me you didn't enjoy what happened back there at the farm? That it means nothing to you?"

"Yes," Annajane said. "That's what I am telling you."

"You've got a funny way of showing it," Mason muttered.

"That's not the point," Annajane said, feeling wretched. "What we just did . . . that was bad . . . it wasn't right. You were mad at Celia, and I was, I don't know, I guess, maybe just feeling vulnerable and sentimental. For the way we used to be. What happened back there, it was just . . . revenge. And horniness."

"What?" he exclaimed, nearly swerving off the road.

"We have no right to be alone together like this," she continued. "I admit, I still have . . . feelings for you. I guess I always will. But there was a reason we split up. It was ugly and awful. We patched things up, yes, and figured out how to go on with our lives, separately, but I can't pretend, Mason. Our divorce nearly killed me."

Mason's hands gripped the steering wheel so tightly his knuckles turned white. "If you'll recall, I never wanted the divorce. That was your idea. I just gave you what you wanted."

Annajane felt the bile rising in her throat, all the old pain stirred up again. "What I wanted was a marriage based on honesty, but that's beside the point now. And it's been so damned hard to make myself give up and move past all that, to move forward. But the things that ended our marriage were real. And as much as I care about you, I can't go through all that again. There's no going back."

"Annajane," he started, then stopped, shook his head. "Maybe you're right. Maybe nothing has changed. You didn't trust me then; you won't trust me now."

"You cheated," she exclaimed. "And maybe I could have gotten past that, if you'd just told me the truth."

"I did tell the truth," Mason said through gritted teeth. "I never, ever cheated on you. You talk about honesty, but if you were honest with yourself, you'd admit you had some responsibility, too, for our breakup. The first time things didn't go your way, you just took off and ran home to your mama. Who I'm sure helped you figure out what a crappy husband I was. Marriage is a two-way street, you know. You talk about trust, but you never did trust me."

The headlights of an oncoming car lit up Mason's face—his jaw was clenched, his eyes unblinking. She'd seen that look before, and it harkened back to the bad old days when their marriage had come unraveled. What had she been thinking? The answer, of course, was that she'd done just what he'd urged her to do—she hadn't thought at all.

"You're right," she said finally. "It wasn't all you. There's a reason we're not together anymore. We were just too different then. And now the gulf has only widened. It's idiotic to think we could make it work again. It's just too late. I'm sorry, Mason. For everything. Then and now."

"Unbelievable," he muttered. "All this fuss over a damned kiss."

The silence was overwhelming. He punched the button on the tape deck, forgetting what they'd been listening to earlier in the evening. When their song came on, he silently cursed and punched the stop button.

The ride back to town was interminable.

Finally, Mason pulled the car up to the curb in front of her loft. He left the motor running and didn't bother to come around and open her door. She'd barely closed the door before he gunned the Chevelle's engine and screeched away down the dark street.

20

Celia dropped her bag and water bottle on the bench outside the tennis court. She sat down and squinted up at the Monday morning sky. Puffy white clouds floated overhead, and the temperature was already warming up. She unzipped her hot pink Nike jacket and bent down to retie one of her shoes. What with all the wedding planning and hoopla, she hadn't played tennis in weeks. It would feel good to get out on the courts and work up a sweat.

"Well, Celia!" Bonnie Kelsey dropped down beside her on the bench. She cocked her head to the side and gave her an odd look. Bonnie swiveled her legs until their knees were touching, and she took Celia's hand and squeezed it.

"Are you all right?" she whispered, looking around to make sure they couldn't be overheard. They were early though, and DeeDee and Jenn, their opponents, hadn't yet shown up.

"I'm fine," Celia said. "Sophie's fine, too. They may even let her come home today."

"Oh yes, well that's a blessing," Bonnie said. "But, well, I meant, how are you? I'm actually surprised you came this morning. You can talk to me, you know. I'm totally discreet."

"Why would I cancel our doubles match?" Celia asked, puzzled.

"Oh, no reason," Bonnie said. She patted Celia's knee. "You're such a trouper. That's what I love about you, Celia. Such a positive outlook on life."

"Bonnie," Celia said, a note of warning coming into her voice. "I have no idea what you're getting at. So you might just as well tell me."

Her tennis partner had the grace to blush and look away. "I'm not one to spread gossip," she said, fiddling with the clasp of her tennis bracelet.

As if, Celia thought. She'd met Bonnie Kelsey and her dippy husband, Matthew, at a cocktail party at the country club the week after she'd arrived in Passcoe, and after three margaritas and two trips to the lady's room in the space of three hours, she'd gotten filled in on the sexual and social history of every single person in the room. Sex, lies, and innuendo were the coin of the realm in the small world of Bonnie Kelsey.

"I know that," Celia said, trying to sound reassuring. "But if it's something that concerns me, don't you think I should be made aware of it?"

Bonnie bit her lip as though trying to make up her mind.

Tell it, sister, Celia thought. *Before I have to choke it out of you.*

"I'm sure there's a logical explanation for all of this," Bonnie started. "Or maybe the person who told it to me got the names mixed up. Although usually, this person is pretty reliable. And the parties involved *do* have a history . . ."

"Please just tell me, for God's sake," Celia said through clenched teeth.

"And you're sure you won't get upset?" Bonnie asked.

Celia's hand was just itching to reach out and yank the bitch's ponytail as hard as she could.

"I'll be fine," Celia said, trying to sound soothing. "It's always better to know than wonder, right?"

"Riiight," Bonnie said.

"The way I heard it," she said hurriedly, "was that Grady Witherspoon—I guess you don't know him—he doesn't really run in our circles? Anyway, he's retired from the service, the navy, I think, and moved back to town and he's renting Miss Sallie's daddy's farm. He and Gail have fixed up the old homeplace really cute, I hear . . ."

"Bonnie?" Celia said, about out of patience. "How does this affect me?"

"Right. As I was saying, apparently Grady and Gail were watching television last night; it was after dark, and they heard music coming from the field down by the old corncrib. And he's had a lot of trouble with the local kids going down there and doing drugs and vandalizing things and so forth. So he got his shotgun and a flashlight and walked down there to check it out. And when he got down there he saw this big old shiny red convertible, and there were two people in it, and they were, uh, well . . ."

Shiny red convertible? As in that horrible old car of Mason's? The one Sophie called his fun car? What was it, a Camaro, or a Mustang, something like that?

Celia tried to keep her composure. "What were the couple doing, Bonnie? And who were they?"

Bonnie clutched both Celia's hands in hers. "Oh honey," she said, her pale blue eyes brimming with tears. "It was Mason. And Annajane Hudgens. And according to Grady, who I believe, because he is a decorated veteran after all, he caught the two of them. In the act."

"In the act?" Celia needed to be absolutely sure she understood exactly what Bonnie considered the act to be.

Bonnie nodded her head vigorously.

"As in?" Celia prompted, wishing Bonnie would let go of her hands.

"You know," Bonnie whispered. "It. They were naked and they were doing it." She lowered her voice again, just to make sure Celia comprehended. "F-U-C-K-I-N-G."

Somehow, Celia managed to keep her composure. But her mind was whirling, going a thousand miles an hour.

The son of a bitch! She should have known something was up between him and Annajane. She'd seen his face at the wedding—just for a moment—right before Sophie got sick—he'd had that awful deer-in-the-headlights look. She'd chalked it up to nerves at the time. But then afterward, when Annajane had commandeered her spot in the ambulance, conned Mason into driving her home from the hospital, Celia should have put a stop to things right then and there. She should have seen that Annajane was still carrying a pathetic torch for Mason.

But she'd had no reason to doubt Mason's faithfulness. He was honest to a fault, disgustingly loyal. Look at the way he kept resisting Jerry Kelso's perfectly acceptable offers for Quixie. The man just loved a lost cause. She would have to do something about Annajane Hudgens, and she would have to work fast. In the meantime, she needed to throw some water on this particularly volatile piece of gossip.

"Mason and Annajane?" she heard herself say, with a careless laugh. "Are you serious, Bonnie?"

Bonnie looked at her as if she'd just sprouted another head.

"That's the silliest thing I've ever heard," Celia said. "I don't know this Grady person, Bonnie, but I can tell you right now he needs to get himself some new glasses. Mason positively could not have been out in some cornfield doing the deed with Annajane last night. Because he was right there at home with me last night, and I don't like to be indelicate, but honey, for all intents and purposes, it *was* our wedding night. I fixed the two of us an intimate little dinner, and then I modeled that little black lace number—you remember the one Jessica Satterthwaite gave me at the lingerie shower?"

Bonnie, the stupid cow, just nodded her head, wanting desperately to believe her story.

Celia rolled her eyes heavenward. "Well, I hate to think what she spent on it, because Mason took one look at that thing and he was like a man possessed." She gave a self-conscious little giggle.

"I made the mistake of modeling it in the kitchen." She rubbed her backside for effect. "All I can say is, thank heaven for throw rugs."

Bonnie's eyes widened. "You did it on the kitchen floor?"

"The kitchen floor, the living room sofa, the recliner in his study," she giggled again. "I think we figured out a new position that La-Z-Boy definitely wouldn't approve of. And that was just the first floor."

"But," Bonnie sputtered. "That red convertible. The old Chevelle. There's no mistaking it. Everybody in town knows that car. Mason's daddy gave it to him for his twenty-first birthday."

"Well that explains it," Celia said. "Mason keeps the convertible in the garage at the plant, and he leaves the keys under the floor mat. Anybody who works at the plant could have decided to borrow it. Anybody at all. Who knows, maybe your farmer friend mistook Davis for Mason?" She raised an eyebrow, daring Bonnie to contradict her. "Everybody knows what a wild hare Davis is."

"That's true," Bonnie agreed. "Davis does have a reputation."

Celia spotted their doubles opponents walking toward them, racquets slung over their shoulders. "Here come the girls," she said. "Let's forget all this non-sense and play some tennis, all right?"

DeeDee and Jenn never knew what hit them. Celia's typically restrained brand of country club tennis was abandoned. She proceeded to mop up the courts with the other two women with an unexpected combination of killer serves and slashing backhands. She made suicide dives for impossible shots, played the net, and roamed the back court, rifling volleys right back in the other women's teeth. The final score was brutal: six-one, six-love.

The putting green at the club was deserted this early on a weekday morning, which was good, because he was in no mood for company. He had a lot to think about. Mason heard the muted toot on his cell phone, letting him know he had an incoming text message. He laid his putter down on the green, took the phone from the pocket of his golf slacks, glanced down at the readout panel, and saw that the text was from Celia.

WE NEED TO TALK. NOW!!!

He felt his gut twist with dread. So she'd heard already. He shouldn't have been surprised. He looked down at the cell, knowing that modern etiquette, not to mention common decency, decried the idea of breaking an engagement with a text, but secretly wishing the deed could be done with just a few taps of the keyboard on his BlackBerry. He knew better, of course.

He removed his golf glove and tapped his reply.

I'LL BE HOME IN AN HOUR.

Mason let himself in the kitchen door, warily peering around the corner to see if the coast was clear. His heart sank at the sight of Celia, seated at the kitchen island. Her face was pale and tear-streaked, her eyes red-rimmed.

"Hi," he said, setting his golf bag down in a corner. He was looking for a neutral opener, an icebreaker. What he came up with was admittedly lame. "How's your aunt feeling?"

"My aunt?" She raised one eyebrow. "You're telling me you care how my aunt is feeling? How about me? How do you think I'm feeling?" Her voice rose to something approaching a shriek, or the closest he'd ever heard Celia come to a shriek.

"Celia, look . . . I'm sorry . . ."

"Do you realize that you have humiliated me in front of this entire town?" she asked, her voice just barely above a whisper now. "I showed up at the club this morning for my doubles match with Bonnie Kelsey, and I'd hardly gotten my racket out of my bag before she pulled me aside, and with this look of pity on her face, *which I will never forget,* actually suggested that, considering the emotional pain I must be in, we might want to forfeit the match."

So, Mason thought dully, it had been Bonnie. He might have guessed the delight she would have taken in sharing the news with Celia.

"I don't know what to say . . ."

She opened her eyes wide. "Tell me it's not true. Tell me you were not with Annajane last night. In a cornfield. Tell me it's all just a hideous lie." Her lower lip trembled and her huge eyes filled with tears. "Please tell me that, Mason. *Please?*"

"Christ," he swore quietly. "It's not true. Well, not exactly."

She held out her hand, like a school traffic-crossing guard. "Stop!" she cried. "Whatever is going on between you and Annajane, if you love me, you'll stop seeing her. For God's sake, Mason, last night was supposed to be our wedding night. What were you thinking?"

He said the first thing that came to mind. The truth. "I guess I wasn't thinking at all. After you left, I went out for a drive in the Chevelle, and things just kind of happened."

"Happened?" She was weeping again, with her head down on the counter, her petite body jerking with every sob. She raised her head. "You just happened to find yourself in a car in a cornfield with your ex-wife, naked? How does that just happen?"

"Nobody was naked!" he said. The thing of it was, he really couldn't explain how any of the previous night had happened. In fact, this morning, when he'd thought about it, he couldn't say with any certainty that it hadn't all been just a whiskey dream. One thing he did know was, he had to find a way to make things right. With Celia, and with Annajane.

"I still care about Annajane," he said finally. "I'm sorry. I guess I just never really got over her."

There. He'd done it. Said it out loud. He felt better. For about five seconds.

Celia's shoulders slumped and she dropped her chin to her chest, as though somebody had knocked the wind out of her body. "Why did you ask me to marry you in the first place?" she asked, her lower lip starting that trembly thing all over again. "If you still had a crush on her? Didn't you ever love me? Even a little?"

"I don't know," he said miserably. "It just kind of happened. I mean, you and I were spending a lot of time together, business lunches turned into dinners, and we had some fun, and the next thing I know, you're moving in with me, and then, all of a sudden, we're engaged."

"What?" she cried. "Are you saying I railroaded you? That the engagement was all *my* idea?"

Yes, actually, now that he thought about it, the engagement was definitely her idea.

"No," he lied. "That's not what I'm saying at all."

"Then what are you saying?"

He sighed. This was not going well. He'd turned the whole situation over in his mind on the way back to the house, and he'd mapped out a compassionate, logical discussion with Celia. He would tell her about Annajane, and she would be hurt at first, but then, being the practical, logical girl she was, she would shed a few tears and then allow him a graceful exit from this whole marriage thing. But so far, Celia wasn't playing fair. She'd turned on the tear tap, full throttle. It was brutal, is what it was.

"I'm just saying," he started. "Somehow, things spun out of control. I thought I was in love with you. I mean, probably I was. Kind of. At some point, I knew I should man up and tell you how I felt, but then, once you started planning the wedding, it kept getting bigger and more elaborate. And then, there was the country club, and the harpist from Atlanta, and that enormous damned cake, and your aunt was flying in . . . I just couldn't . . . I didn't want to disappoint you."

Celia looked like she'd been slapped across the face. "So this is all my fault? Because I wanted a nice wedding day? A day I would have been able to remember my whole life?"

"It's nobody's fault," Mason said wearily. "It just is. Look, I never, ever meant to hurt you, but knowing how I feel about Annajane, how conflicted I am, well, I can understand that you'd want to call off the wedding for good now. Nobody could blame you after the heel I've been."

"Call it off?" Her face crumpled. "For good?"

"It might be for the best," he said, feeling like more of a heel than ever. "We're just too different. We want different things. I mean, you hate my car, and you don't really like living in a small town like Passcoe, and you hate my sister, well, okay, I guess she's the one who hates you, but you know you never really warmed up to Pokey . . ."

He was babbling, and he wasn't normally a babbler. But then he'd never been in a situation like this before, so really, who could blame him?

Mason laid a tender, caring hand on Celia's arm. "Celia, I know this is pretty rotten right now, but believe me, eventually, you'll agree it's all for the best that we didn't go through with the wedding. It never would have worked out."

Celia pushed his hand away and ran from the room. She threw herself onto the sofa in the den, burying her face in the cushions.

Things were happening too fast. She had to step back and regroup. Call off the wedding? Just because she and Mason had a little tiff and he'd gotten sloppy drunk and sentimental and ended up giving his pathetic ex-wife a pity fuck? Oh, no. This was not happening. She would not allow this to happen. Mason was hers, and she would not give him up without a fight. She had a plan, a whole new life plotted for herself, and she'd be damned if she'd give it up now and end up like her wretched, welfare-cheating, coupon-clipping, snot-dripping coven of sisters back in Nebraska. But how to win Mason back, when he was convinced he still carried a torch for somebody else?

She knew Mason, better than he knew himself. Knew what mattered to him. Honor. Loyalty. Fidelity. Family. Doing the right thing. It was what he lived for.

Mason trudged stoically into the den. Just when he'd convinced himself that they were almost through with this unending agony, things seemed to go from bad to worse. Probably he should just shut up and leave and let her cry it out. But maybe not.

He sat on the sofa and rubbed her back. "Heey," he said softly. "I'm so sorry."

She turned and looked up at him and her face softened. "I knew it," she whispered. "In my heart, I knew this wedding, this marriage was too good to be true. I knew somebody like you could never really fall in love with somebody like me."

Even with tears streaming down her face, Mason thought, Celia still managed to look stunning. Her hair wasn't mussed, her nose wasn't running, and her makeup wasn't streaking. It was the damnedest thing.

"I just thought if I wanted it enough, I could make it happen," she said sadly. "And we came so close."

He felt like a heel. Like a jerk. Like a dickhead.

"This isn't your fault," he said, kneeling down awkwardly on the floor beside the sofa so his face would be level with hers. "Don't blame yourself."

Celia sniffed loudly. "No. It's me. I try too hard. I always have. I don't know. Maybe because my folks moved around so much when I was a kid, and because I was an only child, I always thought if I were nice and friendly, and tried to be everything for everybody, they would like me. And I thought if I worked really hard, harder than anybody else, I'd be a success. When I came to Passcoe, I thought it would be just another short-term thing. I'd sold my company; I didn't have anything to prove. But then I met you and . . . fell in love."

She sat up and dabbed at her face with the hem of her tennis top. "I didn't mean to. I'm so stupid. So naive. I really thought we could do something together. With Quixie. That we could build a life together."

"I thought so, too," Mason admitted. He sat on the sofa beside her, took her hand, and squeezed it. "That's what I wanted for us."

Celia tried to smile. "I don't blame you for wanting Annajane instead of me."

More tears welled in her eyes. "She's sweet, and you've known her forever. I just wish you'd figured out things between you sooner. Before I came here and fell in love with you, and Sophie and your mom ... oh God. Sallie has just been so wonderful. Like my own mom, if she'd still been alive."

Oh, Christ, Mason thought. Sallie. She adored Celia. What would she say about this bizarre turn of events? His temples were starting to throb. What the hell had he gone and done?

Now Celia was patting his knee, trying to make him feel better, which actually made him feel much worse.

"Don't worry," she said, her voice wobbly. "I'm not going to make any more of a scene. I'm sorry I carried on. I don't know what's come over me. I guess maybe it's my hormones."

"You had every right to make a scene," Mason said. "And if you want to hit me or something, I'll go out to the garage and get you a wrench. Or a tire iron."

"If I thought it would change anything, I still might," Celia said. She slumped back against the sofa cushions.

"You don't hate me?" Mason asked cautiously.

"No," she sighed. "Maybe I should, but I don't."

"If it makes you feel any better, Annajane doesn't actually want me back," Mason said glumly.

Celia fixed her huge, luminous eyes on his. "She doesn't?"

"No. She said it was all a mistake. That she really loves this Shane guy. She thinks we were both just ... confused."

"Mason," Celia gripped his shoulder with her fingertips, her nails digging into his flesh. "Is ... is what Bonnie Kelsey said, is it true? Were you two having sex?"

"No!" Mason said. "It was just stupid teenage stuff."

"You say Annajane doesn't want you back. But what about you? What do you want?"

"God, I don't know anything." He looked over at her. "Except that I don't want to hurt you any more than I already have. I am truly sorry I've screwed everything up so badly."

"What about us?" She leaned her head on his shoulder. "What happens with us? With all our plans?"

There is no us, Annajane had told him only a few hours ago. She'd been very clear about that. No going back. What was that saying? Love the one you're with?

He turned and, with his fingertip, wiped away one last lingering tear as it rolled down her cheek. "I don't know, maybe just step back and really figure out what we both want. Take things a little slower this time. We can still be friends, right?"

"Friends?" her laugh was shaky.

"Well, really good friends," Mason said. "I still care about you, Celia."

She grabbed his hand. "Do you mean that, Mason? It's really over with Annajane?"

His face darkened. "It really is."

"Thank God," she said fervently. "Because there's something else. I didn't want to tell you like this. I was waiting until after the wedding. I didn't know how you'd feel about it, but Mason, I just can't keep it from you anymore."

Somehow, he knew what she was going to say before the words were out of her mouth. A sense of dread washed over him.

"I'm pregnant," Celia said. "Mason, we're pregnant."

21

When he was eight years old, he and his friend Stevie Heckart stole a package of firecrackers and a box of kitchen matches from Stevie's older brother. They rode their bikes out to Hideaway Lake and took the firecrackers out onto the dock. It was winter and nobody was around. For a while they amused themselves by lighting firecrackers and flinging them into the lake. But then boredom set in and they began looking for a bigger thrill, a bigger bang. They found a rusty coffee can full of nails in the tin-roofed boathouse. They dumped out the nails and put an entire package of the firecrackers in the can and lit it. The ensuing explosion left him numb and deaf for several minutes, with only a vibrating ringing in his ears.

That was how Mason felt after hearing that Celia was pregnant. It was as if the words she'd uttered had been spoken from the bottom of a well, through a wall of water.

She grabbed his arm. "Say something, please. Tell me you're as happy as I am. Because I'm, well, I'm delirious. I'll finally have a family of my own now."

Too stunned to speak, he simply stared.

"Mason?" She grabbed his arm and shook it.

"I thought you were on birth control," he said, when his brain started to thaw.

"I was using birth control," she said. "The patch. But apparently, sometimes things can happen. Remember that upper-respiratory infection I had this past winter? I took antibiotics? They can counteract birth control. And I guess they did. Because here I am . . . pregnant!"

"But . . . when? I mean, we haven't even really been together . . . like that, since you started planning the wedding."

She wrapped her arms around his neck and kissed him. "I know. Which was another reason I was so upset that my plans for last night were ruined. It's been soooo long. But I promise, I'm going to make it up to you tonight." She laid her head on his shoulder and looked up at him from beneath her uncannily luxurious eyelashes.

He continued to stare at her. "How long, exactly? I mean, if you know."

"The ides of March," she said, snuggling against his chest. "I'm due in December. Just think, a Christmas baby."

He looked at her carefully. She didn't look pregnant. She was wearing tight jeans and some kind of stretchy top and her belly was as flat as the palm of his hand. When Pokey was pregnant, she swore you could tell the minute her egg latched onto a sperm. But Celia seemed to be saying she was at least six weeks pregnant and she was no bigger around than a twig. "And you're sure? I mean, have you seen a doctor or something?"

"Of course I'm sure," Celia said smoothly. "I took two of those home pregnancy tests. Plus I saw a doctor in Charlotte the last time I was there."

"Oh," Mason said. He buried his head in his hands. He got to his feet unsteadily. "Excuse me," he said, ever the southern gentleman. He hurried into the powder room and closed the door firmly.

"We have to talk," Mason said, when he finally emerged from the powder room, pale and grim-faced. While he'd been retching, she'd moved into the kitchen, washed her face, and combed her hair. She looked radiant, if that was possible.

"Yes," Celia said, nodding eagerly. "I agree."

He went to the liquor cupboard, pulled out a bottle of bourbon, poured three fingers into a water glass, and downed it in one swallow.

Celia had never seen Mason drink this early in the day. She slid onto one of the leather barstools at the kitchen counter. But Mason remained standing, his backbone ramrod straight.

"There's no easy way to say this," Mason started. "The thing is, even before, well, the thing with Annajane, I guess I'd started to realize maybe we should rethink getting married."

One large tear rolled down Celia's cheek. She turned her head and brushed it away with the back of her hand.

"I'm sorry," Mason said. His shoulders slumped. "I just don't love you. I thought I did, but I don't. You deserve better than that. Marrying me would be the biggest mistake of your life, Celia."

"But, the baby," she whispered, fighting back the tears. "Our family . . ."

He sighed. "I can't lie. The baby complicates things. You said December?"

Celia nodded.

He looked out the kitchen window. A baby. His own flesh and blood. How could he have been so careless? And not just about that. How could he have let his marriage to Annajane dissolve, without a fight? How could he have let the business deteriorate to the point that it was at risk? How could he get himself engaged to a woman he didn't really want to marry? Had he been asleep for the past five years? What would his old man think of the way he'd screwed things up?

"I will, of course, take care of you and the baby," he started to say. "Financially, emotionally, whatever. You'll never want for anything."

Celia was uncharacteristically quiet.

"You don't still want to get married, do you?" he heard himself ask.

She shrugged. "I don't want to force you to marry me." She sniffled a little. "But I never thought I'd be an unwed mother!" And then she was crying again. Loud, gasping sobs. He put a hand on her arm, and she shook it off angrily, refusing to be comforted. "Just leave me alone," she said.

22

Annajane couldn't sleep. She was haunted by the consequences of her actions. By six that morning, she'd decided on a course of action. She had to go to Shane, tell him what she'd done, and ask for his forgiveness.

She threw some clothes into an overnight bag and text-messaged Davis.

"Won't be coming in today. Maybe not tomorrow either. Sorry."

Celia, she thought wryly, would be delighted.

It was a six-hour drive to Atlanta. She welcomed the quiet, the chance to think, the absence of distraction. She watched the sun come up over an emerald-green pasture dotted with horses and an old sway-backed mule and, finally, at eight, gave herself permission to stop at a Bojangles' north of Greenville, South Carolina, for coffee, a biscuit, and a bathroom break.

The restaurant was busy, with construction workers picking up bags of chicken biscuits, office workers lined up in their cars at the drive-through, and two long tables of elderly men who were obviously members of an unofficial coffee klatch.

Her cell phone rang as she was getting back into her car. She glanced at it warily, praying it wasn't Mason, grateful it was only his sister, Pokey.

"Hey," she said.

"Oh my God!" Pokey breathed. "OhmyGodOhmyGod. I can't believe you did not call me."

"I was going to," Annajane said. "But I left at six. I figured you'd probably still be asleep."

"Left where?" Pokey asked, her voice rising with excitement. "Are you telling me you actually spent the night with him? That is the best news I've had in months. Years maybe."

"Spent the night with who? What are you talking about?" But Annajane had a sinking feeling she knew exactly what her best friend was talking about.

"You. And Mason. Last night. Doing the wild thing out at the farm. In the Chevelle."

"Oh, no," Annajane moaned. "This cannot be happening."

"Oh, yes," Pokey crowed. "Believe it."

"Where did you hear it?"

"What's important is who I didn't hear it from," Pokey said. "You! How could you?"

"This is not exactly my finest moment," Annajane said dully. "How did you hear, anyway? Surely not Mason . . ."

"My brother? Be serious!" Pokey said, laughing. "Of course I didn't hear it from him. I did call him right before I called you, but he's not answering his phone, the jerk."

"Then who?" Annajane asked, bewildered. Her face was in flames. "It's only eight o'clock in the morning. How on earth . . . ?"

"Oh, honey," Pokey drawled dramatically. "It's gone viral. You know I walk every morning on the high school track at seven with Vera Hardy, and she was just agog over the news. And then on my way home, I stopped to get milk and cereal and juice boxes at Harris Teeter, and Bonnie Kelsey, that bitch, stopped me by the Pop-Tarts and wanted to know what was going on with you two. Don't worry, though, I played dumb . . ."

"I'm having a nightmare," Annajane said.

They heard a faint beeping on the line.

"Oops," Pokey said. "That's Pete. I'll call you back."

Ten minutes later, she called back. "Pete wants to know if you two could reschedule the wedding before he has to return his tux to the rental place," Pokey reported. "Save him a hundred bucks."

"Not funny," Annajane said. "Did you have to tell him?"

"I *didn't* tell him," Pokey said. "He already knew."

"How?"

"Kiwanis breakfast meeting," Pokey said succinctly. "You know those men gossip like a bunch of old biddies."

"The whole Kiwanis Club knows?" Annajane felt fine beads of perspiration forming on her upper lip and forehead.

"Rotary, too, apparently," Pokey added. "Pete said Davis called him this morning, about to split a gut over it. Davis told Pete he's furious at Mason for disgracing the family, if you can believe it. Talk about the pot calling the kettle black."

"Davis knows?" Annajane felt a stabbing pain in her abdomen.

More faint beeps.

"Oh, Lord, that's Mama," Pokey said. "I've gotta take this. You know if I don't pick up on the second ring she'll pout for days and days."

Please, please, please, Annajane prayed. *Please don't let Sallie have heard. Anything but that. Please.*

But apparently the gods were deaf to her pleas.

"Mama knows," Pokey said, calling back ten minutes later.

"Davis told her?"

"Afraid not," Pokey said. "She heard it at altar guild this morning."

"What all did she say?" Annajane asked, dread in her heart.

"Don't ask," Pokey said darkly.

"I just don't understand how this got out so fast, and so far," Annajane cried. "Mason would never have said anything to anybody, and I for sure didn't."

"Well, that's easy," Pokey said. "Grady Witherspoon! If you wanted to keep your affair with your ex-husband secret, you should have picked a more private place than the farm."

"We are not having an affair! It was a kiss. One stinking kiss."

"That's not how I heard it," Pokey said. "Pete said Watson Bates saw Grady at the feed and seed this morning. Watson told Pete he heard the two of you were going at it buck nekkid in the backseat of the Chevelle."

"It was the front seat!" Annajane objected. "And we were not naked."

"Were you fully dressed?" Pokey asked.

"None of your business."

"Half-dressed?"

"It doesn't matter now," Annajane said, biting her lip. "The truth doesn't matter, because all of Passcoe is now firmly convinced I was having sex with Mason Bayless last night. So that's it. I can never show my face there again. Thank God my loft is already sold. You're gonna have to finish up my packing for me."

"Come back from where? You never did tell me where you are right now."

"I'm going to Atlanta," Annajane said. "I need to talk to Shane."

"To tell him it's over between you?" Pokey said hopefully.

"To confess my sins and ask forgiveness," Annajane said.

"Bad idea. Terrible idea," Pokey said. "Clearly, something, even if it wasn't full-blown, buck-nekkid car sex, is going on between you and my brother. You need to turn around and come back here and get it all sorted out. And then take another ride in the Chevelle to finish off what y'all started last night. Hopefully to a motel or somewhere twenty miles away from the prying eyes of Grady Witherspoon."

Annajane's phone beeped again. "I'm gonna let you get this," she told Pokey. "But please, don't bother calling me back with any more reports of who said what. I can't take any more."

23

Shane's faded blue Aerostar van was parked in front of the cabin. A beat-up bicycle leaned against the concrete-block foundation, and his yellow lab, Wyley, barked once as she pulled the car under the shade of a huge old dogwood with fading pink blooms.

A minute later, Shane stood on the porch, his face alight with pleasure.

"Hey!" he called, grinning. "Awesome!"

Annajane ran from the car and threw herself into his arms. "I've missed you," she whispered into his neck. "I just had to come to remind myself why."

"I'm glad," Shane said, patting her back reassuringly. "Totally."

He rubbed his cheek on hers, the dark stubble scraping against her skin. He was dressed in rumpled khakis and a faded Doc Watson T-shirt, and his feet were bare.

He pulled back a little. "But I wish you'd called to let me know you were on your way. The place is a wreck. They guys and I have been pulling all-nighters, working on stuff for the tour."

"Who cares?" Annajane said. Wyley bumped up against her leg, nudging her hand with his muzzle until she relented and leaned down to scratch his ears.

"See? We're both glad to see you," Shane said.

He retrieved her overnight bag from the car, and they walked inside arm in arm. The cabin was essentially two rooms: a combined living and dining room with a small kitchen L, and a tiny bedroom with adjoining bath.

It didn't look like it had been cleaned since the last time Annajane was there a month earlier.

Newspapers and books littered the floor and tabletops. A guitar and a Dobro were leaned up against the soot-blackened brick fireplace, and the leather sofa and matching armchair were coated in a fine layer of yellow dog hair. The coffee table in front of the sofa held an open laptop computer, a cereal box, and an empty plastic milk jug. Music wafted from a pair of enormous old stereo speakers that served as Shane's end tables.

The tiny kitchen counter and sink held an array of dirty dishes, and the trash can overflowed with beer bottles and pizza boxes.

Annajane wrinkled her nose. "You really do need a woman's touch."

"That's what I've been telling you," he said. "I'm sorry you had to see the place like this, but the guys and I have been working on new material," Shane said. "Wait til you hear."

He swept the newspapers off the sofa and pulled her down beside him. "We've got almost enough material for a new album." He tapped some keys of the lapboard and turned up the sound.

Banjos and fiddle music and a harmonica and three voices, combined in high harmony, with lyrics about pleasing and sneezing, and summer and bummer.

"Nice," Annajane said, nodding her head to the beat. "What's it called?"

Shane beamed. "Ragweed Rag. I mean, this is just kinda the first pass. Corey wants me to finesse the lyrics some. I'm kinda worried about the bass line. What do you think? Too clunky?"

Without waiting for a response, he started the song over again.

"It's good," Annajane said. "But you know I don't know that much about bluegrass..."

"You'll learn," he said, squeezing her knee. "Let me play you the song we were working on last night. Okay?"

"Actually," Annajane said, catching his hand, "there's something important I need to talk to you about. It's why I came down here today."

"Sure," Shane said, still tapping at the computer's keyboard. "Hang on just a sec, can you? Corey just IM'ed me. He's got an idea for the melody for the bridge for one of the new songs." He grabbed his Dobro and started to strum, nodding and pausing.

She got up and wandered into the kitchen and began putting it to rights without giving it much thought. The space was too tiny for a dishwasher, so she ran a sink full of hot soapy water and scrubbed and rinsed and dried virtually every dish, spoon, or fork Shane owned. When the dishes were dried and put away in the one tiny cupboard, she bagged up the trash and took it outside to the garbage can, which was also overflowing with what looked like a month's worth of bagged-up trash.

The bedroom was a disaster. A plastic laundry basket erupted with dirty clothing. The bedding was a tangled knot of threadbare sheets with a worn green sleeping bag stretched across them. And frankly, she thought, the place smelled like a swamp.

"Ugh." She tugged at the window, finally forcing it upward. But the window had no screen, and a fine film of yellow pollen drifted inside. She sneezed but left it open. With a singular motion, she swept all the bed linens into the laundry basket, took them out to the tiny mud porch at the back of the cabin, and unceremoniously dumped everything into the washing machine.

She would not, she decided, be spending the night at the cabin tonight. She would have to find a tactful way to suggest that a night at a nice motel would be just the thing to reignite their romance.

When she'd done all she could in the way of housekeeping, Annajane rejoined him.

Shane was still noodling around on the Dobro, but now he was talking on his cell to one of his bandmates. She recognized that he was in what he liked to call his "groove," and with a shrug, she found a weather-beaten broom and gave the entire house a thorough sweep.

"You don't have to do that, baby," Shane said, glancing up from his playing. He slapped the sofa cushion next to his. "Come sit down. I'll get that later. Didn't you say you needed to talk to me about something?"

"Okay," Annajane said, feeling a lump in the pit of her stomach. *Just tell him,* she thought. *Don't be a chickenshit. Get the truth out in the open, and everything will be all right.*

She sank down onto the sofa and turned to face him. "First off," she said nervously. "I don't want there to be any lies between us. Remember when we first started seeing each other, the promise we made to each other?"

"Right," he said. "No lies. It's the foundation of our relationship."

"Okay, well, the thing is, some stuff has come up with Mason."

"Your ex? Didn't he just get remarried, like, yesterday?"

She took a deep breath. "He was supposed to get married on Saturday, but his little girl got sick right in the middle of the ceremony, so they had to postpone it."

"I'm sorry," Shane said. "Is the kid okay?"

"She had an emergency appendectomy," Annajane said. "She'll be fine. Mason, on the other hand, may not be getting remarried after all."

Shane frowned. "How come?"

"It's a long story," Annajane said. "Celia's all wrong for him, but he's just figuring that out. Better now than later, I guess, huh?"

"Better now than later," Shane said, nodding solemnly.

"Uh, well, then we went out for a long drive together last night," Annajane continued. "And he had a flask of bourbon in his glove box, and I found an old mix tape I made him, from years ago, and I don't know, it might have been the combination of the bourbon and Journey, but I . . ."

"Wait!" Shane interrupted. His eyes were aglow. He grabbed up the laptop and started typing like a fiend.

"Better late than never," he said, humming. "It's genius! That's the bridge lyric, the one we've been trying to nail down all week!"

Now he grabbed the Dobro and started picking. "Better late than never," he sang in a high, nasal twang. "You never promised me foreverrrrrr."

He leaned over and kissed Annajane's nose. "Keep talking, babe. It's all golden. You're my muse. Just tell me what's on your mind, it's like you're opening up my creative floodgates here."

Annajane started over. "One minute we were listening to Journey, and the next minute, Mason was kissing me, and I was kissing him back . . ."

"Journey? Seriously?" Shane put down the Dobro and frowned. "I'm starting to question your musical judgement."

"I *like* Journey," Annajane said. "Or I did at the time. But that's really not the point. The point is, my ex kissed me, and I kissed him back." She sat back and waited for the realization to hit him.

"I see," Shane said. His face was solemn. "Did you say you'd been drinking?"

"Bourbon," Annajane confirmed.

"Alcohol can cloud anybody's judgment," Shane said. "Sometimes I have a few brews with the guys and the next thing I know, I'm watching old Guns N' Roses videos on YouTube and shooting squirrels with a BB gun."

Annajane reached over and gently took the Dobro from her fiancé.

"I don't think you get what I'm telling you here, Shane," she said. "I was alone out in the country with Mason. I willingly went with him. Yes, I was drinking a little bourbon, but to be perfectly honest with you—and I do want to be honest with you—I sort of knew he was going to kiss me before it happened. And I didn't fight him off. In fact, I enjoyed it."

"Jesus, Annajane." His face fell, and she felt as though she'd slapped him.

"I know. I feel horrible," she said. And she did.

Wyley looked from Shane to Annajane. The dog whined and licked Shane's hand, and Shane scratched his ears absentmindedly.

He looked down at the floor, and then, with hopefulness, at Annajane. "So, it was an of-the-moment kind of thing, right? Not something you'd do again, right?"

"Not if I was thinking rationally," Annajane said.

"And when you're thinking rationally?" Shane asked, taking both her hands in his.

"I know it will never work for Mason and me. There were too many issues when we were married before that never got resolved. I'm done with all that."

"You're sure? Really?"

She took a deep breath and let it out slowly. Her pulse was racing, and she could feel her heart hammering in her chest. Finally, fighting back tears, she nodded.

"Okay then," Shane said. He leaned his forehead and rested it against hers. "You had me worried there for a minute, babe, showing up like that, out of the blue." He kissed her. "It's forgotten. Right?"

"Riiigghhht," she said.

As if, she thought.

"I trust you totally," he told her. "What we have together, it transcends petty jealousy. In a week, you'll be down here, we'll be together, and Mason whats-hisname will be ancient history."

And that's what she wanted to believe. She would have given anything to believe it. But no matter what she did or where she went, she knew Mason would never be history. Not completely.

He stood up, stretched, and yawned. "Wow, I've been so busy, I totally for-got to eat today. So, what's your plan? Wanna get some lunch or something? We're meeting over at Rob's house at two for rehearsal, but there's still time for us to run up to the sandwich joint at the shopping center and grab something before I take off."

She was staring at Shane now, who was standing there, his hand resting lightly on her shoulder, so trusting, so willing to forgive what he considered her minor transgression. She thought of the qualities that had drawn her to him the first time they'd met in Holden Beach.

Shane had no inkling it wasn't cool to call a girl five minutes after she'd driven away from him, and that was part of his charm. He didn't care about cool. He cared about her. The next time they met, in Roanoke, he'd gone to a supermarket and bought pink roses and had them delivered to her table in the club where he was playing. And the next time he was in North Carolina, he called, and even though he was playing in a bar halfway across the state, he drove the three hours over and back just to take her to dinner before he had to drive back and play a late-night set.

He sent her sweet, funny e-mails, links to his music and the band's Web site. He started, but never finished, writing a song called "Annajane in the Morn-ing." The band was a regional success. Shane made enough money to do what he loved to do—making music, hanging with his friends, traveling around in his van with his dog, and then coming home to his little cabin.

The life was enough for him, she thought, and he was blessed that he thought so. The problem was, she saw now, it wouldn't be enough for her. Shane wanted her, she knew. But he didn't really need her. His life was just the right size, just as it was.

She'd been spouting off about honesty—both to Mason and Shane. But if she was being really honest with herself, she knew there was a reason she'd resisted moving in here or setting a date for their wedding.

"Annajane?" Shane was standing at the door, his Dobro in his hand. "Ready to go?"

She covertly twisted the plain ring from her left hand and looked around the room one last time.

"Shane?" He turned to her, and when he saw the somber look on her face, his beautiful, sunny smile clouded over, and then disappeared.

"It's over, isn't it?" he asked, leaning up against the doorjamb. "You're never moving in here; we're never getting married. God. I am so damned dense. That's what you really came to tell me, wasn't it?"

"No," she said, walking toward him. "I mean, I thought I came here to convince myself that you're what I want. To remind myself how lucky I am to have your love. And I know, I must be the luckiest girl in this state. But as much as I want this to work, I just don't think it will."

"We could make it work!" Shane exclaimed. "Once you're living closer, away from all that drama back in Passcoe, things will be different. We'll make them different. If you need some time and space, I get that. You can have all of it you want. Just as long as you stay in my life. Okay?" He reached out, took her hand, and kissed it.

"Your ring?" he asked, dropping her hand.

She dug it out of her pocket, put it in his palm, and gently closed his fingers over it. "I messed up my last marriage. Gave up and ran off when things got bad. It was easier to blame him, his mama, my mama, everybody but myself. But now I've got to stop running. I've got to figure out what I want from life."

"Mason?" His mouth twisted as he said the name.

"I honestly don't know," she said. "He's got a lot of his own stuff to figure out. Right now, I think I'll just concentrate on fixing me."

"You're fine the way you are," Shane said.

"No, I'm not," Annajane said. She picked up her overnight bag and slung it over her shoulder and gave Wyley a final head scratch. "But I'm gonna be."

24

Farnham-Capheart's offices were on the seventh floor of a midsized office tower in midtown Atlanta. Annajane parked in the underground garage and took the elevator to the marble-floored lobby. As she passed a small sandwich shop, her growling stomach reminded her of the breakfast and lunch she'd skipped.

A trio of women, dressed in chic dark suits and heels, stepped out of the elevator as she stepped in. She looked down, ruefully, at her own attire: black slacks, a pale pink ruffled cotton blouse, and quilted black ballet flats. When she'd fled Passcoe before dawn that morning, she hadn't stopped to think about what clothes she'd need. She brushed some dog hair from her slacks, reached in her pocketbook, and brought out a simple pair of pearl earrings and fastened them to her ears.

This would have to do for now, but she'd certainly have to step up her game, fashion-wise, once she started work at the ad agency. Back in Passcoe, she'd dressed much more casually for work, even wearing jeans on Fridays in the summer. Clearly, that wouldn't work in Atlanta. She was in the big leagues now. And, she reflected ruefully, she was single again. Probably destined to stay that way, too.

When she arrived at the agency's office suite, she had to wait a moment for her new boss, Joe Farnham, to meet her in the reception area.

"Annajane?" he said, looking a little flustered. "Aren't you still working in Passcoe?"

"I came into town this morning on the spur of the moment," she said. "Just thought I'd drop by and chat for a minute before I head back home to finish up my packing."

"Come on back to my office," Joe said, guiding her by the elbow. "I guess it's just as well you're here."

When he was seated at his desk with his office door closed and with Annajane sitting across from him, Joe Capheart pulled a foil-wrapped roll of antacids from a desk drawer. He popped one in his mouth and silently handed one across to her.

Her stomach fluttered. News was coming, and it wasn't gonna be good.

"I take it you haven't talked to Davis today?" he asked, frowning.

"Uh, no," she said. "It's been a pretty crazy weekend at home. I left super-early this morning and haven't had a chance to talk to Davis."

"You're gonna want to," Joe said. He chewed the antacid silently and stared out the window. "They've put me in a hell of an awkward position here. Not to mention all the other repercussions."

"What's going on?" Annajane said, trying not to sound alarmed.

"The long and the short of it is, Quixie has pulled their account."

She chewed the antacid furiously for a moment, while she let the news settle in. "Since when?" she asked, when she could speak again. "That's crazy. I talked to Mason yesterday, and he didn't say anything like that."

"Davis e-mailed me about fifteen minutes ago," Joe said glumly. "I haven't even told the rest of the partners yet. An e-mail—you believe that? After all the years the agency's done business with them?"

"Did he give you a reason?" Annajane asked, still dumbfounded. "I mean, Joe, I was just in the office yesterday, going over the new summer promotion plans. Davis had signed off on all of it."

"This came from out of the blue! As far as I knew, we were golden," Joe said. "Thirty years we've been working on the Quixie account. I was just a junior copywriter when Glenn Bayless hired us, and Davis, the little prick—excuse my language, Annajane—was barely potty-trained. All his e-mail today said was that there were some new developments in the company's ownership. Do you have any idea what that's supposed to mean?"

She felt a chill go down her spine. "All I know is that Jax Snax has indicated they're going to tender an offer to buy Quixie. Mason is totally opposed to a sale. And so is his sister. But Davis has been actively agitating for it."

"What about Sallie?" Joe asked urgently.

"According to Mason, she's been on the fence."

Joe crumpled up a piece of paper and tossed it into the trash. "Sounds to me like maybe she fell off that fence."

Annajane took a deep breath. "What does this mean for the agency?"

"It's a huge punch in the gut, of course," Joe said. "Quixie was one of our biggest accounts. I'm gonna try and talk to Davis, and Mason, if I can. But if we don't retain that account, well, that changes everything."

"Including my hire?" She kept her tone deliberately neutral, calm.

"I'm afraid so," Joe said. "We'll still pay for your moving expenses, of course, and any other out-of-pocket expenses you've incurred, but without the Quixie account, we'll have to do some major reshuffling around here."

"I see," Annajane said. She stood up and held out a hand to Joe Farnham. "Well, thanks, I guess."

"Son of a bitch!" he growled. "This isn't right. It just isn't. I wish there was something more I could do. We were all really looking forward to having you join the team, Annajane. I told Davis, right before we offered you the position, he'd be crazy to let you walk away."

Annajane turned, startled. "You talked to Davis about hiring me? Not Mason?"

Joe shrugged. "It was Davis's idea. I mean, if I'd known you were thinking of leaving Quixie, I'd have snapped you up in a minute anyway, but yeah, he mentioned in passing that he thought you'd be uncomfortable staying at the company after Mason got serious with that consultant of theirs."

"Celia," she said. "Her name is Celia." And her grimy mitts were all over this little maneuver, Annajane thought.

. . .

As much as she dreaded going back home, Annajane knew she had no choice. Celia had laid down the gauntlet, and it was too late now to back away from a fight. Before leaving Capheart's parking lot, she called the leasing office for the apartment she'd rented to let them know she wouldn't be moving in after all, and got the not-unexpected news that she would be forfeiting the first and last month's rent that she'd already paid.

She called Pokey as soon as she'd cleared Atlanta traffic and was back on the interstate, headed to Passcoe. "What's going on up there?" she demanded.

"Let's see. Where do you want me to start?" Pokey said. "I think the right rear tire on my Range Rover has a nail in it. Petey has a weird rash all over his body; and Clayton has decided he does not want to be potty-trained, which means he might still be in Pull-Ups in junior high; and, oh yeah, Mama announced a little while ago that she's just fine with selling Quixie to some outfit in Tenafly, New Jersey, that makes jalapeno cheese–stuffed microwaveable tater tots."

"Oh, God," Annajane moaned. "How? Why?"

A loud scream pierced the air from the other end of the phone.

"Hang on a second, will ya?"

Annajane heard the sounds of footsteps, and then the sound of water flushing, and then childish shrieks. "Denning Riggs!" Pokey yelled. "Do not dunk your little brother in the toilet. I don't care if he does smell like poopie. No! I mean it. Put him down this instant."

Pokey came back on the line and sighed. "What was I thinking having all these kids? One more is gonna put me in an early grave."

"You love it," Annajane said, laughing despite the seriousness of the current situation.

"As I was saying, it seems that my darling brother Davis has somehow managed to pull another fast one on us," Pokey said. "And I'll just bet the formidable Celia has been bending Mama's ear, too. She's spent a lot of time over at Cherry Hill these past few weeks, in the guise of making wedding plans, sucking up to Mama."

"So that's it for Quixie? It's a done deal?" Annajane asked.

"Not quite yet," Pokey said. "Mama claims she doesn't want to do anything unless all of us are one hundred percent on board."

"Well, that's something," Annajane said. "Have you talked to Mason about any of this?"

"Not yet," Pokey said. "The shit literally just hit the fan. I've called the office and left a message with Voncile to have him call me, and I left him a voice mail on his cell, but I'm sure he's up to his ass in alligators right now. And speaking of which, how did Shane handle your true confession?"

"He said the right thing for all the wrong reasons. I'm more messed up now than I've ever been."

"You're gonna have to spell this out for me, hon," Pokey said. "I've got baby brain already."

"We're not getting married," Annajane said. "I broke it off with Shane."

"Yippee! I mean, oh, that's too bad," Pokey said. "You sound pretty okay though."

"Definitely not okay. Shell-shocked," Annajane corrected. "But that's not all. I'm having a hell of a morning my ownself. After I left the cabin I went to see my new boss, Joe, at Farnham-Capheart. Who greeted me with the news that I don't have a job there after all, because Davis e-mailed him this morning that Quixie is pulling the account from the agency."

"Shut up."

"It's true. Joe was just as shocked as I was. He'd literally just gotten the news. Since Quixie was one of the agency's biggest accounts, it's a huge blow for them. And since the Quixie account was going to be mine, I am now, officially, redundant."

"Can Davis do that?" Pokey asked. "I mean, Farnham-Capheart has been the company's ad agency since forever."

"He can and he did," Annajane said succinctly. "Although I have an idea this is a plot he probably hatched with Celia's assistance. Joe let it slip that Davis was the one who suggested they hire me—since I was probably going to want to leave the company anyway once Celia was in the picture."

"That conniving little slut," Pokey said. "I'd like to rip her arms off and beat her to death with 'em."

"And I'd help," Annajane said. "Except, knowing her, she'd just grow a second set of appendages."

"What are you gonna do now?" Pokey asked.

"You mean now that I'm both jobless and homeless? We close on the loft sale on Thursday, and I've got to be out of there by Friday at five. Of that I'm certain. As for the rest of it, who knows? I guess I'll start polishing my résumé, for a starter. Celia made it very plain when I saw her at the plant yesterday that she plans to install Tracey, the new girl, in my old office any second. She even suggested I didn't need to finish out this week. Of course, I lied and told her I had some very important business to finish up first. I just didn't tell her the business I needed to finish was her."

"Good for you," Pokey said. "Anything you want to do, count me in. Anything else?"

"Yeah. Back to Celia. Let's get back to destroying Celia. Did you ever ask your friend at Belk's about her?"

"I'd forgotten," Pokey said. "But I'll call her right now. Or right after I get these hellions down for their naps."

25

Mason felt his neck and shoulder muscles tighten as soon as he drove through the wrought-iron gates at Cherry Hill. The smell of freshly mown grass wafted through the open windows of his car, and small birds and large yellow butterflies hovered over the splashy ribbons of pink, white, and purple azaleas that lined the long drive, but he was too distracted to enjoy the sights of a beautiful spring day.

The message Sallie had left on his phone was brief and succinct. "Son, I need to see you this morning. I'll be at home until noon."

He massaged his temples with his fingertips. His mother's agenda could have any number of unpleasant items.

Mason parked his car and trudged slowly up the front steps of the Greek Revival house. The white paint gleamed in the sunshine. He paused at the front door. Normally, he just walked inside and announced himself. After all, this was his family home. He'd lived here right up until shortly before he and Annajane married and had moved back here, briefly, after their split. But somehow, today felt different. He was poised to ring the doorbell when the door opened and his mother greeted him, her voice decidedly cool.

"Since when do you ring the doorbell here?" she demanded, offering her cheek to be kissed.

He kissed her lightly, inhaling the familiar scents, hairspray, Chanel Number Five, and yes, cigarettes with an after-note of cinnamon-flavored chewing gum. His mother had been a closet smoker for as long as he could remember. You'd walk into a room at the house, and there she'd be, guiltily fanning the smoke out opened windows or spritzing the air with room freshener.

He followed her into the high-ceilinged entry hall, and her heels clicked on the black-and-white marble-tiled floor. "You look nice," he said, hoping to establish détente. Her hair had been freshly done and she wore a yellow silk pantsuit and a gleaming gold-link necklace and matching earrings.

"I had altar guild this morning," she said, leading him into the study. She sat down behind the dainty walnut French provincial desk she'd installed there in the place of his father's massive oak desk. "And I can tell you it wasn't a very pleasant experience, walking into a room full of buzzing women, all of whom fell silent the moment I entered. And what do you suppose they were talking about?"

Mason stayed standing. "Is that why you asked me over here? Because of a bunch of gossipy old biddies?" He turned and headed for the door. "You'll have to excuse me, Mama. I've got a business to run."

"I'd like you to stay," Sallie said. Her voice was steady. She seldom raised it, because she seldom had to. All her life, Sallie Bayless had been a force with which to reckon.

He slouched down into the pale blue damask wing chair facing the desk and instantly felt like a schoolboy called into the principal's office.

His mother fidgeted with a pen on the desktop, rolling it back and forth beneath her fingertips.

"Is it true?" she said finally. "You . . . and Annajane? Really, Mason, I can't imagine what you were thinking. Or doing? And out at the farm?"

"I don't know what you've heard," Mason said. "But I doubt much of it is true. Anyway, I don't care to discuss my personal life with you. Or the rest of Passcoe."

"Your personal life, and the way you conduct it, reflects on your entire family.

And on Quixie," Sallie reminded him. "So when you and your *ex-wife* go cavort-ing around out in a public place, of course it's going to be talked about." She shook her head.

"If Celia decides to take you back, it will be a miracle. She should be nomi-nated for sainthood."

Mason felt the muscle in his jaw twitch.

"And yes, I know about the baby," she added.

He jumped to his feet. "That's it. I'm thirty-nine years old. I'm a little too old to have my mother slap my hand."

"And what a shame," Sallie said. "I should have slapped your hand—and your fanny—much more frequently than I did when you were a boy. Maybe if I had, we wouldn't be having this conversation."

"We *aren't* having this conversation," Mason said. "I'm leaving now."

"Before you go rushing off, you should know that Celia didn't volunteer the information about her pregnancy," Sallie said. "I called her just a few minutes ago, and I could tell by the sound of her voice that she'd been crying. Still was crying, poor thing. She didn't want to tell me what had happened, but I persuaded her she needed a friendly shoulder. Mason, Celia doesn't have any family to speak of, except her poor old aunt. We're her family now."

"Lucky Celia," Mason said, not bothering to hide the sarcasm. He glanced down at his watch. "I have to go, Mama. Sophie gets out of the hospital this afternoon, and I haven't even made it into the office yet."

"Mason!" Sallie said, with just a hint of sharpness. "I want all this nonsense stopped. You are engaged to be married to a wonderful, intelligent woman, who will be an asset to this family and our company. You need to remember that and stay away from Annajane Hudgens. Especially now that Celia is carrying your child."

She gave another shake of the head. "I didn't say a word when you brought Sophie home, did I? We welcomed her into our family and treated her just the same as Pokey's children. We all adore Sophie. But Mason, one illegitimate child is the limit! You simply cannot walk away from Celia."

"I never intended to walk away from her," Mason said, his voice danger-ously calm. "But Celia and I are the only ones who can make the decision to get married. I won't be pressured, Mama. Not by you or her."

"Why on earth would you hesitate to marry Celia?" Sallie demanded. "Please explain it to me, because I just don't understand what your problem is."

"I'm not in love with Celia," Mason said. "That's the problem, in a nutshell."

"Love? Don't be ridiculous. As you've already pointed out, you're thirty-nine years old, Mason. You tried marrying for love once. How did that work out for you?" She arched one eyebrow as a dare.

His neck began to flush red.

"You see?" Sallie went on. "Annajane was all wrong for you. I know you think it's snobbish to say so, but it's the truth. There's a reason these kinds of marriages never work out. Ruth Hudgens is little more than white trash. Annajane's real father was a high school dropout, and Leonard, bless his heart, never was the sharpest knife in the drawer. I'll give her credit for this: Annajane was always determined to marry up. And she succeeded in that, even though the two of you had nothing in common. But Celia is different. She's perfect for you. She's clever, she's ambitious, a hard worker, and she sees the big picture. It's a brilliant match. It will be a horrible tragedy for you and Quixie if you let this girl get away from you."

"A brilliant match?" Mason repeated. "What did you do, Mama? Set up an Excel spreadsheet with all the attributes of a corporate wife, and then set out to find her?"

"No," she shot back, "but if I had, I couldn't have done better than Celia. Nor could you." She leaned across the desk, her dark eyes snapping with intensity. "Mason, your daddy and I did not raise you to shirk your responsibilities. You have got to marry Celia and be a father to her child. And the sooner you do, the better. Celia's not going to wait around for you forever, you know. If you don't marry her, she'll surely leave Passcoe, and take my grandchild with her. Is that what you want?"

Mason winced involuntarily, and Sallie saw that her last remark had hit home.

Sallie opened the drawer in the desk and slid out an opened pack of cigarettes, an engraved silver lighter, and a heavy cut-crystal ashtray. She closed the drawer, lit the cigarette, then sat back in her chair and inhaled deeply.

Mason stared. He'd never actually seen his mother smoke. She saw him watching her, and she smiled, tilted her head back, and blew a perfect smoke ring.

"What? You think I'm too old to be misbehaving?" She held the cigarette at eye level for a moment, then tapped the end neatly into the ashtray.

"Did you ever smoke in front of Dad?" Mason asked.

"Of course not," Sallie said. "And don't change the subject. We're not talking about my marriage; we're talking about yours."

"No, we are not," Mason said. "Was there anything else, or can I go back to work now?"

"Just one other thing," Sallie said. "We'll find out the final disposition of the estate when we meet with Norris Thomas next week, but I think we can pretty much anticipate how Glenn will have divided up the company. In the meantime, I want you to give serious consideration to the offer from Jax Snax."

He started to protest, but she waved him off.

"Your father is dead, Mason," Sallie said. "I know he had some sentimental notion about keeping the company in the family, but five years have passed, and the state of the economy has changed, drastically, and not for the better. Glenn could not have anticipated the way our costs have escalated while our sales have dropped. And if you won't consider it in light of your own best interests, think about me. You and your brother are young enough to go out and start new businesses. On the other hand, I'm a widow. If Quixie fails, what am I left with? This house? It's a damned mausoleum. Do you have any idea of what it costs in maintenance? Seven bedrooms, five bathrooms? For a woman who lives alone? The pool needs to be relined, the tennis court needs resurfacing, and my heat and air man tells me we barely have enough BTUs to cool the living and dining room. I need a whole new system, dual heat pumps, the works. Twenty-five thousand dollars! I'd sell it in a minute, but to who? We're the only people in this town with any *real* money."

Mason looked around the study and tried to see it through his mother's eyes. There was a somewhat threadbare oriental rug on the wide-planked wood floor. The heavy linen drapes that hung at the windows had been there as long as he could remember. An oil portrait of his grandmother Bayless hung over the fireplace. He'd never once considered that Sallie might have come to resent the family homeplace. But clearly, she had.

"Now," Sallie went on. "I've talked to several people in the industry, and they assure me that the Jax offer is a good one, probably the best we'll ever get."

"I disagree," Mason said. "We should hold onto Quxie. It is what Dad wanted. That's why he put that five-year moratorium on a sale. We've had challenges, I know, but I really believe we can turn things around now, especially if we expand our brand with the new drinks Dad was considering. I won't support you on a sale, Mama. And neither will Pokey."

She took another drag on the cigarette. He found it fascinating and unsettling to watch a parent indulge in such a taboo. It felt like watching Santa Claus read a copy of *Hustler*. Unseemly.

"Davis is in favor of it," Sallie said. And Celia knows it's for the best, too. You should try listening to her, Mason. She has a really fine head for business, you know. Don't discount her just because she's a woman."

He stood up. "If we're done here, I need to go pick up Sophie."

"Oh yes," Sallie said, stubbing out her cigarette and stashing the still-smouldering ashtray back in her desk drawer. "Poor little Sophie. I have some ice cream for her, out in the kitchen."

She came around from behind the desk and gave her son an awkward hug. "Think about what I've said today, Mason, will you? Patch things up with Celia, and let's get this wedding rescheduled." She gave his cheek a pat that was very nearly a slap. "And whatever you do, stay away from Annajane Hudgens."

26

When he finally made it into the office, Mason found a thick pile of phone-message slips and an endless stream of e-mails. He was exhausted, guilt-wracked, and pissed off at Annajane Hudgens, whom he blamed for plunging his usually well-ordered life into a maelstrom of doubt and indecision. He was clicking his way through the e-mails, when he came to a long one from Joe Farnham, expressing his regret about the termination of the Quixie account and wishing the family well, that set his blood boiling. He called Farnham and had a brief conversation with the ad-man. As soon as he hang up, he stormed into Davis's office without knocking, slamming the door closed behind him.

"Hey, bro," Davis was dressed in his customary custom-tailored suit, heavily starched white dress shirt, and an expensive Italian knit tie. He was on the phone.

"We need to talk," Mason said, and he felt his jaw muscle twitch. He glanced at Davis's computer screen—and saw what looked like a page of real estate listings. Davis quickly tapped the mouse and the Quixie logo appeared on his screen saver.

"Hang on a minute, can you?" Davis said, covering the phone with his hand. He gestured toward the wingback chair in front of his desk.

"Look, I'll get back to you on that," he said and hung up. He swiveled his chair around and gave his brother a searching look.

"Dude," Davis said, with a merry chortle. "I hear you had yourself quite a night last night. So. You and ole Annajane out at the farm, scaring the livestock. Congratulations, buddy. Didn't know you had it in you."

Mason clenched the sides of the chair with both hands. "Shut the fuck up," he said fiercely. "I mean it, Davis."

"Okay," Davis said, shrugging. "Don't get so bent out of shape. I was just messin' with you."

"You've been messing with a lot of people lately, haven't you, Davis?" Mason said. "I just got an e-mail from Joe Farnham. He tells me you've terminated our account with them?"

"Well, hey-yullllll," Davis drawled. "You know, it's just one of those things. It we do this deal with Jax Snax, they've got their own in-house agency. And I know you've been on a cost-cutting tear, so it seemed to me that now was the time to cut Capheart loose. We've got the summer promotion plans, and it's no biggie for me to cherry-pick the best parts . . ."

"It is not just one of those things," Mason said. "We've been working with Farnham-Capheart for years. They've done a good job for us. More importantly, this Jax thing you keep harping about is not a done deal. You know damned well we don't have any idea of how Dad's trust arrangement is going to shake out. For all we know, he may have left Quixie to the Humane Society."

Davis's eyes shifted nervously. "The old man wouldn't have done anything like that. Anyway, we'll know by next week. I'm just trying to make sure we've got all our ducks in a row once we do know how it shakes out."

"I am not going to let this company be sold, Davis," Mason said quietly. "Not without a fight. I know we've had some philosophical differences in the past, and we've managed to work things out, but this time, I'm not backing down. Our great-grandfather started this business. He and Granddad and Dad managed to keep it afloat during the Depression and the war years. They fought off Coke and Pepsi and half a dozen other companies that tried to put us out of business. But if Kelso and his bunch get their hands on Quixie, you know as well as I do that they won't leave us alone. I've seen how they operate. They don't want us—not the physical us. They just want our brand and our market share. Oh yeah, they'll make promises about keeping things just the way they are, but that's a bunch of bullshit. They'll write us a big check and then show us the door. They'll shut the plant down, ship the equipment somewhere else, and throw everybody in town out of work. Everybody but the Baylesses."

"You got something against making money?" Davis asked. "Or do you just enjoy the idea of being the last noble Bayless to run Quixie—right into the ground? Because that's where it's headed, big brother. Get your head out of your ass! Take a look at what's happening in the business."

"We can turn it around," Mason said stubbornly. "The new flavors, the focus groups loved 'em. And we need some fresh ideas, but we've got a good product . . ."

"I'm telling you it's too late," Davis said, half-shouting. "The brand extensions you're talking about will cost millions. We'd have to retool the plant, add extra capacity, and God knows what all. And I'm tired of flushing good money after bad. If you don't believe me, talk to Celia! She'll tell you the truth. The smart money is on Jax. We make the deal, get 'em to sign an iron-clad agreement not to move the company—at least for four or five years. Maybe milk the state for some tax incentives to stick around . . ."

The muscle in Mason's jaw twitched as though it had been touched with a live wire. "We are *not* going to hold this state ransom and hang around for a government handout just to turn around and double-cross them. That's not how Baylesses do business."

"The hell you say." Davis was leaning back in his leather chair. He clicked his mouse and his computer screen was again filled with color photographs of real estate listings. He swiveled the monitor so Mason could get a look.

"You see this? That's a four-bedroom house on Figure Eight Island." He tapped the screen with his forefinger. "The lot alone cost a million, three, and I know the owner spent another million and a half building the damned thing. Then he lost his ass in the speculative real estate market. Guy is hurtin' bigtime. Now, he's begging me to buy it—fully furnished—including a thirty-five-foot Grady-White. I just put an option on it. Eight hundred thousand. You believe that?"

Mason felt his stomach churn. His brother relished the idea of feasting on another man's disaster. "You could buy that house and boat right now, without taking a dime out of Quixie," he pointed out. "You've got the money. Nothin's stopping you."

Davis leaned across his desk. Beneath the tan, a network of fine red veins threaded across his high cheekbones. "Quixie is stopping me," he said. "Floggin' this dead horse takes up all my time and energy. But now I'm done."

He laid his palms flat down on the desktop. "And before you start in on lecturing me about family duty and all that bullshit, you need to know that I am not the only one in favor of this sale. I know Pokey's dead-set against it, but hell, Pete's got plenty of money, and anyway, our baby sister don't know squat about cherry soda."

He glanced over at a glamorous silver-framed photo of Sallie that rested at the edge of his desk. She'd had the portrait done only a year ago, not long after she'd made a trip to Florida that had been billed as a winter vacation, but which they all knew was for a skillfully done face-lift.

"I wasn't gonna get into this right now, but you need to know that Mama is ready for this deal to happen. She's not getting any younger. She wants to get out and enjoy her life while she still can. And if you let this company go to hell, out of your own stubborn pride, that's on you, buddy."

He pointed at the monitor with the photo of the beach house. "This summer, when you're messin' around out at that broken-down old boathouse and cottage out at Hideaway—that's where I'm gonna be spending my time. Ocean views on one side, views of the sound on the other."

Mason shook his head. "I went to see Mama this morning. You've been telling her all kind of lies about what'll happen to the company if we don't sell, haven't you, Davis? Scaring her, making her think she'll be a penniless widow?"

His younger brother gave a nonchalant shrug. "Mama's a grown woman with plenty of business sense, Mason. She can see the handwriting on the wall without a flashlight."

"I'm done here," Mason said tersely as he stood to go. "Anyway, I didn't come in here to debate the merits of Jax Snax. What I did come in here to talk about is Quixie. Here and now. Today. I've tried to stay out of your side of the business, but I can't do it this time. I called Joe Farnham after I got his e-mail this morning. He told me losing the account meant he couldn't hire Annajane.

Was that your intention? Making sure she wouldn't have a job? What the hell has she ever done to you?"

"Nothing," Davis said. "I'm okay with Annajane. How was I supposed to know he'd let her go? I'm not privy to their internal workings."

"You need to fix this, Davis," Mason said, glaring at his younger brother. "Nobody knows the company history as well as Annajane or understands our market like she does. Rehire her, or I will. Firing Capheart is one of the stupidest damned moves you've ever made. And you've made some pretty stupid decisions in your life."

"You're calling me stupid?" Davis leaned forward. "Take a look at yourself, big brother. I'm not the one lettin' my gorgeous fiancée sleep at Mama's house while I'm out fuckin' my ex-wife in a cornfield."

Mason felt the blood rushing to his head. He stood very still. He jammed his hands into his pockets to keep from slugging his brother.

"I'll call Annajane and let her know she's been rehired," he told Davis. "In the meantime, we need to concentrate on running Quixie, the best way we know how." He turned and stalked out of the room.

27

N *OW ENTERING PASSCOE, N.C. HOME OF QUIXIE BEVERAGE COMPANY SINCE 1922.*
Annajane slowed the car as she passed the city limits sign.

Funny, she'd never really noticed the tasteful green and red billboard before. If Jax Snax managed to gobble up Quixie in the proposed merger, would the town fathers leave the sign standing? The real question, of course, was whether there would be anything left of the town if Quixie got sold.

She'd seen too many other small towns around the state decimated after the departure of textile mills, furniture manufacturers, and yes, even the much-maligned big tobacco. The sight of those abandoned buildings, with their weed-strewn properties; ghostly, boarded-up windows; and forlorn FOR SALE signs never failed to send a shiver up her spine.

They didn't cure cancer or promote world peace at Quixie. They just made fizzy soft drinks. But their product made people happy.

Mason might fret about shrinking market share, but one thing did not change. Their customers felt intense loyalty to a soft drink that had been around for more than ninety years. Quixie employed three hundred people in Passcoe, which made it the county's biggest employer. Quixie, and by extension the Bayless family, had provided most of the funding for Memorial Park, the high school football stadium, and the obstetric wing of the hospital. Quixie and its employees were always the biggest contributors to the local United Way fund, and, of course, their taxes kept county roads paved and libraries and schools funded.

Annajane ran her tongue over her now-straight teeth. As the child of a long-time Quixie employee, the company's health plan had paid for her orthodontia, and Leonard's company-sponsored savings plan had sent her to college.

Quixie, she vowed, could not just up and leave. She might not have a home or a job or a future here, but she couldn't let all of this go. Not without a fight.

Her cell phone rang and she recognized the number on the readout as her real estate agent's.

"Annajane, hey," Susan Peters said. "I'm so glad I caught you."

"Please don't tell me you have bad news," Annajane said. "I've already had enough today."

"Not exactly bad news," Susan said. "But news. We need to move up the closing on your loft to Wednesday. So you'll get your money two days early. Hooray, right?"

"But that's the day after tomorrow. I'm not even done packing."

"Sorry," Susan said. "Your buyer has to leave the country on business Friday, and Wednesday is the only day we can get it scheduled with the lender and the closing attorneys. So it's Wednesday or nothing."

"I won't have to move until Friday though, right?"

"Uh, no. You'll need to be out of there by noon Wednesday, so she can get moved in before she leaves on Friday."

"Susan!" Annajane said, with a moan. "You don't know what you're asking. I just found out today my job in Atlanta fell through. I don't have any place to move to."

"Can't you just move in with your fiancé?"

"Probably not, since we're no longer engaged," Annajane said.

"Oh. Wow. You are having a run of crappy news," Susan said. "Well, look on the bright side. You're making out like a bandit on the sale of the loft. You can afford to buy something really nice now. I've got a darling 1940s cottage over on Mimosa Street. It's a three-bedroom, two-bath, on a huge lot, with tons of potential. You could pick it up for a steal, and have lots of money left over for the restoration."

"Restoration?"

"It's what we real estate professionals call 'a handyman's special.' You know, it'll need a new roof, plumbing, electrical, heat and air, a new kitchen, like that. I can show it to you today, if you want, and if you love it, which I think you will, we can write up an offer by tonight."

"Whoa!" Annajane said. "I'm still processing the news that I'll be homeless in two days. Look. I can't wrap my mind around this right now. I'll have to call you back, okay?"

"Okay, but remember, closing is now at 9 A.M. Wednesday. And you really do have to be out of the loft completely by noon. Call me if you want to see Mimosa Street."

Annajane dropped her phone into her open pocketbook with a sigh. This day was one that would go down on record as one of the worst in her life. Ever.

She slowed the car at the intersection of the county road and the street that led to Mason's house. She would deal with her broken engagement, the job situation, and the moved-up closing later. What she needed now was a little cheering up. Sophie would be home from the hospital by now. Impulsively, she made the turn, and hoped all the turmoil at the office meant she could visit the little girl without encountering Mason. Or Celia.

Sophie's nanny, Letha, gave Annajane a quick hug. "She's been asking about you since we got home," Letha said. "Her daddy told her you'd gone out of town, and she sure didn't like hearing that!"

She found Sophie propped up on the leather sofa in Mason's study, sipping from a glass bottle of Quixie and watching *The Little Mermaid* video. The little girl's pallor was gone, and she was giggling as Sebastian the lobster capered around on the colorful flat-screened television.

"Annajane!" Sophie cried, spotting her. "You came back."

"I did," Annajane agreed, sitting gingerly on the edge of the tufted ottoman that served as a coffee table. She reached over and adjusted Sophie's sparkly pink glasses, then ruffled her hair. "Are you glad to be home?"

"Yeah. The nurses were nice, but Letha is nicer."

"Lots nicer. And you're feeling better, I hear?"

As an answer, Sophie pulled up her pajama top and pointed at her abdomen. A small square of gauze covered her incision. "I'm gonna have a scar," she said proudly. "Nobody else in my whole school has a scar like me."

Annajane laughed. She stuck out her leg and rolled up her pant leg to her knee. "I've got a scar, too," she said.

Clearly intrigued, Sophie ran her finger over the faint strip of puckered flesh and shivered. "Did you have to go in an ambulance and have an operation at the hospital?"

"Nope. My scar isn't anywhere near as cool as yours."

"How'd you get it?"

"It was a long time ago," Annajane said. "I was dressed up in the Dixie the Pixie costume. You remember that from my office, right?"

"Uh-huh."

"Well. I was marching in the Fourth of July parade, and I had a cart full of Quixie to give away to people watching the parade, but then these bad boys ganged up on me, and they stole my cart."

"Oh no." Sophie's eyes widened. "What did you do?"

"I tried to chase after them, to get the cart back," Annajane reported. "But I had on that big goofy pixie head, and I couldn't see very well, and then I was also wearing those silly shoes that were five sizes too big, and I tripped! And that's how I banged up my knee and got this scar."

"You left out the part about how I rode up in the fun car and saved you."

Mason. She hadn't even heard him come into the room.

Annajane didn't turn around. "Actually, I saved myself. But your daddy did give me a ride home that day."

"Don't forget I bought you a hot dog and some potato chips," Mason said. He walked over to the sofa and dropped a kiss on the little girl's head. He held up a white paper sack. "Guess what's in here?"

"Ice cream!" Sophie exclaimed.

Mason pulled a round cardboard tub from the bag. "Your grandmother sent this over. Strawberry shortcake ice cream. Want some?"

Sophie nodded vigorously, sending the pigtails on either side of her face wagging.

"I'll fix it," Annajane volunteered, taking the bag from Mason.

She was out in the kitchen, scooping ice cream into bowls, when Mason strolled into the kitchen. "I'll just fix this for you guys, and then I'll take off," Annajane said.

He leaned with his back against the counter and crossed his arms over his chest, surveying her with studied indifference.

Tell her about the baby, he thought. *Tell her so she can cut and run. Do it now.* But he couldn't. Not tonight.

"Wanna share any news with me?" he asked.

Annajane gave him a backward glance. "Pokey told you I broke up with Shane, right?"

"She mentioned it. I'm sorry, Annajane. So, he didn't take the news of our, uh, encounter well?"

"He didn't take it the way I anticipated," she said, avoiding all the messy details. "As it turns out, it's been a day full of unpleasant surprises."

Mason took her by the shoulders and turned her around to face him. "First things first. I want you to know that I had no idea Davis was going to fire our ad agency, effectively rendering you unemployed. He didn't bother to inform me until it was a done deal."

"What was he thinking?" Annajane asked.

"I have no idea," Mason said with a scowl. "We're basically only communicating by e-mail these days. But that's going to change pretty shortly. In fact, a lot of things are fixing to change."

"You met with Sallie?"

"Yes," Mason affirmed. "We had a fairly long, frank discussion about a lot of stuff. She's still not totally convinced the family should keep Quixie, but that's sort of a moot point at the moment."

Annajane looked over at the bowl of ice cream she'd just scooped out. "Sounds like this could be a long story. So let me just take this in to Sophie before it melts, and I'll be right back."

Annajane came back into the kitchen. "You were saying?"

"My brother and I can't keep working at cross-purposes," Mason said. "It's hurting the company, and it's hurting the family. We managed to hammer out a short-term agreement this morning." He took a deep breath and looked directly at Annajane.

"I told Davis we have to find a way to get you not to leave the company." He clamped his hand over hers. "We need you, Annajane. Need your talent, your energy, your commitment. Davis and I don't agree on much, but it turns out we do agree about that. What do you say? Will you come back?"

She stared down at their hands and sighed.

"Please?" Mason's face looked haunted.

Annajane looked away, struggling to find the right answer, for the right reasons.

"I'm all done." Sophie stood in the kitchen doorway, her tousled blond curls backlit by the sun streaming through the windows. Her pink pocketbook was slung across her chest, bandolier-style. She padded barefoot into the kitchen and carefully placed her bowl on the table where Mason and Annajane were sitting. Without a word, she slid onto Mason's lap.

"Whatcha doing?" Sophie asked, glancing down at the intertwined hands on the tabletop.

Annajane snatched her hand away from Mason's, but she could feel herself blushing.

"I'm trying to talk Annajane into changing her mind about moving away," Mason said.

"Letha says it's a damned shame Annajane got chased outta town by that lil' hussy," Sophie said brightly.

Mason choked. "I'm going to have to have a talk with Letha about little pitchers having big ears."

Sophie cocked her head and regarded Annajane somberly. "Will you stay, pretty please?"

"I'm not sure," Annajane said. "I have a lot to think about."

"Like what?"

"For one thing, I don't have a job anymore," Annajane said, keeping her tone light.

"You can have your old job back," Mason offered.

"Yay!" Sophie clapped her hands in delight.

"Also, I don't have anyplace to live. My loft is sold, and I have to move out by the day after tomorrow," Annajane said.

"Since when?" Mason asked.

"My real estate agent called right as I was driving into town," Annajane said. "The closing had to be moved up to Wednesday, which means I have to be totally moved out of the loft by noon that day."

"You could come live with us!" Sophie said delightedly. "Right, daddy?"

Mason coughed politely. "I think Annajane probably wants a place of her own, Soph."

"Letha told Aunt Pokey that Daddy and Celia had a big ole fight, and now Celia is gone for sure, thank you, Sweet Baby Jesus," Sophie reported, mimicking Letha's slow southern accent with deadly accuracy. "So now, Annajane could sleep in your room, couldn't you, Annajane?"

Mason coughed so violently his face turned purple and tears streamed down his face. Annajane couldn't help herself. Her shoulders heaved with suppressed laughter.

"I am going to have a serious talk with Letha about spreading gossip," Mason said solemnly. "And for your information, and Aunt Pokey's and Letha's, we did not have a big fight. We had an um, discussion. But Celia is not gone."

"Are you still getting married?" Sophie asked, tilting her head to look at her father.

He looked out the window. "It's still under discussion," he said finally. "Anyway, that's nothing for you to worry about."

"Annajane could stay in my room with me. Right?"

"That's a very generous invitation, Sophie," Annajane said, giggling despite herself. "But if I do stay in Passcoe, which I'm not sure I will, I'll need to find a house of my own."

"Why?" Sophie looked puzzled. "Don't you like us?"

"I like you a lot," Annajane said. "But I've lived alone for a long time now. I'm used to my privacy, and doing things my own way. It would be best for everybody if we left it like that."

Sophie yawned widely and leaned her head back against Mason's chest.

"Time for you to go take a nap," he told her, gently sliding her down from his lap.

Sophie threw her arms around Annajane's neck. "Will you come over and watch *Milo and Otis* with me tonight?"

"Hmm," Annajane said. "I wish I could, Soph, but now I've got to go home and get my stuff all packed up to put in storage. But I promise, as soon as that's done, we'll have movie night again."

"Okay," Sophie said, trying to suppress another yawn.

Mason waited until Sophie had gone to find Letha before returning his attention to Annajane.

"Will you at least agree to come back to work at Quixie?" Mason asked. "I'm dead serious, Annajane. I told Davis I want you back on our team. You'd report directly to me. I know it'll be awkward, but that can't be helped. Will you do it?"

He gave her that slow, winning smile that had always worked on her in the past.

"I don't know," she said quietly. "I really don't want to get between you and your brother. Or Celia. I've complicated things enough already."

Tell her, damn it. You're only making things worse by talking her into staying.

"You're not what's between us," Mason said. "Davis and I have been having issues for a long time now. And Mama, she's got her own agenda. But I do want to talk to you about this new marketing scheme; I don't like it."

Annajane bit her lip, hesitant to trash Celia.

"You know," she said finally. "Yesterday, I was cleaning out my office and taking some old file boxes that had been in there for years and years out to the Dumpster. One of the boxes was so old it fell to pieces as I was unloading it. Inside it I found all the old magazine and newspaper mechanicals and tear sheets for Quixie ads from the '40s and '50s. They were so charming, so right, so *Quixie*, for want of a better phrase. For me, they just really captured the essence of what we're selling—fun, refreshment, and yeah, the idea of celebrating the moment. I honestly think that's what we've forgotten with all these slick, sophisticated campaigns we've bought into in the past few years."

Mason nodded thoughtfully. "I remember those old ads. There was one, from the sixties, probably, showing teenaged girls in a speedboat..."

"I saw that one," Annajane said. "It made me want to run out and get a permanent wave and a Jantzen bathing suit, maybe buy a Chris-Craft outboard."

"Mama and my aunt Lu posed for that ad," Mason said. "They took the photo that the illustration was based on, out on the lake, back in the day. Dad had it framed and hanging in the basement playroom for years and years, when we were growing up."

"Those are the ads that *everybody* remembers," Annajane said. "Quixie is never going to be Coke. It's never going to be Pepsi. It shouldn't even try. The brand is iconic in its own way, and I think that's what the message needs to return to. Retro is in again, you know."

"My granddaddy always said he just wanted us to be the best independent regional soft drink company in the business," Mason said. "He never touched coffee, but he drank a bottle of Quixie from his own special Quixie icebox just about every morning of his life, as soon as his feet touched the bedroom floor. As far as he was concerned, our product was unique, and he really believed every bottle of Quixie that left the plant was the thing that would sell the next one."

He grinned. "That and ads with curvy girls in bathing suits."

Annajane stood up. "I better get going. I've still got to finish packing and, I suppose, start looking for a temporary place to live, at least until I figure out my next move."

"Think about what I said, will you?" Mason said, touching her arm lightly. "I think you're on the right track with your ideas about returning to our original brand message. If I can just get Davis to listen, I think he'd realize it's brilliant."

"Maybe," Annajane said. "I will say that if he's dumped the ad agency, he's gonna have to come up with a new summer campaign in a big hurry."

"One more thing," she added, her hand on the back door. "I bumped into Celia as I was sifting through that file box I just mentioned. She urged me to throw all of it in the Dumpster, and not to bother you with any of that old crap, but I told her you might like it for the company archives. There are a bunch of the old original Quixie bottles, too, the ones with the ribbed glass . . ."

Mason looked horrified. "You didn't throw them out, I hope."

"Nope," Annajane said. "I put it all in a new box and stashed it in the trunk of my car, just in case."

"Great," he said. "I'd really like to see those ads, maybe use them to persuade

Davis it's time to go retro. Hell, maybe we'll even resurrect Dixie the Pixie." He did a mock leer at Annajane's legs. "I'll bet you'd still fit in the suit. And the Fourth of July is just around the corner. Right?"

"No. Frickin'. Way," she said succinctly. "But maybe Celia would like to wear it."

28

Pokey picked up a plastic tub of winter clothing and balanced it on her hip. Annajane swiftly snatched it away from her.

"No lifting! Folding, packing yes, lifting no. How many times do I have to repeat myself?"

Pokey stuck out her tongue and took the tub back. "Don't you think that little chunk o' love Clayton weighs waaay more than these clothes? I tote him around all day long, just like I toted Petey when I was pregnant with Clayton. Relax, will you? I'm pregnant, not crippled."

Annajane looked around the loft at the barely controlled chaos. It was Wednesday morning. She was dressed in the only clothes she hadn't packed: a bleached-out Durham Bulls T-shirt and a pair of ratty cutoff jeans. Pokey wore an oversized blue and white oxford cloth dress shirt she'd borrowed from her husband and a pair of stretchy yoga pants. They'd been packing all night.

"I've got to be at the lawyer's office in three hours," she reminded her friend. "And the movers I hired still aren't back from the storage place to pick up the second load yet. I honestly don't know if I'll be out of here by noon."

"You will," Pokey assured her. She held up her cell phone. "I just texted an SOS to Pete. He's sending over a truck and a couple of the guys from the furniture store to give us a hand. This is the last of your clothes to go into storage. So if you'll just get your rear in gear and pack up the clothes and toiletries you need for the next month or so, I think we've got it licked."

"You really think so?" Annajane pushed a strand of hair behind her ear. "I'm so overwhelmed I guess I can't see the forest for the trees."

They heard a horn honking out on the street, and Pokey ran to the plate-glass picture window and looked out. "See here? Pete's guys just pulled up, and your movers are right behind them. Why don't you grab some clothes and head over to our house? The boys won't be back from Pete's mom's house until two. You can get a shower and change into some halfway decent clothes and still have plenty of time to get to the closing. I'll stay here and supervise. You know how I love to boss around men with trucks."

"That would be great," Annajane said. "Are you sure Pete's okay with me staying with you guys for a couple of days? Just until I find a place of my own? I mean, I really could go to the Pinecone Motor Lodge . . ."

"Pete probably won't even notice you're there," Pokey said. "With every-thing going on at the new furniture store, he barely notices I'm there half the time. You, on the other hand, will probably get tired of the wild bunch way be-fore we get tired of you. The boys are superexcited you're coming. Denning even offered to let you sleep in his tree fort, which is saying a lot. You know he's pretty antigirl these days."

"That's the second best offer of a crash pad I've had from a member of your family in the past couple days," Annajane said drily.

"Fascinating! Who made the first and best offer?" Pokey asked.

"Sophie did. I stopped by to check in on her after she got home from the hospital Monday. She heard me telling Mason my tale of woe about having to move out of the loft early, and she just piped up and invited me to sleep in her daddy's room."

"She didn't!"

"Oh yes, she did."

"Out of the mouths of babes," Pokey snickered.

They heard footsteps in the stairwell, so Pokey opened the door with a grand sweep, and the room began to fill with men and furniture dollies.

"Okay, then, I'm outta here," Annajane told Pokey. "Just as soon as I find the carton with all my clean underwear."

At eight that night, Annajane wearily dragged her suitcase onto the front porch of Pete and Pokey Riggs's cheerful pale blue Dutch colonial revival home. She opened the heavily carved mahogany front door with her hip and walked in unannounced, letting the door bang behind her.

The sound of a television echoed in the high-ceilinged hallway. She stepped out of her shoes and left them on the worn rug at the foot of the stairs.

"Is that you?" Pokey called from the direction of the back of the house. "If it is, come on back. We're in the den, and it's cocktail time."

Annajane made her way toward the den, stopping over a spilled box of Legos, a green rubber dinosaur, and an enormous cardboard box of Pampers. She found her best friend sprawled out on her back on an overstuffed bottle-green damask sofa, with her bare feet resting in her husband's lap.

Pete Riggs stood up and gestured toward a silver cocktail shaker resting on a tufted leather ottoman in front of the sofa. "Care for a martini?"

"I would kill for a martini," Annajane said gratefully. She slumped down into a wing chair and looked around the room suspiciously. "It's awfully quiet around here. Where are the heathens?"

"It's grown-up time," Pete said, handing her a pint Mason jar. "Hang on a sec," he added, plunking an olive into her drink. "Now you're ready."

"The rule around here is, everybody under the age of eight has to be in bed by eight," Pokey said. She was noisily slurping on a large chocolate Blizzard. "It's the only way we keep our sanity."

Pete rejoined his wife on the sofa. "So—did your closing go all right? We were starting to get a little worried when we didn't hear from you earlier in the day, but Pokey didn't want to jinx things by calling you."

"We closed," Annajane said. "There was some minor panic when one of the loan documents still hadn't arrived at noon, but by the time we finished signing all the other paperwork, the courier had arrived with it. I'm no longer a home-owner."

"You'll find something else just as nice," Pokey said. "Here in Passcoe—right?"

Annajane sipped her martini appreciatively. "I guess. Susan Peters showed me three more listings this afternoon. That's where I've been all this time."

"And?" Pete asked. His red hair shone dully in the light from a pair of antique brass sconces on the wall behind the sofa, and, close up like this, Annajane noticed with a start that he was beginning to get just the slightest hint of silver around his temples and paunch around his midriff. He wore a pink button-down oxford cloth shirt, rumpled khaki slacks, and oxblood penny loafers with no socks.

She was struck by how much he'd changed since the first time Pokey brought him home to meet her family. Pete Riggs was a twenty-four-year-old stud, a rich, cocky kid from Charleston, who'd started on the varsity golf team all four years at Wake Forest, and he was enrolled in grad school when he'd met Pokey and gotten her pregnant right before the end of her senior year at Chapel Hill.

The Baylesses had been devastated, but Sallie had assured Pokey the family would take care of her and the baby, no matter what. Nobody could have predicted that Pete Riggs would do what he did—drop out of grad school, marry Pokey, and get a job working in his family's furniture business. And the biggest surprise, to everybody, including Pokey and Pete, was that the two of them would make a success of all of it—including marriage, parenthood, and, eventually, running and expanding Riggs Home Fashions.

"It's hopeless," Annajane said of her house hunt. "The cottage on Mimosa—the one she thought I'd be so crazy over? It's Old Lady Harrison's house. If I'd known that, I wouldn't have bothered to take a look."

"Eeewww," Pokey said, wrinkling her nose. "Mama used to make me sell her Girl Scout cookies every year when we were kids. She used to pay for the cookies with nickels and dimes that looked like they'd been scraped up out of a sewer or something. That house was nasty way back then, and she's been dead and gone at least ten years. I don't think anybody's lived in that house since she died."

"Correction," Annajane said. "There's a family of raccoons living there now. Or maybe squirrels. I didn't get past the living room, where they'd been nesting in an old sofa, so I couldn't say for sure."

"What else did you look at?" Pete asked, absentmindedly stroking Pokey's hair. "How about Clay Snider's house? I hear he and Whitney have split up."

"Yeah," Pokey said excitedly. "The Snider's house is fabulous. We went to a Christmas party there a couple years ago. You would love what they've done with the kitchen. They blew out the whole back of the house, and there's a patio and a pool house . . ."

"Susan sent me the link to their Web site. I'd love that house even without the patio and pool house. But alas, I do not have the eight hundred and fifty thousand dollars they're asking," Annajane said. She reached over to the tray on the ottoman and helped herself to a handful of roasted peanuts.

"I looked at a totally mediocre brick ranch over on Rosewood. It's a two-bedroom, two-bath, with a crazy floor plan. You actually have to walk through the master bedroom to get to the living room. But it was only eighty-nine thousand. And then I saw a butt-ugly contemporary house out past the country club. Gray cinder-block walls, smoked plate-glass windows—which were all across the whole front of the house. You'd feel like you were on display for anybody who drove past."

She sighed and took another sip of her martini, smacking her lips dramatically. "If Pete would promise to make me a martini like this every night, I might just threaten to move in here with you guys."

Pete raised his own Mason jar in a mock salute. "I live to serve."

"You know you can stay here as long as you like," Pokey said. "What have you decided about going back to work?"

"You're going back to work at Quixie?" Pete said.

"Maybe," Annajane allowed.

"You are," Pokey said. "You must. For my sake and the sake of my unborn child. Not to mention the rest of my whole nutty family."

"It's gonna depend on Davis," Annajane said. "If he won't listen to any of my ideas for a new marketing plan, it's a waste of my time to go back to work. And I really, really do not want to be around Celia. Especially now."

"Whooo," Pete chuckled. "I hear old Celia is pretty fired up about you, Annajane darlin'."

"What did you hear?" Pokey demanded, tugging at Pete's arm. "Tell!"

"Aw, no," Pete demurred. "I didn't really hear anything. Just a little trash talk in the men's grill at the club today."

"Peterson James Riggs, you better spit out what you heard at the club right this minute," Pokey exclaimed. "It's no fair teasin' us."

"Yeah, Pete," Annajane urged. "Tell. Come on, sticks and stones may break my bones and all that."

"You know I don't usually listen to that mess," Pete groused. "I was walking past Matt Kelsey at lunch, and I just heard him tell Ben Gardner that Celia was accusing you of being a home wrecker."

"You know Bonnie Kelsey is the one spreading that talk," Pokey said. "Her and Celia, that little bitch!" She pounded Pete's knees for emphasis. "Who does she think she is, coming into town and trying to take over Quixie and my brother?"

"Hey!" Pete protested. "Don't kill the messenger. I'm not agreein' with her. I'm just reporting. Anyway, who cares what those two girly men Matt Kelsey and Ben Gardner gossip about over lunch?"

Annajane plucked the olive from her half-empty drink and sucked on it. "It's a small town," she said finally. "And Mason is running the biggest business in it. People are always gonna talk about him, and the Baylesses. Face it. It comes with the territory."

"I might have to face it, but I don't have to like it," Pokey said. "Every place I go in town, somebody comes up and asks me if the boys are gonna sell Quixie. I'm getting really sick of telling people it's just a rumor."

"Jax Snax is no rumor, baby," Pete muttered. "They want Quixie, and they want it bad. The question is whether Mason or Davis is going to prevail. And how your mama's gonna vote."

"What about me?" Pokey demanded. "Don't you think Daddy left me any say in what happens to Quixie?"

"I sure hope he did," Pete said. "But let's face it, honey—you've not worked for the company since you were a teenager, and you never worked in management. Knowing your daddy like I do, I've got a feeling that when he divvied up the pie, he saved the biggest, juiciest pieces for your brothers. And your mama."

"I guess we'll find out who gets what next week," Pokey said. "But I called Davis today, and I told him flat out, if he lets Quixie close down, or move from Passcoe, I will never forgive him."

"What did he say to that?" Annajane asked.

"Oh, he just tried to bullshit me," Pokey replied. "Said nobody's discussin' closing it down or moving it. He says Jax Snax will only make the company better."

"And him richer," Pete quipped.

Pokey picked up the remote control from the tray on the ottoman. "All right y'all, enough talking about business. I am ready for some mindless television for an hour or so before I call it a night. Which is it—HGTV or Food TV?"

"You mean food porn or decorator porn?" Pete grabbed a pillow and wedged it under his wife's head. He stood up and dropped a kiss on Pokey's forehead. "I think I'll go watch baseball upstairs."

Annajane experienced a familiar pang of jealousy at Pete's tenderness toward Pokey. Her friend had so much—a home and a husband who adored her—and three rowdy but healthy children, with a fourth on the way. Did Pokey appreciate just how blessed she was? Or how hollow and envious Annajane sometimes felt in her company?

"Check on the boys, will you?" Pokey called absentmindedly while she flipped channels. "Make sure Denning isn't up there messin' with one of those doggone video games."

An hour later, after they'd both grown bored with *Real Housewives* and *Bridezilla* shows, Pokey handed off the remote to Annajane.

"It's all yours," she said, yawning.

"Nope," Annajane said. "I'm going to bed, too. I've got to save my energy for going back to Quixie in the morning."

"Good for you," Pokey said, nodding her approval. "And what about Mason? What's going to happen with you two?"

"Leave it be, Pokey," Annajane warned. "Everything is happening too fast. We're friends, okay? Can we just leave it at that for now?"

"Friends with benefits?" Pokey chirped. "Look, I just don't want you to let Celia Wakefield screw things up by guilt-tripping you," Pokey said. "You and Mason didn't do anything wrong. Not deliberately anyway. You acted honorably, so just hold your head high and ignore Celia."

"Celia, ugh," Annajane said. "I am not looking forward to running into her tomorrow."

"Oh my God," Pokey said suddenly. "I forgot. I finally did call Angela—my sorority sister, the one who's a buyer for Belk?"

"Does she know Celia?" Annajane asked.

"She'd heard of her, but she didn't really have any dirt on her. However, she did give me the name and phone number of a friend of hers who might know more about the details of Celia's clothing business," Pokey said. She reached in her pocket and handed over what looked like the page from a Bob the Builder coloring book that had been written on in red crayon.

"Her name is Katie Derscheid," Pokey said, yawning widely again. "I wasn't sure how to spell it. Just call her and mention Angela Hooker's name."

At some point in the evening, Annajane dimly recognized the sound of rain on the roof and the brush of tree limbs against the windowpanes. She opened one eye and saw a jagged flash of lightning streaking across the deep blue sky outside. She snuggled deeper into the down comforter and pulled a spare pillow over her head to drown out the noise, glad not to be out in the storm.

She drifted off to sleep again, but maybe an hour later was aware of a shaft of light streaming in through the doorway. She lifted her head off the pillow and spied a small, forlorn little body standing in the doorway.

It was Petey, clad in his cotton Thomas the Tank Engine pajamas, sucking his thumb and trailing a bedraggled but much-loved blue silk bordered blanket.

"Hey, buddy," she said groggily. "What's up?"

"I'm scared," he said, moving his thumb aside only long enough to speak.

"Want me to walk you back to your bed?"

He shook his head side to side, vigororously.

"Want to go sleep with your mommy and daddy?"

"The baby is with Mommy and Daddy."

She sighed and scooted over on the queen-sized bed. "Come on, then."

Petey favored her with a tremulous smile before crawling up into the bed beside her. Annajane rubbed his back the way she'd seen Pokey do so many times, and a few minutes later, she heard his breathing become soft and rhythmic. Smiling to herself, she turned on her side and fell back asleep herself, only dimly aware of the warm little body spooned up against her back.

Maybe an hour later, she heard the bedroom door creak open. Looking up, she saw Pokey silhouetted in the doorway.

"Hey," Pokey whispered. "Pete's in there snoring so loud I can't sleep. Okay if I bunk in with you?"

Annajane lifted the edge of the comforter to reveal the sleeping form of Petey.

Pokey laughed softly, and walked around to the other side of the bed, yawning widely as she shifted her young son into the middle of the bed. Moments later, mother and son were breathing in tandem.

Once again, Annajane managed to fall back asleep. The rain began to beat at the windows, heavier now, and the howl of the wind became ominous. She shifted in the bed and now felt a warm, damp spot where she'd been sleeping moments earlier. She sniffed the sheet, sniffed Petey.

"Crap," she muttered softly. Wrapping herself in the quilt from the foot of the bed, she tiptoed out of the room, headed for the sofa in the den. Tomorrow, she promised herself, she would either find a house to buy or check into a room at the Pinecone Motor Lodge.

29

Annajane felt small hands lightly patting her face. Opening one eye, she spied Petey, staring at her intently. *"Curious George,"* he said.

Sleep deprived, she turned over so that she was facing the back of the sofa. He shook her shoulder. *"Curious George,"* he repeated. She felt her head being struck with something, and reached back and caught his hand, which was holding the remote control.

"Petey! Leave Annajane alone."

Annajane rolled onto her back. Now Pokey stood over her, holding an out-stretched mug of coffee.

The room was still in half darkness. "What time is it?" Annajane mumbled.

"A smidge after seven," Pokey said. She sat on the edge of the ottoman, and Annajane, with effort, managed to pull herself upright.

"Curious George," Petey said loudly. "I want *Curious George."* He slung his damp, pee-scented blanket across her knees and climbed into her lap.

"Sorry," Pokey said, deftly scooping the child off Annajane and onto the ottoman. "Petey is our early bird. I've tried everything to get him to sleep late and let us alone in the morning, but it's no use. Little guys don't know numbers, and they have no concept of time. So now I've trained him to wait until the streetlights go off outside. Then and only then, he can come downstairs to the den and turn on PBS. He loves *Curious George* and *Dinosaur Train*."

"Those are television shows?" Annajane took the mug and inhaled the hot coffee fumes.

"His favorites," Pokey said, clicking on the television. "How come you wound up sleeping down here?"

Annajane handed her the damp blanket. "Your son sprung a leak last night."

"Sorry about that," Pokey said with a laugh. "Welcome to my world."

"Yeah, about that," Annajane said. "It won't hurt your feelings if I find myself someplace else to stay?"

"Not in the least," Pokey said. "I'd stay someplace else if I were you. Hell, I'd stay someplace else if I were me, but I think my husband might object."

Annajane reached out and tousled Petey's strawberry-blond hair. "Don't kid yourself, sweetie. You've got the world on a string. A beautiful home, loving husband, great kids. I'd trade places with you in a New York minute."

"I know you would," Pokey said softly. "But you'll have all that pretty soon, too, Annajane. I know you will, if you just hang in there and make up your mind that he's worth fighting for."

Later that morning, Annajane swung her car into the parking lot at the Quixie plant and groaned when she saw the familiar silver Saab parked in its customary slot.

You can do this, she told herself. *Celia is not the boogeyman. And you are not a quitter.*

Heads turned to stare at her as she walked through the reception area and into the back office. Obviously, everybody had heard the rumors about her and Mason.

She smiled and ignored the stares and whispers. She found Voncile at her desk, stationed right outside Mason's office. Voncile was on the phone, but when she looked up and saw Annajane, she waved her into Mason's office.

He'd just slammed down the phone and was staring intently at the computer monitor on his desktop, frowning, when she walked in.

"Hey," she said, feeling unaccountably shy. Hadn't she come just a flashlight beam away from hot messy car sex with this man just a few days ago?

"Morning," Mason said.

"Something wrong?"

Mason rubbed his chin and looked away. "Not good news. I've asked Davis to stop in for a chat, and I'll fill you in when he gets here."

He held up a can of Quixie. "Want one?"

She shuddered. "It's a little early for me to start on the red stuff. What gives?"

He took a long chug of the soda. "Just getting myself back to the brand, like we talked about yesterday. I hadn't realized how long it had been since I'd actually really stopped and tasted our product."

"Did you come to any conclusions?"

"As a matter of fact, I did," he said, leaning back in his chair. "For one thing, I think it's a pretty darned good waker-upper."

"Better than coffee?"

He shrugged. "I don't think we can claim that, based on the amount of caffeine in Quixie, but it's just as good as some of these high-priced energy drinks that are killing us at convenience stores."

"Hold that thought," Annajane said, grabbing a pen and a yellow legal pad from his desktop. "What else?"

"You were right about the taste of celebration. I'm thinking Quixie reminds people of good times, happy occasions, boat rides on the lake, summers at the beach, campouts under the stars. Fun, wholesome stuff. That's what we started out selling, that's what we need to get back to."

"Riiiight," Annajane said. "We're on the same page so far."

They heard a tap on the door, and the sound of a throat clearing.

Davis leaned into the office, glancing from his brother to Annajane. "You wanted to see me?"

Mason stood up and walked around his desk, clasping his brother's hand. "Come on in."

"I'll talk to you later," Annajane said, making for the door.

"No, stay," Mason said. "But close the door behind you, please."

. . .

Davis, Annajane thought, was clearly uncomfortable being in a room with her. He tugged at the too-tight starched collar of his pale blue button-down shirt and made a point of taking a chair as far from hers as possible.

His face was jowly and sunburned, and his dark hair, already starting to recede, still bore damp comb marks. Unlike Mason, who usually wore khaki slacks and a Quixie logo shirt to work, Davis was, as always, impeccably turned out in an expensively tailored dark suit, a red silk tie with repp stripes, and black wingtip shoes polished to a low luster. A pair of flashy gold cuff links twinkled from the French cuffs of his shirt. He looked like a refugee from Madison Avenue.

When the three of them were seated, Mason solemnly handed cold cans of Quixie to his guests.

"Is this a stunt?" Davis asked, putting the can, untouched, on the edge of the desktop.

"Not at all," Mason said, edging the can back toward his brother. "Come on, Davis, at least take a sip. It won't kill you. You've been drinking it your whole life, for Chrissakes."

Davis rolled his eyes, sipped, and put the can back on the desk. "Happy now? Actually, I never liked the stuff. I'll take a Sprite or ginger ale any day."

Mason leaned back in his chair. "Well, that's one of the roots of our problem, right there."

"I resent that," Davis snapped.

"It's not meant as a personal criticism. I just don't see how you can sell what you don't like and don't believe in," Mason said, his voice mild.

"I believe in the company," Davis said. "I believe in profits. And I don't need a marketing lesson from you, thanks just the same."

Mason leaned across the desk, raising his hands, palm out, in a gesture of surrender. "Can we just have a friendly, nonconfrontational business discussion here?"

"You're the boss," Davis said. "What's on your mind?"

"Our marketing plan," Mason said. "Or the lack of."

Davis's face reddened. "Look, if you want to second-guess me and rehire Farnham-Capheart, I guess you can do that, since you're the CEO. But I don't see the point in doing an end run . . ."

"I'm not second-guessing you," Mason said crisply. "And I have no intention of making an end run around you, which is why I asked you to meet with Anna-jane and me this morning. But I would like to point out that it would have been good if you, as a courtesy, had informed me that you intended to fire the ad agency we've been working with for more than thirty years."

"As vice president of marketing, that was entirely my decision to make," Davis said, glancing nervously over at Annajane. "If this Jax Snax deal hap-pens, we'll be working with their agency, which happens to be the largest in the country, and anyway, Annajane, you said yourself you didn't like the tone of the new campaign . . ."

It was Annajane's turn to clear her throat. Her stomach roiled with nervous-ness, but something else was boiling up inside her. Anger.

"You deliberately sabotaged me," Annajane said quietly. "You and Celia sug-gested to Joe Farnham that he should hire me, because you were sure I would be 'uncomfortable' working with Celia after she and Mason got engaged. And then, as soon as I'd quit my job here, and days before I was to start there, you made sure I wouldn't have a job in Atlanta. That was petty, Davis. It was mean and it was low-down, and I really can't believe I've ever done anything to you to deserve that kind of treatment."

"Hey!" Davis said sharply. "This was nothing personal. It was business."

Mason looked stunned. "Is this true?" he asked Davis. "You angled Joe to give her a job—to get rid of her, because Celia didn't want her around?"

"I assumed you wouldn't want your ex-wife around," Davis said easily. "Because your fiancée sure as hell didn't. I just did what I thought you would have done—if you had any balls, which you apparently don't."

Mason's face darkened. "Annajane and I had managed to get along quite nicely for the past five years, without any help from you. She's been an impor-tant part of our team . . ."

"Oh please!" Davis broke in. "She came to work here because Dad thought she was a cute kid and she was married to you, and she stayed on after the di-vorce because you somehow felt guilty about the breakup. Well, that's on you, brother." He gave Annajane a pitying glance. "She hasn't had an original idea in years. Once Celia came on board, it was clear—to everybody but you—that we needed a new direction. I did what needed to be done. And I'd do it again."

Annajane felt her hands clench and unclench with barely suppressed rage. Tears sprang to her eyes, and she blinked them back helplessly.

"That's enough," Mason roared. He pointed at his computer screen. "If you're such a marketing genius, explain to me why our sales have been sliding every quarter for the past two years. Also, explain why we're paying a six-figure promotional fee to a scumbucket Nascar driver like Donnell Boggs, who not only hasn't placed in a race since we hired him, he's had two DUI arrests in the past six weeks." Mason flung a stack of autographed glossy photos of Boggs, wearing a cap emblazoned with the Quixie logo, across the desk at his brother.

The photos fluttered to the floor. "That's the face you hired to be the face of Quixie?" Mason thundered. "Check the front page of today's *Charlotte Observer.* Or you can find the story online. It's on all the wire services, The Mecklenburg County Police arrested Boggs at a motel in Concord last night, where he'd checked in with a sixteen-year-old high school dropout, a quart of Tecate, and eleven hundred dollars' worth of Ecstasy."

Davis's ruddy face paled. "What? No. That's not possible. I talked to Donnell last night. He was heading to Spartanburg for the opening of a new Piggly Wiggly; then he was throwing out the first pitch at a minor league game in Greenville. It was Quixie night."

"He never made it to Spartanburg, or Greenville, thank God," Mason said. "He was too busy hooking up with a teenager he met online. I want him fired. Today."

"I can't fire him. He's got a contract," Davis said. "We've got all the summer promotional materials set. Cardboard cutouts of Donnell for all the displays, models of the number eight Quixie car. Supermarket openings, theme park promos. His picture is gonna be on the twelve-pack cartons. They go to the printers tomorrow. It's all set."

"Unset it," Mason said bluntly. "Do whatever it takes. Call our attorney and have him start the paperwork. I want that contract canceled based on the morals clause. I want the sponsorship deal ended, and I want our name painted over on his cars, even if you have to do it yourself. I don't want that degenerate turd's name mentioned in the same breath as Quixie."

"God," Davis said, burying his head in his hands. "We've spent thousands on this campaign. Hundreds of thousands. We'll have to do new ad buys, shoot new commercials . . . There's no time to create a new campaign from scratch."

"I can help with that," Annajane said.

Davis gave her a sour look.

"It's what Mason was just talking about. Returning to our roots. Retro. I've got all the old mechanicals and illustrations for the Quixie ads from the forties through the sixties," she said. "And I bet if I call Farnham-Capheart they've still got footage of the old commercials. We just clean up the graphics for the print ads, maybe reshoot some of the commercials, cut out the footage of Donnell and the Quixie car, maybe substitute with novelty bits from the old commercials. Make the new ones look like those old Dr Pepper ads everybody used to love. We can do Facebook pages, the works. If we get started right away, we should be able to pull it off."

"Fine," Davis said tersely. "You seem to have it all figured out. I'll leave it to you."

"Davis, enough!" Mason snapped. "Annajane didn't hire Donnell Boggs because she wanted to party with a bogus celebrity. You did. Now stop with the pissy attitude and let's get this fixed."

Davis stood abruptly and dumped his nearly full Quixie can into a metal trash can, where the sound of metal meeting metal made a hollow clang.

"You can't fire me," he told his brother. "And you can't stop the inevitable. You can slow it down, but only until next week, when old man Norris gets off his ass and tells us how the trust works. But we both know how it's gonna go down. Mama's tired of watching this company slide into the dumper. She'll vote to sell. And when that happens, you'll be out. I guarantee."

Mason watched his brother's exit with a pained expression on his face. He turned to Annajane. "Fun times, huh?"

She winced. "That was pretty brutal."

"At least we cleared the air," Mason said. "No more of this bullshit passive-aggressive radio silence. He knows how I feel, and I definitely know where he stands on things. Also, it's gonna be expensive, but at least we're shed of that slime-dog Donnell Boggs. I knew that guy was trouble the minute I laid eyes on him."

"I guess we're just lucky he got arrested before the new campaign rolled completely out," Annajane said.

"Luck had nothing to do with it," Mason said. "I've had a private investigator following him for weeks. As soon as he saw Boggs pull into the motel parking lot with that girl yesterday, he called me, and then he tipped the cops."

30

An unfamiliar woman's voice on the other end of the line asked, "Is this Annajane Hudgens?"

She glanced at the caller ID screen on her phone, but it said UNKNOWN.

"Yes," Annajane said cautiously. "Who's calling?"

"My name is Katie Derscheid. I'm a friend of a friend of your friend, Pokey Riggs. I understand you're interested in knowing something about Celia Wakefield and Gingerpeachy?"

Annajane's pulse quickened. She got up from her desk and closed and locked her office door. Just in case. She'd been working furiously all day, trying to rebuild and rebook the summer Quixie promotion, had even worked straight through lunch, so she'd fortunately managed to avoid Celia. But she wouldn't put it past Celia to be lurking somewhere nearby.

She sat back down at her desk and straightened her shoulders. "Hi Katie. I was actually going to call you today, until I got involved in putting out assorted forest fires around here." She lowered her voice til it was just above a whisper, and still deliberately avoided saying Celia's name out loud. Just in case. "So . . . you do know her?"

"Ohhhh yes," Katie Derscheid said. "She's, uh, not a friend of yours, is she?"

"No," Annajane said, a slight shiver going down her spine. "Definitely not."

"Oh goodie," Katie said. "Now we can really talk girl to girl."

Annajane laughed ruefully. "She's a bit of an enigma, isn't she?"

"She's a scorpion," Katie said. "Absolutely deadly. And not in a good way. She screwed my former company, Baby Brands, big-time."

"Interesting," Annajane said. "The company I work for, Quixie, hired, um, that person, as a consultant, based on her reputation as a sort of girl genius with branding and business development."

"Yeah, what's genius about Celia is her ability to totally bullshit her way through life," Katie said.

"Did she really sell her company for ten million? That's what we all heard. In fact, I think she kind of alluded to that herself."

"The purchase price was actually just under half that—five million," Katie said. "The deal was structured so that Celia would be paid in staggered amounts. She did take Baby Brands for more than a million in cash, but she'll never see another dime of their money—not if their lawyers have their say."

"Oh my," Annajane breathed. "So . . . what happened?"

"Smoke and mirrors," Katie said cryptically. "That was the essence of her company. When Baby Brands bought Gingerpeachy, they were told she had millions in orders from several chain retailers—Gymboree, Pottery Barn Kids, Macy's. We bought everything—the name, the outstanding orders, the inventory. And all of it was bogus. The order numbers were wildly inflated, and as for inventory—there was none. A couple bolts of fabric and a ton of factory seconds that were unsalable as far as we were concerned."

Annajane's eyes widened. "How did she manage to pull that off?"

Katie's laugh was the deep, throaty chortle of a woman who'd seen a lot. "Celia Wakefield has ESP—extrasensual perception. She meets a guy, and within a couple hours, he's begging her to 'beat me, hurt me, make me write bad checks.'"

"And that's what happened at your company?"

"She met the president of Baby Brands, Reeve Sonnenfeld, in the lobby bar at the Mansion at Turtle Creek, in Dallas, during the Winter Mart week. Celia was repping her own line in a little showroom at the time."

"I think I know where this is going," Annajane said. "She met my boss in the exact same way."

"Gotta love a gal who trolls hotel bars, right?" Katie said with a chuckle. "She's one step up from a whore, that Celia. Anyway, she strikes up a conversation with Reeve, tells him she's got this great line of dresses, reversible, all cotton—she even whips a sample dress out of her purse to show him. And then she acts all surprised when he tells her he IS Baby Brands. They have a couple more drinks; then Celia gives him her business card and takes off, leaving Reeve begging for another look, if you know what I mean. Of course, they meet later that night, after Reeve's wife Sandee has gone back to the suite."

"Right there in the same hotel with his wife?" Annajane asked.

"Oh, it was all business," Katie said. "At first. Reeve came back from Dallas raving about this brilliant young entrepreneur he was going to 'mentor.' It was revolting. I mean, she's two years younger than his daughter, for God's sake. Pretty soon, he's flying off to meet Celia in Atlanta and LA for Marts there, only those times, he made sure Sandee stayed home. Everybody in the company knew what was going on with those two. Everybody but Sandee."

Annajane leaned back in her desk chair and looked out her office window. It was getting late in the day. The parking lot was emptying out. She got up and walked over to the window. If she stood at just the right angle, she could see Celia's parking space. It was empty. She exhaled noisily.

"Hey, are you still there?" Katie asked.

"I'm here," Annajane said. "What happened next?"

"The inevitable," Katie said. "Reeve got the brilliant idea to buy Gingerpeachy. As soon as the deal was inked, Celia and Reeve were history. And we were left holding a big bag of Gingerpeachy crap. It couldn't have happened at a worse time. You know what the economy's like."

"Is Baby Brands in trouble?" Annajane asked.

"They'll survive," Katie said drily. "Of course, it meant some belt tightening. Which meant I lost my job."

"Oh, wow, I'm sorry," Annajane said. "So, how does she get away with something like that? I mean, isn't what she did fraud or something?"

"Or something," Katie said. "It's all been kept pretty hush-hush. But yeah, I think Baby Brands has started legal action against Celia."

"You mentioned Celia met your vice president at a hotel bar," Katie said. "Are they having a fling?"

"No. Davis was infatuated with her, but strictly on a professional basis, as far as I know," Annajane said. She was somehow reluctant to reveal to this stranger that Celia had targeted a much bigger fish at Quixie, in the form of Mason. "He brought her into the company as a consultant, based on what he thought was her marketing expertise and, of course, because of her track record starting and selling a successful retail business like Ginger-peachy."

Katie's laugh sounded sour. "Let me just fill you in on Celia Wakefield. First of all, is she still peddling that line of crap about how she designed the original PopTot dress?"

"Yeah," Annajane said. "I've seen the dresses. They really are adorable."

"They're very adorable," Katie said. "But there's some question of who actually came up with the idea for them."

"Really?"

"After Baby Brands bought out Gingerpeachy, *Parenting* magazine did a nice spread on the dresses," Katie said. "Not long afterwards, the reporter who did the piece called to let us know that *she'd* had a call from a woman claiming that Celia stole the idea from her."

"Why do I have a mental image of the theme music from *Jaws* in my head?" Annajane asked.

"A shark would be insulted to be compared to Celia," Katie said. "Celia happened to be working at a boutique and she got hold of one of this girl's sample dresses, which she was sewing at home with her mother. So Celia, sniffing an opportunity, drew up a business plan, hired a sewing room, and turned out a line of dresses exactly like the ones from the boutique. The next thing you know, she's the girl genius of retailing."

"Did you do anything to check out the other woman's claim?" Annajane asked.

"Nope," Katie said. "It's not like she trademarked the dresses. Anyway, there wasn't anything we could do about it. We listened to her story, but what could we do? We'd been victimized, too. By then, Celia was long gone."

"I know," Annajane said, putting down her pencil. "By then, she was here."

There was a knock at Annajane's office door. Her pulse quickened. "Katie, I have to go now. There's somebody at my door. Thanks so much for the information."

Mason stood in the hallway outside her office, his laptop case slung over his shoulder.

"Hey, you," he said, looking puzzled. "You're locking yourself in now?"

"Sorry," Annajane said. "I had so much going on; I just couldn't deal with distractions today."

"Wish I could lock myself in. Or other people out," Mason said. "Look, it's nearly six. Wanna go get some dinner?"

Annajane looked up and down the hallway. "I don't know," she murmured. "I've still got a ton of work to catch up on."

"Let it go until tomorrow," Mason said firmly.

"It's not just that," she said. "You know how people are. If they see us out together, it'll just fire up the rumor mill again."

"So?" He brushed his hand through his hair, impatient. "I've got news for you, Annajane. People in this town already think we're having some big flaming affair."

"I hate being the topic of gossip," Annajane said.

Mason rolled his eyes. "Me, too. Especially when I'm not even getting to do the things people suspect we're already doing." He caught her hand. "Come on. Please? We've wasted five years pretending we don't care about each other. I don't want to waste any more time. Do you?"

She felt so torn. She wanted to see him, be with him. Why was it so hard to say yes to making herself happy?

"Annajane?"

"All right," she said finally. "But I've got to finish up a couple things. I'll meet you. Where?"

"There's a new place, Blueplate, in Creekdale. Where the old Emile's used to be? But it's silly to drive all the way over there in two separate cars. I'll go home, check on Sophie, shower and change, and meet you back here—in an hour?"

"It's a deal," Annajane said. On impulse, she leaned in and kissed him on the cheek.

He raised an eyebrow in surprise. "Now you're talking."

31

Blueplate was located in a small wood-shingled cottage set back from the road in Creekdale. Annajane had eaten there once when it had been Emile's, but hadn't cared for the ersatz French menu—or the haughty waiters.

Now, though, the place had been transformed. Rough whitewashed plaster walls replaced the overblown red damask wallpaper, and the furnishings were a friendly mélange of wooden tables and mismatched chairs. A small bar took up most of the entryway, and, beyond, they could hear the clatter of dishes and the hum of conversations in the dining room.

The hostess, a slender brunette with pale skin and tattoos wreathing both wrists, identified herself as Tabitha, the owner and wife of the chef, as she gathered up a menu and silverware for them.

"It's such an awesome night; I think we have a table out on the patio, if you want," Tabitha offered.

Annajane looked to Mason for approval. "That'd be great," he said. "We've both been cooped up in an office all day. It'll be nice to have some fresh air."

As they were led through the dining room, Annajane kept her face lowered and stayed a couple steps ahead of Mason. Realizing that she still felt awkward and self-conscious about being seen in public with him, she gave herself a mental scolding.

Stop hiding! You've done nothing wrong. Anyway, it's only dinner.

The patio was just as charming as the interior of the restaurant, with a rough-beamed peaked ceiling lined with twinkling white lights and a flagstone floor. Despite her earlier internal scolding, Annajane was grateful when the hostess seated them at a table shielded from the rest of the room by an enormous potted hydrangea whose platter-sized blue blossoms formed an effective screen.

They ordered drinks. Mason looked surprised at her order.

"Since when do you drink martinis?" he asked, sitting back in his chair and regarding her with interest. "You always used to like those girly drinks— what, cosmos?"

"Tastes change," she said lightly. "People change. But I know you still like bourbon."

"I've changed in other ways," Mason said. "Older and wiser, I hope. More cynical, definitely."

A single candle in a low jar in the center of the table illuminated his face. She studied it now. His thick blond hair had a few streaks of gray, and crow's feet etched the corners of his eyes, which somehow seemed a deeper blue, not the clear blue she remembered from their youth. His jawline was still firm, and she realized, with surprise, that he seemed to have lost weight, his cheeks somewhat hollow, his worn blue blazer hanging awkwardly from his shoulders. And now that she thought about it, his khaki slacks bunched at the waist where his belt cinched them too tightly.

She wrinkled her forehead. "How much weight have you lost?"

He shrugged. "I don't keep track. Maybe twenty, twenty-five."

"You're not dieting, right? You never used to have a weight problem."

He shrugged. "Not dieting. Just kind of distracted with everything going on in my life."

Annajane laughed. "I wish I had that problem. I can't think of too many foods I don't like."

"Don't say that." His voice was sharp. "You're fine exactly the way you are."

The waiter brought their appetizer, a sizzling skillet full of sweet briny shrimp sautéed in garlic and olive oil, swimming alongside tiny Greek olives and feta cheese. A loaf of hot crusty bread accompanied the shrimp, and they busied themselves dividing up the shrimp, dipping the bread into the fragrant juices.

"Mmm," Annajane said appreciatively between bites. "Heaven. I like this place so much better than Emile's. I'll have to come back here."

"How was the rest of your day?" she asked, after the waiter removed the remains of the shrimp and brought their entrées.

Mason took a bite of his flounder, chewed, and considered. "Difficult. Davis is determined to battle me on every issue, large and small. Business decisions that should be routine, things like truck maintenance or contracts with vendors, all of a sudden, he's questioning, objecting to, second-guessing."

He shook his head. "It's like he feels like he has to stir every pot."

"Maybe he's trying to prove himself."

"To whom? He's family. It's not like I can fire him, as he so aptly pointed out today."

"I don't know," Annajane admitted. "Being an only child, your family dynamic is kind of hard for me to read. Maybe he feels he has to prove himself to himself. Or your mom." She took a sip of water and had another thought. "Or Celia."

"Celia," Mason put his fork down and frowned. "Much as it pains me, I think this is a topic we can't keep avoiding."

"You don't have to talk about her," Annajane offered.

"Yeah. I do." He picked up his fork and took another bite of fish. And then another.

"It's like she casts this giant shadow over us. I can't get around it. Can't seem to get away from her."

Annajane giggled. "You make her sound like this huge presence, when in reality, she's this teeny-tiny little person."

He grimaced. "Her physical size is one of many deceptive aspects to Celia. I guess I found that out the hard way. It's like she . . . wills something, and it happens. She showed up at Quixie, and she was smart and hardworking . . ."

"And sexy," Annajane put in. "Glittery and fascinating and compelling."

"On the surface, maybe," Mason agreed. "But when you get her alone, one on one, after a while, you realize there's just nothing much there. She doesn't read, except business stories, doesn't watch movies or television, except CNBC. Really, the only thing I think she's passionate about is money. Making it, and spending it."

Annajane took a sip of the wine he'd ordered her, gathering courage. "You two did seem like an odd match to me."

"She was ... different. I guess that's what fascinated me about her," Mason admitted. "And okay, I was surprised she didn't go for Davis, the lady's man of the family. Maybe I was flattered that she was so openly pursuing me."

"Or your money," Annajane said, wondering if she should share what she'd just learned about Celia's business dealings with her ex-fiancé.

"Davis has as much money as I do," Mason pointed out.

"But maybe not as much power over the company. Anyway," she added, "I get what she saw in you—besides the financial aspect."

"And what would that be?"

She gave him a gentle smile. "Now you're just fishing for compliments."

"No. Seriously. Are you still attracted to me?"

Color crept into her cheeks and she looked away.

"Annajane?" His knee touched hers lightly under the table.

Another sip of wine. "I never stopped being attracted to you, but then you knew that. Even ... when my world fell apart, it was so hard, being around you, seeing you, knowing what you were capable of."

He looked stricken. "How would I know what you were thinking back then? You deliberately cut yourself off from me. You wouldn't return my calls, or talk to me, or even listen to reason. And then Dad died . . ."

She sighed. "I was crushed. I couldn't stand to see you. It was so painful, knowing . . ."

"Annajane," his voice was even. He pushed his half-eaten dinner aside. "You've spent five years dodging me, hiding from me, even though all that time, I was right there. You told me earlier tonight that you've grown up. Matured. Are you finally ready to listen to me now?"

Her eyes met his. "Are you ready to tell me the truth?"

"I never lied to you about that night," he said, returning her gaze. "I was never unfaithful to you. Never even considered it. I loved you, and you were all I wanted."

She felt the old shame, the bitterness welling up in her throat. Unbidden, the memories of that night—the last night of their marriage—came flooding back.

"You never came home!" she said urgently. "You knew it was the company Christmas party, that I was counting on you. But you didn't even bother to call. I was humiliated. And then I really thought you'd been in an accident or something. You have no idea how terrified I was. But when you came home and acted as if I should have known it was 'just business' that you were out with that woman . . . Eva."

"Christ," he muttered. He leaned over and dabbed at her eyes with his dinner napkin. "I'd completely blocked her name from my memory."

"I'll never forget her name," Annajane said, her voice wobbly. "Or her hand-writing. On that CD I found in your car."

"Can I tell you something?" He took her chin and cupped it between his palms. "I couldn't tell you this that night. I wanted to, but I was so mad at you for thinking I'd cheated, my damned pride wouldn't let me."

"Tell me what?"

"You found that CD, but it wasn't mine. It was the company car, remember? I drove it to Atlanta and back, but it was the company car."

She stared. "Then, whose?"

"Dad's. God help me, it was Dad's."

She sat back, stunned. "Your father? He was the one having an affair with that Eva woman?"

Mason nodded sadly. "That's why we were so late getting back that night. We signed the papers for the Maxi-Mart deal, and we were all supposed to meet up afterwards at the Ritz-Carlton in Buckhead for dinner. Dad offered to drive Eva back to her hotel so she could change for dinner, and he made it clear to me that he didn't need me riding shotgun. So I stalled for a while, and finally caught a ride over to the Ritz with one of the Maxi-Mart guys. We had drinks in the bar, and waited . . . and waited. I kept excusing myself to go to the men's room, so I could call Dad's cell, but he wasn't answering. I didn't know what the hell to think."

"You had no idea he was seeing her?" Annajane asked.

"None," he said bitterly. "He knew I wouldn't put up with that crap. I caught him, once, years ago, with another woman. At the cottage at Wrightsville Beach.

Pokey was with me. I confronted him; we had a huge blow-up. That's the summer I left town. I couldn't stand to look him in the face for nearly a year; I was
so disgusted with him for cheating on Mom. On us."

"Pokey told me about that," Annajane admitted.

It was his turn to get taken by surprise. "She swore she'd never say a word.
We both did."

"Relax," Annajane chided him. "She only told me the other night, at the
hospital, while we were waiting for Sophie's surgery. She said that was how
she knew you wouldn't have cheated on me. Because you didn't want to be like
your dad."

Mason let out a long breath and sat back in his chair. "He was a hero to me
in so many ways, you know? He was a great dad. As busy as he was with Quixie,
he always had time to spend with us kids. And I know he loved my mother. You
saw them together. He was devoted to her! So how could he? It made me sick to
think about it."

"Your dad was a good man," Annajane said. "He did so much for this community, in Passcoe. He could have spent his time being just another rich prick,
but he wasn't like that. He genuinely cared about people. And he did love your
family. Especially Sallie. I guess maybe some men just compartmentalize
things. They think sex and love are two different things, and it's okay to sleep
around, as long as their wife doesn't find out and nobody gets hurt. I can't explain it, but I believe it's so."

"I'm not like that," Mason said evenly. "I'm not like him. Not that way."

"Tell me about that night," she urged. "I'm ready to listen now. I want to
understand what happened."

He took a sip of wine and closed his eyes, remembering the evening. "It was
getting late, so we finally ordered dinner," Mason said. "I was beginning to think
I might have to cab back to the hotel and spend another night, because I had
no idea where Dad and Eva were. Finally, at around ten o'clock, the two of them
came strolling in, acting like nothing had happened. It was ten o'damned clock!
We were the last party left in the dining room. The waiters were literally sweeping the floors and polishing the glasses in the bar."

"Did they have some kind of an explanation for where they'd been?"

"Dad had some lame-ass story about how they'd stopped for a drink on the way over and just lost track of time," Mason said, his lips curling in disgust. "It was a load of crap. He reeked of gin, and her hair looked like she'd just gotten out of bed. They were screwing their brains out in her hotel room. It didn't take an ace detective to figure it out. We ordered coffee, and finally, at eleven, I managed to drag him out of there. And then, on top of everything, it really did start snowing. The farther north of Atlanta we got, the icier the roads were."

"You should have called," Annajane said. "Just to let me know."

"I know I should have. Now," he said. "I was a selfish, self-centered idiot. I was so furious with Dad, I couldn't even speak. And he was half in the bag. He fell asleep as soon as he got in the passenger seat. I swear to God, more than once, as I was driving, I had the urge to reach over and throttle him. For what he'd put me through. And what he was doing to Mom. I didn't give a thought to you."

Annajane sighed. "Why didn't you just tell me that night—as soon as you got home?"

"I don't know," Mason admitted. "I remember how tired I was, and then you were so pissed at me; I just wasn't in the mood for a fight right then. I'd made up my mind, the next day, to have it out with Dad. I was seriously thinking, on that long drive home, maybe it was time to leave Quixie. Get out from under all the family drama, and see if I could make it on my own someplace else. I hated his guts that night."

"I wish I'd known," Annajane said.

"I shook him awake when we got to Cherry Hill that night," Mason said. "I didn't even cut the engine. I just said, 'We're home.' He got out of the car. He couldn't even look me in the eye. He could tell how angry I was. I think he said something like, 'Talk to you tomorrow,' and he staggered toward the front door. And I just drove off. Of course, the next time I saw him, he was barely alive. All I could think about was how I'd left it with him. 'We're home'—that's the last thing I ever said to my father."

"Oh, Mason," Annajane began.

Just then, Mason's cell phone began to ring. He looked annoyed but pulled it from his pocket and looked at the readout screen.

His expression softened as he saw who the caller was. "Hey, Soph," he said. "Everything okay?"

Mason listened for a moment, then laughed. "No, afraid not, punkin. Letha is the boss, and if the boss says you have to go to bed, then you'd better ske-daddle. Okay? Hmm? Yeah, actually she's right here."

He handed the phone to Annajane. "Sophie would like a word with you."

"Hi, Sophie," she said.

"Annajane, Aunt Pokey says you spent the night at her house last night."

"That's right," she said cautiously.

"No fair!" the girl cried. "Petey and Denning and Clayton get all the fun. I want you to spend the night at my house."

"Not tonight," Annajane said. "Maybe the next time your daddy has to go out of town, I can come over and we'll have a spend-the-night party. Girls only! How would that be?"

"Come tonight," Sophie said

"I can't tonight, sweetie," Annajane said. "It's a school night for you, and a work night for me."

"But Letha says I'm not going to school tomorrow, because I had an opera-tion."

Annajane rolled her eyes at Sophie's logic. "I forgot about that. However, I still have to go to work. We'll have our slumber party. Soon. Okay?"

"Oh-kay," the child said reluctantly.

She handed the phone back to Mason, barely suppressing a yawn. "Speak-ing of skedaddling. Guess I better call it a night, too. I didn't get much sleep last night, and tomorrow, I think, is gonna be another killer day."

"We need to talk about something else," Mason said, keeping his voice low. "It's ... about Celia."

Annajane put her wineglass down carefully. "I'm listening."

"First, we need to talk about us," Mason said. "The other night, you told me—there was no us. There never could be. But then you broke your engage-ment to Shane. I'm kinda getting mixed signals here, Annajane."

She gave a wry smile. "I could say the same thing about you."

"Let me ask you something," Mason said, leaning forward so that his knees were touching hers under the table. "In a perfect world—where we hadn't split up, where there was no Shane and there was no Celia—do you think we'd still be together?"

"No," Annajane said.

His face fell.

"Not the answer you wanted, I know. But I just think our lives were veering so off track, we probably wouldn't have made it—even without the things that broke us up. Your family—mine—our jobs, our own selfishness, pride and insecurity, we had to work through all those things. I don't know about you, but I think I'm only just now really starting to figure out how to be a grown-up. So maybe now I'm almost ready to have a mature, committed relationship." She laughed. "Of course there's just one thing standing in the way of that."

"Celia."

Annajane shrugged.

"I can't," he started to speak, and then reconsidered.

"No matter what else happens, I want you to know that I love you. I always have. That's never changed. Do you believe me?"

"I guess." Her pulse was racing. She glanced up at him, then looked away.

"No, that's not good enough," Mason said, taking her hand and looking directly into her eyes. "I need you to understand that there are things that are out of my control. Situations . . ."

She lifted her chin. "Why don't you just come right out and tell me what's going on?"

"She's pregnant," Mason said.

Annajane picked up her glass of wine and sipped slowly. She was aware of the hum of voices around them, the smell of a sizzling steak being carried to a table next to theirs, the easy jazz playing on the restaurant's sound system, the breeze rifling the fronds of the potted fern next to their table. A tiny piece of her brain noted these things and filed them away. *This is how it felt the night I learned I would never win the man I loved. I drank this wine and ate these foods, and I will never see or smell or taste these things again without thinking of that night.*

"What will you do now?" she asked, putting the wineglass down because her hand was starting to shake. She rested her left hand on top of her right, to keep it from trembling.

"I don't know yet," Mason said. "She just told me a couple days ago."

Annajane bit her lip and looked away. "And she's sure?"

"So she claims," Mason said bitterly. "At first I couldn't believe it. I mean, we've been living apart for weeks now. She was obsessed with all this wedding stuff, and Sallie decided it didn't look right to Sophie for us to be living together, so Celia has pretty much been staying at Cherry Hill. Plus, I guess maybe I subconsciously knew I didn't want to go through with the wedding, because I just didn't have the desire..." His face colored briefly and he looked genuinely ill. "I couldn't even remember the last time..."

"I'll bet Celia could," Annajane said. She felt bile rising in her throat. Had Celia done this on purpose? Deliberately gotten pregnant just to make sure Mason would marry her?

"March," he said glumly. "She was on birth control, the patch. She claims it sometimes happens. But..."

Annajane was having a hard time catching her breath. It felt as though she'd been punched in the chest. She held up her hand, struggling to regain her composure. "I don't want to hear this, Mason. It's too personal."

"My God," he said, his voice breaking. "I never saw this coming."

Annajane sat back in her chair, easing her hand out from beneath his. She folded her hands in her lap, just for something to do.

"So now what?"

"Celia knows I'm in love with you. But she doesn't seem to care. She says she can't raise a child by herself. Not that I would let her. Celia's not really... maternal." He straightened his shoulders. "This is my responsibility. I'll just... have to figure out how to make it work."

Annajane could only nod. She felt her eyes filling with tears and was sure that everyone in the room was watching them. She fumbled with her napkin and tried to push her chair away from the table. But the chair caught on the edge of the tablecloth, and her glass of wine tipped over, sending a rivulet of sauvignon blanc flowing across the table and into his lap. "Damn. I'm sorry," she said, desperate for a way out. But her chair was stuck on the edge of a flagstone. "I need to leave. Right now. Please, Mason."

He caught the waiter's attention and asked for the check. In the car, he looked at her expectantly. "Where to? Pokey's?"

"No," Annajane said. "I don't think so. I'll just get a room at the Pinecone Motor Lodge."

He frowned. "A motel? Come on, that's crazy. I'll take you back to my place; you can have the guest room. It'll all be very circumspect. And if you're worrying about Celia, don't. She's been staying over at Cherry Hill."

"The Pinecone will be just fine for now," Annajane said. "It's under new management. It's clean and it's cheap, and that's really all I require for right now."

He gave it some thought. "That place is in the middle of nowhere. I don't like the idea of you driving out there at night like this. At least let me follow you there."

"Mason," she said calmly. "You forget I've been single for five years. I'm used to traveling alone, driving places by myself, checking into motels by myself. I appreciate your concern, but this really is no big deal."

"I don't like the idea of you staying in a motel. It's . . . seedy."

"This isn't really up to you," Annajane pointed out.

"I'm following you out there," he said, and the stubborn set of his jaw told her it was no use arguing.

The Pinecone Motor Lodge had been the only motel in Passcoe for as long as anybody could remember. Consisting of semicircle of a dozen small whitewashed frame cottages, it was set amid a thick grove of its namesake pine trees, and reached by a winding driveway leading off what had formerly been the main route into town.

Built in the postwar years as a tourist court, the Pinecone did a respectable business up until the 1980s, when the state built a bypass around it, traffic dwindled, and the Pinecone lost some of its luster. It changed hands a couple of times, then languished in foreclosure for two years, until a semiretired couple from Florida bought it to run as a hobby.

Mason had driven past the motel often in the past, duly noticing its slow deterioration. Now, though, he was relieved when his headlights revealed the changes brought about by two gay men and what must have cost several hundred thousand dollars.

The little cabins were gleaming white, with freshly painted dark green shutters with pine-tree-shaped cutouts. A neatly clipped boxwood hedge lined the front of each unit, and window boxes with perky red geraniums and trailing ivy flanked the doorways. Lanterns shone above every door, and on each miniature porch stood a pair of red-painted spring-back motel chairs.

She parked in front of a white bungalow with a small neon OFFICE sign. Mason pulled his car alongside hers. "Okay," Annajane said, when he rolled down his window. "See? It's perfectly respectable. You can go now."

"Nuh-uh," Mason said stubbornly. "Not til I see you safely inside."

The look she gave him was bleak and full of despair. "Just go," she said quietly. "Please?"

A small brass plaque on the office door requested that visitors RING BELL AFTER 10 PM. It was five past, so she hesitated, but then pushed the doorbell. A moment later, a lean man with a deep mahogany tan and a shiny bald head opened the door.

"Come on in," he said, before she could ask about a room.

She found herself in a small entry hall. Her host, who was barefoot and dressed in a wildly flowered Hawaiian shirt and baggy white shorts, stepped behind a tall antique oak reception desk.

"I'd like a room, if you've got one," Annajane said.

"One? I've got eight or nine," he said. "You can have your pick."

"Oh," she said. "I'm sorry. Is business that slow?"

"Don't mind me," he said. "Thomas—that's my partner—he says I'm a chronic complainer. Actually, business is a little better than we'd expected. We've been full every weekend this spring, and word is starting to get around about our little restoration project and the new management."

"I've been hearing good things," Annajane said.

"Just a single tonight?" he asked, peering over her shoulder out the window, where Mason sat patiently in his car.

She blushed. "Yes. My, uh, friend just wants to make sure I get checked in all right."

"Ain't none of my business," he said airily. "We're strictly don't ask, don't tell around here. Now. We're an entirely smoke-free facility, but from the looks of you, I'd say you're not a smoker anyway. Also, all the cottages have kitchenettes, with refrigerators and microwaves, a coffeepot, and toaster. But we also have a coffee hour here in the office-slash-reception area, from seven to nine every morning. We do fruit, and whatever kind of muffins Thomas feels like baking that day. And coffee and tea, of course."

"How nice," Annajane said.

He pushed the registration book toward her and turned to get a key. "Here you are," he said, pushing an old-fashioned brass skeleton key with a silken red tassel hanging from it across the desktop. "You'll be in unit six. It's my favorite— so quiet, and there's a pink rosebush just blooming its head off right outside your window. If you do decide to have company, there's a new pullout sofa and a spare set of sheets and pillows in the top of your closet."

"Fine," Annajane said absentmindedly as she tried to remember her car's license number. She handed him back the registration book, and he glanced down at it.

"Oh. You're from Passcoe?" He peered at the book through the wire-frame glasses perched at the end of a long, bony nose.

"Yes," she said. "I just sold my loft, downtown, and we had to close much quicker than I'd anticipated, so I'm sort of homeless for the moment."

He nodded. "I can offer you our weekly rate, if you like. It'll save you about twenty-five dollars a night."

"All right," she agreed. "I'm sort of in transition right now. I'm not really certain whether I'll even decide to stay in town, or for how long."

She opened her billfold, took out her credit card, and handed it to him.

"Annajane Hudgens," he said, reading the charge plate aloud. He stuck out his hand, and she shook it. "Welcome home, Annajane. I'm Harold, and I run the place. Have you always lived in Passcoe?"

"Just about," she said. "I'm a native."

"You're lucky to be from such a beautiful place. Thomas and I just love it here," he confided. "As far as we're concerned, you can have Miami."

Annajane put the credit card away. "You might change your mind come February, when it's fifteen degrees here, and in the eighties in Florida."

"Never," he declared. "Now, don't be a stranger. We'll expect to see you in the morning for coffee."

"Maybe," she said. "I leave for work pretty early."

"Where do you work?"

"Quixie. The soft drink company?"

"Quixie, we adore it! We've even been talking about buying cases of it, so we can put a bottle in every room. Guests love that kind of local stuff."

"Let me know if you want to pursue that," she said, ever the marketing professional. "I can get one of our sales reps to talk to you about adding the Pinecone to one of the regular routes."

"Perfect!"

She picked up her key. "Good night, Harold."

"Good night, Annajane."

32

Mason kept watch until he felt certain Annajane was safely inside her unit at the Pinecone Motor Lodge. Finally, when he saw lights blink on inside the cabin, he reluctantly drove home.

Letha had left the porch light burning for him. He didn't bother to drive around to the garage, instead parking by the front door and leaving his car there.

He went into the kitchen and saw that she'd left him a paper plate of food neatly covered with aluminum foil, which he dumped into the trash.

Stepping softly, he climbed the stairs to the second floor. He opened Sophie's bedroom door and peeked inside. A pink-shaded nightlight shone from an outlet beside her bed, and he could see her blond curls spilling out on her pillow. Mason sat lightly on the edge of the bed and looked down at her. Five years ago, he'd been terrified at the idea of raising a baby. She'd been so tiny, so sickly, so helpless.

He'd been lucky to find Letha, who was Voncile's sister-in-law and, like Voncile, a widow. She'd raised three of her own children and taken care of numerous grandchildren. She was as skinny as Voncile was stout, with improbably dyed frizzy red hair and pale blue eyes. Letha was calm and loving and untroubled by Sophie's bouts of colic and sleeplessness. But even with Letha hovering nearby, Sophie seemed to prefer Mason's presence to her nanny's. For the first six months after he'd brought her home, he'd fallen asleep in a chair beside her crib more nights than he could count, with the fretful infant hugged tightly to his chest.

Mason wondered what Sophie's reaction would be to having another baby supplant her in his affections. Sibling rivalry? And how would Celia treat Sophie after her own baby was born? She'd never really seemed the maternal type to him. He'd somehow managed to sublimate that during the short time they'd been dating. Celia was fun, she was lively, she was undeniably attractive, and undeniably attracted to him.

But there was an undercurrent there, a layer of dark and cold he could never pierce, and didn't actually care to try.

Sophie stirred and he laid a hand on her back. Her face relaxed, and he felt himself responding in kind. He wound one of the silky corkscrew curls around his finger. Finding out about Sophie's existence had been a shock, but now he couldn't imagine his life without her. He had to believe that he would come to feel this way about Celia's baby, too. Even if he knew he would never actually love her the way he'd always expected he would one day love the mother of his children. That love, Mason thought, belonged to another. To Annajane.

Sophie turned slightly, and the shift exposed her pocketbook, which she'd hidden beneath her bedsheet. It had been a birthday gift from Annajane last year and had quickly become his daughter's most treasured possession, which she rarely let out of her sight. Whenever anything small disappeared around the house, they all knew to check Sophie's pocketbook. She was especially fond of anything shiny. More than once he'd had to retrieve from the pink plastic purse a favorite silver Mont Blanc cartridge pen, various keys, and even a small an-tique sterling silver penknife that had been a high school graduation gift from his grandfather.

Soon now, he thought, they would have to discourage her unauthorized acquisitions. But for now, Sophie's hoarding of trinkets was harmless. He leaned down, planted a kiss on the top of her head, and stood up. He was suddenly ex-hausted.

Inside the master suite, he placed his watch, wallet, and cell phone on the bathroom vanity. He brushed his teeth and stripped to his boxers, leaving his clothing in a heap on the floor, reverting to his messy bachelor habits.

Mason dropped onto his unmade bed and pulled the sheet up at the same time he glanced at the clock radio on the nightstand. It was just after 11:00 P.M. He bunched his pillow under his head. The pillowcase was warm! He turned on his side and a pair of sinuous bare arms wrapped around his own bare shoulders.

"Surprise!" Celia whispered.

"Jesus H.!" Mason exclaimed. He sat bolt upright in the bed and switched on the lamp. "What the hell are you doing here?"

Celia blinked rapidly. "For goodness sake," she said, laughing. "It's not like I broke in. I have a key, remember?"

She gave him a lazy smile and raised the hem of the sheet to show him that she was completely nude. "I didn't think you'd mind," she said, propping herself up on one elbow to give him an even better vantage point. She reached for his hand and placed it on her right breast.

He snatched it back.

"This isn't funny, Celia," he said.

Her eyes narrowed. "It's not supposed to be funny, darling," she said slowly. "It's supposed to be a turn-on. Do you have any idea how many men fantasize about coming home and finding a nude blonde in their beds?"

"I am not one of those guys," Mason said flatly.

She sat up in the bed, allowing the sheet to fall around her waist to give him a better understanding of the extent of her endowment. And she was admittedly gifted in that particular department. Celia's breasts would probably be considered one of the seven wonders of the modern world to any other man with a pulse. But right now they didn't do a thing for him. God help him. She parted her lips slightly and gave him a come-hither look that had once had an appalling effect on him. Now? Nada.

"Don't do this," he said.

"Do what?" She slid closer to him on the bed and casually rested her hand on his crotch. He jumped as though he'd been bitten by a rattlesnake.

He picked her hand up and dropped it onto the sheet. "That," he said, frowning. "I've had a hell of a long day, and I am really not in the mood for this kind of a stunt."

"It's not a stunt," she said, looking hurt. "I'm trying to remind you of why we got together in the first place. It's been so long. I love you and I've missed you. Is that a crime?"

He shook his head. "Does Sophie know you're here?"

"No," she said. "She and Letha were both sound asleep when I let myself in an hour ago. Which reminds me. Where have you been all night? And don't tell me you were at the office, because I checked, and your car was gone." She leaned in closer and sniffed. "You've been drinking wine?"

"I was out," Mason said. "Having dinner with Annajane." Maybe, he thought, his mood black, if he infuriated her enough, Celia would leave.

"Oh Annajane," Celia said with a dismissive shrug. "Did you tell her about the baby? Or are we going to let Bonnie Kelsey break the news to her?"

"She knows," Mason said. He stood up, looked around, and saw where she'd neatly folded her clothes on the armchair at the foot of the bed. He snatched them up and threw them at her. "Come on, Celia. Get dressed. I don't want Sophie to wake up and find you here."

"Darling, please come back to bed and stop being such a prude," Celia said, patting the mattress. "We've made love lots of times right here in this bed with her in the next room, and it never bothered you before."

It actually *had* bothered him, he thought ruefully. But not enough to induce him to turn Celia out of his bed.

"I was a hypocrite," Mason said. "That stops now." He jerked his head in the direction of the door. "Please go."

"And what if I won't?" Celia said playfully. "Are you going to pick me up and bodily throw me out of the house? With Sophie and Letha sleeping right next door?" She gave a look of mock horror.

Mason's face hardened. He stomped into the bathroom and pulled on the clothes he'd just removed. He went back to the bedroom and sat on the armchair.

"Look," he said. "Don't make this any more difficult than it has to be. You and I are going to have to come to some kind of an arrangement."

"I can't wait to hear this," Celia said. "Do explain."

He hesitated. "I am willing to marry you, and be a father to our child. But that will be the extent of my obligation to you. I'm not in love with you, and I won't pretend to be."

She arched an eyebrow. "So . . . you're telling me you'll live with me, but you won't make love to me?"

He recoiled for a moment. "If that's how you choose to put it, yes."

Celia laughed. "That's so noble of you, Mason. So gentlemanly. And what if I tell you I don't want to marry you under those conditions? In fact, what would you say if I told you I might decide not to have the baby after all?"

He felt his heart contract. "You wouldn't do that," Mason said. "Because that baby is the only hold you have over me." He looked at her coolly. "I no longer kid myself that you're infatuated with me. I realize you only got involved with me because you had some notion of a payday."

"You have such a low opinion of yourself," Celia said. "It never occurred to you I fell in love with you?"

"It did," he admitted. "But then I realized what a fool I've been."

She leaned forward. "I really do love you, you know. I could make you happy, if you'd let me."

"Don't insult my intelligence," Mason said. "Just go, would you?"

Celia's eyes blazed. "If I leave here tonight, Mason, it will be for good. I mean that. You won't see me, or our child, again. Ever. You see, I'm an all-or-nothing kind of girl."

It was the one threat he feared, the thing that had gnawed at his gut since the moment she'd told him about the baby. He knew Celia would think nothing of depriving the baby of a father, if it meant getting vengeance against him. The idea of her raising his child, his own flesh and blood, gave him a sick, terrifying feeling. He would do anything in his power to keep that from happening. And she knew that, of course.

Celia knew she'd won. She leaned back against the headboard, allowing the sheet to slip downward again. "I'm tired," she said, raising her arms over her head for an exaggerated stretch. "It's much too late for a woman in my condition to be driving around at night. Anyway, we have a wedding to plan, don't we? How's Saturday for you?"

"I'll leave that up to you," Mason said. "But no church. No reception, none of that. Just you, me, and a justice of the peace."

"You really know how to romance a woman," Celia said bitterly.

"This isn't about romance. It's about duty. And decency," he added. "If you won't leave, I will. Just make sure you're gone before Sophie wakes up in the morning."

"Where do you think you're going?" Celia demanded.

"Anywhere but here," Mason said.

33

Annajane smelled baked goods as she opened the door into the Pinecone's office-slash-lounge. "Well, hello!" Harold was dressed in a different Hawaiian shirt and baggy blue jeans. He wore a faded baseball cap, and he was setting a tray with mugs and saucers on one of two bistro tables by the window. "I'm so glad you came in."

"Thomas?" he called out.

Another tall, skinny, bald man with a long nose came bustling out from what must have been the kitchen. He looked enough like Harold to be his twin brother, but he was wearing a white butcher's apron, and he held an enormous napkin-covered basket of muffins.

"You're just in time; these are still warm from the oven," the baker said, setting the basket down on the table with the mugs. "These are date-nut muffins. My grandmother's recipe."

"Thomas, this is Annajane, the young lady I told you about earlier. She's going to stay with us for the week. And she works at Quixie. Isn't that fun?"

"Very fun," Thomas agreed. He held out his hand, which was dusted with flour; wiped it on his apron; and then extended it again. "So nice to meet you. I guess Harold told you we're complete Quixie fanatics. I'm serious. It's . . . so essentially southern tasting. Like grits or homemade peach ice cream. It tastes like Dixie, right?"

Annajane's eyes widened. "What did you just say?"

"What? The part about it being better than grits? Or the part about it tasting like Dixie?" Thomas asked.

"Ohmygod!" Annajane breathed. She reached for the pen on the reception desk and started scribbling. Then she turned around, waved the paper under Thomas's nose, and proceeded to kiss him on the mouth.

"What was that for?" he asked, clearly startled.

"I think you just came up with our new slogan," she told him. "Quixie—the Taste of Dixie!"

"I did that?" Thomas said, looking pleased.

She nodded enthusiastically.

"I did that!" Thomas told his partner.

Harold rolled his eyes. "There'll be no living with the man now. He's been tinkering with making Quixie muffins, you know. He's gone completely bonkers over the stuff."

"Totally kooky, right?" Thomas said. "So far, I can't get the consistency right, but I'm not giving up. I know there has to be a way to bake with that stuff."

Annajane sat down at the table, and Harold and Thomas joined her. Thomas poured her a mug of coffee, and she inhaled the fumes gratefully before taking a sip.

It was funny. Her life had come apart at the seams last night, and yet here she was, calmly having coffee and muffins with a pair of total strangers, still chatting about Quixie, selling the product for all she was worth.

Later on today, she would have to figure out how to start rebuilding a life for herself. But for right now, indulging in a decent cup of coffee and some hot sugary treats wasn't a bad beginning to a new day. Plus she had a new slogan. So maybe the day didn't totally suck. Yet.

"You know," she said, reaching for a muffin and peeling the paper liner off. "The company did a Quixie cookbook, way back in the '60s, I think. It has all kinds of crazy recipes in it—Quixie Jell-O salad, Quixie layer cakes, Quixie barbecue sauce. I'm sure there must be some kind of muffin recipe, too.

I think there's still a box of them somewhere around the office. I'll bring you one if you like."

"I'd love that," Thomas said. "How long do you think you'll be staying with us, Miss Annajane?"

"Just long enough to figure out what comes next."

34

Annajane sat at her desk and forced herself to go through the motions of doing her job. It was the one thing she was good at. Doing her job. She dashed off a memo to Davis about her proposal for the new Quixie slogan and sent another to route sales, asking them to drop off six cases of soda at the Pinecone Motor Lodge.

Celia Wakefield had taken her man, but, so far, she hadn't succeeded in destroying that last piece of her life.

She had decided on the drive in to work that she would keep her promise to Mason. And she intended to go out with a flourish. The summer campaign, she'd decided, would break all sales records. And then she would hit the road. Annajane had no intentions of hanging around to watch Celia's belly grow and expand with Mason's child.

As luck would have it, she was just pulling into her slot in the parking lot when Mason drove up. There was no time to duck down in the seat or pretend she hadn't seen him. She took a deep breath and got out of the car and locked it. She could maintain her dignity and act as though nothing had happened between them. Because essentially, nothing had. Or would.

"Good mor . . ." she started to say, but she thought better of it when she got a good look at him.

Mason's eyes were heavily shadowed, his hair uncombed. He obviously hadn't showered or shaved, and he was dressed in the same clothes he'd worn to dinner the night before.

"Are you all right?" she asked, picking a pine needle from the sleeve of his shirt.

"Fine," he said, hoisting the strap of his briefcase onto his shoulder.

"You look like hell," Annajane said. "Didn't you go home after you left me last night?"

"I did," Mason said, trying unsuccessfully to smooth his hair. "But Celia was there. In my bed," he added, with a scowl. "So I took an impromptu camping trip."

"Camping?" Annajane asked, bewildered.

"I slept at the lake house," Mason said, his tone sour. "Or tried to, anyway. Between the raccoons and the pigeons roosting in the rafters, I didn't get much rest."

He eyed her warily. "How about you? How was the Pinecone?"

"Delightful," she said. "I slept like a baby."

"Glad to hear somebody did," he muttered. They were standing at the employee entrance to the plant. He held the door open for her.

"Annajane," he started.

"Mason, I really need to get in and get started on my work," she told him. She squared her shoulders and headed down the hall. "We've gotta sell some cherry soda today."

Once at her desk, she spent half an hour scanning online job listings for marketing positions. She e-mailed her résumé to a couple of former colleagues from her Raleigh days and called Joe Capheart to let him know she'd used him as a reference.

Then she got back down to soft drink business. She went to the break room and begrudgingly fed four quarters into the vending machine for a can of Quixie, hoping for some kind of inspiration.

As always, the combination of carbonation and the sharp-sweet taste of cherries gave her a start. Quixie was something special, she reminded herself, something worth saving.

She got a begrudging "Good idea" e-mail back from Davis, approving the new "Taste of Dixie" slogan. Then she spent the morning on the phone, talking to bottle manufacturers about copying the Quixie glass bottle from the '50s. She'd located the old molds from the bottles in a dusty corner of the warehouse, and now her challenge was to find a company willing to copy the old molds and start producing new bottles immediately.

There was a soft tap on her office door. Before Annajane could call out, the door opened and Voncile stepped inside. "Annajane? Can I talk to you?"

"Sure," Annajane said, rolling her chair away from her desk. "What's up?"

Voncile closed the door and locked it, then sat nervously in a chair opposite the desk, pulling the skirt of her sensible brown cotton skirt even farther down over her knees.

She folded her hands in her lap and blinked rapidly, opening her mouth, then closing it again, before finally the words came out in a torrent, her voice shaking with fear and indignation.

"I have worked for this company since I was fifteen years old. I worked for Mr. Glenn, God rest, and then I was so happy to go to work for Mason. And when he brought Sophie home, I prayed about that, and I called up my sister-in-law, Letha, and told her he needed a good woman to take care of that precious baby. And I have been with this company for thirty-two years."

"I know that," Annajane said reassuringly, wondering what this was all about. "And I know Mason and the rest of the family appreciates you and Letha's dedication."

Voncile nodded. "Last year, Mason said he was gonna have to quit naming me Employee of the Month because I'd already won it so many times it was making some people jealous. He said he was just going to go ahead and name me Employee of the Millennium and be done with it. But I never did get a certificate or anything."

"I think that was just Mason's idea of a joke, Voncile," Annajane said.

Voncile shrugged. "You know, Annajane, I've been praying for you and Mason to get back together. It was a sad day for all of us when you two split up. Miss Celia is nice, and she certainly seems to know a lot about business, but just between the two of us, I think you would make a better mama for Sophie. Not that it's any of my say-so."

"That's very sweet of you to say," Annajane said demurely. "And I appreciate your prayers. But I think it's best if Mason and I go our separate ways."

Voncile gave Annajane an appraising look. "You know I do not listen to gossip. The Bible says, 'A gossip betrays a confidence; so avoideth a man who talks too much.' That's Proverbs 20:19. You could look it up. But Troy Meeks is a good man, and he said the talk around town is that you and Mason have gotten back together again. Is that true?"

Annajane felt herself blush. "Well, uh, not really. I think maybe Troy misunderstood. Mason and I are just friends."

"But you didn't marry that boy down in Atlanta." She nodded pointedly at Annajane's left hand. "You're not wearing your engagement ring. And you didn't take that job down there," Voncile protested. "I thought that meant Mason was going to ask you to marry him."

"I'm afraid not," Annajane said, fervently wishing for an end to the conversation. "Was there something specific on your mind, Voncile?"

The older woman stared down at the floor. "One of the girls in accounting told me the company is in such bad shape, we might get sold off. She said she heard Davis is already talking to some company in New Jersey that wants to buy us."

Mason had sworn her to secrecy, but obviously news of the Jax Snax offer had begun to leak out. She didn't want to lie to Voncile, but she also didn't want to keep the rumor mill going.

"Yes," she said finally. "I do know that there is a company that's approached the family about selling Quixie. But as you may know, Glenn Bayless established an irrevocable trust shortly before he died that prohibited a sale for five years after his death."

"It was five years this past Christmas that Mr. Glenn passed away," Voncile pointed out.

"Right. And next week, I think, Thomas Norris, Glenn's attorney, is going to let the family know how Glenn wanted the company left to his heirs. Until the family finds that out, any talk of a sale is premature," Annajane said, trying to choose her words carefully.

"Mason wouldn't sell us out," Voncile said flatly. "He knew what this company meant to his daddy. And his granddaddy. He wouldn't let that happen. Right?"

Sometimes, Annajane thought, *doing the right thing means doing the wrong thing for the people you care most about.*

"Mason cares deeply about his responsibilities," Annajane said. "But I'm afraid it isn't just up to him. Davis and Pokey and Sallie will probably all have a say in what happens."

Voncile's breathing grew rapid, and two bright pink splotches appeared on her heavily powdered cheeks. "I was afraid of that. If outsiders buy Quixie, what will happen to all of us?" She nervously chewed her lower lip. "I need this job, Annajane. My Claude, rest his soul, didn't leave me hardly anything when he passed. If we get bought out, those New Jersey folks won't want a fifty-nine-year-old like me with bad knees and fallen arches, even with all my Employee of the Month certificates. And I'd lose my health care. Annajane, I have the sugar diabetes. And hypertension. I can't afford those pills without my health care plan."

Annajane nodded in sympathy. "Nothing's been decided yet, Voncile, so please don't go getting yourself all upset. It's true that Davis is in favor of the sale. But Mason doesn't want to sell, and neither does Pokey."

"And what about their mama? Miss Sallie? She wouldn't let them sell Mr. Glenn's company, would she?"

"I'm not sure," Annajane admitted. "Really, nobody knows how this will all be settled until Mr. Thomas meets with the family next week to explain about Glenn's trust."

Voncile clucked under her breath. "Rest his soul. This company was Mr. Glenn's baby. I just pray he fixed it up good with the lawyers so things can stay the way he intended."

Annajane stood up and patted the older woman's shoulder. "I hope your prayers get heard, Voncile."

Voncile raised her eyes heavenward. "My faith is in the Lord," she said solemnly. "But sometimes, the lambs of the flock have to rise up and take care of themselves. Sometimes, it is up to the righteous to do the Lord's work here on earth for him."

"Okay, then," Annajane said, walking Voncile back out into the hallway. She wondered, for only a brief moment, what kind of measures the righteous would take to cast somebody like Celia out of Passcoe. And then she got back to work.

At midmorning, she ran to the ladies room down the hall, pushed open the heavy door, and ran smack into Celia herself, who was standing in front of the mirror, touching up her already-flawless makeup.

Annajane nearly did an about-face. But after drinking all that Quixie, she desperately needed to pee, and there was only one lady's room in the plant, and this small, two-stall bathroom was it.

She nodded curtly at Celia and went to open the door of the nearest stall. It didn't budge. She glanced downward and saw that it was occupied. As was the one next to it. There was nowhere to hide. Annajane crossed her arms over her chest and stood with her back to the paper towel dispenser, staring up at the ceiling as though it were the Sistine Chapel.

Celia was in no particular hurry. She took a large brush and dusted her face with tinted mineral powder. Rummaging in her cosmetic bag, she brought out an eyebrow pencil and applied short, feathery strokes to her pale brows.

A toilet flushed, and Patsy, one of the girls from accounting, emerged from the stall. She looked from Annajane to Celia and scurried out of the bathroom without even stopping to wash her hands.

Grateful for a reprieve, Annajane ducked into the stall. The toilet next to hers flushed, and she watched while a set of cheerful red ballet flats walked out of the stall. She heard water running, and then the sound of the bathroom door closing. She waited for another two minutes, just to make sure the coast was clear, before emerging.

Her heart sank when she saw Celia, standing at the mirror, fully made up, an odd, fixed smile on her face.

Annajane stood at the sink and washed and dried her hands. She stepped past Celia and reached for the door handle, but Celia neatly stepped sideways, effectively blocking her exit. "Excuse me," Annajane said.

"I'll only take a moment of your precious time," Celia said. "And then I'll let you get back to packing up your shit and getting the hell out of this company."

"This is not happening to me," Annajane muttered. She reached for the door again, but Celia slapped her hand away.

"Oh, honey, it *is* happening," Celia said. "So you better pay attention. Because I need to have a few words with you."

"Whatever," Annajane said. "What's on your mind, Celia?"

"*You* are on my mind," Celia said, poking her index finger into Annajane's clavicle. "Every time I turn around, Annajane Hudgens, there you are. At my wedding," she poked Annajane. "In the ambulance on the way to the hospital." Another poke. "At the freakin' hospital." Yet another poke. "Fucking my fiancé in a fucking cornfield. And, oh yes, at a restaurant, last night. Did you think I wouldn't find out about that?" She poked Annajane again. "Did you?"

Annajane caught Celia's hand roughly. "Do. Not. Touch. Me," she said. "Ever." She squeezed Celia's fingers together tightly and then released.

Celia laughed. "You have been messing with Mason's mind for months now. Making an exhibition of yourself. The whole town is laughing at you. Yeah. But that ends right now. I saw the two of you talking out in the parking lot this morning. Very touching. Heartbreaking, almost. Was he telling you good-bye? Did he mention that we've rescheduled the wedding for tomorrow?"

A wedding? Saturday? Annajane felt as though she'd been slapped across the face, but she would not give Celia the satisfaction of registering her shock.

"No," she said lightly. "He didn't get around to a wedding announcement. But he did tell me that last night he slept on the floor of the lake house, with the raccoons and the pigeon poop and the mildew and the roaches, rather than share a bed with you."

"Don't kid yourself that he's had a change of heart, Annajane dear. One little night apart won't hurt me. Because he'll be sharing my bed for years and years to come," Celia gloated. She stepped aside and held the bathroom door open with a flourish. "And don't bother to wait on an invitation to the wedding. This time, it's strictly a private *family* affair."

35

"Voncile," Celia said, walking into Mason's outer office. Her voice dripped saccharine. "Don't you look nice today? I love that shade of chocolate on you. So flattering with your coloring."

Mason's assistant looked up at Celia. "Thank you," she said, preening just a little, patting her hair and straightening the collar of her blouse. "You look nice, too. But I'm afraid Mason asked me to tell people he can't be interrupted today. He's trying to catch up on work."

"Actually, I came in here to speak to you," Celia said. She perched on the edge of the chair opposite Voncile's. "I'm so excited," Celia confided. "We've re-scheduled the wedding for tomorrow."

"Congratulations," Voncile said politely.

This traitorous Bible-thumping cow will be the first to go after we get back from the honeymoon, Celia told herself. *Mason needed a younger, smarter, more attractive woman for an administrative assistant. Although . . . not too much younger. And not much more attractive. At least he could find somebody with two years of college, for God's sake. Mason might put up a little resistance, but after he realized how much more time he would have for his personal life, once the office was running efficiently, he would be grateful for her input.*

"But I need your help," Celia said. "I have a million things to do to get ready by tomorrow and we don't want Mason to be bothered with the trivial details of a wedding, do we?"

"Well," Voncile said, reluctantly.

"Fine," Celia said. "I'll e-mail you the checklist. It's nothing really. We've already gotten the marriage license, of course. We're just going to have a very small, private ceremony, at Cherry Hill. Very cozy. So I'll need you to line us up a justice of the peace, and then you can call the florist and arrange for flowers. I've sent you a detailed memo about the flowers, so don't let them talk you into some tacky daisy and carnation horror. And talk to the caterer from the country club, see if they'll just do some nice appetizers and deliver them to the house. And wine, we'll need some champagne—I doubt if Sallie has anything decent at her house, so I need you to go to that nice wine shop over in Southern Pines. Get a couple bottles of Vueve Clicquot, and maybe a nice red. I'll research it and e-mail you what we need . . ."

Voncile had been dutifully scribbling notes, but now she put down her pen. "No ma'am," she said.

"Excuse me?" Celia said, staring.

"I am a godly woman. A deaconess. I've never set foot in a liquor store in my life," Voncile said. "And I'm not starting now."

"Oh, Voncile, of course you don't have to go into the store," Celia said sweetly. "I'll arrange to have them bring it out and put it in your car. All right? They can put it in your trunk so you don't even have to look at it."

"Well," Voncile said, not convinced. "What if somebody saw those men putting liquor in the trunk? I have people in Southern Pines. It wouldn't look right."

Celia narrowed her eyes. "Voncile, I really, really need you to do this. I'm sure Mason will be happy to give you a little time off so you can drive over there to pick it up for our wedding. And of course, we'll pay for your gas and mileage."

"All right," Voncile said reluctantly. She'd been outmanuevered and she knew it. "Since this is for your wedding, I will make an exception this one time."

"Fine!" Celia said brightly. "It will mean a lot to Mason to know you're doing this for our special day. And you'll let me know right away, won't you, as soon as you've lined up the justice of the peace?" She gave a self-satisfied little smile. "Since you work so closely with Mason, I guess it won't hurt to let you in on a little secret. I'm expecting! And I want the ceremony done before I start to show."

Voncile's expression remained wooden. "Yes, ma'am."

Gone, Celia told herself, *as she hurried back to her office. That woman is so gone.*

She sat down behind her desk and went back to the list she'd been working on. Flowers. A bouquet for herself, something elegant but understated to go with the dress she'd actually intended to wear to the wedding reception before the church wedding was postponed. A boutonniere for Mason, and a corsage for Sallie, of course. Sophie? Definitely not. She wouldn't give the little brat a second chance at spoiling Celia's big moment.

Her cell phone rang, and she picked it up and answered without a second thought.

"Well hey, Lil' Sissy," a familiar voice said. "Long time, no talk to."

"Veronica? How the hell did you get this number?"

Her older sister laughed unpleasantly. "Our dear cousin Mallery gave it to me. Wasn't that thoughtful? She called me last week because Aunt Eleanor is in a bad way, and she just happened to mention that dear old Aunt Ellie had gone down to North Carolina to see you get married. Funny thing. I guess my invitation must have gotten lost in the mail."

Dammit. She should have known better than to have invited even one member of her wretched family to the wedding. But she'd thought it would look too odd not to have any family there, and Aunt Eleanor, her mother's aunt, was reasonably presentable. She should have left well enough alone.

"What do you want, Veronica? I'm at work, and I've got a million things going on today, so I'd appreciate it if you'd make it brief."

"Oh, Sissy," Veronica said mournfully. "You're about to hurt my feelings. I was just calling to catch up on old times. Hey, Mallery says you're quite the businesswoman. Had your own dress business, sold it for ten million dollars. Mama and Daddy and the girls and me, we hear you're rolling in the dough. Mallery says you even paid to fly Aunt Eleanor down for the wedding."

"Mallery doesn't know dick," Celia said. "I did sell my business, but there were . . . complications. The money's all tied up in stock options and stuff like that, so if you're calling to hit me up for a loan, you can forget it."

"A loan?" Veronica laughed. "No, see, I was calling you about the money you *owe* me. Remember? When you blew town, you stole my car? I'd say the car alone was worth six thousand. And in the glove box in that car was quite a bit of cash that belonged to Eddie? Like three thousand dollars?"

Celia clicked her fingertips impatiently on the desktop. "That piece of shit Cutlass had a hundred and sixty thousand miles and leaked oil like a sieve. It was worth maybe six hundred, tops. As for the cash in the glove box, it was only eighteen hundred. And since we both know the money was the proceeds from your ex-husband's sideline of selling oxycodone you stole from your nursing home patients, I figure he's probably not going to call the cops and report it missing. Six years later."

"Fine, you wanna quibble?" Veronica said. "We'll call it four thousand dollars even. And I won't even charge you interest, since you're family."

I have no family, Celia thought. *I am an only child and an orphan. And I intend to stay that way.*

"And what if I say I'm not giving you a dime?" Celia challenged.

"Well, then, I guess I'll just have to call up your ritzy-titzy *new* family, the Baylesses, and tell them all about your real family—the one you left back here in South Sioux City," Veronica said.

"Do that," Celia said, lowering her voice. "And I'll call the owners of that shithole nursing home you work at and suggest they check your personnel records at that hospital you got fired from in Lincoln. And then I'll call the sheriff in South Sioux City. Now, Veronica, I really do have to go. And I suggest you lose this phone number. Immediately."

She clicked End on her cell phone, tapped the Block Caller icon on her phone, and went back to work on her to-do list.

Celia looked down at her list and frowned. Mason had been adamant about no guests, but they had to have two witnesses. Davis? No. He and Mason had been at each other's throats all week long. And anyway, she thought, allowing herself a very small, very secret smile. She had another task for Davis. A very private task.

Matt Kelsey? She frowned. If she invited Matt, she'd have to include the insufferable Bonnie. You couldn't very well not invite the wife if you invited the husband, could you? She shrugged. After they were married she could tactfully unfriend the Kelseys. But for the immediate future, she needed them. In fact, she might as well put Bonnie's skills to work right now. She picked up her phone and tapped the icon for Bonnie's cell phone.

"Bonnie!" she cried. "Please tell me you and Matt don't have any plans for tomorrow afternoon."

"Well," Bonnie said. "Let me think. I've got a tennis lesson in the morning, and I don't know whether Matt's playing golf yet."

"I can tell you that Mason won't be playing golf on Saturday," Celia said. "Because we've rescheduled the wedding."

"Oh, Celia!" Bonnie said. "I'm so happy for you. So . . . everything worked out with that unfortunate rumor about you-know-who?"

Celia held the phone away from her face and smirked. "Just ugly innuendo," she said. "I don't know how that kind of talk gets spread around town, do you?"

"I have no idea," Bonnie said. "But I bet I know who's behind a lot of the gossip."

"Who?" Celia asked, crossing her eyes. She knew damned good and well that the font of all gossip in Pasccoe was on the other end of the line.

"Don't be mad at me for saying this, but I think Pokey Riggs has been telling all kinds of stories on you, Celia."

"I wouldn't be surprised," Celia agreed. "She and you-know-who are thick as thieves. Anyway, I choose to rise above all of that petty stuff. And I know you do, too."

"Absolutely," Bonnie said. "Now tell me about the wedding."

"It'll be tomorrow afternoon at Cherry Hill," Celia said. "Very, very private and exclusive. In fact, we're not having any attendants at all. Just Mason and me, the justice of the peace, and Sallie. And our two very *dearest* friends. If you're not too busy."

"Really?" Bonnie squealed. "We would be honored."

"Thank heavens," Celia said, rolling her eyes. "I was praying you didn't have any prior commitments."

"We'll clear our calendars," Bonnie said. "But why such a rush?"

Celia lowered her voice. "You'll keep this in strictest confidence, won't you, Bonnie?"

"You know me," Bonnie said. "Whatever you tell me, I'll take to my grave."

"I can hardly believe it," Celia said. "We really hadn't planned on starting a family this soon, but sometimes, you know, life intervenes . . ."

"Really? Celia, you aren't. I mean, are you? Pregnant?"

"I am," Celia said. "And Mason is over the moon. You won't tell a soul yet, right? We haven't even broken the news to Sophie."

"I won't breathe a word," Bonnie promised.

Celia hung up and laughed out loud.

"As if." The news would be all over town within a matter of minutes. Just a little additional insurance, in case Mason had any second thoughts about backing out on the upcoming nuptials.

36

Annajane sat at her desk and clenched and unclenched her fists. The encounter with Celia left her breathless with the kind of fury she'd never experienced before. She wanted to kick something, smash something, break something. Preferably something related to Celia. The bitch had actually ambushed her in the lady's room.

Poor Mason, Annajane thought. A life sentence with Cruella de Vil.

She busied herself with more work, more phone calls and e-mails, but couldn't manage to completely put aside the white-hot anger seething inside.

Pokey was already sitting at their usual table when Annajane arrived at Janette's Tea Room. She waved a carrot stick in Annajane's direction as a greeting.

"Sorry," she said, between chews. "I got here early, and I was starving, so I went ahead and ordered for us. You're having the chicken salad, yes?"

"Of course," Annajane said. There were no menus on their table, but after meeting her best friend at Janette's for lunch nearly every week of their adult life, they didn't need menus. Pokey always had the special salad with strawberries and pecans and chicken pot pie, while Annajane had the chicken salad plate. They always split a slice of chocolate silk pie.

Janette's dining room was a pink and green confection, a Lilly Pulitzer dress come to life, humming with feminine conversation conducted in sugary southern drawls. All the tables in the room were filled with women their age or their mothers', dressed in floral sundresses or summery pants outfits. Annajane recognized most of the women in the room and smiled and nodded at all of them.

Pokey sighed contentedly and patted her midsection when the waitress set their plates in front of them. "This baby has got to be a girl. I was hungry when I was pregnant with the boys, but this time around I am ravenous all the time!"

Annajane took a sip of her iced tea and laughed. "Well, I hope it is a girl, for your sake. When do you find out?"

"Next week," Pokey said. She ate a forkful of potpie and frowned. "Mama called right before I left to come over here. She told me about Celia's baby. I kinda threw up a little in my mouth."

"Bad news travels fast," Annajane said, nibbling at a grape that was part of the fruit garnish. "Did Sallie also tell you about the wedding tomorrow?"

"No!" Pokey threw her fork against the side of her plate. "You really are doing your damnedest to ruin my appetite, aren't you?"

"At least you didn't have to hear about it the way I did," Annajane said. "I went to the lady's room at the plant and Celia was lying in wait for me. Just had to tell me the happy news to my face."

Pokey gaped. "She didn't."

"She certainly did," Annajane said. "She as much as told me to get my ass out of town before she kicked me out."

"Tell me you slapped the sass out of her," Pokey said.

"I should have, but I didn't," Annajane admitted. "I was too shocked to do anything more than stand there with my mouth hanging open. It was unnerving!"

Pokey took another bite of her lunch and chewed thoughtfully. "We're not gonna take this lying down, are we?"

"What can we do?" Annajane asked. "Celia's pregnant, and she just happened to have picked the one baby daddy on earth who actually feels obligated to do the right thing and marry her."

"I've been thinking about that ever since mama shared the happy news,"

Pokey said. "Sallie is deliriously happy, by the way, at the thought of a Bayless grandbaby with a capital B."

"She already has four grandbabies, your three boys and Sophie," Annajane pointed out.

"Nuh-uh," Pokey said. "I'm just a girl. My babies are *Riggs* babies. So they don't really count as far as my mother is concerned. Even though Denning is named for Daddy. And then, of course, Sophie is what Sallie thinks of as a 'yard baby.' Although she would never dare come out and say so to Mason's face."

"A 'yard baby'?" Annajane looked puzzled.

"You know. Yard baby. Do you remember that housekeeper we had when I was little? Cora? I overheard her telling Sallie one day that she had six children at home, but two of them were actually her oldest daughter's 'yard babies.' Later on, I asked Mama about that and she told me a yard baby was a child born to a woman who wasn't married to the baby's father."

Pokey grinned suddenly. "Which prompted me to ask how a lady could *have* a baby if they weren't married. Let me tell you, Sallie Bayless was not prepared to have that conversation with an eight-year-old."

"I'll just bet," Annajane said, laughing.

"Back to Mason, though," Pokey said. "If he didn't feel obligated to marry Sophie's mama, why is he going ahead and marrying that bitch Celia? You know she deliberately got herself knocked up so she could trap Mason into marrying her."

"I don't know," Annajane said. "He never really talks much about Sophie's mother. All he told me was that they'd had a very brief fling, right after we were separated, and that the girl wasn't able to raise a child on her own. I think he's only agreed to marry Celia because he knows she'd totally be an unfit mother if he weren't around."

"We just can't let him marry her," Pokey repeated. "We have to do something."

Annajane poked at her chicken salad with her fork, separating out the bits of chicken and almonds and diced celery, but eating little.

"I think it's a lost cause, Pokey," she said sadly. "Unless we find out Celia is a convicted sex offender or bank robber or something by tomorrow, she's going to be your new sister-in-law."

"We can't give up now," Pokey said. "Did you find out anything else about her dress company?"

"I did talk to that woman, Katie Derscheid, who knows your friend Angela," Annajane said. "She confirmed our suspicions that Celia is a crook. After Baby Brands bought out Gingerpeachy, they discovered that she'd wildly inflated the value of the inventory and her orders. They're suing."

"Hmm," Pokey said. She finished off her potpie and pointed her fork at Annajane's plate. "Are you going to eat that chicken salad, or perform an autopsy on it?"

Annajane pushed it across the table toward her best friend.

"A lawsuit? That's pretty interesting. Wonder if we could get a copy of it?"

"I doubt if it would make much of a difference to Mason," Annajane said. "I'm pretty sure he has no more illusions about his bride to be."

"And this is the woman who's going to raise his child," Pokey said, making a gagging motion. "And Sophie. Perfect."

A pained expression crossed Annajane's face. "I can't bear thinking about that. You're just gonna have to shield Sophie from Celia, as much as you can."

"If she'll let me," Pokey said. "Remember, Celia hates me even worse than she hates you."

"You gotta give Celia credit for smarts," Annajane said. "Once she'd started up her own company, she immediately started looking for a way to trade up. She stalked the president of that other company, and then showed up in the hotel bar where he was staying during a trade show."

"Isn't that how she met Davis in the first place? In a lobby bar?"

"Sort of. According to Davis, Sallie actually tracked Celia down after buying a couple of dresses for Sophie. And then they just happened to be at the same conference in the same hotel at the same time." Annajane lifted a skeptical eyebrow.

"Yeah, I don't think there are a lot of coincidences where Celia is concerned," Pokey said.

The waitress came by and dropped off their chocolate silk pie, but Annajane shook her head when Pokey offered her a slice.

"Could you bring me a glass of Chablis instead?" Annajane asked the waitress.

"Hey, what goes?" Pokey asked. "You never drink on a workday."

"Extreme duress calls for extreme measures," Annajane said glumly. "Anyway, I doubt that anybody at Quixie is going to notice if I come back to work a little later than usual today."

A moment later the waitress was back with her wine. Pokey took the glass from her, waved the glass under her nose and sniffed appreciatively. "This is the thing I miss most when I'm pregnant. A nice little midday buzz. That, and seeing my own ankles."

"A midday buzz is just what the doctor ordered for me," Annajane declared, taking a sip of the wine. She looked over at her best friend. "As soon as I get the summer campaign lined up, probably next week, I'm gone."

Pokey started to protest, then changed her mind. "Where will you go?"

"Not sure yet," Annajane admitted. "I've got a little bit of a financial cushion, with the money from selling the loft. Maybe I'll travel for a while."

"You better come back here in time for my little girl to be born," Pokey threatened, blinking back tears. "Or I'll send the boys to live with you, wherever you are."

Annajane handed Pokey her napkin. "Don't be such a crybaby. Of course I'll come back."

37

Sallie Bayless beamed at her future daughter-in-law as Celia walked into the den on Friday night. They'd had an early dinner together at the country club, just a salad and some broiled flounder, although Celia had only picked at her food, pleading the case for morning sickness.

On their return to Cherry Hill, Celia had excused herself, saying that she needed to make a few quick phone calls. Now she had changed into form-fitting black slacks and a low-necked silver-gray halter top that showed off her tanned shoulders and slim, muscular arms.

"You look lovely, dear," Sallie said. "But won't you be chilly in that top?"

"Not at all," Celia said. "It's eighty degrees out."

"It's a shame Mason isn't here tonight to see you all dressed up. Have you talked to him this evening?" Sallie asked.

"Several times," Celia lied. The prick was deliberately avoiding her, barricading himself in his office for the past few days, ignoring her e-mails, texts, and phone calls. He had Voncile aiding and abetting him in this subterfuge, and Celia was damned if she'd just break into her own fiancé's office. "He asked me to send his regrets. He's got so much going on at the office, he didn't think he'd get away for dinner tonight."

She'd tried once more to lure Mason into having sex, showing up at his house, their house, at dawn just that day, dressed only in a raincoat, a black garter belt, and her highest spike heels. It had been one of the more humiliating and ultimately futile encounters she'd ever had with a man. He'd laughed and slammed the door in her face.

Time was running out. She'd quit taking her birth control pills as soon as she'd hatched her plan and now felt sure she was about to ovulate. And if Mason wasn't going to cooperate, she was going to have to put plan B into action.

Celia picked up her car keys and slung her tote bag over her shoulder.

"Going out so late?" Sallie asked, with a slight frown.

Jesus, the old lady watched her every move. It was like she thought she was Celia's chaperone.

"Bonnie Kelsey and a couple of the girls from the tennis team are having a little get-together in my honor," Celia said. "Sort of a bachelorette thing. But don't worry. I warned them, absolutely no male strippers!" Her giddy laugh echoed in the high-ceilinged room.

"I should hope not," Sallie said, looking horrified. She went back to reading her magazine. "If Mason calls, I'll tell him where he can find you."

Like that's going to happen, Celia thought. *But what if, by some chance, he did call his mother, and went looking for her? That could prove to be extremely embarrassing.*

"Now don't you go spoiling my fun by telling your son where he can find me tonight," Celia said gaily. She patted her tote bag. "This is strictly just us girls. Since it's probably going to be a late night, I'm planning to spend the night with Bonnie."

"Really?" Sallie shot her a disapproving look. "Aren't you a little old for that type of thing? I realize we're only having a small ceremony, but you do want to look your best on your wedding day, Celia. The photographer I hired is going to shoot a wedding portrait of you and Mason, and I know you don't want any dark circles or unfortunate puffy eyelids."

"The ceremony isn't until four o'clock," Celia said. "Don't worry, I swear, I'll get my full eight hours of sleep, and I'll be fresh as a daisy for the ceremony." She kissed Sallie warmly on the cheek. "Tomorrow's the day!"

She waited until she was almost to the gates of Cherry Hill before taking the phone out again.

"Heey," she said softly. "Are you busy tonight?"

"Not really. What did you have in mind?" he asked.

She was fairly sure he knew exactly what she had in mind, but if he wanted to play games, so could she.

"I was hoping we could get together to talk strategy. About the deal."

"Fine with me," he said. "Where and when?"

"Hmm," Celia said, playing along. "Someplace private?"

"I know just the place," he said.

38

Friday night. Annajane had listened to the tapes of the tinny recordings of the old Quixie radio ads a couple dozen times, trying for inspiration for a new jingle. Despite her gloomy mood, the vocals, done by what sounded like a group of midgets huffing helium, gave her an unstoppable case of the giggles.

> *Ask for Quixie in your glass*
> *for a summer filled with sass!*
> *It's the quicker fun-time drink*
> *it's cool, it's cold, it's pi—iiinnk!*

She glanced over at the tableau she'd set up on the desk opposite her bed at the Pinecone Motor Lodge.

She'd had one of the vintage magazine ads with the new "Taste of Dixie" sell-line on it blown up to poster size and dry mounted on a foam-core board with an easel backing. In front of the board she'd arranged smaller similarly mounted mock-ups of the summer fun ads from the '50s and '60s. And as a finishing touch, she'd filled one of the old green throwback Quixie bottles with a can of the cherry soda she'd picked up on the way out of the plant.

Shaded by the vivid vintage fringed barkcloth lampshade on the desktop, the green bottle gave off an eerie glow. The old jingles were funny and catchy, Annajane decided, but definitely stretched the truth. Quixie was not pink at all. It was definitely, decidedly red. Unless you added a scoop of vanilla ice cream, in which case it would lighten to an obliging pink.

She reached for the martini glass on her bedside table, took a long drink, and smacked her lips. She'd worked late, only stopping in the early evening to eat a bag of chips from the break room vending machine, and had been the last one to leave the plant at 9:00 P.M.

When she pulled into the parking lot at the motel, she'd been surprised to see that every slot in the parking lot was full, and most of the vehicles were vans or box trucks. Lights shone from all the units, and smoke curled from a barbecue grill that had been set up in the courtyard. Music drifted out from several of the units, and casually dressed men sat in front of several cottages, chatting and sipping from Styrofoam cups. The place was hopping. She followed the blacktop around to the back of the units and finally found an empty space behind the office.

Annajane was trudging back toward her own unit when the door of the office opened and Thomas, one of the owners, beckoned her inside.

"You're just in time for happy hour," Thomas informed her. He pointed to an overstuffed green chintz armchair. "Sit. I'll get you a drink. You can have anything you want as long as you want a martini."

"A martini would be fabulous," Annajane said. "But what's going on around here? Did you book a convention?"

"Kind of," Harold said with a grin. He was wearing a different Hawaiian shirt, and neatly starched beige linen pleated-front slacks. "There's a big florists' trade show that starts in Southern Pines tomorrow. One of Thomas's old boyfriends saw our Pinecone Motor Lodge ad in the North Carolina Pink Pages, and he sent out a few e-mails and voilà! We're nearly sold out with a full house of florists."

"He is not an old boyfriend!" Thomas protested with a blush. He handed Annajane an oversized glass and poured her drink from a bullet-shaped glass and chrome cocktail shaker. "He's just a kid. It was years ago. We had maybe one date before I realized he was too immature for me."

"Immature?" Harold said with a hoot. "They went out to dinner and Harold had to order him a Happy Meal."

"Would you stop?" Thomas said. "Annajane doesn't want to hear about my old flames." He went into the kitchen and came back with a dish of cheese straws.

"Yum," Annajane said gratefully. "I didn't have any dinner tonight."

"Were you at work all this time?" Harold asked. "We were beginning to wonder if you'd changed your mind about staying."

"I've got a big project I'm trying to wrap up," Annajane said quietly. "I've resigned effective next week."

"Oh, no," the men said in unison. "Does that mean you're leaving Passcoe, too?" Harold asked.

"For now," Annajane said. She stared into her cocktail glass. "I need a change of scenery."

Thomas exchanged a meaningful look with his partner. "Man troubles?"

She nodded. "You could say that."

Harold patted her on the shoulder. "Whoever he is, he's an idiot."

"Thanks," she said. She stood to leave and held out her half-empty glass. "He's getting married tomorrow. Would you mind pouring this into a go-cup for me? After the day I've had, I think I need a nightcap."

"Here," Thomas said, handing her the cocktail shaker. "Just take the whole thing with you."

The bad thing about staying in a genuine retro '50s motel room, Annajane decided, was that all that authenticity meant that she didn't have a television. She'd finally given up on her jingle project after an hour of staring at the old ads and listening to the old commercials.

Instead, she reached into the box of old Quixie recipe booklets she'd rescued from one of the boxes that had been headed for the Dumpster. She decided to look for anything approaching a muffin recipe that Thomas could use.

The booklets had apparently been produced in-house and given away at grocery store displays or as mail-in premiums. She was leafing through a booklet called "Quixie Entertaining Tips" when she came to a page featuring recipes for "Summer Quix-E-Que." Among the dishes was a Quixie-marinated barbecued chicken, the baked beans recipe Annajane had seen in an earlier advertisement, and a chocolate sheet cake recipe with "Choco-Quixie frosting."

On the page facing the recipes was a full-page black-and-white photo of teenagers enjoying a summer cookout. As she was marveling at the teenager's clean-cut outfits, she realized, with a start, that the perky brunette who was holding an upraised bottle of Quixie in her hand was none other than a teenaged Ruth Hudgens.

"Oh my gosh, Mama," she said softly. Her mother's dreamy-eyed smile was directed at a trim lad dressed in a madras short-sleeved shirt and sharply pressed khakis. He looked enough like Mason to take her breath away, but as she looked closer, she realized she was staring at a teenage Glenn Bayless, who had his arm around the very young, and very adorable, Ruth.

Annajane knew the photo had been staged, but as she studied the faces of the other teens, she realized that Sallie Bayless was not among the partygoers.

"Mama and Glenn?" she murmured. Had the two of them ever dated? Emboldened by the martinis she'd been sipping, she picked up the phone and called her mother.

"Hey, Mama," she said softly. After a few minutes of chatting about her job prospects and some sharp questions about why she didn't come to her senses and make up with Shane again, she finally managed to get to the point.

"Listen, Mama," she said, staring down at the recipe booklet spread out on her bed, "I was going through some old Quixie ads, and I found one with a photo of a barbecue layout that you were in. Do you remember that?"

"That old thing?" her mother chuckled. "Good Lord, honey, I haven't thought of that in years."

"You were wearing a little cotton shift dress and had your hair in a flip; you looked so cute, a little bit like Jackie Kennedy back in the day," Annajane said.

"People did used to tell me that," Ruth admitted. "I bet I wasn't but eighteen when they took that picture. I made that dress myself. It was my favorite."

"It'd be right in style today," Annajane said. "Mama, in the picture, Glenn Bayless has his arm around you. And the two of you look pretty lovey-dovey."

"What?" Ruth sounded startled. "Annajane, the photographer posed all of us like that."

"You're looking at him like he hung the moon," Annajane said. "And he's looking at you the same way. Mama, did the two of you have a thing, back then?"

She heard Ruth sigh. "We went out a few times that summer, yes. I wouldn't call it a thing."

"Was this before or after Glenn started going with Sallie?"

"Now, why are you digging up all this ancient history? You are good and done with that family, I hope."

"Humor me, Mama, please?"

"I can't remember back that far," Ruth groused. "I think that was the summer after our senior year. Glenn and Sallie dated all through school, but then I seem to recall that they broke up right before the prom. And I ended up going with Glenn, and then we went out a few times that summer. But then your daddy came home from overseas, and I never gave Glenn another look. He and Sallie got back together right before he went off to college. And I ended up marrying your daddy. Now, can I please go on to bed?"

Annajane ran her finger over the old photograph. "Why didn't you ever tell me you'd gone out with Glenn?"

"It was years and years ago," Ruth said. "Way before you were born. What difference does it make?"

"I thought you hated all the Baylesses," Annajane said.

"I never said I hated them," Ruth corrected. "I just said I didn't care for the family. Especially the mother."

"All these years, I've wondered why Sallie didn't like me; this explains everything."

"Sallie Bayless didn't like you because she thought she was better than you and me and everybody else in this town," Ruth said.

"But she hated *you*, probably because she had some idea that you stole Glenn from her," Annajane said.

"Stole him! I did no such thing. Glenn was a nice enough boy, but even back then he had a wandering eye. I wasn't the only girl he was seeing that summer."

"But I bet he only went running back to Sallie after you threw him over for my daddy," Annajane guessed. "And to somebody like Sallie, that would be unforgivable. And unforgettable."

"That woman is bad news," Ruth said flatly. "How we were ever friends is beyond me."

"You were friends?"

"Best friends. In grade school," Ruth said. "Like you and Pokey always were. Although I will say that Pokey is nothing like her mother, thank the Lord."

"And then what happened to break up the friendship?" Annajane asked, fascinated.

"Boys!" Ruth said. "Sallie Woodrow was boy crazy. She didn't have any time for girlfriends once she discovered boys."

"Wow," Annajane said. "Just . . . wow."

"If that's all you wanted to know, I'll say good night," Ruth said. "It's too late for an old lady like me to be up this time of night. But honey?"

"Yes, Mama?"

"Send me a copy of that picture, would you?"

After talking to her mother, Annajane couldn't settle down. She'd tried reading, but couldn't concentrate. And her iPod was packed away in boxes with all the rest of her belongings. She could hear voices outside from the courtyard. People having a good time. It made her deepening depression even worse. Everybody in the world, it seemed, had a man. Except her.

The room did have an old hi-fi, though. Annajane lifted the console lid and picked up a half-dozen old record albums. Most of the artists were ones she recognized only because her step-father had inherited his father's old record collection. She wrinkled her nose in distaste at the selection: the Ray Conniff Singers, Perry Como, Brenda Lee. Pat Boone? Harold and Thomas were dears, but their musical taste definitely ran to midcentury cheese. She considered the last album in the stack, *Johnny's Greatest Hits*, by Johnny Mathis.

What the hell, she decided. She had to study the console switches and knobs for a few minutes to figure it out, but then she put the record onto the turntable, turned up the volume, and dropped the needle on the record.

Lush strings and background singers filled the room. Annajane stretched out on the bed, propped her head up on the pillows, and poured herself another martini.

"You ask how much I love you," Johnny crooned in his velvet voice, "Until the twelfth of never." She managed to make it through two more syrupy ballads,

"Chances Are" and "Wonderful Wonderful," before she broke down in great, sorrowful sobs.

"That's it," Annajane cried, lunging for the hi-fi's on-off dial. Much better. Thank God the proprietors of the Pinecone Motor Lodge's tastes didn't include vintage Journey, or she would have slit her own wrists with a dull nail file. She poured herself a little more martini and decided that was better yet.

The twelfth of never, she reflected, sipping her drink, could have been the theme song for her relationship with Mason, with never the operative phrase. They'd been so close this last time to finding their way back to each other. But close, her mother had always warned, only counted in horseshoes and hand grenades.

She found the old snapshot in her purse, where she'd stashed it while packing for her move, and studied it again, hoping to find a clue to that happy place they'd inhabited so long ago. Mason's eyes were shadowed by his sunglasses, but his lips curled in a carefree, unaffected grin that was nothing like the guarded, hesitant half-smile he'd affected these last few years.

And what about her own face? The Annajane of the photo gazed up at Mason in unabashed adoration that made her cringe today. Back then, she'd hidden nothing, held back nothing. Stupid, vulnerable girl. Couldn't know then what she wished she didn't know now. How she missed that girl.

Annajane heard a small ding come from the direction of her cell phone. It was a text. From Mason.

I need 2 see U.

She glanced at the photograph again, looked at the happy face of that stupid, unguarded, vulnerable nineteen-year-old version of herself. One more time, she decided. One more chance. And the hell with the consequences.

Annajane grabbed her purse and her car keys. She opened the door. Mason stood on the threshold.

"I'm sorry," he said, but he never got to finish his sentence, because Annajane was kissing him.

. . .

"Don't say anything," she cautioned, when he managed to pull back from her. "Don't tell me you're sorry again."

"I won't," he promised, taking her face between his hands. "I tried to stay away tonight. But I couldn't. I had to see you."

"I know," Annajane said. "I've been sitting around here moping and crying all night long." She managed a laugh. "I was listening to an old Johnny Mathis album, for God's sake."

"I've been standing here for ten minutes, listening," Mason admitted. "Trying to get up the nerve to knock."

"I couldn't take any more," Annajane said. "He was killin' me. My tear ducts are totally dry."

"I don't want you to cry," Mason said. He pointed toward the door. "Come on. Let's get out of here. I brought the fun car. For old time's sake. I'm selling it after tomorrow."

Annajane gasped. "You're gonna let her make you sell it? But you love that car."

"Not anymore," Mason said. "What's the point of keeping it? I think I'm done with fun."

"Sophie loves that car, too," Annajane pointed out. "And you promised to take her for a ride in it. All the way to the coast."

"She'll forget," Mason said with a shrug. "She's just a kid."

"Stop that!" Annajane said. "I can't stand being with you like this."

"I'm . . ." he started to say. And then he caught himself. "One more ride."

Annajane pulled away. "I don't think so," she said slowly.

His eyes widened. "Look, it's my last night. I've told her I love you. But after tomorrow, I can't come to you like this. I won't cheat. Not even with you."

"I know that," Annajane said. She turned her back to him and lifted her hair to expose the nape of her neck. "I think we should stay in tonight. Could you please help me with my zipper?"

He held her hair up with one hand and kissed her neck. He inched the zipper down slowly, following its track with his lips.

Mason turned her around. He kissed her lightly at first, his lips brushing hers, almost a brotherly kiss, she thought, somehow dismayed at the casual nature of his embrace. But then he bent, and his lips strayed to her bare collarbone and the warm hollow of her neck. He pulled her closer, and Annajane's arms twined around his neck. Finally, his lips found their way back to hers. He kissed her slowly, gently, deeply, his tongue teasing as she opened her lips to him.

I remember this, Annajane thought, as she melted into Mason. She inhaled the scent of him, his soap, his aftershave. She was intoxicated with the scent of him, his nearness, dizzy with wanting him. With her fingertips, she traced the smooth skin of his jawline.

"I've missed you," Annajane started to say, but he kissed away whatever else she might have said. His hands cupped her butt, and then they finger-walked their way up her spine, and the shiver that worked its way up her body made him chuckle, as it always used to.

He eased his thumbs under the band of her bra, pushing her breasts upward, until they spilled out of the gaping neckline of her dress, and then he bent his head, raining feathery kisses at first, and then, nipping and kissing and caressing her exposed nipples, until her knees buckled and her brain idly telegraphed, *I remember this. Oh. My . . .*

Somehow, her dress slipped to the floor. She pushed Mason's polo shirt up, and then over his head, and tossed it aside. A moment later, her lacy coral bra joined his shirt, and she pressed herself against him, wanting the sensastion of his nipples pressed against hers. She hooked her fingers briefly inside the waist of his jeans, and then ran them up his belly, laughing to herself as she felt his sharp inhale of arousal, and pleasing herself, running her fingers through his chest hair, over his now-taut nipples.

He buried his hands in her hair, kissing her so deeply, with such passion, he literally lifted her out of her heels. Then he set her gently back down, pressing her with his hips, until her back was to the cabin wall. Without her heels, she was four inches shorter than Mason. He braced one hand on the cabin wall, looking down at her with such ineffable tenderness it took her breath away. He bent, kissed her forehead, nuzzled her ear, traced the nape of her neck with his tongue, murmuring under his breath. "So sweet, so sweet . . ."

All the while, he worked his knee between hers, his hands roaming over her bare torso. He bunched the fabric of her lace panties with one hand, and then the other, effortlessly sliding them from her hips. She gasped as he slid his fingers into her, and ripples of pleasure flooded her body. *I remember this. Oh. My. God. I want this.*

She slid her hand down his chest again, feeling the hard strain of him against the fabric of the worn jeans. She let her hand linger there for a moment, before unfastening the metal button. She inched the zipper down slowly with her thumb, letting the palm of her hand rest against the hardness for another long moment.

Mason's breath caught as she langorously unzipped his fly. She tugged at his waistband, and then, lifting one leg and wrapping it halfway around him, she pulled at the jeans until they puddled around his ankles, and he was forced to pull away, kick off his shoes and step out of the jeans.

She gave him a lazy appraisal. "Still a boxer man, I see."

"I'm the same as I always was," he said, taking her by the hand and leading her to the bed.

She pulled the covers down and slipped beneath them, and a minute later, he was beside her. He propped himself up on one elbow, and gazed at her so intently, she found herself blushing.

"What?" she said nervously.

He kissed her. "I've been waiting for this a long time. Five years. I tried to make myself forget you, but it didn't work. Nothing else worked. Nobody else was you."

Annajane kissed him back. She laid her cheek on his chest. "I know. Some nights, I'd leave work, and driving home, if I had the radio on, and a certain song came on, I'd completely lose it. I'd go to meetings at work so I could be near you, but then you seemed so cold and distant; I knew you hated me. It was all I could do to stay in the same room."

Mason ran his hands down the length of her body, and she shivered in delight, curling toward him as he stroked and caressed her, and she did the same, reacquainting herself with the contours of his body, the flat plane of his belly, his muscled thighs, even the smallpox vaccine on his upper left arm.

His voice was husky. "I never hated you. I couldn't. It was just . . . a defense mechanism, trying to keep you at a distance because I knew I'd blown my one chance with you. I never thought I'd get you back again."

"Tonight's the twelfth of never," she laughed, with a catch in her voice, as he rolled on top of her. And it was that easy, as they moved together, the dark, empty years receded, the cold place in her heart melted, and all was light and joy and pleasure, as their rhythms matched and their bodies coupled so easily, so naturally.

"Annajane," he said it over and over again, as though he'd just discovered the name of his long-lost love. "Annajane." His voice faltered, as they climaxed, in unison, waves of ecstasy washing over her as she arched her body to meet his. *I remember this. This is mine. For one last time.*

The soft buzz of Mason's snore awoke her. He was curled on his side, one hand cupped over her breast, the way he'd slept so many nights of their marriage. She smiled sleepily to herself and glanced at the clock radio on the nightstand. One o'clock.

"Mason!" His snores drowned out her whisper. She'd forgotten what a heavy sleeper he was. "Mason." She turned and shook his shoulder. "Mason, wake up."

"Why?" he said groggily, rolling over onto his other side, facing away from her.

"It's after one. You have to go home." She shook his shoulder again. "Come on. Get up, now."

"Sleepy. Stayin' here."

"No, you're not staying here." She hopped out of bed and rummaged in her suitcase for her robe. Knotting the belt around her waist, she gathered up the clothes he'd dropped on the floor earlier in the evening and took them around to the other side of the bed.

He was snoring again. "Mason!" Her voice took on a new urgency. "Look, you can't stay here. You need to go home."

"Celia's at Mama's house," Mason said.

"You need to go home to Sophie," Annajane insisted.

"Letha's there," he mumbled.

"I don't care. Sophie will wonder where you've been. I don't want her to think you're playing spend the night with me, when you're marrying Celia this afternoon. It's . . ." She searched for the right word. "Trashy."

He tugged at the shoulder of her robe. "Not trashy. It's romantic. Now come back to bed."

"Absolutely not," she said, yanking the covers off him. "You're going home." She shoved the bundle of clothes at him. "Here. Get dressed."

39

She followed him out of the cabin, missing him already, wanting him to stay, knowing she couldn't ask him to.

"Where's the Chevelle?" she asked, looking out at the quiet parking lot, half-empty now.

"I had to park clear out in back, right near your car," he said. "Just as well. Everybody in town knows the fun car by now."

"Are you worried about the gossip? About what Celia will think?" Annajane asked.

His jaw muscle twitched. "I don't give a damn what Celia thinks. But I'd rather not have another lecture from Sallie."

She nodded. "I'm not going to kiss you good-bye."

"Better not to," he agreed.

"I'm almost done with the promotion," Annajane said. "By midweek, I'll have it wrapped up. By the time you get back from your honeymoon, I'll be gone."

"Honeymoon?" He nearly spat the word. "I said I'd marry her, but there's just so far I'll go with this farce. I never said anything about a honeymoon. If she wants to take one, she's going solo."

There was so much she wanted to ask him, but the time had slipped away.

They'd only had a few hours. She was glad they'd spent them loving each other. One last time.

"Have you told Soph you're leaving after all?" he asked, stuffing his hands in the pocket of his jeans to keep from touching her again.

"Not yet," Annajane said. "I'll figure something out. One good-bye at a time is all I can manage right now." She swallowed hard. Her tear ducts apparently hadn't dried up after all.

It was chilly out, and she was barefooted. She hugged herself and hopped up and down to keep warm. "Okay. I'm going in now."

"See ya," Mason said. Then he turned and walked right out of her life.

Sunshine flooded in through the slats of the wooden window blinds. She heard the slam of a car door and the murmur of voices from outside.

Annajane sat up in bed and peered groggily at the alarm clock. It was only seven o'clock. Her head throbbed dully, leading her to wish, too late, that she hadn't finished off the shaker of martinis after Mason's early-morning departure.

She showered and dressed in a pair of jeans and a pale blue Dandelion Wine T-shirt. Her mouth felt dry and cottony. Coffee, she thought, heading toward the motel's office, might be her only hope of salvation.

"Good morning," Thomas called, as she pushed into the little lounge area. He held up the coffee pot, and she nodded gratefully.

"You're an early bird this Saturday," Harold said, looking up from the computer screen behind the check-in desk.

"Too early," Annajane said, taking the mug of coffee Thomas offered. She looked out the window at the quiet courtyard and half-empty parking lot. "What happened to all your florists?"

"The Stallion Club happened," Harold said.

"It's an after-hours gay bar they discovered in Pinehurst," Thomas explained.

"They have gay bars in Pinehurst?"

"Bar. Singular," Thomas corrected. "Apparently it's quite the scene. A couple of the boys came knocking on our door at two, asking if we wanted to go along."

"Honey, we are too old for that kind of nonsense," Harold said.

"Now," Thomas added. He raised an eyebow. "But there was a time . . ."

"Annajane is a nice girl," Harold told his partner. "She doesn't want to hear about the scandalous behavior of our youth."

"You mean your youth," Thomas shot back. "I'm not the one who traveled with a Village People tribute band the summer I turned twenty-four."

"Were you the Indian chief or the construction worker?" Annajane asked.

"Both!" Harold said. He smoothed his hands over his nearly bald head. "But that was back in my drinking days. The strongest thing I drink now is your delicious Quixie."

"That reminds me," Thomas said. "We've got another guest staying here who works at Quixie."

"Really?" Annajane took another sip of her coffee. "I wonder who it is?"

Harold looked down at the old-fashioned ledger book on the reception desk. "Hmm." He laughed. "It says here his name is Harry Dix. And he paid cash for the room. Whoever he really is, he has a delightful sense of whimsy."

"Harry . . . oh, I get it," Annajane said, blushing slightly. "He used a pseudonym. But how do you know he works at Quixie?"

"He asked for the corporate rate," Thomas said. "Seemed like a nice guy. Dark hair, late thirties, getting a little bit of a paunch, drives a Porsche Boxster. There can't be that many of those around here."

"A dark-haired guy driving a Boxster?" Annajane said, her eyes widening.

"I'm surprised you didn't run into him when you came over here this morning," Harold chimed in. "He's staying in unit twelve, on the end. It was the only room we had when he checked in last night."

Annajane felt the blood drain from her face. Davis Bayless drove the only Boxster in Passcoe that she knew of. And of course, according to Pokey, he'd been using the Pinecone Motor Lodge to shack up with his girlfriends for years. She'd totally forgotten he had a history with this place.

What if Davis had seen Mason's car here last night? Was he aware that Annajane was staying at his favorite motel?

Her head pounded. She took another gulp of coffee, and tried to reassure herself. Mason had parked on the other side of the complex, in the unlit back parking lot. And he'd left in the middle of the night. He'd been gone for hours now. Where was Davis's car?

She stood and gazed out the window, and, as she did, the door to unit 12 opened. Annajane's head was muddled, but her reflexes were fine. She hit the floor.

"Do I sense some drama?" Harold asked.

"Don't worry, hon, she's not even looking this way," Thomas said.

"She?" Annajane pulled up to her knees, crawled over to the window, and peeked out.

A petite woman in tight black slacks, a slightly askew silver halter top, and high-heeled silver mules peeked out the door of unit 12. She had short, white-blond hair and a large overnight bag slung over her shoulder.

Annajane gasped and ducked again.

"Oh my God," she whispered. "Is she looking this way?"

Harold walked over to the window and looked out. "Not really. She's talking on her cell phone. Do you know her?"

"Afraid so," Annajane said. "Her name's Celia. She's the one who's marrying my ex-husband today."

Now Thomas was standing at the window, too. "Hmm. She's certainly blessed. Do you think those are real?"

Harold went back to the reception desk and fetched his bird-watching binoculars. He studied the set in question. "Ooh, look, here comes Mr. Harry Dix."

Annajane's heart was pounding in her chest as she poked her head high enough to see out the window. Sure enough, a man had stepped onto the tiny porch of unit 12. His dark wavy hair looked damp. His white dress shirt was rumpled and untucked, and he carried his expensive pin-striped suit jacket over one arm. He glanced around furtively, ducked his head, and headed around to the back of the unit, in Celia's wake. A moment later, the black Boxster came roaring from the rear of the unit.

"Oh. My. God." Annajane breathed. "I should have known."

"So you do know him?" Harold asked. "What's his real name?"

"His name is Davis Bayless," Annajane said, standing slowly, hoping her head would stop pounding. "He's the groom's baby brother."

"Uh-oh," Thomas and Harold said in unison. They did a well-choreographed fist-bump. "Undercover lovers!"

40

P okey was fifteen minutes late, which was actually early by her own standards. She slid onto the cracked orange vinyl dinette bench opposite Annajane and automatically reached for the oversized laminated menu.

"I already ordered your french toast and sausage," Annajane said.

The Country Cupboard was jammed as usual on a Saturday morning. There
were other breakfast spots in Passcoe, but none as popular as the CC, as everybody in town called it. The long counter at the bar was filled with people tucking into their runny eggs, country ham, bacon, hash-browns, grits, and biscuits,
and every table and booth in the restaurant on the town square was full.

"What's up?" Pokey asked.

Annajane took a sip of ice water and looked around nervously. She should
have picked a quieter, more private place, she realized. The tables were set close
together, and everybody in the CC knew everybody else.

"I have news," Annajane said, trying to keep her voice low.

Pokey eyed her best friend with unguarded curiosity.

"You look different this morning," she said.

Annajane blushed.

"Wait a second. Oh, yeah. I remember that look. You've got afterglow!"

Pokey exclaimed. "Or maybe it's beard burn. You did it, didn't you? Finally."
She clapped her hands excitedly. "Yay! I'm so glad."

"Shh!" Annajane whispered. "Lower your voice! Everybody in here knows
us, and they all think they know what we're talking about. So, can we *not* talk
about what they think we are?"

Pokey leaned forward. "Okay, we won't discuss. Just nod your head, or tap
your glass once for yes, two for no. Did you or did you not? Do it with you-know-
who?"

"All right," Annajane groused. She tapped her glass once with the side of
her spoon.

"Was it amazing?" Pokey demanded.

"Pokey! None of your business," Annajane said, and then, with a shrug, she
tapped her glass once. "Now, can we change the subject? Because that is not
what I need to talk to you about."

"Sure, after you tell me where the deed was done."

Annajane looked away. "Some things a lady doesn't discuss."

"I'm no lady," Pokey replied. "Despite Sallie's best efforts. Did you do it at
his house? Or did you go back out to the farm?"

"No! God, no."

"Where? You might as well spit it out, because you know I'll get it out of you
eventually."

Annajane did know. "All right. It was at the Pinecone."

"Oooh," Pokey said, rubbing her hands together gleefully. "Perfect. Your
own little love nest."

Annajane glanced around the room and leaned her head toward Pokey's.
"Not as perfect as you might think. Guess who else was checked in at the love
nest?"

"The baby mama? For real?"

Annajane tapped her iced-tea glass once with her spoon.

"And she had company! When I saw him sneaking out of her unit this morning I almost wet myself."

"Who?"

"It was almost a family reunion," Annajane whispered.

"Davis?" Pokey's eyes widened.

Annajane tapped her spoon once against her glass. "And he'd signed the guest register with a pseudonym. Harry Dix!"

A plume of ice water erupted from Pokey's nose.

"Oh my God!" Pokey said, dabbing at her face with a paper napkin. "You can't tell me that kind of stuff without a warning."

"I know," Annajane whispered.

"Day-yummm!" Pokey exclaimed. "Harry Dix! That must be his porn name."

Annajane snickered. "Wonder what Celia's is?"

"Lotta Lays?" Pokey offered. She reached for the basket of biscuits in the center of the table, selected one, and sliced and buttered it. She took a bite and chewed slowly.

Annajane sipped her coffee and waited.

"You have to tell Mason," Pokey said.

"No way," Annajane said.

"Somebody needs to. We can't let him marry that, that, woman. Not now."

"I can't be the person to tell him his brother betrayed him like that," Annajane said. "And neither can you. He and 'Harry' might not get along all the time, but it would destroy Mason to find out that 'Harry' slept with 'Lotta.' Anyway, we don't really know for sure what they were actually doing there."

"Oh, please. You saw good old Harry coming out of a room with you-know-who at the Pinecone Motor Lodge this morning. And we both know that's where Harry has always stashed his girlfriends over the years," Pokey said.

"Maybe he was just dropping off some papers to her," Annajane said. "Or they were plotting how to overthrow Mason at Quixie."

"And maybe I'll be the cover model for next year's *Sports Illustrated* swim-suit edition," Pokey said. "We always knew she was a skank. And now she's a double skank—sleeping with brothers. Eeeewww."

The waitress brought Pokey's french toast and set it down on the table. Pokey carefully drizzled maple syrup across her plate. "You're not eating?" she asked.

"Not hungry," Annajane said. "I'm just so . . . sad and mad. And maybe a teensy bit hungover. I wish I knew how to save Mason. I wish he wanted to save himself. But he's resigned to marrying her and making the rest of his life miserable."

"Don't forget he's ruining your life, too," Pokey added.

"I don't have to live with her," Annajane pointed out. She slumped against the back of the vinyl bench. "Are you going to the wedding?" she asked.

"I'm not invited," Pokey said. "Not that I'd go even if I were invited. I'm going to go pick up Sophie after I leave here and take her over to spend the night at my house."

"Sophie's not going to the wedding, either?" Annajane asked, raising an eyebrow.

"Nope. According to Mama, it'll just be her and the happy couple. Oh yes, and Bonnie and Matt Kelsey, who will be the witnesses."

"Interesting that old Harry Dix won't be performing best man duties today," Annajane said.

Pokey gave a smirk. "My guess is, he's already performed for *Lotta*."

41

Mason sat behind the desk in his study, stone-faced, as his sister made one last attempt to change his mind.

"Don't do this, Mason," Pokey begged. "Please? You do not have to do this. You do not have to marry Celia."

"I appreciate your concern," he said quietly, "but I have to do what's best for the child."

"You don't even know that the child is yours," Pokey said bitterly.

"That's enough," Mason said, scowling. "You're talking about the woman I'm marrying. I know you've never liked Celia, but you won't make things any better for this family if you keep up this kind of talk."

"I don't care," Pokey said. "She's a liar and a phony, and I'll risk pissing you off if it means keeping you from marrying her."

"I have obligations," Mason pointed out. "And I won't run from them."

"Fine! Wait til the baby's born. Get some DNA testing. Pay Celia a shitload of child support and buy her a house. But don't, for God's sake, marry her. Look, you never married Sophie's mother, and nobody cared," Pokey said.

Mason clenched and unclenched his jaw. "That's different. For one thing, Sophie's mother didn't want to marry me. She barely knew me. I took Sophie because her mother wasn't equipped to raise her on her own. Maybe it was self-ish of me, deciding to become a single father, I don't know. But I know now that Sophie needs a mother and a father. Two parents. And so will this baby."

"Jesus, Mason!" Pokey shouted. "Do you always have to be the big brother? Always have to look out for everybody else? Always have to know what's best? For me, Davis, Mama, the company? You're so worried about doing the right thing and keeping up appearances, have you even noticed what you're doing affects other people? And that maybe this one time you actually *don't* know what's best? What about Annajane? She loves you and you love her, and you're going to just throw that away? You're going to let her walk away—from you and her friends and her job?"

"Annajane understands," Mason said.

"Bullshit!" Pokey cried, her hands on her hips. "Bullshit. Bullshit. Bullshit."

"Aunt Pokey?" a small voice called from the hallway.

Sophie peeked around the doorway. Her blond ringlets were a tangled mess, she had hot pink lipstick smeared around her mouth, and her sparkly pink glasses slid down her nose. "Are you and my daddy having a fight?" she asked timidly.

Pokey held out her arms to the little girl. "No, punkin," she said, looking shame-faced. "We weren't really fighting, we were just discussin'."

"And cussin'," Mason added. "But we're not really mad at each other. Right, Aunt Pokey?"

Sophie tiptoed into the room. She had obviously dressed herself in her second-best dress, a hand-smocked pink batiste dress she'd worn to her little cousin's christening, which she'd managed to put on backward, so that the tiny mother-of-pearl buttons fastened in the front. She wore a pair of unbuckled white sandals on her feet, and slung across her chest was her pink plastic purse.

"Don't you look nice," Mason said, looking down at her. "Are you all dressed up to go see your cousins?"

"I'm dressed up for the wedding," Sophie said. "But I can't wear my wedding dress, 'cuz Letha said she had to throw that nasty thing out after I got sick on it."

Her impression of her nanny was, as usual, uncanny, and both Mason and Pokey laughed.

Mason picked the little girl up and sat down on the sofa with her on his lap. "I'm sorry, Soph, but you're not going to the wedding today. This is just for grown-ups. Me and Celia and your Nana. That's all."

Sophie's face crumpled. Her lower lip pooched out.

"I'm not even going to the wedding," Pokey said. "Who cares about a stinky old wedding, anyway? I bet they aren't even gonna have any cake."

"We're not," Mason assured her. "Not a lick of cake."

"But I wanna gooooo," Sophie wailed, huge crocodile tears running down her cheeks. "I wanna go with Daddy!"

Pokey plunked down on the sofa beside her brother. She patted Sophie's back. "Come on, punkin, don't cry. You and me are going to have a girl's night out. Do you know what that is?"

"Nooooo," Sophie sobbed. "I wanna go to the wedding. I don't wanna go girl's night out." She buried her face in Mason's starched white dress shirt. "I. Don't. Wannna. Idonwanna," came her muffled chant. "I donwanna. I donwanna!"

"Sure you do," Pokey said, attempting to shift Sophie onto her own lap. "It'll be lots of fun. We can bake some cupcakes. Pink ones. I bought pink sugar sprinkles just for us. And we can watch *The Little Mermaid*. And I'll make Uncle Pete sleep with the boys and it'll be just you and me in the big bed. I'll even make us pancakes for breakfast in the morning!"

But the little girl wrapped her arms tightly around Mason's neck and clung to him like a small, determined barnacle.

Mason looked stricken. "Help," he mouthed.

Pokey reached over and gently disentangled Sophie's arms, wrapping her in her own. "It's just for one night, Soph," she said. "And then tomorrow, Daddy will pick you up at my house and take you right back here to your own house and your own bed."

"Noooo," Sophie cried. "I donwanna."

Mason looked down at the hot pink smears on his shirt. "She's breaking my heart," he said. "What should we do?"

Pokey looked over Sophie's head at her brother. "Let's see if we can distract her," she whispered.

"Hey Soph," she said brightly. "Let me see that pretty dress of yours, will you?"

"No," the little girl said. But after a moment she slid out of Pokey's lap and did a slow twirl.

"It's bee-you-ti-full!" Pokey said encouragingly. Sophie did a faster spin, and the flap of her pocketbook opened, and a strand of silver chain slipped out and onto the carpet.

"You dropped your necklace," Mason said, picking it up to examine it. He frowned down at the chain. "Where did you get this, Soph?"

"It's my jewels," Sophie said, tucking the pocketbook protectively under her arm.

"Hmm," Pokey said, reaching out her hand to take the chain. "This is white gold, and that's a nice-sized sapphire stone. That's an expensive-looking jewel for a five-year-old."

"It's Celia's," Mason said. "I bought it for her at Christmas."

"Oh, Lawwwd," Pokey drawled. "If Celia finds out Sophie's been looting her stuff, you're gonna have hell to pay, brother."

"Christ," Mason muttered. "Like I don't have enough to deal with."

"Sophie," he said. "Have you been borrowing Celia's treasures? You know you're not supposed to get into her things."

"No," Sophie said petulantly.

"Sophie?" he said, a warning note in his voice. He held out his hand. "Can I see what's in your pocketbook?"

"It's my treasures," the little girl said, taking a step backward. "I found 'em."

"Okay," Mason said pleasantly. "But can I see what you've found? Please?"

Reluctantly, Sophie unwound the strap of the purse from her neck and handed it over to her father.

"Let's see," Mason said, reaching inside. He held up a silver-cased pink lipstick with a missing cap.

"Not mine," Pokey said. "I don't wear slutty shades like that."

Mason shot her a warning look, but reached back inside the purse and brought out a handful of silvery objects, which he dumped on the sofa cushion. "Let's see what we've got here," he said, taking inventory.

"Couple sticks of chewing gum, some Quixie pop-tops, an earring . . ."

Pokey picked up the hand-tooled silver hoop earring. "I was wondering where that had gotten to."

Mason continued with the inventory. "Nail clipper, some kind of eye makeup thingy . . ." His voice trailed off and he held up a flat foil-wrapped package. "Pills!" He looked panicky. He grabbed his daughter's hand. "Sophie, you didn't swallow any of these pills, did you? Tell daddy the truth. Did you swallow any of these pills?"

Pokey reached over and took the packet, turning them over and reading the fine print of the label. A slow smile spread across her face.

"I didn't swallow any," Sophie said. "I only take pills Letha or Daddy gives me."

"Thank God," Mason said. "What are they, anyway? I wonder where Sophie got 'em?"

"They appear to be birth control pills," Pokey said, holding up the back of the packet so Mason could see. "And according to the prescription label, they belong to Celia Wakefield."

"What?" Mason said, taking the packet from his sister. "These must be an old prescription. Celia told me she was on the patch. That's how she got, er," he looked over at Sophie, who was listening attentively. "You know."

Pokey took the package back. "They're not that old," she told her brother. "According to the label, these were dispensed from the CVS Drugs out on the by-pass, to Celia Wakefield, on April 1. That's two weeks ago. She picked them up a week before your wedding. And look," she said, pointing to the empty perforations in the foil. "There are ten pills gone. Seems to me Celia was on the pill, right up until three days ago."

She gave her brother a piercing look. "Isn't that when she told you she was pregnant?"

They heard the sound of the lock turning in the front door, and the sound of it opening and closing, and then the tap of high heels on the wooden floor.

Celia stood in the doorway of the den, with a plastic dry-cleaner's bag across her arm. "Mase? I picked up your suit from the cleaners. I knew you'd . . ." She saw Pokey sitting on the sofa beside Mason, and saw Sophie, seated on the floor, refilling her pocketbook with her treasures.

"What's going on?" she asked, sensing the hostility radiating from every pore of Pokey's body.

"Just a family conference," Pokey said.

"Giving it one last try, to convince your brother not to marry me, are we?" Celia asked, trying to sound lighthearted. "Mason's a better man than you give him credit for, Pokey."

Pokey held up the silver package of birth control pills. "And he's a smarter man than you give him credit for."

Celia snatched the pills from Pokey's fingertips. "Where did you get these?"

Pokey pointed to Sophie's pocketbook, which was once more slung across the child's chest. "Sophie has apparently been helping herself to some of your most secret treasures. We found these in her pocketbook, along with one of your lipsticks and some other things she picked up around the house."

"That's absurd," Celia said, but her laugh was hollow. She turned the package over. "I don't know where she found these, but I haven't been on the pill in months and months."

Mason stood up and took the package from Celia. "According to the label, you had this prescription filled two weeks ago." He pointed at the perforations from the missing pills. "What does this mean, Celia?"

Celia pulled herself up to her full five feet one inches of height. "It means I don't appreciate being interrogated like a common criminal." She shot Pokey a glance of unmitigated venom. "For your information, I *was* on the pill, months and months ago, but I switched to the patch right after Christmas. Anybody could have called the CVS and had this prescription refilled, and then planted it with Sophie to make me look bad. Darling, this is obviously some farce your sister has cooked up, to keep you from marrying me. But it won't work."

She turned on Pokey. "I just bet Annajane Hudgens is in on this nasty little plot of yours, isn't she? She'd do anything to try and get Mason back."

Mason glanced down at Sophie, who was watching the brewing storm with interest.

"Pokey," he said, keeping his voice pleasant. "Maybe you and Sophie should get started on that girl's night out."

"I don't wanna," Sophie protested, even while Pokey was taking her by the hand and attempting to lead her out of the room. "I wanna go to the wedding."

"Come on, Sophie," Pokey coaxed. "I don't think there's gonna be a wedding today."

"Over my dead body," Celia called.

Pokey turned and gave her a dazzling smile. "Oh, trust me, that can be arranged."

42

Celia stood by the fireplace, still clutching the plastic bag of dry-cleaning. But Mason had retreated to his desk. He had the package of birth control pills, and he kept turning it over and over. "Mason," she said, pleadingly. "You can't believe I would lie about the baby. Pokey did this. And Annajane. I swear, they refilled that prescription just to make me look bad, and then planted them with Sophie, so that you would find them. They'd do anything to keep us apart."

"Enough," Mason said. "You lied. Please don't make it worse by blaming my sister."

"You don't know them," Celia said, flinging the suit onto the back of a leather wing chair and marching over to the desk. "You think your baby sister is so perfect. And Annajane! You have no idea what that woman is capable of."

Mason kept staring down at the birth control pills.

"There never was any baby, was there?" he asked, when he finally looked up at her.

"Of course there was!" Celia cried. "Would I make up something like that?"

The muscle in Mason's jaw twitched. "I think you did," he said, in disbelief. "I don't know why, but I do believe you cooked up a phony pregnancy because you knew that was the one way in the world I would go ahead with marrying you."

"No," Celia insisted. And then, her voice fainter. "No. This is Pokey and Annajane. They're out to get me. They refilled those pills . . ."

He sighed. "What would you say if I asked you to take a pregnancy test? Right now?"

"I'd say that proves you don't trust me," Celia said, her face growing pale. "That you'd take the word of your sister and ex-wife over mine."

"Unfortunately, I don't think I can trust you," Mason said. "I just can't understand why you would do something like this. You know I'm in love with another woman, but you'd go to this kind of lengths to trap me into a loveless marriage?"

"It wouldn't be loveless," Celia said. "Once we're married, and you see how good we are together, how happy I'll make you, you'll forget about Annajane. We'll sell Quixie, start a new business, have a family. I'm perfect for you. Everybody says so."

"No," Mason said. "Enough lies, Celia." He picked up the telephone.

"Who are you calling?" Celia asked, her voice panicky.

"I'm calling Sallie," Mason said. "To tell her the wedding's off." He held up the receiver to her. "Unless you want to call her yourself?"

43

Mason Bayless was a man who lived up to his obligations. And the one he dreaded nearly as much as he'd dreaded going through with his wedding was telling his mother that he hadn't.

By four that afternoon, he'd arrived at Cherry Hill, removed the festive wreath of orange blossoms and hydrangeas from the front door, and poured his mother a stiff scotch and water and briefed her on the most salient details of the breakup.

"I don't understand," Sallie repeated, for the fifth or sixth time. "How could this happen? Are you sure this wasn't just some misunderstanding between the two of you?" She took a deep drag on her cigarette, tamped the ashes into the kitchen sink, then turned on the tap to wash them down the drain.

"No misunderstanding," Mason said drily. "There was never any pregnancy. Celia made it up, because she knew that was the only way I would marry her."

"That's just not like Celia," Sallie protested. "Such a lovely girl. With a wonderful head on her shoulders. I'm heartbroken. Really devastated." She studied her oldest son's lack of expression.

"Aren't you the least bit upset? About the baby, at least?"

"Relieved is the word I would use," Mason said. "Relieved and grateful."

Sallie sighed deeply. "And I was so looking forward to a Bayless grand-child."

"You have four grandchildren," Mason said sharply. "Remember?"

"Of course," she said quickly. "But Pokey's boys aren't Baylesses. They're Riggses. And Sophie, well, you know what I meant."

"No, Mother," Mason said, his voice icy. "What did you mean? That Sophie isn't a Bayless, because I never married her mother? Is that another reason you were so hot for me to marry Celia, so that you'd have a legitimate grandchild from me?"

"Stop it, Mason," Sallie demanded. "I won't have you speak to me like that. You know perfectly well that I've accepted Sophie as one of our own. I've always treated her exactly as I have Pokey's children. And I wanted you to marry Celia, and for her to have your children, because I believed she would make you happy and be an asset to this family. Is that so wrong for a mother to want?"

She took another drag on her cigarette and let the smoke curl from her nos-trils, waving it away, as though she could wave away anything unpleasant or displeasing in her life.

"Whatever," Mason said. "It's done."

"But where will she go?" Sallie asked. "You'll let her stay on at the company, won't you? She has a consulting contract."

"Celia is gone," Mason said emphatically. "She's moving her things out of my house as we speak. As for Quixie, no, of course I'm not going to keep her on. We'll pay out what we owe her, but under the circumstances, it would be dis-ruptive to business to allow her to stay on."

Sallie's eyes flared. "And yet you kept Annajane on. Even after the divorce."

"Yes, and thank God I did," Mason said. "No thanks to Davis. Or Celia."

Realizing that she was on shaky ground, Sallie quickly changed tack. She flicked a fingertip at the tray of plastic-wrapped crab bundles, the caviar-topped deviled eggs, and the bacon-wrapped chicken livers. "All this food," she said with a sigh. "For the second time in a week. And there are six bottles of cham-pagne in the refrigerator and half a case of expensive-looking red wine in the dining room. And should I even mention the wedding cake? What on earth am I supposed to do with yet another wedding cake? I still have the top layer of the first one in the freezer down in the basement."

Mason shrugged. "I don't give a damn. I told Celia I didn't want any of it in the first place. Feed it to your bridge club. Throw it out. Or better yet, send it over to the nursing home, why don't you?"

Sallie winced. "I am not looking forward to explaining to the girls in bridge club about this latest debacle in your personal life. And as for sending caviar and chicken livers to a nursing home? Certainly not." She picked up the telephone on the kitchen counter. "We'll just have a particularly extravagant family dinner instead. Pokey and Pete and the children will come, of course, and I'll call Davis, too. You'll stay, of course."

"No thanks," Mason said. "There's somebody I have to see tonight. If she'll see me."

When she finally stopped laughing, Pokey hung up the phone.

"Was that Sallie you were talking to?" Pete Riggs asked, looking up from the DVD player he was trying to repair on the kitchen table.

"It was," Pokey said, still chuckling.

"What makes your mother such a laugh riot this afternoon?" Pete asked. He stabbed the Shuffle button, but the machine didn't move.

"Poor Mama," Pokey said, sitting down beside her husband. "I know I shouldn't have laughed right in her face like that, but she's really so clueless."

"What's she so clueless about this time?" Pete asked.

"Life. Family. All of it. She actually wanted me to call Mason and try to 'make him see the light' about his breakup with Celia."

"Like that was gonna happen," Pete said. He picked up a screwdriver and jabbed at the DVD player.

"And then when I told her I was thrilled that the bitch had been caught in her own web of deceit, she invited us all over to supper tonight—to eat the appetizers Celia ordered from the country club, for a wedding to which we were specifically uninvited."

Pete sniffed the DVD player and wrinkled his nose. "Does this thing smell funny to you? I think it smells like something crawled up here and died."

Pokey inhaled. "Eew. Rancid peanut butter. Probably Petey. I don't know what it is with that kid and peanut butter."

"So what did you tell her about dinner?" Pete asked.

"I said *hell* to the no," Pokey retorted. "Then she got her panties all in a wad because I told her I didn't think caviar and deviled eggs and chicken livers were ideal food for three little boys."

"But I love caviar and deviled eggs and chicken livers," Pete said plaintively.

"Pete! We are taking a stand here. We are not eating any food that has any connection to Celia Wakefield or her foiled attempt to drag my poor brother to the altar. Besides, we're having pizza tonight. And then Sophie and I are baking cupcakes. Pink ones."

"Okay, fine," Pete said. "I'm good with pizza. Also cupcakes, pink or otherwise. What does Sophie think about her father's canceled wedding?"

"Not fazed in the least." Pokey said. "She's really more upset about the fact that Mason made her give back that sapphire necklace of Celia's that she had in her pocketbook."

"Not to mention the birth control pills," said Pete, who'd already heard his wife's triumphant blow-by-blow account of the demise of Celia Wakefield. "Soph really saved the day, didn't she? If the kid hadn't found those pills and stashed them in her purse, and you guys hadn't found them when you did, poor old Mason would be celebrating his wedding night right now."

"Not a chance," Pokey said, jabbing at the back of the DVD player with a butter knife. "If Mason hadn't called off the wedding himself, I still had plan B."

"Do I want to know what that was?" Pete asked.

"Probably not," Pokey said. She got up, sat on her husband's lap, and patted his cheek. "Know this, Riggs. When it comes to messing with my family, Pokey don't play."

44

Celia Wakefield was an unholy mess. Her eyes were red and puffy from crying, and a nasty patch of acne had spontaneously erupted on her chin and was working its way north toward both her cheeks. She was hot and sweaty from lugging all the belongings she'd packed up from Mason Bayless's house and cramming them into the back of her Saab. She'd broken two nails and twisted her ankle.

And the very cherry on her parfait of personal misery was that she had gotten her period within the past hour. Two weeks early.

She'd been examining her options, and they didn't add up to much. If it weren't for the money she'd be losing out on, she'd have been positively giddy at the prospect of seeing Passcoe, North Carolina, in the rearview mirror. Where to next? Not Kansas. The lawyers from Baby Brands were making noises about a lawsuit, so she wouldn't be launching another children's clothing business anytime soon. Hmm. Texas? Or maybe Florida? Lots of wealthy men with lots of lovely money. It was something to ponder. Now, she was already late for her meeting. Her cell phone rang and she snatched it up and answered without checking the caller ID, an impetuous decision she immediately regretted.

"Hey, honey," Cheryl's voice, coming live over the phone from South Sioux

City, Nebraska, sounded like she'd been gargling with broken glass and battery acid. "Vernonica tells me you're living in North Carolina now. I hear it's real nice down there."

"How did you get this number?" Celia demanded.

"Veronica give it to me," Cheryl said. "But that's not a very nice way to talk to your mama."

"Sorry, I'm having a really shitty day," Celia said. "What do you want?"

"Why do you assume I want something everytime I call you?" her mother asked.

"Because you always do. What is it this time? I hope it's not money, because I don't have any to spare. I just lost my job."

"Oh." Silence. "I wasn't calling to ask for nothing," Cheryl said, sounding hurt. "I just wanted your new address, so I could send your birthday present. Gene's got these real nice Louis Vuitton purses now, and I know you like that kind of stuff."

Her mother's boyfriend for the past ten years was a grifter named Gene, who spent more time in lockup than he did in the house he shared with Cheryl.

"My birthday isn't until November," Celia said. "And how would Gene get his hands on Louis Vuitton handbags?"

"He's got his ways," Cheryl said airily. "Anyway, it's too bad about your job. I was thinking it might be nice to come visit you. I've never been to North Carolina."

"Why would you suddenly want to visit me now?" Celia asked. "Did Gene kick you out of the house?"

"Hell, no!" Cheryl said. "I just thought it would be nice to see you. It's been a real long time."

Not long enough, Celia thought. It had been six years and counting. She'd dropped in and out of college and was waitressing at a steakhouse when a good customer there offered her a job as a traveling sales rep for a company that sold a line of hospital linens. She'd "borrowed" her sister Veronica's car and headed out that night for St. Louis, with nothing more than the clothes on her back. The wad of cash she'd found in the glove box was a pleasant and unexpected bonus.

"Now is not a good time," Celia said flatly.

Never would be the perfect time to be reunited with her family.

"Maybe you could come on back here, while you're between jobs," Cheryl suggested. "There's plenty of room in the house. You hadn't even seen Jaymie's twins, and they're almost six. And Terri's boy Richie, he's a big old thing. Nearly twelve, I think. He's already started shaving, you believe that? And Jasmine, she's nine and just as tall as her mama."

"Are they all still living with Daddy in the double-wide?" Celia asked.

"I don't ask," Cheryl said. "Those girls don't care nothin' about their mama. I don't even get a card on Mother's Day. Doyle's the only family they care about."

Most likely, Celia thought, *what her two youngest sisters cared about was their father's latest disability check. Neither Jaymie nor Terri had bothered to graduate from high school, or to marry the various fathers of their children. Instead, they'd gotten an early and thorough education in the art of scamming from Doyle Wakefield.*

Celia peered through the Saab's windshield, at a booth near the window of the restaurant. "Look, Mama," she said. "I gotta go now. I'll give you a call with my new address when I get settled."

And when hell freezes over, she thought. *She really was going to have to get a new phone number now.*

"You do that, precious," Cheryl said. "And you know, if you did happen to have a few extra bucks laying around, you could send 'em my way."

Davis Bayless sat across the table from Celia at the Waffle House on the bypass and wished he were somewhere else.

"You have to do something," she told him.

"What?" Davis said. "I can't hold a gun to his head, Celia. I can't make him marry you if he doesn't want to."

"He did want to," she insisted. "Right up until the minute that Annajane Hudgens crooked her little finger and decided she wanted him back."

Davis shrugged. "What can I say? My big brother is a big sap. Ole Annajane must know some tricks in the sack that we ain't heard of. Anyway, I'm the last person he's likely to listen to these days. My advice is, take what you can get and move on down the road. He offered to buy out your contract, right?"

"That's peanuts. If we'd gotten married, and the Jax deal had gone through, it would have been worth millions. To all of us. Now, I walk away with what? Maybe fifty thousand dollars? Screw that!"

Celia glared at Davis. "You have to make this right, Davis. I'm the one who brought Jerry Kelso and Jax to the table for this deal. Kelso had never heard of Quixie until I met him in that hotel bar in Atlantic City. I'm the one who made them understand what this brand is worth. Most importantly, I'm the one who sucked up to your mother, gained her trust, and then hammered it into her silly southern belle head just how much cash she will get out of this sale, and just how much she needs to get out of the godforsaken town of Passcoe, North Carolina."

"I know what all you did, and I appreciate it, Celia, I really do," Davis said soothingly. "And don't you worry. Once we get that deal with Jax inked, getting Celia Wakefield on board in an executive position, that's gonna be my number one priority. Jerry and I have already discussed it." He winked and then reached under the table and squeezed her thigh. "Davis is gonna take good care of you, baby."

She slapped his hand away. "I don't need taking care of that way. The only thing I want from you is an ironclad, signed agreement that I will be fairly compensated for my participation as a go-between in Jax's acquisition of Quixie."

"Sure thing," Davis said. "You have my word."

Celia's laugh had a nasty edge.

Like I would take the word of a man who'd fuck his brother's fiancée?

"I'd prefer to have it in writing," Celia said. "Just so there won't be any misunderstandings."

"Hey, now," Davis said, rearing back. "I'm on your side, remember? Didn't I help you out with that little problem you were having?"

"I don't know what you're talking about," she said.

Davis slid his hand over Celia's, trapping it on the tabletop. "Why, trying to get you knocked up, what else? Don't you think I figured out why you were in such a hurry to get in my pants Friday night? And me without a condom? I'll admit, my feelings were a little hurt when you first came to work at Quixie and immediately set your sights on Mason, instead of me, but I got over it eventually. Hell, I was even willing to take one for the team and let you pass off my baby as Mason's, if that's what it took to seal our little deal."

He glanced around the restaurant. It was only eight o'clock, past the dinner hour, too early for the night owls, and nobody he knew ever frequented the Waffle House, which was why he'd agreed to meet there.

"Hey, uh, you don't think Mason knows, do you? You know, about us? I mean, you didn't happen to mention that, right? Because that could make things kind of awkward. Him being my brother and all."

The seed of an idea took hold in Celia's imagination. *If you got right down to it, they were both from the same gene pool, so one Bayless was as good as the other, wasn't it? Davis wasn't the man Mason was. He never would be. But once the Jax deal was inked, he'd be just as rich.*

"It's our little secret," she assured him.

She was about to pay for her coffee and leave when her cell phone rang. She grabbed for it, still not totally convinced Mason wouldn't have a change of heart. She saw the caller ID too late.

"Sissy! Is that really you?" Her baby sister Jaymie sounded drunk.

"Hey, Daddy! I got Sissy on the line," Jaymie called. "Hang on, hon, Daddy needs to talk to you real bad."

"Where did you get this number?" Celia said through clenched teeth.

"Veronica gave it to Terri and me," Jaymie said. "Listen, Sissy. Daddy's not doing too good. That last accident, he messed up his back. For reals. He's in a wheelchair . . ."

"I'm sorry, I'm afraid you have the wrong number again," Celia said pleasantly. She clicked the Disconnect button and dropped the phone into her purse. Davis was staring open-mouthed at her.

Celia took a deep breath. She really had to work on keeping her cool. "On top of everything else some lunatic keeps calling me over and over again. I'm going to have to get a new number."

"Yeah, tough luck," Davis said. He pushed away the money Celia placed on the tabletop. "I'm glad we got together to talk tonight. Cleared the air. No hard feelings, right?"

She sighed and tried to look forlorn. It wasn't her strength. "Maybe it's for the best," she said, giving her imitation of wistfulness, standing to go, giving him the shot he was hoping for. She leaned over and gave him a lingering kiss, just to remind him of the good times.

"Good-bye, Davis. It's been fun."

"Well, hey," he said, confused. "It doesn't have to be good-bye, now, does it? I mean, I've got the evening free, and there's always the Pinecone Motor Lodge."

"That's so sweet," she said. "But I've had a really long day. I think I'll just drive over to Pinehurst and get myself a motel room and try to figure out my future."

"You do that," Davis said, beaming. "And give me a call when you get your new number."

"Don't worry," Celia promised. "You'll be hearing from me."

45

The florists were having themselves a high old time at the Pinecone Motor Lodge. A long banquet-sized table had been set up in the grassy courtyard and draped with a gauzy white cloth. A series of elaborate silver candelabras marched down the middle of the table, punctuated by raised epergnes of gorgeous centerpieces spilling lilies, hydrangeas, roses, tulips, and flowers whose names Annajane didn't know. The men, and a few women, were dressed in spring finery, milling about the tables, sampling from dozens of platters of appetizers and sipping wine from plastic champagne flutes.

She'd been holed up in her motel room most of the day, her phone turned off, all her focus turned toward the Quixie summer ad campaign, until, finally, Harold and Thomas had coaxed her out for a glass of wine shortly before dusk.

"I'm not really dressed for a cocktail party," she'd said, trying to beg off, but the men had insisted, so she'd changed out of her yoga pants and T-shirt into a somewhat respectable flowered, cotton ankle-length sundress and a pair of teal ballet flats. The dress dipped deeply in the front and criss-crossed with buttons at the shoulders. She pinned her hair up in a modified french twist and, in lieu of any real makeup, applied a quick bit of peach lip gloss.

"You look adorable," Thomas had assured her, handing her a glass of rosé and a stuffed mushroom cap. After polishing off the appetizer in two bites, she realized she hadn't eaten all day and gratefully accepted the plate full of food Harold fetched for her. "Much lovelier than that hussy who spent the night with your friend Harry Dix last night," Harold said. "You're like something out of *The Great Gatsby*."

"Thank you," Annajane said, squeezing his arm affectionately. "Is flattery part of the package deal at the Pinecone Motor Lodge? If so, I might have to rethink my checkout date."

"We wish you would," Thomas said. "You're the first real friend we've made in Passcoe. People are curious about what we've done with the motel, but they seem a little standoffish. I mean, where's all that famous southern hospitality we've always heard about?"

"We've got to do a little marketing and networking for you," Annajane said. "Get you out and about and meeting people in town. Seriously. If you haven't done it already, you should join the Chamber of Commerce. And either the Kiwanis or Rotary. And have you thought about hosting an open house here? People need to see what you've done with the Pinecone. Most of them probably still think it's this slightly sleazy no-tell motel it was for years and years."

"We *should* do that," Thomas said.

"This would be the perfect place to have out-of-town guests for weddings or the holidays," Annajane enthused. "It would be a great function space, too, especially if you built some kind of covered gazebo or pavilion. Passcoe doesn't really have that many places to hold gatherings, outside of the country club and the church social halls. You'd probably want to get a pouring license, too."

She gestured toward the elegant cocktail party spread out before them on the grassy courtyard. "You should take some photos tonight and put them up on your Web site and use them in all your marketing materials. The gorgeous flowers and food, and the light is so beautiful right now."

"Web site?" Harold said.

"Marketing materials?" Thomas said. "Annajane, we don't know anything about that kind of stuff. It's all we can do to keep this place up and running."

"If only we knew a good marketing person!" Harold said, shooting a sideways glance at Annajane.

"Somebody with taste and talent and energy," Thomas said, looking squarely at Annajane. "You know anybody like that?"

"Sorry," she said. "I'd like nothing better than to work for you two. But I'm moving away after this week. Remember?"

"You said you were quitting your job," Harold said. "You'll need a new one, right? That doesn't mean you have to move away, does it?"

"I'm afraid so," Annajane said. "I've already given notice . . ."

"Ooh," Thomas said, interrupting. "Look at this cute car!" As he spoke, a flashy vintage red Chevelle convertible came cruising toward them. The top was down, and the driver's dark blond hair glinted in the late-day sun.

Harold turned toward Annajane, who had the oddest look on her face. "Somebody you know?" he asked.

"I used to know," she corrected him, watching as Mason parked the convertible in front of her unit. He spotted her in the courtyard, waved, and began to walk over.

"Excuse me, fellas," Annajane murmured.

Mason glanced around the courtyard at the men who were strolling the grounds, laughing and chatting and sipping wine. "What's all this?" he asked.

"It's a florists' convention of sorts," Annajane said. "Mason, what are you doing here? I thought we agreed not to see each other alone again."

"Don't you ever answer your phone?" he asked, sounding irritable. "I must have left you half a dozen messages this afternoon. And I'm pretty sure Pokey left a bunch. The wedding got called off."

She dimly heard her own breath catch. "Is that so?" She was trying for non-chalant, but her voice was shaky. She sucked at nonchalant.

Mason didn't look like much of a bridegroom. He wore a faded and rumpled pink oxford-cloth button-down shirt tucked into a pair of threadbare old jeans that rode down on his hips and sagged in the seat. His sockless feet were jammed into a pair of beat-up Top-Siders that she was sure he'd owned since his high school days. He was paler than she could ever remember seeing him before. Celia seemed to have sucked all the life out of him.

He nodded. "We need to talk. Will you go for a ride with me?"

Annajane looked dubious.

"Not to the farm this time, I swear," Mason said. "Please?"

Her heart was thudding in her chest. She wanted to go, wanted to ride off into the sunset with him, but what happened after sunset? She'd been Mason's second choice, after Celia. What made this time any different?

He must have guessed what was on her mind.

Mason took her hand and swung her around to face him. His mouth softened, and his eyes took in the flowered dress that swirled around her ankles in the late-day breeze and the graceful arch of her bare neck and slim arms. Annajane wasn't model-thin. She had curves, real hips and thighs that he could see silhouetted through the thin cotton of her dress, and breasts that were round and promising. Her full lips were slightly parted, her large green eyes serious and sad. He'd hurt her badly, and had no right to ask for another chance. But how could he not?

He looked puzzled. "Have you always been this beautiful?"

Annajane cocked her head. "Mason? You've seen me five days a week every week for the past five years. I look like I've always looked. Except maybe a few pounds heavier and a few more wrinkles," she said ruefully.

"No," he insisted. "You're different. I can't describe it. Like a peach, perfectly ripe. Wait, that's no good. You were always pretty before. But now, it's like, you've grown into who you were supposed to be. Luscious. Yeah, that's it."

She blushed and looked away. "What am I supposed to say to that?"

"Say you'll come with me," he said. "One more time."

The sun was slipping toward the glowing green horizon as the convertible bumped slowly down the dirt road, washboarded by rains and tree roots. Overgrown branches slapped at the sides of the car and kudzu vines scratched Annajane's bare arm. She knew, of course, where they were headed as soon as they passed through the wrought-iron gates at Cherry Hill.

Annajane glanced at Mason's profile. He seemed more relaxed, steering with his left hand, his right arm slung casually over the seat back.

"I need to get out here with a sling-blade and cut back some of this stuff before it completely blocks off the road," he said. "I had to stop the car twice the other night to drag fallen trees out of the way. And, I swear, I think I saw a glimpse of a coyote."

She shivered and tucked her legs beneath her and turned toward him. "When was the last time you were out here before that?"

He looked chagrined. "Probably the day I moved the last of my stuff out. How about you?"

"The second anniversary of our breakup," she said. "I was in a particularly melancholy mood. Guess I just wanted to torture myself. I was shocked by how fast everything went to seed."

A moment or two went by, and then they turned a curve in the road and the stone cottage came into view. Annajane gasped.

Vines completely covered the stone façade, with the exception of the doorway, where Mason had obviously cut a path through the growth. Part of the chimney had tumbled down, and the camellia bushes had reached nearly roof height, completely obscuring the front windows.

"This is so sad," she said softly. "Much sadder than when I was here last."

He pulled to the side of the house, driving as far forward as he could, until the nose of the Chevelle protruded from a thicket of privet and they could see the glint of the lake in the fading daylight.

Mason got out of the car, went around to the trunk, brought out a long-handled pair of loppers, and proceeded to spend ten minutes shearing off enough of the privet until they had an unobstructed view of the water.

"It's a start," he said, wiping his hands on the seat of his jeans before climbing back into the driver's seat.

"Looks like you'd need a backhoe and probably a bulldozer, too, to get all the way to the edge," Annajane observed. She half-stood in the seat, trying to get a better look.

"It's getting so dark, I can't see the dock and the boathouse," she said. "Is it even still there?"

"It's there, but it's gotten so rickety it's not safe to walk out onto it," Mason said. "Guess I need to post warning signs. Now that the weather's warming up, I'd hate for somebody to come over here by boat and try to explore—and wind up getting killed when the dock collapses under them."

Annajane shivered involuntarily at the idea. Mason reached into the back seat of the car and handed her a blanket. "Here," he said, drawing it around her shoulders. "I'd forgotten how quickly it cools down out here after dark."

"What, no flask?" Annajane asked.

He reached under the seat and produced a leather-wrapped thermos. Uncapping it, he poured a drink into the cup-shaped top, and the sound of crushed ice chinked against the worn silver. "I wasn't sure you'd come tonight," he said. "But I thought if you did, considering what happened last time, maybe I should mix up a proper drink."

Annajane took a tentative sip and laughed. It was Quixie and bourbon. "Very nice. So. What did you want to discuss?"

"I have a proposal I'd like you to consider," Mason said, turning toward her. "And I know I have no right to ask. But I have to anyway. I came so close today to ruining my life, it scared me. Pokey was trying to talk me out of marrying Celia, and she said something that hit home. She said Celia would ruin my life if I went through with the wedding. But I knew, as soon as she said it, that I'd already damned near ruined it myself. Worrying about what other people think. About my mother, about people in town. I was so concerned with *my* image, *my* responsibilities. All I could think about was my big, selfless sacrifice. And how noble I was. Marrying a woman I'd come to detest, just because I thought she was having my child."

"Go on," Annajane said, taking another sip of bourbon and handing it over to him.

Mason took a long drink. He looked at Annajane. Her cheeks were pink, and her pinned-up hair had come undone. He reached out and touched a tendril of windblown hair. "You didn't listen to any of your voice-mail messages today?"

"No," she said. "I decided to just shut out the whole world, since the world seemed such an unfriendly place to be in. I was determined to get the Quixie promotion plans nailed down. I think I've got the radio and television ads figured out . . ."

Mason put his fingertips across her lips. "There isn't any baby," he said. "Celia faked the pregnancy."

Annajane's eyes widened. "How did you figure it out?"

He rolled his eyes. "When Pokey came over to pick up Sophie before the wedding today, we just happened to see a necklace that had slipped out of her pink purse."

Annajane nodded.

"You know how Sophie does. She's a little magpie, always picking up shiny stuff and hiding her treasures in that purse. Anyway, the necklace somehow fell out, just as they were about to leave, and it was an expensive thing I'd given Celia for Christmas last year. So we checked out the rest of the contents. Low and behold, we found a half-empty package of birth control pills, with a prescription label that said they were Celia's."

"I don't understand," Annajane said.

"I wouldn't have either," Mason said with a chuckle. "Celia told me she'd been on the patch—that's how she got pregnant, because she'd been taking antibiotics, and they'd counteracted the hormones in the patch. But as Pokey helpfully pointed out, the drugstore label said the prescription had been filled just two weeks ago, and it looked like Celia had been taking the pills—right up until the day she claimed she was pregnant."

"Ohhhhh," Annajane said.

"When Celia showed up at the house, I confronted her with the pills," Mason said. "She tried to lie her way out of it. It wasn't very pretty."

"What was her explanation?" Annajane asked.

He shrugged. "She tried to say it was an old prescription and that anybody could have had it refilled. She even suggested that you and Pokey had gotten the pills and planted them on Sophie."

"Me!" Annajane said indignantly.

"Doesn't matter," Mason said. "She's an expert liar, but this time, she really couldn't talk around the truth. And so . . . it looks like I'm not going to be a father again. Anytime soon." His lips twisted into a sardonic grin.

"Not a very convincing smile," Annajane observed.

He ran his fingers through his hair. "I never said I didn't want more children," Mason said. "I do want more. Sophie needs brothers and sisters. I'd almost convinced myself that everything would be okay with another child, as long as I was around to make up for Celia's shortcomings."

"But you changed your mind?"

"It's not enough to have a husband and wife living in the same house," Mason said. "If those people don't really love each other, it's not a family; it's a fraud, with or without a marriage license. And a child will eventually see through that. I don't want that for Sophie. Or any child."

"That's pretty deep stuff there, Mason," Annajane said.

"Jesus," he said. "I came so close to blowing it. You'll never know how close."

Annajane was almost tempted to tell him the full extent of Celia's deception. But she knew she wouldn't. It was a hurt he didn't need.

"What happens next? With Celia, I mean?"

He glanced at his watch. "She and her stuff should be gone by now. And her contract with Quixie has been terminated. I'll pay out the rest of the money she's due. And hopefully, that will be the end of it."

He took a long drink from the cup and passed it back to her.

She shook her head and handed it back. She needed to keep a clear head. "You said you had a proposal for me?"

Mason rolled to the right and reached into the pocket of his jeans. He turned toward Annajane, opened his fist and revealed a ring on the flattened palm of his hand. It was the engagement ring he'd given her their first time together. He waited for her reaction.

Nothing.

"I want," he swallowed hard. Mason didn't think of himself as a big talker. He wasn't really effusive. That was his brother's gift. He'd never had a problem talking to Annajane before. But tonight the words stubbornly resisted being formed into sentences. He'd been thinking about this moment off and on for five years, since the day she'd left. He'd rehearsed the scene in his mind, trying to make it perfect.

She slapped at a bug on her neck and waited. He couldn't read what she was thinking. That had changed, too. Once, her face had been an open book, vulnerable, patient, expectant. Now, she was a mystery to him. Somehow it was frightening and sexy at the same time.

He took a deep breath. "I want to ask you for a do-over. I know I don't deserve it. And I have no right to ask for it. But I love you, Annajane. I can't lose you again. I just can't. And I know I'm doing this all wrong, blurting out stupid stuff, and it's crazy to think you'd take me back, after everything I put you through, but I can't help it. I'm going nuts here."

Annajane was still staring at him.

"Anything?" he asked.

"I'd like for you to kiss me," Annajane said quietly.

He carefully put the ring in the ashtray, then pitched the rest of the drink out the open window and tossed the cup into the backseat. Mason held her face between his hands. He rubbed his thumb across her lower lip, and then he lowered his face to hers.

Annajane's lips were warm and full and sweet, reminding him of ripened cherries. He teased his tongue into her, and laced his fingers in her long, thick hair. Her arms went around his neck, and he slid out from beneath the steering wheel, drawing her closer, letting his hand trail down the smooth skin of her bare arms. She smelled different than he remembered, not the girlish floral scent she'd worn during their marriage; this perfume was spicy, citrus, even exotic. He kissed her earlobes, and her throat, and the hollow of her neck, and his hands drifted downward; slipping one strap of her sundress from her shoulder, he nudged it the rest of his way with his chin, kissing her breast while she raked her fingers through his hair and down his back.

There were buttons on the straps of her dress, and he fumbled, trying to unbutton one, hoping she'd help him out, but instead, she sat back and assessed him with cool green eyes, before catching his hand in hers. She kissed him deeply, then drew back.

"What was the question again?" she whispered.

"I want you to marry me," Mason said urgently, his hands going to her other shoulder, tugging uselessly at the buttons. "But first, could we take this dress off?"

She kissed him, and nipped his lower lip with her teeth. "I'm afraid not. Not tonight anyway."

46

Mason wasn't used to being told no. He wasn't even used to maybe. He grinned that lazy grin of his, knowing full well the effect it had always had on her. "No, we can't take this dress off, or no, you won't marry me?"

She slapped at another mosquito that had landed on her arm and kissed him lightly. "Hmm. As much as I love this place, I really don't love getting eaten alive by mosquitoes. In case you haven't noticed, they are currently feasting on my flesh."

He looked stricken. "I'm sorry. I didn't stop to think. I mean, you always loved it out here at the lake. It was our special place. I just wanted to be out here with you, again, when I, you know . . ."

"Asked me to marry you?"

"You're really not going to make this easy on me, are you?"

"Not this time." She kissed him again, this time, slipping her tongue into his mouth, pressing herself against him, flattening her breasts against his chest.

He groaned and tried to pull her onto his lap, but she laughed again and moved away. She curled her arms around his neck. "I want you, Mason. I really do. I guess I never stopped wanting you, even after I should have known better."

"Annajane," he started, but this time she was the one doing the shushing.

"I'll give you a do-over. But this time, I need to feel wanted. I want to be courted and flirted with. I need to believe I'm the only woman in the world you want to be with."

He gripped her arm. "You are. You always were. I was just too stupid to realize it, and to realize that you needed to hear it from me. And you will. I swear, I will never take your love for granted again. I'll spend the rest of my life reminding you what you mean to me."

Annajane propped one elbow on the seat back and sighed contentedly. "God, I've missed you."

He took her left hand and tenderly kissed each finger, and then he slid the engagement band onto her ring finger. She cupped his chin in her hands and kissed him deeply, and then handed the ring back.

"I haven't finished," she said sweetly. "If I marry you . . ."

Mason frowned. "You mean, when. Right?"

"If," she said, lifting her chin. "I definitely mean if. If I marry you, we can't go back to the way things were. I won't be the little woman back at the house waiting for your phone call that never comes."

"Annajane, I've changed," Mason said.

"Good, because I've changed, too," she said. "At least the divorce did that for me. I'm good at what I do, Mason. I mean, really good. If you'll let me, I think I can help save Quixie. This summer promotion, if we can get the production started on the ads and commercials and Facebook campaign right away, I think it might really work. And I don't care what Davis says; I know you're right about adding the new Quixie flavors. We've got to expand the brand, not retrench. But you're going to have to really trust in me and believe in my professional abilities. The way you trusted Celia."

He looked shame-faced. "You're right. I totally bought into her vision for the company. Until the shine began to wear off, and I saw what was beneath."

"It was a pretty beguiling package," Annajane said.

"All of it was sham," Mason said. "Me, the company, we were just a commodity to her, something she could pluck, polish, and then peddle."

"Was that pluck, or fuck?" Annajane asked, laughing at the shocked look on Mason's face. "See? I told you you've been underestimating me."

"Never again," he pulled her into his arms. "Are we done here?"

"Not quite," Annajane said, trying to sound stern, which was difficult while he was nuzzling her neck. "Do you get what all this means, Mason? I want us to be full partners. In everything. I won't be like your mama. I'm not interested in bridge or in running the altar guild. There's nothing wrong with those things, but they're not me."

He was kissing her again. "I am not marrying my mother. And you are not marrying a man like my father." He tipped her chin up. "I love you, and only you. I will never cheat on you, Annajane. You are the only partner I will ever want, or need."

She kissed him back. "I've been trying not to think about it, but what happens after next week? You'll find out how your father divided up the company. What if Davis gets his way? What if you have to sell the company after all?"

"Worrying about that now won't change whatever is in my dad's will," Mason said firmly. "And if we have to sell the company, at least I'll have a kick-ass partner to help me start a new one. Right?"

"Right," she said. She held out her hand and held her breath while he replaced the ring. She held it up to the moonlight to admire it. "I'd forgotten how much I loved this thing," she said.

"And me," he said helpfully, sliding her onto his lap.

"Yes," she said. "You, too." She pushed herself off his lap. "Now can we please go back to the Pinecone? You were going to court me, remember? If we're going to do it, let's do it right."

On the way back to the motel, she found the cassette tape she'd made and slid it into the player. When Steve Perry sang the opening lines of "Open Arms" she looked over and saw that Mason was singing right along with Journey at the top of his lungs. Shane had said Journey was cheesy. She didn't care. This was their song. They were getting a do-over. For once, their timing was flawless.

47

Annajane looked around the conference room of the law offices of Thomas and Fleishman, attorneys at law, and saw that the lines had already been drawn in what looked like a troubling Bayless family feud. Sallie, dressed in a chic black St. John Knits suit, black and bone Ferragamo spectator pumps, and her ever-present pearls, had seated herself at the head of the sleek glass and chrome table.

Davis sat at her right hand, in his customary navy suit and striped rep tie. He'd scooted his chair over until it was only inches from his mother's, and their heads were bowed together as they shared a whispered confidence.

By contrast, Mason had seated himself at the far end of the table. He looked remarkably composed, Annajane thought. His pale green dress shirt and khaki slacks were crisply pressed and he wore a hunter green tie with the red Quixie Pixie logo woven into it. Annajane smiled to herself when she saw that tie.

She'd custom-ordered the ties for all the Bayless men: Glenn, Mason, Davis, and even Pete, the first year of her marriage. Mason, who seldom wore a dress shirt, let alone a tie, swore he loved his Quixie tie. But she couldn't remember ever seeing him wear it again. The tie, she knew, was Mason's subtle way of letting his family know where he stood. With Quixie.

He glanced over at her, saw what she was looking at, and gave her a wink. Annajane looked away. How could he be so relaxed, knowing the company's fate—their fate—would be revealed in just a few moments?

She'd been a bundle of nerves all morning, trying on and discarding outfits until her room at the Pinecone was strewn with clothing, shoes, and jewelry. In the end, she'd decided on a slimly cut pale aqua sleeveless sheath with a matching jacket. She'd twisted her hair into a modified french knot and, on a whim, chose Grandma Bayless's diamond engagement ring as her only piece of jewelry— an unspoken declaration of her loyalty. To him. No matter what the day's outcome.

Annajane had nearly turned her car around when she arrived at Norris Thomas's law office above the Mid-State Bank. Why should she be here, she asked herself, for the tenth time that morning. This was Mason's battle, not hers. But when she saw Davis and Sallie drive up together in Davis's Porsche Boxster, she knew why she'd come. For him, yes, but mostly for herself.

Glenn Bayless considered her part of his family. He'd made that clear the day of her wedding to Mason, when he made a special trip to her house to tell her about his gift of stock in Quixie. No matter what Davis or Sallie thought, she too had a stake in Quixie's future.

She waited until Sallie and Davis went into the bank, gave them a five-minute head start, and then followed them in. Sallie's greeting to her when she entered the conference room was decidedly frosty.

Annajane was surprised to realize that for the first time she could remember, she wasn't fazed by Sallie's hostility toward her. "Hello, Sallie," she said sweetly.

The conference room door opened, and all eyes were riveted in that direction. Pokey rushed in, her face flushed, her hair mussed.

She wore a brightly flowered red, yellow, and purple linen maternity tunic; yellow slacks; and spangly purple thongs, and the oversized tote slung over her shoulder was actually a green and navy quilted diaper bag.

Sallie's eyes flickered briefly but meaningfully over her daughter's outfit. "There you are," Sallie drawled. "We were about to send out an all-points bulletin for you. You do know you're ten minutes late?"

"Sorry, Mama," Pokey said, sinking down into the empty chair between

Annajane's and Mason's. "The sitter was late, and then I couldn't find the car keys because Clayton had hidden them in the potty chair, and then I got stopped at the railroad crossing by a train that I swear was a mile long . . ."

"Never mind," Sallie said, waving away any other excuses. "Just so you're here. Did you tell the receptionist to let Norris know we're all present now?"

"She knows," Pokey said, reaching for the bottle of water sitting in front of her place at the table and taking a hefty swig. "She said to tell you he's on the phone."

"He needs to let one of his junior associates tend to the phones so he can tend to business," Davis snapped. He glanced down at his watch. "I'm about over all this waiting."

"Relax, Davis. We've been waiting five years," Pokey said. "Another five minutes won't kill us."

"Some of us give a shit," Davis shot back. "Some of us have a business to attend to."

"Davis!" Sallie said sharply, laying a warning hand on his sleeve. "That's enough."

But Pokey was undaunted. "It's not even ten thirty yet. No worries, Davis. You can sell off the company after lunch, and then you can hightail it to Figure Eight Island and still have plenty of time to spend your new fortune."

"Pauline," Sallie said sternly. "I want this unpleasantness stopped immediately."

"Whatever," Pokey said. "I guess we know whose side you're on, Mama."

"I'm not on anybody's side," Sallie said, struggling to retain her majestic bearing. She looked around at her three grown children. "We are all here for the same reason, and I'd appreciate it if you would all remember that. Your father would not have tolerated this petty bickering."

"Not so petty, Mama," Mason said. "Davis wants to sell to Jax Snax for thirty million. That's a lot of pepperoni popcorn."

Pokey giggled, but before Sallie could admonish her again, Norris Thomas walked into the room, a thick file folder clutched tightly under his left arm.

Annajane had met Thomas on several occasions and reflected now that he didn't seem to have aged in the past ten years, despite the fact that he must be in his late seventies. His build was storklike, with long legs and a slight paunch in the belly. His wiry white hair stood up in tufts above his high, patrician forehead, and the silver aviator-frame glasses he'd favored for the past thirty years had come and gone back into fashion again without his notice.

Davis and Mason got up and shook hands, and Sallie, still seated, coolly offered her own hand in greeting, deliberately making the elderly attorney a supplicant, rather than the trustee of a multimillion-dollar family fortune.

Pokey stood and gave the older man a hug. "Uncle Norris," she said. "How is Miss Faye?"

"She's good, spoiling the grandchildren rotten, and she sends her love," Thomas said. He turned and greeted Annajane warmly, before making his way to a chair in the middle of the table on the far side.

He cleared his throat twice, took a sip from the bottle of water at his place, and cleared his throat once more.

"All right, y'all," he started, flipping the file open on the table. "I do apologize for being tardy." He peered down his nose through the spectacles at the file, and then at the family members ranged around the table. "I'm happy to see that everybody is here today, and I trust that you all are enjoying good health?"

"We're fine, Norris," Davis said impatiently. "Busy, but fine."

Sallie shot him a look, but Davis shook it off. "The trust, Norris. We really need to know the details of the trust Dad set up for us."

Looking unperturbed, Norris began handing around five sheaves of stapled documents. "This is a copy for everybody concerned," he said. "The document you now have in your hands is the irrevocable trust drawn up by Robert Glenndenning Bayless. The trust provides for the division of stock in the legal entity called Carolina Carbonated Beverage Company, or Quixie."

As Glenn Bayless's widow and children bent their head over the document and began leafing furiously through the pages, Norris went on.

"As you all know, Glenn was proud of his family's ownership of Quixie, and of Quixie's contributions to this community. His greatest wish was that the company would always stay in Passcoe and that it would be run by his heirs. This was the reasoning behind the provision mandating that the company could not be sold for a period of five years following his death."

Norris was speaking, but Annajane was the only one listening. The others' eyes were glued to the thick document in their hands.

Norris took a deep breath. His gaze fell on Sallie's elegantly coiffed head, bowed over the trust agreement.

"Glenn wanted the division of the trust kept confidential for that same period of time," he said, "for reasons he did not divulge to me, but which I might guess at. It was always his intention to have the company run by his sons, Mason and Davis."

Davis nodded but didn't look up, still scanning the fine print.

"But," Norris went on, "Since you, Sallie, were provided for quite generously through Glenn's will, with ownership of real estate, stocks, cash, jewelry, and other real property, Glenn decided to divide ownership of Quixie amongst his children."

Sallie's head shot up, and her eyes widened. "What exactly does that mean?"

Norris coughed again. "Well, uh, the children inherit the company."

"Not me?" Her eyes narrowed. "Are you telling me I have no ownership in my family company? No vote in how it's run?"

"Glenn felt," Norris said, apologetically, "that since your commitment was to rearing your family and being active in the community, that you would not desire to be burdened at this stage in your life with ownership in the corporation."

"That's crazy!" Sallie cried. "Glenn depended on my advice. I was his partner, in everything!"

"Of course you were," Norris said soothingly. "Nobody questions that."

"Apparently he did!" Sallie cried, shoving the papers away from her. "My God! I can't believe this."

Davis reached over and rubbed his mother's arm lovingly. "It's all right, Mama. None of us will do anything about the company without your approval. You know that."

"Of course," Mason echoed, looking at Pokey, who said nothing.

"Well," Norris said, "that, uh, leads us to the next matter. And I'm afraid this is going to be very awkward, but as trustee it's my duty to follow through with Glenn's wishes, to the letter."

"Awkward?" Pokey looked amused. "More awkward than telling Mama she's out of running the company?

"I'm afraid so," Norris said, two bright spots of red blossoming high on his cheekbones. "So let's just get to it. With the exception of the small, minority portion of stock Glenn left to you, Annajane, as his daughter-in-law, the rest of the stock is to be divided amongst the four living children of Robert Glendenning Bayless."

"Four?" Davis said. "What the hell?"

It was as though a live wire had been poked directly into the skull of everyone sitting around the conference room table. Everyone, that is, but Annajane and Norris Thomas.

"Four," Norris said firmly. "Mason Sheppard Bayless, Davis Woodrow Bayless, Pauline 'Pokey' Bayless Riggs, and, er, the minor child, Sophie Ann Bayless."

Dead silence.

Finally, Pokey spoke up. "Uncle Norris, I don't understand. You're saying Daddy left stock in the company to Sophie? We didn't even know Sophie existed until after Daddy died. And she's Mason's daughter. Daddy didn't leave stock to any of the other grandchildren, did he?"

Davis was leafing furiously through the trust documents. "What kind of crazy shit is this? You're saying Sophie, a five-year-old, for Christ's sake, has a share in Quixie equal to mine? That can't be."

Norris Thomas looked pleadingly at Mason, who had been strangely quiet. "Mason, you're going to have to help me out here."

"Yeah," Davis barked. "Help all of us out. Help us understand how you managed to have your illegitimate child inherit our mother's share of the company. I wanna hear this, *brother.*"

Annajane felt something inside her stir. Mason was staring at his mother, and his eyes, riveted on hers, were filled with a sadness Annajane hadn't seen in him since that day in the emergency room, when he'd learned of his father's death. It was as though a fog had lifted, and she could suddenly see, with crystal logic, the meaning of everything that had happened over the past five years.

"Sophie's not my daughter," Mason said quietly. "Not biologically, anyway. She's Dad's." He looked at Davis, and then at Pokey. "She's our sister." He reached across the table and took Annajane's hand, squeezing it tightly. She squeezed it back and held on for dear life.

48

Every head in the room turned toward Sallie Bayless. "Mason, for God's sake!" she cried, her face drained of blood.

Davis jumped from his chair, fists clenched. "What the hell kind of slimy stunt are you trying to pull here? Ain't no way Sophie is Dad's. And I'll tell you what, we have all had it with your high-handed tactics. Blood or no, I am fixing to give you the ass kicking you have been begging for."

The room was dead quiet.

Mason looked directly at his brother. "Bring it," he said, unblinking.

Norris Thomas looked supremely uncomfortable. He coughed and cleared his throat and stared down at the stack of papers on the table.

Pokey was kneeling down beside her mother, ineffectively patting Sallie's shoulder. "Mama, did you know anything about this? About Sophie?"

"No," Sallie said, flinty-eyed. "And I refuse to believe it. Mason, I cannot believe you would stoop so low. To accuse your father . . . it's . . ." She took a deep breath. "It's an unspeakable, unforgivable lie, and I want you to take it back. This instant."

"Um, Sallie, everybody?"

All heads swiveled toward Norris Thomas.

The elderly attorney tugged at the collar of his shirt. A fine film of perspiration beaded his forehead. "Mason is telling the truth. Sophie is the legal issue of Glenn Bayless. I understand that this is a shock to all of you, as it was a shock to me. Glenn was my oldest, most trusted friend, but I assure you, there is no doubt about the child's paternity."

"But, how?" Pokey asked, her voice catching.

Norris looked beseechingly in Mason's direction. Annajane squeezed his hand and gave him an encouraging nod.

"Mama, I'm sorry," he said, turning toward Sallie, his voice low. "I truly wish you wouldn't have had to find out this way."

"Mason didn't know what was in the trust agreement," Norris said. "I gave my word to Glenn that I would keep everything in confidence until the day I disclosed the details of the settlement."

"Mason?" Pokey asked.

"Dad . . . met this woman at a car rental place. At the Jacksonville airport. Her name was Kristy. They had an, um, relationship. And she got pregnant. With Sophie."

"Glenn was made aware of the pregnancy shortly before his death," Norris volunteered. "We had already drawn up the trust mechanism some months earlier, after he'd experienced some cardiac issues."

"Wait," Pokey said. She glanced over at her mother. "Daddy had heart problems before?"

Sallie only shrugged, tight-lipped. "Of course not. Glenn was perfectly healthy, as far as I knew."

Norris Thomas did not contradict the widow, but it was obvious that he was working from his own set of facts.

"Glenn came to me, at that time, and he was, naturally, quite embarrassed about the, um, child. We drew up a confidential document that would provide financial support for the child's mother, and the child, of course. And at that time, Glenn determined that he wanted that unborn child to have an equal ownership share in the family company."

"Unbelievable!" Sallie cried. "He wanted some bastard to have what belonged to *my* children, his real family? And you went along with this lunacy, Norris?"

"Dad would never do anything like that," Davis said. "He would have never cheated on Mama. Never! This is the biggest cock-and-bull story I've ever heard." He looked to Pokey. "Are you gonna let Mason sit there and defame your father like this?"

"But Daddy did cheat on her," Pokey said sadly. "Mason and I caught him, years ago. And that's why I can believe he cheated on her again."

"What the *hell* are you talking about?" Davis said fiercely. "He would never. Goddamn it, Pokey! Are you in cahoots with Mason now, too?"

"It's true," Pokey said, watching her mother's drawn face. "It was years and years ago. Mason and I went down to the house at Wrightsville Beach on the spur of the moment. Daddy was there, with a woman. I was just a kid, but even I knew what they were up to."

"I don't believe it," Davis said. "You've got no proof."

"The Chevelle," Pokey said, blinking back tears. "Dad said he was giving it to Mason as a twenty-first-birthday gift. But it was a bribe. So he wouldn't say anything to Mama about that girl."

"Not that I would have," Mason said. "I hoped she'd never find out. About any of this."

"Mama?" Davis said.

"I will not have this," Sallie said, her voice strained. "I will *not* have you children dishonor your father's memory this way. Do you two hear me? Do you?" Again, she didn't raise her voice. She didn't have to.

Sallie fixed Norris Thomas with a withering stare. "How dare you? How dare you make these grotesque allegations about a man who is not here to defend himself? Norris, I would never have expected this of a man of your reputation."

"This bullshit trust won't fly," Davis added. "We'll hire our own lawyers and challenge it." He thrust out his chin aggressively in Mason's direction. "That bastard kid of yours won't get a nickel of Dad's money."

Thomas opened the folder in front of him and brought out a single sheet of paper. "Davis, I can't stop you from doing what you think is best. But you should know that your father was very specific about the trust agreement. I did try to convince him he might provide for his unborn child in other ways, but he was adamant that each of his children would have an equal share in Quixie.

And I should also tell you that we've done DNA testing, and it absolutely proves that Glenn Bayless was Sophie's father."

He handed the paper across to Davis, who angrily batted it to the floor.

Thomas retrieved the paper without comment. He'd been a small-town estates and trusts lawyer for five decades. He'd witnessed more colorful dramas than this. He coughed, and his face colored slightly. "After Glenn's death, I contacted the child's mother, to let her know about the provisions of Glenn's will. Unfortunately, it was the first she knew that he'd passed away."

Pokey winced.

"The mother's pregnancy was normal and seemed to be going smoothly," Thomas went on, "but the baby was born somewhat prematurely."

"Sophie was in the neonatal intensive care unit at University Hospital in Jacksonville for six weeks," Mason said. "They really weren't sure she would make it and, even if she did, whether or not she would have lingering developmental problems." He reached across the table and took Annajane's hand again.

"Norris, uh, thought that somebody in the family should be aware that this baby, our half sister, was fighting for her life in the neonatal unit," Mason said. "It was a risk, but he confided in me. I went down to Jacksonville several times to check on her.

"She was so tiny," he marveled. "I'd never seen a baby that small. Theoretically, I could hold her in the palm of my hand. Except I couldn't, because they had her hooked up to all the tubes and monitors. They wouldn't let me hold her until shortly before they released her. But the first time I did, I knew she was ours."

He gave his weeping sister a pleading look. "She had Dad's blue eyes. My damned high forehead, and just the barest fuzz of blond curls. Just like Pokey's baby pictures."

"Stop it," Davis shouted, pounding the tabletop with his fist.

Sallie stood abruptly, pushing her chair back with such force that it went crashing to the floor. "I won't listen to another word of this," she said. She got to the door and looked over her shoulder at Davis.

"I'm leaving, too," he announced. The conference room door slammed behind them.

"Pokey?" Mason asked.

She shook her head and settled back in her chair, arms crossed over her chest. "I want to hear it. All of it."

Mason got up and walked around to the chair next to hers, the one Davis had just vacated.

"Kristy, that's Sophie's mom, isn't a bad person," he said. "She was only twenty-six when she got pregnant."

Pokey buried her head in her hands. "Oh God, Daddy," she moaned. "A twenty-six-year-old? How could you?"

"She looks a lot older," Mason said. "I thought she was about thirty-five when I met her. She's divorced, and she's smart, but she hasn't had an easy time of it. I think she really cared about Dad. He was good to her, you know?"

"Whom," Pokey said, sniffing. "How long do you think he was seeing her?"

"Kristy told me they'd been dating for about a year," Mason said. "He met her at the Hertz counter at the airport in Jacksonville, and he'd call her whenever he was in Florida on business, which was pretty often that last year he was alive, because we were chasing that Maxi-Mart deal. But I was totally in the dark about her. He knew I wouldn't put up with that crap."

Pokey wrinkled her forehead. "Wait—back up a minute. Uncle Norris, are you sure Dad told you he'd been diagnosed with heart problems?"

"Yes, Pokey," the lawyer said. "We had the same cardiologist. Blaine Mc-Namara. Max Kaufman referred both of us to him. Glenn and I talked about it several times."

"But how could Mama not know Daddy was sick?" she asked, looking bewildered. "He wouldn't have kept that a secret from her, would he? I mean, was he on some medications?"

Norris Thomas looked distinctly uncomfortable. "We discussed the prescriptions he'd been given. He was, uh, worried about potential side effects."

"What kind of side effects?" Pokey asked. "Could that have been what killed him?"

Thomas tugged at his collar. "Well, um, I don't know that would be something he'd want me to discuss with his daughter, Pokey."

"He's been dead five years now, Uncle Norris," Pokey said flatly.

Mason chuckled. "I think Norris probably doesn't want to tell you that Dad didn't like the fact that his heart meds affected his sexual performance," Mason said. "Does that about sum it up?"

"Well, uh, in a manner," Thomas said. His face was the shade of a glass of Quixie.

Pokey turned her attention to her older brother. "You two traveled a lot together. Did he talk to you about having a heart condition?"

"No," Mason said. "I know he had a bunch of pill bottles in his shaving kit, but we usually didn't share a hotel room." His face darkened. "His excuse was that he snored too much and didn't want to keep me awake. In hindsight, I suppose the real reason was that he had company in his room some of those nights. Like Kristy."

Pokey's eyes softened. "Tell me how you ended up with Sophie."

"The medical bills were pretty steep," Mason said. "But Dad had taken care of that. He'd put Kristy on the company payroll, so she'd have insurance coverage."

His sister rolled her eyes. "Oh God. If Davis found out about that he would blow a gasket."

"Yeah, especially if he heard her title. Taste Ambassador."

"Oh, no." Pokey giggled. "Taste Ambassador. That's just . . ." The giggle turned into a guffaw, and even the stern-faced Norris Thomas managed a nervous chuckle, and then Annajane joined in, and soon the conference room echoed with the Bayless family's grief-tinged hilarity.

"Oh, God, Daddy," Pokey said, wiping her eyes with a tissue from the box in the center of the table. "Who knew you had such a delicious sense of irony?" She patted her brother's hand. "Thanks, I needed a little comic relief to cut all this drama. Finish telling me about Kristy. What's she like?"

"She's not a gold digger, or your typical home wrecker," Mason said. "I think she really thought she would be able to raise Sophie on her own. Her mom lived nearby and was going to help with the baby. But then her mom was diagnosed with breast cancer, and she was going through chemo, and Kristy was terrified and totally overwhelmed. That last time I was down in Jacksonville, I ran into her in the neonatal unit, and she just . . . came unhinged."

"The doctors had been trying to explain to her about the special care Sophie would need after she was discharged from the hospital and to warn her about the possible developmental issues," Mason said. "I walked into the nursery, where she'd been standing by the isolette, just looking down at the baby. Kristy was scared to touch her, to hold her, even though the nurses told her that's what Sophie needed most. 'You take her,' she said. 'I can't do this.' And she ran off."

"Not permanently ran off, right?" Pokey asked.

"No. She called me later that night and asked if we could meet. We did, and that's when she told me she couldn't take Sophie home. She was living with her mom in a tiny one-bedroom apartment, and it just wasn't going to get any better. Even with the money Dad left her, Kristy was not equipped to care for a baby on her own, especially a baby as sick as Sophie had been."

Mason shrugged. "What could I do? She had already started calling adoption agencies to try to get Sophie placed. I couldn't let strangers take her, Pokey. She was ours. And I couldn't tell Mama. She wouldn't have stood for me bringing home Dad's child by another woman. You saw her reaction today."

Pokey leaned over and hugged Mason. "You big dope. You know I would have taken her and raised her as my own. Everybody knows how badly I've wanted a little girl."

"No," Mason said. "Anybody who saw Sophie would know she was a Bayless. There would have been questions. And we'd be right back at square one. This was the only way. I adopted Sophie and Kristy gave up all rights to her. That's how she wanted it."

"You could have told me the truth," Pokey said. "I would have been shocked, yeah, but I could have handled it."

"I wanted to tell you," Mason said. "But if Mama ever found out you were in on it, she would have never forgiven you."

"Well, hey-yull," Pokey drawled. "It wouldn't be the first time I got cross-wise with Mama." She looked over at Annajane. "Did you know?"

"Not until Sunday night," Annajane said. "He told me right after he proposed."

"Lying to Annajane was the worst of it," Mason said. "Letting her think I went out and got some chick knocked up even before our divorce was final. And her having to put up with all the gossip and crap going around town, everybody assuming we split up because of Sophie."

"You did what was best for Sophie," Annajane said. "That's what matters."

"Man, oh, man," Pokey said. She gazed down at her belly, then pantomimed a telephone call. "You hear that, baby mine? We just found out your cousin is really your aunt. And that my niece is actually my sister. Or half sister. Crazy, huh?"

Norris Thomas looked pointedly at the clock on the conference room wall. "Well, I guess our family conference can probably be concluded, since half the family has decamped."

"Sorry about the histrionics," Mason said. "And I guess we can expect that the issue is not closed as far as my mother and brother are concerned. Should we be worried?"

Thomas was putting papers back in the file folder. "I don't think so. Glenn was very thorough with these kinds of things. He had me research the issues, and we reviewed every sentence of the trust agreement backwards and forwards."

"Davis won't care," Pokey predicted. "He just wants his money out of the company, and he'll do anything to get it. You watch, he probably left here and went right across the courthouse square to hire himself another lawyer." A new thought occurred to her. "Uncle Norris, could he get Dad's trust thingy overturned, on some kind of incompetency thing? It's ridiculous to even think about, but I wouldn't put it past Davis."

"Glenn Bayless, incompetent? Absurd," Thomas said. He stood up and touched Pokey's shoulder. "I'll tell you how incompetent he was. When we drew up the agreement, and the documents setting up the financial arrangements for Sophie's mother, he hired a videographer to record the meeting. At the time, I thought he was being overly cautious, but now, I suppose he was anticipating what your mother's reaction would be when she learned of the child's existence."

"Daddy might have had a wandering eye, but his mind never wandered," Pokey said. "Nobody was sharper. Lucky for Sophie. And us."

49

I'm hungry," Pokey announced. "Let's get lunch."

"It's not even eleven o'clock," Mason protested.

"You can have coffee or something, but I am pregnant and starving, and I need to eat. Annajane?"

"Lunch sounds fine," Annajane said. "Where shall we go?"

Pokey looked around the courthouse square, past the gazebo and the confederate memorial statue. "The Country Cupboard," she decided.

They easily found a booth near the back of the room and placed their orders. After the waitress brought their drinks, Pokey put both elbows on the table and gazed across at her brother. "I've still got a lot of questions," she said.

Mason sipped his coffee. "I swear, I did not know anything about how the trust was set up. Norris never said a word to me, and I certainly had no clue Dad would leave Sophie part of the company."

She waved away his disclaimers. "I saw your face when Uncle Norris spilled the beans. You were as surprised as all of us."

"Not as surprised as your mother," Annajane said. "It's too bad it had to come out the way it did. She looked so hurt."

"Hurt?" Pokey said with a hoot. "Sallie wasn't hurt. She was red-hot furious.

I haven't seen her that mad since the day I told her I was pregnant and dropping out of Carolina."

"She'll either get over it, or she won't," Mason said. "I can't be worrying about her hurt feelings. I've got a daughter to raise and a company to run." He nodded at Annajane. "And a wedding to plan."

"Yay!" Pokey said, clapping her hands. "When's it gonna be?"

"Soon." Mason said.

"After Memorial Day," Annajane said, at the same time.

They looked at each other and burst out laughing.

"I can tell y'all have spent a lot of time discussing this," Pokey said. "Do I get to be the maid of honor again?"

"Of course," Annajane said. "But I don't think we're gonna have anything elaborate. Just family."

"Half of our family isn't currently happy with you two," Pokey pointed out. "So that ought to make for a real intimate affair." She looked at Annajane. "Have you told your mama?"

"Yes," Annajane said. "She told me I'm crazy as a bedbug. She's still furious that I broke it off with Shane. So I guess we can cross her off the guest list, too."

"More cake for me," Pokey said. "What did Sophie say?"

"Yippeee!" Mason said, in a girlish, high-pitched squeal. "She can't understand why Annajane won't move in right now. And I happen to agree with her."

"Nope," Annajane said, shaking her head obstinately. "You've got a whole lot of courting to do yet. Besides, I happen to love staying at the Pinecone Motor Lodge."

Pokey looked at Mason thoughtfully. "Will you tell Sophie about her real father?"

"Eventually," Mason said, reaching for Annajane's hand. "When she's old enough to process it. And hopefully before she hears it from somebody else. She does know that her biological mother lives down in Florida and that her mother couldn't take care of her and thus gave her to me. She has a picture of Kristy, but at this point she hasn't asked a lot of questions about her."

"Do you ever hear from Kristy?" Pokey asked.

"No," Mason said. "We kind of lost touch after her mother died and Kristy moved. The last time I talked to her, about two years ago, she'd gotten remarried. Her new husband is actually her supervisor at the airport, and he knows about Sophie. So I think that's probably a good thing. She'll have some stability in her life."

"And she's never asked to see Sophie?" Pokey said, shaking her head. "I can't even imagine that."

"Me neither," Annajane agreed. "But then I haven't had the challenges she's had."

"Kristy knows how to reach me if she wants to," Mason said.

"Mason," Pokey said, toying with her straw, "Did you think Mama's reaction today was, well, odd?"

"She was furious that Dad didn't leave her any stake in the company. I think it's understandable that she'd be hurt," Mason said. "I guess we all assumed he'll leave her controlling interest. Instead, he completely cut her out. I was stunned. Weren't you?"

"I guess," Pokey said. "Although, when you stop to think about it, Mama was never all that interested in or involved in what went on down at the plant. And we all knew he wanted you and Davis to run the company. I guess I'm having a hard time wrapping my head around all of it."

"We all are," Annajane said. "Imagine finding out your husband had a child with another woman—who was being raised as your grandchild?" Annajane said. "That's a pretty big shocker."

The waitress brought their food, and Pokey sighed happily as she contemplated her club sandwich and french fries. She dipped a fry in the fluted paper cup of ketchup and nibbled. Annajane reached across the table and helped herself to a fry, too.

"I wonder," Pokey said, midbite, "if it really was a big shock to Mama that Daddy fooled around on her."

"You think she knew?" Annajane asked.

"They were married for forty-five years," Pokey reminded her. "Sallie was never naive. I can't decide if she just chose not to notice, or if she knew and chose to look the other way."

"Don't guess we'll ever know for sure," Mason said.

50

Annajane found Voncile in the break room, eating her lunch at a small table in the corner of the room: a tuna-fish sandwich on neatly sliced and trimmed white bread, a huge dill pickle in a plastic baggie, and a small container of baby carrots. Two route drivers sat at a table in the opposite corner of the room, arguing about the merits of Fords versus Chevys.

"Annajane!" Voncile motioned her over. The older woman's face was wreathed in smiles. Her hair had been freshly permed and colored, and she wore a muted navy print rayon dress.

"Mason tells me you have happy news," Voncile said, her voice low. "Praise the Lord!"

"Thank you, Voncile," Annajane said, twisting her engagement ring around to face her palm. "We're not really making a public announcement yet, but I know Mason couldn't wait to tell you himself."

"He was grinning ear to ear when he came in on Monday morning," Voncile said. "I don't know when I've seen him that happy."

Annajane laughed. "I'm pretty happy myself, to tell you the truth."

Voncile sighed and shook her head. "That Celia sure had me fooled. I thought she was just about the nicest, sweetest girl Mason had ever dated—except for you, of course."

"She fooled a lot of people," Annajane commented.

"She took a nice check with her when she left, too," Voncile said indignantly. "Some people have no shame."

"Maybe so," Annajane said. She watched as the two route drivers gathered up their fast food bags and tossed them in the trash on the way out of the room.

"Say, Voncile," Annajane said, trying to sound casual. "Did you know anything about Glenn Bayless having heart problems before he had the heart attack that killed him?"

"Why do you ask?"

"Something came up today," Annajane said vaguely. "And it started me wondering. So, had he had symptoms in the past?"

"Oh, yes," Voncile said. "You know he had a spell here in the office, a few months before he passed. It about scared me half to death."

"Really?" Annajane said, leaning closer. "I didn't know that. When was this?"

She had to think. "I know it was summertime. One afternoon, he'd had a big steak lunch, probably at his Rotary meeting. He came back here, and his face was so pale; he looked awful. He swore he felt fine, but I knew he didn't. I got him a glass of water and some antacids, but it didn't seem to do much good. I'll tell you, Annajane, I fussed at him so much that day, he threatened to fire me. He finally did call his cardiologist, Dr. McNamara, over in Pinehurst, and of course when the doctor heard his symptoms, he wanted to call an ambulance for Mr. Glenn. Instead, I drove him over to Pinehurst myself."

"Was it a heart attack?" Annajane asked.

"I don't think so. But you know how Mr. Glenn was. He was that vain about his age. Never wanted to admit anything was wrong. I'll bet he never stayed home sick more than once or twice in all the years I worked for him."

"Mason is the same way," Annajane said. "Never gives in to a cold, flat denies the possibility he could ever get sick. So, Glenn had been seeing a cardiologist?"

"Sure," Voncile said. "You know, I made Mr. Glenn's appointments, business and personal. Even doctors, dentists, barbershop—everything. That way I kept everything on one calendar, so I could remind him. I made his appointments with Dr. Kaufman, and Dr. McNamara. And I got his prescriptions filled. I had to keep after him to take those pills every day."

"For his heart condition?" Annajane asked.

"And his high blood pressure," Voncile said. "We had the same prescription."

Voncile folded and unfolded a paper napkin. "Annajane, why are you asking me all these questions about Mr. Glenn?" she asked. "He's been gone all these years. Five years now. Are you going to tell me what happened at that meeting with the lawyers today? Mason looked kinda funny when you all got back from lunch."

"I'd prefer you to hear it from Mason," Annajane said.

Voncile's face fell.

"All right," Annajane said. "I know Mason had to get on a conference call after lunch. And I know he'd probably tell you this himself. So here it is. Glenn's trust left equal shares of the company to his children, but not to Sallie. His *four* children: Mason, Davis, Pokey, and Sophie."

Voncile raised an eyebrow. "You're saying Sophie is Mr. Glenn's child? Not Mason's? My goodness, that must have taken everybody by surprise. But how can a five-year-old own part of the company?"

Annajane sat back in the hard plastic chair and regarded Voncile. She had the best poker face she'd ever seen.

"As her legal guardian, Mason will control Sophie's share of the business until she comes of age when she's twenty-one," Annajane said.

Voncile processed that for a moment, then nodded her head slowly in understanding. "So, if Pokey and Mason, and Sophie, don't want to sell off the company, they outvote Davis, is that right?"

"Essentially," Annajane said.

"Praise the Lord!" Voncile said, raising her eyes heavenward. "My stomach has just been in knots all this week, thinking about what might happen to all of us if we got sold."

"Mine, too," Annajane admitted.

"And Sallie doesn't have a say in what happens to Quixie?"

"Nope," Annajane said. "According to Mr. Thomas, Glenn didn't think Sallie would want to be bothered with running the company at her age. And, after all, he'd already left her pretty well-fixed in his will."

"My, my," Voncile said. "I'll bet there were some fireworks when all of that came out. Especially the part about Sophie."

"You already knew about Sophie, didn't you?" Annajane asked.

The older woman allowed herself a small, private smile. "I guessed," Voncile admitted. "But I never said a word to anybody. And I never will. I'll take it to my grave."

"I know Mason will appreciate that. But how did you know?"

Voncile cut her sandwich half into quarters, and then eighths, but she didn't eat them. "Mr. Glenn had me handle the paperwork to put that girl on the company payroll. We never had anybody working for us in Jacksoville, Florida, before. And then she'd call the office, sometimes, looking for him." She pursed her lips in disapproval. "Just how old a girl was she?"

"Young. Just twenty-six when she had the baby."

"Mercy." She shook her head. "Mr. Glenn knew I didn't approve of that kind of thing. He was a good man in so many ways, Annajane. He helped people in this town in more ways than you'll ever know. Paid doctor bills, got folks out of jail. Had to get a few folks put *in* jail, too. He bought people cars, gave them jobs."

Annajane smiled. "He gave me my first real job when I was fifteen, remember?"

"I sure do, honey. You were so serious and business-like. Such a good little worker. Mr. Glenn noticed that, too. You were always his favorite."

"And he was mine, too," Annajane said, feeling a little weepy. "Even before Mason and I got married, he always treated me like one of the family."

"Unlike some folks," Voncile commented. "Miss Sallie just never did take to you, did she?"

"Sallie . . . had an old, silly grudge against my mother," Annajane said. "And she always thought Mason could have done better. Maybe she was right."

"Never," Voncile said. "I always thought you were Mason's one true love, even though I did get hoodwinked by that Celia. Mason is a good man, like his daddy. Did you know Mr. Glenn helped us buy our house? My husband, Claude, had been out of work, so the bank wouldn't give us a mortgage. Mr. Glenn held the paper on the house and let me pay off a little bit every week. Interest-free. He didn't go to church like Miss Sallie, but he was as fine a Christian man as I ever knew. Not perfect, though. He just had a weakness for the flesh is all. I used to pray about it all the time."

"Voncile," Annajane hesitated. "Well, maybe it's none of my business. Never mind."

"Go ahead and ask, honey. You're wanting to know if Sallie knew about the other women, aren't you?"

"Yes," Annajane said.

Voncile rewrapped the remnants of her sandwich into a neat wax-paper bundle while she thought about her answer.

"If she knew, she never let on to me," she said finally. "But she wouldn't have. She is a proud lady, and of course we didn't really have that kind of relationship. As far as Sallie was concerned, I was just somebody who worked for her husband at the plant."

"Did Sallie know about Glenn's heart condition?"

"I don't see how she couldn't have known," Voncile said. "With them living in the same house. I sure knew about my Claude's cancer. That man didn't have a hangnail or a hemorrhoid that I didn't have to take care of."

That made Annajane laugh. She remembered Voncile's husband. He was a skinny stick of a man, who always seemed to have an ailment of some kind. He'd taken early retirement from the plant in his late forties.

She decided to confide further in Mason's administrative assistant. "At the lawyer's office today, Sallie said she had no idea Glenn ever had any heart problems."

"That's not right. It can't be right," Voncile said. "Why, Annajane, that Saturday, the day he died, I talked to him on the phone that morning. With him not making it to the Christmas party the night before, I got a little worried that maybe he wasn't feeling too good. So I called to see if he was all right."

"What did he say?" Annajane asked, intrigued.

"He sounded funny; his voice was kind of weak," Voncile said. "He kept insisting he was fine, but he didn't sound fine. He sounded like he did the last time he was having chest pains. I told him he needed to call Dr. Mac or get over to the hospital."

"Did he agree to do that?" Annajane asked.

"He kind of laughed at me and said I was overreacting. He said Sallie was right there, and she'd take good care of him."

"What time was that?" Annajane asked.

"Hmmm." Voncile folded and refolded her paper lunch sack while she tried to remember. "It must have been around ten o'clock, because I needed to go out and do some last-minute Christmas shopping."

Annajane felt a chill go up her spine. "Did you check back later in the day to see how he was?"

"I tried," Voncile said. "I called his cell phone before noon, when I got back from the store, but my call went straight to voice mail, so I called the house. Sallie answered right away, and I asked her how Mr. Glenn was feeling. She told me he was fine, which kind of surprised me. He sure wasn't fine when I'd talked to him earlier."

"Did you tell her he'd been having chest pains earlier in the day?"

Voncile's face crinkled up in concentration. "It's hard to remember—it was so long ago. I think I asked to speak to him, but she said he was taking a nap or something."

"So you never did talk to Glenn again?"

"No," Voncile said, frowning. "I tried later in the day, around three, maybe, but all I got was a busy signal. I tried and tried, for half an hour or so, but then I kind of forgot about it because we were getting my granddaughter's angel costume ready for her Sunday School pageant. And then we drove over to Garner to spend the night with my daughter."

Now it was Annajane's turn to think back on that Saturday, with all its painful memories. She'd run into her mother-in-law at noon, at the country club, and Sallie had been oddly insistent that Annajane join her group for lunch.

She wondered whether Sallie was aware that her husband was having breathing problems and chest pains earlier in the day.

Voncile looked stricken. "Oh heavens. He must have had his heart attack right after I talked to him."

"I don't think so," Annajane said slowly. "Sallie said she found Glenn unconscious at around six that evening. That's when she called the ambulance. They worked on him at the hospital, but the doctors said it was too late."

"But that was hours and hours after I talked to him," Voncile said. "I thought . . . I mean, I always assumed he'd gone to the hospital earlier in the day, right after we talked. Are you sure that's right, Annajane?"

"Very sure," Annajane said soberly.

Voncile crumpled her paper bag into a tight ball. "I just don't understand. Why didn't Sallie call the doctor? Or take him to the hospital that morning?"

"That's what I'd like to know," Annajane told her.

51

Pokey Bayless Riggs stood on the doorstep of her brother's bachelor pad, a contemporary two-story wooden structure with soaring beams and weirdly jutting angles located on the grounds of the Cherry Hill estate, just out of Sallie's line of vision. She'd called in advance and left numerous voice-mail messages, but she had gotten no response. Now she was determined to have it out with him, face-to-face.

She'd been ringing the doorbell and pounding on the door with no luck. Finally, she took a step backward and, cupping her hands into a makeshift megaphone, began hollering, "Davis Bayless! I know you're in there, you weasel, so you might as well let me in.

"Davis! I'm not going away. I'll stand here all night if I have to."

Finally, she walked around to the back of the house, tried the kitchen door, and found it unlocked. She stepped inside and found Davis, seated at the smoked-glass kitchen table, eating a microwaved chicken potpie and washing it down with what looked like a very large tumbler of Dewar's.

His suit jacket hung from the back of his chair, and he'd loosened his tie and rolled up the sleeves of his dress shirt.

"Go away," he said sourly.

"Nope," she said, seating herself at the table, opposite him.

"I got nothin' to say to you," he said, fishing a large green garden pea out of the potpie and lining it up on the edge of the plate with a lot of other discarded green peas.

"Then don't talk," Pokey said. "Just sit there and listen."

"This is my damned house. I don't have to sit here and take any crap off of you," Davis said. "Why don't you go on home to your husband and kids?"

But Pokey had had a belly full of her brother. Now she had fire in her eyes and was ready for a showdown.

"Don't do this, Davis," she said, crossing her arms across her chest and regarding him with a mixture of regret and disgust.

"Do what?" he asked, innocence itself. "Eat a potpie for dinner? You should try one." He pushed his plate in her direction. "They're really good. Jax Snax just bought this company. Maydene's Home-Style Frozen Diner Dinners. Jerry sent me a big ole carton full of 'em. They got frozen pot roast, frozen chicken and dumplings, frozen mac n' cheese. I may never have to go out to dinner again."

"Stop trying to change the subject," Pokey ordered. "Everybody in town knows what you've been up to. You've hired a lawyer to contest Daddy's trust arrangement, and you're already starting to drag our family's name through the mud. And for what? More money?"

Davis placed his fork on the side of his plate with elaborate precision. He wiped his mouth with a paper napkin. "Look here, Pokey. I don't see why you're so hot and bothered about selling Quixie. I mean, let's face it. You ain't never really had to work a day in your life. Sure, you played at working for Daddy summers in college, and a little bit after you married Pete, but you're just a stay-at-home mama. And that's fine. You've got three swell little boys and another on the way. Pete makes a good living. Why do you wanna go messin' around with stuff that doesn't even really concern you?"

"Don't you dare patronize me, Davis Bayless," Pokey snapped. "I am not one of your stupid bimbos. I may not have worked in the day-to-day end of Quixie, but you better believe I know what goes on with our business, and I do care. I care deeply. Daddy knew that, even if you don't, which is why he left me an equal share of the business."

"Yeah, well, I wouldn't count on that trust agreement standing, if I were you," Davis said lazily. "My lawyer says there's loopholes in that thing big enough to drive a Quixie truck through."

Pokey clenched and unclenched her fists and finally clasped them tightly together in an effort to keep herself from slapping the smile right off her big brother's jowls.

"Your lawyer is a jackleg Yankee just dying to take you for every dime you've got," Pokey said. "And in the meantime, you need to know that I will fight you every step of the way if I have to. Because I will be damned if I will allow you to sell off my heritage. And my sons'. I've taken a look at that Jax Snax offer, and it's a load of garbage. You know what happened to that family-owned pretzel business they bought? They shut it down. Yeah. Spun off the one product they really wanted, shifted production of it to one of their own plants, laid off two hundred and fifty workers, then sold the equipment for scrap metal. That town was already hurting, but losing the plant was like putting a stake through its heart. Half the houses in town are in foreclosure, and I read on the Internet that they've closed the town's only high school. They have to bus the kids forty-five minutes away to the next town over. I am not gonna sit still and let that happen here."

Davis shook his head. "You and Mason just don't get it. Frankly, Daddy didn't get it either. Even six, seven years ago, the handwriting was on the wall. But he refused to believe it. Twenty years ago, there were nearly a dozen other family-owned soda companies operating in the Southeast. Now? You've got what? Three or four? If that many? You know why? Because it's a lost cause. Quixie is a dinosaur. We can't compete with the big boys. Not unless we become one of 'em."

"See!" Pokey said. "When you think like that, it's a self-fulfilling prophecy. We're still operating in the black, still have a good product, but I believe you actually *want* the company to fail. That's why you resist any kind of change in the product line or spending any money to update the plant or the distribution network. You're deliberately sabotaging Quixie."

"Me?" Davis laughed. "I don't have to do a goddamn thing to make that happen. All I have to do is sit back and let Mason keep on the way he's keeping on. Which I don't intend to do."

Pokey took a deep breath. "What's the matter with you, Davis?"

"Me? Nothin'. I am fine as frog hair."

"No, seriously," Pokey said. "You're my brother, and I love you, but I don't understand one thing about you. We were raised in the same house, by the same parents, but sometimes I wonder how you got to be the way you are. Don't you have an ounce of loyalty towards our family?"

"I'm a businessman," Davis said, shrugging. "Family loyalty's got nothing to do with it. I love my big brother, but I have serious doubts about his abilities to run Quixie the way it needs to be run in this economy. I've tried to talk sense to him about that for the past five years, but to Mason I'll always be the dumb baby brother. The wannabe."

"You say you love your brother?" Pokey asked. "Is that why you slept with his fiancée?"

"I don't know what you're talking about," Davis said. He took a long drink of the scotch, and she noted that his hand shook. Just a little. "And this conversation is beginning to bore me, little sister. What say you get the hell out of my house?"

"I'll go when I've had my say," Pokey retorted. "And I believe you do know what I'm talking about. You and Celia have been in cahoots over this Jax Snax deal for a long time now. I just wonder how long you've been in bed together, literally."

"You're crazy," Davis said.

"Not as crazy as you," she said calmly. "Let's talk about Friday night, shall we? The night before Celia was supposed to marry Mason. Remember him? Your beloved big brother, the one you're so loyal to? How crazy could you be, Davis, taking Celia to the same motel you always take your sluts to? How stupid could you be, paying cash but making sure to ask about the Quixie employee discount? And what kind of lowlife, slimy horndog struts around calling himself Harry Dix?"

Davis looked away and closed his eyes slowly.

"You don't know anything," he said. "You're bluffing."

"Really?" She reached into her pocket and pulled out a photocopy of the registration book from the Pinecone and waved it under his nose. "That's my proof. Your handwriting, and the place where you wrote down the license number of the Boxster. Dumb shit. And you should know, Celia was seen coming out of that room with you the next morning by more than one person. You are so busted."

He opened his eyes. "Does Mason know?"

"No," Pokey said. She put the photocopy back in her pocket. "He already knows she's a lying, cheating piece of crap. I really don't have the heart to let him know his own brother is just as bad. Or worse."

"So, what? You're gonna blackmail me now?"

"No. I'm going to appeal to your long-dormant sense of decency. And your greed. Pete and I have had a long talk. We want you to sell us your share of Quixie."

"As if." Davis drained the scotch in his glass and poured himself another tumbler full. He took a long drink, smacked his lips, and drank again.

Pokey reached over and took the glass out of his hand. "Listen to me, Davis. We're serious. Jax was prepared to pay the family thirty million for Quixie. You own a quarter interest. Pete and I want to buy you out. We'll pay you seven and a half million cash. You take the money, go do whatever you want to do. Buy that house on Figure Eight Island, take a job with Jax Snax, or whatever. Or just sit back and count your money. But you walk away from the company. And you drop your challenge to Dad's trust agreement."

Davis got up and walked over to one of the gleaming ebonized kitchen cupboards. He got himself another tumbler, grabbed the Dewar's bottle, and poured himself another dose. He leaned up against the black granite countertop. "What if I don't take your offer? What if I decide to stay around and fight?"

"You'll lose," Pokey said, her chin jutting out. "And in the process, you will have antagonized everybody in this town. You will have trashed Daddy's good name, and you will have estranged yourself from your entire family. Including Mama."

"Mama . . ." he started to say.

"Mama is feeling hurt and betrayed right now, finding out about Sophie the way she did. Although I'm not really certain she didn't suspect all along that she wasn't Mason's child. She'll get over it, eventually. And when she does, she will not want that piece of news broadcast all over some lawsuit and the Bayless family name dragged through the mud. And you had better believe she would never, ever, forgive you for the way you betrayed Mason by sleeping by Celia."

Davis jiggled the ice in his glass and smirked. "All of y'all are gonna have to get over this thing you have against Celia."

"And why is that?" Pokey asked.

He chewed on the ice for a moment before answering. "What would you say if I told you we're together now?"

"You and Celia? Is this a rhetorical question, or is this your ass-backward way of telling me the two of you are an item?"

He shrugged. "It was probably inevitable. We both tried to pretend we weren't attracted to each other, but hell, it is what it is."

Pokey shuddered. "What it is is grotesque, Davis. The two of you together? It's a bad reality show on a third-rate cable channel. But the sad thing is, the two of you deserve each other. I just hope Mason doesn't find out when the two of you hooked up."

"You just said you'd never tell Mason," Davis pointed out.

"I wouldn't. But if Mama were to find out . . ." Pokey shrugged. "You know what Passcoe's like. It's a small town."

"It's a shithole," Davis muttered into his scotch. "A two-horse, two-traffic-light shithole."

"All the more reason you should take the money and run," Pokey suggested. "Delta's ready when you are."

"Maybe I will," Davis said. "Tell Pete to give me a call in the morning, if he's serious."

"No need to talk to Pete," Pokey said. "I handle all our family finances. I'll have our lawyer draw up an agreement, and I'll send it over to you in the morning."

52

The kitchen table was set with placemats and blue and white checked napkins and blue glass water goblets. A perky bouquet of daisies in a red bowl sat in the center of the table, and tall white taper candles burned from blue glass candleholders.

Mason stood at the stove, long-handled fork poised over a cast-iron skillet full of frying chicken, while Annajane sat at a high stool at the counter, preparing the salad.

Sophie came clomping into the kitchen and her eyes widened. She was wearing a pink ballet tutu over her purple pajamas and pink cowboy boots. "Are we having a party?" She climbed up on the stool beside Annajane's and plunked down a picture book, some paper, and a box of crayons.

"Yep," Mason said. "It's a Friday-night party. And you're invited."

"Who else?" Sophie asked, noticing that the table was set for three.

"Just us," Mason said. "It's a very exclusive gathering. We used to have Friday-night parties a lot when I was your age, Soph. It was the only time my daddy ever cooked. And he only knew how to cook one thing, so we always had fried chicken."

"I don't like fried chicken," Sophie said, her eyes sparkling behind the thick glasses. "I love it!"

"Me, too," Annajane said. "How about we start the party with a cocktail?"

"For me?" Sophie looked puzzled.

"It's a kiddie cocktail," Annajane explained. She took a plastic highball tumbler from the cupboard. She poured in a couple inches of Quixie, added a splash of ginger ale, then topped it with a maraschino cherry before presenting it to the child. "Ta-da!"

"Mmm," Sophie took a delicate sip. "Am I allowed to have Quixie?"

"In very small amounts," Mason said. "For very special occasions. Like tonight."

Annajane reached over and picked up the well-loved picture book. By her own estimation she had read *The Runaway Bunny* to Sophie at least a couple hundred times. The edges of the board book were dog-eared, and the cover bore a couple of purple crayon doodles, but nothing had ever diminished Sophie's love for her favorite book.

Sophie picked up her crayons now and began to draw on the sheaf of printer paper she'd borrowed from Mason's office.

"Whatcha drawing?" Annajane asked, looking over.

"I'm ill-luss-stra-ting," Sophie said proudly, drawing out the word. "Miss Ramona lets us make new illustrations for books in school. This is my homework. I'm illustrating *The Runaway Bunny.*"

The child's pink glasses slipped down her nose as she bent over her picture, painstakingly drawing a very small bunny. She glanced over at Annajane. "In school, Miss Ramona reads the stories to us while we draw."

"Then allow me," Annajane said, putting her paring knife down, pushing away the salad bowl and the wooden cutting board, and picking up the book.

"Once there was a little bunny who wanted to run away," Annajane read. "So he said to his mother, 'I am running away.'"

Mason flipped the pieces of chicken over in the pan and covered it loosely with the lid. He stepped behind Annajane and, looking over her shoulder, read, "'If you run away,' said his mother, 'I will run after you. For you are my little bunny.'"

Sophie poked out the tip of her tongue as she concentrated on drawing the rabbit's ears. "I would never run away from my mama, if I was the little bunny," she commented, filling in the middle of the rabbit's orange ears with a brown crayon.

"Even if it was just a game, like hide-and-seek, like we play sometimes?" Mason asked.

"No," Sophie said solemnly. "If I had a mama, I would never, ever run away."

Annajane glanced over at Mason, who looked stricken. "Sophie," he said gently. "Remember, you do actually have a mama. I told you that, remember?"

Sophie continued coloring, using a gray crayon to draw a lumpy version of the rabbit's body. "My real mama's name is Kristy. She lives in Florida now, and she loved me a lot, but she couldn't take care of me, so she asked my daddy to take care of me." Her voice was singsongy, but matter-of-fact.

"You're killin' me here," Mason muttered. "You know, Sophie, when you came here to live with me, I decided I would be your daddy *and* your mama for a while. Then I asked Letha if she would come and help take care of you while I'm working. And your aunt Pokey helped out, too, and also Annajane. So you're a lucky girl, because you have lots of people to love and help take care of you, instead of just one mama."

Sophie looked up at him thoughtfully. "The runaway bunny only needed one mama. The kids in school all have one mama. Except Lucy. She has two mamas. And Clayton and Denning and Petey all have one mama—Aunt Pokey. That's all I need, too."

Annajane and Mason exchanged worried looks, but Sophie, who knew the book by heart, was already onto her next illustration, drawing a fish, swimming in a stream. "Read some more, please," she told Annajane.

So Annajane read, " 'If you become a fish in a trout stream,' said his mother, 'I will become a fisherman and I will fish for you.' "

Sophie gave the fish a green body and a yellow tail and a red dorsal fin. She drew wavy blue lines to represent the blue trout stream, and beside the stream she drew a stick figure with long brown hair, wearing a dress and red high heels, holding a fishing pole.

"Who is that?" Mason asked, tapping the figure in the picture.

"That's the mama," Sophie said, rolling her eyes at her father's ignorance. "Duh."

"But she doesn't look like a bunny fisherman," Mason said.

"This mama is a real lady. Like Annajane," Sophie said. "See, she has brown hair like Annajane."

"And red shoes," Annajane added. "I have a pair of red shoes that look like that."

Mason wrapped his arms around Sophie. "We were thinking, Annajane and me, that when we get married, Annajane will be my wife. And she'll be your mama. Your only mama. What do you think of that idea, Soph?"

"We're not gonna marry Celia, right?" Sophie asked, adding a pink bow to her fisherwoman's hair.

"Nope. Celia and I decided that wouldn't be a good idea, because I love Annajane best," Mason said.

"Letha said Celia is gone for good this time," Sophie said.

"That's probably true," Mason conceded.

"We should marry Annajane," Sophie said, without hesitation.

Mason left one arm around Sophie, and put the other around Annajane's shoulder. "I think so, too. Definitely."

"See?" Sophie said, as if that settled it. She put the fish drawing aside and started on another one. "Keep reading, please."

Annajane read the next few pages, and Sophie's crayon flew over her paper. At one point, she looked up at Annajane. "What's a crocus? And why do they have a hidden garden?"

"I guess they have a hidden garden because the little bunny and the mother bunny are playing hide-and-go-seek," Annajane said, leafing ahead in the book. "And a crocus is a little flower that comes up from the ground in very early spring," Annajane said. "We can look online and find a picture of one, if you want."

"No, that's okay," Sophie said, reaching for another sheet of paper and drawing a daisy. "Keep going."

So Annajane read on, about the baby bunny morphing into a rock, then a bird, and a sailboat, and even a trapeze artist.

Mason hovered over his stove, adjusting the heat under the skillet and putting a pot of peeled potatoes on to boil. He poured a glass of wine for himself and one for Annajane, who nodded her thanks and kept reading aloud.

Near the end of the book, Sophie put her crayon down and sighed dramatically. "I hate this part," she announced.

"Why?" Annajane asked, almost afraid to hear the answer.

Did Sophie resent the fact that she didn't have a real mother like the bunny in the book? Or had she been dwelling on the fact that her own mother had, in a way, run away from her? Maybe they should think about having Sophie see a child psychologist. Especially since at some point, before Sophie got too much older, they would need to explain the complicated story behind her real father as well as her real mother.

"Yeah, Soph," Mason said, placing his hands protectively on the little girl's shoulders. "Do you hate this part of the story because you're sad about the runaway bunny and his mama?"

"No," Sophie said, frowning down at her picture. "I hate this part because I can't draw a tightrope walker, like the one in the book." She looked up at Mason. "You draw it."

"Hmm." Mason picked up a crayon and sketched a brown rope, and then added an extremely detailed sketch of a little girl with eyeglasses and blond curls, wearing a pink tutu with a pink pocketbook slung over her arm and one dainty foot placed on the rope, the other poised above it. "How's that?"

"It's me!" Sophie breathed. "You drew me!"

"Not bad," Annajane said, regarding Mason with new respect. "I didn't know you could draw that well."

"I am a man of many talents," Mason said, bowing first to Sophie and then to Annnajane.

"Draw the next one," Sophie ordered. "The one with the bunny turning into a little boy and running inside the house."

Mason glanced over at the stove. "Can't," he said. "My dinner is just about ready. I've got to get my potatoes mashed. Are you two almost finished reading your book?"

"Almost," Sophie said, glancing over at the book. "Read the end, Annajane. That's my favorite part."

Annajane liked the ending, too. "'If you become a little boy and run into a house . . . I will become a mother and catch you in my arms and hug you.'"

She stood and folded Sophie into her arms. Sophie wriggled contentedly and picked up her cue like a seasoned pro, reading in an uncannily baby-bunny-sounding voice.

"'Shucks,' said the bunny. 'I might just as well stay where I am and be your little bunny.'"

"Come on, you two," Mason called, dumping his mashed potatoes into a serving bowl. "My dinner is getting cold. Annajane, you need to finish making that salad."

"In a minute," Annajane said. She knew the last two lines of the book by heart. As did Sophie.

"'And so he did,'" Sophie said.

Annajane reached into the salad bowl and snagged one of the vegetables she'd been cutting up.

"'"Have a carrot," said the mother bunny.'"

Sophie took the proffered carrot and munched happily. "The end," she announced.

Annajane's cell phone rang just as she was wiping the skillet clean with a paper towel. Sophie had gone to bed, and they'd been discussing whether or not to watch a movie. She looked down at the caller ID. "It's your mother," she told Mason. "I didn't even know she knew I had a cell phone."

"This can't be good," he said. "Don't answer."

"I can't not answer when Sallie calls me," Annajane said. She punched the Connect button.

"Hi, Sallie," she said brightly. "This is a surprise."

"I'm sure it is," Sallie drawled. "Annajane dear, I was wondering if you could come over to Cherry Hill tomorrow morning for a little chat."

Annajane put her hand over the phone and lip-synched to Mason, "She wants to see me."

Mason shook his head vigorously. "Tell her no. Tell her hell no."

"Well, um, let me think what my morning is like," Annajane said, stalling for time, fishing for an excuse.

"I won't take up much of your time," Sallie said. "Just a quick little visit."

Put like that, she couldn't very well decline, Annajane thought.

"What time?" she asked.

"Ten would be perfect," Sallie said.

"Perfect," Annajane said gloomily.

53

They discussed the visit to Cherry Hill until midnight, right up until the moment Annajane reluctantly got in her car to drive "home" to the Pinecone Lodge.

"You do not have to go over there tomorrow," Mason said, his lips lingering at her collarbone. "She can't just call you up and issue a command performance."

"I'm going," Annajane murmured, her arms wrapped around his waist.

"She's still mightily pissed about me breaking up with Celia," Mason said. "Even after I told her about the fake pregnancy."

"And she's just as mightily pissed at me for marrying you years ago—and agreeing to marry you again," Annajane said.

"Which is why you should politely decline," Mason said.

"Nope," Annajane kissed him one last time. "I'm not running away from your mother anymore. I'm here to stay, and she can just like it or lump it."

In the bright light of Saturday morning, Annajane began to doubt the wisdom of a visit to the lioness in her own den. But it was too late to back out now. She played various scenarios over and over again in her head, planning a strong, assertive, take-no-crap offensive against Sallie Bayless.

She dressed carefully for the occasion, but not in the clothes she might formerly have worn for an audience with her mother-in-law. This time, she wore what she'd wear any other Saturday morning around town: a pair of red cotton capris, a red and white striped oxford-cloth shirt, an off-white cable-knit sweater, and a pair of navy-blue skimmers.

After she rang the doorbell at Cherry Hill, she repeated her mantra under her breath, as she'd done countless times on the drive over. "She is not the boss of me."

Annajane heard footsteps approaching from the other side of the heavy carved door. It swung open, and Sallie offered her a chilly smile. "Right on time. How nice."

Sallie was dressed in what passed for casual wear for her: black slacks, a peach silk blouse, and a black cashmere sweater that was looped across her shoulders. "It's such a beautiful morning; I thought we'd sit out in the sunroom."

Annajane followed her down the wide, marble-tiled central hall and out through a set of tall french doors onto the sunporch. She hadn't been out here since the divorce, but she doubted that anything had changed in five years. The room stretched the length of the back of the old house, with large, arched windows that gave a stunning view of the back garden and pool area. The floors were made of muted pink and gray brick pavers that had come out of the old smokehouse on the property, and the ceiling was high, with thick cypress beams. Fringy potted palms and ferns filled the corners of the room, which was furnished with comfortably battered white-painted wicker with flowered cushions. A ceiling fan whirred lazily overhead.

Sallie seated herself on a high-backed wicker armchair and gestured for Annajane to sit on a matching armchair opposite hers. A silver tray on the wicker coffee table held a pitcher of iced tea.

"Tea?" Sallie asked, pouring a glass. "Or I could open a bottle of Quixie. Glenn always thought it was so cute how much you enjoyed the stuff."

"Nothing for me, thanks," Annajane said. "I do still love the taste of Quixie, but I try to limit myself to one a day, and I had one for breakfast already."

"Oh," Sallie said, looking faintly nauseated at the idea. "How sweet."

Annajane looked uneasily at her surroundings, wondering how long it would take for Sallie to get down to brass tacks.

"The garden looks beautiful," she said, looking out at the sweep of emerald lawn and the blooming flowerbeds. The turquoise of the swimming pool dazzled in the sunshine. It was a storybook setting, Annajane thought, as she had so many other times in the past.

Sallie waved away the compliment. "This is not our best spring. My tulips were anemic-looking, and, I swear, Nate's gotten so old and blind I believe he mistook most of my perennials for weeds and dug them up back in the fall. But that's not what I wanted to discuss with you today."

Annajane steeled herself. "What did you want to discuss?"

"Family," Sallie said, without hesitation. "I want to talk about my family. You know I love my children, unconditionally."

"Of course," Annajane murmured. Although she might have argued about the unconditional part. She'd seen how stingy Sallie could be with her affection if one of her children—especially Pokey—didn't measure up to her impossible standards.

"I never thought you were the right kind of girl for Mason," Sallie said flatly.

Wow, Annajane thought. *Way to get the niceties out of the way.*

"You've made that pretty clear over the years," Annajane said.

"Glenn felt differently about you," Sallie said. "He admired your 'spunk,' whatever that is."

"Glenn was lovely to me," Annajane said.

"And I . . . wasn't." Sallie reached under the cushion of her chair and brought out a pack of cigarettes and lit one. "Someday, if you ever have children of your own, Annajane, you'll understand what it's like, as a mother, to stand by and watch your child make a decision that you're positive they will regret. And maybe you'll understand why I treated you as I did."

Annajane felt her face go hot. "*When* I have children, and they grow up, I hope I'll trust their decision-making skills. Mason wasn't a child when we fell in love and got married, Sallie. He was an adult, and he was fully capable of deciding the qualities he wanted in a wife."

"Maybe," Sallie said, conceding nothing. She inhaled and then exhaled a long plume of smoke through her nostrils, waving ineffectively at it. She got up and opened the glass door that led to the patio and pool area. A cool wind swept the room, sending the pale green fern fronds swaying. "Better," she said to herself.

She gave Annajane an assessing look. "You know, you're much more attractive than your mother ever was. Your features are softer; you wear your hair in a much more flattering style; and of course Ruth, bless her heart, never did know how to dress."

For real? Annajane thought. *She expects me to sit here and listen to her insult my mother?*

"I disagree," Annajane said. "Mama was much prettier than me at her age. She had a way better figure, and if she didn't have the nicest clothes, well, that's because her parents never had a lot of money." She smiled. "It's funny you should mention my mother. Do you know, just this week I came across an old Quixie recipe booklet that had a photo of her at a cookout. In the photo, they had her posed with a bottle of Quixie, and Glenn was standing there, too, with his arm around her. They looked like a real couple. Funny, I'd never seen that photo before."

Sallie exhaled another stream of smoke, and her eyes narrowed. "Your mother never told you she dated Glenn?"

"No. She didn't even want to admit it when I called her that night to ask about it."

"I'm not surprised," Sallie said. "It's nothing to be proud of, stealing a friend's man."

That made Annajane laugh out loud. "Mama had a different perspective. She told me she went out with Glenn only a few times that summer, after he'd already broken up with you, but before my father got back from the army."

"That is *not* how it happened," Sallie said sharply. "Glenn and I were engaged to be engaged, and everybody knew it. But your mother had a huge crush on him. And why not? He was the best-looking boy in school, from the best family. He and I had some silly fight that spring, and I broke up with him. To get back at me, to make me jealous, he asked your mother to the prom. The biggest dance of the year, and I'd already bought my dress. Of course, Ruth knew all that, but she went with him anyway."

"And you never forgave her, or me, by extension," Annajane said. "She never forgave you, either, although she refuses to talk about her reasons."

"I wouldn't know either," Sallie said airily. "Ruth was always full of spite. Your mother is not a happy person, Annajane."

"Mama was in her early twenties when my father died. Driving a Quixie truck," Annajane said, her tone mild, pleasant even. "She was widowed with a young toddler. She had to go back to night school to get a nursing degree so she could support us, and she worked days to pay for the tuition. She hasn't exactly had an easy life."

"Oh, yes," Sallie said, rolling her eyes. "Here we go again, poor, poor Ruth Hudgens. The twice-widowed martyr with a chip on her shoulder the size of a two-by-four."

"Knock it off, Sallie," Annajane warned. "I'm used to your criticism, but I don't have to sit here and listen to you ridiculing my mother."

Sallie shrugged, unrepentant. "The point is, I knew what kind of girl your mother was, and I figured you'd be the same sort. I didn't want that for Mason. And besides, you two came from two very different worlds."

Annajane stood up. "Is there a point to all of this? Because if not, I can think of a more pleasant way to spend a Saturday morning."

"I'm almost finished," Sallie said. "Sit down, please."

Annajane glanced at her wristwatch. "Five minutes. That's how much more of my time you've got."

Mason was right again. She shouldn't have come. Despite all her best intentions, Sallie was getting to her yet again, needling, criticizing, and, yes, pushing her around. Annajane felt all the years of long-simmering resentment coming to a boil.

Sallie took a deep drag on her cigarette and flicked the ashes into the nearest potted palm. "All I wanted to do . . . all I wanted to say, is this: if you're going to become a part of this family . . . again, I want you to stop trying to tear us apart. That's it. In a nutshell."

"I'm tearing your family apart?"

"You think I don't know what you've been up to?" Sallie asked. "Pokey is furious with me over this mess with Celia, which she somehow thinks is my fault. Mason won't return my phone calls. He actually has Voncile running interference for him. And just last night, Davis came over here and announced that he was selling his share of the business to Pokey and possibly moving away." Sallie blinked rapidly, fighting back tears. Her voice cracked. "This is all your doing."

Annajane was speechless. For nearly a minute.

"You are unbelievable," she said, when she could finally gather her thoughts. "Me? Wreck your family? Let me clue you to the real world, Sallie, since you refuse to face it for yourself. Your daughter is furious with you because you let her know you don't consider her children to be 'real' Baylesses. Also, you treat her like shit, always criticizing her clothes, or her weight, or her housekeeping, always letting her know she isn't quite good enough."

"I never!" Sallie said. "Pokey knows I love her. And if I've given her constructive criticism, she knows it's because I want her to be the best she can be."

"I don't know what's going on with Davis," Annajane admitted. "It's news to me that Pokey and Pete are going to buy him out. But it's good news. He hasn't been happy at Quixie in years, and it's time for him to move on to something else if he doesn't believe in the company anymore. Besides, if he leaves Passcoe and quits trying to prove what a hotshot he is, maybe he'll finally grow up and become half the decent, compassionate, loyal man his father was and his brother is."

"You have no right," Sallie said, stubbing out her cigarette in the palm. "I want you to leave this house right now."

"You asked me over here, and I listened to your bullshit, so now it's my turn," Annajane said. "Do you want to know why Mason won't return your calls? Why he avoids coming over here like the plague? It's because he's tired of having you tell him how to live his life. You helped destroy our marriage, years ago, and then you came damned close to pushing him into marrying a pathological liar. Earlier this week, you as much as accused him of lying when he finally told you the truth about Sophie. A truth you already knew."

"How dare you!" Sallie jumped up from her chair and stormed into the house. Annajane found her in the kitchen, unsteadily trying to open a bottle of wine.

"It's not even noon yet," Annajane observed, taking the corkscrew from her and applying it to the bottle herself. "But go ahead and have a snort. You're gonna need it by the time I've had my say." She took a goblet from the cupboard and poured the glass nearly to the brim.

Sallie gulped the wine, spilling some down the front of her blouse, a rare sight. "He had no right to tell those lies, to talk about his father that way," she said.

"He's telling the truth and you know it," Annajane said. "Mason loved his dad, more than you'll ever know. He loves you, too, which I don't think you fully appreciate. That's why he went down to Florida and brought Sophie back here after Glenn died. It's why he adopted her, rather than let her be raised by strangers, and why he let everybody believe he'd cheated on me. He did it out of respect for you and Glenn, because he couldn't stand the idea of a scandal. I don't think he had any idea he'd fall in love with Sophie as quickly or as deeply as he did."

Sallie took another gulp of wine. "This is unforgivable."

"You knew all about the cheating, didn't you?" Annajane asked. "You knew all about the other women, but it was convenient to look the other way, wasn't it, Sallie?"

"I didn't know anything," Sallie said, unconvincingly.

"But you guessed."

Sallie stared down into her wineglass. "The first time he cheated, I told myself it was just a slip. The children were so young; Pokey was still in diapers. He went to a ballgame in Chapel Hill for the weekend, and I stayed home with the children. When he came home, I just knew. The phone would ring at night, and if I picked up, she'd hang up."

She gave Annajane a tremulous smile and fingered the pearls around her neck. "He bought me these, afterwards. And the phone calls stopped, and I told myself all was well. Until the next time. It was years later. He'd gone up to Virginia to visit Mason, when he was in boarding school up there. I think he was actually sleeping with one of the teachers. That went on for three or four years."

"Why didn't you have it out with him?" Annajane asked. "Threaten to leave him if he didn't stop fooling around?"

"I didn't want to leave him," Sallie said. "I was in love with him. You knew Glenn. He was a good person. A wonderful father to our children. And so generous. He never denied me anything."

"Except your self-respect."

Sallie raised an eyebrow. "A highly overrated commodity, Annajane dear. We had a good marriage for a long time. It worked for us."

"Until things changed," Annajane said. "Like that last Christmas. The night of the company party."

"It was outrageous behavior!" she said, her nostrils flaring. "Even for him. I waited up all night, wondering whether he and Mason were even alive. He came stumbling into our bedroom way after midnight, still drunk. And Glenn rarely got drunk. He stripped down to his underpants and fell into bed. I slept in the guest bedroom. In the morning, I found his clothes on the bathroom floor, where he'd left them. His clothes reeked of her perfume. That was a first. Before, he'd always been very careful to hide his . . . affairs. And then I went to unpack his overnight bag, to put the rest of his clothes in the laundry. I was emptying his pants pockets before I put them in the wash. He always left loose change and his pocketknife in his pockets, and I've ruined more than one load of laundry that way. But this time I found all that and a little bottle of blue pills I'd never seen before."

"His heart medication?" Annajane asked.

"Sildenafil citrate. Ever hear of it? I hadn't. I had to look it up on the Internet." Sallie put the glass carefully down on the counter, then picked up a sponge to wipe down any traces of the spilled wine. "He'd gotten himself a prescription of Viagra so he could perform like the young stud he thought he was. He didn't care if he couldn't get it up for his wife," she said bitterly. "But his girlfriends were a different story."

Sallie opened the cupboard under the sink and brought out a bottle of spray cleaner. She sprayed the already-immaculate formica countertop, then wiped it briskly, using nearly half a roll of paper towels, while Annajane stood, transfixed, waiting to hear the rest of the story.

"You think I'm a bitch," she told Annajane. "A mean, withered-up, spiteful old bitch."

Annajane shrugged. "Mean and spiteful, yes. But not so withered up."

That made Sallie laugh. "I spend a lot of money to look this good. I had a face-lift last year, did you know?"

"I wondered," Annajane admitted. "You had it done down in Florida?"

"Yes. There's a surgeon down there who does amazing work. I'm thinking of having a tummy tuck next. In fact, I've put in a contract on a little bungalow down in Palm Beach, and that's where I'll be wintering next year. I'm going to sell the Wrightsville Beach cottage. I never cared for it there anyway. It's much nicer in Highlands, and most of my friends have places there. A much more interesting social scene."

"Sounds like you won't be spending much time in Passcoe," Annajane said. "How long has this been in the works?"

"I've been thinking about it for a long time. And now, since I don't have any ties to Quixie, well, there's really no reason to stay around here. This house is beyond depressing. I'm only sixty-six, did you know that, Annajane? Glenn left me very well-fixed, so I intend to go out and live my life for myself now. Maybe even date. Who knows? I might even decide to remarry."

"Go for it," Annajane said. "But you were telling me about Glenn. About the day he died."

"I put the Viagra bottle on the bathroom counter, right beside his shaving kit, and then I waited for him to wake up and find it," Sallie said. "He came downstairs, still in his bathrobe. Glenn never left the bedroom unless he was fully dressed. It was a pet peeve of his."

"I remember, Pokey always had to get dressed before she came downstairs, even on Saturday mornings," Annajane said.

"I should have known he wasn't feeling well," Sallie said. "But I was so angry!"

"Did you confront him about the Viagra? About the woman he'd been with?"

"Eva. Her name was Eva," Sallie said. "He said it was just a . . . mild flirtation. We had a fight. I told him I wouldn't stand for being humiliated anymore. I asked him if he wanted a divorce, and he said no, of course not. He apologized, and I left shortly after that, to go to the country club for my bridge date. And when I got home," she said, biting her lip. "He was on the floor, unconscious." She opened a cookie jar on the counter and brought out yet another pack of cigarettes and a lighter. She lit a cigarette with trembling hands and blinked back tears.

"That's a nice story," Annajane said. "Too bad it's not true."

"You're calling me a liar?" Sallie asked, her face deadpan.

"I guess I am," Annajane said.

54

Sallie flicked her cigarette into the sink, then turned on the tap to wash away the telltale ashes. She regarded Annajane as she might have regarded a cockroach who'd had the bad luck to wander into her immaculate kitchen.

"Why don't you tell me what you think happened?"

"I know for a fact that Glenn was having chest pains that morning," Annajane said. "Voncile called him on his cell phone, because she was concerned that he'd missed the company Christmas party."

"Did she now?" Sallie asked.

"Even she could tell, just from his voice on the phone, that he was having problems breathing. He admitted that he wasn't feeling well. Voncile begged him to call his cardiologist or to go to the emergency room, but he told her you were right there, taking good care of him."

"Cardiologist?" Sallie said. "I wasn't aware at the time that he had a cardiologist. Just one of the many secrets Glenn kept from me."

"You're a liar," Annajane said. "You knew he was on heart medication. Blood pressure meds, too. You had to know. If he was having . . . whatever, that he couldn't perform in bed . . ."

"Who said he was having problems in bed?" Sallie asked. "Didn't your mother ever tell you to have respect for your elders?" She tsk-tsked. "This is really not a topic for polite conversation, Annajane dear."

"I'm tired of polite conversation," Annajane said. "So let's get down to the nitty-gritty."

"Oh, please do," Sallie said.

"Voncile talked to Glenn at around ten o'clock that morning. He was having chest pains, which you had to have known. But you did nothing. I ran into you at the country club when you were arriving around noon. You knew he was probably having a heart attack. Did you hide his meds from him? Did you watch him gasping for breath, Sallie?"

"Absurd," Sallie said. "Glenn was fine when I left the house. He was watching the Carolina game and cussing a blue streak about the defense."

"The Carolina game? At noon? Really?" Annajane said mockingly. "That's interesting, because Mason was watching the game much later that afternoon. You know, it would be easy to look it up on the Internet, what time that game started. Are you sure that's right?"

"It was some football game," Sallie said. "I was so mad; I was distracted. But I do know that Glenn was fine when I left that house. He was alert and watching the game. And that's all that matters."

"Voncile told me she tried to call Glenn's cell again before noon," Annajane said. "But the call went right to voice mail. So she called the house and she talked to you. Don't you remember that, Sallie?"

"It was an awful day. My husband died that day, remember?"

"Voncile remembers it, because she was so worried about Glenn. You told her he was fine, but he was taking a nap."

"I just told her that to get her off the phone. He was watching the game!" Sallie repeated. "Glenn hated to be disturbed when he was watching football. The whole house could have burned down around him, and he wouldn't have noticed."

Annajane shook her head. "I don't think so. I think he was in full-blown cardiac distress. I think you knew it, and you were so pissed at him, you deliberately left him there to die."

She stood inches away from Sallie, whose back was to the sink. "Did he ask you to get his heart meds, Sallie?"

"No!"

"Did he ask you to call 911?"

"No!"

"Did you stand there and watch him dying? Was he already unconscious when you left to go play bridge at the country club? Were you surprised to come home that afternoon and find him still alive? Is that why you called 911 when you did? Because you knew it was already too late?"

Sallie stubbed her cigarette out in the sink and turned on the tap and then the garbage disposal. The metallic rattling filled the room until she switched it off. She washed her hands, dried them, then carefully applied moisturizing cream to each of her elegantly manicured hands.

"I loved my husband," she said calmly. "I took care of him until the very end. And you can't prove otherwise."

"You're right. I can't prove a thing," Annajane said. "But I don't have to. Mason and Pokey are already asking themselves the same things I just asked you. They don't want to believe what you're capable of. But I know. And you know. And that's good enough for me."

Annajane left Sallie standing in the kitchen. She let herself out the front door and didn't look back. It was, she'd already decided, her last trip to Cherry Hill.

55

Mason pulled around to the front of the Pinecone Motor Lodge and parked in front of Annajane's unit. It was Friday night, the week before Memorial Day, and she was still putting the wedding off, still refusing to move out of the damned Pinecone Motor Lodge. It was a nice enough place, he guessed, but he was tired of playing this cat-and-mouse game. He honked the horn twice. Nothing. He was going to have to do this the hard way. Her way. He strolled up to the door and knocked.

"Who is it?" she called.

"It's the big bad wolf," Mason answered. "Open up, or I'll huff and I'll puff..."

The door swung open. Annajane was barefoot, dressed in a pair of white shorts and a beat-up Braves jersey. His lucky jersey. "And then what?" she asked carelessly.

He smiled and tugged her by the hand. "Come on," he said. "There's something I want you to see."

"Right now?" she protested. "Mason, I've got stuff to do. I told you that earlier today. I'll come over in the morning, and we'll fix bacon and pancakes for Sophie, but right now..."

"Right now, you're coming with me," he said. "Please?"

"Just let me change," Annajane said. "I'm a mess. I was going to wash my hair."

"You're fine the way you are. In fact, perfect. Now let's go."

She finally managed to talk him into letting her put on a pair of sneakers and grab her phone, but five minutes later they were rolling through town in the Chevelle with the roof down, Journey blasting on the tape player.

"Are you going to tell me what the surprise is?" she asked.

"Wait and see," he said.

When they approached the gates to Cherry Hill, the sight of the discreet FOR SALE sign gave her pause. It had been six weeks since Sallie had announced she was putting the estate on the market and abruptly decamped for her new house in Highlands, North Carolina.

The rusted wrought-iron gates were open, and Mason easily swung the car down the driveway.

"Mason," Annajane said uneasily. "Look, I know it's your childhood home and all, but I really don't want to go up to the house tonight."

"Relax," he said, pulling her across the bench seat toward him. "I have no interest in going there, either."

"Ever?"

His jaw muscle did that twitchy thing. "Mama offered to sell it to me. I told her no thanks. Pokey doesn't want it either."

"What about Davis?"

"Don't know," he said. "I haven't talked to him. But I doubt Sallie would sell it to him. They might be thick as thieves, but she has to know that if Davis did get the house, he'd tear it down in a minute, probably build mini-warehouses or something. Sallie's funny about the place. She doesn't want to live there anymore, but she doesn't want it torn down, either."

"I'm still shocked she put it on the market," Annajane said.

"Yeah, well, she knows nobody around here has got three point two million to buy Cherry Hill. Listing it, that's her way of thumbing her nose at everybody in Passcoe."

"Especially me," Annajane said.

He turned the car onto the dirt road leading to the lake house, but, to Annajane's surprise, the road wasn't dirt anymore. It had been paved so recently she could still smell asphalt and tar. The underbrush had been cleared, too; the huge old oaks picked clean of their coatings of kudzu; the shoulders stripped of the privet and weeds, with sod laid down; and ribbons of new shrubbery planted. She could see islands of azaleas and rhododendrons and camellias.

"Hey," Annajane said, craning her neck to see the new landscaping. "What's going on here?"

"The new owner made some improvements," Mason said.

"Sallie sold off the lake house?" Annajane didn't bother to hide the disappointment in her voice.

"She never came down here anyway," Mason said, a bitter edge to his voice. "It was too primitive for her taste."

"You were the only one in the family who ever really cared about the lake or the lake house," Annajane said. "I wish you'd told me before it closed. It would have been nice to come back and look around again, for old time's sake."

"That's what we're doing now," Mason said. "Once more, for old time's sake."

She caught a glimpse of something bright blue through the treetops as they got closer to the caretaker's cottage.

"What's happened here?" she asked, half standing in her seat.

"You'll see," he said.

Without the tangle of fallen pine trees, kudzu, and privet, the old stone cottage stood proudly now on its point looking out over the lake, which could also be seen now. The blue she'd glimpsed earlier turned out to be a huge tarp that had been secured over the roof.

Annajane breathed a sigh of relief. "At least they didn't tear the house down," she said, turning to Mason. "If they're fixing the roof, maybe they're planning on trying to save the house?"

"Maybe," he said, bringing the fun car to a stop at a new graveled parking court that had been laid to one side of the cottage. "Whoever bought the place has obviously got more dollars than sense." He pointed past the house, and, even in the twilight, she could see the stacks of lumber and building materials and, beyond that, what looked like new pilings stretching out into the lake. "They've started rebuilding the dock. You believe that?"

"We used to talk about doing that," she said quietly. "Remember? We were going to build a two-story boathouse? With a fireplace and a deck on the top level?"

"And a screened-in sleeping porch," Mason added. He got out of the car and came around and opened her door. "Come on. Let's take a peek inside."

"No," she said. "I don't want to see. This was our special place, Mason. Even when it was rotting and falling down, I always thought, at the back of my mind, maybe someday we'd find our way back here. Knowing that can never happen now, even if it wasn't ever really realistic, it's just so unbearably sad."

"Just one look," Mason cajoled. "Aren't you the least bit curious?"

"No," she said stubbornly. "Honestly, can we just go back to the Pinecone now? So I can wallow in self-pity for an hour or so?"

"Later," Mason said.

She reluctantly allowed herself to be escorted to the door, noticing, along the way, the new flowerbeds; the new walkway constructed of worn, antique bricks; and, finally, the cottage's front door, which had been newly sanded and painted a gleaming periwinkle blue.

"At least they kept my color for the door," Annajane said. She pointed at the worn brass hardware, which had been buffed up, not to a garish bright gold, but to the mellow color of good old brass. "And they saved the old hinges and even the old knocker."

Mason produced a key from his pocket and, noting her surprise, said only, "The new owner's a decent guy."

He let her walk in first. If the outside of the cottage was mostly unchanged, it was a different story inside. The tiny, cramped entry hall was gone. In fact, all the walls were gone.

She was standing in one large, airy room. It smelled of sawdust and cut pine, and what remained of the day's light poured in through a wall of new windows overlooking the lake. The windows were open, and a slight breeze blew in off the lake. The water-stained plaster ceilings were gone, exposing age-darkened ceiling beams, and the old wooden floors were scarred and dusty, but intact.

"Oh my God," Annajane said, her voice echoing in the empty room. "They've gutted it!"

"Look at the views of the lake," he suggested. "Pretty cool, huh?"

"Unbelievable," she agreed. It was then she noticed a large old brass bed, situated in the right corner, near the fireplace, which looked like it had been recently reworked. The bed was dressed with white linens and an old quilt, which was neatly folded at the foot. A table had been fashioned from two-by-fours laid over a pair of sawhorses, and a couple of bright orange sheetrock buckets had been upended to use as chairs. There was a picnic basket on the table and a stub of a candle stuck into an empty wine bottle.

"Mason, look," she said, pointing at the bed and table. "The new owners must be staying here. Now I really do feel like a trespasser. We need to go, before they come back."

But he wasn't listening to her. He walked over to the table, picked up a box of matches, and lit the candle.

"What?" But she knew. Maybe she'd suspected as soon as she saw the bank of new windows.

"The new owners are right here," Mason said, giving her the brass skeleton key he'd used to open the front door. He took her by the hand and seated her on one of the buckets. He began extracting a number of foil-wrapped packets from the picnic basket, opening each one for her inspection. It wasn't the stuff of a romantic picnic. No imported cheeses or fresh fruit, pâté or crusty french bread. Instead, the meal he offered consisted of ham sandwiches on mushy white bread with bright yellow mustard and crunchy pickles, individual bags of potato chips, and store-bought chocolate chip cookies.

"You remembered," she marveled.

"Our first meal out here," he said. "You packed the food and I brought the beer. A very deliberate seduction on my part."

"Except the cookies I brought were oatmeal raisin. That was before I knew you were a raisin hater."

"A rookie mistake. Could have happened to anybody," he said graciously.

He sat on the bucket opposite hers and reached into the picnic basket one more time, bringing out two chilled bottles of Quixie. He unscrewed the caps and handed her one.

She took a drink. The essence of cherries lingered on her tongue and the bubbles tickled her nose. This taste thrilled her just as much as her first one had, nearly thirty years ago, at Pokey's birthday party. It still tasted new and full of promise. Mason was watching her. He held up his bottle, and they clinked them together.

Annajane got up and walked over to the windows. The sun was setting on the horizon, and the calm waters of the lake reflected the last amber glow of daylight. Mason stood by her side, and she nestled her head against his shoulder. They could hear the thrum of cicadas through the open windows and, from nearby, the soft hooting of an owl.

"You bought the cottage?" she asked. "And had all this work done?"

"Actually," he said. "Sallie gave it to us. As a wedding gift."

Startled, she turned to stare at him. "No way. She hates me. After the things I said the last time I went to Cherry Hill . . ."

"I was as shocked as you were when she sent the deed over," Mason said. "When I called to ask her about it, she just said she'd had a change of heart about us. And she said something about a down payment on self-respect, which I didn't get, but which she said you would."

Annajane shivered, and he put his arm around her, thinking she was cold. She'd actually been thinking about Sallie Bayless and her self-imposed exile from Passcoe. Was this, the gift of the lake house, Sallie's passive-aggressive way of admitting her guilt and asking forgiveness? Or was it the genuinely kind and thoughtful act of a loving mother?

"I didn't want to do too much to the place before I brought you out here," Mason was saying. "Mostly I've just been cutting back the jungle, planting some trees, and shoring things up. I knew you'd always wanted bigger windows looking out at the lake, so I went ahead and did that. And I had to evict the raccoons and have the fireplace relined and the masonry redone. All the rest, I thought we'd plan together."

She turned and kissed him. "You did all this for me? And kept it a secret?"

"For us," Mason corrected her. "But Sophie was in on it. She's already picked out the paint color for her bedroom. Princess pink."

"What would you think about adding a second story?" Annajane asked. "We'll need more bedrooms. And bathrooms. And a home office for both of us . . ."

They stood and looked out at the lake for a long time, eventually switching out the Quixie for a bottle of good red wine. As they watched the new moon come up over Hideaway Lake and marveled at the clarity of the stars in the night sky, they talked about their plans. For their new old house; for the company, for their all-new life together. When Annajane shivered again, this time from the chill seeping in off the lake, Mason went to the fireplace and lit the wood he'd already stacked there.

When he turned to remark on the lateness of the hour, he found that Annajane was already standing by the brass bed. She'd pulled back the covers, slipped off her shoes, and was pulling the lucky jersey over her head. He admired her smooth bare skin as the candlelight began to flicker out.

"Come to bed," she said.

And so he did.

Epilogue

The ruckus in the hospital room was close to deafening. Pokey Bayless Riggs was making a valiant but fruitless effort to look beatific while surrounded by her brood. Three little boys clambered onto the hospital bed, pushing and elbowing each other out of the way in hopes of being the first to hold their new sibling. "I wanna hold her." "No, me. I'm the oldest," "You're too little." "Mama! Make him stop!" while their father, who was trying to capture the whole scene on video, called out directions. "Look at the camera, Petey. Clayton, take your finger out of your nose. Denning, be careful, you're squishing your mama."

"Peterson Riggs, don't you dare shoot a second of film with me looking like this," Pokey cried above the din. She reached for her lipstick and a hand mirror and gasped when she saw her reflection. "I look like I've been rode hard and put up wet."

"You look beautiful," her husband declared, zeroing in on his wife's face. "Now hold her up a little higher, so I can get a shot of those big blue eyes and all that gorgeous red hair."

Pokey grinned and gently cradled the baby in the hollow of her shoulder. "Isn't she amazing?" she cooed, looking directly into the camera. "World, meet our daughter. Olivia Pauline Riggs."

Sophie stood close to her aunt's bedside, holding Annajane's hand tightly in her own. "My first girl cousin," Sophie said, not for the first time that day.

"That's right, Soph," Pokey said. "And you're going to have to help me figure out what to do with a little girl now. You can help me shop for dresses, and dolls, and all that girly-girl stuff for Livvy."

"I brought her a present," Sophie said, her eyes shining with pride. She reached into her pink pocketbook and brought out a lumpy package of pink tissue wrapped in what looked like a mile of cellophane tape. "I wrapped it myself."

"She wouldn't let me help at all," Annajane put in, squeezing Sophie's hand.

"I wanna open it," Petey clamored. "No, me," Denning hollered, shoving his younger brother completely off the bed, which set off a fresh set of howls from the injured party.

"That's it," Pete said, putting the camera down. "We're outta here." He leaned over and kissed Pokey and his brand-new daughter and extended a hand to the two boys remaining on the bed. "Come on, guys. Thanksgiving is only three days away. We've gotta get to the store and buy our turkey."

"And pies!" Denning said. "I want pecan. And pumpkin."

"And coconut custard," his father said, swinging Clayton onto his shoulders. "That's my favorite. Your mama makes me one special every year."

"But everybody's eating at our house this year," Annajane reminded him. "And I've already bought the turkey."

"Pete has to cook his own turkey, remember?" Pokey said. "He hordes his leftover turkey like it's a treasure from King Tut's tomb."

"My turkeys are a treasure," Pete proclaimed. "Wait til y'all taste what I'm doing this year. Deep-fried and injected with my supersecret sauce. Sweetest, juiciest thing you ever put in your mouth."

"Nuh-uh," Mason said. "Wait til you see what I've got up my sleeve. I bought a farm-raised free-range beauty from a farmer near Carthage. Then, I'm brining it for two days ahead of time. Kosher salt, cracked peppercorns, a bunch of other herbs Annajane's got out in the garden, and a whole liter of white wine. I got a bastin' sauce worked up with just the right essence of Quixie, too. You might as well leave that pitiful bird of yours at home, Riggs, because nobody's going to want it after they get a load of the bird from Maison de Mason."

"A brine?" Pete said derisively. "That's all you got?" He looked over at Pokey. "Honey, would you please tell this fool why my turkey rules?"

"Oh, good," Pokey said. "Dueling turkeys for Thanksgiving. This oughtta be interesting. Nothing like a good old-fashioned family food fight for the holidays."

"Speaking of family," Mason said, "What have you heard from the rest of our clan?"

"Sallie has been calling on the hour, demanding pictures and videos of Livvy," Pete said. "Says she's thrilled about us naming her Pauline after her mama."

"But not thrilled enough to leave Palm Beach to come see her new grandbaby," Pokey added, not bothering to hide her disappointment. "She wants us to come down for Christmas, even offered to buy us first-class plane tickets. As if! Like I'm going to load up all of us, plus a newborn, plus all the Santa Claus stuff, for a quick trip to Florida just to see her new house and meet her new boyfriend."

"She's got a boyfriend?" Mason asked, startled. "She's never said anything about that to me."

Pokey made a face. "Sallie doesn't come right out and call him that. His name is Brewer, and she claims he's her investment guy. But every time I talk to her, it's 'Brewer took me to this fabulous new restaurant' or 'Brewer thinks I need a nicer car' or 'Brewer and I are taking a cruise in February.' From what she says, he's semiretired, and, I gather, just a teensy bit younger. Most importantly, to Sallie, anyway, he seems to have his own money."

"What about Davis?" Annajane asked, "Has he been by to see the baby yet?"

Pokey sighed and gestured toward a mammoth flower arrangement sitting atop a dresser near the window. It was a towering affair of pink lilies, orchids, tulips, and roses that was only dwarfed by the five-foot-tall stuffed bear sitting beside it.

"He sent those last night," she said. "With a very sweet card. Signed Davis and Celia." She wrinkled her nose. "Although I'm certain Celia has no idea her name was signed to that card."

Annajane shrugged off the mention of her former nemesis's name. Although Celia and Davis were living in a grandiose new subdivision on the outskirts of Passcoe, she rarely ran into either of them, and when she did, she managed to grit her teeth and smile graciously. "Do you think Davis will ever actually marry her?"

"Gawd, I hope not," Pokey exclaimed. "He'd never admit it to me, but I get the feeling there's trouble in la-la land. He stopped by the house last week, and I got the distinct impression he was running away from home because he'd had another big fight with you-know-who. After a couple drinks, he told me that lawsuit the Baby Brand people brought against her is starting to heat up. He was complaining about the huge legal fees, which, of course, she expects him to help pay. And, he mentioned, her daddy and her two trashy sisters showed up out of the blue two weeks ago for a 'visit,' and, so far, they don't show any signs of leaving. The poor sap. Her mother and her mother's boyfriend only just went back home to Nebraska. After showing up uninvited, eating them out of house and home for nearly a month, to top it all off, they backed into Davis's car on their way out of town and never offered to pay for the damage."

"Wait a minute," Annajane said. "Didn't Celia tell everybody she was an orphan? And an only child?"

"Wishful thinking, apparently," Mason said.

"Davis did call the house this morning while I was in the shower," Pete said. "He left a message on the answering machine with some lame excuse about why he wasn't going to be able to get over to the hospital to see you and the baby for the next few days. Something about his pool contractor and a gigantic screwup."

Mason scowled. "He's adding a pool now? Because a tennis court and a stable and a riding ring and a frickin' guesthouse aren't showy enough for two people?"

"He *had* to add a pool," Pokey said. "Because *we* had a pool growing up at Cherry Hill. And he *had* to build the biggest, gaudiest, most ostentatious house this county has ever seen, just to show everybody how rich and successful he is, since we bought out his share of Quixie. And to house all these freaky relatives of Celia's who keep showing up."

"And to demonstrate that he has the biggest pecker in Passcoe," Pete said.

"Way bigger than mine," Mason added, with a wink.

Annajane clamped her hands gently over Sophie's ears. "Little pitchers!" she reminded her husband and brother- and sister-in-law.

"Sorry," Mason said, glancing over at his nephews. "Sorry, guys."

But the boys and Sophie were busily helping themselves to the gift box of chocolates that had come with their Uncle Davis's flower arrangement and hadn't heard a word the grown-ups were saying.

"I better get these kids outta here before they start eating the flowers," Pete announced. "Sophie, would you like to come help us pick out the turkey that's gonna make your daddy's bird look like a Colonel Sanders reject?"

"Okay," the little girl said, polishing off a piece of candy. "But can we wait til Aunt Pokey opens my present?"

"Of course!" Pokey said, tearing at the multiple layers of tissue. A moment later, she held a small yellowed cardboard box in her hands. Lifting the top, she found a glittering object nestled on a bed of cotton.

She held it up for the others to see. It was a green rhinestone brooch in the shape of a pixie—a pixie holding an uptipped and intricately wrought ruby-red Quixie bottle.

"Sophie!" Pokey squealed. "Where on earth did you find this? I haven't seen one of these since my daddy gave me one when I was a little girl just your age. Of course, I lost it almost immediately. It's perfect. I love it."

Sophie beamed and wriggled with delight at her aunt's praise. "I have one, too," she said, reaching back into her pocketbook to produce an identical pin.

"Annajane found a box of them when we were going through stuff from the attic over at Cherry Hill," Mason said, his arm thrown across his wife's shoulders. "According to Sallie, Granddad had them made as Christmas gifts for the top distributors' wives back in the sixties."

"There are only a half-dozen left in the box," Annajane added, "but we found a jeweler in Asheville who's copying them for us. They'll be great little holiday giveaways for the women at the office."

"Along with cash bonuses, right?" Pete added. "After that kick-ass summer promotion upped sales forty percent, I think everybody in the company deserves something extra in their Christmas stocking this year."

Mason nodded in agreement. "Bonuses are definitely on the agenda for the next board meeting."

Pokey was busy pinning the brooch to her hospital gown. "Now that you mention it, I think I remember Grandmama Bayless wearing a pin just like this one at Christmas."

"Only hers was the real thing," Mason said. "Emerald and diamond chips and rubies. Sallie said she still has it but never wears it because she thinks it looks tacky."

Sophie looked up at Annajane with interest. "What's tacky?"

"Tacky is in the eye of the beholder," Annajane told her. "It's a word some people use for something they think is in poor taste."

"But this pin is not in poor taste at all. It's just beautiful," Pokey declared. She reached for her niece and gave her a hug. "And you're beautiful for thinking of me and giving it to me. And when Livvy gets as grown up as you, I'll let her borrow it for special occasions."

"Oh, we've got another one for Olivia back at the house," Mason said. "And we've got this, too, for a special toast."

He reached into a shopping bag he'd set on the floor and brought out a bottle of champagne and a sleeve of plastic cups.

"Yippee!" Pokey said, grabbing the bottle and giving it an exaggerated smooch. "Hello, my old friend. Welcome back to my world."

Mason took the bottle and popped the cork, which brought a small "mew" from the startled Olivia, who looked around, took in the scene, and then promptly dropped back to sleep. He handed cups all around, and even poured a tiny bit for the children.

"To Pokey and Olivia," Pete said. "My two favorite girls in the whole wide world." He went through the motions of touching cups with the grown-ups and the children, and then settled on the bed next to his wife, dropping another kiss on the top of her head.

"Here, here," Mason said.

Pokey raised her own glass and took a huge gulp of champagne. "Come on, everybody," she urged. "Don't make me drink alone. I've been waiting nine months for a taste of something stronger than iced tea."

Denning, the oldest, took a wary sip. "Gross!" he said. "Quixie's lots better than this." He took his cup and dumped it into the sink, and Sophie and Petey loyally followed suit.

"Annajane?" Pokey said, pointing at her friend's empty glass.

"None for me, thanks," Annajane said, with a barely suppressed grin, looking over at her best friend and sister-in-law. "But if you had some skim milk—and some prenatal vitamins, I could go for that."

"What!" Pokey screeched. "Seriously? Does this mean what I think it means?"

"Yes," Annajane said, leaning her head on Mason's shoulder. "I'm pregnant. We just found out. Can you believe it?"

Pokey looked from her beaming brother to her teary-eyed best friend. "What I can't believe is that it took you this long."

Sophie giggled, and Pokey gave her a look of mock outrage. "You already knew, didn't you? And you kept it a secret from all of us?"

"Yup," Sophie said. She proudly removed her bulky quilted jacket to display the T-shirt she'd been hiding underneath. I'M THE BIG SISTER! was written on the white shirt in glittering silver letters.

Pete was pumping Mason's hand. "Congratulations. When's the big day?"

"Fourth of July," Mason said.

"Give or take a day or two either way," Annajane cautioned.

"It'll be the fourth, no matter what, as far as I'm concerned," Mason said. "The most important day of my life."

"Why's that?" Pete asked, looking from Annajane to Mason.

"Because that's the day Daddy saved Mama," Sophie volunteered. "It was a long time ago. She was dressed up like a pixie, that's an elf, kind of, for the Fourth of July parade, and some bad boys pushed her down, but then Daddy rode up in the fun car and saved her."

"And she saved me right back," Mason said, wrapping his arms around Annajane's waist.

"And they lived happily ever after," Sophie declared. But Annajane snaked an arm around Sophie's waist and drew her into an embrace that had finally, finally come full circle. "*We* all lived happily ever after," she said, gently correcting her daughter.

1. The book opens with Annajane attending the wedding of her ex-husband. Do you have any exes with whom you have maintained a relationship? Have you ever successfully rekindled a relationship you thought was long dead? Could you attend the wedding of an ex? Discuss potential gift ideas.

2. Annajane was never accepted by Mason's mother, though Sallie seemed to take to Celia right away. How do you explain Sallie's rejection of one and acceptance of the other? What does Sallie have in common with each?

3. Ruth Hudgens made her distaste of the Baylesses clear from when Annajane was a child and first befriended Pokey—even going so far as not to allow Quixie in her house. How did your interpretation of Ruth's ties to the Baylesses evolve over the course of the novel? Have you ever had a friend that your mother didn't approve of? How did you manage the situation?

4. Discuss the significance that the lake house at Cherry Hill held for Annajane and Mason. What parallels do you see between the house and the way it was tended to and Annajane's relationship with Mason?

5. Annajane assumed that Mason had been unfaithful once she discovered the mixtape in his car. In your gut did you feel she was correct in this assumption or did you think she jumped to conclusions? Discuss the ways that their first marriage fell apart and how it could have been different. Who was at fault and how?

6. Mason and Davis are quite different despite being brothers close in age. How do you account for their different personalities and approaches to life and business? Does each man get what he deserves?

St. Martin's
Griffin

7. Do you think Glenn redeemed himself as a husband and a father? In the end, were you sympathetic to him as a person? Why or why not?

8. Quixie's survival as a family-owned company was in peril at certain points in the novel. Would you have been tempted to sell? How does Quixie exemplify our current economic issues? Discuss examples of the struggles faced by local businesses and the responsibilities that companies have to their employees and the towns where they are based.

9. What were Celia's motivations when it came to Quixie? To the Bayless men? Imagine and discuss Celia's future with Davis and the rest of the Bayless family.

10. What role does Sophie play in Mason and Annajane's relationship and how does her role evolve as the novel develops? If you were in Annajane's shoes, how do you think you would have reacted to Sophie at first? Sophie's favorite book is *Runaway Bunny*. What parallels do you see between that children's book and Sophie's own life? Between Mason and Annajane's relationship?

For more reading group suggestions, visit
www.readinggroupgold.com.

Read on for an excerpt from
Mary Kay Andrews's novel

Ladies' Night

....

If Grace Stanton had known the world as she knew it was going to end that uneventful evening in May, she might have been better prepared. She certainly would have packed more underwear and a decent bra, not to mention moisturizer and her iPhone charger.

But as far as Grace knew, she was just doing her job, writing and photographing *Gracenotes,* a blog designed to make her own lifestyle look so glamorous, enticing, and delicious it made perfectly normal women (and gay men) want to rip up the script for their own lives and rebuild one exactly like hers.

Achieving effortless chic took hours and hours of mind-numbing fiddling.

On the evening her life imploded, Grace Stanton had already spent half an hour tinkering with a recalcitrant burlap table runner, inching it slightly to the left, then to the right, before peering at it through her camera lens. She fluffed the raveled ends of the runner and checked the image. Better, but not perfect. She deliberately rumpled the stiff fabric, and immediately hating the effect, smoothed it back out again.

She stared down at the table. The hammered copper chargers were topped with square, hand-thrown pottery plates in a mottled blue-green, which were themselves topped with round wooden salad bowls she'd picked up on clearance at Target. Unfortunately, she only had five of the salad bowls, and this was supposed to be a dinner party for six.

"Damn it," she muttered. She fanned the nubby green and yellow striped linen napkins atop the bowls and resigned herself to shooting from the end of the table, which would leave the place setting without the salad bowl off camera.

From the sideboard behind the table, she grabbed an armload of avocados she'd picked up at the farmer's market earlier in the day. She plunked one down on top of each salad bowl.

She was studying the effect when a hand snaked around her waist.

Startled, she gave a small squeak.

"Looks great," Ben said, planting a kiss on top of her head. "Are we having guests for dinner?"

"What?" she said, distracted. "Dinner?"

Her husband gestured at the table. "You've been out here messing with this table for two hours. I was just wondering who's coming over. And what are we having? I don't smell anything cooking."

"You're kidding, right?" she asked, frowning.

"I never kid where dinner is concerned," Ben said. "So—no dinner party?"

Grace glanced out the dining room's gleaming expanse of windows. Just another sunny Florida afternoon. Not even a cloud on the horizon. "What time is it, anyway?"

"After six," Ben said. He waved his hand in the direction of the table. "If we're not having a dinner party—or dinner, for that matter, what's all this stuff for?"

Grace rolled her eyes. "For Tablescape Thursday, remember? Danielle— from *Dining with Danielle*'s blog party? It was your idea to link up with her."

"Ohhhh," Ben said, suddenly enlightened. He snapped his fingers. "That's right. I'd forgotten. Your first Tablescape Thursday. Pretty exciting stuff, huh?"

"I don't know," Grace said. "You don't think it's weird—me setting up a phony dinner party to show fake friends online?"

"Noooo," Ben said. "Have you seen Danielle's Google Analytics? She's got 140,000 unique visitors a month, and 750,000 page views. And since she had the triplets she's got huge crossover with the mommy blogging crowd. Lots of people would kill to be invited to guest blog with her."

"But it's so artificial," Grace protested. "There's not even any real food. Just these big dumb avocados. I mean, I love avocados, don't get me wrong. I love the shiny green peel and the voluptuous shape. Like a Modigliani nude. But who plunks a whole avocado down on a salad bowl in real life?"

"Look at any lifestyle blog on the Internet, Grace," Ben said, putting on the professorial voice that so annoyed her. "It's not about reality. It's about aspiration. Your job is to create an experience so gorgeous, your readers will want to run away from their own crappy little double-wide life and move into yours. It's like we always used to tell our clients in the ad business—you're not selling steak, you're selling the sizzle."

He thumped one of the avocados. "This is the sizzle."

Grace tucked a lock of her hair behind one ear. "I guess," she said reluctantly. She picked up her Nikon D7000 and fiddled with the lens. Ben picked up one of the pottery plates from the table and examined it.

"What?" She studied his face, as always, craving his approval. "You don't like the pottery? It's hand-thrown by an artist in town. Each one is different."

"They're nice. In an artsy-fartsy kind of way," he said. "What's with the centerpiece?"

Her face fell. She loved the centerpiece she'd put together, an old wooden dough bowl piled high with different varieties of heirloom tomatoes in every shade of yellow, pink, orange, red, and green.

She pushed a strand of light brown hair off her forehead and took a step back from the table. She'd spent over an hour putting the table together, and she'd been fairly pleased with the effect she'd achieved. But now she was looking at it in a different light.

"Too country-cutesy?" she asked, glancing at her husband. Ben's trained eyes missed nothing. He'd been in the ad business forever, and no detail was too small or too insignificant. It was why they made such a great team.

"It's your blog," he reminded her. "And your name is on it. I don't want business stuff to impinge on your editorial freedom. But . . ."

"But what?" she said, trying to survey the table through his eyes. "Come on. I'm a big girl. I can take it."

"The Aviento folks sent us a big crate full of pieces of their new fall line," Ben said, hesitating. "Treasures of Tuscany, the new pattern is called. It's for the giveaway you're doing next week. I was thinking maybe you could put the tomatoes in one of those bowls they sent."

Grace wrinkled her nose. "That is seriously the ugliest pottery I have ever seen, and it looks about as Tuscan as I do."

"You don't have to set the whole table with it. Just maybe put some of those tomatoes in one of the bowls," Ben countered. "They are spending a lot of money advertising with us now, and it would be good if they could see their product . . . you know."

"Stinkin' up my tablescape," Grace said, finishing the sentence for him. "Did you promise them I would use it editorially? Tell me the truth, Ben."

"No!" he said sharply. "I would never try to influence you that way. I just think . . . you could maybe try a couple shots with one of the bowls. Or a plate. Would that hurt?"

"I guess," Grace said. "I'll try it out. But if it looks as crappy as I think it will, I'm not going to run it. Right? I mean, you promised, when we monetized the blog, we wouldn't be whoring me out by using the advertiser's product in a way that would compromise my aesthetic."

"It's your call," Ben said, picking up one of the tomatoes and examining it. "These are weird-looking. What kind are they?"

"Don't know," Grace said, gently taking the tomato from him and replacing it on the table. "J'Aimee picked them up at the farmer's market. She said one of the organic farmers was selling them."

"Kid's got a good eye," Ben said. He glanced back at the table. "How long before you're done here?"

"Maybe an hour? I guess I'll try some shots with the Aviento stuff. Then I need to edit, and I've still got to actually write the piece. And in the meantime, I guess we need to do something about dinner. I've been piddling around with this tabletop for hours now."

"Since you brought it up, is there any actual food to go on these pretty plates?"

"Nada," she said apologetically. "I'm sorry. I completely lost track of the time. Look, I'll just take a couple more shots with the Tuscan Turds, then I'll run down to Publix and pick up some sushi. Or maybe a nice piece of fish to grill. I can have supper on the table by seven. Right?"

"Finish your shots," Ben said easily. "J'Aimee can go pick up supper."

"No, I'll go. I've had J'Aimee out running errands all afternoon."

Ben dropped a kiss on her forehead. "That's what assistants are for, Grace."

"But I hate to bother her," she protested. "She just went back over to the apartment an hour ago."

Grace gestured in the general direction of the garage, which was at the back of the "motor court" and the apartment above it, where her twenty-six-year-old assistant, J'Aimee, had been living since she was hired three months earlier. J'Aimee's battered white Honda Accord was parked in the third bay, beside Ben's black Audi convertible.

Their builder had referred to the apartment as a mother-in-law suite, or even a nanny suite. But Grace's mom lived only a few miles away on Cortez and she wouldn't have moved to this "faux chateau," as she called it, at gunpoint. Ben's mother lived quite happily down in Coconut Grove. And since the fertility specialist still couldn't figure out just exactly why Grace couldn't get pregnant, the apartment, for now, was the perfect place to stash an assistant.

"Finish your shoot," Ben said, settling the matter. "I'll walk over there and roust J'Aimee. In fact, I'll ride to Publix with her."

"Thanks," Grace said, going back to her camera. "You're the best."

Ben gave her a gentle pat on the butt. "That's my girl," he said.

Grace went into the kitchen and found the heavy wooden crate with the Aviento shipping label sitting on the polished black granite countertop, pausing, as she always did, to flick a crumb into the sink. She hated the black granite. Even the tiniest fleck of sea salt showed up on it, and she seemed to go through a gallon of Windex every week, keeping it shiny.

But Ben and the builder had ganged up on her to agree to use it, after the granite company offered the countertops at cost, with no labor, in exchange for a small ad on *Gracenotes*.

Brushing aside a mound of brown excelsior, Grace lifted out various pieces of the Aviento pottery. Truly, it was the ugliest stuff she'd ever seen. There were outsized dinner plates, salad plates, soup bowls, and mammoth coffee mugs.

Finally, she extacted a soup bowl and set it on the granite countertop. It was huge, the size of a hubcap, with garish cobalt, green, and yellow zigzag designs circling concentric rings of red and yellow glaze. Her homely little farmer's market tomatoes would get lost in this thing. Rolling her eyes, she grabbed a bowl and a handful of the excelsior, and went back to the dining room.

She set it in the middle of the pine table, mounded the excelsior in the bottom, and piled on the tomatoes, tucking the brown paper strands out of sight. She stood back and took a look.

"Freakin' ugly," she muttered. She opened a drawer in the sideboard and took out a selection of dinner napkins: creamy damask banquet napkins, homely red and white checked ones, yellow and white striped homespun napkins, and even a pair of her favorite blue and white striped grain sacks.

She unloaded the tomatoes from the bowl and draped a yellow and white striped napkin diagonally across it before returning the tomatoes to their nest.

"Hmm," she said, gazing into the viewfinder. "Better." The napkin managed to obscure all but a few inches of the offending pottery. She reached over and plumped up a tomato, and tugged the edge of the napkin slightly to the left.

"Doesn't suck," she grudgingly admitted, clicking the motor drive. The light was actually a little better now, and she was liking the way it further bleached out the tablescape.

Behind her, she heard the familiar roar of Ben's car as it backed out of the garage. She turned in time to see that he'd put the Audi's top down. He did a neat three-point turn, and gave her a carefree wave before he sped down the driveway, his forearm casually thrown across the back of the passenger seat, and J'Aimee's long red hair flowing gracefully in the wind.

Ben reminded her of Cary Grant in *It Takes a Thief,* a golden boy, elegant, aloof, mysterious, maybe even a little dangerous. Watching him drive off like that, she reflected briefly on how unfair life really was. At forty-two, Ben was six years older, but you'd never know it from looking at him. He could drink a six-pack of beer and devour an entire Sara Lee cheese Danish all by himself (not that he would, of course—or at least, not in front of her) and never gain an ounce. He kept his tennis tan year-round. His gloriously glossy dark brown hair still didn't show a speck of gray, and those crow's feet around his eyes lent him the look of wisdom, not imminent geezerdom.

Grace, on the other hand, was beginning to spend what she thought of as an alarming amount of time on maintenance. At five-four, even five extra pounds seemed to go right to her butt or her belly, and she'd begun coloring her sandy brown hair two years earlier, at the suggestion of Ruthanne, her hairdresser. Her face was heart shaped, and only thirty minutes in the Florida sun left her round cheeks beet colored, giving her even more of the look of a little Dutch girl when Ruthanne got carried away with the blonde highlights. Ben insisted she was still as gorgeous as the day they'd met six years earlier, but they both knew that with Grace's blogging career about to take off, she would have to be that much more vigilant about her appearance.

Blogging A Career?

If anybody had told her two years ago that she'd make a living out of journaling her quest for a more beautiful life, she would have laughed in their face. And if anybody had told her that she would become enough of a success that Ben would quit his career to run hers? Well, she would have politely written that person off as a nutcase.

But it was all true. She and Ben were right on the very verge of the big time. This house, a 6,500-square-foot Spanish Colonial located in a gated golf course community, had been one of the subdivision's model homes, and the builder, whose wife was a *Gracenotes* reader, had given them an incredible deal on it in exchange for a banner ad across the top of the blog. Most of the expensive upgrades on the property—the landscaping, the pool and spa, their amazing master bath—all those had also been trade-offs for advertising.

She'd always loved writing, and had tinkered with photography for years, but once the blog took off, it had somehow caught the eye of magazine editors and television producers. In addition to having their own house featured in half a dozen magazines, writing, photography, and decorating assignments had begun coming her way. She'd become a contributing regional editor for *Country Living* and *Bay Life* magazines, and next month, they were going to start working with a production company out of California to shoot a pilot television show of *Gracenotes* for HGTV.

Some days, when she woke up with the Florida sun streaming through her Belgian linen drapes and spilling onto Ben's muscled bare shoulders, she had to remind herself that she was finally living her dream.

She couldn't say why she awoke so suddenly. Normally, Grace fell asleep the moment her head hit the pillow, and she slept so soundly Ben often reminded her of the time she'd slept through Hurricane Elise, not even stirring when the wind tore the roof totally off the screened porch of their old house in a slightly run-down Bradenton neighborhood. That night was no exception. She'd retreated to her office after dinner, writing and rewriting her *Gracenotes* post and fussing over the photographs, before finally, shortly before eleven, pushing the SEND button and crawling into bed beside her already slumbering husband.

For whatever reason, she sat straight up in bed now. It was after 1 A.M. Her heart was racing, and her mouth was dry. A bad dream? She couldn't say. She glanced over at Ben's side of the bed, hoping she hadn't woken her husband, who was a light sleeper. But she needn't have worried. He wasn't there.

She shook her head. He was probably downstairs, in the media room, watching a tournament on Golf TV, or maybe down in the kitchen, pawing through the fridge, looking for a late-night snack. Grace yawned and padded downstairs, already planning her own snack.

But the downstairs was dark, the media room deserted. She went out to the kitchen. No sign of him there, either. The kitchen was as spotless as she'd left it three hours earlier, after finishing up the last of the dinner dishes and packing up the faux-Tuscan pottery. Not even a cup or a spoon in the sink.

Grace frowned, and this time she didn't bother to worry about wrinkles. She checked the downstairs powder room, but the door was open and there was no sign of her husband. She ran back upstairs and checked the two guest suites, but they were empty and undisturbed. She walked slowly back to the bedroom, thinking to call Ben's cell phone. She was starting to get a little worried. But when she saw his cell phone on his dresser, along with his billfold, she relaxed a little. And then she noticed the keys to the Audi were missing, and her heart seemed to miss a beat. She went to the window and peered out, but saw nothing. There was only a quarter moon that night, but it was obscured by a heavy bank of clouds. The backyard was wreathed in darkness. She couldn't even see the garage.

"It's nothing," she told herself, surprised to realize that she was talking out loud. She shrugged out of her nightgown, pulling on a pair of shorts and a T-shirt, slipping her feet into a pair of rubber flip-flops. "He's fine. Maybe he's out by the pool, sneaking a midnight cigar."

The sandals slapped noisily on the marble stairs, the sound echoing in the high-ceilinged stairway. She ditched them by the back door, carefully switching off the burglar alarm before stepping out onto the back patio. She paused, put her hand to her chest and could have sworn her heart was about to jump out of her body.

"Ben?" She kept her voice low. It was pitch-black, except for the pale turquoise surface of the pool and eerie green uplights on the date palm clusters at the back of the garden. Cicadas thrummed, and in the far distance, she heard a truck rumbling down the street. She crept forward, her hands extended, feeling her way past the pair of chaise lounges perched at the edge of the patio, feeling the rough-textured coral rock beneath her feet.

Gradually, her eyes adjusted to the dark. There was no glowing cigar tip anywhere on the patio or the garden. She glanced toward the garage. No lights were on in J'Aimee's upstairs apartment, and the garage doors were closed. Was Ben's car there?

For a moment, a train of scenarios unspooled through her imagination. Ben, passed out, or even dead, at the wheel of his car, an unknown assailant lurking nearby. Should she retreat to the house, find some kind of weapon, even call the police?

"Don't be an idiot," she murmured to herself. "You're a big girl. Just go look in the garage. You live in a gated community, for God's sake. The only crime here is dogs pooping on the grass."

She didn't have the remote control to open the bay door, so instead she walked around to the side door of the garage, trying to remember whether or not it would be unlocked.

Luckily, it was. The knob turned easily in her hand, and she stepped inside the darkened space, her hand groping the wall for the light switch.

And then she heard . . . heavy breathing. She froze. A man's voice. The words were unintelligible, but the voice was Ben's. Her hand scrabbled the wall for the switch. She found it, and the garage was flooded with light.

A woman squealed.

Grace blinked in the bright lights. She saw Ben, sitting in the driver's seat of the Audi. He was bare-chested, his right hand shielding his eyes from the light. His hair was mussed, and his cheeks were flushed bright red.

"Grace?" He looked wild-eyed.

And that's when she realized he wasn't alone in the car. Her first instinct was to turn and run away, but she was drawn, like a bug to a lightbulb, to the side of that gleaming black sports car. The top was retracted. She looked down and saw that distinctive mane of flaming red hair.

J'Aimee, her loyal, invaluable assistant, was cowering, naked, making a valiant effort to disappear into the floorboards of the car.

"What the hell?" Grace screeched as she yanked open the passenger-side door.

"I'm sorry, Grace, I'm so sorry," J'Aimee blurted, her eyes the size of saucers. J'Aimee's clothes were scattered on the floor of the garage, and come to think of it, that was Ben's shirt—his expensive, pale-blue, custom-tailored, monogrammed, Egyptian cotton shirt that Grace had given him as a birthday gift—that was flung over the Audi's windshield.

With the passenger-side door open, Grace saw, at a glance, that her husband was nearly naked, too—if you counted having your jeans puddle down around your ankles as naked.

For a moment, Grace wondered if this was some bad dream she was having. Hadn't she just been asleep a moment earlier? This couldn't be happening. Not Ben. Ben loved her. He would never cheat. She shook her head violently, closed her eyes and reopened them.

But this was no nightmare. And there was no mistaking what she'd just interrupted. Suddenly, she felt a surge of boiling hot rage.

"Bitch!" Grace cried. She clamped a hand around J'Aimee's upper arm and yanked her out of the car in one fluid, frenzied motion.

"Ow," J'Aimee whimpered.

Grace flung her against the side of the car.

"Stop it," J'Aimee cried. Her face was pale, with every freckle standing out in contrast to the milky whiteness of her skin. For some reason, Grace, in an insane corner of her mind, noted with satisfaction that J'Aimee's breasts were oddly pendulous for such a young woman. Also? Not a real redhead.

"You stop it!" Grace said, drawing back her hand.

"Jesus!" J'Aimee screamed. She raised her arms to cover her face, and for a moment, Grace faltered. She had never hit anybody in her life. She dropped her hand and glared at the girl.

"Now, Grace," Ben started. He was wriggling around in his seat, trying in vain to surreptitiously pull up his pants. "Don't get the wrong idea. Don't . . ."

"Shut up, just shut up!" Grace shouted, her eyes blazing. For a moment, she forgot about J'Aimee. She flew around to his side of the car, but before she could get there, Ben had managed to slide out from under the steering wheel, zipping up his pants as he stood.

"How could you?" she cried, raining ineffective punches around his head and shoulders. She was aware that her high-pitched shrieks sounded like the howls of a lunatic, but she was helpless to stop herself. "You? And J'Aimee? My assistant? You were screwing her? Under my own roof?"

He easily caught her fists and held them tight in his own. "No!" Ben lied. "It's not what you think. Look, if you would just calm down, let's talk about this. Okay? I know this looks bad, but there's a logical explanation."

"Like what? The two of you snuck out here to the garage while I was asleep and you decided to have a business meeting in your car? A clothing-optional meeting? And suddenly, J'Aimee decided to give you mouth-to-penis resuscitation? Is that the logical explanation for this?"

"Calm down," Ben repeated. "You're getting yourself all worked up. . . ."

They heard a door open, and Grace looked over just in time to see J'Aimee scoop up her clothing and make a run for it out the side door.

"Oh, no," Grace said. "You're not getting away from this." J'Aimee was out the door like a flash, and Grace went right after her.

"Get away from me," J'Aimee cried, running in the direction of the house. "I'll call the police if you come near me. . . . It's aggravated assault."

"You don't know the meaning of aggravated," Grace shouted. She flinched as her bare feet hit the lawn, damp from the automatic sprinklers, but loped after J'Aimee, who was surprisingly slow for a young woman unencumbered by clothing. She picked up her speed until she was only a few yards behind her former assistant. She reached out to try to snatch a handful of J'Aimee's hair, but she was too slow, and her prey danced out of her reach.

"Don't you touch me," J'Aimee cried, backing away. "I mean it."

But Grace was quicker than even she expected. She managed to grab J'Aimee's arm, and the girl screamed like a stuck pig.

Lights snapped on at the house next door. A dog began barking from the back of the property.

"Get away," the young woman screeched, dropping her clothing onto the grass and windmilling her arms in Grace's general vicinity. "Get away."

Now they heard the low hum and metallic clang of the garage door opening. Grace glanced over her shoulder to see Ben come sprinting out of the garage. "Are you insane?" he called. "For God's sake, Grace, let her go."

In her fury, Grace turned toward her husband, and in that moment J'Aimee slipped out of her grasp. While Grace watched, speechless, J'Aimee scampered naked around the patio. A moment later, she'd disappeared behind the thick hedge of hibiscus that separated the Stantons' property from their nearest neighbor.

"Go ahead and run, bitch!" Grace screamed. "You're fired. You hear me? Your ass is fired!"

Ben was walking slowly across the grass, his hands raised in a cautious peace gesture. "Okay, Grace," he said, making low, soothing sounds at the back of his throat, the kind you'd make to coax a cat out of a treetop. "Oh-kay, I know. You're upset. I get that. Can we take this inside now? You're making a spectacle of yourself. Let's take it inside, all right? I'll make us some coffee and we can sort this out. . . ."

"We are *not* going inside," Grace snapped. "Coffee? Are you kidding me? You think a dose of Starbucks Extra Bold is going to fix this? We are going to stay right here. Do you hear me?"

Ben was shaking his head. "The whole neighborhood can hear you. Could you lower your voice please? Just dial it down a little?"

"I will not!" His calmness made her even crazier than she already felt. Grace megaphoned her hands. "Hey, people. Neighbors—wake up! This is Grace Stanton. I just caught my asshole husband screwing my assistant!"

"Stop it," Ben hissed. "I was not screwing her."

"Correction," Grace hollered, lifting her voice to the sky. "She was blowing him. My mistake, neighbors."

"You're insane," he snapped. "I'm not staying around listening to this." He turned and stomped off toward the house. "We'll talk about this when you've calmed down."

"One question, Ben," Grace called, running after him. She grabbed him by the shoulder to stop his progress. "You owe me that."

"What?" He spun around, rigid with anger. She noticed three small love bites on his collarbone. Hickies? Her forty-two-year-old husband had hickies? A wave of nausea swelled up from her belly. She swallowed hard.

"How long? How long have you been fucking her?"

"I'm not . . ." He shrugged. "Come inside. All right?"

"How long?" Grace felt hot tears springing to her eyes. "Tell me, damn it. This wasn't the first time, was it? So tell me the truth. How long?"

"No matter what I say, you won't believe me," Ben said quietly.

"Tell me the truth and I'll believe you," Grace said.

"No," he said softly. "Not the first time. But we can fix this, Grace."

"Fix it?" Grace stared at him for a moment, at a total loss for words. A moment later, a fiery scarlet mist descended over her eyes and she exploded with pure, senseless rage.

"Fix it," she said, lifting her voice to the heavens. "He's been screwing her for a while now, and he thinks we can fix it."

"That's it," Ben said. "I won't stand here and let you humiliate the both of us like this."

"Don't you dare walk away from me," Grace called.

"I'm gone," Ben said, not bothering to look back.

She followed him to the back door, to discover that he'd locked her out.

"Let me in, damn it," she screamed, pounding on the kitchen door.

Nothing. She kicked the door. Still nothing.

She looked around for something, anything, to break the glass in the door. Just then, she spied the heap of clothing J'Aimee had discarded in her hasty escape.

Grace scooped the clothes up and stalked around to the back patio. She craned her neck in the direction of the hibiscus hedge, hoping she might spot J'Aimee's bony white ass back there, hiding in the foliage or, better yet, being gnawed on by the neighbor's dog, a foul-tempered cocker spaniel named Peaches. But nothing moved.

She had an idea. She stepped onto the patio and found the switch for the outdoor kitchen, with its granite counters and six-burner gas-fired barbecue.

Earlier in May, her *Gracenotes* blog had dealt with barbecues.

Mr. Grace and I are fortunate to live in Florida, where grilling season never ends. But just because we're dining outdoors doesn't mean I serve burnt hot dogs on spindly white paper plates. I love to spread a white matelesse bedspread diagonally across our glass-topped patio table, and anchor it with a pair of heavy black wrought iron candelabras, or, if it's a windy day, I'll place votive candles in old Mason jars anchored with a layer of bleached-out seashells. Especially for casual occasions like this, you do not have to have a set of matched plastic dishes. I'll let you in on a secret: I hate matchy-matchy! Instead I have an assortment of mismatched Fiestaware plates picked up at junk shops and yard sales over the years, in bold shades of turquoise, green, pink, yellow, and orange. Paired with silverware with ivory-colored Bakelite handles, and oversized plain white flour-sack dish towels bought on the cheap from Ikea, and a bouquet of brilliant zinnias cut from the garden, they telegraph the message to guests: the fun is about to begin!

Grace chortled as she tossed J'Aimee's clothes—a T-shirt, pair of shorts, bra, and pink thong panties—onto the counter and then reached into the stainless steel under-counter refrigerator and found herself a perfectly chilled bottle of Corona. She didn't really like beer all that much, and there were no lime slices handy, but she'd have to just make do. She twisted off the bottle cap and took a long, deep swig, and then another. She pushed the ignite button on the front burner and the blue flame came on with a satisfying whoosh.

The beer wasn't bad at all. She took another sip and tossed the panties onto the burner. The tiny scrap of synthetic silk went up in flames and was gone in a second or two, which was a disappointment. The shorts made a nicer display, and she watched the blaze for two or three minutes, reluctantly adding the T-shirt, and then, after another five minutes, the bra. The bra, which had heavy padding, smoldered for several minutes, sending up a stinky black fog of smoke.

She looked around for something else to add to the fire, and remembered Ben's shirt, his favorite shirt, still draped over the windshield of his Audi.

Ben loved expensive things. But Grace, raised above her parents' working-class bar in the nearby fishing hamlet of Cortez, could never quite get comfortable with the luxury goods that her husband had grown up with as the pampered only son of a Miami bank executive. The day she'd bought the shirt at Neiman Marcus, for $350, she'd walked away from it twice, finally forcing herself to pull the trigger and buy the damned thing.

Grace stood in the open doorway of the garage, scowling at the Audi. If the shirt was Ben's favorite, the Audi, a 2013 Spyder RX convertible, was beyond his favorite. It was his obsession. He'd purchased the Audi right after they signed the pilot deal. One day he'd left the house in his sedate Lexus convertible, a perfectly good two-year-old model with less than 8,000 miles on it, returning hours later with the Audi. Ben wouldn't disclose what he'd paid for the car, saying only that he'd "worked a deal" on it, but when she checked the prices online, she'd discovered that the thing retailed for $175,000! She'd somehow managed to swallow her resentment over not being included in the decision to buy the new car, telling herself that if Ben, who handled all the family finances, thought they could afford the car, then she shouldn't worry.

She walked around to the driver's side, snatching the shirt off the windshield. Looking down, she noticed the keys were still in the ignition.

The next thing she knew, she was using the shirt to wipe down the bucket seat's leather upholstery—just in case. She slid beneath the wheel and turned the key in the ignition, smiling as the powerful engine roared to life.

Ben didn't exactly prohibit her from driving the Audi, but he didn't encourage it either, telling her it was "a lot of car" for a woman, and pointing out that her experience driving a stick shift was limited, although she'd learned to drive on her father's beat-up Chevy pickup truck.

Maybe, Grace thought, she'd just take the Audi for a spin around the block. Wouldn't that just fire Ben's rockets? She hoped he was watching from one of the upstairs windows. He'd have a stroke when he saw her behind the wheel. She eased the car into reverse, carefully backing it out of the garage.

Manuevering what she thought of as an expert three-point turn, she was about to head down the driveway when the kitchen door flew open.

"Grace!" Ben yelled. "What do you think you're doing?"

"Going for a drive," she said cheerfully, raising the beer bottle in a jaunty salute.

"The hell you are," he barked, walking toward her. "You've been drinking and you're in no shape to be driving. Get out of my car."

"Your car?" she raised an eyebrow.

"You know what I mean," he said. "You've had your fun. This is taking things too far."

She gave it not another moment's thought. Grace revved the Audi's engine and slammed the car into first, screeching past Ben, who was a shouting, raving blur. Now she was at the edge of the patio, knocking over chaise lounges and the wrought iron table with its jaunty green umbrella. The limpid turquoise surface of the pool was straight ahead. She closed her eyes, held her nose, and stomped the accelerator. The shock of the water was a final reminder. This was no nightmare. She was awake.